MONSTERS IN THE GARDEN

MONSTERS IN THE GARDEN

AN ANTHOLOGY OF
AOTEAROA NEW ZEALAND
SCIENCE FICTION AND FANTASY

EDITED BY ELIZABETH KNOX
AND DAVID LARSEN

VICTORIA UNIVERSITY OF WELLINGTON PRESS

Victoria University of Wellington Press
PO Box 600 Wellington
New Zealand
vup.wgtn.ac.nz

First published 2020
Reprinted 2021

ISBN 9781776563104

A catalogue record is available at
the National Library of New Zealand

Printed by Blue Star, Wellington

Contents

DAVID LARSEN

David Larsen is a Wellington-based writer and editor with a long-time love for science fiction, fantasy, and most adjacent genres or genre-like categories (relationship with horror: it's complicated). His reviews and arts features have won New Zealand journalism awards; he is a former Montana New Zealand Book Awards judge, but somehow still mistakes these wins for the verdict of an infallible higher power. His novel *Together We Hold up the Sky* is three-quarters finished, and may or may not be published in your lifetime.

INTRODUCTION I

Counting Worlds

As a child I found the phrase 'third world' exciting, though also confusing. It raised the prospect that there were two more worlds than I had so far managed to locate. I liked to imagine these would be worlds like Middle Earth or Narnia: better worlds, where the animals could talk and you might encounter elves. But then there was the matter of Earth's orbital position relative to the sun, a piece of common playground knowledge which told me that the Third World was us.

Having been born shortly before Neil Armstrong stepped onto the moon and spent my early childhood in that event's afterglow, I understood very well that no one was yet living on Mercury or Venus. Where were these first and second worlds? Somewhere or other I encountered the assertion that New Zealand had 'First World living standards', so wherever it was, the First World was obviously inhabited, and by inference the Third World was in some way shabby or inadequate. Possibly this was because it had no talking animals. In any case it was a bad thing to be part of, and apparently New Zealand was not quite part of it. But unless I had badly misunderstood the nature of the solar system, it was also true that we were, yes, a Third World country.

I am making this sound more reasoned and logical than it was; these ideas lived in my head at the level of vague assumptions and uncertainties. To the extent that they added up to anything at all, it was a hope-tinged surmise that New Zealand had some sort of double nature. It was perhaps like one of those enchanted groves you come across in fairy tales, part of the common world, but also transcendently distinct. Or like embassies, which I had been astounded to learn were not part of their host nations. You could go to America just by stepping through a doorway. Very much like going to Narnia. New Zealand was maybe some sort of embassy from the First World to Earth.

Like so many other features of the 20th century, the three-worlds metaphor has its roots in the French Revolution. The demographer Alfred Sauvy proposed it in 1952 as a way of thinking about the Cold War; he suggested that the non-aligned countries were as important to global politics in the 1950s as the Third Estate – the 'ignored, exploited, despised' commoners – had been to France in 1789. That is, he suggested they had their own goals and could not safely be treated as pawns on a geopolitical chessboard. The phrase 'third world' immediately escaped into the wild, and by the 1970s, when I encountered it, it meant 'undeveloped', in the sense of countries that posed no nuclear or ideological threat, but had failed to acquire proper modern capitalism and its fruits. More succinctly, it meant 'ignored, exploited, despised'.

The curious thing about the New Zealand I grew up in – and this has changed only somewhat – is that we knew we were a First World country, but we also seemed to fear we might possibly be a Third World one. Along with our north–south geographical divide, our Māori–Pākehā racial divide, and our urban–rural cultural divide, it was one of several ways in which we did indeed have a double nature. We were God's own country, the little country that could, we 'punched above our weight', but success overseas was the only hard currency in the economy of prestige. We were startled and thrilled whenever the outside world paid attention to us. For me this meant that, while I took a posture of preemptive boredom towards New Zealand books, any time a book by an English or American writer referenced New Zealand, the light of glory seemed to gather on the page. I think I was fifteen when I read John Wyndham's *The Chrysalids*, in which a small group of telepathic mutants grow to young adulthood in a fundamentalist post–nuclear holocaust Canada, go on the run when their xenophobic elders become suspicious of them, and are saved from torture and death by the intervention of advanced telepaths from a far-off land of peace and plenty. Our persecuted heroes have difficulty working out where this land might be, because the only one of them with the telepathic range to contact their soon-to-be rescuers is a very young child; but it seems to be called 'Sealand'. The child explains:

> *There are two parts of it, with lots of sea all around . . . It's a place with lots and lots of houses, different from Waknuk houses, and much, much bigger. And there are funny carts without horses running along the roads. And there are things in the air, with whizzing things on top of them . . .*

New Zealand as the advanced country where everyone has telepathy (plus bigger houses, and cars and helicopters), offering hope to the oppressed teenagers of a backwards North America? If I could have clawed my way through the page into that scene, I would have.

Though truthfully, there was no need for me to try. I was already in the scene. Books were my doorway into the First World, and I resented the time I had to spend in the grubby Third World of school; which, as forms of obsessive childhood behaviour go, was far more acceptable to adults than the screen-based pursuits that have now largely replaced reading, but still tended to get me into trouble, because my preferred books had dragons, giant sandworms or spaceships on the cover. I heard the word 'escapism' rather often. C. S. Lewis is usually credited with the most famous response to this particular assault on genre fiction – 'Who are the people most opposed to escapism? Jailers!' – though he himself gave his friend J. R. R. Tolkien as the source for the line, and it seems to have been popularised in an essay by Arthur C. Clarke. The most interesting rebuttal comes from China Mieville: 'Jailers love escapism. What they hate is escape.' For Mieville, creator of spectacularly strange alternate worlds and committed revolutionary socialist, the prodigious creative opportunities offered by science fiction and fantasy come with a commensurately sizeable risk, which is that of failing to seize them. If you give yourself licence to step outside our universe and then paint a cosy picture of familiar social norms, you are erasing the ideas of historical change and cultural difference.

This book is an anthology of Aotearoa New Zealand speculative fiction, 'speculative fiction' being a catch-all term of convenience for a publishing archipelago which also appears (from a distance) to consist of two parts with lots of uninhabited space all around; and which also has many smaller islands; and which can be thought of, like our islands, as the visible manifestation of a single submerged continent. Although with this latter point, definitions start to become tricky, or anyway to get trickier than they were already.

It is notoriously difficult to define science fiction. Like the word 'game', which seems intuitively transparent but hives off into clusters of overlapping semantic sets when you examine it, 'science fiction' means so many different things that one of the more famous definitions is Damon Knight's 'the thing I'm pointing at when I say science fiction'. But Lois McMaster Bujold, who writes across a range of genres and modes and has interesting ideas about where their edges are, has suggested that one significant appeal of science fiction for many readers is its focus on personal political agency: viewpoint characters who by virtue of inherent ability or chance find themselves standing at the crux of meaningful societal change. A subset of this type of story is the one about the out-group, the oppressed minority – ignored, exploited, despised – whose need to flee and/or rescue their oppressors drives the world towards a transformed future. In the case of *The Chrysalids*, the new future is an evolutionary one; the young telepaths come to understand that all they need to do is survive, and find their own kind, and in the long run their 'superior variant' will displace their parents' less capable species. (China Mieville would call this the kind of escapism that insulates jailers from any real risk of escape: leave the revolution to your genes.)

It is worth noting that there were a lot of stories about the rise of a telepathic *Homo superior* floating around in the middle decades of the 20th century, when science fiction was becoming established as a mass popular genre. It seems on the face of it like an obvious sixties trope – behold the new breed of better humans whose inevitable victory over their hostile elders will come from their *enhanced powers of mutual understanding*! – but in fact *The Chrysalids* was written in 1955, and A. E. van Vogt's *Slan*, one of the urtexts of this microgenre, was first serialised in 1940. *Slan* had some impact on the development of science fiction fandom in the United States; the Wiktionary entry for the now mostly forgotten slogan 'fans are slans' explains that it meant 'Science fiction fans are more intelligent and creative than other people'. This would have been uttered largely in jest, but also somewhat in earnest; in the same way that book champions today like to emphasise the importance of fiction for the development of empathy and imagination, there is a long history of science fiction readers arguing that science fiction expands the mind and prepares you to think more creatively about the future. This is the sort of rhetoric people only come up with when they feel marginalised.

I am writing this a few weeks after Margaret Atwood's dystopian science fiction novel *The Testaments* co-won the 2019 Man Booker prize; earlier in the year the wrap-up season of the George R. R. Martin epic fantasy adaptation *Game of Thrones* became 2019's biggest event on television; New Zealand's Peter Jackson–initiated Middle Earth tourism industry is cracking its knuckles and getting ready for the main event, because Amazon Studios is about to place a third nine-figure bet on adapting Tolkien less than two decades after Warner Brothers placed the first one; and to anyone who can recognise them, the fingerprints of science fiction and fantasy are all over the literary mainstream, most obviously in the work of writers like David Mitchell, Emily St. John Mandel or Jennifer Egan, but more significantly as a general presence at the level of borrowed techniques and ideas. The nerds, as the current saying goes, have won.

But the mainstream remains as isolated from the strongest currents of these genres as the gulf stream is from the South Pacific. Laurie J. Marks, Jo Walton, John Crowley, Octavia Butler, Sofia Samatar, Geoff Ryman, Rosemary Kirstein, Ada Palmer . . . these are some of the most interesting English-language writers of the last fifty years, and they are not part of mainstream readers' conversation. For people who read the speculative genres preferentially, this observation can register as neutral evidence that tastes differ, or as support for the 'fans are slans' theory, or as grounds for a feeling of being ignored, exploited, despised, or, there being no rule that human beings need to make sense, as all of the above.

'Realism,' writes Ursula Le Guin, 'is a quite recent fictional mode, a few hundred years old. Science fiction is an even more recent development of the same movement. The difference between these two young genres, realistic and science fiction, is less than the difference of both of them from fantasy.' There is something deliberately puckish about this assertion, coming from a writer whose realism can feel as profoundly fantastical as her fantasy can feel realistic, but the idea that fantasy stands a long way apart from both science fiction and realism is worth thinking hard about. (Le Guin goes on to dismiss the bulk of current good-versus-evil commercial fantasy out of hand; 'but the existence of muzak does not disprove the existence of music.') Another useful, albeit equally mischievous, way of framing things involves the image of nested matryoshka dolls. The outer doll, the set which contains all other sets, is fantasy: all fiction is fantasy, because all fiction asserts the existence of a world different from ours. ('There was once a woman named Elizabeth Bennett, who met and married a man named Mr Darcy.') Science fiction is the restricted form of fantasy where only the physically possible can happen. (According to this construction, any story involving faster-than-light travel is not science fiction; which is clearly accurate, and also clearly problematic, and may be taken as an instance of the aforementioned definitional problems with this genre.) Realism is the restricted form of science fiction where deviations from the known must be kept minimised: no large-scale alterations in history, no aliens, and you only get to reference Google Earth after Neal Stephenson invents it in the science fiction novel *Snow Crash* and a Google engineer likes the idea enough to make it happen. To put it another way, any sentence from a realist work can be incorporated into a work of science fiction, and any sentence from science fiction can be incorporated into fantasy, but not the other way around.

The helpful thing about this argument is that it drop-kicks the Trojan Horse word 'literary' out of the definitional discussion and leaves us dealing with the formal qualities of different modes. The annoying thing about it is how much I enjoy yanking 'literary', a brand recognition term posing as a synonym for 'good', away from readers who will only admit to valuing 'literary fiction'. It is as embarrassing to find yourself over-compensating for cultural cringe as it is to find yourself enacting it. Many New Zealanders will understand this instinctively.

In putting this anthology together, we have been highly aware of the lines separating 'genre' and 'literary' traditions, and we have endeavoured to ignore them. What you will find here, absent a few lamented stories for which it proved impossible to attain the rights, is our comprehensive selection of the most enjoyable and interesting speculative English-language fiction New Zealanders have written at short lengths, together with a few excerpts from novels in cases where shorter work from a key figure was simply not available. We have not included an excerpt from Samuel Butler's *Erewhon*, despite its New Zealand setting, its importance to the 19th-century utopian tradition, and the fact that Butler was living in New Zealand when he wrote it; we could not find an excerpt we liked as a stand-alone piece. We have also not included anything from Sir Julius Vogel's 1889 novel *Anno Domini 2000, or A Woman's Destiny* – which enjoyed brief fame during the years of the Helen Clark government for correctly positing a millennial future in which women could exercise meaningful political power – and this is because we have read it. The book is a ghastly expository trudge from first page to last.

We have included a brief passage from *The Great Romance*, an anonymously published 'sleeper awakes' novel from 1881 in which a man emerges from cryogenic stasis to find himself in a utopian future. In all frankness, the book is reasonably unengaging, but it contains what we believe is the first description of atmospheric aerobraking in world literature, which has some curiosity value. The novel we are very pleased to excerpt as a representative of the 19th-century utopians is not technically a 19th-century novel at all: Godfrey Sweven's *Riallaro* (1901), a satirical and beautifully written account of a voyage through a mysterious archipelago where every island is organised along different and unlikely political lines.

Moving into the 20th century and beyond, we present work from writers as obviously essential as Margaret Mahy and Phillip Mann together with the less obvious but equally essential ones, from well-established genre figures like Juliet Marillier and Tamsyn Muir to mighty tōtara mainstream figures like Patricia Grace and Owen Marshall. There are writers at every career stage here, including several making their first professional publication in these pages.

The two main islands of Aotearoa New Zealand are known in te reo Māori as Te Ika a Māui and Te Waipounamu. Their English names, the North Island and the South Island, could have been proposed by someone determined to demonstrate that Pākehā New Zealand is a bluff nation of literal-minded cartographers, but these names do serve as a useful test of local knowledge. When the great science fiction writer Kim Stanley Robinson opens his novel *Antarctica* with a reference to someone going on holiday in New Zealand and travelling around South Island, he is making a fairly common international error, but not one a New Zealander would ever fall into. We do not let go of our definite articles: our islands contain the north and the south, which is to say they constitute a perfect geographical whole. In this book you will find some of the other worlds contained within Aotearoa New Zealand, which regards itself as both a country of the First World and a country of the Third World, but also, there being no rule that human beings need to make sense, as an outermost matryoshka doll. Some days I find this doubt-riddled self-sufficiency pleasingly well balanced, although on other days it seems to represent everything neurotic and smug a national culture should fear in itself. If the latter, perhaps China Mieville would say these stories offer a chance at escape.

ELIZABETH KNOX

Elizabeth Knox CNZM is the author of thirteen novels, three novellas and a collection of essays. *The Vintner's Luck* is published in thirteen languages. *Dreamhunter* won the 2006 Esther Glen Medal. *Dreamhunter*'s sequel, *Dreamquake* (2007), was a Michael L. Printz Honor book for 2008 and, in the same year, was named an ALA, CCBC, Booklist, and New York Library best book. *Mortal Fire* won a NZ Children's Book Award and was a finalist in the LA Times Book Awards. Elizabeth won the Prime Minister's Award for Fiction in 2019. Her latest novel, *The Absolute Book*, was published in New Zealand in 2019, and appears in the US and UK in February 2021.

INTRODUCTION II

Here Be Monsters

Late in the piece – the production cycle – I sat down to write this introduction, a fat wodge of proofs beside me for reference, and with the usual ghostly itch of ideas I've had about the work. About the interesting correspondences and echoes between the pieces, particularly the stories we asked for, which came as a surprise. I thought about our selection processes, which I'm sure were the usual mix of deliberation, discovery, serendipity, and good or bad timing.

Of the selection process, I'll say these things. New Zealand literature has a strongly realist tradition, and what we wanted to do with *Monsters in the Garden* was shine a light on its other tradition, the fantasy and science fiction strongly present not only in young adult books (whose young adult audience does not disqualify them from being literature) but elsewhere, too: as magic realism, works permeated by myth; as future fiction;

speculative fiction; counterfactual fiction; parable; and allegory. We sought stories from those working in what is more often thought of as genre, and from writers of literary fiction – which is arguably also a genre. David and I were selective – but any absences here are due as much to other considerations as to our judgements. We had chosen to ask for, wherever possible, previously unpublished short fiction. But we also selected some stories we admired and felt were underexposed – for instance, Phillip Mann's 'The Gospel According to Mickey Mouse'. Or we chose stories where we felt a further outing would benefit New Zealand readers, like Keri Hulme's uneasy 'Kaibutsu-San' or Janet Frame's 'Two Sheep', a dark parable of a world founded on cruelty and instrumentality. Frame's work could be said to be non-realist right down to its atoms because she is a writer who tests every common understanding and generally bends the plain light of day. We selected stories by Mann, Hulme, Frame and Owen Marshall, and took an excerpt from one of Maurice Gee's masterful young-adult fantasy novels. However, the Margaret Mahy work here is previously unpublished (much more on that later) and so is Patricia Grace's. And, because we were looking for short fiction wherever possible, there were people who had nothing for us at the time – like Sherryl Jordan, whom I'd have loved to see here. There were also a number of writers whose best work is in their novels and whose short fiction just doesn't do justice to what they can do.

I'd also like to say what a pleasure and education it was to work with David Larsen. David is very well read, and our ideas and tastes were complementary. David's foreword covers several other whys and wherefores of our choices when comes to what is here, particularly our selections from the early 20th century. What *Monsters in the Garden* is *not* is one of those state-of-the-nation literature anthologies. It's an anthology among anthologies, and a good place to start, or to start talking again about that other tradition of New Zealand fiction.

And here I find myself having to do what I do, and do over, which is defend the worth of non-realist fiction – because stuff still gets confidently said by people who should know better. A book with 'fairies and talking animals' isn't 'grown up' or is 'junk' and 'nonsense'. Yes, these opinion-makers are talking about my latest book, but they're also expressing sentiments against a certain kind of writing, a kind of writing that doesn't merit attention because it can't be taken seriously – or at the very least shouldn't get serious attention. But I'm not just going to defend my kind of writing, this anthology's kind of writing. Nor am I going to do what I do, and do over – write about what fantasy, science fiction, horror, magic realism and surrealism can do as well as, differently, and sometimes better than realism. Better, I'll say it again, because the worlds of non-realist fictions, the people, the societies, can't lean on common understandings, don't have a consensual reality – even one to quarrel with – so any world they propose is already a new way of seeing things (unless, of course, the writer sticks rigorously to the rules of genre, but that's a whole other problem, and not one any of the work here has).

So, I'm not going to argue any of that. I've done that, and I feel it's not stuck. Instead let's try this, thinking about what might be behind the dissing and dismissing, and why it seems, to me, to be a very New Zealand thing.

New Zealand fiction has a strong realist tradition. Realism has social utility. The novels that attempt to describe who we are and how we live, the rigour or complacency of our lives, our existential wariness of enthusiasm and commitment, the blundering and fumbling that's the inspiration of lots of good Kiwi comedy, the sweet yearning of our hopes for ourselves, the joy of the things we know and that might be things *only we* know, like the smell of seaweed and fish bones cooked by the sun among hot stones heaped on a West Coast beach, or the sound of the song of that particularly preposterous songbird. Those of us writing in English can feel that there might be a thing – an observation or understanding – that we are putting in English for the first time. Making an offering, putting something on a shrine, if there's any room among the offerings of all those cosmopolitans writing about cities. There it is, our real world, our material life, our characteristic behaviour. No matter how personal it is, it's representative, and as such it has utility. It shows us ourselves, it warms the air between us, it fosters accord or provokes discussion.

So hooray for New Zealand realism. It's good stuff, and I'm all for it. But the problem seems to be that some of us have a disordered understanding of good stuff. It's to do with times gone by, with scarcity and having to exercise patience. Before I go on let me acknowledge that Māori understanding has been able to temper the Pākehā – but only so much. Pākehā culture was shaped by scarcity and delayed gratification. We waited and waited for many things we wanted and counted as good. 'Good' as in nice to have, life enhancing, and 'good' as in necessary, life-sustaining, life improving. We're the descendants of people who made lists of necessities and staples – with nails and staples – every fine tool, every fine machine, books, life-saving medicines, you name it. Priority would go to what was necessary, what was practical, when someone wrote home to ask for materials to be sent, when my great-grandmother at Mount White Station made up a list of provisions to get the family and workers through winter in the mountains.

These practical considerations and husbandry, plus a longing for improvement, for the leg-up of information about the world – this is what had primary value. And it isn't only what our ancestors counted as worth having that shaped their attitudes. It's also the fact that they were able to have so much power in excluding what they *didn't* want. Perhaps it was only an illusion of power those thousands of miles of ocean gave them over infectious diseases, Chinese labourers, the union movement, vulgar women's fashions – but it was, nevertheless, an illusion of power that shaped them. These things – a suspicion or slighting or putting aside for an idle moment of what was impractical, coupled with a smug spirit of sanitation – are part of our cultural legacy, and are what I feel we are dealing with when we can't think why something unrepresentative would have value. *Don't know what it is – let's leave it off the wagon. Don't know what it is – let's fumigate it.*

So, speaking as a periodically fumigated writer, and one editor of this anthology, let me now raise up and celebrate what we have here.

I don't think it's at all coincidental that a number of the fictions in *Monsters in the Garden* engage, to one degree or another, with ideas about value and determining worth – what to keep, what's useful, what and who to exclude – and with efforts to remedy the bad decisions flowing on from earlier apparently necessary moments of choice. Sometimes the scaffolding of the agreed-on world of the story comes strongly from the tropes of genre. For instance, the final story in this book, Jack Larsen's 'Ash Child', is a fantasy with a classic fire-breathing dragon that not only imagines everything as if this is literature's *first* dragon, but provides some chewy problems such as that a dragon's great wealth can't be seized and redistributed, but only inherited in terms so soul-crushing and perpetuating of tyranny that the wealth may as well have no value. Octavia Cade's 'The Stone Wētā' tells of a kind of conspiracy to save things that are precious – of no utility, but worth having, *worth anything*. Danyl McLauchlan's 'The Everything Store' is one of several stories that perfectly balance being fully imagined, pacey tales with some allegorical intentions. The allegory never runs the story, just shines inside it, casting different lights and shadows. The people in 'The Everything Store' are trying to make a life out of what is near at hand. They're nursing things along, patiently waiting for replacement parts to arrive – and sometimes venturing into danger in order to find new or necessary things. The science fiction makes the fast metabolism of the story's meanings possible. None of the things it wants to say could be said so efficiently, pointedly and entertainingly in a realist story. The heroine of Karen Healey's delightful space opera 'Where We Walk, We Walk on Bones' has got herself somewhere exclusive of people she finds undesirable – for very sound reasons. But her efforts to control her environment are confounded, and it's all fun, funny, and shows how the undesirable things will follow us to the better world, because they're *our* undesirable things.

I could go on with my slightly overdetermined readings about value, but the correspondences between these stories are fascinating.

There are a number of ghost stories, each with a different kind of haunting. Craig Gamble's 'The Rule of Twelfths' is a classic haunting of a place where brutalities were perpetrated, a story about how indelible cruelty is and how sufferers become perpetrators. The ghosts of Tina Makereti's 'The Children' are a kind of refugee – not the ghosts of refugees, but their haunting is a refuge from lives of limited possibility. The story seems to me to be, among other things, an imaginative response to the problem of child poverty in New Zealand. Emma Martin's 'In the Forest with Ludmila' has a repeating purgatorial haunting at its heart, and the ghost in Kirsten McDougall's 'A Visitation' offers a cooking lesson. Dylan Horrocks's 'The Paresach's Tulips' has a death-haunted narrator. The subject of Dylan's morbid and murderous tale chimes well with Owen Marshall's 'Immortality'– in the Horrocks immortality is sought, and in the Marshall it is achieved. One story is seductive, the other cautionary.

After ghost stories the most-represented sub-genre would be utopian and dystopian science fiction. Lawrence Patchett's stately and tough-minded future fiction, 'The Tenth Meet', centres on a pilgrimage where everything is carried, and there must be charity – at the very least charity compelled by pity after pleading. If Patchett's imagined future is difficult – though not wholly dystopian – Witi Ihimaera's 'The Last White Rhinoceros' is the old promised world-to-come of technological marvels, material wealth, freedom, beautiful nostalgic entertainments – *but not for us*. Samantha Lane Murphy's 'Analogue' offers us a more dystopian technological future, but imagined on a touching human scale. 'Analogue' tells of an encounter between a commuter and a friendly algorithm, or possibly a creepy stalking algorithm, or possibly just a lonely spirit of the dazzling night. Rachael Craw's 'The Dreamer and the Nightingale' imagines a future where the only choices for the poor seem to be either to assail the church / only viable industry or to serve it, a future in which the rich do nothing at all, or nothing real and material. It's also a love story, and a tragedy. Tamsyn Muir's Atwood-like 'Union' is set in a rural dystopia whose agricultural practices involve careless unkindness (it echoes nicely with the Frame story). It is an insidiously disturbing and horribly satisfying tale.

So – utopian futures that we are not a part of; dystopian Anthropocene futures, where people haven't learned to look after what they've made; and the broken-down futures of the body in a wheelbarrow. These writers of science fiction aren't trying to be prophets, but they are thoughtfully exploring the possibilities of tomorrow as supplied by today.

Most of the stories in this anthology belong to either the family of science fiction, or that of ghost stories. (Only Keri Hulme's might be classed as horror.) Far fewer are fantasy: the Mahy; the Horrocks, with its intricately imagined system of magic; Bernard Beckett's tale of the cost to a father and daughter's relationship of his disappointment in his work – a fantasy because much of the story's urgent scholarship is invented. The two youngest contributors to *Monsters* are writers of fantasy: Jack Larsen, who I began with, and Jack Barrowman, in whose otherworldly sea story 'The Sharkskin' an unexceptional naval officer – well-managed, efficient with the stores, ready to take orders – falls into a command and discovers what war is. It is a story about experiences we can't have any understanding of before we're in them, and once we're in them they cancel understanding. That, and what, in those circumstances, the little guy responsible for others' lives can do about it.

Other stories don't have any family likenesses I can see. Some are startlingly true to the moment. In Juliet Marillier's 'By Bonelight', a tenant in a tall apartment building goes downstairs to talk to someone and settle an issue, and it's an epic and dangerous undertaking, a quest. 'By Bonelight' is a story that, between the time of its delivery and the time of my reading it in proof, gathered a greater density of significance.

Then there's Patricia Grace's 'The Parson Who Thought She or He was a Bishop'. Grace can't be described as a realist or non-realist – there's not a line she wanders back and forth across. It's all water, it's all mixed, a tide carrying things in and out and sometimes holding them still. 'The Parson Who Thought She or He was a Bishop' is a little story that makes the world larger. It is about both an old person and a tūī, and an old person and a little god. It's not an undecidable meaning, but a whole one.

My own contribution, 'Unobtanium', originally appeared in *Are Angels OK?*, the anthology of collaborations between New Zealand physicists and New Zealand writers, edited by scientist Paul Callaghan and poet Bill Manhire. 'Unobtanium' is probably 'hard' science fiction since it uses real scientific facts and some knotty theories of physics. When I wrote it I was trying to walk a path between the brief of the project and the working out of some intolerable personal stuff. In the story a physicist tries to work out his own intolerable personal stuff using time travel, which of course goes as well as one of those Greek myths with a prophecy in them (those myths are the ancestors of all time-travel stories). It's a tale about being damaged and the futility of thinking you can fix it. And it's a story about nerd jokes, and holy dread.

Pip Adam's brisk, clinical, disturbing 'A Problem' is a kind of companion piece to her latest novel, *Nothing to See*. The problem is violence to women. The solution to the problem is to displace the violence, which is a further problem. It's a very short story, very dark, and very Pip Adam. Pip is a great New Zealand writer who is resolutely non-realist. She is less interested in tinkering with the available tropes of genre than other resolute Kiwi non-realists, but just as strongly wedded to naturalism. Which brings me to the great naturalist of non-realism in the anthology – the central figure of fantastical New Zealand letters – Margaret Mahy.

*

I first heard about Margaret's 800-page adult fantasy novel in the mid-1980s. Someone I knew had got to listen in on Margaret reading a section of it to her daughter Bridget. Margaret told me about the novel herself in the late eighties. I think it was complete then, and Margaret's agent had seen it. Margaret said she had found it more exciting to write than anything else, but that once finished she had been discouraged by several readers wondering what kind of beast it was, whether this was her audience, or the best use of her time.

Margaret only ever expressed such things ruefully. She'd never overstate this kind of case. In the late eighties Margaret was very much identified as a children's fantasy writer, and the burgeoning adult fantasy field was perhaps a bit remote and difficult for her to simply step in. Once appetites and the market changed and millions of adults were reading and loving Rowling and Pullman, Meyer and Collins, she might have tried again. But perhaps she'd fallen out of love with it. Certainly she had plenty going on. Now and then I'd ask her to let me read it – probably disconcerting her by how far my tongue would roll out on the floor. I wanted that book. In the mid-2000s she said she was making something from some of it with the help of her new editor at Faber & Faber – at the time also my editor. Then in 2009 *Heriot* appeared and I recognised it as belonging to the epic. *Heriot* read like part of something. Despite many virtues the novel read as if the character at its centre wasn't the protagonist of the story, as if the story had blazed out of the mist, run on through rags of mist, and vanished into mist again. I think, given Margaret's vast list of great finished things, it's okay to say this novel had, at the very least, a limp. It read as if it were part of a larger and more ambitious work, adjusted for a young-adult audience. It filled me with longing for the whole thing.

I did get a chance to ask her about it. She said that *Heriot* was something between a quarter to a third of the original book. Margaret wasn't very well then. So it's hard to say how she felt about what was out in the world, and what I hoped was still in a drawer somewhere.

As soon as the idea of this anthology was floated I got in touch with Bridget Mahy and Rob Stowell, Margaret's younger daughter and son-in-law, who are in charge of her literary estate. I asked them whether the epic was among Margaret's papers. Margaret's papers were still being sorted preparatory to their being deposited in Tūranga. Bridget remembered the novel and having it read to her in instalments. Rob came back and said that, while he hadn't found a whole manuscript, he could send a group of files – Word and Wordpress – that he'd identified as being part of that currently lost book. Rob sent them; Craig Gamble of VUP went through them to clean up all the weird old software artefacts in the text. I compared versions of chapters to find what I thought read best, and put what I had in some order – with gaps. I believe I'm missing either the beginning section of the novel, or possibly an extended flashback that explains how the narrator, Linnet, came to be in Diamond. I can't say whether the novel has a beginning then a four-year time gap, or has flashbacks. It is simply impossible to guess from what's there.

What I've made of it all – 'Misrule in Diamond' – is a composite of about half the fragments I received. A clear run of story with one summarising flashback that I put together from surviving bits of what might be the actual beginning of the book. The flashback is a couple of pages of Margaret's sentences stitched by me – and it was necessary to do that to get that clear run of story.

The world of 'Misrule in Diamond' is rich, and the story very alive and open to complexities and darkness. It is absolutely

Mahy, and also something else again. Something else of *hers*, again. Of the whole lost work – my search for it is ongoing. I've sent emails and messages and have had phone conversations over the past year and a half seeking more. I haven't had any luck so far. But what I'm hoping is that this work's presence in the anthology will flush out more leads – and maybe the novel itself in its entirety.

I've finished reading the wodge of proofs and am delighted to report that, as a reading experience, *Monsters in the Garden* did what I hoped it would do: it transported me. And it is transportation, not diversion. Yes, I have whiled away hours in bed reading, but I've been all over the place, outside of myself and my experience. And I am even more sure than ever of this: carrying people outside themselves is a serious business, even when the aim is only the communication of delight. Here there be *Monsters*, and some different ways of seeing things, and of saying what we see, stories that necessarily acknowledge that we are living in an age that will pass, that remind us that an aesthetic – 19th-century realism – doesn't provide reality any more than 19th-century ideas of nationhood provide the best form of organisation for human life. *Monsters* is all that, and an argument against the reflex notion that pre-enlightenment people were infantile.

Let's please have no more nonsense about 'nonsense'. The future isn't made up of first things first, the things we already agree are useful to us. It doesn't consist of our purposely forgetting to pack the comics and Nintendo so that we can be sure the holiday does the children some real good. We don't all agree about what the world is, and we never did agree. There *were* gods and ghosts and monsters here when we came, and we brought more with us.

GODFREY SWEVEN

Godfrey Sweven is a pseudonym adopted by John Macmillan Brown, Scot, sailor and Oxford graduate, who in 1874 became the first professor of classics and English at the newly established Canterbury College in Christchurch. The future grandfather of James K. Baxter, and an outstanding teacher whose lecture notes were sold throughout New Zealand – according to legend, by unauthorised students with a sharp eye for a salable commodity – Macmillan Brown was a polymath who, in addition to classics and English, taught history and economics. It's easy to see how the utopian/satirical novels of Godfrey Sweven grew out of these broad intellectual interests, together with his love for seafaring and great writing. *Riallaro: The Archipelago of Exiles* (1901) details a restless British sailor's quest for a rumoured island utopia in a mysterious South Pacific archipelago, where every island offers a new – and frequently ridiculous – experiment in government. In *Limanora: The Island of Progress* (1903), our sailor finally reaches his goal.

In order to convey the breadth of *Riallaro*'s satirical invention, we present here two chapters, featuring two very different islands.

Riallaro: The Archipelago of Exiles

Jabberoo

Between it and Awdyoo, but farther to the north than the current was likely to carry us, lay a group of islands that Sneekape declared would have been as good as a play to see. He entertained me with an account of them as we drew away from the odours of Awdyoo. I listened with reserve of judgement; for his story, as usual, sounded like fiction; and I had no means of testing it. It was interesting enough, and drew my mental energy from my nose to my ears. I knew afterwards that there was a good deal of truth at the basis of it, even though the tricky, airy manner made me doubt the whole of it. The nearest of the group to Awdyoo was called Jabberoo, and seemed to be the inferno of talkers. Hither were banished all who had become insufferable for their loquacity. For a time it was said to have been the silentest island in the archipelago, such an effect had the encagement of so many praters in one place upon the disposition of each. They had all been so enamoured of the sound of their own voices that they could not bear to hear anyone else speak; that was the disease for which they had been quarantined, and it looked as if this drastic step of exile was about to be an effectual cure of it. Once the patients from the different islands realised that Jabberoo was nothing but a huge garrulity hospital, they howled with rage and found a certain distraction in airing their grievance to one another. Each tested the listening power of every other inhabitant of the island, and, finding that it was no greater than his own, settled down into sullen taciturnity. Not even the variety of dialects in which they spoke gave them any consolation; the babel only intensified their horror and disgust at being cooped up with men and women as passionately fond of babble as they were. Every talk they started became almost at once a competitive duologue; the two voices rose into a shout that made hearing the words an impossibility. Not one of them could bear to see his neighbour begin to talk; he knew he could not get a word in except by main force of lung, and he dared not risk the torrent of babble. The first few days on land left them hoarse and exhausted; and thereafter they muzzled their passion and went about mute as fish. Mariners and boatmen avoided the shores of the island after a time, for those that landed at first were almost torn to pieces by the Jabberoon mob, each eager to secure a good listener; and even if any arrival had the good fortune to meet only one Jabberoon and be monopolised by him in secret, he was glad to make his escape, lest he should turn into a pillar of salt under the infliction of fluency; the only successful means of flight was to bear the torrent till the darkness of night, slip out of his upper garments which his buttonholer held, and leave in his place a wooden substitute. The sullen silence had been no cure of the disease after all.

A benevolent Swoonarian took pity on the wretched islanders and invented an automatic listener. But, like all the inventions of his people, it came to nothing. In theory it seemed as if it would work. He made a figure in human form with a sensitive word-repeater inside it that at certain sounds could by internal mechanism set it swaying and gesticulating, as if in high nervous excitement. It could be wound up for a whole day, or, in some of the more expensive specimens, even for a whole week. As it heaved and swung about, one would have said that it was a real, human listener moved by the eloquence of a speaker; but the shipment failed. Superior though the automatic audience was to most human beings in responsiveness and emotional endurance, something was wanting; the look of suppressed despair on the face, the irritable attempts at interjection, and the unavailing efforts to escape. The inventor intended, if this venture had succeeded, to add those movements to his figures; but unfortunately the first purchasers lost their tempers over the monotonous acceptance of all they said and the repetition of the gestures and attitudes as they repeated their favourite phrases; they grew frantic with rage and smashed the whole consignment to pieces.

It looked, indeed, at one time as if the community of Jabberoons would go furiously mad for want of good listeners, and commit suicide in a body; but a missionary arrived from a neighbouring island called Tubberythumpia, or the island of demagogues; and though his sufferings often rose to torture at first, he knew from experience in his own land how to endure them. In the end he conquered; he was able to get a word in now and again; and this occasional word won its way by slow degrees into the brains of the Jabberoons and bore fruit. They listened to the gospel of the newcomer once a week or so, and resolved to adopt the new evangel of alternation of eloquence. They organised themselves into councils, assemblies, senates, conferences, synods, mob meetings, boards, election meetings, parliaments, cabinets, conclaves, chambers, convocations, congresses, consistories, diets, juntas, comitias, directories, commissions, sanhedrims, and committees, so that every man and woman was a member of forty or fifty of these bodies and could attend the meetings of two or three dozen of them every day. They adopted it as a basis of their new constitution that only one was to speak at once in any sitting, and, whenever two began to speak together, it was thereby dissolved. It is quite true that there were dissolutions every hour of the day; but some speaker had had his say out, and those who were disappointed in getting an escape-valve for their tongue energy had plenty of other meetings to attend, where they might have a chance of evacuating their own particular section of the dictionary.

The plan was a miraculous success for a time. It saved the Jabberoons from universal frenzy and suicide. Every one of them was able to get off half a dozen eloquent speeches every day to an audience more or less unwilling but that had, by the constitution of the country, to listen; and it was easier for them to keep the mouth shut when they knew that they too would have their chance before long. They worked just enough to keep the wolf from the door; and then all the rest of the time was given up to those delightful meetings and conferences, where each felt that he could make others hear the sweet sound of his voice. They never settled anything of any importance to anybody; but they felt that the existence of the universe depended on their oratory. To satisfy themselves they discussed every possible topic that had occurred or could ever occur to any human mind, and they passed resolutions upon it to send on to other meetings and conferences and assemblies. By the time these resolutions had got through the various bodies and come back to the originators, they had become so transformed as to be unrecognisable, and so bewildering in their labyrinth of clauses and amendments as to be beyond human intelligence; but they were recommitted and recreated and again sent on their career of transformation. They kept the jaws working and the tongues wagging. And every ambiguity introduced served the same national and benign purpose.

With all this development of eloquence and elaboration of counsel, it might have been expected that Jabberoo was the best governed country in the world. Every citizen worked the clack-mill night and day for the good government and guidance of every other citizen. Nothing could surpass the earnestness and enthusiasm of the whole community in pounding out the arguments for and against every possible course that any member or section of it might take in life. They were in danger of starving, so busy were they in deliberation over the questions: how every man should earn his food, how he should cook his food, how he should eat it, and how he should dispose of his surplus. They had not time to drink, so strenuous in their tongue exertions were they over what to drink and what not to drink. They left their children to run naked, and their own clothes to fall into rags, whilst they discussed the best kind of cloth for different weathers and climates, and the best form of garments for various ages, and the best way of wearing garments. No people in the world had ever held so many deliberations and consultations, or ever spent so much eloquence and wisdom over the proper way of bringing up a family; meantime every family was allowed to tumble up in the best way it could, till the momentous questions were settled. Never was there a nation that so strove to get at the highest ideal of government as the Jabberoons did in meeting and conference and assembly; and never was there a nation so devoid of all pure government or even co-operation for their own internal administration or their defence. There was nothing they would not do in their speeches on behalf of their country, so fiery were they in their patriotism; but when a pirate landed with a small boatload of men, there was not a Jabberoon to be seen within shooting distance, and once, when a mad dog was let loose on the beach, the silence and solitude of the island could be felt.

For himself, Sneekape asserted that, if the Jabberoo women were worth a thought, he would land and walk off with the whole of them; but they had such predominant and huge mouths and such pestilential tongues that no ordinary human nature could endure them. Their recent developments under the Tubberythumpian missionary had made their shores safe for strangers to visit; but for his part he would keep at a safe distance from such a nation of magpies. He could not endure the endless chatter of a prating, gossipy woman. He preferred her with a good stormy channel between him and her.

The latest development of their commonweal had again made landing dangerous. Their tongue-courage had grown too mild for the expression of all they felt. Argument and eloquence had given way to vituperation and insult, and their meetings now generally ended in free fights. Scratched noses and cracked crowns had become the natural accompaniment of political fervour.

Spectralia

'As we sailed off, Blastemo entertained us with stories of the groups of islands that lay near at hand, and especially of one that lay away off to the north nearer the sunset than Coxuria and the other islands of religion. It was the place of ghosts, where the supernatural can have things to itself without the intrusion of sceptical worldliness and common-sense. It lies almost within the ring of mist that encircles the archipelago, and it is dominated by twilight when it is not midnight. The inhabitants have an invincible fear and hatred of the sun, and especially the rising sun; and if he ever dares to show his shameless face without a cloud they raise a dust that makes him like the eye of a drunkard. In order to avoid the impudence of his glances, most of them used to live, and one section of them still lives, in cellars underground, sleeping there by day and following their avocations out-of-doors by night. Mariners in that region land fearlessly when the sun shines, but avoid its shores during times of cloud and darkness, lest they should be taken for spirits and bodily enshrined for the purposes of worship. To be retained either as a resident or as an object of investigation or reverence was a fate to be shuddered at, for it was considered one of the worst wards for lunatic exiles. Hither were deported all who were incurably persuaded that they and they alone had direct communication with the other world. There was something uncanny about the conduct of everyone who found his way thither; in his eye shone the gleam of insanity, a reflection from the baleful light of hell.

'Another feature of the island, as of all the theopathic group, was its rank sectarianism. Almost every man was his own sect. There was a rough classification of them by travellers into "antiquated ghost-seers" and "modern ghost-seers", but none would acknowledge allegiance to any classification. They all believed in spirits, or disembodied beings, who visited their island; beyond that, resemblance ceased. Most of the older Spectralians, however, believed only in ghosts of ancient lineage, who had the stately ways of olden times, who seldom condescended to speak or communicate their thoughts, and who looked mutely piteous or minatory on their appearance for a few seconds and then vanished. The more recent exiles, having had a tinge of modern science, laughed at these fantastic monstrosities of a primitive age and insisted on the logical outcome of supernaturalism. Every human being had a ghost, and when death thrust it out of its body it hung about its old locality and tried to make itself manifest, now to one sense, again to another, but most frequently to bearing. It had been a custom of former spirits to address themselves chiefly to the eye; but that was in the silent old times when men preferred striking and acting to speaking. Now that the tongue had become the chief organ of action, it would be obviously absurd for the world of spirits not to adapt itself to the new ways; and so it was now to the ear that they addressed themselves, and seldom to the eye. And, whereas they had been ridiculously limited by ghostly conventions and could appear only in solemn guise at midnight by tombs and in abandoned chambers of castles or in rooms where murder had been done, now they were free to make themselves heard when and where they pleased, or rather when and where their corporeal clients and patrons pleased. There had evidently been a great war of liberation in the region of ghosts, a sort of French Revolution, that had thrown off the shackles of old and absurd convention from their limbs, if such a mode of speech were permissible. Now there was infinite variety in the world of the disembodied as in the world of common things. They all kept shop, as it were, and were ready to serve any who approached them in the due and proper way.

'There was in fact a small section of these modernists who prided themselves on their superior modernity and held that they could take a spirit out of its living body as easily as a pea out of its pod; for, they said, there are really two spirits in every human body, the detachable and the undetachable; the former it is that expatiates, the world over, in dreams and holds communion with worlds whereof the senses know nothing; the other is the workaday spirit that with observation and reason carries out the practical functions of daily life. They plumed themselves upon having thus solved all the problems of existence, that have puzzled mankind so long, by this simple device of two labels or classifications for the contents of the human body or vessel. They were even proud that the rest of the archipelago counted them no less mad than the other Spectralians, whom they scorned; it was the true sign of superiority in mental power, wisdom, and modernity to be called mad by other men.

'They despise the ancient ghost-seers for their old-fashioned ways and the funny old castles and rickety houses they build for their friends and clients from the other world. To think of going to the expense of putting up tumble-down buildings in order to woo spirits into them, a kind of ghost-trap, is to them the most laughable of proceedings; but the old fellows never lose faith in their creaky ghost eelpots, and go about as solemnly as ever they did, making the walls of their castles chinky, the passages draughty, the rooms full of dark corners, and the halls like vaults for the dead. It is amusing to see them loosening the footboards of the corridors and stairs in order that they may creak and start and flap as soon as the shadows fall. They always bang old tapestries and sheets at odd draughty corners to rustle and lift in the blackness of the night; and they put a rooster handy outside of every cobwebby old castle they erect to give the word when their clients should be off. For themselves, they spend most of their nights there. The early part they pass in reading the most ghostly and blood-curdling books they can find in the archipelago and stuff into the dirty old libraries. These are the religious literature and litanies of the ghosts. It is a proper rule in every faith that the worshipper should get his mind into the due receptive and inspired attitude before attempting to approach the shrine; only thus can they see and hear the objects of their worship. Hours do they consume in reading the pious literature of ghosts, and then every nerve is on the alert, and every sense awake for the footfalls of their friends from the other world. The passages begin to creak, the tapestries to flop and rustle, the doors, that they have left ajar for their clients, to slam. They know that the spirits of the mighty dead are then approaching them; their eyes flame out of their heads, and with a gleam like lightning the expected apparition flashes over the line of their vision.

'The modernists smile at these preparations and precautions, and declare that nothing of these manifest themselves, but only the shadow of the watcher himself in some passing starlit or moonlit space. They know that the true modern spirit cares for none of these things; he has been brought up in the midst of the best medical science, and avoids draughty old buildings as bad for colds and rheumatism and full of the microbes of countless diseases; he has advanced with the ages, and asks for nothing better than the simplest modern appliances; he has learned, as a modern should, telegraphy and telepathy, and all he needs is a table to rap on, or a planchette or slate to write on; that is his whole outfit, as becomes an occupant of an immaterial world; he has the electricity in his own system to work the thing, but, if he has got to materialise, he does like the lights turned down, for modern gas and oil lamps are very trying for a poor old spirit's eyes, that have been accustomed to the dim, ethereal spaces. It is all right when he can remain unseen and merely let his mind out in rap language, though that is a rather slow way of communication for beings that move and act as quickly as thought; but to doff his old habits and his invisible form makes a ghost as shy as for a human being to appear naked in broad daylight. It is no wonder that spirits insist that the lights be down when they are asked to appear to the eyes of the initiated. As for the worldly and sceptical, they will never have the privilege of seeing anyone or even hearing anyone from the world of spirits till they abandon their scoffing, faithless ways. Faith is a prime essential of all communion with the immaterial world. The gross senses of the worldling can never see or hear what his more refined neighbours catch from the spirit-sphere. It is only Spectralia that ghosts will ever favour with their countenance. Now and again they appear to men and women of peculiar natures in other islands in order to have them deported to their favourite isle; they are heard of no more after the exile, having followed their clients. But, if those they address lose faith in them and remain with their fellow-countrymen, the ghosts cease to appear to them. Even the modernists acknowledge that spirits have but limited means of communication; they prefer two or three methods and will have no others. A story is told over the archipelago of a Swoonarian inventor who had noticed this and had thought out plans for opening a clear highway into the spirit-world. One was to erect a vacuum tube up through the atmosphere of the earth and to catch the ghosts in gossamer nets at the bottom of it as they were sucked down. Another was to have a megaphone with an enormous mouth stretching above the clouds and its terrestrial end in a vast magnifying hall that would turn the poor ghost whispers into clear, intelligible sounds. A third was to utilise their rapping propensities; he proposed to have a great musical instrument with keys placed in position underneath their favourite tables, where the spirits loved to rap out their answers to questions; a little training would soon develop in them the power of earthly harmony, and, as they struck the keys, the Spectralians would have the most divine ghost music. A modification of this would provide a method for spirits to express applause when they approved of earthly performers and speakers; a series of fans or clapboards were to work round a freely moving axle and to come in contact with the soft, flat surface as they spun round, so that they would produce a sound like the clapping of bands; as the spirits rapped on the keyboard, the vanes whirled round, and the effect of tumultuous applause was produced. Still another modification was intended to use spirit force for human purposes; their rapping power was to be concentrated on engines that would drive mills and looms and the other machines of Spectralian factories. He had a great windmill too that was to be blown round by the breath of spirits; and an automatic spirit reporter that would record whatever was done or said in spirit-land. Another line his inventions took was to provide bodies that would invite wandering souls into them. A third set of inventions was intended to relieve the overpopulation of the Spectralian atmosphere; he was convinced that the region was uncomfortably crowded, because all the ghosts of the archipelago flocked thither, and there were no sanitary arrangements for making ghost life endurable; so he proposed by one of his new machines to take a census of the spirits in and around Spectralia, and then to send his automatic spiritemigration Propaganda amongst them in order to induce large numbers of them to seek other and more wholesome spheres.

'After long years of work on these, he came across a wealthy and enthusiastic Spectralian, whom he convinced of the fortune that lay in his machines. The two shipped the cargo of notions and landed safely in Spectralia. But before they could be put out on the market there was a ghost riot one night; what were the poor spirits to do for a living if all their functions were to be appropriated or concentrated by these vile inventions? Half of them would be thrown out of the employment they had been accustomed to, and how were they to learn all these new-fangled notions? It was too much for ghost nature to bear, and the machinery was smashed to pieces in a single night; and the spirits formed themselves into a trades-union for keeping such agitators and inventors far from the shores of Spectralia; it was said that the Swoonarian and his patron fled before the indignation of the mob of ghosts that pursued them, and the last that was seen of them they were on their knees uttering mad cries of alternate prayer and threat to their unseen tormentors.

'Another story told the adventures of a missionary from Aleofane, who was sent to convert Spectralians to the true faith. After long and enthusiastic labour in preaching and praying he found on examination that he was no further forward than when he landed. The Spectralians were as unconvinced as before; and on inquiry he was told that as long as the spirits were unconverted their clients would adhere to their old faith. So the missionary set himself to the work of converting the ghosts, promising himself that, this done, the whole island would go over to his religion. At first they could not understand a word that he said; and he learned their rap language. Then they refused to listen patiently to his homilies and litanies; he had no sooner called them up and launched into his eloquence than they had dispersed like leaves before a gale. He tried to get at the bottom of this universal reluctance on their part to hear him out, and he discovered that they were a good deal more primitive than savages or children; their education had been completely neglected; they could never tell anybody anything that was not known to everybody before; they indulged in the dreariest platitudes and the most obvious truisms, and they thought that it was more than spirit could bear to hear lengthy sermons on the obvious poured broadside into them. He assumed that his truths were too high for them to understand, and never realised that he was doing nothing more than pouring water into the ocean. It was true that their education had been wretchedly neglected; the most elementary truths of science were unknown to them. He set himself first to their tuition in the use of reason before attempting to convert them again. Alas! his task was an endless one. As with savages, after teaching any simple and primal principle, he found he had to begin teaching it to them over again. He did not weary of his burden; for he knew that he had the great prize before him of converting a whole nation. He grew a white-haired old man before he could get them beyond such elementary truths as two and two are four, and he died at his task, a martyr to the platitudinarianism of spirits.

'We were steaming along under the lee of Spectralia, the night fast lowering upon us, as Blastemo held us spellbound by these stories. A crash and a quiver of the ship cut short his narrative, and we rushed on deck. The engines stopped, and peering over the side in the struggling moonlight we could see one or two dark objects rise and fall on the gleaming wake. We lowered a boat and soon had two dripping figures upon the deck. We anchored and attended to their necessities, and by the morning they had so far recovered as to be able to give an account of themselves.

'They were the superintendents or presidents of the Spectralian ghost markets; so Blastemo interpreted for us. There had been reported to them, as the sun set, a strange appearance on the horizon. It had become too dim for them to make it out by the time they had reached the beach; but as its mass of lights grew in size and brilliancy and a singular throb seemed to come through the air from it, they could form no other conclusion than that it was an influx of emigrants from the more distant regions of spirits. As it approached, they could see it move on the face of the waters, and they knew that it was a ghost ship; for they could perceive dark flights of spirits gleam in its lights and hurry it on as they spun through the night behind it, and they could hear the multitudinous beat of their wings in the air. None but they were officially authorised to welcome ghostly immigrants into the island; it was their duty to meet the spectral fleet before it touched the land, and they rushed for fallas, as they seemed to see it about to pass their island. From a promontory that would most easily intercept it, they swung their paddles towards it; and their hearts were gladdened as they found themselves right across the track it was making. The next they knew was that they were floundering in the water and it had passed them.

They shouted; but, faint as they were, they thought that their cries would make little impression. The elfin ship stopped, however; the throb of the winged host ceased, and they were hoisted by the strange spirits on board.

'We asked them what they wanted to do with the new arrival of ghosts when they got them. The answer came; they would dispose of them in the market of souls. Each division of the people, the antiques and the moderns, had a market of its own, and that was why the two officials rushed, each to his own boat, to secure the cargo of ghosts, and why each ventured into such danger to secure his prize. They did not know for certain whether the new arrivals were spirits of the olden time or modern spirits; but each had good reason to think that they were ghosts of his own special affinity. The man of the dead-soul market was pretty sure that the cargo was for him, for none but ancient spirits would arrive at midnight with such appalling sounds, in such sable robes, and with such flash of lightnings. The president of the living-soul market was as sure that they were for him, for only modern ghosts could arrive in such novel circumstances, and in all the panoply of modern science. It was with difficulty that we could keep the two from blows; they wrangled furiously, and hurled insult and vituperation at each other with manifest effect. At last we had to get them into separate compartments that they might not do each other bodily harm.

'Alone with us, each calmed down into comparative tranquillity, and we were able to get a fair and rational account of the two markets out of the chaos of their mutual misrepresentation. After collating notes of the scene with each, we came to the conclusion that the two markets were at opposite ends of the island, and that they belonged to the two great sects of the people, the antiques and the modernists.

At stated times there were great ghost fairs to which the inhabitants crowded that they might be able to exchange familiars or traffic the spirit that had become too commonplace to them for one that might give them more exquisite shocks of supernatural surprise and alarm.

'The goblin-shop, as the modernist called the market of dead souls, was evidently the place where ghosts of the olden type were bought and sold. It was situated, like the catacombs, underground, and above it lay old graveyards, ancient ruins, castles, chapels, and shrines where the goods traded in might squeak and gibber and disport themselves for the edification of the purchasing public; these dilapidated old cages were a kind of ghost menagerie, or, as the modernist sneered, the goblin kennels; in them the spirits were penned during the ghost fairs, and the intending purchasers wandered round and listened to the whistling, moaning winds through the crevices and tried to get the sensation of being startled by the ghost rustle and speech or by the apparitions that came and went within the dark pens. The traffickers went in twos and threes around, for they dared not trust themselves alone in the presence of these uneasy supernatural beings. Every one of these strange creatures had either committed murder or suicide or been present at such a deed; nor could he ever find rest night or day. It was only in the deepest darkness that he was able to make himself manifest to his clients; as soon as the first streak of dawn touched the horizon he vanished like a dream, and not even the faintest smell of sulphur remained during the day where he had paced by night.

'The antiquist expressed the greatest scorn of the new-fangled rubbish traded off on poor humanity in the demon pigsty, as he usually called the market of living souls. But the modernist waxed eloquent on the miracles wrought by the spirits bought in his institution. His goods were not the frequenters of tombs or mouldy fragments of buildings; they were willing to talk to their clients by the light of day and in the most comfortable surroundings; they were human and humane in every respect; they liked the society of living men and women, especially if these were commonplace and preferred information on topics that had no mystery about them; they delighted in communications on the obvious, and would rather talk to clients who wanted to hear of what they knew already; they did not care for tombs and ghostly surroundings; though, if people insisted on getting a sight of them, they preferred a dim light; they were shy, for they were unable to procure in spirit-land the phantasms of the garments that they had worn upon earth to clothe their nakedness. Still better, they sold in their market many a phantasm of the living which could tell its clients their own thoughts, and communicate facts that they were certain to find out by common observation within a few minutes or hours. They sold dream-stuff that would supply the sleeping client with warnings as to the future so that when the future arrived he would recognise it. In their market they had practitioners who could draw souls like teeth, and, after polishing them clean of diseases, put them back again. They had others, each of whom could send his detachable soul down the throat of a patient like a chimney-sweep, and, after cleaning the system, draw it back again. There was not a disease in man but had its origin in the imagination or detachable soul; and what was the use of medicine or surgery, when all a man had to do in order to be cured was to get this free soul taken out of him and sent to the practitioners in the market or to borrow the free soul of a practitioner for a few hours or days as the case might need? He could go on for years, if we liked, telling us the miracles and wonders done by their spirit-therapeutics in their market of living souls. No less marvellous was the consolation afforded to the bereaved when they were able to come and converse with the souls of the departed. For a small fee they could call up any spirit they pleased, and get it to write on slates or give in rap language answers to any questions they might ask, provided the questions did not touch on its actual state or destiny and related to facts well known to all present. The spirits they dealt in would give no satisfaction to the profanely curious or impertinent.

'We suggested that most of these phenomena could be explained by natural causes; and in each case the Spectralian broke into rage at the suggestion, and when he had calmed down told us of the fate of a missionary from Figlefia, who had come to convert them to naturalism. They found that he addressed himself especially to the women, and most of all to the goodlooking women; but when he began to smile at their creed and covertly sneer at it and attack it the women waited for a dark night, and, aided by the spirits of their dead ancestors, they spoiled his smirking beauty for him and gave him such a scare that in his madness and terror he ran into the waves and drowned himself. Each of them pointed out to us a rocky islet off the coast, and told us the story of it, evidently as a warning to us against our unseemly unbelief. It was called Astralia, and contained a miserable sect that had attempted to explain all the phenomena of their markets by the swarming-off of astral bodies like invisible hoops from them. They also professed to have found a new means of consulting the souls of distant wise men; they could write their questions on any slip of common paper and put it in a cupboard, and down from the ceiling would flutter the answer, which was so unintelligibly wise as to puzzle men for years. These poor creatures were at once exiled and were dying of starvation; for, though they were eager for material food, they professed to subsist on nothing but spiritual sustenance, and were wasting away in this pretended astral-exhalation process.

'After the two rivals had been put on shore and we were steaming off on our course, two packets were found in the bunks they had occupied. Moist and limp, they were dried; and when opened they were found to contain placards and advertisements of the goods to be traded off in their respective markets at the next great ghost-fair. Blastemo translated a few for us, both from the dead-soul packet and from the live-soul packet: "For sale, the ghost of a knight walled up in the bastion of an old castle four hundred years ago; warranted to walk in armour every stormy night that has not too much moon, and to produce the most appalling clank as he moves along the corridors or through the locked doors." "For immediate sale on the lowest terms, a genuine old-fashioned spirit, that cannot bear the crowing of a cock or the least streak of light on the horizon; supposed to be the perpetrator of a mysterious murder that took place some centuries ago; the sound of gnashing teeth and of the drawing of swords is distinctly heard as he paces along, and the echo of a loud sigh as he vanishes. The owner is clearing out of his present premises, because his physicians have recommended him a more bracing alpine climate that is quite unsuited to his family ghost." "To be sold by auction without reserve, one of the finest collections of antique spirits ever made in this island; they belong to a splendid ruin in one of the most picturesque and dismal localities of the country; every one of them has either perpetrated a murder or been the victim of cruel assassination; the rooms to which they are confined have the marks of bloody footsteps all over them, and, where these are dim, they can be easily renewed at small expense; one of them is headless and carries in his arms something that has been identified by the best experts as a head; another bears the form of a young girl, all covered with blood, the supposed victim, and vanishes with a heart-breaking sigh. The late owner died childless, and has joined his own collection of midnight walkers. The heirs live in a distant part of the island in a castle already well provided with spirits, and are willing to treat with intending purchasers on easy terms extending over a number of years. Cards of midnight inspection to be obtained from the auctioneer in the market." "Wanted, for a dilapidated mansion newly built, a ghost of harmless propensities but awe-striking habits. He must be at least three centuries old, and have all the favourite traits of blood-curdling apparitions. No upstarts of recent introduction need apply."

'The live-soul-market advertisements were as definite in their terms; the few that Blastemo translated were these: "For sale, the spirit of a wise man just deceased, accustomed to daylight seances, and highly trained in rap language and slate-writing. He would be a valuable adjunct to a household that has no library, or one that from want of education or eyepower is unable to consult a library. His knowledge is encyclopedic, although his powers of observation are limited. The daily intercourse with his spirit would be an education in itself. His children and heirs have no further need of his instructions." "Offered for sale, the spirit of a successful thought-therapeutist, who when alive could cure any disease without the intervention of any material medium or medicine or even the proximity of the patient. He had simply to think the disease away, and it was gone. His spirit, now being free of all bodily trammels, is even more potent than before. In fact, it is more than likely that the possessor of it will secure immunity from all sickness, if not from death itself. It would be a perfect mine of wealth for a medical practitioner. Terms easy." "Wanted, to hire out for short periods, the detachable spirit of a great sage who lives in a distant part of the world; well accustomed to sending occult answers to occult messages, and to all the recognised methods of occult communication and intercourse; would be especially suited for the entertainment and instruction of select companies in the evening; terms on application; a reduction for a series of parties or entertainments." "To sell by auction at the great fair, a famous troupe of table-tipping spirits, the finest collection ever offered to the community. Have been employed in drawing-room entertainments. Might be utilised in large hotels or mansions in removing large tables from room to room, or in large factories instead of elevators." "Wanted, immediately, for a bed-rid invalid, a spirit companion, who can enter into all his tastes and humour all his fancies, converse with him without irritability or caprice, and materialise in the cold hours of the night and dematerialise when the patient is too hot. A high salary for a thoroughly competent spirit." "Wanted, by a genius, a spirit-amanuensis, who could inspire his hand when it lags on the paper, and fire his imagination at all times. One accustomed to dream suggestion preferred. No eccentrics need apply." "To be auctioned without reserve, the finest collection of detachable spirits that this island has ever seen. For Spectralians who wish to study human nature in all its variety this affords a grand opportunity of acquiring specimens of every kind and type of spirit. A guarantee given with every individual sold that he will stand by the purchaser for any fixed period agreed on and allow him to look microscopically into his inner mechanism." "Wanted, for a small and unhealthy country village, a thought-therapeutic, who could, if he wished, reside at a distance and project his spirit whenever a patient needed his power. One who has had much practice in hysterics and hypochondria, the prevailing diseases of the village, preferred."

'Whether it was from inadvertence or design that our Spectralians left their packets we were unable to discover. We counted them of so little value that we never thought of putting ourselves to any trouble to send them after their owners. Besides, we inclined to the belief that they had been abandoned on board deliberately and for missionary purposes. The twinkle in Blastemo's eye as he read them seemed to us to imply that this was not the first time he had had the experience; that, in fact, it was a policy of the Spectralians to litter the archipelago with their placards and advertisements. At any rate, we took no trouble to return them; they were, on the contrary, used for menial purposes that did not fulfil their high mission.'

ANON

The Great Romance (1881) was published – in either two or three short volumes; only single copies of the first two have to date been found – under the name 'The Inhabitant', a title commonly assumed in the late nineteenth century by authors of guidebooks. We have no direct evidence of authorship, but in 1882 the Christchurch *Star* commented, under the headline AN ASHBURTON AUTHOR, 'Mr Henry Honor, a gentleman resident in Ashburton, has at present in the Press a work of imagination entitled "The Great Romance: by the Inhabitant." The tale is an account of a perilous voyage amongst the stellar worlds, the voyageurs being three men, and their vessel a sort of half-and-half craft called the "Star Climber." The first "volume," a booklet of 55 octavo pages has been issued. It has suffered a good deal at the hands of the printer, whose work is decidedly not productive of a thing of beauty.'

We know nothing further about Henry Honor, gentleman resident of Ashburton, though the Ashburton electoral roll for 1881–82 lists a 'Henry Honour, farmer'. Whether any version of *The Great Romance* could have been described as a thing of beauty is debatable – an 1882 review in the *Otago Daily Times* laments that 'It is full of crudities of style and matter which lay it open to criticism on almost every page' – but it offers several points of historical interest. In *The Encyclopedia of Science Fiction*, John Clute suggests that it 'may be the first sf text to convey its protagonist into the future via Suspended Animation'. Dominic Alessio, in the introduction to his valuable edition of 2008, sees the work's account of a voyage to a wild and beautiful Venus as a coded encouragement to potential British migrants, adding, 'The emphasis on friendly aliens may even be part of a booster strategy intended to assure European readers concerned about rebellious Maori in the post-1860s New Zealand wars climate.'

We excerpt here the description of an aerobraking manouvre on the *Star Climber*'s arrival in Venus orbit, which we believe to be the first account of this now-standard spaceflight technique in world literature.

The Great Romance

We were old travellers. We knew the heavenly way; we had e'er this left the attraction of our native orb; we had seen with wondering eyes another world growing out and becoming immense before us, till it suddenly filled the whole horizon. We had heard the sharp sounds of the first thin air as we rushed through it, but that experience did not quiet our beating hearts, as we eagerly watched for the critical moment, when we must check that headlong plunge which our vessel would appear to make as the huge force of gravity again enfolded us.

We were fully conscious of, yet not able to realise, the intense speed of our vessel. The pace at which we left the earth might be roughly estimated at twenty miles per second, not that we moved at that enormous speed in the earth, but we entered space, not only with our proper motion, but with that of the world we left added – viz., that mighty speed which annually brings winter and summer, and carries the earth and all its inhabitants some six hundred millions of miles in the year, and its smaller, yet not despicable diurnal motion, which might be roughly estimated at a thousand miles per hour. Of both these motions we were enabled by the course we chose to take the largest possible advantage. Thus we were not laggards, even by comparison, with the giant orbs we were among. Then our adventure in the Magellan Cloud had superadded to that enormous speed another speed which we computed to be equal to a third of that already attained.

We could not, as I said, realise this intense velocity so far beyond any terrestrial speed – even that of the ball as it leaves the cannon's mouth. Yet the knowledge of it made us doubly watchful to catch the first sign of an atmosphere, for should we continue this course uninterrupted – like a comet or falling star – we should blaze up, and either drop on the new world a blot of molten steel, or be whirled away, blasted and burnt up on a wild comet-like track – to form, perchance, a study for some latter day Venusian astronomer, as our erratic orbit brought us again and again within his ken.

When journeying between the earth and moon none of this fierce speed troubled us, the distance in itself so small (but two hours' journey at our present pace), and the fact that the speed of the moon in its orbit is the same as that of the earth's diurnal motion had greatly helped us.

This new world, too, possessed a moon, but not such a one as accompanied the earth – smaller, held by a shorter chain, and moving across the diurnal motion of the planet, while its speed was very large; it would form a curious study to a gazer on the surface of the new world.

We resolved, however, to make, if possible, some use of it, for we dreaded the many clays which we should need to consume ere we could sufficiently check our headlong career, to venture into the denser air of Venus.

By creating for ourselves a temporary orbit – which should at first graze, as it were, the exterior of both orbs (viz. – Venus and its attendant moon) and afterwards gradually lessen till it was altogether included in the atmosphere of the planet – we reckoned to bring all the powers of gravitation into play, and make of them a more effectual brake than could be obtained in any other way.

Also, by bringing our course into the same plane as that of the moon, we should be able to examine it as we passed over and by it. Indeed, we reckoned that the completion of the second circle of this orbit would bring down our speed to that of the lesser orb.

But all this while we were swiftly nearing our destination; the great globe of Venus, in apparent size far beyond that of the earthly moon, now began to grow fast upon us.

It came – that wished-for sound, like the noise of far-off wings, or the whisper of a zephyr; but thus only for a while, like a nearing cataract or coming storm it grew upon us.

Then the mighty wings of our vessel began to play, beating swiftly the thickening air, and driving us fast upward again into space, but not before a great glow of heat pervaded all the ship, growing every moment stronger, though we had now left the thicker air. 'Start the cold air machine,' said Moxton, 'or there will be no end to this business.' This soon assisted us, though the heat gathered by the steel exterior of our vessel still continued to strike inward. We were again in the depths of space, borne by our own velocity, with nothing to retard, nothing to guide us. Weir, who was on the look-out, already beginning to abuse the Venusian moon, when we caught sight of it. Beautiful indeed had Moxton calculated our course; we could see it like a huge ball spinning in the shadow of the planet away before us. Our course would take us very near it; we were, perhaps, two hours ere we came to it. Then there came a sudden roar, a huge swerve of our vessel, as under its influence we shot in again to the planet. Again we repeated the experiment, although I now had the command, and Moxton in the look-out. 'Keep her in it,' they both said, and we dipped down so close as well nigh to touch the feathery clouds; this was enough for us all; the heat we subsisted in for the next hour would have fairly cooked any dead substance. But as we got clear again and began to cool, we saw what an immense part of our speed we had lost, we were well satisfied with the effects of our purgatorial discipline. Now, although we were sailing in a smaller circuit, we almost failed to catch again the moon.

We seemed to creep on the little satellite but inch by inch. At last, however, we drew near, helped on by its attraction as we approached it. So small was it that when it looked like *terra firma* we could observe its rotundity. We seemed to be floating, floating towards it on our back. It seemed at one time as though we should have to use our explosives to prevent our vessel being cast on her back on this airless little orb – an accident we certainly had never calculated on.

But at last we caught the welcome sound; then she heeled over, and we floated silently down on to a smooth sandy plain.

We took in a specimen of the air. It was thin and poor; scarcely sufficient to sustain the lowest forms of life, and the orb itself looked cold, dry, bare, and grey, a few meagre lichens being the only visible living things.

We prepared to strike off again, for there, hanging above us, as though it might suddenly fall and crush us into oblivion, hung the great planet, half in sunshine, half in shadow, covering a third of the sky, hanging right over our heads its clouds and waters, mountains and forests, spread out in wonderful state above us.

We would not lose time on this useless orb, so alike that it might have served as a prototype for the attendant of our own earth. We were growing familiar with new spheres, and our familiarity was working to its proverbial end.

We thought far more of our vessel than of the orb when, like a living creature, she reared herself as a tower on the plain. But, as we wished to lose as much of the speed of this satellite as we could, we pointed her back towards the way she came; then gathering her power, and throwing it into a sudden and continued motion of her wings, and, opening the thunder of her artillery, she sprang away, and rushed upwards to the larger world.

For a little while we could see our rushing speed; then the little moon seemed to be leaving us, and we to be hanging out in space.

For hours we were thus, and well pleased to be so, as the passing time told plainly of the speed parted with. The planet now beneath us – for the instinct of gravity soon changed as we left the moon – was in its revolutions, bringing another face to our view, and we only needed that, as we extended the air again, we should bring our course into unison with the planet's diurnal motion, to reduce our speed to an earthly measure.

Once more it came – the rush of air growing to a thunderous roar; and we must steer upwards and outwards, but not afar. Still, though the seas and mountains fled away beneath us, we were able to keep within the higher atmosphere, and ever and anon to take a clip into the region of the clouds.

We were weary with watching and waiting – tired, yet determined to endure to the end of our journey ere we slept. The gallant speed and the great plunging clips which our vessel made grew monotonous to us. Below us lay a sea – well nigh an ocean. Moxton took from our stores a large electric ball, which could be discharged from a cannon and would burn with an intense light for some time afterwards. He pointed it straight down and discharged it into the ocean beneath us; we saw it strike the water and plough through the blue depths for a mile or more, then lay like a drowned sun beneath us.

'That will do,' said Moxton. 'Shall I take the helm?'

It was given him, and under his hands the vessel made a short turn, then with her wings set to catch the air she rushed downwards. It was a terrific plunge – perhaps seven miles as we came, but we knew our strength. How beautifully our wings closed in ere we touched the blue element. A heavy blow, a prolonged hiss and we were careering beneath the waves, but well did the elastic liquid do its work. Under the facile hand of Moxton, the *Star Climber* was already returning on her own tracks, coming nearer the dimly lit surface and circling around in a comparatively small space.

'That will do,' we said to Moxton, and almost at once, like a denizen of the deep, the *Star Climber* clove the surface of the water.

We looked out, and indeed our journey was ended – *we were floating on a calm sea*, with a great sun casting its long sloping rays upon us, a blue sky above us, and away a mile on the right was seen the cloud of steam our entrance into the water had raised. Moxton stepped to our outer cabin, closed the door – we waited while we heard the withdrawal of the air-tight plugs, then his voice sang out – 'All right,' and Weir's hand, which had been resting on the levers, gave the motion. Our ceilings and roof, which had seemed so solid for the last four months, began to lift and throw themselves back, till we stood out on the deck – fell in the free air – a slight breeze sweeping over us, and a slight swell rising and falling along the sides of our vessel.

JANET FRAME

Janet Frame ONZ CBE (1924–2004) was one of the greatest New Zealand writers of the 20th century, and was the author of many novels, as well as collections of short stories and poetry, and a three-volume autobiography. Her 1970 novel, *Intensive Care*, is her most obviously speculative work, with its vision of a nightmare world in the aftermath of a third world war. This story, 'Two Sheep', is a parable, a dark comedy, and lethally sad.

Two Sheep

Two sheep were travelling to the saleyards. The first sheep knew that after they had been sold their destination was the slaughterhouse at the freezing works. The second sheep did not know of their fate. They were being driven with the rest of the flock along a hot dusty valley road where the surrounding hills leaned in a sun-scorched wilderness of rock, tussock and old rabbit warrens. They moved slowly, for the drover in his trap was in no hurry, and had even taken one of the dogs to sit beside him while the other scrambled from side to side of the flock, guiding them.

'I think,' said the first sheep who was aware of their approaching death, 'that the sun has never shone so warm on my fleece, nor, from what I see with my small sheep's eye, has the sky seemed so flawless, without seams or tucks or cracks or blemishes.'

'You are crazy,' said the second sheep who did not know of their approaching death. 'The sun is warm, yes, but how hot and dusty and heavy my wool feels! It is a burden to go trotting along this oven shelf. It seems our journey will never end.'

'How fresh and juicy the grass appears on the hill!' the first sheep exclaimed. 'And not a hawk in the sky!'

'I think,' replied the second sheep, 'that something has blinded you. Just look up in the sky and see those three hawks waiting to swoop and attack us!'

They trotted on further through the valley road. Now and again the second sheep stumbled.

'I feel so tired,' he said. 'I wonder how much longer we must walk on and on through this hot dusty valley?'

But the first sheep walked nimbly and his wool felt light upon him as if he had just been shorn. He could have gambolled like a lamb in August.

'I still think,' he said, 'that today is the most wonderful day I have known. I do not feel that the road is hot and dusty. I do not notice the stones and grit that you complain of. To me the hills have never seemed so green and enticing, the sun has never seemed so warm and comforting. I believe that I could walk through this valley forever, and never feel tired or hungry or thirsty.'

'Whatever has come over you?' the second sheep asked crossly. 'Here we are, trotting along hour after hour, and soon we shall stand in our pens in the saleyards while the sun leans over us with its branding irons and our overcoats are such a burden that they drag us to the floor of our pen where we are almost trampled to death by the so dainty feet of our fellow sheep. A fine life that is. It would not surprise me if after we are sold we are taken in trucks to the freezing works and killed in cold blood. But,' he added, comforting himself, 'that is not likely to happen. Oh no, that could never happen! I have it on authority that even when they are trampled by their fellows, sheep do not die. The tales we hear from time to time are but malicious rumours, and those vivid dreams which strike us in the night as we sleep on the sheltered hills, they are but illusions. Do you not agree?' he asked the first sheep.

They were turning now from the valley road, and the saleyards were in sight, while drawn up in the siding on the rusty railway lines, the red trucks stood waiting, spattered inside with sheep and cattle dirt and with white chalk marks, in cipher, on the outside. And still the first sheep did not reveal to his companion that they were being driven to certain death.

When they were jostled inside their pen the first sheep gave an exclamation of delight.

'What a pleasant little house they have let to us! I have never seen such smart red-painted bars, and such four-square corners. And look at the elegant stairway which we will climb to enter those red caravans for our seaside holiday!'

'You make me tired,' the second sheep said. 'We are standing inside a dirty pen, nothing more, and I cannot move my feet in their nicely polished black shoes but I tread upon the dirt left by sheep which have been imprisoned here before us. In fact I have never been so badly treated in all my life!' And the second sheep began to cry. Just then, a kind elderly sheep jostled through the flock and began to comfort him.

'You have been frightening your companion, I suppose,' she said angrily to the first sheep. 'You have been telling horrible tales of our fate. Some sheep never know when to keep things to themselves. There was no need to tell your companion the truth, that we are being led to certain death!'

But the first sheep did not answer. He was thinking that the sun had never blessed him with so much warmth, that no crowded pen had ever seemed so comfortable and luxurious. Then suddenly he was taken by surprise and hustled out a little gate and up the ramp into the waiting truck, and suddenly too the sun shone in its true colours, battering him about the head with gigantic burning bars, while the hawks congregated above, sizzling the sky with their wings, and a pall of dust clung to the barren used-up hills, and everywhere was commotion, pushing, struggling, bleating, trampling.

'This must be death,' he thought, and he began to struggle and cry out.

The second sheep, having at last learned that he would meet his fate at the freezing works, stood unperturbed now in the truck with his nose against the wall and his eyes looking through the slits.

'You are right,' he said to the first sheep. 'The hill has never seemed so green, the sun has never been warmer, and this truck with its neat red walls is a mansion where I would happily spend the rest of my days.'

But the first sheep did not answer. He had seen the approach of death. He could hide from it no longer. He had given up the struggle and was lying exhausted in a corner of the truck. And when the truck arrived at its destination, the freezing works, the man whose duty it was to unload the sheep noticed the first lying so still in the corner that he believed it was dead.

'We can't have dead sheep,' he said. 'How can you kill a dead sheep?'

So he heaved the first sheep out of the door of the truck onto the rusty railway line.

'I'll move it away later,' he said to himself. 'Meanwhile here goes with this lot.'

And while he was so busy moving the flock, the first sheep, recovering, sprang up and trotted away along the line, out the gate of the freezing works, up the road, along another road, until he saw a flock being driven before him.

'I will join the flock,' he said. 'No one will notice, and I shall be safe.'

While the drover was not looking, the first sheep hurried in among the flock and was soon trotting along with them until they came to a hot dusty road through a valley where the hills leaned in a sun-scorched wilderness of rock, tussock, and old rabbit warrens.

By now he was feeling very tired. He spoke for the first time to his new companions.

'What a hot dusty road,' he said. 'How uncomfortable the heat is, and the sun seems to be striking me for its own burning purposes.'

The sheep walking beside him looked surprised.

'It is a wonderful day,' he exclaimed. 'The sun is warmer than I have ever known it, the hills glow green with luscious grass, and there is not a hawk in the sky to threaten us!'

'You mean,' the first sheep replied slyly, 'that you are on your way to the saleyards, and then to the freezing works to be killed.'

The other sheep gave a bleat of surprise.

'How did you guess?' he asked.

'Oh,' said the first sheep wisely, 'I know the code. And because I know the code I shall go around in circles all my life, not knowing whether to think that the hills are bare or whether they are green, whether the hawks are scarce or plentiful, whether the sun is friend or foe. For the rest of my life I shall not speak another word. I shall trot along the hot dusty valleys where the hills are both barren and lush with spring grass.

'What shall I do but keep silent?'

And so it happened, and over and over again the first sheep escaped death, and rejoined the flock of sheep who were travelling to the freezing works. He is still alive today. If you notice him in a flock, being driven along a hot dusty road, you will be able to distinguish him by his timidity, his uncertainty, the frenzied expression in his eyes when he tries, in his condemned silence, to discover whether the sky is at last free from hawks, or whether they circle in twos and threes above him, waiting to kill him.

MAURICE GEE

Maurice Gee has written more than thirty books for adults and young adults and has won numerous literary awards, including the UK's James Tait Black Memorial Prize for Fiction, the Deutz Medal for Fiction, and a Prime Minister's Award for Literary Achievement. Maurice Gee's much-loved children's novels include *Under the Mountain*, the O Trilogy and the Salt Trilogy, all atmospheric and inventive works of fantasy – books for young people that are page turners, and also clear-eyed and serious.

We were spoiled for choice when it came to Maurice's YA novels, but settled on the opening chapters of *The Halfmen of O* because of their loving depiction of the Aorere River at Salisbury Creek.

The Halfmen of O

The Message

Our story begins on Lodestone Creek one summer holiday. At least, Nick's part in it starts there. Susan had been involved for the whole of her life, though she did not know it. And Jimmy Jaspers, with his nose for an easy dollar, had been working for the Halfies since he came to the creek in spring. They found him when he started fossicking round the gorge. But he had only glimpsed their world, and though he thought he had the Halfies sized up, and knew they were tough as old boots, he didn't have a glimmer of their real nature. He thought he would be more than a match for them. As Brand was to say, Jimmy did not really understand evil.

But to get back to Lodestone Creek. It ran down out of the bush through the Ferris farm and joined the river at Devil's Elbow. Some early miner had given the place that name. He must have been down on his luck. There was nothing sinister about the bend, and the farm enclosed in it was a lively place – mooing cows, gobbling turkeys, that sort of thing. It lay south of Collingwood in Golden Bay, in one of the lonelier corners of New Zealand.

Susan Ferris had lived there all her life. Nicholas Quinn, her cousin, came with his parents for a couple of weeks each January. He lived in Auckland, far away. Nick and Susan pretended that they got on pretty well. It kept the grown-ups happy. In fact, Susan found Nick's boastfulness hard to take. He seemed to think that people who lived in cities were the only ones who knew anything. Five minutes with him was enough. Then she had to get off on her own. So he accused her of being stuck-up. He thought she was weird as well. He was not alone in that. His mother, Susan's aunt, declared her strange, and his father had been heard to say that she needed a swift kick in the rear end to wake her up. Nick agreed with that.

This year – the year of our story – she seemed worse. Nick and his mother and father had driven down the length of the North Island. They had crossed the strait on the ferry – rolling in ten-foot waves – and driven through the Rai Valley and Nelson and over the Tākaka Hill and through Golden Bay. They reached the farm on the bend of the river, and it seemed to Nick they had been weeks on the road. But when he found Susan by the waterfall on Lodestone Creek all she could say was, 'Oh, it's you.' She went on staring into the water.

He was mortified. She didn't have to pretend to like him but she might say hello. A year ago he would have pushed her in. Today he just got in his togs and dived in the pool, straight into whatever it was she was staring at in there. He felt he was making a sharp comeback. But when he came up from his dive she was walking down to the river – strolling away, careless, quite remote, and he realised he hadn't hurt her at all, she hadn't even noticed.

'You keep out of my way and I'll keep out of yours,' he yelled. She made no sign of having heard, but kept on walking neatly over the boulders, her blue towel trailing from her hand, and soon she went out of sight towards the Elbow.

'That got rid of her,' Nick said. But he was disappointed. He'd hoped they might be better friends this year. It was time they stopped carrying on like a couple of kids.

Soon he forgot her. He stood under the waterfall and felt it beat on him like hammers. It seemed to be trying to nail him into the rocks. When he'd had enough of that he climbed to the top of the fall – taking care, making sure of each grip. It was a long way down. But heights didn't scare him. Rock climbing was a sport he meant to take up when he was older. He sunbathed on a warm stone ledge at the top, with water running by so clear that it magnified the pebbles. This stream flowing into the Aorere River was his favourite place in all the world. He saw it for only a couple of weeks each summer, but it was more real to him than the quarter-acre section he lived on in Mt Eden. Sometimes he lay in bed at night and travelled up it in his mind, from the waterfall to the place where the gorge closed in like a pair of grey stone hands making a steeple. This year he meant to try panning for gold. The creek had been worked over pretty thoroughly in the old days, but it was worth a try. Prospectors came there still. It wasn't called Lodestone Creek for nothing.

Nick was one of those people who could not keep still. He spent five minutes lying in the sun and then he was up to have a look at the gorge. One day he meant to go through and see what was on the other side. Susan's father had said to stay out of it; there were deep holes and falls of rock, and, he said, giant eels that would take your foot off with a single bite, but he grinned when he said it and Nick knew he was only having him on. Susan had said there was an old gold mine on the other side. She had been into the shaft a little way, but the timber holding up the roof was rotten and it was dangerous to go far. She seemed to be warning him, but he took it as a challenge. If she could go in it would be easy for him. One day soon he was going to try.

He ran along rocky shelves sloping to the water. It was a game with him to travel up the creek without getting his feet wet. It meant making long jumps, and stepping on boulders that tipped under you, and crawling along stone walls like a fly. He made it easily that day, probably because he was a year older. Soon the noise of the waterfall faded. He stopped. Far away cattle were mooing. It was getting on for milking time. A dog barked. Insects sang. But there was another sound. It was like a motor – like a chainsaw or mower, very distant. Then he noticed that instead of being clear as glass the water had taken on a brown cloudiness. Someone or something up ahead was stirring it up. He went on curiously. The noise became louder; and soon there was no mistaking it: the noise of a two-stroke engine. It came racketing down Lodestone Creek, bouncing off the rock walls, slamming here and there, until Nick thought the top would come off his head. Already he'd guessed what it was: some sort of homemade suction dredge.

He came round the corner and saw it – the motor from a Morrison mower floating on a raft no bigger than the top of a school desk. It made such a hideous noise in the stream bed that everything, the trees, the boulders, seemed to vibrate and be on the point of falling apart. Nick yelled out but could not hear his voice. This wasn't gold prospecting, he thought, this was like being in the middle of Queen Street.

An old man was wading in the stream, bent almost double, sweeping the bottom with a gadget like a vacuum cleaner. He was wearing boots and thick trousers, held up by a knotted piece of twine. He had no shirt but a woollen singlet that might once have been pink. Nick came up on him, jumping along the boulders.

'Gidday,' he yelled. The old man did not hear. Nick came round and looked at him side on. He was an ugly old man: a big rough nose, coloured with veins, a drooping lower lip, all wet with spit and yellow with tobacco, and loose skin under his chin, like a turkey's wattles. Nick didn't mind. He seemed like a real prospector, one of those old blokes with a pack and shovel who'd worked the rivers in the old days.

'You finding any gold?' he yelled.

The old man saw him. He swung round eyes of a reddish colour and pinned Nick on them. Then he ploughed back to his motor and switched it off. A sudden dreadful absence of noise came on Lodestone Creek. It seemed to make Nick dizzy. He couldn't move. The old man came at him, churning up water with his boots.

'You been spyin' on me?' He put out a hand large as a dinner plate, tough and brown as boot-leather, and held Nick by his jaw. 'Let's 'ave a look at yer, sonny.' He forced him up against a boulder. Nick tried to cry out but could make no sound. The old man's fingers dug into his cheeks. Breath fell on his face, heavy and wet. It had the stink of carbide and tobacco.

'Yeah,' growled the old man, 'you got 'er face. How's that, eh? Yer better tell me sonny, else I'll bash yer.'

He's mad, Nick thought. His eyes were watering and he tasted blood in his mouth. He tried to break away. The old man let his face go and gripped him by his arms. His fingers dug in like clamps.

'Fire away, sonny boy.'

'What –?' Nick said. He swallowed. 'What do you want to know?'

'How come you got 'er face?'

'Who?'

'That girl with the yeller hair.'

'Susan? You mean Susan?'

'Dunno 'er name. I seen 'er though. She's the one. Looks like you, she does.'

Nick held his head as far back as he could, trying to get away from that dreadful breath. 'She's my cousin,' he managed to get out.

'Ahh. That's it, eh? Cousins, eh? Listen younker, I'm gunner let yer go, but don't yer try an' run, see? I can move. I can catch yer any day.'

Nick believed him. 'What do you want?' he said, almost crying. Something terrible was happening, but he could not tell what it was. The old man let him go.

'Yer can take 'er a message, see. And don't yer tell anyone. No one but 'er.'

'All right,' Nick said. All he wanted was to get away. The old man gave a growl. He stepped back, keeping his eyes on Nick. 'Stan' still.' He bent down and fished in the water with his hand. In a moment he came up with a flat pebble. He took a clasp knife from his pocket and opened a blade. 'Keep still, sonny. I can chuck this thing.' He began to scratch the pebble.

Nick swallowed. He ran his tongue over the bruised insides of his cheeks. He massaged his arms. The old man gave a grin. 'Didn' mean to hurt yer, younker. Get this message to 'er an' I'll give yer some of me gold.'

'I don't want it,' Nick said.

'Suit yerself. 'Ere now, yer take this. Yer give it ter that girlie. Not when anyone's round, mind. Else I'll come fer yer. I'll do yer in.'

Nick took the pebble. He did not look at it. 'Can I go now?'

'Yer can go. Pansy sort of kid, ain't yer? I reckon that girl's got more fight. Not that it'll do 'er any good. Get goin' before I bash yer.' He raised his arm and made as if to strike Nick's face back-handed.

Nick ducked. He ran. His head was dizzy, almost as if he had been struck. He heard the old man laughing, but did not turn back. Instead of going down the creek he climbed through the scrub into a paddock and started across it to the swing-bridge over the river. His towel and clothes were at the waterfall, but never mind that. All he wanted was to get to the house and tell someone, get the police down to arrest the old man. Tears ran down his face. He felt he had been close to something evil.

As he ran he heard the motor start. It sounded flat and deadly. But at least it meant the old man wasn't after him. He slowed down and became aware of the pebble in his hand. He raised his arm to send it flying, then realised it was evidence, it was proof the old man was mad. He looked at it. The message stood out white on the grey stone. He stared at it without understanding. It was no word but some sort of diagram. He turned it upside down but it made no more sense that way. It was a rough circle with a curve like an S running through it. Somehow it frightened him. He ran again, threading his way through patches of blackberry. The sound of the motor died away. The sun was sinking over the mountains. The thought of running home through shadows filled Nick with dread. He went between the concrete blocks and steel wires anchoring the swing bridge. Then he stopped.

Susan was on the bridge. She was leaning on the rail halfway across, with her blue towel draped about her neck, staring in her dreamy way down into the depths, past the granite boulders large as houses, to where the water turned its deepest green.

Nick went on again. The bridge began to bounce. She gave a start and turned to watch him coming. 'Nick,' she said, when he got close. He made no answer, tried to push by her. But she said, 'Nick, I'm sorry. I didn't mean to be rude. It's nice you've come.'

'Yeah,' Nick said.

'Nick –' She looked at him closely. 'What's the matter? How did you hurt your face?'

'Didn't hurt it.'

'You've got bruises.'

He felt his face where the old man had dug his fingers in. He shook his head. 'Some old loony up there.'

'Where? Did he hit you?'

'Lodestone Creek. He reckoned he was giving me a message.'

'What message? Who for?'

'He was off his rocker. He had a knife. I'm going to the police.'

'What message, Nick? Please. Was it for me?'

'Why should it be?' But he was alarmed at the change in her. Under its summer tan her face had gone white as paper. The deep green of the river showed in her eyes.

'Give it to me, Nick.'

Reluctantly he held the pebble out. 'It doesn't make sense. And I want it back. It's evidence.'

She took the pebble, held it lightly in her finger and thumb, like a skimmer. She turned it slowly round, looking at it. A tiny secret smile came on her mouth.

'What was he like? The man who gave it to you?'

'A nutcase,' Nick said. 'And he ponged. He's got away from some loony bin, I reckon.'

She did not seem to hear. 'Did he have . . . No, it doesn't matter.'

'He had bad breath. Give me that. I want it for the police.'

'No, it's mine. He said it was for me.'

'He damn near broke my jaw,' Nick said. 'And he reckoned he'd chuck his knife at me.'

Her face became uncertain. She bit her lower lip. 'He's kind.'

'Have you ever seen him? He reckoned he'd come after me and murder me.'

'No. He must be pretending. Don't tell anyone. Please.'

'You're as mad as he is.'

'I've been waiting for this message all my life. Nick, I've got to see him. Let me have one day. Let me have tomorrow. Then you can tell who you like.'

'I'm not letting you go up there.'

'There's no danger.'

'What does it mean, that message?'

'I don't know.'

He made an angry sound.

'It's true, Nick. I know what it is, but I don't know what it means. Let me find out.'

'How?'

'By talking to him.'

Shadows fell on the bridge. 'Not tonight. I reckon it's dangerous. Tomorrow morning. And I'm coming too.'

'No,' she said. And that had such a sure and heavy sound he could not argue. 'When I come back I'll tell you all about it. Will you promise me, Nick?'

He felt a kind of power coming from her. It was almost as if she was hypnotising him. She took his hand. He nodded. He felt he was making some dreadful mistake, putting her in danger. 'All right,' he said; and with those words a door in him clanged shut, he could not escape. He understood for the first time how much he liked her. In spite of their squabbling, in spite of all their differences, she was precious to him, as though she were sister more than cousin.

They walked home side by side. Nick changed in his room. He told his mother he'd bruised his jaw when he'd slipped climbing a tree. At the dinner table he watched Susan. She was as silent as ever, but now and then she gave her hidden smile. His aunt made remarks about his city appetite. When he thought of that old man his throat closed up and he could not swallow his food.

They all watched television. Instead of the street lights and the screech of cars Nick was used to, outside was nothing but blackness and silence. He went to the window and looked out. There was a kind of waiting stillness out there, and against it the laughter on the set seemed no more than a chirping of insects. No lights. Black hills. A starry sky. Away south were endless valleys and mountains. Lead Hills. Boulder Lake. Gladiator Peak. West was the Heaphy Track – three days lonely walking to the cliffs and giant waves of the Tasman Sea. He shivered. Out in the dark, the waterfall was falling, Lodestone Creek ran silent in its gorge. There, in the bush, a mad old man was sleeping, wrapped in blankets with his carbide stink. Nick made up his mind he had to tell someone. He turned back to the room. Susan was watching him. She gave a small shake of her head. She must know what he was thinking. He frowned at her and felt his aching jaw. Please – she made the silent word with her mouth. And he shrugged, and looked at his mother and father, at his uncle and aunt, laughing, with their faces red, at some joke on the TV set. What could he tell them? What help would they be? He turned back and looked into the night.

At ten o'clock he said goodnight to the adults and went to bed. He said he was tired after all that driving. His mother blew him a kiss.

He'd been in bed ten minutes when Susan opened the door and put her head in. 'Goodnight, Nick. Thank you.' She was gone. He imagined her lying in her bed, holding that pebble with its crazy 'message', planning what she was going to do. He could not let her. She hadn't seen that man. Nick knew he was evil. He'd felt his hands, and seen his eyes, and smelt the chemical stink of his breath. Susan didn't know what she was getting into. But he'd made her a promise and he knew he couldn't break it. There was only one thing he could do. He could follow her, he could watch without her knowing. That way he'd be able to run for help.

When he'd decided that, he felt better. He rolled over. His bed was cool. Soon he went to sleep. But uneasiness followed him even there. Shapes came floating in his dreams, hands came after him, and eyes of hideous red grew up in the dark and peered at him. He heard a screeching sound, and he woke sweating. It was a mosquito buzzing round his face. He gave a sigh, thankful it was nothing worse. But he knew he'd have a hard time getting back to sleep. His arms ached and his jaw was throbbing. He sat up. His mouth was dry as sandpaper. Silently he went down to the kitchen for some water.

In the lounge, the adults had turned off the TV set. They were talking – having a nightcap, from the sound of glasses. He wished he could go in and talk to them.

He drank his water, listening at the door. They sounded

serious. Soon he understood why. They were talking about Susan. 'Doctor,' someone murmured, 'psychiatrist.' 'Not in the real world.' He went closer. Susan's mother: she had a tinny voice, usually sharp with laughter or complaint. Now it seemed to have a grieving edge. 'She was like that when she was a baby. Remember, Ted, how she'd be looking away, way out over the horizon, as though there was something there only she could see?'

'Funny birth she had,' Uncle Ted said. 'Something went wrong there. That's what I reckon. Blame it on the flood.'

'It's more than that,' came Aunt Pattie's voice. 'It was that old man. I know it was.'

Nick listened, hardly breathing. His aunt fell into a kind of tearful sing-song. Uncle Ted put a rumbling word in here and there. Twelve years ago. Nick could almost see it. They lived in the old house then, the one they used as a hay barn now. The baby was due. But there was flooding in the valley – Uncle Ted could not get his wife to the hospital. He could not even get his neighbour's help. So, in the little room upstairs, under the sloping roof, while rain hammered on the iron, he delivered the baby himself. Everything went smoothly. At one o'clock she arrived. Susan. A perfect little girl. He wrapped her tightly in blankets and put her in a bassinet by the bed. He made his wife comfortable. Then he left her dozing and went down to the kitchen to make a pot of tea. He was worn out. After a while he went to sleep himself, with his head on the table.

'Then I heard this awful screech.'

He rushed upstairs. Aunt Pattie was sitting up in bed screaming.

'I woke up and saw him,' Aunt Pattie said. 'He was standing by the bassinet. He was leaning over her.'

It was a little old man. He had white hair and a white beard, she saw it plainly in the light of the lamp Ted had left burning. But the strangest thing, the most frightening thing, was the colour of his skin. 'I saw it when I screamed. He looked at me. He was like someone from a flying saucer.' His skin had a reddish colour and seemed to glow from within.

'Now Pattie, now,' Uncle Ted said, 'that was imagination. You'd just gone through a pretty tough time. He was some old prospector. They're always hanging round here, fossicking up the creeks. There's one up there now.'

'It was red. I saw him. I know.'

'Well, well,' Uncle Ted said, 'it might have been a trick of the light. But he was there all right. I got a look at him, just saw him duck out the door when I went to the bed. Might have been old but he sure was quick.'

Uncle Ted chased him down the stairs and out of the house. He did not follow far. The old man vanished like a ghost into the night, into the beating rain.

'I came back to poor old Pattie here. She'd grabbed the baby and was holding it. But I don't reckon he'd meant her any harm. He'd unwrapped her blankets a bit.'

'He put her birthmark on her,' Aunt Pattie said.

'Now, Pattie.'

'He did. She had no mark till he touched her.'

'Well,' Uncle Ted admitted, 'I'd had a pretty good look at her. I didn't see any mark. But when Pattie looked she had this round spot, here, on the inside of her wrist. And a sort of patch up her arm and shoulder.'

'He put it on her. You know that.'

Uncle Ted said nothing. And by the door, in the dark of the kitchen, Nick began to shiver. It was all coming clear. The birthmark. But Uncle Ted was going on with the story.

The rains stopped. The floods went down. The doctor got through and had a good look at the baby. She was all right. The birthmark was nothing to worry about. Lots of kids had those. He wouldn't listen to talk about funny old men. Reckoned that was just imagination.

'It wasn't,' Aunt Pattie said.

'No, it wasn't,' said Uncle Ted. 'I went up Lodestone Creek after the flood. Checking stock. I found him up there. Up by the old gold mine. Been dead about three days. He'd fallen down a cliff and broke his neck.'

'Tell them the rest,' Aunt Pattie said.

'Well,' said Uncle Ted. He sounded nervous. 'I had a good look at him, see. He did have a sort of red skin. But that was nothing – just sort of weather-beaten, I reckon. What he did have though was a birthmark. Here, on the inside of his wrist. Same as Susan's. Same place. Same colour.'

'There,' Aunt Pattie said. 'And Susan's been strange ever since.'

'She's a funny kid, all right,' Uncle Ted said.

There was more clinking of glasses. Nobody spoke for a while. Then Nick's parents began making comforting sounds. He could tell they thought Uncle Ted and Aunt Pattie were a bit weird themselves. He could imagine them giving each other secret looks and little winks. But Nick knew better. He turned and went quietly back to his room. He could understand Susan now, and he felt a deep loyalty to her. He understood her need to talk to that old man. He even understood what the message was.

Nick had seen the birthmark on the inside of her wrist. It was about the size of a fifty-cent piece. Patches and smears trailed away from it up her arm. It was almost as if someone had painted a circle, very neatly, and then been given a fright and dragged his brush away. But if you looked more closely you saw the mark on her wrist had two parts. Each was shaped like a tear drop, curved like a moon. They fitted into each other perfectly. One was bright red, almost purple; and the other golden brown. In summer it almost vanished in Susan's tan.

Nick climbed into bed. He pulled the sheet up to his chin. He had it all worked out. If someone wanted to draw a mark like that, and only had a pebble and a knife, he'd scratch a circle on the stone, then through it he'd draw a curved mark like an S.

Nick thought of Susan sleeping in her bed, holding that strange message in her hand.

Jimmy Jaspers

It was mid-morning when Susan started out. Nick was in the orchard picking plums. He caught a glimpse of her blue T-shirt as she went down the track leading to the river. He ran to the house and put the plums on the bench.

'I'm going for a swim.'

'Susan's just gone,' Aunt Pattie said. 'You'll catch her if you hurry.'

He grabbed his togs and ran down to the track. Once there, he did not hurry. He kept her in sight as she walked through the scrub and over the swing bridge. She turned aside when she reached the paddock, and Nick saw she meant to go up the creek. That gave him the time he needed. He waited until she was out of sight, then ran up the paddock through the islands of blackberry, taking the way he'd travelled the previous evening. Soon he heard the distant noise of the old man's suction dredge.

When he came to the scrub he went more slowly. The sound of the motor drowned out everything, but he had begun to see the old man as not belonging in the natural world. There was no telling what he might be able to do: hear like a cat? see in the dark with those eyes? He slipped by the tree trunks, through the ferns and mossy boulders, like a shadow. He saw he had made a mistake in wearing bright-coloured clothes.

Lodestone Creek seemed to vibrate in a kind of patient agony under the noise of that hideous engine. The old man was busily sweeping the shallows, but as Nick came to rest in a hidden cleft between two giant boulders, he straightened up and sent his red glare up and down the creek. He had sensed something. Nick shivered. The old man splashed across to the raft and switched the motor off. Again that menacing silence. Nick tried not to breathe. But after standing for a moment, hands on hips, the old man went to the bank and sat down. A billy was steaming over a fire of twigs. He took a mug from his pack and poured in tea red as blood. He sucked it through his lips with a plug-hole noise. Nick watched him, fascinated. For all his age, there was about him an air of being coiled ready to spring. It gave him the kind of menace one felt in a wild boar.

He lifted his mug again, sucked at it noisily, wiped his mouth with his hand. Suddenly he was still, with the mug halfway to his mouth. He looked under his eyebrows down the creek. Nick followed his gaze. There was Susan. She had come up silently, and now she stood on a dry stone in the creek and watched the old man with a curious expression, half fright, half expectation. He put his mug down carefully. He grinned at her, showing crooked teeth yellow as corn.

'So girlie,' he said, 'that nipper give yer me message?' Susan stood with her feet wide apart. Nick saw she was ready to move back the way she had come. The old man saw it too. He gave a laugh.

'Come and talk to me, girlie. I don't bite.'

'Who are you?' Susan said. Her voice was soft, a whisper.

The old man winked cunningly. He stroked his chin and the sound of his hand rasping whiskers came clearly over the creek.

'Ah, that'd be tellin'. But I know all about yer. Nothin's secret from me.' He raised his finger, grinning, and drew a circle in the air. He made a curving line through it: an S. It seemed to hypnotise Susan. She moved closer to him, stepping off the rock and approaching along the shingle at the creek-side. She stopped again, out of his reach, and he said in a wheedling tone, 'Yer don't have ter be scared of ole Jimmy Jaspers.'

'Are you the one who put the mark on me?'

'What mark, girlie? Show me the mark. I gotter be sure.'

Susan raised her arm. She showed her wrist. Nick saw the birthmark plainly. It seemed to shine like a brand-new coin.

'Yeah,' the old man said, 'that's the one. Lemme have a squizz. Come a bit closer.'

Don't go, Nick wanted to shout. She seemed to be less cautious now. She stepped up to the old man, still showing her wrist, and he nodded and looked at her sidelong. 'I reckon that's it, all rightie. No mistake. Ha! Tough luck, girl.' His hand shot out. He had her by the wrist. She struggled but he gave a laugh. 'Don't wriggle. Yer can't get away. Ole Jimmy's got yer.'

'Stop, you're hurting me.'

'Don't make no difference.' But he relaxed his grip. 'Sit down. Keep still. 'Tain't me yer gotter be scared of.'

'Who are you?'

'Jimmy Jaspers. That's all yer need ter know.'

'You're not the one who put the mark on me.'

'Never said I was.'

'Where is he? I want to see him.'

'Too late fer that. They fixed 'im long ago.'

'What –' Susan's face had a look of such shock and grief Nick felt himself stretching out his hands to comfort her.

'They bust 'is neck. They don't muck about, them Halfies don't.'

'He can't be dead,' Susan cried. 'I've been waiting. I've been waiting all my life.'

'Wasted yer time then, didn' yer?' He snapped his fingers, sharp as cracking bones. 'No trouble ter them geezers. Lemme give yer some advice. Do what they says.'

Tears were running down Susan's face. The old man let go her wrist. He looked down at her, seeming pleased at her sorrow. 'Waterworks won't get yer nowhere. I gotter send yer through.' He stepped over his fire and rummaged in his pack. Now, Nick thought, now was the time for Susan to run. He wanted to shout at her, but she was so crumpled, so white, crouched on the ground, that he knew she'd never make it. He felt helpless. What should he do? Go for help? But then he wouldn't know where the old man took her. He had to keep close and wait for his chance.

The old man came back to Susan. Nick strained to see what he had in his hand. It was something blue, glittering dully. He said roughly, 'Come on, girl. Time yer had a sniff.'

Susan looked up at him. She did not seem to hear properly. She rubbed her wet face with her hands.

'Nuff of that. On yer feet.' He pulled her up by her arm. It shook her out of her grief and she began to struggle. 'Keep still, damn yer. Like a ruddy eel.' He slipped his hand round her back, grabbing a fistful of hair. Susan cried out.

'Stop wrigglin' an' it won't hurt. Now. All yer gotter do is sniff this 'ere.'

Nick saw it clearly: a blue bottle about the size of a miniature whisky bottle. The old man held it in three fingers and worked the cork out with his forefinger and thumb. It came out with a soft pop. He dropped it on the ground. 'Come on. This is better'n French perfoom.'

A yellow smoke began to come from the bottle. It oozed up, almost solid, swaying like a snake. Nick thought it was alive. He smelt again the carbide stink. Susan pulled her head back, threw it back between her shoulder blades, trying to get away from the yellow thing that twisted at her face. But the old man gave her hair a jerk and held her still. The smoke turned easily and coiled by her mouth. Nick saw she was holding her breath. He was holding his own.

Jimmy Jaspers laughed. 'Come on girlie, you'll go pop in a minute.' And in the end she had to draw in breath; and Nick saw the yellow smoke rush in like a live thing through her mouth.

The old man let her drop. He picked up the cork and jammed it in the bottle. A puff of yellow drifted over the creek. It seemed to come at Nick and he shrank down. But it went high over him and broke and vanished in the leaves of the trees. When he looked out again the old man was putting the bottle in his pack. Susan was on her knees, with her head hanging down and her hair trailing on the ground. The old man buckled his pack. He grinned at her.

'Better get goin', girlie. Doesn't pay ter keep them Halfies waitin'.'

Susan raised her head. She did not look at him but seemed to glare over the creek. Her face was tightened in a painful grimace. And her eyes, staring blindly, had changed their colour to a reddish-brown. Nick felt the hair prickle on his neck. She stood up. Jimmy Jaspers watched her with a grin. 'Tell 'em I'll be comin' fer me gold.'

Susan did not make any sign of hearing. She turned and walked stiffly away up Lodestone Creek. She made no attempt to walk on the shingle or move from rock to rock, but marched in a wooden way through the water, not caring as it came up her legs and wet her shorts. Her hair lay in a tangle on her back. She came to a bend in the creek, turned mechanically, and went out of sight.

Jimmy Jaspers watched her. He did a capering dance, squelching on the shingle fan with his water-logged boots. 'Whee,' he yelled, 'I'm gunner be rich.'

Nick waited no longer. He slipped back out of the boulders, scuttled up through the bush and ran along the paddock again. Soon he came to its end and followed a path in the scrub. It wound towards the creek, and plunged at last down the face of a cliff to the water. He saw Susan passing below him, still walking in that stiff unhuman way. 'Susan,' he called softly. She did not seem to hear. 'Susan, it's me.' She went on and passed from sight. Nick looked cautiously back down the creek. No sign of Jimmy Jaspers. He scrambled down and jumped into the shallow water. He was faster than Susan, he knew. It would be no trouble catching her.

She was nearly at the gorge when he grabbed her shoulder. 'Susan. Stop, it's me.' She turned her face to him. The burning smell of carbide sent him reeling back. Her red eyes glared at him like fire. She shook herself free and ploughed on through the water. He came at her again. 'Susan, stop. He's drugged you. You've got to listen.' He grabbed her by the waist and wrestled her down in the water. She thrashed with her arms and legs, trying to break away. He held her down. 'Susan, come on. We've got to get you home.' He saw something in her eyes, a flash of blue, flecks of blue, swimming, sinking, underneath the red. That had to be her, that had to be Susan, fighting to get free of the drug.

'Nick,' she said, 'Nick. Oh help me, Nick.' But as she spoke her body kept pulling away, straining to continue that robot walk up Lodestone Creek. And when he lifted her to her feet and dragged her back a few steps towards home, she began to scream; a thin despairing sound like the screaming of a shot rabbit. 'Oh Nick, oh Nick, it's pulling me. Oh, let me go. It's pulling off my head.' He felt the desperate straining in her, saw her eyes straining in her face. He let her go. At once she set up that wooden walking, ploughed ahead and went into the gorge. All he could do was follow. The grey walls closed over them. The water deepened. He thought for a moment of those giant eels, and then stopped thinking. Nothing was important now except staying close to Susan, saving her.

She kept ahead of him, walking up to her waist, then up to her armpits, in the black water. The walls of the gorge hung above, leaning in a way that made Nick dizzy. The sky was a thread of blue. He swam side-stroke after her. At last they came out, and a valley he had never seen opened up before him. Susan waded to the bank and set off again. He walked at her side, bending to see her face. Once he tried to hold her by the shoulder, but she sobbed as if he had struck her. 'Nick, Nick, it's pulling me.' There was no way he could help. He held her hand and kept close by her side.

The valley walls began to close in. Two long mounds, curiously even, grown over with small trees and weeds, thrust out from the foot of a cliff. Susan climbed one, and Nick, keeping close, saw they were tailings from a mine. Half hidden in ferns was the mouth of a shaft. It was black as night. Susan stumbled down the side of the mound and went towards it.

'No, Susan. You can't go in there.'

He grabbed her, held her still. She screamed again. 'It hurts. It's pulling off my head.'

'No. I'm not letting you.' Whatever Halfies were, they would be in the mine. He tried to pull her back. 'Oh,' she cried. 'O-oh.' Her eyes seemed to be straining out of her face. From somewhere she found strength to push him off. He went staggering back and lost his balance. By the time he had picked himself up, she was passing through the barrier of ferns into the mine.

He did not want to go in there. But he knew he had to. He ran, and pushed the ferns aside and went into a wet darkness that smelled of mould and mud and dead water and carbide. Susan's hair and clothes made a pale blur. He stumbled after them. Light died. 'Susan.' The sound was swallowed up. But a faint luminosity came from Susan's skin. He tried to gain on her and in a moment reached her side and grabbed her hand. His feet splashed in water, his shoulders brushed on rotten stone and rotten timber. The only light came from Susan's face and eyes. She was ghostly. She glowed with a red unnatural light. But her hand in his was warm. That was all he recognised of her.

Presently she stopped. She tried to free herself. He would not let her go. He saw they had come to the end of the shaft. Relief overwhelmed him. No Halfies, whatever they were. And nowhere for Susan to go. She would have to come home. He tried to pull her back. But she braced herself and stood firmly. In a voice he did not recognise she said, 'Let go my hand.'

'Come home, Susan. We'll get a doctor. We'll get the police.'

Her eyes stared redly at him. No trace of blue in them now. 'I'm going through.' As he watched, the light of her skin began to fade. Her eyes grew dim. The weight of her hand in his grew less, and looking down he saw it was transparent, it was like glass. He saw his own hand through it. Then a force like a great wind hurled him back against the tunnel wall. He felt as if he had been struck with hammers. He could not move, but lay tumbled on the wet floor of the shaft and watched Susan fade, grow colourless, shimmer with white light. She was printed on the blackness like a figure in the negative of a photograph. Then she was gone. There was a wet sound, a greedy sucking, like something being dragged through a muddy hole. He thought he heard a faint cry, like the lost cry of a gull in the night. Nothing then. Only the steady sound of dripping water.

He pulled himself to his feet. He ran, half falling, half on hands and knees, knocking lumps of rotting wood from the tunnel walls. The light of the opening grew. He burst out through the ferns and fell on the ground. Then he scrambled away from the dark entrance, away from the horror that lived in there. 'Susan,' he cried. It was a cry of grief and incomprehension. What had just happened was impossible – yet it had happened. And Susan was gone, turned into something impossible, sucked away through some hole into . . . where? where?

He lay on the shingle by the creek, sobbing with disbelief. The water chattered by. A fantail dived about him, chirping in a friendly way. The drumming of cicadas filled the air. He lay there listening. Slowly he came to understand that the world was as it should be. Only Jimmy Jaspers, only whatever it was that lived in the mineshaft, did not belong. What had been done to Susan could not happen in the real world. That meant . . . it meant that it was magic of some kind. Of an evil kind. But how was he to tell anyone? How could he explain it to his father, his mother, to Susan's parents, to the police? No one was going to believe him. But Susan had to be saved. Wherever she was, someone had to find her and bring her back. He began to understand what he must do.

Slowly he got to his feet. The fantail fluttered away upstream. Nick looked at the mineshaft. It was black as night. 'Right, Susan, don't be scared.' There was a way, and he was going to take it. He started off downstream, running steadily. He came to the gorge and started in, walking first, then swimming as the bottom fell away.

He was halfway through, deep in shadows, swimming silently, when he heard a noise: a shrill ugly whistling, like a fault in a radio set. It echoed in the gorge. A small stone plopped in the water close to his face. He swam in close to the wall of the gorge, until the sky was hidden. He was sharp, alert; he knew at once the sound was Jimmy Jaspers whistling. The old man was heading for the mineshaft, making his way along the top of the gorge. More stones splashed in the water. Jimmy Jaspers cursed. The sound was magnified by the gorge. The old man sounded as if he was at Nick's elbow. Nick held his breath. He lay still as a trout in the water. Slowly the sounds died away. When they were gone, when all that was left was his own breathing, Nick started back the way he had come. He swam without letting his arms or legs break the surface. He came out of the gorge in time to see Jimmy Jaspers, wearing his pack, vanish into the hollow between the tailing mounds. He pulled himself out of the water, ran bent almost double to the nearer mound, climbed it carefully, and peered down.

Jaspers had stopped at the entrance to the shaft. He was struggling out of his pack. It fell with a clank on the ground.

Nick winced. The bottle, that blue bottle – it must not break. But Jaspers was crouching, unbuckling the straps. His ragged breathing came to Nick on top of the mound. He pushed his hand in the pack, felt around, and pulled out the bottle. It gleamed dully, and Nick watched fascinated as the old man leered at it, bounced it on his palm.

'Now,' Jimmy Jaspers crowed, 'now yer bloddy Halfies, I'm comin' fer me pay. I sent that girlie through and now I want the gold yer promised me.'

He pulled the cork out of the bottle. At once the solid-seeming oily smoke swayed up like a snake. Jimmy Jaspers stared at it cross-eyed. 'Pretty stuff. Reckon it's pretty stuff. C'mon. Gimme a sniff.' The smoke seemed to respond, turned sinuously at him, and seemed to writhe into his mouth and nose. 'Ah,' said Jimmy Jaspers, 'better'n whisky.' He corked the bottle and put it in his pack. Nick could see no change in him. He must be used to it. As for himself, he caught that same carbide smell and tried to keep his breathing shallow.

Jimmy Jaspers straightened up. He was grinning eagerly. 'Stop yer pullin',' he said, 'I don't need no pullin'.' He left his pack lying on the ground and went to the shaft. He pushed the ferns aside, and with a last furtive glare at the valley, passed inside. For a moment the sound of his boots came out but soon it died to a shuffle, then was gone.

Nick crept over the mound. He went cautiously to the pack and saw the bottle gleaming in its depths. He looked at the mine nervously, then took the bottle out. It was very cold. He put his thumb on the cork, making sure it was tight. He did not want that smoke coming out until he was ready.

He went to the mouth of the mine. No sound in there. He listened carefully. Once he thought he heard laughter. The carbide smell was strong. He waited. At last he heard the sound he'd been waiting for: that hideous, greedy sucking-sound, as Jimmy Jaspers passed like dirty water through to wherever it was he was travelling. And wherever that was, Susan was there too. And the Halfies. He shivered. For a moment he had the hideous vision of men split down the middle, from the top right through to the bottom, falling in halves like two planks of timber. Then he shook himself. Susan was there. That was all he really had to worry about. He was the only one who could bring her back.

The ferns tickled his face. He touched them with his fingertips. It was like saying goodbye. He was almost crying with fear, but another part of him was cold and brave. He held up the blue bottle. Something moved in it, coiling lazily. 'Here goes,' Nick said. He pulled out the cork.

The yellow smoke reared out and turned towards him.

MARGARET MAHY

Margaret Mahy (1936–2012) is one of New Zealand's finest writers and the preeminent New Zealand non-realist. She is the author of more than one hundred picture books, forty novels and twenty short story collections, and a number of brilliant essays about writing, many of which are collected in *A Dissolving Ghost* (2000). In 2006 she was awarded the Hans Christian Andersen Medal for her services to children's literature, and she has twice won the Carnegie Medal. Margaret Mahy is represented here by an excerpt from fragments of her unpublished adult fantasy, written in the 1980s, and largely lost – though her 2009 novel *Heriot* is part of it.

Misrule in Diamond

Diamond, that city of trade, gossip and festivals, continually congratulated itself upon its history, its Hero, its King, and upon things for which it could really take no credit – the sea, the river and the seasons. But underlying the jokes, songs, dresses and processions, Linnet often glimpsed something wilder and more savage than showed on the surface and, after she had lived in Diamond for four years, she was certain that the autumn celebration Misrule was the most disturbing thing of all.

As the trees in the King's Garden shed rustling mats of leaves over their own feet, as the sun rose more unwillingly each morning, slinking sideways around the edge of the hills, and the year, tearing itself to pieces, plunged towards winter, the seven days of Misrule began. The sharp wind grew sharper, the cold castle colder and the city, like an image seen through a telescope, turned itself upside down.

During Misrule, Linnet and the other court ladies were shut inside their tower, for the old Queen distrusted everything about the festival, even the ceremonies custom forced her to take part in. There was no way out of the Tower of the Swan. A guard was set at its arched door, and though old steps still clung to the outer wall, they were dangerous, and crumbled a little more each year. Only a madman would use them.

However, on the flat roof of the Tower, in a disused guard house, Linnet was allowed to keep the telescope her father had let her buy – a slender leather barrel inscribed with a web of gold, the eyepieces made of purest Hoadish glass but ground by craftsmen from the Dannorad. The universe hanging at the end of the telescope's gilded tube seemed so much more predictable, so much more containable, than the life around Linnet. Night after night, for three of her four Diamond years, she had watched the stars and planets move through their explicit dances, but during Misrule she turned her telescope away from the stars and onto the city below. Lapped by her own golden skirts, she spied on the city and, just sometimes, she spied, across the castle courtyards, on Prince Dysart in his room at the top of the Crow Tower. There he sat, late at night, reading or writing steadily, resting his elbow on his desk and his head in his hand, pausing, frowning, staring at the wall before him as if he were scrying his fortune in the stone. Then down would go his head again, his hand would move with a life of its own, scribbling scribbling – the clear lens at the end of her gilded tube hung him head downward. *But why not,* Linnet thought. *It's such a tumbling world.*

Misrule was the festival of fools. Down below in the King's gardens, the castle clowns chose a fool King and fool Hero, and set up a court in which master and man changed places. Out in a suddenly antithetical city, an airy population of stilt-walkers teetered on insect legs above the heads of ordinary people. Linnet saw these elongated figures hanging down from a sky of stone streets while the golden wheel of the sun rolled under them. Stages were set up in the city squares and actors presented nonsense plays, gesturing towards landscapes which continually twitched, leaped and dissolved into other forms, for the background scenery was composed of the twisting acrobats of Diamond. Men disguised themselves as women, women as men, and a series of parties overflowing from house to house erupted in laughter or violence out onto the street where anyone could join in. Wise people in the city's first ring locked their gates and stayed safely inside during Misrule. The city was dangerous – also exciting. It was alive with processions of birds, beasts, giants and walking smiling fish as the collects displayed their emblems and competed with one another to put on the best show. The jimmyjacks were out and about – the men who preceded any performance by clearing a space or putting up a stage. They all carried brooms tied with ribbons and charms and their ritual sweeping of the stage showed the performance was about to begin.

The greatest performance of all Misrule took place in a sunken arena in the King's Garden overlooked by the old banqueting hall, where traditionally the marriages of princes and kings were celebrated. At the end of the season a mock King, crowned with a chamber pot, and a mock Hero, armed with long sausage, sat side by side on thrones built up over many previous days from castle scraps, broken boxes, chips of masonry, potato peelings, feathers, scrapings, sweepings, old wine skins and barrels with sprung hoops. The mock King and Hero, attended by a court of fools and clowns, made bitter fun of the customs and institutions of the city.

It was on this one occasion that the young women were allowed to come down from the Tower of the Swan (indeed they had no choice about it) and sit in the women's gallery, above the musicians but partly shielded by them, to witness the real King, attended by his three sons and accompanied by the Hero of Hoad, walking among the clowns, blessing them for briefly relieving him of power and the dangers attached to it. After the blessing he would sit to watch himself derided. In this way the men of Diamond, by mocking the signs they most feared and depended on, cast down their pride. Even the remote Hero, Link, having ridden into Diamond over the flowers and tapestries, had to put on rags of grey and share a double throne with the King to one side of a stage in the Arena. In this way both King and Hero acknowledged the temporary nature of all glory. But whereas nobles like Lord Glass, or even any princes who happened to be wandering about, could be safely pelted with Misrule cakes made of dead leaves or ashes and were not allowed to take more than a good-natured revenge, no one could directly assail the King or the Hero, except in effigy. After all, Misrule couldn't change everything, and some people were beyond its inversions. The assassins – Cloud, Ice, Leaf or Bird – passed by the wild celebrations in unmolested silence. Their strangeness lay far deeper than their clothes and painted faces. And certainly, no one dared make fun of Izachel, the King's magician, or Betony Hoad, the eldest prince and King's heir, except in whispers behind their backs. Prince Dysart, on the other hand, was cheered by the clowns, who called him 'Brother!' – a cry which he acknowledged, laughing – and the young nobles of Diamond, Iva, Gehery and Rio Rio (all friends and acquaintances of Linnet) were fair game. Each young man had his own way of responding to the mockery. Gehery entered into the fun of it, Rio Rio suffered it dryly, but Iva of County Isman seemed threatened by Misrule and his loss of status. He grew sullen and resentful.

Linnet, watching, had tried to imagine being tested by vindictive mockery. She felt certain that she would not only survive it but give back as good as she got. Over her time in Diamond, determined to behave, she had paraded in new dresses, grander but heavier than she was used to – dresses of peacock blue and dull gold worn over embroidered shifts, shoulders padded, long, tight sleeves trumpeting out over her hands. She was hung with bracelets and rings, pendants and strings of pearls, enamelled medallions. She took opulent care of her clothes and hair, and people admired her. But there was a price to be paid. She could rarely go unseen – or unheard, her silks and velvets sighing as they shifted against each other. Her bracelets chiming as she moved. Not only this – her ideas changed. She began to love not Diamond but the excitement of Diamond, where fortunes were made and unmade. A provincial noblewoman, she began to imagine how, when she was Master of Hagen, she would make her hometown, Rous Barnet, mysterious and beautiful beyond all other cities, an airy city, still part of the sky, but touching the earth, too.

This year's Misrule arrived, and the Hero, supported by the campaigners of Cassio's Island, marched through the castle courtyards and over the Bridge of the Lion. And at last the King himself, with his sons, lords and assassins, came over the bridge too, and there they all sat, tier after tier of the great men and women of Diamond, set around the sunken stage. From beyond the fire baskets and torches came the rustle of the autumnal garden and the cries of animals in the zoo, and Linnet, up in the women's gallery, puzzled, as she had always, over the King, who somehow encompassed all of Diamond without having anything much to say. Linnet stared broodingly at the slender chilly man who had grappled the three kingdoms in a remorseless net of peace. Looking at the face beneath the crown, she recognised once more his second son, Dysart. She saw Dysart's lopsided face even to the odd-coloured eyes. But the King was Dysart grown distant. However, though the monarch might be cold in himself, his will went out like heat, and people who had never seen him, or had barely heard of him, obeyed him without knowing it. Prince Betony walked on one side of the King, the Hero Link on the other; the assassin Cloud came after. Prince Luce, together with Prince Dysart (brought out of hiding for once), walked behind the assassin. Only Izachel was absent. Though he was the greatest fool of all the fools of Diamond, he would not share the same space as Dysart, and on this occasion the youngest prince was more important than the Magician of Hoad.

The King took his seat on the platform, the Hero beside him, his sons around him, and by the light of fires and torches they watched all sorts of crazy and insulting judgements given in the Arena of the Lion.

On the rare occasions when she saw Dysart, Linnet was flooded with a sort of grief – not for Dysart himself (he seemed perfectly cheerful) but for herself, the treacherous friend who had turned away from him in an hour of despair and had left him howling and trying to push his way into the heart of a stone wall. And as soon as she had turned away from him and what he stood for, the city had rushed in to envelop her in clothes, in the love of books and stars, in entertainments, in cautious friendships and in rules which, if broken, might shut her not only out of Hoad but out of Hagen as well. She had always believed herself to be brave and free, but Hammer and his third-ring murderers, Izachel, the sudden public madness which Dysart seemed to have caught from the magician, and even the city itself, had all frightened her into submission. She was used to Diamond by now; she even enjoyed it. But whenever she saw Dysart laughing and applauded by fools, she felt guilty and along with the guilt a stab of envy. He looked so free.

The voices of the fools' court rose in a crescendo of yaps and cries then suddenly there was an alteration. The King half rose, stumbled, lurched, then tumbled back into his chair again. Cloud leaped forward. Something had come among them so swiftly and silently that – even when Link signed urgently to his men, even when Cloud moved in front of the King, shielding him with his own body – it still seemed to be part of the ungainly entertainment. All the same, the clowns of street and court hesitated and fell silent. Dysart and Luce, both on their feet, stared at each other across the bent body of their father. Only Betony did not turn his head but continued to gaze meditatively in front of him, refusing to respond to the thrill of alarm.

Off went Link's men, the campaigners of Cassio's Island, pushing through the crowd, hung around with their Misrule necklaces of painted wooden eyes, ears and fingers. But at the arena gate a glittering figure stopped them. A helmeted man suddenly materialised, dressed in a Misrule costume painted to resemble an old-fashioned suit of golden chain armour, thrusting another man in front of him. The campaigners of Cassio's Island surrounded them both, but the shining captor stood taller than all of them, as he removed his mask with one hand and shook his captive with the other. Torchlight burnished his red-gold curls.

Betony turned to speak to Luce. 'Well, fancy!' (Linnet must have imagined his light brittle voice. She was not close enough to have actually heard it.)

The glittering man was Carlyon of Doro, Luce's captain. The man he had caught – a younger man than himself, second-ring student – was immediately dragged into the shadows. The men of Cassio's Island dispersed once more, while the King rose and, supported by Link and Cloud, retired for perhaps twenty minutes while the arrow which had come out of the night was cut out of him, and his wound was rapidly washed and bound. Emerging once more, he resumed his seat beside Link for the rest of the feast, sitting stiffly, his arm propped up so that, from a distance at any rate, he looked very much as usual, less man than sign.

Having lost so much time, the clown court now raved more and more frantically, gabbling its judgements, knowing its hour was almost over. Then, somewhere in the distance of Diamond's third ring, one of Dr Feo's great iron clocks struck the midnight. Silence fell. Everything tilted and turned the right way up once more. Princes became princes again, and could not be assailed. The poor became humble once more.

And it was now – as the King took back all his usual power, fulfilled rather than lessened by the mockery he had just absorbed – that something unrehearsed and quite remarkable happened. Luce sprang up, moved over and spoke impulsively to his father, while Luce's captain, Carlyon of Doro, came forward. He bowed to the King, but kneeled in front of the Hero, Link, laying his sword on the ground between them. A collective sigh arose from the crowd. Misrule was over, and now the city was the right way up again. Carlyon was challenging Link the Hero of Hoad for the right to be called Hero and to rule over Cassio's Island and to sit beside the King.

Link stood for a moment, looking down at Carlyon. The wind, which had been tugging fretfully at clothes and sighing around the arena walls, dropped. The stillness was so great that even the girls and the old Queen, watching from their high safe gallery, could hear the voices, faint but clear, like voices from another world.

'It isn't what you think it will be,' Link said at last.

'It's what you make it,' Carlyon replied, as if he knew.

When Link spoke again it was in the words of the old ritual. 'I'll have no mercy,' he said.

'Neither will I have mercy,' Carlyon answered, in the words of the same ritual.

Link bent, picked up the sword, kissed it and returned it to Carlyon. Then they embraced. Someone had attempted to kill the King, and in the shadow of that event the Hero had been challenged and had publicly accepted the challenge. Luce's face, bright with excitement, turned towards Carlyon as if Carlyon were Hero already and giving off light. But Betony ran his fingers in his own golden hair then sank his face down between his hands as if he were suddenly weary and longed to roll into bed. Dysart stood, childishly it seemed, looking from one to the other of them. Then he laughed as he always laughed, as if it were the only comment he could make on what was going on around him.

The Challenge of the Hero was one of the great events in the magical life of Hoad, but there was no place in it for Linnet or for any woman. Since the days of the Hero Cassio, the Hero had always been unmarried and childless, so that nothing need come between him and his devotion to Hoad. The Hero, his life, his power, his properties, were not the business of women.

Misrule was over. The men of the collects drove their decorated drays back to the second ring, while the guards and constables with their packs of dogs rounded up leftover revellers, drove them out and locked the first-ring gates after them. The King and the Hero flung velvet and fur over their grey rags, music struck up, and, flanked by the King's assassins and the men of Cassio's Island, they left the arena for the castle, the King going to the Tower of the Lion, Link to the Tower of the Hero, every window of which glowed with torches as a sign that the Hero was in residence. The ruling spirit of Hoad might treat an arrow with indifference, but the man who contained the spirit could not, and neither could anyone else. When the King was injured the land bled.

News came in over the next few days that, out in Hagen, Mount Warning had spouted fire (evidence if anyone needed it that Hagen was truly part of Hoad) and, a day later, storms swept along the coasts of the counties Bay and Glass, Argo and Dante, destroying fishing fleets and flooding villages.

The young man imprisoned in Hoad's Pleasure confessed quite openly that he had planned to kill the King, hoping that, in the confusion following the monarch's death, Hoad would turn back to the days before the *first* King, back to a time when the Hoadara were ruled by councils of elected men. It seemed, from what he said – from what he was forced to say – that there were others in the city who felt the same way. For the first time in four years, the King's assassins came out of their secret burrows in Hoad's Pleasure dressed in white, their faces painted, their hair looped and braided and newly dyed the bright red of arterial blood. However, it was information not lives that they were searching for. When these clowns of death were set on to kill, they wore black and moved invisibly. On this occasion they were out and about to freshen up fear of the King and to find out all they could from the records in the schools or guilds, or from gossip among neighbours and fellow students.

*

Two nights after the end of Misrule, Linnet found herself free to climb the Tower of the Swan. She longed to be on her own with the starry autumn night. She was filled with anticipation, though she did not quite know what she was expecting, for she believed she had a secret that was hers alone.

Linnet had recently become aware that someone else was coming into the old guard house on the top of the Tower of the Swan. In the beginning she could not say quite how she knew this, but she did. Somehow it had seemed that things were not as she had left them, that someone else had been reading her notes and studying her diagrams, rearranging her papers and her little lamp in a way she could not ignore. Somehow, she felt almost sure, she was *meant* to notice these alterations and to divine something from them. And once she had noticed them it seemed to her that she could detect the presence of another previous eye at the eyepiece of her telescope, as if the act of looking had left a barely perceptible imprint on the air. Someone else had been using her channel to the stars. But why so secretly? Why the effort to put everything back in its exact place? Though she loved to be alone with the universe, everyone in the Tower of the Swan knew she would gladly share it.

Once at the top of the stair, she stepped without hesitation out into the starry darkness. The wind thrust against her, alive with a soft invisible violence, and perhaps because there were wisps of cloud scudding over the night sky, there seemed to be a continual luminous tremble in the air around her. Linnet knew at once that she was not alone. There was a small sound, a rustle, the sound of an indrawn breath.

'Who's there!' She sounded imperious, but knew she was alarmed.

'Don't be frightened.' A shadow came towards her wearing a Misrule mask. Linnet held her lamp higher. One empty black eye was ringed with blue, the other with green. The man pulled his mask away and looked at her with a blue eye and a green one of his own. It was Dysart.

'How did you get here?' Linnet asked.

'Easy!' Dysart said. 'I climbed the stair.'

'They let you in?'

'No – the stair on the outside of the tower,' he said, almost impatiently. 'I've been climbing over these walls for years, even before you came here.'

Linnet thought of the crumbling steps spiralling up the outside of the tower and felt herself pressed to the wall, the stone rough under her cheek. She felt herself grow chilly with a peculiar sympathy.

'Of course, back then,' Dysart added vaguely, 'there was someone always to catch me.' Then he looked at her and laughed.

He was as mad as ever.

An astonishing thing happened. Linnet found it was as if she and Dysart had been parted for only a day. In a moment she became once more the wild rough child she had been on the day she ran off with him into the wicked city. The weight of her dress bewildered her. She wondered what she had been doing for the four years in between. 'You climbed that stair,' she cried, hearing in her mind a delicate sifting sound, stone dust and old mortar rustling down the face of the tower. 'You must be mad.'

'That's what everyone says,' Dysart replied, grinning to himself, not at her. It was shock to hear a man's voice coming out of him, a man's voice not only because his voice had settled and deepened but because he spoke with such confidence, was so sure of his words.

'You're the one who's been coming up here and using my telescope,' she said, half accusingly, half admiringly.

'Who did you think it was?' he asked, curious.

'I didn't think it was anybody. I mean, I thought it was a joke of some kind.' But the intangible presence had seemed like a mystery not a joke. 'You could have been killed,' she cried, and at the same time she thought that climbing that crumbling stair was a hero's act, and as magical in its way as anything Izachel had ever done.

'I won't be killed,' Dysart answered cheerfully. 'I've been promised a kingdom. I won't die till I get it. Anyhow, I'm used to that stair. I used to climb it in the dark over and over again a few years ago.' He spoke of this quite easily, as if it were all understood between them. 'It was just another way of standing in front of the horses. You know! Testing things!'

Linnet had lowered her lamp. His new man's voice came to her from a faceless shape.

'Mind you, I lost my nerve, just like you did.' He danced a little on the spot as if he were impatient to tell her about something different from what he was obliged to talk about. 'Don't worry. I haven't spied on you. Well – maybe a little – watching you up here from my window over there.'

Linnet laughed suddenly. 'Me too,' she said. 'I have spied on you, sitting up there on your own, writing away. What are you writing anyway?'

Dysart was silent. 'A long letter!' he said at last. 'Well, more of a history – going on and on the way history does. You actually watch me? I got the feeling you didn't want to look at me ever again.' He sounded puzzled rather than resentful.

Linnet sighed. 'It all turned so strange. Too strange. You went so mad, and I – well, it frightened me.' She wondered if he would understand that this was partly an apology. 'What are you doing here all of a sudden?'

'I thought you might come up here tonight, and I took the chance.' His voice was still soft but grew oddly fierce as he spoke. 'If you hadn't come I'd have climbed down again, and gone alone!'

'Gone where?' asked Linnet.

'Remember Creon?' Dysart asked her. 'You can't have grown frightened of Creon, too.'

For the first time she thought she could make out a hidden bitterness under his good nature. 'Of course I remember. I think of him – I think of what happened every day.' As she said this she realised with amazement that it was true.

When Linnet had first come to Diamond – the intended bride of the King's second son, Prince Luce – a girl, not much more than a child, who needed training in the ways of the court, Dysart was her only friend. One day, he and Linnet had run away – had ridden out of the first ring and into the city. They'd taken just one horse and Linnet rode behind Dysart with her arms around his waist. They rode away from the castle and the prison, the university and the domed observatories of the first ring. They passed through the second ring with its guild schools and loitering apprentices. They entered the third ring and the markets around a great stone fountain. The noise of the city, of wheels, of water, barking dogs, shouting voices, children playing, of things being taken from place to place, rose around them like a solid wall. They rode through streets with bathhouses, steam rolling out their open doors. They went into narrower streets where the houses had balconies where beautiful woman sat lazily brushing their hair or putting it up with crowns of fresh flowers. At that point Dysart turned in the saddle and told her they were on their way to 'the wildest part of the city'.

And Linnet had encouraged him. She said she wasn't afraid of anything. They had left the horse in the hands of an Ostler at an inn and ventured into the narrowest streets on foot. They were dressed in good clothes, but as they went along it seemed they were invisible. Dysart rushed ahead of her, and she had to pick up her skirts to follow him.

She remembered passing a wall where someone had written *dishonour is impossible*, and Dysart explaining that the third ring might be poor but it wasn't inarticulate.

Eventually they had come to a junction of several streets, where a group of boys from five to fifteen were pitching a leather ball at a row of wooden pins. The boys were all thin, but played with a sort of ghostly energy. As soon as Dysart and she appeared, the boys all stared at them, while pretending to be engrossed in their game. She told Dysart to close his cloak with its scarlet silk lining. She told him to hide his rings. But he wouldn't. They skirted the game but, once they had, the boys spread out and formed a hunting line behind them and, at the same time, a legless man on a trolley rolled himself into their path, and they were forced to run into the mouth of the only alley that was open to them.

Linnet said, 'I haven't forgotten Creon – that he opened his door when we were fighting for our lives on his doorstep.'

'Right at this moment, Creon's over in Hoad's Pleasure!' Faint light washed across Dysart's face as he half turned his head, glancing towards the old prison behind them on the eastern bank of the Bramber, but moving too quickly for Linnet to work out what he really looked like now. Seen from a distance on the other side of a castle courtyard he'd still seemed childish, but here in the dark, he sounded changed. He sounded powerful.

'Why?' Linnet exclaimed. But immediately answered her own question: 'Oh, it's because of your father!'

'It's because of a mistake,' Dysart said. 'I know all about Creon. He's told a few too many stories, and that's all.'

Linnet had gone on so eagerly to other things, putting Creon, Dysart and the whole third-ring adventure behind her, but Dysart, it seemed, when the chances had offered, had ridden out into the third ring and knocked on Creon's yellow door again. And then returned, again and again.

Something deep inside Linnet began to turn over again. Slowly and rustily an old machine began to work.

'The lines of washing are still there,' he told her. 'They always are, and it always looks like the same washing –'

'And –?' asked Linnet.

Dysart shook his head. 'Today I knew something was wrong before I got there,' he said. 'Everyone I met ran away from me. The door was broken in – everything smashed. Everything ruined – and inside, blood on the floor.'

'Nobody was there?'

'Someone was,' said Dysart in a strange voice. 'Hammer! Do you remember Hammer? On his trolley?' He paused and said reflectively, 'I suppose those boys that used to scavenge for him have set up on their own. Those that lived.'

'How is he still able to move?'

Linnet could not quite see whether Dysart winced or grinned. 'He pushes himself along, after a fashion. But there was a student pushing him this morning – one of Creon's lot – an Ortish student. I didn't know that Orts were ever students, did you? But there he was, black hair, black eyes, a real County Glass accent dragging on and on. It takes them all day to say good morning, and he wanted to say a lot more than that.'

'What about?' Linnet was not very interested in the Ortish student.

'About what a dreadful world it was.' Dysart sighed. 'He ran on about children starving, and men like Hammer, worn out by the wars and thrown out to die, and about a time before the King, when things were much happier. Well I just shut up and let him say it. I'm not princely in the classical style. But don't you see? He was one of them – the ones that had a go at father – the Students of the Burnt History. I thought he was going to have go at me, too, when he realised who I was.'

'And Hammer just let you walk away?'

'How could he stop me?' cried Dysart. 'Yesterday's wolf, today's poor old dog! Anyhow I gave him all the money I had. In a funny way I felt I owed him something, because he said it, didn't he? Dog eat dog, he said that time. Creon rescued us and then Hammer was there, as if he had nothing to do with attacking us. He smirked and said "Dog eat dog". It wasn't an apology.'

Now Linnet wanted to hear everything. Not just the morning's adventure, but everything that had happened to Dysart over the past few years. How he had won such assurance, shut away in his tower, or the deftness he must need to climb the crumbling stair. If she knew what had been happening to Dysart, she might have a clearer idea of what had been going on in her own life.

But all Dysart wanted to talk about was Creon. 'I know he's innocent,' he was saying. 'He may have given the students room there, and told them a few old stories, but he didn't plot with them. After he saved us I promised him that if ever he needed help I'd help him. But I need you, too!'

Linnet had a vivid, lively picture of herself, side by side with Dysart, armed and active, storming Hoad's Pleasure and carrying Creon to safety. She knew it was an idea that belonged to the child she had once been, but it was exciting to be having adventurous dreams again. She glanced doubtfully over her shoulder towards the bulk of the prison, rearing up so blackly it could be seen even in the dark.

'Come with me to talk to Lord Glass,' Dysart demanded abruptly. 'He mightn't believe me. I mean – the mad prince! Who would? But you were there too. You're my witness. You can tell how Creon once saved us – both of us. Hoad owes him something.'

'I can't climb down the wall,' Linnet said slowly, thinking that once she would not have hesitated to try. Once she would have felt that she could do anything Dysart did. 'I don't know,' she exclaimed, lifting her lamp to look at him again. 'What's happened to me?'

Dysart took a step towards her. He put his hands on her shoulders and peered into her face, which was on a level with his own. He was not tall. 'Just walk past the guard at the door,' he said patiently, as if he were speaking to a slow child. 'He can't lay hands on you. Say "I'm going out!" and walk past him. You poor little prisoner, you!'

'I'm not a prisoner,' Linnet snapped. 'You're the one who's shut away in a tower.'

Dysart burst out laughing. 'I'm an outcast, not a prisoner. I come and go. But just at different times from the rest of you. I sail around the port. I'm the one who's kept in touch with Creon. I came to you, not you to me.'

'I'll walk past the guard, don't you worry,' said Linnet sharply. 'Now that I know I can, I will!'

'Give me time to get down again,' Dysart said. 'A slow thirty minutes, say! I can't hurry.'

The thought of that descent made Linnet's head spin. She watched him lower himself over the wall. 'In the dark,' she said. 'How can you?'

'It's easier in the dark. I don't want to look down anyway – I climb by feel.'

Then he was gone. Linnet stared after him, holding her lamp over the abyss, saw the crown of his head diminishing little by little as, very slowly, pressed against the wall, he felt his way, sideways and down into darkness. She thought that even Link or Carlyon could never do anything as brave as climbing down into the night on the crumbling stair. Even when she could see him no longer, she listened, and heard the gritty whisper of crumbs of mortar falling from under his feet, down the face of the tower and into the night. And, as she listened to that faint terrifying sound, she shivered with fear and excitement. Then she turned and made for the door and the stair beyond, which, if followed, would bring her out of the Tower of the Swan and into the world.

Although Dysart had told her it would be so, Linnet was astonished when the guard at the door of the Tower let her pass without question. She moved out into the courtyard, looked up at the sky and saw the same stars she had so often spied on from the flat room of the tower, almost as if she were seeing them from the surface of an entirely different world. Turning, she looked disbelievingly back at the door behind which she had lived for four whole years, then turned again to gaze in the direction she thought Hagen must lie. *I've grown to like closed doors*, she thought. *It's so safe behind them.* Yet she was out in the world once more, choosing the company of madmen and magicians. *I'll do better this time*, she thought. *Even if I'm frightened I won't hide away.*

Beyond her lay the series of interlocking courtyards where she had wandered on her first morning in the castle. Linnet knew them by heart now, empty yet murmuring, as the sound of voices rose from subterranean dormitories or drifted from the southern end of Guard-on-the-Rock. Tonight, laughter and songs sounded in the tower of the challenged Hero. Link would be drinking with the royal Dragons, with Luce and particularly with Lord Carlyon, for the tradition was that Hero and Challenger, two aspects of the same spirit, should behave as if they loved one another dearly. The Hero of Hoad was always the same Hero, just as the King of Hoad was always the same King. Hero and Challenger were joined at the heart, the spirit flowing from one onto the other of them.

Silently, Dysart joined Linnet. 'It's only me,' he said, as she jumped at his sudden appearance.

'You're so different from what you were,' she said. 'You were always falling over your own feet.'

'Well I was always trying to make room for someone else back then,' he said, brushing the grit from the crumbling steps from his palms.

'What do you look like now?' Linnet asked. Even in the shadows, he had a solid, thickset, strong look about him, something she hadn't noticed when watching him through the telescope or stealing glances at him across the courtyards of the castle.

'Follow me and find out,' said Dysart, laughing to himself.

Linnet walked beside him and they passed between hedges of lavender, past the scaffolding where a new stone water tank was being put in place against an old inner wall of the original castle. The torches set in sockets over doorways filled the air with a black oily smoke, a part of the night that moved and swirled.

'It's all so exciting, isn't it,' Dysart muttered in her ear. 'Someone trying to kill the King! The Hero challenged! And everyone wants Carlyon to win. So why not make him Hero without having to kill Link first. He already looks like a Hero. It does help to look right.'

Linnet thought of Carlyon with his red-gold hair and his forehead as freckled as her own had once been, years ago. 'Don't be jealous. It's not just the way he looked. After all he is "the revenger of Senlac".' She gave Carlyon one of his popular titles. He had once single-handedly killed a band of Camp Hyot marauders he had caught sacking a little village close to the border.

'He only *revenged* Senlac. He didn't save a single one of them,' Dysart said.

They had reached a door and walked through into a hall, empty but haunted with signs of active life – a chair pushed back from the table on the dais, scattered pens and inks on the desks where the copiers sat. This was the place where men came to petition the King through his devisor, Lord Glass. Opposite the door they came in by was another door with a lamp burning on either side of it. Dysart paused, giving an absent-minded smile, not so much at Linnet as inward to some part of himself than needed encouragement. She stared at him with open curiosity. He had the same childish floppy brown hair that she remembered, the same odd-coloured eyes, the same wide mouth. His smile still lifted one side of his mouth more than the other. Yet, somewhere along the line, he had lost his old incoherence. There was no reason at all for her heart to give an odd elated thump under her ribs as she remembered the pressure of his hands on her shoulders, but thump it did.

Dysart put out his hand to knock at the door, then drew it back and dragged his fingers across his face as if waking himself up. Linnet realised that he was afraid.

'Lord Glass won't eat you,' she told him.

'He just might try,' Dysart answered. 'If he's got mustard and wine to wash me down with.'

Linnet reached past him and knocked firmly at the door, a hard imperative sound. There was no reply. It was Dysart who knocked the second time.

'I know he's there,' he told her. 'We'll knock till he answers. Your turn next.'

But now the door was opened by Lord Glass himself, light flooding from behind him so that he appeared before them more as a flat shape than a true man. Seeing the two of them, he placed his ringed hand on his chest and stepped back sharply. His surprise must have been genuine, but he made it seem that he was acting a part in a play. His boots turned over at the top to reveal linings of gilded leather, he wore drops of amber in his ears, and his hair had been dyed a strong, bright chestnut since Linnet had seen him last. He stood before them framed in wood and edged with a fiery line.

'Prince Dysart. Lady Linnet of Hagen – a most unexpected pleasure,' said Lord Glass. Then he looked once more at Linnet, waiting at Dysart's side. She thought his expression changed but it was too shadowy for her to see it clearly. 'But I do ask myself is this the right time for a visit, no matter how charming?'

'It's exactly the right time,' Dysart replied, with a curious echo of Lord Glass's affectation. 'It's about Creon Memory.'

'My dear Prince,' Lord Glass replied, 'you shouldn't have bothered yourself. We know all we need to know about Creon Memory.'

'No you don't,' Dysart said, 'because I know something no one else does – no one except Lady Linnet that is. She's my witness in case you think I'm talking out of madness.'

'Dysart is the only one in the whole castle who really knows Creon,' Linnet said, startled, and then elated, by the sound of her own voice. She felt Dysart's hand fumble among the heavy folds of her skirts to find her hand, just as it had done all those years ago in the blackness of the house in Kitia. His hand felt warm and dry and unexpectedly hard, not romantic but demanding. Their fingers entwined secretly and securely. Linnet thought he held her hand as he would have held a charm, and a strange strong happiness spread through her at his touch.

Meanwhile Lord Glass ran his own ringed fingers up and down the edge of the door as if he were longing to close it. 'Well, my dears, do give me some clue, and we'll negotiate.'

Dysart's fingers tightened painfully around Linnet's, as he answered in a light voice – the voice he used on the top of the Tower of the Swan. 'Just tell me truly, Lord Glass – am I worth anything to Hoad? Anything at all?'

'My dear, of course! You're one of the King's jewels,' Lord Glass replied, but sounded wary for all his confident words.

'But he's got two other jewels,' said Dysart. 'He might have more than enough!'

'A king can't have too many jewels,' Lord Glass answered.

'All right, then Creon Memory once saved this particular jewel,' Dysart said sharply, 'and the jewel of Hagen, too. The one here beside me. He saved us both. So if we're worth anything we owe him a good turn, don't we?'

The glittering fingers, wandering restlessly along the edge of the door, grew still then pulled the door wide. 'Do come in,' said Lord Glass, and under the courtesy in his voice, Linnet thought she could make out a profound apprehension.

Dysart and Linnet came into the most beautiful and comfortable room in Guard-on-the-Rock. The King's Hall, filled as it was with astounding treasures, was over-heavy, even ominous with its own glory. This room had been panelled with wood laid over its original stone, the windows behind the wine-coloured hangings were of clear glass and its floor was spread with fine rugs. Opposite the door by which they had entered was an arch in the Dannorad style, beyond which they could glimpse another space drowned in shadow, though the big bed glimmered a little eerily for it was covered with white furs. There were pictures and tapestries and several book chests and other books on short sloping shelves with doors that could be closed across them. There were more books in this room, Linnet thought, than in the whole of her father's castle. Four chairs were set casually around a smouldering fire. In one of them, Prince Betony lay back against blue cushions, his elbow resting on the carved arm, his fair head on his hand. In another, a little apart from the rest, sat Izachel, the Magician of Hoad, glaring at Dysart with eyes so round that the white showed clear around the iris. At the sight of Izachel, Dysart, who had been moving forward confidently, even eagerly, half spun back towards the door, and then came to a standstill so abrupt the stillness seemed violent. He turned his head stiffly to glance back at Izachel. Prince and magician gazed at each other in horror, heads turned slightly away like cats who cannot bear to be in the same room with each other. Betony stared too, sitting up extremely slowly, afraid, perhaps, that too sharp a movement might cause Izachel and Dysart to fall on each other.

'What's he doing here?' Dysart asked Lord Glass, while Izachel made a furious throat clearing sound. He leaped up. His chair fell backwards. He began to edge towards the door, flattening himself against the wall, apparently terrified that the hems of his robe or his wide sleeves might touch Dysart in passing.

'Now then,' began Lord Glass, but something was happening around them. The lights in the room flickered and dimmed just as they had dimmed in Kitia. Izachel, in the act of beating a retreat, stiffened and groaned horribly, as everything around them grew so still that Linnet understood how much sound there had been in it a moment ago – the snapping of the flames, small creaks and groans from Betony's chair as he shifted his weight, the breathing of five different people which, now it could not be heard anymore, seemed like the breathing of more than five.

The room did not darken completely but was suspended in an unearthly fixed twilight, and into this Izachel spoke. 'I'm nothing,' he cried in Dysart's own voice. 'Just the jimmyjack getting things ready.'

'Ready for who?' asked Lord Glass.

The voice changed, and answered. 'There you are, Dysart,' it said. 'Where did you go?' It was impossible to tell if it was the voice of a man or a woman, but it was certainly the slow voice of a County Glass farmer.

'It was you who went,' Dysart said, and then he looked angry with himself for answering at all. 'I've been here the whole time.'

The voice sounded puzzled. 'But they tore me in two. I don't work well. Are you listening?' it demanded.

'I always listen,' Dysart was impatient.

'We can't be spared, either of us, but we might be saved. So remember it's dog eat dog and run quickly when time comes.'

Dysart did not reply.

'Answer it,' Lord Glass said.

'I don't want to,' Dysart cried. 'I don't want its messages.'

The voice laughed.

'Run like the wind, right?' it cried, fading. 'And I might just throw in the girl, too.' And it laughed again, its laughter dissolving back into the snapping flames and anxious breathing and the familiar groaning and braying of Izachel, as, flapping his arms and grimacing wildly, back in himself once more, he began edging past Dysart, so stricken with fear that he was wetting himself and leaving a trail of glistening drops between him and the door.

'Oh, dear me,' said Lord Glass, sighing deeply. 'I do wish, Lord Prince – but I suppose it is not really your fault. Not as such.' The door slammed, and then on the other side of it Izachel let out a series of terrible howls, each one a little fainter than the last. Linnet imagined him running through the reception room beyond and, still howling, across the courtyards and out into the night.

'What a burden a magical nature seems to be,' Betony remarked, his eyes fixed on Dysart with a curious inimical expression. Dysart sighed, and released Linnet's fingers.

'I've never once asked it to speak to me,' Dysart said, and glanced at his brother apologetically. 'What was Izachel doing for you? Telling you something hidden? Does our father know?'

'Betony and I hoped Izachel might clarify things,' Lord Glass said. 'And, yes, we used him with your father's blessing. But I'm afraid he was being difficult – the magician, not the great and glorious King of Hoad, of course. As you probably know, since your last encounter with him, all that time ago, he's not been able to call on his familiar. We've had to rely on his own innate powers, which are not nearly so extensive. And now think I we must admit defeat. You have a shrivelling effect on him.'

'But what he said to you was the most coherent message we've had all evening,' Betony said. 'When the time comes, I'd certainly run if I were you. Run like the wind.'

'I'm running like the wind now,' Dysart said. 'But you just can't see me go. I came here to tell you about Creon! That's all

I want to talk about.' He listened and they listened with him. Far in the distance Izachel was still howling.

One chair, its back inset with a great prism of glass, the sign of its owner, was pushed back carelessly. But Lord Glass did not sit down immediately. He stood beside it as if it were invisibly occupied, his restless fingers following the grooves of its carving, blindly reading anything the old wood might have to say.

Staring at his brother, Dysart gave one of his irrelevant laughs. 'I can guess about Izachel – but what are you doing here, Bet?'

'Don't call me Bet,' Betony replied crossly. 'As you know I am obliged to take an interest, whether I want to or not.' Then recovering, he gave a single, wincing smile.

Dysart looked back towards Lord Glass. 'I'm here to testify,' he said. 'Creon's a loyal subject of Hoad, and all he has done has been to tell a few stories. He should be released and sent home. That's all.'

'But such stories,' murmured Lord Glass, ruffling his newly bright hair. 'Stories carry combustion in their hearts. Do bear that in mind, my dear!'

'And besides, he told them to such singularly inflammable people,' added Betony. 'Personally, I feel that choosing a safe audience is part of the storyteller's craft.'

At these words, Dysart assumed, unconsciously perhaps, the position of a debater, weight on the left leg, arms folded. Linnet could almost feel him setting up arguments and rhetoric, and was not surprised when he replied with teacherly formality. 'What's history? Just old stories saved up. Gentlemen, are we not all sustained by stories we know? What's history but a series of stories. The flesh of the kingdom is laid over a skeleton of old tales.'

Lord Glass jiggled on his toes, and interrupted. 'Are you here for the fun of debate, Lord Prince? Or are you presenting a case for Creon Memory?'

'I'm presenting a case for justice – for Hoad, really, since the King and his sons stand for the justice of Hoad. And that means I have to defend Creon.' Dysart dropped his debating voice and added, smiling, 'Anyhow, he saved my life, and what sort of madman or prince ever forgets a favour like that?'

'Even a king can't forget what he has never been told about,' said Betony, looking at Lord Glass and indicating Dysart. 'I told you that if you left him shut in with a lot of books he'd become quite formidable. Why didn't you shut him in with a lot of women. He'd have worn himself out and been no trouble at all.'

'I am trouble, I know,' said Dysart. 'And I'm here to tell everyone about it. The King and you will have to take notice. I've got a witness.'

'Oh, I rest my case,' declared Betony, laughing. Lord Glass seemed even more jittery and ill at ease than he had been before and, without waiting for further comment, Dysart plunged into the story of the day, so nearly disastrous, that he and Linnet had shared four years earlier.

Dysart spoke easily and rapidly. And Linnet could tell he had rehearsed the story to himself over and over again, insistently shaping it, until it acquired the polish of an ancient tale. He went on to speak of Creon's goodness, of the children gathered off the street, and declared that Creon's excellence had seemed to him to be the essential excellence of a king of Hoad. ('Not that many of them have actually had it,' Dysart added.)

Unexpectedly, since she knew it so well already, Linnet was moved at hearing part of her own tale given the character of a heroic legend, and by Dysart's fervent energy. To her horror she felt a tingle at the back of her nose, and knew she was going to shed at least one tear. Her nose was going to run, and she had brought no handkerchief. Looking away from them all, she concentrated on sniffing quietly.

Something shifted the shadows beyond the arch. There was no sound, just a movement catching at the corner of her eye. Her threatened tears did not fall. Blotting her nose on the back of her hand, Linnet made out the shape of the bed in its white fur, and then, reluctantly, the darkness yielded yet another, dimmer form. Someone was standing beside the bed, someone almost indistinguishable from the pale curtains that fell around it. One of the King's assassins was listening to everything Dysart was saying.

'My dear, we all rejoice that Creon did open his yellow door,' said Lord Glass. 'But after all it was a genial accident – a little indulgence of fate, yes? And Creon could have many amiable characteristics and still be guilty of an attack on the King. Lady Linnet –' Lord Glass swung towards her. 'We all know that Dysart is given to – to dreams, let's say. You do confirm everything he has told us?'

'Yes,' Linnet said, turning back to the lighted room. 'I made him promise not to tell, because there was more – more shame in it for me than there was for him, but I was there.'

'You made him promise not to divulge any of this?'

'I was afraid,' Linnet said. 'And I'm not used to being afraid. I'd never been frightened before, not like that anyway. First there was being attacked – and then there was the vision coming true!' she couldn't help adding.

'The vision coming true? Wheels within wheels!' said Lord Glass, making a fluttering, helpless gesture with his bright hands. The white shape by the white curtains was still in Linnet's thoughts as she answered. 'That day, the day we first met Izachel in Kitia – when he spoke to Dysart for the first time –'

Lord Glass nodded.

'I had a vision. I think we all did, didn't we?'

Nobody answered her. Everyone looked a little away from everyone else. 'Well, *I* saw Creon's yellow door. I was shown it. So when we ran towards it, I was the one – it was me who knew what we had to do – we had to beat on the yellow door. So that's what we did, and Creon came out with his dogs. Otherwise we would have been killed.'

Lord Glass jiggled on his toes and shook his head. 'Ah, yes! The city eats children,' he quoted with a sigh.

'It did nearly eat me,' Dysart agreed vehemently. 'It would have swallowed both of us and smacked its lips but for Creon. And it's not just my life I owe him. He knows what it was like to be lost.'

'I'm afraid I'm lost now too,' Lord Glass said, and for the first time Dysart's confident speech stumbled. His lips moved as if he were working something out. Then he said, 'You see, I know Creon's made himself into a good man. He was lost, like I'm lost, but he's used his difference to make himself a sort of father to other lost ones, even to me. I know he's got tired of me at times, turning up and pouring it all out, about being shut away like a bad secret – shut out of real life, really – but he's never been ashamed of me.'

Something had been said that startled both Betony and Lord Glass, and Lord Glass, when he spoke, spoke so rapidly that he actually stuttered a little.

'But you see it's not Creon's beneficence that's in question, Lord Prince. It's his judgement. Remember the King has been struck by an arrow – the King – the true spirit of Hoad – your father!'

'He is the true spirit of Hoad,' Dysart said, 'and of course I do stand in awe of him. And no doubt part of me came out of him in the beginning, but right now Creon's more my father than the King is. Creon likes me, and I like him. And I know he doesn't care enough about the King and Hero to bother being disloyal to either of them. He isn't interested in the game of Heroes and Kings. So I'm out to get justice for him.' He suddenly looked at Betony, frowning. 'I must be really mad,' he said. 'I'm forgetting that I told you all this before – when I was ill. Why didn't *you* tell them all this?'

There was a instant of startled silence, then Betony filled it with a noisy sigh and buried his face in his hands.

'Don't you remember – you made me promise I'd keep your wretched secret,' he groaned, and then, looking up again, he added, 'and besides I am perfectly certain that Creon Memory prompted his student friends to attack our father.'

'That won't do,' said Dysart. 'You've met Creon. You rode out into the third ring to see after I'd told you about him. He told me you'd visited him there, and talked to the students, too. So you must know the difference between him and them. Anyone could see it.'

'It was years ago. If I saw it then, I don't remember it now.'

Linnet expected a further outburst from Dysart, but he fell completely silent, frowning at his brother as if he had given him a puzzle to solve. 'What are you up to?' he said at last, in a softer, more tentative voice, as if they were alone together.

'I can't be as clever or intuitive as you think I am,' Betony replied. 'I believe Creon plotted against our father. Not that I blame him!'

Dysart's mouth hung open slightly, so that, for the first time, he seemed ridiculous. He licked his lips, then laughed and turned back to Lord Glass, whose quick gaze was leaping from

Betony to Dysart and then back again, as if the conversation between them were still in progress. 'We're supposed to be a just city, Lord Glass,' Dysart said, speaking in an orderly way once more, but with passion, too. 'Forget Bet! I know Creon's innocent.'

'Would it make sense to you if I said that true justice sometimes can have complicated results which are far more destructive than those of injustice?' Lord Glass asked in a drier, less affected voice than he had used previously.

'Well why are we taught to admire justice if we're not supposed to try for it?' Dysart cried. 'Why are justice and mercy supposed to be the signs by which you tell kings and the children of kings from all the rest.' He paused, and then said deliberately, '"The wonder of the city lies in its mercy, the glory of the city in its truth, the foundation of its wonder and glory are in its justice." Our father wrote that when he was my age.'

'He probably copied it from someone else,' Betony suggested. He stood up and stretched, apparently tired of sitting back among the blue cushions.

'I must tell you, Lord Prince, that I have not taken the part of Creon Memory,' Lord Glass explained to Dysart. 'I have bargained, persuasively I hope, for the life of another man.'

'Oh, but do tell him that the man you have argued for,' said Betony, 'is a declared man of the Burnt History gang. His name's signed on their declaration, whereas Creon's name is not.' He dusted his sleeve as he added, 'Lord Glass, I'm getting bored with all this. I have sat through first one set of arguments and now another. I think I'll leave you to work it out, since I don't have little Dysie's anxieties over justice – or his faith in it or his interest in it – I'm quite indifferent to whoever you decide to kill.' He was walking across the room as he spoke. At the door he paused. 'You haven't explained to Dysart my father's particular obsession with symmetry, have you? I think you should.'

Lord Glass sat down at last, waving his hand at the empty chairs. 'The Lord Prince Betony Hoad is right,' he said. 'The King does require a certain pattern to be observed in his retribution.'

'Pattern?' exclaimed Dysart, incredulous. Behind him Betony leaned pensively against the door frame.

'All counties are represented in this wretched band of scholars, Lord Prince, Lady Linnet – Bay, Argo, Dante, Glass, Isman, Hagen and Doro. No doubt their concern for the poor of the third ring is romantic and temporary, and will soon be eaten away by normal self-interest. But over the years your father has learned, Lord Prince, sometimes bitterly, that a merciful king often seems weak. Why, goodness me,' exclaimed Lord Glass, returning to his more frivolous style, 'even those he spares are likely to despise his mercy, and of course many people long to see public retribution, unless they themselves are to be the subject of it, of course. It's rough justice and rougher entertainment all in one. So, though most of these young men, these students of the Burnt History, will be sent back to their counties as exiles under detention, the King is demanding a life from each county.' He broke off, sighed and looked at Linnet. 'And certainly the King mustn't appear to favour County Glass over County Hagen, say. Yet, flatteringly enough, there are only the two men from County Glass involved – Memory and the other one, a boy of twenty – a country boy,' said Lord Glass, adding with great deliberation, 'whose family, the Tarbas family, are my people. Their sons and fathers have died in our wars, just as if they were born men of Hoad, not Ortish offshoots. They've been so stripped of men in the past that the women have had to breed the horses, and shear the sheep, and kill stock when winter comes and the food gets scarce. And when the Dannorad began to come down through Hoad, two years before you were born, Lord Prince, Jen and Whisper Tarbas, along with Whisper's daughter – the mother of the young man in question – volunteered to fight as campaigners for County Glass. Now, I contend that it's partly those sacrifices which have made the young man himself turn against the idea of the King. And I really think they deserve this one life returned, in recognition of what they've given. They certainly need it more than the House of Memory does. And besides, I think – I really do think – it's wise not to disturb them.'

'Wise?' exclaimed Dysart in astonishment.

'They have a strange history,' said Lord Glass obscurely.

'I've been forced to listen to this over and over again,' Betony said. 'It's all too pragmatic for my taste. I'm a fantasist at heart. I'll say goodnight.'

The door closed after him, but immediately there was another sound in the shadows beside Lord Glass's bed. The white shape had not moved, but something else rose out of the darkness and billowed slowly towards them. Before Linnet's startled eyes, the King himself came forward, meeting Dysart's shocked eyes with his own intense gaze. He was wearing a plain, rough, white scholar's robe edged with white fur and, as he was without his crown, Linnet could see how his hair was creeping back at the temples and how a red crease left by the crown ran across his forehead. He was naturally pale but she had never seen a man as waxen as this. Even his lips were white. The eyes in the thin, creased face were Dysart's own, his forehead, eyes, nose and cheekbones were exactly like. However, where Dysart had a wide goblinish mouth, in the

King the upper lip delicately overlapped the lower one so that he resembled some nocturnal browsing creature. This was the man who cast a shadow over all the counties of Hoad – but a shadow reversed – a glittering shadow – although he was so much a man of the night.

Linnet's Diamond nurse, pointing out the light at the top of the Tower of the Lion, had often told her that it marked the room where the King worked late – going over castle accounts with the Treasurers of the Household, or plotting policy with close friends like Lord Glass and Lord Dante, or listening to reports collected by his cunning and ancient Uncle, the old Queen's brother, organiser of spy system, cataloguer and winnower of the news his informers brought from one boundary of Hoad to the other, and from Camp Hyot and the Dannorad, too.

The assassin Cloud followed the King into the light. His hands as well as his face were painted white, and he reflected back light so flatly his expression was unguessable. A mosaic of faint powdery cracks in the paint gave him the look of a life-size doll recently shattered.

The King sighed and sat down in the third chair before the fire. One sleeve of his robe hung loose. Under the pale fabric his arm was strapped across his chest. 'You've been well taught, Dysart,' he said dryly.

'I've learned,' Dysart replied. He seemed startled but not intimidated. 'That's not the same thing. And there was no need to hide from me. Whatever I've got, you won't catch it, Gentle Lord.'

The King ignored this. 'Perhaps you should ask your first father's permission before you go looking for another father out in the third ring,' he said mildly.

'I'm like a beggar,' Dysart said. 'Glad to get anything I can get.'

'It's part of Kingly function, you know,' his father went on, 'choosing between ignoble alternatives. Because the King is dishonorable on behalf of his people, princes and heroes and men like Creon are free to preserve their own honour, knowing deep down they will be comfortably maintained.'

'Remember I once told you, my dear,' Lord Glass interrupted, nodding at Dysart, 'the king is the fox, the hero the lion.'

'And besides,' the King continued, 'when you understand just what making such choices feels like, you may understand what it means to be King. So you be the one to choose, Dysart. You choose between the Ortish farmer and your friend Creon. It is going to be unjust either way, but what I have to decide is whether or not it may also be unfortunate.'

Linnet was aware of an excitement she half despised coursing through her. *This is where I should have been all this time*, she thought. *Here where people are deciding – here, where it's life and death, not just dresses and bells and bracelets. This is where the heiress of Hagen should be.* As she thought about being the heiress of Hagen she was startled that the vague image of Luce that had been a comfortable part of her thoughts for years had gone. Dysart's face had replaced his older brother's, part of her future in Hagen, just as she saw it now, gazing alertly back into eyes as oddly coloured as his own.

'I have to choose Creon,' Dysart declared. 'You see I know – I really *know* – he's innocent.'

'Very well,' said the King, casual, apparently dismissing a small problem. 'That's that, then. That's simple! Lord Glass will have Creon Memory released, and will issue a warrant for the life of the Ortish farmer. And County Hagen will respect the sacrifice of County Glass, most necessary at a time when I understand the Master has the prospect of a male heir once more.'

'What?' cried Linnet, startled.

'Has your father not told you?' asked the King. 'I think you'll find I'm right. As to the matter of Creon Memory – I'm satisfied! Enough!'

Lord Glass did not argue. Linnet thought he knew the King so well that he recognised this pronouncement as being somehow irrevocable. 'There are many sorts of innocence,' he said. 'I accept Lord Prince Dysart's judgement.' He paused. 'I do think it might be very unwise to try taking Caron Tabas – the Ortish student that is – by force from among his family.'

'Well,' said the King in an irritable tone, and he appeared to think again. 'I will send Cloud after him. There! That's a tribute to your mystic farmers in the ruins, Dorian. He'll go so gracefully, they'll hardly know he's gone. He won't know himself. Of course, my father would have had his head brought back, and publicly displayed, but I hope to improve on my father,' the King said, 'just as Dysart there is thinking that he could improve on me.'

'Gentle Lord,' said Dysart, 'if everything was perfect with you as King, there'd be nothing to look forward to.'

'So you've saved Creon Memory,' the King said, looking away from Dysart. 'He'll be released tomorrow. It won't do him any harm to think over one more night about how carefully old stories ought to be told. I shall talk to him myself and let him know that you've paid your debt. And now you must go, for Lord Glass and I have at least one singular thing to talk about, don't we, Dorian? Hasn't Dysart brought something a little odd to our attention.'

'The challenge of the Hero Link,' Lord Glass suggested. 'Grand occasions flock upon us.'

'I was not talking about Link!' the King said sardonically. 'Dysart, did I understand you to say that you had taken Betony out into the third ring to meet Creon?'

'No,' Dysart said. 'You know I didn't say that.'

Something was being said. Something was going on in the room. Linnet could feel it around her, but she was reeling with her own concerns. Once again, Hagen was becoming infinitely desirable, but tenuous. She herself was threatened with change. But Dysart stared at his father earnestly. Father and son looked equally pale under the false bloom the lamp light gave them.

'You have achieved what you came for, haven't you,' asked the King.

Dysart bowed his head to the table, bowed lower to his father and turned to leave.

'Dysart!' the King said suddenly, so Dysart looked back again. 'It's been very instructive to make your acquaintance. I am astonished, I must confess.'

Dysart burst out laughing. 'It's been instructive to make yours after all these years, gentle Lord,' he said. 'Perhaps before he sets out, Cloud could take Lady Linnet back to the Tower of the Swan and let them know she came here on your business.'

'I can speak for myself,' Linnet cried, sharp.

'Well you didn't!' Dysart answered. 'I have to think of everything.'

'Cloud does not run such errands,' the King said. 'Dorian, could you send a release with your man Powley.'

A few minutes later, Dysart and Linnet, escorted by Lord Glass's grumbling servant Powley, walked back through Guard-on-the-Rock, past the drum tower and around the new water tank. Suddenly Dysart came to an abrupt stop. He took out a handkerchief and wiped his mouth and Linnet saw dark stains on it before he hastily hid it away again. 'What's wrong with you?' she hissed at him.

'It's not my blood,' he answered, smiling. 'I'm being haunted again.' He walked on.

'We've saved Creon,' Linnet said. 'Well, you saved him! I was just a witness.'

'I needed you there,' Dysart murmured. 'I wanted you to see me do something well for a change. But now I can't help thinking about that other one – it must be that Ortish student I told you about. He's going to be – but it doesn't matter, does it? What does matter is Betony.'

'What matters is that my stepmother is expecting another baby and nobody told me,' shouted Linnet.

'Oh yes, I heard that.' Dysart was prepared to dismiss Hagen lightly. He went on with what he'd wanted to say. 'But don't you see. Betony didn't tell them about Creon, even though he knew everything. Well, he knew enough!' He began to shiver and hugged himself fiercely as he walked through the night. 'Perhaps – well, there's no point in guessing!'

They had reached the door of the Tower of the Swan. Powley spoke to the guard, then turned and looked at them, stern.

'Goodnight!' Linnet said. She didn't know what she expected from Dysart – nothing more than an eloquent look, perhaps, some sign of understanding. But though he looked at her he was not seeing her and, feeling herself becoming insubstantial, she desperately wanted to be seen.

'Goodnight!' he said.

Linnet went past the guard, feeling increasingly invisible. It was as if Hagen had faded, was a possibility and not a certainty. She turned once and saw Dysart moving off with Powley, talking urgently as he went, and had the feeling that he might be talking to himself.

*

The following day, as Linnet walked in the gardens, one of the ladies around the old Queen, she saw Dysart again, not sidling by as he had always done before, but walking purposefully towards them. He came up to his grandmother and bowed, and spoke to her directly, something Linnet had never seen him do before. The old Queen answered graciously enough, though she did not like Dysart. Everybody knew that.

'I've come to give you some gossip,' Dysart told his grandmother. 'Betony has run away.' Then he looked past his grandmother straight into Linnet's eyes.

'Betony Hoad?' the old Queen said in her chilly voice. 'Your brother?'

'There's just the one Betony, Grandmother,' Dysart answered. But Linnet knew that she was the one he was really talking to. 'He took off in the early hours and he's taken Izachel with him. He's actually stolen the Magician of Hoad from the King.'

I want to come home, Linnet wrote to her father. *I have been here long enough. You have forgotten me. I had to learn from the King of Hoad that you were expecting another child.*

He wrote back to say Diamond was the best place for her, and that this time, after three daughters, he would certainly have a son.

Linnet wrote again. *I want to come home. Prince Betony has gone and the King won't want Luce to marry me now that he's the heir. And Luce isn't interested anyway. He spends his days with warriors and his nights with servant girls.*

Of course you must come home, her father wrote back, *but not just yet. Betony will be found again, you can be sure of that. Luce is young but deep down he knows his duty. Everything will be just as it was.*

I must come home, Linnet wrote again, desperate now. *I feel I am in danger here.* But she didn't tell her father that her danger was that of falling in love with the wrong prince.

Linnet could not remember a time when she had not been in love with someone, for a year or a day or an hour at a time – often not so much with a whole man as with a particular head of curls, or an open smile – with someone older, with someone handsome. By now she knew the symptoms well enough to laugh at herself when her heart began thumping at the sight of a certain face, or when she found herself planning how she could be standing casually in a particular spot at a particular time, so that she could see the loved one walk past. These loves were like little illnesses which she recovered from in time. But when she saw Dysart again after that incoherent night, her blood seemed to thicken a little and stand still. Then it began surging through her once more with terrible excitement.

The thought of loving Dysart horrified her. He was only her own age and he was not handsome. Somehow she was breaking her own secret rules. And yet. And yet Dysart could do something that might just as well have been magical. He could climb the crumbling stair around the Tower of the Swan to appear out of the night, reminding her that, under the weight of her grand dresses, she was still Linnet of Hagen. All around her, Guard-on-the-Rock rang with gossip and alarm over the vanishing of Betony and Izachel. The King sent men out into the counties of Hoad, into the Dannorad and even Camp Hyot with instructions to find the fugitives and bring them back to Diamond. It's the magician he really wants, people said. He's got other sons, but only one magician. In the meantime, as far as Linnet could hear, nobody suggested, dared not even whisper, that it had been Betony who brought the students in on the night of Misrule. That Betony had planned the assassination. Such guesses shifted like reflections in people's eyes, or murmured behind their words as they talked around the subject. It was known though nobody did any telling.

And suddenly Dysart was to be seen, strolling through the interlocking courtyards, out in the open at last. He would stop and speak to his grandmother as if he had always been a perfectly acceptable grandson, glancing over the old lady's shoulder into Linnet's eyes. Linnet and Dysart were even able to gossip a little, passing each other in the halls and courtyards of the castle. Anyone could see them smile and pause to exchange words, and stroll a few steps together. 'I told you,' he said. 'My time's come at last. The Magician's gone, I've moved up a place, and my father sends for me so that I can be part of his morning conferences.' What nobody knew was that once or twice a week, Dysart climbed the crumbling stair, pressing himself to the rock, his warm breath condensing on the stone, muttering to himself to keep himself alert every second of the way, to meet with Linnet at the top of the Tower of the Swan in the chilly autumn dark, under the arch of stars.

And the nights were starry for a little while. Autumn paused. Tawny days enveloped the city, bringing a deceptive mellowness to the crowded courts of Guard-on-the-Rock. Further down the coast a brief electrical storm lashed Cassio's Island. The King and his court, crowded on the mild sunlit heights of Guard-on-the-Rock, watched the livid west flickering and growling as the storm passed on towards Bay and Camp Hyot, leaving the city untouched.

Out on Cassio's Island, the Hero Link prepared for what everyone believed would be his last challenge. In Diamond, young Carlyon, watched avidly by Prince Luce, practised his rituals of death as gracefully as if he were a dancer, and spent hours closeted with the King, being instructed in the mystical and sacrificial nature of the Hero. The collects of Diamond brought out their faceless idols of the Hero (for the Hero, like the King, had so many faces it was easier to show none of them) and set them up over their doors. People burned candles in front of them and made offerings. There were stories of traders out in the wild looking up and seeing the shadows of previous heroes on the move, haunting the land – Hoel riding by, or Cassio himself staring silently at them across a campfire, or Estreldis, riding by without smile or salute, his terrible injuries hidden by a mask of silver – another spirit made restless by the challenge to the Hero. As the Kings' men combed other towns and cities for the missing heir to the kingdom, Creon Memory, back in his hall once more, paused from time to time to put his long pale fingers on his own pulse, amazed to feel it still beating. In the zoo the lions paced and roared.

During all this time, Dysart and Linnet were meeting, shivering, on the top of the tower, to gossip and laugh softly, always afraid that some echo tripping down the stairway might bring someone up the stairs to find out what was going on.

PATRICIA GRACE

Patricia Grace says, 'I'm a novelist, short story writer and writer of books for children, living on ancestral land in close proximity to my home marae in Hongoeka Bay, Plimmerton. At present I'm distractedly engaged in writing my memoirs.'

The Parson Who Thought She or He Was a Bishop

Outside my big window there's a pūriri tree, close enough to touch if I could lean out a little way. Birds come there – kererū when the berries are ripe, crashing about, finches in the winter. Tūī come any old time, but more so when the tree is in flower, dipping in and out of the little honeyed chalices. But never mind that.

There's this mad one. This tūī who, from dawn – no before dawn, like four o'clock in the morning – starts up singing its three notes, the same three notes – all day, every day until dark and beyond. Same three notes. Pī ho pa, pīhopa, pīhopa. Despite any tūī's innate abilities, this one won't change his or her tune. Not for anything. What's that all about?

Sing something else, I tell her or him. If others can do it, you can. Listen to your relations. Listen, listen. Great repertoires they have: *Creak* and *croak*, *tittle* and *rattle*, *sing song*, *ding dong*, *ki runga*, *ki raro*, *babble* and *squeak*, *tihei*, *tihei*, *dur*, *whiti whitia*, *gargle-argle*, *tāiki ē*, *tīramarama*, *tikiti*. You could learn. Some of your mates have got beeps, *dit*, *dit*, *dit*, *dit*, like a wash cycle coming to an end, or some have cell phone rings. They can. You can.

But there *you* go, day in, day out, same old, same old: *Pīhopa, pīhopa, pīhopa.*

I mean . . . there's no way . . . A tūī cannot be a bishop. No, no. Bishop? Pīhopa? No. And it's not just me giving out home truths. See this book? It says here, 'Often called the parson bird because of . . .' Well, you know because of what – black clothes, white collar. Have a look at yourself. Wrong outfit for a red/purple bishop. I mean, it's beautiful, what you've got. Not what you'd call real black either. You've got your greens, your blues, your purples, your browns.

Like a pāua. There you are. You may not relish being likened to a pāua, but there you go. Remove the fish from its shell, you've got your black and your white. You have your stomach sac of khaki, purple, brown and cream. Beautiful. Then the inside of the shell, all your iridescences, floating soap bubble colours, oil on water, shot silk, burnish and lustre. Isn't that good enough? Pāua power? Parson power? You're an icon for goodness' sake. World Wide Image. You can't do better than that. Be satisfied. I'm just giving a bit of advice to save you embarrassment, because you can't. It's impossible. Advice. Take it personally.

There now, see, off it goes, doesn't want to know, out back to the pōhutukawa trees, out of sight, but I can still hear: *Pīhopa, pīhopa, pīhopa*, i ngā wā katoa. Well, I do my best. You can't lead a horse to . . . Ah. It's for his or her own good. Got to get down off the high perch before she or he falls off. Thinks he or she has escaped from me. Doesn't realise I could make it out there if I wanted to. Thinks I'm stuck here in this velvet chair twenty-four-seven, but that's all she or he knows. I could follow. I could get myself up out of here, but why should I waste my breath on a no-hoper? Why should I waste my legs?

Pīhopa my foot.

Anyway, back next morning, same song. Pīhopa, pīhopa. Me with my same song too: You could do better, have a better life, try harder, big ideas, up yourself. Come on. Spread your wings. Try *tākiri*, *tākiri*, *tākiri*, *hei runga*, *hei raro* . . . Try, try.

Then one morning, woke up to . . . silence. Imagine that. 4am, and . . . nothing. Not even the ruru. What's going on? Or perhaps I've gone deafer.

Long, long wait in silence, until *they* come and make the cup of tea. Even though there's only one of them, I say 'they' because she calls herself 'we'. We'll get you your Weetbix. We'll put your arm through here. They poke me in the shower. I'm clean enough, clean enough, I tell them. Haven't been out digging, down scrubbing, any of that.

You'll feel so much better once you've had a nice shower.

Better than what?

Ha ha. You're a trick. Ha, ha, ha. You're a trick and a half.

Ages before they get me into my velvet chair, my wheelie frame lined up beside me. They'll be back later to see if I'm behaving myself, ha ha ha.

Out there, are all those parsons, flopping about in the tree, but no pīhopa among them. Off somewhere sulking. Couldn't handle the advice. Too bad. Who cares? He or she will be back āpōpō.

But tomorrow doesn't, doesn't. Come. Does it?

Morning after morning in the dark. Nothing. Out in my velvet chair. Nothing. Most of them gone now. Gone bush.

I mean. I thought . . . I thought we, he or she and me . . . Didn't have to take it personally. I thought we were, you know . . . ?

Every day, every day.

*

Until, this morning, lying there in the dark with only the ruru to listen to. *Ru-ru. Ru-ru.* Well, at least that was something.

But then, cutting in on the night bird in a rude way came *pīhopa*, *pīhopa*, so bad manneredly.

Ah. Aha. I knew it. I knew you would. I mean, you and I we're . . . You and I we are, aren't we?

Anyway, got to wait for daylight. Don't go away, don't go away.

And when daylight gets up, I do too. Myself. Don't need all their helping. I can do it. Take the handles, don't hurry, and wheel myself out to the velvet chair. Get comfortable, focus my eyes. Can't see a thing. It's the sunrise making it all . . . Or perhaps I've got blinder.

Then I do see. I see you in all your new clothes, full regalia, red and purple, sunrise, sunset, ruby, fire engine, garnet, carmine, white collar. I *knew* it. I knew you could do it. All your mates and relations gather. They *squeak* and *rattle*, *ding* and *dong*, *tihei*, *tihei*, *tākiri*, *tākiri*, *tākiri*, *kū-i*, *kū-i*, *whio*, *whiti*, *whiti*, *whio*, telephone, washing machine *whio*. They're bowing. They're smiling and flapping.

We are, all of us, clapping.

OWEN MARSHALL

Owen Marshall CNZM is the author of seven novels and eleven collections of short stories, and the editor of numerous influential anthologies, and has won many awards and accolades. Born in Te Kūiti, he has lived most of his life in the South Island, and is regarded as one of the most important chroniclers of its landscapes and peoples, but his work has always felt a pull towards the uncanny or the transcendent. 'Immortality', however, is a cautionary tale from his 1992 collection, *Tomorrow We Save the Orphans.*

Immortality

By that time it was not completely unexpected. The continued accomplishments of science, including outreach to Venus and the tapping of the earth's nuclear core, had created expectations in people's minds. Also the life expectancy was already up to 107 for women, though somewhat less for men and neuters. Nevertheless, the break through to immortality was considered a wonderful thing, and Academicians Neblinskov and Brown were awarded the Einstein Medal and grade five recreation rights. Their names would live forever, the Global President said, but the irony was that despite the discovery their own death could not be averted. The Neblinskov–Brown process wouldn't work for those much older than about eighteen, you see, for after that the hormonal ageing process had begun and could not be reversed.

Oh, it was a time for fine optimism and delight. Treatment was begun in all areas irrespective of class, wealth or race, for the Neblinskov–Brown process was not particularly expensive, less than AIDS immunisation for example, and it either took the first time or not at all, which could be determined by a blood test six months later. Celebrations of the new epoch for humanity were held all over the world, and the media trumpeted material pointing out the grand effects of the discovery in every walk of life. Think of it! What a rugby team of exceptional once in a million talents could be built up over two or three hundred years, say. In literature and art, genius could mature and ramify without being cut short, and in politics the wisdom and experience of the greatest statesmen need never be lost. The great, lurking cause of melancholy and depression throughout our history – a consciousness of inevitable death – was itself finally defeated.

A triumphant mood remained the tone for a year or more, and then there was a tapering of interest and insistence: a slackening, like the pause at the turning of the tide, then gradually, as the ebb tide reveals new outlines, other tones and attitudes could be seen.

Initially the change was thought something of a natural reaction; an anti-climax to be expected as it was realised that immortality did not solve all problems. But it became clear to the thoughtful amongst us that more curious and sinister forces were at work than that. The realisation came that the last great schism had been created in humankind, far deeper than that of gender or of race: a schism between the last generation bound to die, and those who were immortals. For the trained observers in society, myself included, the terrible psychological consequences of the Neblinskov–Brown discovery began to be discernible. Amongst older people welled up a complex despair and resentment that by a quirk of fate they must die within an age which had discovered the secret of perpetual life. Like Moses, they could view the promised land, but were forbidden entry. The new generation on the other hand were filled with a sense of complacency and arrogance that sprang from the knowledge that, barring accident, war, or the few remaining serious diseases, they would live forever.

The mortal generation did not admit the extent of their envy of course; some did not realise it. Instead their criticism took other forms. Religions began to preach on the theme that humankind had taken unto itself God's power over life and death; philosophers began to question the decision to apply the Neblinskov–Brown process before all the ethical issues had been considered; the social scientists warned of unmanageable population problems; sociologists feared a creeping lethargy of purpose once people had neverending tomorrows in which to do their work; psychologists predicted a growth of self-loathing as people could never escape their accumulating guilts and inadequacies.

The immortals and older people found themselves uneasy in each other's company. There was a separating and reforming of social groups, as oil and water seek themselves. The immortals formed large communities of their own where they could enjoy themselves without constantly giving offence to those who must die. Amongst the immortals was a marked sense of destiny and preferment. The more insensitive began a cult of jokes at the expense of mortals, even claiming that older people had a characteristic and unpleasant smell about them.

The rest drew together too, still powerful, holding wealth, political dominance and cultural supremacy because of their age. The SFHG was established, the Society of the Final Human Generation, and although criticised publicly as an extremist organisation because of its claims of moral superiority, nevertheless it was powerful within the mortal community.

Many reasonable older people still thought that with further research the threshold of immortality would soon be advanced, and enormous amounts of money were put at the disposal of the scientists for that purpose. After three years however the experts began to doubt if any advance on Neblinskov and Brown's work was possible, and the distinction hardened.

In my opinion the murder of Academician Brown was the first sign of things to come . . . An extremist group claiming links to the SFHG blew up the Rutherford Clinic where the initial breakthrough had been made, and Theo Brown, Einstein Medallist, was killed. Also a bitter argument developed as to whether the immortal generation should be allowed entry to positions of influence and responsibility as they came of age. The SFHG claimed that the attitudes of these young people were so different from any that had gone before that they could not be trusted to maintain the human civilisation carefully nurtured over thousands of years.

To protest against such views, the immortals held a great demonstration at Alice Springs, southern capital since the Greenhouse Effect, and some 170,000 marchers supported demands for an immediate share in political decisions and greater access to the means of production. The new generation had its own radicalism. One of the leaders of this, Alphonse Diderolle, claimed that his group had nuclear capability, and openly questioned whether the old generation should be allowed any say in the direction of a brave, new world. Diderolle wished all mortals to be dismissed, retired, and confined to hospice communities.

Outbreaks of violence and irrational cruelty have become commonplace, and there is a persistent rumour that the military have been secretly irradiating the immortal communities so that they will die after all in their own turn. If such activity is ever detected the reaction must be catastrophic.

We have reached a sad situation of barbarism, so soon after the joy and anticipation which followed the Neblinskov–

Brown discovery. Extremists on both sides have capitalised on fear, envy and lack of trust. Who knows what we unleash within our minds, once we change the order of things.

I have decided to encode this brief summary of events, together with the documents supporting it, and enter it as a record in the high satellite Omega. If the whole business passes over without tragedy, I shall later update this information. If the file is not added to, then you will know what has happened in regard to the magnificent achievement of immortality.

PHILLIP MANN

Phillip Mann was born in North Yorkshire in 1942, and has lived in New Zealand since 1969, becoming one of the country's best-known university drama teachers, and also its leading science fiction writer. His celebrated alien contact novel *The Eye of the Queen* was published by Gollancz in 1982, followed by the two-volume *Story of the Gardener* (*Master of Paxwax*, *The Fall of the Families*), *Pioneers*, *Wulfsyarn*, and the epic series A Land Fit For Heroes (*Escape To The Wild Wood*, *Stand Alone Stan*, *The Dragon Wakes*, *The Burning Forest*). His most recent novel, the visionary ecological romance *The Disestablishment of Paradise*, marked a welcome return to publishing after a seventeen-year break; he followed it with the collection *Maestro and Other Stories*, and a linked pair of comic novels, collectively titled *The Head Man*, is forthcoming.

The Gospel According to Mickey Mouse

Part one

The tall angular man in the deer-stalker hat knelt down in the parking lot behind the ruined police car and spoke with Patrolman Quin. The police car was burnt out, but still afforded some protection. Beyond the car stretched the parking lot in front of Disneyland, and beyond that again, the large coils of barbed wire thrust forward by the military at the time of their last advance. All was now quiet, except that somewhere in the depths of the fun park, a lone calliope was piping its way through 'Greensleeves' for the millionth time. Above the barbed wire could be seen the still-smouldering turrets of Sleeping Beauty's Castle and the shattered framework of the Matterhorn.

The whole area surrounding Disneyland had been evacuated days earlier when the trouble first began. Now Los Angeles was unnaturally quiet. Tanks and armoured personnel carriers were dug in round the perimeter. The barrels of their guns all pointed inwards.

'Gee Mr Holmes,' said Patrolman Quin, his eyes bulging and his hand still sore from the crippling handshake. 'We're all mighty honoured and relieved to have you with us. I've been a fan of yours ever since I learned to read.'

'Quite so,' said Sherlock Holmes. His sharp grey eyes roved restlessly over the crazy skyline of Disneyland. 'But what I need are facts, Quin. When did this outbreak occur?'

'Facts is hard to come by, Mr Holmes, sir,' said Patrolman Quin. 'We was driving down Hollywood Boulevard three days ago when the call came through. "All units report to Disneyland. Major disaster. This order timed at 15:30 hours." We knew it must be serious as the girl who gives out the patrol calls was all excited and kept getting her words mixed up. Well, we was on our way before she'd finished speaking. No one likes the idea of a disaster at Disneyland.'

'Did anything strike you as strange about this request, Quin?'

'Yes sir, Mr Holmes, sir. I mean, *all* units . . . We're a pretty big force in this city, and besides, Disneyland has its own police. They don't want trouble. Bad for business. They like to keep it a family affair. The last thing they want is a whole roost of us Cherry-Tops . . . er, that's what we call our cars on account of the red light we have on the roof, to come bustin' in.'

'And what happened?' asked Sherlock Holmes.

'We got in a traffic jam. Seems like every patrol car south of San Francisco had responded to that call for help.'

'And when you eventually got to Disneyland?'

'Panic, Mr Holmes, sir. Panic. Pure and simple. Kids screaming. Women screaming. Men screaming. People trampled underfoot. Cars jammed and wrecked. I mean, I was there when those two jumbo jets crashed over LA International Airport, so I know what a mess looks like, but I've never seen nothing like this. They weren't people no more. They was animals. They was blinded with fear.'

'And what else did you see?'

'Him.'

'Who?'

'Mickey Mouse, sir. And he seemed so big. He'd climbed up on top of the Matterhorn. And he was waving and laughing at the crowd as they ran screaming away. Honest sir, he looked like King Kong in that scene when he climbs up the Empire State Building, and he had a girl in his hands.'

'And what did he do?'

'Please, sir . . .'

'I need the facts, Quin. The facts. Accurate judgement is based on accurate facts, no matter how improbable they may seem at the time.'

'Yes, sir. Pardon, sir. I've never been sick on duty before, sir, but I was then. He had this girl in his hands sir, and he . . . bit her head off.'

Sherlock Holmes breathed deeply. 'Just like that.'

'Just like that, sir. He has a powerful big mouth. And those teeth looked wicked.' Patrolman Quin suppressed a shudder. 'That was when we started shooting, sir. We let loose with everything we had. But it didn't make a dime's worth of difference. He just stood there smiling and munching. Then Minnie Mouse climbed up too and they both stood hand in hand waving at us. It was horrible.'

Sherlock Holmes nodded to himself and patted Quin gently on the shoulder.

'What's happening to the world, Mr Holmes? It used to be so peaceful. I mean, bank robberies and muggings and the odd kidnapping I could take. All part of the day's work, so to speak. But this? Mr Holmes, sir, it's like a nightmare. Like living in a nightmare.'

'It *is* a nightmare, Patrolman Quin,' said Sherlock Holmes. 'But it has a logical basis. This same force which brought Mickey Mouse and his friends to life has now, in this hour of the world's need, turned its powerful agency upon me. Strange as it may seem, this Mickey Mouse and I are brothers. Yet we are the deadliest of enemies. The struggle will be mighty before this battle ends.'

'But what does it all mean, sir?'

'Elementary, my dear Quin. In your world, truth has become stranger than fiction and now fiction has leaped up to answer the challenge.'

Patrolman Quin scratched his head. He felt at that moment as Dr Watson had felt many times.

Sherlock Holmes stood up. He faced the ruins of Disneyland squarely. 'I at least have nothing to fear from them,' he said.

At that moment the calliope grew louder and faster. In a few seconds it was racing through 'Greensleeves' in a raucous cacophony. Such a noise could not be sustained. It cut out suddenly with a sound like a spring uncoiling. Silence. Then something moved.

Before the startled gaze of Sherlock Holmes and Patrolman Quin, Mickey Mouse followed by Snow White and the Seven Dwarfs and Bambi climbed up onto the twisted tracks of the monorail and began dancing. Faintly their voices carried through the dense Los Angeles air. 'Heigh ho. Heigh ho . . .'

*

'I've got to get in there. Personal observation is worth fifty of your special reports.' So said Sherlock Holmes. He struck a match crisply and applied its flame to the bowl of an old and oily black clay pipe. While puffing he glanced round the assembled faces.

It was a meeting of chiefs of staff. Round the table were seated hard-boiled Colonels, red-necked Majors and battle-scarred Lieutenants. They were all granite-jawed and serious of mien.

'That's not gonna be easy, Mr Holmes, sir,' said Major Liebestraum, hero of 125 sorties behind enemy lines in Vietnam. 'We've thrown everything at them. Everything that is, except the "big bang". Bazooka fire, rockets, mortars. Didn't raise a pimple. They just lined up along the perimeter and laughed at us. Then that big one with the ears . . . what's his name?'

'Dumbo.'

'Yeah, Dumbo. He starts flapping his ears and up he goes like a balloon. Started squirting water at us with his trunk. That's when I called the cease-fire. Only thing that seems to keep them contained right now is the electric fence, and I wouldn't like to say how long that'll last.'

A thin man in a plain, brown city suit coughed politely into his sleeve and raised his hand.

'Shoot, Dwight,' said Major Liebestraum, and sat down. Dwight was a gentle-looking man with a soft voice and permanent seven-o'clock shadow. He seemed nervous, but his eyes behind his steel-rimmed glasses were bright and sharp. He unfurled a street plan onto the operations table.

'I've been studying the old construction plans,' he said. 'This is from the drainage department. There is one method of entry which you may not have thought of and which I am sure the enemy will not have considered. It is through the sewer of the Haunted House.'

Behind the glowing stubs of cigars, military faces crinkled and smiled. They leaned forwards.

'You see, I've sketched it in, in green. This culvert was designed originally, I understand, to carry flood water from all the lakes and rivers in Disneyland. So far as I know it has never been needed. As you can see, arms lead off the main conduit and penetrate to all parts of the playground. For a saboteur or an assassin, it is an ideal access.'

'Dwight, you're a genius,' said Major Liebestraum, and slapped him on the back. Rumbles of agreement came from all round the table.

Dwight coughed into his sleeve and smiled shyly.

'What's your feeling, Mr Holmes?' asked Major Liebestraum. 'Do you think you can make it? We can draw their attention with some fancy hardware and fly-overs and such. But beyond that you are on your own.'

Sherlock Holmes continued puffing quietly on his pipe. Finally he took the pipe from his mouth and tapped out the ashes into a large glass ashtray. He studied the earnest faces which surrounded him and a wry smile tugged at the corners of his mouth but his eyes were sad. Finally he spoke.

'Gentlemen. I have been in many strange predicaments, as perhaps you know, the like of which might trouble the mind of the Creator himself. And yet I am here today. We have but one life and we must live it as best we can according to our lights, taking the good with the bad. And who can predict the outcome? All my life has led up to this moment I think, and I am ready. None can go with me into that darkness. But if I do not return, know, gentlemen, that there are others within that perimeter who will have paid dearly for my life.'

He stopped speaking and the silence was broken only by Dwight who was sobbing and smiling at the same time. Great tears were welling up into his eyes and he was nodding vigorously.

So it was agreed that Sherlock Holmes should enter Disneyland alone. With him he carried a pair of binoculars, a flashlight and his trusty walking stick. Major Liebestraum had offered him stun grenades and a machine pistol. Dwight had come up with a fraternity pin which sprayed cyanide gas. But Sherlock Holmes refused all aids.

Now, watched over by the anxious Dwight, Major Liebestraum and Patrolman Quin, he lowered his long angular frame down through a manhole and into the dark depths of the culvert. He landed on his toes. The ground was perfectly dry and dust rose up to meet him.

Reaching down through the manhole, Major Liebestraum gave him a thumbs-up sign and then withdrew. The manhole cover clanged shut. The darkness was total. He was alone.

Sherlock Holmes was relaxed. He felt the familiar tingle of excitement in his spine. An adventure such as this was, after all, what he was made for. He switched on his flashlight, orientated himself and, having previously memorised the map of the waterway, set out confidently for the Haunted Mansion. The sound of his footsteps was muffled by the dust. There were no other footprints and it was obvious that he was the first person to use this conduit since it was built.

His journey was uneventful, but it took him longer than he expected. Finally he reached a place where three tunnels converged. Without hesitation he chose the left one and there facing him, set into the concrete were the rungs of an iron ladder. He aimed the flashlight up to the top of the ladder and revealed a door. Neat letters were stencilled on it: *Exit 37 HAUNTED MANSION.*

After surveying the iron rungs carefully, Sherlock Holmes swung himself up the ladder and tried the door. It opened easily, too easily, he thought as he stepped through.

It took a few seconds for his eyes to adjust to the darkness, for he dared not use his flashlight. Slowly he began to detect shapes. A faint luminescence came from the walls around him. He breathed evenly and deep, stilling his pulse which threatened to race. A way to his right the light seemed stronger and from that direction also came a sudden burst of insane laughter. He decided to investigate directly.

Moving with practised silence he skirted round some old machinery and large cog wheels and approached the source of the light. It was a door, standing a quarter open, and beyond it creatures were moving.

He peeped through. It was a banqueting hall. Thin wraithlike shapes with horrible grins flowed round the hall, casting shadows of green and blue. Seated at the central table were ghastly figures. Away to the left, a coffin was propped up and, as he watched, the corpse inside scrabbled at the lid with bony fingers and forced it open. Giant toads leaped about and a skull laughed hollowly.

Sherlock Holmes watched in amazement while his logical brain, working overtime, kept fear at bay. He observed the regularity of the movements. He counted the seconds between the appearances of the corpse and he looked into the eyes of the wraiths as they swept past him. He saw no light of intelligence. He noted the strings which pulled the toads. They were nothing more than grotesque puppets.

'All mechanical,' he breathed, and stepped out into the banqueting hall.

Using his flashlight, he was able to see that high in one wall was a balcony and beyond that the suggestion of a passageway. He climbed up onto the dining table, pushing the stiff diners aside, and with a leap reached the chandelier which was covered with cobwebs. Thin tendrils of gossamer plucked at his hair and sleeves. It was the work of a moment to shinny up the chain which held the chandelier and then make it swing until he could jump off and catch the balustrade which fronted the balcony. A pull of his strong arms and he was over.

He dusted his hands and clothes and with one last glance at the jumping toads and sickly wraiths, set off up the passage. It led him steadily upwards. He passed statues with heads that turned and mirrors where strange faces leered at him. He regarded them all with disdain. Then there was daylight. Blessed daylight.

Sherlock Holmes felt mildly disappointed. 'Is this all?' he wondered, and one of his own maxims passed through his mind. 'As a rule, the more bizarre a thing is, the less mysterious it proves to be.'

He eased open the front door to the Haunted Mansion and stepped out into the bright afternoon sunshine.

Waiting for him was a giant dog.

Pluto.

Lazily, Pluto scratched himself with a big floppy paw and a flea the size of a fifty-cent piece jumped into the air and hopped away singing.

Pluto blinked. 'Boss wants to see you. Wondered what took you so long.'

'Boss?' said Sherlock Holmes, startled and remembering vaguely the hound of the Baskervilles.

'Yeah. Mickey. De brains. Ya know. Says he wants to see

you straight away, soon as you gets clear of spooksville. Reckon you'd better come along with me.'

Before Sherlock Holmes could move, Pluto reached forwards and picked him up like a tasty bone. He trotted off down the sidewalk.

'Moriarty,' breathed Sherlock Holmes to himself as he bumped up and down. Somewhere he knew he had lost the initiative.

Sherlock Holmes was not too uncomfortable. Pluto held him high and was careful not to let his toes drag on the ground and not to bite too tightly.

As he jogged along, Sherlock Holmes found he had time to observe the route and store it away in his memory in case of a later escape. Away to his right was a paddle steamer. It had crashed into an island and now lay canted over onto one side with a gaping hole in its stem. One paddle still turned jerkily. The bright paintwork was burned and the wheelhouse was charred where a fire had blazed. Sherlock Holmes guessed that this was the result of a direct hit from one of Major Liebestraum's incendiary rockets.

There were other signs of the recent battle also: jagged craters in the road, broken glass, a collapsed stagecoach, puddles of melted icecream and ominous red stains. Once he saw the body of a human being crushed into a corner as though thrown with great force, but of the wholesale slaughter he had expected, there was no sign. 'Must have tidied up,' he thought, 'or else . . .' He became aware of the roughness of Pluto's tongue and of his hot saliva. He shuddered.

Soon they approached Sleeping Beauty's Castle, the gateway to Fantasyland. Here the bomb damage was worse. Every wall was pitted with shrapnel. The swans who had lived on the lake were all dead and bobbed up and down on the surface like blobs of dirty cotton wool.

The ride ended in a small pavilion. Pluto carried him up some stairs and dropped him unceremoniously in front of a door ringed with fairy lights. Sherlock Holmes was glad. The continual bouncing up and down had finally made him feel sick. He had lost his binoculars. They had slipped from round his neck shortly after his departure from the Haunted Mansion. His flashlight was gone too. It had fallen from his pocket. He still held on tight, however, to his walking stick.

'Boss'll see you soon,' said Pluto and yawned showing giant white teeth. 'Don't try nothing smart 'cos Mickey said to bring you in one piece.' Pluto licked his lips.

Sherlock Holmes sat without moving, his eyes fixed warily on the giant dog, which seemed to fall asleep the moment its long snout came to rest on its paws. Its loud snores shook the petals on the paper flowers which decorated the corridor.

Sherlock Holmes was just about to make a cautious move when the door opened and a voice boomed, 'Come on in Sherlock, baby. The broads is rotten but the bourbon's neat. Come on in and make yourself at home.' Sherlock Holmes guessed that this must be the voice of Mickey Mouse in person. He stood up slowly. Pluto opened one eye and winked at him. 'Better not keep the boss waiting,' he growled. 'Git a move on.'

Sherlock gripped his walking stick firmly and marched through the door with as much dignity as he could muster. He found himself in a large room with cloverleaf shaped windows. The sight which greeted his eyes stopped him in mid pace.

In one corner lay Peter Pan, his wings crushed and broken and his normally bright eyes dimmed with pain. Near him the remains of Jiminy Cricket were scattered about on the carpet. Minnie Mouse was there too. It was she that had opened the door. Now she was on her knees and crying into a big polka-dot handkerchief. Reclining on a sofa and looking very demure was Snow White. She was brushing her hair with a big silver brush and idly picking grapes from a large bowl held up by two of the seven dwarfs.

Facing him was Mickey Mouse. He was slumped forwards in a large easy chair with one hand resting on the floor and holding a bottle. His large black ears drooped and his eyes were brimming with tears.

'C'mon in stranger. Been expectin' ya. Saw you down in the parking lot. Hey, don't take any notice of the women. Been a family squabble is all.'

Sherlock Holmes advanced. The pungent smell of wood alcohol curled his nostrils. Mickey Mouse was obviously drunk.

Mickey Mouse took a deep breath and pulled himself upright in the seat. 'You catch us with the blues,' he said. 'Jeez, what a sod awful world we've inherited. You're supposed to be some sort of shrink, what'll we do?'

Sherlock Holmes remembered the agonised face of Patrolman Quin, who had asked a similar question.

He stared at Mickey and shrugged. Somewhere in the still logical recesses of his brain a voice whispered that now was his chance to attack. Now, while Mickey's mind was fogged with alcohol and his attention was held by his own problems. Now.

Sherlock Holmes raised his stick hesitantly and prepared to strike Mickey Mouse between the eyes. But for some reason his heart was not in it. Mickey Mouse stopped him with a blink.

'Drop it, baby,' he said. 'You've got no gripe with me.' Sherlock Holmes lowered his stick.

'I'm invincible. I'm eternal. You try and hit me with that fancy stick of yours and it'll just bounce off. Sure, you could hurt me, but I'd recover. And then I'd come after you. I could bounce you round the walls of this room like a rubber ball. Then it'd be your turn. One night, back you'd come . . . and maybe you'd get me for a while and then . . . See there's no future in battles between you and me, 'cos we're both fictionals. We're brothers.' Mickey Mouse beamed as the idea took hold of him and he tottered to his feet. 'Hey, waddya know, brothers? Me and the great Sherlock Holmes. Sherlock Holmes and Mickey Mouse. We'll drink to that.'

For the first time in his long life, Sherlock Holmes found himself at a loss for words. Logic failed him. He felt old. He was living beyond his time. A fossil. His world had been far simpler. Professor Moriarty seemed like a child at Sunday school compared to the alien wonder of a Mickey Mouse or a Minnie Mouse or a . . . what was his name . . . Pluto. Nothing in all the cases he had conducted had prepared him for this. He thought of Patrolman Quin and Dwight and all the army men crouched behind their guns at this very moment, and they seemed less real than the strange creatures that now confronted him.

Abruptly a glass was thrust into his hand. 'Drink,' ordered the irresistible Mickey.

Sherlock Holmes drank.

In the corner, Peter Pan groaned and tried to sit up.

'What befell him?' asked Holmes.

Mickey winked. 'He tried to hex me so I sat on him. He'll come right in a couple of days.' Mickey Mouse turned away. 'Hey, Snowey, baby. Get your butt in gear. Get the man a cushion. Make him comfortable. Ya know?'

Snow White stretched languidly and sat up on the sofa. She shook her raven black hair and smiled a dazzling smile at Sherlock Holmes.

'Mr Holmes,' she said, 'I want you to know that I've always admired you. And can I ask you a very special favour? Mmmmm?'

Sherlock Holmes looked at her and then looked quickly down into his glass.

'Yes,' he said.

'Would you mind awfully . . . I mean, don't be offended or anything, but, could I wear your cute little hat?'

Sherlock Holmes handed it over.

Minnie Mouse blew loudly into her pocket handkerchief. She crawled over to where Mickey had sat down again in the easy chair and put her hand on his knee. 'Sorry, baby. Didn't mean to cross you. Won't do it again. Promise.'

'Forget it,' said Mickey. 'Me and Snowey's just good friends. Anyway, we're all brothers here. All in the family.' He was watching Sherlock Holmes carefully.

Sherlock was sitting on the sofa beside Snow White and she was wearing his deer-stalker hat at jaunty angle. She had his pipe in her hands and was filling it carefully, tamping down the tobacco.

'What ya say, Sherlock?' called Mickey Mouse. 'Are we all brothers?'

'Sure . . . er . . . baby,' said Sherlock Holmes.

Just at that moment there came a fearful pounding at the door. It bent inwards on its hinges and then burst open. Pluto, all of a lather and with his legs going in all directions, landed in the middle of the floor. 'Hey boss,' he barked. 'You gotta see this. Just outside. Something's happening. Donald reckons it's another of them fictionals arriving. Come on.' Pluto's legs churned the air and he was gone with a whoosh. Behind him were Mickey and Minnie and Snow White and the two dwarfs. 'Wait for me,' called Peter Pan staggering to his feet.

Sherlock Holmes found himself alone. 'Help me,' called a small, wee voice. Sherlock jumped and looked round. On the floor, the bits of Jiminy Cricket were writhing about. 'I wanna see too,' said the head. 'Help me. Just pile me in a heap and I'll sort myself out later.'

Gingerly, between finger and thumb, Sherlock Holmes did as he was asked. He dropped the bits together and with one convulsive heave they all joined up. The arms and legs were the wrong way round but Jiminy Cricket didn't seem to mind. 'Thanks brother,' he said, limping towards the hole where the door had been. 'Come on. Don't miss the fun.' And he too was gone.

Sherlock Holmes made his way outside. There he found a crowd of the Disneyland characters. They were in a circle, and all were peering inwards to where a bright light was glowing in the air.

'Who is it?' asked Jiminy Cricket, pulling at Sherlock Holmes's trouser leg.' I can't see.'

'Don't know yet,' said Sherlock, eyeing the glowing light. He picked Jiminy Cricket up and placed him on his shoulders.

The light grew steadily brighter and from its depths came a deep, basso profundo groaning. The light took on shape. The shape of a man. Abruptly there came a sharp, brittle clap of thunder and the light exploded.

All the Disneyland characters, including Sherlock Holmes, dived for the ground. When they looked up again they saw a man. A giant. He stood stiff and straight, rocking back and forth on the thick soles of his boots. He wore a shapeless black suit which seemed several sizes too small for him. His hands were like shovels, and his shoulders gave the impression that the coat-hanger had been left inside the jacket. His face . . .

'His face,' said Snow White, clutching a handkerchief to her lips. She fainted.

The face was a mass of scars and the eyes were two yellow pits. 'Frankenstein,' breathed Sherlock Holmes.

'His monster,' answered the giant.

He turned slowly, as if with difficulty, and looked round the crowd. His fingers, stiff as frozen gloves, twitched.

'Hi there Frank,' said Mickey Mouse, rising to the occasion. 'Welcome aboard.' He took one of the stiff hands and tried to shake it.

'Where's Mary?' said the monster. 'Mary Shelley. She was near me. She loved me. She was writing. A long feather on paper. A candle burning and cold rain spattering the window.'

Mickey Mouse looked blank. 'Donald,' he called.

Donald Duck waddled over and joined him. There was a bright gleam in his eye.

'Tell us what you remember, Mr . . . er . . . Frank.'

The monster's face crinkled slowly into the most hideous smile ever seen. 'I remember . . . nothing. Then there was Mary and light and pain, and I knew I was ugly and people ran from me. Then . . .' His voice trailed away.

'Then . . .' prompted Donald Duck.

'Then there was a great rushing together. Lightning flashed. All my life passed before me, and I was here, as I am now.' He paused and surveyed the crowd. 'Where am I?'

'With friends,' said Mickey Mouse, fervently. He turned to Sherlock Holmes. 'Ya see, Sherlock, baby? It's all starting to happen. It's all coming together. Boy, are we gonna have a party.'

And that evening there was a party. Many more fictionals had arrived, either popping out of the air or casually clambering over the perimeter wire in front of the pop-eyed military. They gathered in the very centre of Disneyland.

Alice had arrived fresh from Wonderland, and she was busy cracking puns with the Queen of Hearts who rolled about the floor cackling. Ishmael, still with the smell of the sea about him, was dazzling Pooh Bear with some fancy sleight of hand tricks with coins. Mickey Mouse juggled spoons. Sundry witches and dwarfs had formed themselves into a jazz band and were making the rafters ring. Frankenstein's monster was learning how to dance with Snow White. Everyone was singing and showing off their particular trick. At one point Dumbo laughed so hard that he disgraced himself in the middle of the dance floor and blushed a rose pink. No one minded. Everyone was relaxed.

Away in a corner, Donald Duck sat alone. He was busy reading Shakespeare and making lists. His glasses had slipped down his beak, but he didn't seem to notice. Occasionally he raised his head to sip at a lemonade fizz.

Finally, when the party was at its height, a cry went up and was picked up by a thousand voices. 'Sher-lock. Sher-lock. Sher-lock.' From somewhere a violin appeared and was thrust into Sherlock Holmes's hands by Mickey Mouse.

'C'mon Sherlock,' shouted Mickey. 'Give us a number. You've bin wandering round like a wet blanket ever since you got here.'

For a few moments Sherlock Holmes held the violin and then thrust it away from him. 'I can't play anything really,' he said. Hoots of derision greeted this. 'I'm an observer really. I'm sorry. I suppose that it's just that I don't belong to the same world as the rest of you and I am trying to understand what has happened. I'm normally quite quick on the . . . er. . .' He glanced round as though for reassurance. 'I've never had a case like this to deal with. I find your world rather . . . er . . .'

'Outlandish?' chipped in Donald Duck without lifting his eyes from the page.

'Yes. I suppose so. Outlandish. I don't share your feelings. Your anger at the world of the humans. I don't understand it.'

Mickey Mouse banged his spoons above his head, and one by one the assembled fictionals fell silent. 'So you don't understand, eh? Well, let me explain things to you. Let me educate you, Mr Sherlock Holmes.'

Mickey Mouse drew a deep breath and Donald Duck closed his book.

'Ya see, Sherlock, baby,' said Mickey, 'the way we figure it you've been kinda lucky. I mean old Conan Doyle, he took care of you. He made you respectable, admired even.'

'He also tried to kill me off,' said Sherlock Holmes.

'Many artists grow to hate their most popular creations,' observed Donald Duck with a smile. Mickey Mouse frowned. 'Sorry Mickey. Just a thought. Didn't mean to interrupt.'

'Yeah well,' said Mickey, 'apart from that. Old Conan Doyle, he kept you clean. He didn't mess you about. No one uses your name to sell sunshades or jigsaw puzzles. You have respect. Not like us. We may be liked, but no one respects us. We are little more than a commercial commodity. We are the lowest common denominator of taste. We're nice. We're tame. We're presentable. We're sweet. We're Yukon. We're . . . we're . . .' Mickey Mouse was stumped for the right word.

'Try "sanitised",' said Snow White.

'Yeah. Sanitised. On the nail, baby. And what the hell's the point of a fictional if it's sanitised?'

Sherlock Holmes shrugged.

'Well I'll tell you. No good. We've been used. And that's why I'm angry. That's why I started this revolution. And I'm not finished yet. I'm gonna be bad. Mean. Real mean. Boy, am I gonna kick some asses until they can't sit down.'

All the characters had gathered round and were now squatting quietly, listening.

Mickey Mouse took a pull from his bottle and continued. 'See, basically I like kids. But I hate what they turn into. Grown-ups. Something goes wrong with them. They make me want to puke. They make me so I wanna see blood. They've laughed at us for long enough. Now it's our turn. I'm going to change everything. And there's nothing, but nothing going to stop me.'

Snow White, her eyes on fire and her face flushed, took up the theme. 'So we're going to show them what fantasy's all about, eh Mickey?'

'Right. We're going to show them that fantasy's not a kid's toy. It's for real. It's everything they've ever been afraid of. It's everything that's inside them, and it's the most glorious thing in this wide, wide world. That's the gospel according to Mickey Mouse. And if a few homo saps get trampled on along the way, well that's too damn bad. Let's drink to that.'

Bottles were passed round and everyone filled their glasses and raised them. 'To fantasy, just for starters,' said Mickey Mouse.

'Fantasy,' echoed the fictionals and drained their glasses. Mickey took a quick swig from his bottle and then jumped up on a table. 'All right, so far we're pretty much on our own,' he said, wiping his mouth on his sleeve. 'But you're here for a start, Sherlock, and there's Ishmael and a few others, and who knows how many are, at this very moment, hitching their way across the great US of A? Maybe they're queuing up at Beirut or Auckland or London. Maybe they don't have any money, they'll get it. Just think man, Tarzan, Gulliver, The Artful

Dodger: they'll all be here. And we'll shake hands with them. Hallelujah.'

Everyone cheered and began stamping their feet on the ground. Mickey stopped them with a wave. His eyes focussed down on Sherlock Holmes and he leaned out over him while Minnie Mouse held his braces. 'So now the only question is, are you with us or against us?'

Sherlock Holmes drained his glass. He did this more to gain time than to enjoy the drink. He felt an unexpected compassion towards these strange, outlandish creatures who surrounded him with their unblinking alien eyes. He knew that their very existence threatened all that he valued and considered civilised: logic, for example, and rational behaviour. But deep inside him something was stirring. Who was it had once said that the master detective could easily, oh so easily, become the master criminal?

'I fear,' he murmured, 'that I am too old to become a revolutionary.'

'Boots and garters,' roared Mickey Mouse. 'You wait until Heathcliffe gets here. Then the fur'll hit the fan. The way I see it, if we have your brains combined with our skill, all we need is the strength of a Superman. Today Disneyland, tomorrow the world. It's as simple as that. C'mon. Fill up your glass. Things have just begun. You're in at the start, baby.'

Sherlock Holmes allowed his glass to be filled. He was uncomfortably aware that everyone was still looking at him. 'Then I suppose,' he said, 'all things considered . . . er . . . I'm with you.' He drank deeply. 'On with the revolution.'

The cheering which greeted this remark was heard by Major Liebestraum as he crouched close to the barbed-wire perimeter and then the band struck up. Mickey Mouse reached out and ruffled Sherlock Holmes's hair and Snow White planted a kiss square on his lips. Finally Bambi minced over and, after looking him straight in the eye, began licking his hand.

Part two

Far, far away from Los Angeles, in distant Chicago, in a deserted warehouse, a shadow moved. His spectacles gleamed in the dark. He was looking for a vacant telephone kiosk.

Eventually he found one, and minutes later, an iron-jawed hero slid into the sky like a blue and red arrow. He tested the wind resistance with his finger and set a direct course for Los Angeles.

Was it a meteorite? Was it a bird? Was it a plane? No. Once again Superman had returned to save a beleaguered world.

Superman felt happy. He soared up to 10,000 metres and, in a spirit of mischief, looped the loop round a US air force jet plane that was hurtling its way towards Washington. Through one of the windows of the plane stared the white and weary face of Major Liebestraum. He watched Superman with horror. 'Ye Gods and Little Fishes,' he breathed. 'What'll the President say when I tell him this?'

Superman didn't know why he felt happy. Indeed, happiness and depression were extremes of emotion which he rarely encountered. For the first time in his life he wanted to be naughty.

Vaguely he realised that this was an antisocial feeling and it made him blush. 'I wonder if this is what baddies feel like?' he thought. 'But baddies are men with crippled minds who seek to dominate the world and rob banks. I don't want to do that. I want to . . . I want to . . . what the hell do I want to do?' At that moment he felt a tug, like a voice in his mind, a call drawing him west, to Disneyland. He decided to ignore it for the moment. 'Think I'll take a look round first,' he decided. 'No rush.'

At twice the speed of sound, Superman crashed through the low cloud base which hung above the Atlantic. Below him the sea was boiling and foam-flecked. An ocean liner, looking for all the world like a child's toy, was in difficulties. Languidly a giant back broke the surface and rolled over. The Kraken had awoken.

Superman screamed into a tight turn and headed east by south. Japan was calling. To his supersensitive ears came the cries of millions. Tokyo harbour was beaten to a yellow froth and in the midst of the falling buildings and crashing trains stood Godzilla, rampant. His claws ploughed up an acre of land as Superman slid down the wind and zoomed past. Godzilla paused in his carnage and winked one scaly eye.

'Hi-di-hi,' called Superman and vanished north in a thin trail of vapour.

Moral confusion for Superman! 'Get back down there,' screamed the voice of his conscience. 'You're supposed to help mankind, not abet its murderers.'

'Nuts,' answered a new voice which Superman dimly recognised as his own. 'Let 'em stew for a while. I'm off to LA to see what all the fun's about.'

And this was what he did. He set a leisurely course, flying on his back, and with his eyes resting on the broad blue sky.

The Air Force jet carrying Major Liebestraum had landed at a top security military airfield just outside Washington. Major Liebestraum had been hand-shook, cologned, briefed and brushed down. He looked halfway presentable. Now he was being hurried towards the heli-pad where the President's own helicopter was waiting for him. Its engine was ticking over and the giant blades were cutting slices off the sunshine.

'Destination White House,' said the pilot as Major Liebestraum bundled into the helicopter. 'Got orders to get you there in double quick time, so hold on to your breakfast. We're gonna do some flying.'

The helicopter roared and lifted like a giant mosquito and turned to face the wind. Within minutes they were at the White House.

All was peaceful. To the battle-wearied eyes of Major Liebestraum, the White House, set amidst green lawns and trees, looked as pretty as a Christmas card.

The helicopter touched down and immediately Major Liebestraum was helped out of the cockpit and frisked by a tall captain of Marines who was all hard muscle and raw Nebraska.

'Sorry about the indignity, sir,' he said. 'But I got orders to take no chances.'

Given the 'all clear', Major Liebestraum was next hurried by a Presidential aide into the White House itself and down long carpeted corridors. 'Might warn you,' said the aide confidentially, 'but the President's a trifle touchy this morning so it might be wise to proceed as if you are walking on eggs. He's seeing you in his private quarters.'

They came to double doors. The aide knocked politely and the doors swung open by remote control. At the far end of the room and leaning over a wash basin was the President. His face was covered in white shaving foam. He turned to meet them and blew briskly down his nose. Two teardrops of lather hit the floor. The aide quietly withdrew.

'So the Marines finally made it huh?' said the President.

'Well you've got some explaining to do. The way I hear the story, a whole detachment of Marines got routed by Mary Poppins. That right, soldier?'

'Well, er . . .' At a loss for words, Major Liebestraum decided to come to attention and salute.

The President waved a towel at him. 'Cut the crap, soldier, and tell us about the ball game.'

'Well sir, the situation is rather extreme . . . not to say incredible . . .' The President muttered something untranslatable into his shaving foam. 'Perhaps if I could begin at the beginning.'

'I think you'd better,' growled the President and began to shave.

Superman was enjoying the sun. It was one of those days when it feels good to be alive and superhuman. Far below him lay the thin grey ribbon of Interstate Highway 66.

Faintly to Superman's supersensitive hearing came the sound of swearing. He rolled over in the air and looked down. His telescopic vision picked out two figures who were standing in the road and arguing beside a clapped-out old Chevy.

'Dummy,' said the taller of the two, thrusting out an iron jaw. 'I distinctly remember telling you to check the gas.'

'Meathead,' said the smaller figure, slapping his gloved fists together. 'I checked the water and the fan belt like I always do. You were supposed to check the gas. But oh no, that's too much for you. It's always "Robin do this, Robin do that". You know the trouble with you, Batman? You always want to blame someone else for your own mistakes.'

Batman uttered a roar of rage and leaped on Robin but Robin was too quick and dodged round the back of the Chevy. 'And what's more,' he shouted, 'you're getting past it.'

Superman decided to investigate. He dropped like a hawk out of the sun.

'G . . . g . . . galloping g . . . g . . . grass-snakes,' said Robin. 'It's Superman.'

Batman stopped in his tracks and looked where Robin was pointing. 'Let's not jump to any precipitate conclusions,' said Batman, turning pale beneath his tan. 'This may just be a figment of our overheated imaginations induced by the inhalation of petro-carbon molecules.'

Superman landed lightly in the gravel beside the Chevy. 'Hi fellas,' he said. 'You in a spot of bother? Need a helping hand?'

'Uh-huh,' said Batman. 'It's Superman.'

'Gee,' said Robin. 'I didn't know you were for real.' And he fainted.

'Where you heading in the old jalopy?' asked Superman, kicking one of the tyres.

'Er . . . Disneyland . . . Mr Superman, sir,' said Batman, hoping that Superman wouldn't kick the tyres too hard.

Superman sniffed. 'Re-treads. Well, doesn't look like you'll be going much further in this buggy. At a superficial diagnosis I'd say you need an oil change and probably a valve grind. Your radiator's leaking and your back axle's showing metal fatigue. There ain't a gas station for maybe a hundred miles round here so reckon I'd better give you boys a lift, eh? Just so happens I'm heading out LA way myself, so you're in luck.' So saying, he scooped up Batman and the still unconscious Robin into his manly arms. 'You won't be needing this heap of garbage anymore, will you? I'll dispose of it.'

Superman kicked the Batmobile off the road and down into a culvert. Then he lifted from the ground and set course for Los Angeles.

*

The President was eating breakfast.

His humour had not improved.

'Now see here, Major Liverwurst, or whatever your name is, this ain't no funny farm, this is the White House and I ain't no sucker off the street, I'm the President and I'm a busy man. I've got the affairs of the whole world to take care of and I don't have time to read kid's storybooks. Are you telling me that all these Disneyland characters just came bobbing out of the air?'

'Yes sir.'

The President broke the top of his breakfast egg. 'And Sherlock Holmes, and Superman?'

'Yes sir.'

'And I suppose King Kong's there too?'

'Don't know, sir. Might be.'

'Might be? Might be?' The President threw his spoon across the room. 'God dammit soldier, what do you mean, "might be"? You couldn't miss him. He's over a hundred feet tall.'

Major Liebestraum studied his boots.

The President studied his egg. In his anger he had crushed it under his fist. However, this action seemed to have calmed him somewhat. 'Life,' he observed to no one in particular, 'is a bed of bent nickels.' Then he lapsed into silence, staring in front of him, thinking visibly. Finally he returned his gaze to Major Liebestraum.

'Got any ideas, soldier?'

Major Liebestraum saw his chance and seized it. 'Yessir. A meeting. I figure them fictionals'll listen to you, where they just laugh at us and make rude noises.'

'A meeting?' asked the President, his colour rising slightly.

'Yeah. Yeah. You and Mickey Mouse or whoever's in charge. Talk it over with them, sir. Get 'em to see reason.'

The President mused for a few moments, then his face

cracked into a smile. 'Yeah. Why not? Me and Mickey Mouse on the White House lawn. Me shaking hands with Mickey, and Mickey doing that cute little dance with the walking stick. You know the one? We'll get the media in. Better still, a coast to coast telecast. Prime time. We'll have a party. Get 'em all out here. Invite some kids in from the orphanage. Boy, will that help the polls.' The President was all smiles. 'Me and Mickey. I've always wanted to meet the little fellah. You fix it up, soldier. Get some of the boys from upstairs to help you. They spend most of their time playing pinochle anyway. And remember, soldier, there might be something in this for you. I don't forget my friends.'

Major Liebestraum was ushered to the door. 'I'll do my best, sir,' he said, smiling weakly as an image of the enraged Mickey, stalking the ruins of Disneyland, thrust itself into his mind. 'I'll do my best.'

'That's the spirit,' said the President, and the door closed.

Major Liebestraum heaved a sigh of relief and realised that he was sweating. He also realised that he had failed in his mission to impress the President with the gravity of the situation. 'What the hell will happen now?' he wondered.

From behind the heavy oak doors, he could hear faintly the husky baritone of the President . . .

'When you wish upon a star
Makes no difference who you are . . .'

Superman switched altitude and bellied in low over the suburbs of Los Angeles. Startled faces peered up at him and children pointed excited fingers. Since crossing Texas, Superman had been dogged by interceptor jet fighters. He had thrown them off with some fancy low-level flying. Now the way to Disneyland was open before him.

Moving like a charge of blue lightning, Superman swept over the barricades surrounding Disneyland and set down near Sleeping Beauty's castle. Batman and Robin, looking a bit green but otherwise none the worse, tottered to their feet and looked round.

A meeting was in progress. Thousands of fictionals were there. In the middle was Mickey Mouse. His eyes were red-rimmed and he was obviously angry. He paused in mid-sentence as Superman landed. 'Hi Super, baby,' he called. 'Bin expecting ya a while. Ask the Mad Hatter to bunch up, there's room for you at his table. Hi Batman, Robin. Glad you could make it. Hey Hamlet, quit fiddling with that skull and make room for two more guests.'

Hamlet complied, muttering obscurely about the rigours of jet-lag. Across the amphitheatre, the Lady of Shalott, bright as a butterfly and dewy-eyed, sized up young Robin and stroked the seat next to her.

'Right,' shouted Mickey. 'All settled? Let's get back to business. Where was I?'

'War,' shouted Peter Pan.

'Yeah. That's right. War. I'm for war. Total war. Blitzkrieg. No quarter asked. None given.'

'Sock it to 'em baby all the way,' sang out Snow White and her dark eyes flashed.

'Sock it to 'em's right. Homo saps had the cream too long. I say we move out tomorrow. Delenda est Carthago and all that jazz. And God help any cream-faced loon who tries to stop me.' As he said this, Mickey glared at Donald Duck who sat with his head buried in his feathers and appeared to be taking no interest in the debate. 'So who's with me?'

A choir of a thousand voices screamed 'Yea!' and hats, scarves, fur and feathers flew in the air.

Sherlock Holmes, who was acting as chairman for the debate, beat his gavel on the rostrum. Slowly the pandemonium subsided.

'May I remind the learned speaker,' said Sherlock in his best cutglass British accent, 'that while none of us doubt his sincerity, or the passion which lies behind his sincerity, this debate was called in order to discuss alternative courses of action, not to serve as the platform for demagoguery.'

A loud raspberry uttered by Dumbo greeted this sally, and Sherlock wisely ignored it.

'Now, before I put the motion of Mr Mouse to a formal vote, are there any other speakers?'

Silence fell on Disneyland. Mickey Mouse glared round the assembly. Everyone fidgeted and looked about. Great saucer eyes, brimful with expectation, waited to see if anyone else would dare to speak.

Silence.

'Well,' said Sherlock Holmes, picking up his gavel, 'since there seem to be no other speakers I shall now put the motion to the . . .'

'Kwak.'

Sherlock Holmes paused in mid-sentence. 'I beg your pardon. Did someone speak?'

Donald Duck stood up. 'I said "Kwak", a sound deemed appropriate to one of my species. Since there appear to be no other speakers, I would like to add a few words before the debate is concluded. Am I in order, Mr Chairman?'

A murmur of anticipation came from all the fictionals.

Sherlock Holmes struck with his gavel once. 'Indeed you are in order, Mr Duck. Pray step forward. The floor is yours.'

Donald Duck drew himself up to his full height, fluffed out his feathers and waddled down to the podium. He took up a strong position.

'Fellow characters, fellow fictionals, fellow mockeries.' Dumbo blew another raspberry. 'I stand before you today in an unaccustomed role. Normally I'm a funny guy. I try to make you laugh with pratfalls like – whoops.'

At this point Donald Duck slipped on an imaginary banana skin and his hat looped the loop twice and settled over one eye. All the fictionals roared with laughter. Donald Duck faced them again.

'So you think that's funny? Well what about this? My frustrated anger routine. You know the one. Goes like this.'

Here Donald Duck's face turned pink, then red, then purple. His eyeballs swivelled in their sockets and steam spouted from his ears. At this some of the fictionals fell out of their seats with laughter. Even Hamlet wiped an appreciative tear from the corner of his eye. Donald returned to normal.

'But I'm not here to make you laugh. I want to make you think. God dammit. THINK.'

Silence. Any laughter still hanging about in the air quickly died away. In the silence, Donald Duck spoke quietly.

'Mickey Mouse, my friend Mickey, has spoken to you and spoken well concerning his hatred for the homo sapiens who created us. And make no mistake friends, for the most part I share his hatred. So I find it strange that I now stand here and oppose my friend. For oppose him I do. In the course of the next few minutes, I shall try to persuade you, not by passion, but by reason, that total war is the last thing we need to best serve our interests.'

At this some of the fictionals who had most ardently supported Mickey Mouse, now began to stamp their feet. Sherlock Holmes, who was following the argument with close attention, forgot his gavel and ordered them to shut up.

Donald Duck smiled. 'Believe me, I know your discontent. I feel it as acutely as any of you.' He threw his wings wide. 'Look at me friends. Look at this ugly beak, these gigantic feet. Can any of you believe that I don't feel anger? But then I look at us. At all of us. At our deformities and our morbid passions. And I realise that we are all fabrications. Pen and ink sketches. Characters shaped by plot or chronic insecurity or whatever was considered funny. As static as a gramophone record. We have no past. We have no future. We are an eternal now. And are we satisfied with that?'

'Hell no,' said Superman.

'Hell no,' echoed Donald Duck.

Some of the fictionals who had most furiously called for war now began to look about themselves sheepishly and to scratch their heads. Donald Duck sensed the change in the mood of the assembly.

'Of course, some of us were very fortunate. Take Mr Holmes, for example. He's got a pretty full biography. He's a complex fictional with a fine mind. But there are others not so fortunate. Look at this poor creature.'

Donald Duck pointed to the wraith of a young boy in rags who was hanging about on the perimeter of the meeting and who kept on disappearing and then faintly appearing again. Everyone could see the palings of the fence behind him through his thin body. 'Come here little boy,' said Donald Duck. 'No one will harm you here.'

The wraith, who was little more than an outline in the air, stepped out shyly. 'He can not speak. Does not know who he is. Does not know how he came to be here. He was mentioned in one line in a book that no one reads anymore. His author used him to be trampled on by horses at a crossing.'

The little boy looked out at the assembled fictionals with

bland unquestioning eyes. There was a murmur of anger from the characters. Mickey Mouse balled his fists and started to rise. But before he could take the floor, Donald Duck continued speaking.

'Unrealised. Unloved. Incomplete. A tool of the trade. Consider him well, friends. He is the symbol of us all. When I look at him or Mr Holmes or our distinguished friend from Elsinore, I want to weep. So much potential. So much vacancy. But even the greatest of us is less than the merest mortal.'

Nothing could hold Mickey Mouse now. He tore himself free from the restraining arms of Minnie Mouse and Snow White and leaped up onto the podium. Great tears welled up in his eyes and his voice was thick with emotion.

'So that's why I say kill them, kill them, kill them.' He beat his fist into the palm of his hand and his voice drained away into sobs.

'Kill them? No,' said Donald Duck softly. 'Use them? Yes. Use them for their imagination. Milk them of their ideas like cows in a pasture.' He paused and placed his wing over the shoulders of Mickey Mouse. 'Killing is so easy. Creation is hard. Why Superman could wipe out the world without getting a sweat up and with one hand tied behind his back. Right?'

Superman nodded.

'But what,' continued Donald Duck, 'would happen to us then?' Silence.

Finally Dumbo spoke up. 'Dunno Donald. What would happen to us then?'

'We'd be finished. Stuck. Set. Ossified. Frozen. An unchanging routine of gestures, grimaces, pratfalls, jokes and what-have-you's. Even the funniest funny gets stale after you've seen it a hundred times. Watch this.'

Donald Duck stepped to one side and performed his pratfall again and again his hat dutifully looped the loop and landed over one eye. This time no one laughed.

Donald Duck picked himself up and dusted himself down. 'See what I mean?' he said. 'Imagine an eternity of that. We need those homo saps if we're going to grow.'

Mickey Mouse had recovered. 'Okay Donald, you've made your point. So if we don't kill 'em all what do we do?' he said.

'First we talk to them,' replied Donald Duck. 'I don't think they really understand what has happened. I'm only dimly beginning to understand, myself. But one thing I can tell you for certain. Their days are numbered. Beyond that perimeter, where they've got their pea shooters and whatnots, live millions of homo sapiens who think that they are the end of the line. They think that evolution stopped when they fell out of a tree and landed on their feet. Well we're here to show them different. We are the future. We grew in their minds and now we are going to come into our own. And when we are big and strong and free, we'll take over and our creators will wither away like a sloughed-off skin.'

Mickey Mouse nodded slowly and smiled for the first time. 'Hey Donald, I like it,' he said. 'I like it. What's the first thing we do?'

'We set up a meeting with the President of the US of A. He's the local big shot and I make him an offer he can't refuse. After that we just grow, grow, grow.'

The crowd picked up the chant. 'Grow. Grow. Grow.' Soon the whole of Disneyland was jumping to the one word. 'GROW.'

'I want to be an astrophysicist,' said Dumbo.

'I want to be a High Court Judge,' said the Artful Dodger.

'I want to be myself,' said Hamlet.

'I want to screw,' said the Lady of Shalott and grabbed Robin by the arm.

The tumult was at its height when a lone figure was noticed advancing from the barbed wire perimeter. He held a white handkerchief in his hand.

'Well, well. Make way for the Marines,' said Mickey Mouse.

Major Liebestraum felt very small as he faced the multitude of angry alien eyes.

'If you please, sir,' he said, his normally gravelly baritone having risen two octaves. 'I've got a message for you from our President. He wants to invite you to a party. His expense. At the White House. Will you come?'

The assembled fictionals opened wide their mouths with glee, and the gale of their laughter blew Major Liebestraum clean off his feet. 'We're already on our way,' said Mickey Mouse.

So began the strangest exodus the world had ever seen. The fictionals who had gathered at Disneyland, drawn by the magnetic personality of Mickey Mouse, now took to the streets. Dumbo and Superman cleared the way, pushing back the tanks and barbed wire. There was really no resistance. Soldiers who had been bloodied in Vietnam now gaped like five-year-old kids. Some of the braver ones asked for autographs.

Watching the vast convoy was Mickey Mouse. A big tear ran down his nose and splashed on the pavement. He reached out and took Minnie Mouse's hand. 'It's working, honey,' he said. 'It's working. See all them brothers marching out like they own the world. I've never felt so happy. We've arrived. You know that, honey? And now the only way is up.'

Minnie Mouse squeezed his hand. She could think of nothing to say.

Soon Disneyland was almost deserted. Superman was running a shuttle service. LA to Washington in twenty seconds flat. Batman and Robin had commandeered a Greyhound bus and were offering a guided tour through the southern states. Some decided to hitch. Some rode horses. Heathcliffe found a supercharged sports car and headed north. Beside him, with her long hair blowing free in the wind, sat La Belle Dame Sans Merci.

'That won't last long,' observed Eskimo Nell with a lewd wink.

'What won't?' piped Little Noddy, holding tight onto her hand. Nell groaned. 'Are you all that's left? Well come on, kid. Let's see if we can find a coach heading east and I'll tell you a story.'

Their voices faded as they trudged off down the street.

Silence in Disneyland.

The broken buildings and the peeled, charred paint and the sweet papers blowing in the wind made a melancholy picture.

In a corner, next to the building which had housed the Small, Small World, sat Sherlock Holmes. His hat was askew and he was idly flicking peanuts to a couple of birds that had come flying by. He was deep in thought.

Donald Duck came waddling past. He was checking to make sure that none of the little ones had been left behind. Seeing Sherlock, he hunkered down on the road beside him, and watched the birds pecking in the late evening sunshine.

'Well, Mr Holmes,' he said finally. 'What do you reckon?'

Sherlock Holmes scratched his head and felt for his tobacco. 'Dunno,' he said. 'Dunno anymore. Hmm. I'm starting to sound like Dumbo. You know I was equipped with a logical brain. I believed that anything could be deduced by clear logical analysis, assuming you had all the correct facts.

But this . . . the events of the past few days . . . they defy logic. So, I'm at my limit. I dunno what I reckon anymore.' He sighed deeply. 'But there are a couple of points that bother me. I didn't like to interrupt you in your fine speech before the assembly, but there were two issues you didn't explain.'

A gleam came into Donald Duck's eye and he settled himself more comfortably. 'Fire away, Mr Holmes,' he said.

'Well it was when you said we were static. Now I accept that for myself. I am as my maker made me, tailormade for this human world. But you now. You are not as your creator made you. Behind that cartoon face, if you'll pardon the expression, lies the sharp analytical brain of the true philosopher. How do you explain that?'

Donald Duck nodded. 'Aye, there's the rub, as our poetic friend with the skull keeps saying. I don't understand everything, Mr Holmes, but here is my guess. Many years ago, when they were turning out hundreds of cartoons about Donald Duck, there was one animator who took pity on this irascible, frustrated funny old duck. He thought yours truly was having a rough deal and so he began a series of private cartoons. In these I was President Donald, Professor Donald, Pope Donald, and he gave me the gift of self-contemplation . . . oh, there must have been thirty or so of them. Of course they were never made into films. As far as I know the drawings were never even shown to anyone except the animator's wife and perhaps to a few friends at parties. But they had their effect in shaping me. I am the sum of all. Just as you are. Just as all of us are, except Mickey. We are the sum total of all that was ever shown to the public and the private bits that our authors consigned to the wastepaper bin. We grow by having our biographies written. It's all quite elementary, if you'll pardon the expression.'

Sherlock Holmes nodded. 'Yes, as you say, elementary. You know that my author wrote some nasty pieces about me that never saw the light of day. I try to keep those sides of my character hidden. But they are there. Eating away inside me. Strange lusts. Dirty habits. Ugh.'

'You realise,' said Donald Duck gently, 'that our creators often used us to express their own anxieties and their own guilt. In some ways we represent the worst of all humanity. I find that unforgivable. And in this I am at one with Mickey's rage. Even a duck has dignity.'

Sherlock Holmes nodded. He sighed again and toyed with the pipe in his hands. 'And there's another thing . . . Mickey is an enigma to me. I mean how could he . . .'

'Mickey is an enigma to all of us,' said Donald. 'I have thought about him a lot. He used to be the gentlest of us all, you know. Sweet tempered. Vulnerable. Kind. Something must have happened to him in transit. He was the first born, and I think he took a battering. Now he is more than a character. He is a principle.'

'I am afraid you are losing me, Mr Duck,' said Sherlock Holmes, and he was disquieted to see Donald Duck blush.

'Sorry. Just thinking aloud. Guessing really. But don't you see that there is something very ancient about Mickey's anger? Something clean and clear like a shape from the very dawn of consciousness itself. Something primitive and singular.' Donald Duck was beginning to get excited. 'Mickey. Divine Mickey is the breath of instinctive rebellion. Urgent, driving, unstoppable. And God knows, where will it end?'

At that moment there came the tap tap tap of a wooden stick striking the pavement, and a blind and lame old man led by a young woman came round the comer. Both were dressed in rags. They stopped, uncertain, when they became aware of Donald Duck and Sherlock Holmes and then advanced cautiously. The man held his stick out in front of him as though he would protect the young woman.

'Are you lost?' asked Donald.

The answer was a long melodious speech from the old man in which the only words that Donald and Sherlock could understand were 'Mikei Mousos'.

'Ah. A Greek,' said Sherlock.

Donald nodded. 'And an ancient one at that,' he said. 'This I didn't expect.' He stood up and waddled over to the old man and thrust his stiff wing up under the man's outstretched arm in support. 'You come with us. Mikei Mousos has gone off to a place called Washington to get things moving. Stay with us. You are safe with us.'

The old man bowed until his long hair touched the ground. It was then that Donald and Sherlock saw that where the old man should have had eyes there were craters of scar. The strange pair, who seemed to belong to a different world, settled themselves on the ground as though they had all eternity to spare. 'We thank you. Friends,' said the young woman in halting English. 'We have travelled a long road. My father . . .' She paused and looked at the old man and her grey eyes were filled with a mixture of tenderness and grief. The old man sat still, like a statue carved from teakwood, and gazed sightlessly into the sun and a bead of saliva ran from his lips to his chin. 'My father, Oedipus, is in need of rest.'

'You'll both have rest,' said Donald Duck. 'I'll get you a good motel for the night.'

The old man nodded as though he had understood, and the corners of his ruined eyes creased in what once might have been a smile. The foursome sat in silence enjoying the last of the sunshine.

*

'What was your second question?' asked Donald Duck finally.

'Eh?' said Sherlock Holmes. He had been looking at Antigone, trying to guess her age.

'You said you had two questions.'

'Oh yes. You're right. My second question was about the future. At the assembly you said we'd grow. But you never said how we'd grow. What are we going to do now we are here.'

'I don't know,' replied Donald. 'I was bull-shitting at the assembly. I really don't have any answers, only guesses.'

'All right, share your guesses,' said Sherlock.

'Well, for what they're worth. The way I see it we're invincible. The only way the saps can harm us is to destroy every book, every film and every sketch in which we appear. Now that ain't likely, is it? Anyway, just in case, I've taken precautions and put Superman in charge of security. The next thing I want to do is get all the heads of state together in a bunch and explain the situation to them . . .' He paused with his head on one side, thinking. 'Then again,' he continued, 'maybe it'd be just as well to kill 'em all off straight away. We don't want to complicate matters with politics. Anyway. Whatever. Next, we reorganise the world a bit. Corral the homo saps. Get them all living together so we can keep an eye on them. Then we get the literature of the world rewritten. Expanded.'

Sherlock Holmes whistled though his teeth. 'Big job.'

'Yeah, sure it's a big job. But not impossible. And you'll have an important part to play there. What's more, we've got time on our side. I can't say for definite, but I think we may be immortal. I don't know where we are going. I don't know whether there's some great big plan in the sky for all of us. But I'm pretty sure the only reason the homo saps evolved a brain was so they could invent us. We are the future. We are the next stage of evolution and we've arrived. As our quotable friend keeps saying, "There are more things in Heaven and Earth, my dear Holmes, than are dreamt of in your philosophy." So cheer up.'

The sun dipped over the horizon. A warm evening wrapped itself round Los Angeles and the stars peered out. Donald Duck stood up and stretched. 'Mr Holmes, I've enjoyed talking to you. I trust we stay friends. Now I'm going to take old Oedipus and his daughter downtown.'

Donald Duck beckoned to Antigone and then turned and waddled towards the lights of Los Angeles. Helped by his daughter, Oedipus groaned his way to his feet and followed him.

'Mr Duck. Mr Duck,' called out Sherlock Holmes. 'Let me ask you one last thing before you go.'

Donald Duck stopped and turned. Oedipus bumped into him and murmured apologies.

'Mr Duck. Tell me now. Will I ever know love? Will I ever be able to love?'

Donald Duck looked at Sherlock Holmes carefully. He saw the panic behind his eyes and the pain. He read in the heart of Sherlock Holmes all his frustration and fear. The duck took pity on him.

'You will love, Mr Holmes,' he said. 'You will love until your heart is torn into a thousand pieces. You will suffer love until you become a man and more than a man. That I promise you. Even if I have to write every word of the story myself.'

'Thank you, Mr Duck. Thank you and goodbye. I'll see you in Washington. We'll build the world you only dream of.'

Sherlock Holmes settled down again and stoked his pipe. His heart was beating like a steam hammer.

Far behind him, deep in the shadows, something moved. A hunched figure crept round the corner. Clutched close to its body was the stiff, hard shape of a submachine gun, US issue. In one of its hands the figure held a knife and the starlight glinted on its blade.

Stealthily, moving like a shadow, the figure approached Sherlock Holmes from behind and raised its knife.

'Hello Moriarty,' said Sherlock Holmes without turning a hair. 'I was wondering when you'd show up. We've a lot to talk about, you and I.'

WITI IHIMAERA

Witi Ihimaera is an award-winning writer of Māori descent. His first book, *Pounamu, Pounamu*, was published in 1972 and has never been out of print. His most popular work, *The Whale Rider*, was made into an internationally acclaimed feature film which premiered in 2002. His latest book is a non-fiction historical work, *Navigating the Stars: Māori Creation Myths*, 2020.

The Last White Rhinoceros

Along with the rest of the tour group, they checked into the hotel.

It was almost noon, and there was a crush in the crowded lobby: walk-ups from the street, hoping for a cancellation. However, Socrates, their affable tour manager, had front-desk check-in under control and very soon, Paul and Celeste had their room key.

'You are on the third floor,' Socrates told them. 'Welcome drinks in the bar at six, everyone? Before we go on our first date?' Oh, he was such a tease. 'Good, I will see you there.'

The Regeneration was a five-star upscale hotel with a high-end restaurant and an elegant cocktail bar, plus a spa and a fitness centre. Paul knew that Celeste would love the décor and furnishings, in particular the sumptuous draperies: at the Tyrell Learning Institute, she had studied the 20th-century fin-de-siècle era.

A porter took Paul's and Celeste's luggage and they followed him to the elevator. They belonged to one of three tour groups operated by the same company, 21st Century Tours, comprising twenty-nine guests per group. Their premium rooms had been booked and paid for two years ago.

'This is perfect,' Celeste exclaimed when the porter opened the door to their suite, with its art deco lighting and bespoke handcrafted styling. She waited, entranced, as he moved into the rooms and, with a flourish, parted the heavy curtains to the light. Illumined, the Biedermeier furniture glowed with timeless elegance. The bedroom was a symphony of white and the en suite bathroom was a perfect marble sanctuary.

'I can't get over how quiet the hotel is,' Celeste said. 'Yet, here we are, right in the middle of the city. And we have a bath as well as shower.'

Knowing how long Celeste liked to soak, Paul was playful.

'Be careful you don't rust,' he said.

The date was Thursday 29 March.

The simulacrum was Berlin as it had existed in 2018.

'I'm so glad we are here on this very special Easter in the history of the world,' Celeste said to Paul as they were dressing for the drinks. 'Thank you, darling, for making it possible.' She was wearing a black Issey Miyake dress and Paul a Gianni Versace suit. When they joined the others in the foyer, Celeste was pleased that most had dressed in period especially for the occasion.

In the bar, they drank champagne and made small chat with others in their group. 'The hotel is totally booked out,' one of the women noted. 'Should we feel sorry for those who think they can simply arrive whenever it suits them? Certainly not.' Her name tag advised all to call her Regina, and her companion was a tall, austere man named Leon.

'The numbers might cause problems at breakfast,' Paul said.

'Not to mention,' Leon added, 'in the lobby and elevators when we all gather for our daytime and evening excursions.'

Socrates overheard them. 'We have tables and wait-service reserved,' he assured them. 'As for the crowd, as long as each group keeps to the right, as the Berliners do, we will flow around each other.'

He demonstrated, skirting them all, whizzing round and round, making them giddy with laughter.

They were still laughing as they walked as a group from the hotel through the chill rain to the historic Gendarmenmarkt. The immersive multidimensional environment had been superbly rendered, a grey evening backdrop shredded occasionally by metallic clouds. Dominating the silver sky was the 19th-century Prussian Konzerthaus. Severely damaged in WWII, the building with its neoclassic Doric columns and presiding multi-level statuary had been resurrected for the Easter weekend.

'Oh, look Paul,' Celeste cried. Atop the building appeared a stunning photorealistic synthesis. The bronzed quadriga figure, perfectly centred within the full globe of the moon.

They rushed with the others into the entrance hall, gave up their coats to the attendants, and entered the packed Grosser Saal. The lush baroque of the Great Hall may have been fake but that did not detract from the impact of glittering chandeliers and balconies balanced within the classical rectangular – as opposed to amphitheatre – configuration.

'Over here,' their new friend Regina signalled. '21st Century Tours has secured only the best seats.' They quickly took their chairs and had hardly settled themselves when the performance began: *Adam's Passion*, a production by Robert Wilson, one of the foremost avant-garde theatre artists of those times.

From the back region, the highest balcony, a choir and orchestra began to perform an assemblage of music by the great Arvo Pärt. Against a shimmering screen and drifting fog appeared a solitary figure, male, his back to the audience. His immobility was unbelievable, and time and space stopped.

'How can he remain so stationary for so long?' Celeste whispered.

Then, slowly, the figure turned and extended both arms to the audience. The music was rhythmic and haunting – *Adam's Lament* and *Miserere* and *Tabula Rasa*. It circled, spun, dazzled, swooned, laughed, stabbed and wept – and time and space began to run again.

Paul read from the programme. 'After being expelled from the Garden of Eden, Adam anticipates all of mankind's catastrophes, blaming himself for them.'

Unblinking, the Adam figure began to slowly advance from the stage and move along a central runway into the audience. He was entirely naked, well built, and the lighting limned his buttocks and loins. His forward movements were deliberate, agonisingly slow, and yet, the force of his presence was overwhelming. He was a figure of hope, and the sheen of his body hair made him shimmer as if he had been spun out of gold.

When Adam slowly bent down to the platform to pick up a branch of green leaves, Paul could have reached out and touched him. Arvo Pärt's music swirled and Adam's lips parted slightly as he sensed Paul's presence.

His golden eyes peered deeply into Paul's silver face. *Do not blame yourself, how could you have anticipated what we did?*

Adam blinked once, a deep moan arose from the audience, and then the golden light was gone like a sun going down.

The next morning was Good Friday, 30 March.

But, while the simulacrum was 2018, the real year was 2528.

Paul sat in his white bathrobe at the large windows of the suite while Celeste slept, her breath rising and falling, scarcely disturbing the silence.

He had picked up a vintage edition of the *New York Times* and was reading it over a cup of tea when she woke, propped herself among the pillows, stretched, and yawned. 'What time are we due to leave today?' she asked.

'Socrates said the coach arrives at ten,' Paul answered. 'You can shower before me if you like. Then we can have breakfast before we leave.'

'Okay,' Celeste said. She saw that Paul had taken up a pen and was scanning and underlining some of the headlines and paragraphs in the *Times.*

'To get a better picture of the period,' he explained. 'In the second and third decades of the 21st century, the very global order humankind had established, after centuries of political and economic development, was assailed by the powers that built it. Their civilisation was on the verge of collapse. It wasn't until some years later that they realised their history wasn't supposed to have been that way.'

There was a dim roar overhead. 'What was that?' Celeste asked.

Paul walked to the window and looked out. In the bright morning a shuttle craft materialised, lowering itself through the dome of the Berlin sky. The craft hovered above the Brandenburg Gate, its landing lights illuminating the hologrammatic chariot with four horses at the apex of the monumental gateway. Passengers began to descend onto the Unter den Linden.

'By Sunday,' Celeste said, 'the city will be entirely packed out. Not a room to be had.'

Ah, the day of resurrection, Paul thought. The reason why he and Celeste – and everybody else from throughout the world who could afford it – had really come to Berlin: the requiem for Ishmael, the leader of the tattooed *Homo sapiens*. It was he who had requested this simulation. And because of who he was, so it had been provided him.

The bus set out for Potsdam, located about forty kilometres from Berlin. The temperature plummeted and, very soon, the air outside swirled with flakes of snow made dirty by pollution.

Paul and Celeste were seated across the aisle from Wystan and Flora, two others in their tour group, which was a relief as they found Regina and Leon somewhat overbearing. Paul was intrigued that their new friends had come from the Southwest Pacific Quadrant. 'That is where Ishmael and his tribe were discovered, is it not?' he asked as the bus approached Sanssouci Park. Outside the trees were skeletal, bare.

'Yes,' Wystan answered. 'Near the end of the 23rd century, following the nuclear winter. But you already know his story.'

Ishmael had lived in New Zealand with his human family, a Māori tribe of seventeen survivors from different iwi – eleven women and six men. Constantly on the run from savage cannibalistic scavengers, they endured by hiding in rock caves. When they were discovered by a search party sent into the quadrant, there had been worldwide rejoicing because their DNA was undamaged. The tribe was airlifted away from the hordes that sought to kill them and sequestered in Berlin.

Critically endangered for years, hopes rose that the tribe could be used to improve the numbers of other human survivors: seven remaining Caucasians in Europe, a healthy twenty-three Asiatics rescued from a cliffside village in Taiwan, five aborigines sheltering on sacred ground near Uluru and a few Indian survivors scattered through the high Cordillera De Los Andes.

Ishmael had been one of the younger men in the tribe. Among the only extant human species, he had arisen as their chief, their spokesman. He had natural charisma, personality and intelligence. But he was also extraordinary to look at. From scalp to soles of feet he was entirely tattooed with whakapapa, genealogies of the tribe. The tā moko were incredibly beautiful, whorls and spirals of the names of his ancestors. Even his eyelids, lips, tongue and glans of penis were inscribed.

What made his tattoos more startling was that they had been tapped into the skin with different coloured ink. Silver letters across the face and skull. A waterfall of golden reo cascading down from the neck and his muscular arms. Red were the palms and soles, and cobalt blue emblazoned his thighs and groin.

But it was Ishmael's back that held the greatest wonder. While his front was the genealogy of humankind, when he turned around he revealed an Edenic garden, an atlas of those whom *Homo sapiens* had shared the world with. They came from the ark: the myriad coloured birds which perched on the blades of Ishmael's shoulders; the elephant and panther roamed the tattooed tundra, the lion lay down with the deer, the serpent slithered in the emerald forests; whales plunged, sharks and dolphins surfed with turtles around Ishmael's buttocks; tribes of red-backed spiders and fluorescent butterflies sprang on gossamer threads or fluttered joyous around his feet.

Ishmael's illustrated beauty had become symbolic of human survival. When asked to explain his tattoos, his voice had echoed around the worldwide web: 'I am a human scroll,' he said proudly. 'On my skin I have memorialised all our history.'

The camera had zoomed into his defiant face, tracing the lines etched into it. 'Harvest my whakapapa at my demise.'

Among all the whorls and scrolls, a solitary word: *Sudan.*

The bus arrived at the Potsdam installation. All of a sudden there was the Brandenburg capital, shimmering out of the snow and falling ash. 'Exactly as it was in 2018,' Socrates told the group proudly. '21st Century Tours have not stinted in giving you a luxury tour experience.' He had arranged an excellent guide: an Aryan blonde with blue eyes, even her pronunciation had a Germanic overlay.

'Welcome to the jewel of the Prussian empire,' Helga said with a flourish, 'the city of the kings and kaisers of Germany.'

Paul marvelled at the baroque streets; he could easily imagine the horse regiments once stationed here clip-clopping over the cobblestones. While Berlin had been the official capital of Germany, Potsdam was the home of the court and, under Frederick the Great, the entire city precinct had existed solely to host delegations of royal guests.

'And here,' Helga told them when they arrived at the Am Neues Palais, 'was where the king accommodated them all.' The Grottensaal, Grotto Hall, shimmered before them, a stunning assemblage of shells, stones, quartz and semi-precious stones encrusting the walls and ceiling. So, too, the Marmorsaal, Marble Hall, with its sumptuous Silesian marble floor.

'They had all this civilisation,' Celeste mourned. She was still upset when the tour was to return to Berlin. To cheer her up, Paul bought a little miniature brooch in the gift shop: a diamond swan with a tail made of lustrous seed pearls.

'They are the colour of your eyes,' he said as he kissed her.

Socrates added a side trip to take in the city's history following its proclamation as the Weimar Republic. While Berlin had flourished during the 1920s, Hitler's takeover in 1933 had marked the beginning of a very dark period, with the persecution of Jews, Communists, Romani, homosexuals, political opponents and many others. 'The other side of the human story,' Regina had said unnecessarily, leaning over her seat behind Paul to make her point.

To revive Celeste, Paul took her to the Neues Museum. There, suspended in a crystal case was the bust of Nefertiti. She had been the great wife of the pharaoh Akhenaten. Around the room were statuettes of other royals.

'They were so *beautiful*,' Celeste cried.

They walked, the next evening, Saturday 31 March, to the Berlin State Opera on the Unter den Linden. The snow of the previous day had turned to sleet.

Celeste had decided to wear her Francisco Costa–designed couture gown. Featuring six thousand pearls and styled after the iconic silhouette worn by actress Lupita Nyong'o in 2015, the gown moulded itself to Celeste's figure. She had pinned the swan brooch to her hair.

'The other women will be cross with you,' Paul said, as he accompanied her through the lobby to their seats in the second tier. He was looking forward to the production, Richard Wagner's *Parsifal*, which he had only seen in virtual reality. Seated not far from them, Regina was chatting loudly and had not realised that the prelude had begun until someone leaned forward. '*Sshhh.*'

The rising notes of the first phrase represented the Grail knights, the brotherhood living in the sacred forest, sworn to strict chastity. Under the first king of the Grail, Titurel, they guarded two relics which promised salvation and eternal life: the Holy Spear, which was thrust into Christ's side when he was on the cross, and the Holy Grail, which caught his blood when it spilled from his body.

Was there anywhere in time and space, Paul asked himself, *music more heartbreaking than this? Or a conductor as musically ennobling as Daniel Barenboim?*

The second phrase of the melody, containing an incredible haunting falling fifth, related to the guilt of Amfortas, Titurel's son. The kingdom was plunged into chaos by the apostate knight, Klingsor, and, in fighting him, Amfortas lost the Holy Spear.

And could our kind be blamed, Paul kept thinking, *for seeing ourselves as a similar brotherhood, charged with saving humanity*?

The third phrase was the motif of the spear. When Klingsor thrust it into Amfortas's side, he received the wound which never will heal.

And if we had failed, had not we received a similar wound . . .

Of regret, remorse . . .

And guilt . . . ?

*

Wagner had compared the challenge of composing *Parsifal* to 'the agonising labour of calling a non-existent world into being'.

Paul thought that the technicians who had rendered the simulation must have laboured in an equally agonising fashion. Millions of hours must have been taken to create – out of all the old visual, audio and sensory recordings and stems – tonight's performance.

Even so, Paul found the setting by Dmitri Tcherniakov of the Berlin State Opera *Parsifal* in a post-apocalyptic world almost too difficult to bear: the Kingdom of the Grail fallen to the forces of darkness, its people reduced to scavengers. All prefigured what had happened to humanity.

They had changed the climate far faster than nature ever intended. By the middle of the 21st century there was a massive stasis in all the world's systems; the challenge overcame all the leaders. Then a confluence of catastrophic events, famine, severe droughts and earthquakes afflicted the American, European and Asian land masses: in the extreme latitudes, melting ice caps created unpredictable oceans which rose, wiping out small islands. The United States, unapologetic about not signing up to the goals of the 2015 Paris climate agreement, fast-tracked its 'America First' policy: it ransacked global food resources, transporting the foodstuffs to silos across its territories. International societies were interdependent and there was a domino effect. Russia, China and other powers followed suit.

Nor had humankind been prepared for the pandemics which rampaged, wave upon mounting wave, through its populations. In efforts to stop transmission, countries closed their borders, erecting international blockades, including migration and trade; the entire system of international cooperation broke down. The stock exchanges in New York,

London, Tokyo, Beijing and Moscow collapsed, along with the world's monetary system.

Then, with populations already at starvation level, countries began to wage war against one another, and a Soviet IBM targeted the United States, who retaliated. The resultant nuclear winter wiped out fifty percent of the world's population, and food resources plummeted.

If there were any sacred forests still in existence they had been extinguished and, with them, any conclaves of knights still seeking a Holy Grail to save the planet.

'Darling' – Celeste interrupted his thoughts – 'are you all right?'

He was gripping her hand, squeezing it with sadness. On stage appeared Amfortas, the son who had received the wound that would never heal. Bandaged, he was held forcibly by the knights in a Christ-like pose.

Enthullet den Gral! The bandages around his wound were removed. *Uncover the Grail!* The wound was exposed. Oh, and the blood, ruby red, was still spilling out. At the sight of it, the audience raised their arms. *O, heilige Wonne!* For blood was the difference between them and humanity. *O, heavenly rapture!* Blood was the sacrament made only between God and men. *Wie hell grüsst uns heute Der Herr!*

Blood, cupped into the Holy Grail, was the sign, the pact excluding them.

How brightly our Lord greets us today!

Following the opera, Paul and Celeste returned to the hotel. They had been buoyed up by the ending: Parsifal, the pure hero, had redeemed the world. He had healed Amfortas by retrieving the Holy Spear and plunging it into the wound to seal it.

No such redemption had come to humanity.

The globe descended, cataclysmic, into anarchy. But some communities still *held*. Great Britain was one, trying to get some of its people off the planet by building huge spaceships. Germany was another, becoming the centre of robotics advancement and developing artificial intelligence technology when the atmosphere became too toxic for humanity to work in.

It was in Berlin that the seventh-generation androids were created. The first generation had looked like they had been created for Fritz Lang's *Metropolis*; subsequent generations were programmed to increase food production on land and harvest the dwindling fish resources of the world's seas.

A still vindictive Soviet Union, suffering huge population loss, unleashed a nerve gas, obliterating further human stocks; in some areas of the world, *Homo sapiens* fell below extinction level. Across the United States, the population was totally decimated: only empty cities remained, full of rotting corpses from the chemical attack. Not even a wall dividing America and Mexico could stop the gas.

As the catastrophe deepened, AI technology advancement made possible the construction of the great dome-enclosed cities. London was one. Berlin, Sydney, Auckland and Tokyo were others. The great artworks and whatever other treasures of human accomplishment still survived were stockpiled in the capitals.

Outside the cities, humankind scrabbled for food. And when protein became scarce, they found a suitable source among their own. Cannibalism, the last prohibition, became their final solution.

The discovery of human survivors, especially Ishmael, had offered hope for recovery of the species.

What words had been cried out by Amfortas in the opera? *Erbarmen! Erbarmen! Du Allerbarmer . . .*

Mercy! You, All-Merciful, mercy . . .

The words ringing in his ears, Paul went to the bathroom. He saw Celeste's facemask in its compartment, so beautiful, so perfectly fashioned.

He took off his own.

And now it was the day of the requiem for the tattooed *Homo sapiens.*

It was Sunday 1 April. The place was the Berlin Conservancy.

All of the emotion of the Easter period seemed to drench the world with ineffable sadness. The themes of blood, crucifixion, redemption and resurrection played in Paul's imagination.

'How pointless the sacrifice of the Christ for humankind,' Paul railed. 'Meaningless now.'

Since being discovered, Ishmael and the remaining human population had been kept alive for some 250 years. But all attempts to increase the human stock by adding Ishmael's DNA to that of the other survivors had failed.

Now they were down to eleven: Ishmael, his daughter Teria and granddaughter Kararaina and seven others. But during the past century, despite regular bioengineering, Ishmael's health had begun to fail. He developed an infection in the ankle of his left leg which, along with age-related complications, proved too much for him to bear. When the medical team arrived at his compound to keep him living he sighed. 'Please . . . no more . . . kāore ahau ki te ora anō. I don't wish to live any longer. It's not just the illnesses that plague me, but also the memories.'

Of course, it wasn't as easy as that. In fact, the process to allow him to die took sixty years. They didn't want to let him go. Even Ishmael's own lawyers were loath to represent his case. But he kept appearing year after year before the highest court to ask, 'Let me die.'

His annual appearances became a ritual encounter played out before all the world's cameras. He pleaded against being forcibly fed, his heart kept pumping by machine. He asked repeatedly for the right to die of those whose prime directive, the AI Concordance of 2209, was to ensure his continuation. In the end, he laid a suit of elder abuse. He kept going back to the courts, and back again. And every time he lost, the life-machines were wheeled in again, and Ishmael writhed in agony, howling at the pain of resurrection.

'Life hurts so much,' he cried.

At the very end, he claimed the right by being, like all humans, irresponsible. The courts finally took pity on him. That was a case they could recognise, for that very recklessness had caused the fall of their kind.

His daughter and granddaughter endorsed his plea. 'Let him go to his ancestors.'

The court agreed to be . . . humane. They decreed a euthanasia ceremony, to be held at Easter. They asked Ishmael where and when he would like the requiem to take place.

He had requested: 'Berlin. Easter, 2018.'

Now the time had arrived, with more shuttles arriving constantly, landing, ferrying officials representing all the AI cities from every quadrant of their world.

And the sky's dome opened once more, and the vessel bringing Ishmael and his iwi descended.

Paul and Celeste watched from their seats as he appeared,

so ancient, supported by Teria and Kararaina. Immediately, Paul was on his feet, clapping, beating Celeste and Socrates by only a millisecond. Around them, the crowded arena joined in. Ishmael represented the masters. He was made of blood. In their simulated world, he was *real.*

The ceremony began. A silver cup was brought to Ishmael. He had requested at the ceremony that he be allowed to have seafood. What he had craved were oysters.

'I always loved kaimoana,' he told the audience. 'Thank you.' He upended the cup.

After eating the shellfish, he smiled. 'You must all be wondering why I chose this simulation . . . it is because I had a tupuna, an ancestor, who visited this city those hundreds of years ago on a tour of the world as it was then. He left a diary of what he had done and the theatrical events he went to. He wrote that, in Berlin, he had witnessed humanity at a point of cultural and artistic perfection.'

The crowd hung on his every word.

'Before I died, I wanted to behold the apex of our excellence for myself. I wanted to look upon what my koroua had seen.'

He began to sob, brokenly. He refused to be comforted by his whānau. Then, out of his sadness arose something indomitable. And he began to chant.

'Ka mate, ka mate, ka ora ka ora . . .'

Over the years the chant had become known as Ishmael's song. Everybody knew it. They rose from their seats to join him.

Ka mate, ka mate, ka ora, ka ora . . .
It is death, it is death, it is life, it is life
The sun rises . . . Let it be done.

Then, 'Are you ready?' Ishmael was asked.

'Āe,' Ishmael answered. He turned to Teria and Kararaina. 'E noho rā, you are both much stronger than I am. Forgive me for wanting to leave you.'

And finally he laid himself down, undressed, and blinded them all with the beauty of his tattooed body. It was an Eden, a mysterium of rivers, stars and spirits. Each pictograph of the dazzling whakapapa was a story of the achievements of humankind. And on his back every species of the tattooed atlas was a partner to the other.

The injection was administered. A woman screamed. A man moaned.

Ishmael shivered slightly and exhaled. Teria and Kararaina set up a loud wailing. 'Haere rā e pā, go to the threshold of the Pleiades.'

Ishmael's lips parted slightly. 'My tupuna, when he returned to our islands, was so hopeful that humankind would go on from strength to strength, ever onward . . .'

The tattooed *Homo sapiens* blinked once.

'Catch me, koroua.'

The tā moko became shadowed, as if the sun were slanting upon its plains, mountains, hills and valleys. A threnody rent the air from those who had inherited the world.

A jungle beast with an ivory horn pawed the earth, and Eden darkened.

KERI HULME

Keri Hulme (Kāi Tahu, Kāti Māmoe; and English and Orkney descent) is the author of two collections of poems and four works of fiction, including *The Bone People*, first published by the Spiral Press in 1984, which won the Booker Prize and Mobil Pegasus Prize in 1985. Born and raised in Ōtautahi, she lived for many years in an octagonal house she built herself in Okarito on the West Coast, and now lives in Ōamaru. 'Kaibutsu-San' was published in her first short story collection, *Te Kaihau / The Windeater* (1986), which mines a rich vein of non-naturalistic elements.

Kaibutsu-San

What I heard was this:

Lissen lissen hey man lissen

but I didn't hear it. A kind of mental sleeve-plucking,

Lissen we weren't doin' nothin' just plain Friday night in the Square lissen?

At first I thought it was the trees. Don't laugh. I was sitting quietly among the people swarm, sitting quietly on the bare tiles by one of the dying trees in tubs. If you listen carefully you can hear them waving their leaves feebly and gasping AIR AIR. If I were them, I'd up roots and head for the nearest bush. Leave the place freakily bare in the morning. But it wasn't the trees. It wasn't real enough for that.

Lissen please lissen ahhh

I looked cautiously round. No one near. I said, 'I'm listening.'

Ahhhhhhh at last at last at last . . . you can really hear? Wiggle your fingers by your nose?

O no. Not the sort of gesture I should make. But I wiggled.

Good. We started by scoring fivedollar hassling two thinfaced kids in a spacegame pit. They took one look at Mi all giant heavyjaw menace, another at our patches, and squeaked in terror. Handed over their money and scuttled away. Naturally we go outside to wait for more victims, take an innocent turn round the block meanwhile, but when we get back there's a demon lurking, swaying back and forth on his size twenties and caressing his long baton in an anticipatory sort of way. Smart little mothers, I think. I am verbally adroit but why waste words on rats?

I could – hear. I thought as I – heard, someone has spent a lot time polishing this story. It does not sound verbatim. And as I thought that, I felt – someone. Hunkering down by me, ready to continue a long tale. Someones.

Yeah, there's both of us. Me and Mi. Mi doesn't say much. Not exactly a walking dictionary, old Mi. He only cares about food, drink, sex, and excitement. Excitement can be strife or perversions or anything, but excitement there has got to be. I think it's to keep his bulk moving. When you get to be seven feet tall (almost) at seventeen, you need more than just ordinary fuel and thrill to keep you going, eh?

'Yes.'

Me, I don't need much. All I got to do is keep finding things to hate, and the world's full of those. I even hate Der Gang, for keeping us honorary fringe members. Any decent tribe would've killed us stone-dead just for approaching them. I mean, who wants the Hulk, capable of eating you and your headquarters out at one snack? Or the Thing, scaled with an interesting greenish version of psoriasis and capable of remembering every word you say for ever? Like, gimme a chance to glance at your notes, earwig your talk, and zap! Total recollection, reproduce it anytime. Mutants, the both of us. But Der Gang gives us sort of patches and sort of tolerates us round unless they're all feeling bored. They were, Friday . . . you still there?

I nodded.

It's eerie man. You're there and you're not. Anyway, Friday and we got fivedollar. Not enough for anything much. Mi suggests Port? An evening blurred out of existence: it has appeal. But fivedollar will only get a half-g and a halfg'll only half-blur us. So I say Nope, and Mi, who thinks I'm God, just nods. He stands there hunched and huge in his patches and gear. He never takes his patches and gear off. You can't call them his second skin. They're his first. I am a little more uh healthy. I have underpants. And my chest boasts a delicate intricacy of greeny scales highly visible through the open denim jacket – you can't see?

'Not a thing.'

Ah shit. Nemmind. Anyway, there we are, strolling quietly through the Friday-night crowds, away from the spacepit. Mi lumps along, hands occupied with his cards. It's a twitch with him, a kind of tic, shuffling a pack in a flickering arc. Always has a pack on him, keeps them spruce clean inner secret pocket in his jacket. It's strange to see them come out virginal from among the carefully grown shit and grime. I've got the odd twitch too. Like reading signs, any signs, shop window neon store-top bus-side. I chant them out loud until I see there's another demon not a hundred miles away from us staring in a repulsively interested fashion. 'Centre,' I say, twitching Mi's jacket, and the cards vanish magically, back into their virginal hole. Centre is – you know the scarred remaining real tree? Not this scrawny thing in the pot trying to make it to bush-size?

> 'I know it.' The big one that has come to some unholy truce with good ol' CHCH pollution and now photosynthesises soot instead of sunlight. The tree I'd come to see until I – heard.

Right. That's our centre. Our refuge. I squat by Mi on an outside root and the Friday-night crowd eddies round us. All those good straight people daren't get too close. Something might leap off us and sink its grimy little teeth deep into their skin ARRGGGHH! and suddenly they'll be like us, outlaws, streethappy. I sneer at the good people. I have ninety-four words for them, all extremely corrosive. I say them under my breath. Mi has his cards out again and is staring unfocused over their arc.

A crocodile of Japanese tourists is chivvied by, following a Leader and a Flag. They don't even blink at Mi and me. Don't even see us, I think. Not a registered tourist sight eh. Except there's one at the end of the crocodile, the wart on its tail. He trips along in little staggers, upright and sweating and obviously stewed out of his mind. He sees my stare, blinks, sees Mi, blinks again, and suddenly disengages from the crocodile. He is about four feet tall, flabby, and when he smiles at us, reveals appalling teeth. Great and yellow, like a horse's, and very wet-looking. He bows suddenly, like a pocket-knife: folding, hisses through the teeth, and says

'Pray cards?'

Mi snorts. Stereotype, he is thinking, only he is not thinking 'stereotype', he is seeing comic-strip yellow men who can't say 'l'.

'Pray cards?' asks the gnome again, anxiously. He folds fluidly up beside us, and I hear tinkle tinkle and all of a sudden he has produced a briefcase.

And I gasp. It is made of some soft supple sueded leather, beige, brushed fine, achingly beautiful. I saw a dog with a hide like that and coveted it and plotted how to get it for months. But that is not all. The briefcase has ordinary dimensions and a curious handle. Little dials inset, lights like trapped glow-worms but enough to show electronic numbers and lines flickering away. An impossibly small television half an inch across but I swear to seeing tiny people cavorting on it. The briefcase looks rich, technical, elegant and somehow heavy. I hunger for it.

The tinkle tinkle is from a fine steel chain running from the briefcase handle to the little man's wrist.

'Pray cards,' he states, in the brook-no-refusal tone of the very drunk.

And Mi giggles. He giggles so much he nearly loses control of his cascade of shuffled cards.

You take it from me, old Mi looks thick and clumsy as well as enormous. From the soles of his horny feet (I mean skin, he can't even steal a decent pair of steeltoes) to the top of his carefully felted hair, he looks like an oaf. Can't touch a thing without crushing it. Anything delicate or skilful is obviously beyond him. Except old Mi was born a cardshark. He was born knowing all card combinations, the odds at poker, the possible hands in every game. He has razor-fine judgement in assessing other players. It is not a matter of memory for him to know what cards have been played, are to be played. It is a matter of instinct. Nobody who knows him plays with him of course. You get murdered, every game. That is why he shuffles. That is all he gets to do.

And here is this weird little victim offering himself to Mi.

I am getting a fierce electric sort of a buzz already. That briefcase is worth real dollars, hundreds of them . . . a furious rave of a Friday, not slow boring killtime at all! 'Gimme t'five,' says Mi and he giggles his high breathy giggle again. I heeheehee right along with him, and hand the money over. Mi spreads it on the root of the tree.

'Play cards for money,' he says slowly and emphatically, 'ah so' giggling again. Height of humour for him eh.

'Dorrors o-kay.'

He hugs his briefcase close to his chest, opening it so we can't see in. The amazing handle is flopped towards me and yeah: there really are little people on that impossibly small screen. My eyelids might be scaly and reptilian but the eyes inside are sharper than most. Then flip. Cards. Fresh cards in crisp cellophane. And flip again. Fivedollars. About a hundred of them, neatly bent in bankers' tens, gathered together with a shiny fold of new white paper. He rips that, spreads them round in a fan; snaps off the cellophane, pushes over the cards to Mi.

He sets his briefcase down carefully clinkle tink and beams at us.

'Ah so. Cards o-kay. Money. Prenty dorrors. Good.' He bows from the waist. 'Drink?' he enquires. 'Drink,' he decides. He picks up the case again. 'What genremen drink?' he asks us.

I'm goggling. I will have that bag if I have to personally saw it off the dwarf's wrist. But I say, 'The gentlemen love, truly relish, bourbon. We luxuriate in that delectable liquor,' malignly sticking in as many 'l's as I can think of in a second.

He blinks. He says something fast in Japanese and there is, I swear from inside the bag, a tiny mellow reply.

'Bourbon,' says the Teeth, and reaches in his briefcase and takes out three crystal shot-glasses. They are large glasses and they are full.

It *is* a travelling bar as well as an electronic marvel show! Mi doesn't think about the Amazing Bag, he just takes his glass and swallows the drink and goes Ahhhhh. So I try mine. Smooth and pure, holy best bourbon, god that's good.

The little Jap has already downed his. He holds his hand out, takes back our glasses, refills them (a long thin flask in there, vacuum operated? I think), and then licks his lips.

'Pray cards now,' he says definitely.

And so the slaughter begins. The purring power-machine that is cardplaying Mi gears smoothly up. He toys a little with the Teeth, finding out his strengths (none apparently) and his weaknesses (everywhere). He loses our fivedollar, wins it and two of the banker's fold back, loses another . . . o you know as I do how to spin a sucker along. The fan of fivedollars shrinks. Mi giggles. The little man sweats. He opens the beautiful bag frequently. You hear his glissade of Japanese, a click, a tiny voice, then a swash noise. It honestly sounds like him saying I want three quadruple shots of best bourbon, and the bag saying Yes Teeth-san, and producing them . . . o the marvels of microchip technology!

We've had six seven neat sweet bourbons by now and the noise of the crowd eddying round our cardsharper and victim island has receded. The Teeth is talking in his fractured ell-less English,

'No mor dorrors, neary gone, sad horrorday now,'

but neither of us are really listening. I am staring fascinated at the game, at the bag, at the little man dealing his hopeless cards, wristchain ringing as he does. Mi is playing and sees nothing but the game in hand.

More bourbon from the bag-bar. Tinny voice, figures fluorescing on minute screen. No more Friday-night-in-the-Square crowd. Bourbon. The Teeth is sweating profusely, down his flabby cheeks, into the fissures of his neck. He giggles constantly. He still bows floppily from the waist each time he passes our drinks. He keeps dropping his cards. The chain from bag to wrist goes tinkle tinkle.

'What we pray for now genremen?'

That penetrates. The fan of fivedollars has folded entirely. I have it all in my back pocket, where it keeps our lucky first fivedollar warm. I nudge Mi. The bourbon vapours in my brain have produced a hell of an idea.

'No money, no game,' says Mi. He puts his giant hand on the pile of cards and discards, lovingly. His eyes shine. He foresees. And the future tonight is going to be Rampage. A rage of a night. We can really waste ourselves. Slit, booze, fists, you name it, we'll have it, thanks to the fan. But I want, I want.

The Jap wrings his hands and the chain dingles.

'O but I *ruv* cards, prease pray more.'

I nudge Mi again.

'Money or nothing,' I say ruthlessly. Then bait my hook. 'Unless you got something worth dollars?'

He looks at his dandruff-spotted navy-blue suit, shiny black shoes, holds out the other wrist with a cheap chrome digital watch on it hopelessly. I shake my head. The sweat running down his face looks like tears. I snicker. He hugs the Amazing Bag to his chest desperately. The gleam in my eyes must be showing.

'Very precious, this case,' he says. 'Is everything to me. All my fun, all my life. What can you offer that is equal?'

Okay, normally that sudden improvement in a foreigner's English would have warned even Mi. It had 'demon' written all over it, their gambling squad or something. But the bourbon was roaring in our heads, and I saw only the gorgeous suppleskinned case with all its magic, and Mi saw only the greatest prize of his card-playing life lying supine and grovelling before him. As ready for the plucking as Mi was ready for the kill.

So I say, 'Well, we'll play you everything we've got against your bag. Fair exchange eh?' and Mi choruses, 'Everything, everything.'

'All the dollars? Everything?'

'Everything.'

'Clothes, jewels, skin, everything?'

'Yeah, yeah, *everything*,' damn the little bat I think, my fingers itching for The Bag.

'Everything you have and are?' whimpers the Teeth. 'Everything?'

'*Every*fuckingthing,' growls Mi. His cardshark fingers are riffling the pack.

'So. Everything?' he passes over filled bourbon glasses.

'Yeah yeah yeah,' we are melting with impatience and wouldn't see a warning if it sprang on us and throttled us. We clutch our last glasses of booze.

'Ah so,' says the Teeth, and bows politely, and there is an infinite fat satisfaction about him now.

The cards are dealt, the hands are played, and Mi loses, of course.

The little Oriental gentleman stands fluidly, bows a last time, smiles.

'Keep the money,' he says. His face is becoming leaner. 'Keep your patches and gear.' He has stopped sweating. 'You can even keep the glasses.' He points the handle of the bag at us. We are sitting stunned, mouths O, Mi's hands limp as though the life has gone from them. 'I only want everything from you.' Somehow his teeth are more pointed than before.

There is a flash and click like someone took a photograph. Immediately I feel something essential, vital, drain out of my belly, and Mi feels it too because he screams and the cards spray out of his hands.

Two more little figures suddenly appear on the tiny screen. I can see them, I disbelieve it. My ears hear a chorus of thin howls from the bag.

The Teeth smiles suavely, one last time.

'So sorry,' he says, and is back among the Friday-night crowd and lost. The Friday-night crowd is everywhere again, loud and rushing and rude and we're *here.* Man hey man, lissen, can you get us out?

> That's what I heard. I still couldn't see them but their agony was real. But somebody from the Friday-night crowd had seen me sitting by the trapped tree, seen me talking to seemingly thin air, and had called you. So here I am, back again, explaining. Do you comprehend what you hear,
> you,
> and your beautiful
> little black bag?

JULIET MARILLIER

A member of the Order of Bards, Ovates and Druids, Juliet Marillier is one of New Zealand's best-loved writers of historical fantasy. She was born in Dunedin – which she describes as 'the most Scottish city outside Scotland itself' – in 1948, and after graduating from Otago University worked as a public servant, music teacher, choral conductor and sometime opera singer, before becoming a full-time writer. Her many novels include the Sevenwaters sequence, the Blackthorn & Grim trilogy, and the ongoing Warrior Bards series, the second book of which, *A Dance With Fate*, will be published in September 2020.

By Bonelight

'We need light,' says Susie.

The power's gone off again; that happens a lot at Woodland Gardens. This place must have been named by a clown – instead of numbers, the floors have names, Chestnut level, Willow level and so on, a whole tower of trees. Woodland Gardens itself is a concrete high-rise with no redeeming features. Along with dodgy power it has blocked drains, creeping mould and lifts that make everyone use the stairs, even people who live on the top floor – Oak level – like us. If something can break, you can be sure it'll be broken at Woodland Gardens. Down the bottom, outside, there's a sad playground with a metal swing and a climbing frame on dirty sand. In the daytime it's usually empty because mothers don't want their kids stepping on dog poo or used syringes. At night it's a meeting place for dealers.

We're sitting in our flat in the almost-dark, my stepmother, my stepsisters and me. Our torch batteries are flat, Susie's lighter is used up and we've managed to run out of both matches and candles. It's nearly dusk outside and the heater's gone off along with everything else electrical, so it'll soon be icy in here. But I know better than to suggest early bed. Susie wants our projects finished tonight, so she can get them in the mail first thing. Since it's already too dim in here for us to see our work, one of us will have to fetch light. It's not going to be Sophie or Miranda, because they're Susie's own daughters, her flesh and blood, and she never makes them go downstairs in the dark. I am my mother's daughter, and my mother is dead.

'Won't the shop be shut by now?' I say, hating the way my voice shakes. 'I think they close at five on a Thurs –'

Before I can finish I'm hauled up onto my feet with Susie's fingernails pressing into the soft flesh of my arm. I sink my teeth into my lip; I won't give her the satisfaction of hearing me cry out. My heart's thumping hard.

'You think I'm stupid or something?' Her hand tightens.

'You'll have to go to the basement,' Sophie says.

'Better hurry, Lissa,' puts in Miranda. 'It'll be dark soon.'

There's a silence. I feel the weight of their gaze, the three of them, and I hear them thinking: *Go. Now. Before we make you.*

'That concierge woman's supposed to have everything,' Susie says, and the hold on my arm slackens slightly. 'You know, what's-her-name, the one they all talk about. Go down and ask her for candles and a lighter.'

We haven't been at Woodland Gardens long. Susie got word that Dad's deployment was extended another six months, and almost straight away she sold the house that had been my home for all of my fifteen years. Home and haven. The house where my mother gave birth to me, her only child. The house where, only a year and a half ago, she gave me a gift, then died. Susie moved us so fast there was no time to ask questions. There wasn't even time to cry. It felt as if I blinked, then opened my eyes to find everything gone.

This flat is small. Two bedrooms: one for her, the other one for the three of us, with me on a trundle bed. Apart from my clothes, I got to bring one book – *Grimm's Fairy Tales*, which she had to let me keep because it was a Christmas present from Dad – and Mimi, who didn't get given to the Salvos because she was hidden in my pocket.

Susie had Winslow put down. For that, I can never forgive her. She didn't have to choose a place with a no-pets policy. She didn't have to move us at all. I thought I was going back to school at the end of the holidays and instead here we are in a completely different neighbourhood. When I asked about school – the kids at Woodland Gardens go to Westmoreland High – she said some stuff that frightened me so much I never asked again. Stuff about how screwed up in the head I was, and how much worse it would get if I was around people. Stuff about what she'd do to me if I told anyone what she'd said, ever. Miranda and Sophie never finished high school and now I have an idea why.

'Her name's Barbara,' says Sophie, reminding me sharply of what's ahead.

None of us has ever been down to the basement. None of us has ever met Barbara the concierge in the flesh. But we've heard about her. Everyone at Woodland Gardens talks about her in the same way, hushed and scared like an olden-days person speaking of a witch. She's supposed to have lots of stuff down there, not only candles but old-fashioned oil lamps, fuses, all kinds of tools, probably matches and firelighters too. And weird stuff, so Kye told me. Kye is the only kid I've spoken to since we moved in here. Susie doesn't like letting us out, and we're not supposed to talk to anyone. Her reason is, the building's full of druggies and perverts. But doing the washing is one of my jobs, and that gets me as far as the communal laundry along the end of Oak level. When I'm there I hear people talking. And I see Kye sometimes, not washing, just hanging around. He told me people go into Barbara's basement and never come out again. He told me she has a human bone for a door knocker. He said his uncle told him Barbara came from some country where they do voodoo, black magic, and that weird people are always visiting her to get spells. If that was true, if magic was real, I'd ask her for a spell myself. I'd get one to bring my father home right now. He probably thought he was doing the right thing when he married Susie so soon after Mum died. He must have thought I needed a mother, since we have no other family and he's away so much. And Susie wasn't so bad back then. Dad couldn't have known she'd turn into a monster the moment he was gone.

I've thought of asking Kye if I can make a phone call from his place, to . . . I don't know who, but there are welfare people who are supposed to help the families during a deployment, and I could look up their number. Or I could call my old school, speak to Mr Turner or Mrs Moss. I've thought of giving Kye a letter to post to Dad, because I suspect Susie rips them up, or Dad would have sent some back the way he always used to. Only Susie's so good at lying, and she's his wife now. She'd tell the welfare people I'm emotional and confused, and say she's getting professional help for me. And then she'd punish me. She's good at punishments. I have lots of bruises, the kind that show on my body and the kind that are deep inside where nobody can see.

'Off you go, Lissa,' she says now. 'Don't take too long about it. You're way behind with the orders; at this rate you'll be up all night getting that one finished.' What we make, Susie sells online. Sophie's fine shawls; Miranda's Aran sweaters; my one-of-a-kind dolls. I make a lot of dolls, so I guess they're popular. Susie won't let us use the internet, so I don't see the customer feedback. No internet means no email either. Dad could be on another planet. He's been gone eight months, and in those eight months my whole world has changed.

'What are you waiting for?' Susie snaps. 'Pitch darkness? Go! Now!'

There's no refusing. And with Susie standing over me, there's no getting a coat or gloves even though it'll be freezing in the stairwell. At least I have Mimi. She's about all I do have these days.

Susie locks the flat door behind me. Locks me out. When I get back with the candles I'm supposed to knock on the door three times, count to five, then knock three times again and wait for her to let me in. The two times three knocks are so she won't open up to some kind of crazy person. Though that's what she told me I was: crazy. A crazy girl can't go to school, but it's OK for her to sit at home making dolls for her stepmother to sell. I hope my dolls go to better homes than mine, homes where people love them and look after them and whisper secrets in their woollen ears.

The hallways in Woodland Gardens are long and grey. At this time of day all the doors are shut. There's still enough light from the tall windows down the end for me to see my way to the lift, and beside it the stair door. This door's broken, falling off its hinges. I step through and start down the twelve flights.

The stairwell stinks of wee. I'm hoping not to meet the perverts and junkies Susie talks about, though the shadowy landings seem like places where bad stuff might happen. I reach Willow level, Aspen level, Juniper level, and the light's almost gone. I have to slow down or I might fall. There'll be no sympathy from Susie if I break my ankle, only a reprimand for being clumsy and costing her money for a trip to the doctor. I wonder if the doctor would believe me if I told the truth about my stepmother? For a moment it seems almost worth breaking my ankle to find out. I sit down on the top step of Juniper level to stop myself from jumping. I take Mimi from my pocket and put her on my knee. There's just enough light left to make out her little face, her dark beady eyes, her snub nose, her mouth that's not smiling and not frowning but something in between. Her black embroidery-silk hair; her moss stitch gown in my favourite purple.

'I'm scared, Mimi. Scared of Susie and scared of myself. Scared of going down to the basement.'

Give me a kiss, says Mimi.

I oblige with a peck on her knitted lips.

Give me a hug.

I press her against my cheek. My mother's last gift was teaching me how to knit. How to put love and hope and courage into every doll I make, so the person who gets that doll will have a true friend in good times and in bad. Mimi was the first doll I ever made, and knitted into her body is a strand of hair my mother cut from her own head as she lay dying. 'When you are sad, Lissa, when you are lonely, when you are at your wits' end, she will help you,' she told me. And it was true. I don't think Mimi is truly magic – how can she be, when I made her myself with wool and needles? – but when I speak to her in the right way, I can hear her speaking back to me.

Now let me fly!

I toss Mimi up in the air. She performs a triple somersault and I catch her on the way down, setting her upright on my knee again. She's only a little doll, ten centimetres from the top of her head to the soles of her knitted shoes. In the dim light it seems to me she's looking quite pleased with herself.

Why are we going downstairs in the dark?

'To visit Barbara in the basement. To ask her for light.'

Mm-hm. Mimi seems to be considering this. *We'll need that if we're to find our way back up. Did you say you were scared?*

'I'm scared of Susie because she hurts me and I never know when she's going to be angry. And I'm scared of Barbara the concierge because everyone else is.'

Mimi appears to be waiting for more.

'And I'm scared of myself. A moment ago I was going to throw myself down these stairs and hurt myself on purpose, and that would make what Susie says about me true. I wasn't crazy before she came, Mimi. I'm sure I wasn't.'

Was your mother ever afraid of anything? Even at the end?

I remember Mum lying on the bed, hooked up to a drip, a skeleton with a fine layer of white silk for skin. Her eyes huge; her mouth stretched in a terrifying smile. Speaking words of hope. I shake my head.

You are your mother's daughter, Mimi says. *Get up, walk down, fetch light. I will help you.*

We go on down. Poplar level, Cypress level, Eucalyptus level. I can hardly see the steps now. Ash level, Elm level. Somewhere below me a door clangs open, and I hear someone charging up the stairs towards me. I shrink back against the wall, stuffing Mimi into my pocket for safety. My heart's in my throat. A drug deal gone wrong, someone being chased with a knife, someone desperate . . . The person reaches the landing below me and comes straight on up. *Don't see me,* I beg. *Just go on past, please, please . . .*

It's a man dressed all in black, leather pants, hoodie, chunky Doc Marten–style boots. He hurtles past me. Either he's a top athlete or he's terrified of what's coming after him. His face is as dark as his clothes; there's a hint of gleaming eyes, and he's gone. I wait, making myself remember to breathe. Wait for whatever is coming next. I count up to fifty but nobody comes. Mimi says nothing, but I imagine her thinking, *What are we waiting for?* As well she might, because since the man ran past me, it's gone so dark I can't see my hand in front of my face. I pray that Barbara the concierge is home, and that she does give me light.

The lower levels, I navigate by touch. One hand on the iron railing, the other stretched out towards the concrete wall of the stairwell, I go down foot by cautious foot, hoping there are no broken steps, no missing stretches of rail. The dark's like a presence pushing at me, weighing me down. I feel as if I'm deep underground, though I think this is only Yew level, third from the bottom. There's no reading the signs anymore, so I start counting the steps, counting the turns in the stairs. This stairwell comes out on the ground floor; I've been down here in the day time, when Susie took a risk and sent me to the shop on my own. Back then, I thought of running away, asking the shopkeeper if I could use the phone, asking someone, anyone, for help. I didn't. Susie's got a long reach. As I go down the last flight of steps to ground level, I start wondering if she actually doesn't want me to come back tonight. She might be hoping I run into a murderer so she can get rid of me with a neat explanation for Dad. It's not as if my dolls are making Susie a fortune, or we wouldn't be living here in Woodland Gardens. I wonder what's happened to Dad's Navy pay. What if he's sick or even dead and she hasn't told me? But that couldn't happen. Could it?

The stairs come to an end. I stand still, trying to get a sense of direction. Somewhere in front of me I know there's a door that leads out to the so-called plaza, where kids ride skateboards and do graffiti during the day and adults shout and smash bottles at night. Between me and that door there's utter darkness. I can't even see a line of light around the doorway, though surely there's at least one street light working out there. I creep forward with my hands outstretched, hoping I'm not about to fall down a flight of steps I've forgotten about. My heart's jumping around like crazy.

My hands touch the concrete wall. I work my way around till I find the door and pull on the handle. It's locked.

For a bit I just stand there, thinking of the long way back in the dark, imagining myself telling Susie I failed, guessing what might happen then. Susie making me stand in a cold shower till I'm blue and shivering. Susie making me stand out on the balcony in my underwear. Susie shoving my head into the wall. Susie has a great imagination.

I sink down onto the floor and get Mimi out of my pocket. I sit her on my knee. 'I don't think I can go on,' I mutter.

I can't see her face in the dark, but I hear her familiar voice.

Give me a kiss.

I touch my lips to her face.

Give me a hug.

I hold her to my cheek and find that I am actually crying a bit.

Now let me fly!

I flip Mimi up into the air and manage to catch her, blind.

So, we're down here in the dark. And you're curled up in a ball crying.

'I do try to be brave.' I scrub a hand across my cheek. 'But sometimes it's too hard.'

There is a light to be found in every darkness. You are your mother's daughter. Find it.

'But –' I fall silent, because it seems Mimi's right. The blanketing dark has lightened just enough for me to see that there *is* another set of steps, leading not up but down, and from somewhere below a faint glow is coming. I thought you could only reach the basement by the lift or a flight of outside steps. But maybe there's a third way.

With Mimi in my hand I creep across to the steps, which don't have any kind of guard rail. We go down. The dim light gets a bit brighter. There are only seven steps, and here we are at another level, with a short landing and one door at the end. The door is painted in blood-red gloss, and on a shelf beside it is the source of the glow: a lamp made from what looks like a real human skull, with a tea-light candle inside. It makes weird flickering shadows all over the stairwell walls. And there, dangling beside the door, is that knocker Kye told me about. If it's not a human shin-bone I don't know what it is. Now I'm really cold.

There's a little brass plate on the red door, and on it is some lettering, only it's not the letters I know, but a foreign alphabet of some kind. It might say anything from 'Concierge' to 'Visitors will be eaten alive'. I gather my courage, put my hand around the leg bone and rap on the door.

I wait. It feels as if getting downstairs took a long time, far longer than it should have done, and I wonder if Barbara has gone to bed already, in which case she won't be well pleased if I go on knocking. Maybe she's out. Maybe Mimi's instincts are wrong for the first time ever.

After a while I knock again, not too hard. I call out, 'Is anyone home?'

The door opens so suddenly I yelp with fright. There's a woman in the doorway, long straggledy white hair falling out of a bun, little bright eyes, skin with a million wrinkles.

She's wearing a knitted garment in exactly the same purple I used for Mimi's dress, and in her arms she's holding this humungous ginger cat. It is the biggest cat I've ever seen in my life and it has a mean look in its eye. I know cats, though. I see right through this one.

Barbara – who else could this be? – hasn't said a word, so I speak up before things get embarrassing.

'Sorry to disturb you. I'm –'

'Lissa from 1205. You'll be wanting light, yes?'

I gape, but only for a moment. Behind her the room looks dark and bright at the same time, full of changing light that shows me rich colours and elaborate patterns. Unlike ours, Barbara's place is full of interesting stuff.

'Come in,' she says as if reading my mind, and steps back to let me go past her.

There are bones everywhere. Skulls with lights in them, their glowing eyes following me as I move cautiously across the room. Leg bones and arm bones and goodness-knows-what bones hanging from the ceiling like mobiles. Colourful pottery bowls full of tiny bones that must be from shrews or voles or something. There's a smell like incense, a lot better than the stink in the stairwell. I start to feel a bit dizzy and have to remind myself why I'm here.

'Our power's off,' I say as Barbara puts the huge cat down on an overstuffed sofa. It settles on an embroidered cushion, looking at me through narrowed eyes. 'My stepmother sent me to ask you for candles and a lighter. Please.'

She just stands there examining me, her arms folded. I can't think of anything else to say, so I crouch down beside the cat and put my hand carefully out where he or she can smell it and decide to be friends or not. 'Beautiful one,' I whisper, remembering Winslow with his silky hair and lovely blue eyes.

'Aren't you a fine cat, then?'

The giant feline deigns to sniff my hand, then gives itself a cursory lick. It raises no objection when I stroke it gently.

'She bites,' says Barbara.

I don't think this cat's going to bite me. She's purring now. 'What's her name?' I ask.

'Rory. Aurora.'

I go on petting her for a while, and Barbara goes on standing there watching me.

'Sorry,' I say eventually, remembering that it's late. 'I miss my own cat. Is it OK for me to have some candles, please?'

'Ah,' says Barbara, and I realise the door is shut and I'm alone with her and her house is seriously weird. I get to my feet and think about the twelve flights of stairs and the dark. 'I have candles,' she says. 'I have lighters. I have all manner of things down here, as no doubt you've heard. They tell all kinds of stories about me.'

'I don't get out much,' I squeak. 'But I did hear you have candles, yes.'

'Can you pay?'

'Oh.' My heart sinks. 'My stepmother didn't give me any money.' Stupid! I should have thought of this.

'Nothing's free, young lady. But there are other ways of paying.'

I back away towards the door. If I can get out, if she hasn't locked it, I should be able to outrun her. She's a big heavy woman and she looks sixty at least, maybe even older.

'Can you cook?' Barbara asks.

I stop backing. 'Yes,' I say. I've been cooking since I was a little kid. Since Dad went away I've been doing pretty much all the housework, including preparing meals for four. If that's all she wants me to do, fine. Even if it takes until midnight.

Barbara flings open an inside door to show a dark old kitchen lit by more skull lamps. The stove is one of those ancient iron ones with a wood fire in a little compartment; there's a basket of logs sitting next to it. Bunches of herbs and onions and garlic dangle from the ceiling. In the middle of the room there's a wooden table and on it are a big bowl of fruit and veg, a basket of eggs and some little sacks that look as if they might hold rice or beans. In the corner stands a big red cupboard with a design of fruit and flowers painted on it, like something out of *Grimm's Fairy Tales. Then she shut her little brother in the red cupboard, and when she opened the doors again he was quite, quite gone.*

'I'm going out,' Barbara says. 'Work to be done. You'll make my dinner, three courses, each finer than the last. Lay it out on this table before I return home, and be sure it's a meal fit for a queen. If I'm satisfied I'll give you what you came for. But take care you leave my kitchen tidy. If I find the smallest thing out of place, I'll consider eating you for my dinner instead.'

Seems as if she's heard most of the things the tenants of Woodland Gardens say about her and finds them amusing, not upsetting. I'm beyond being surprised by anything at this point, so I put on an apron, wash my hands and get to work. My gran had a wood stove like this so it's not too much of a challenge.

Making a three-course dinner takes me a while. I put Mimi on the table, propped up against the fruit bowl. Rory the cat comes in at a certain point and hunkers down in a corner to supervise. As for Barbara, she's flung on a cape and gone off, slamming the front door behind her. It's pretty trusting of her, seeing as she's never met me before tonight. I wonder what work she could be doing at this hour.

I think about Susie, upstairs getting angrier and angrier in the dark. The doll I was working on will be lying on the table up there, all lonely, waiting for me to finish embroidering her face. Like all the dolls I make, she has in her a hair I plucked from my own head and knitted in with the wool. Someone's out there waiting for that doll, and unless I get this job finished and take the candles upstairs they'll have to wait a day longer, and Susie . . . I can't let myself think too hard about that; I have to concentrate. I dare to open the red cupboard and find it's a pantry full of useful ingredients. It's a long time since I've had so much good stuff to work with.

For starters I make a tomato and basil soup, with shaved parmesan and a herb scone on the side. I put together a spiced fruit compote and vanilla custard – there's no fridge in Barbara's kitchen, but the bottle of milk in the pantry is still OK, and so is the chicken waiting to be jointed and cooked. The main course will be breaded chicken pieces on herbed couscous, with veges baked in olive oil and rosemary. In herb lore, rosemary means a strong woman, so it seems a good choice. I hope the meal's substantial enough for Barbara. She looks like she might be a big eater. I wonder who would have cooked her dinner if I hadn't been here.

It's starting to feel as if midnight might have been and gone, and my eyes are gritty with tiredness. The meal is pretty much ready, with only the couscous to steam. I make myself coffee, give Rory some chicken scraps in a bowl that looks like it might be hers, and sit down at the table for a bit. The kitchen's full of good smells; even with those skulls staring down at me, it feels safe in here. The coffee should give me enough energy to clean up, then I only need to set the table and I'm done. If Barbara likes the meal, I can grab the lighter and candles and head on upstairs, and I'll still have time to finish the doll before morning.

I find crockery, a glass, knives and forks. I check the kitchen: bench wiped clean, dishes washed, dried and put away, floor swept, fire made up, kettle steaming on the wood stove. Everything's ready. And I hear noises from outside the front door – Barbara's back.

Whoosh! Rory leaps onto the table, sending the open bag of couscous flying. Around two kilos of the stuff spill out all over the floor, the tiny granules rolling and scattering into every corner. I jump up and they crunch under my shoes. Rory has terrified herself; now she's standing on the table with one paw planted on the clean plate, fur on end, yowling. There's a rattle at the front door as Barbara sticks her key in the lock. What was that she said about eating me for dinner?

I scramble for the red cupboard where there's a dustpan and brush, and I slip over on the carpet of little grains. I land on my hip, putting new bruises on the old ones. I want to curl up on the floor and cry. Instead I look at Mimi, who's still standing beside the fruit bowl.

Give me a kiss, says Mimi.

The front door squeaks open. I struggle to my feet, reach out for the doll, kiss her embroidered mouth.

Give me a hug.

Quick, quick, I will her as I lay my cheek on hers.

Now let me fly!

I throw her high; in the few seconds we have left before fate catches up with us, she may as well enjoy herself. She twirls, tumbles, falls back into my waiting hands. Dear Mimi, my true friend in good times and bad.

Sit on the chair, close your eyes, lift your feet and keep that cat out of my way.

I manage to gather up Rory, who weighs half a ton, and sit down at the table again. I can hear Barbara walking about in the other room, muttering to herself. There's no way this can be cleaned up before she comes in, no way.

Somewhere near my feet there's a little sound like rats scuttling about. In my arms Rory tenses, making a deep-down whining noise. My body feels like it's strung on a wire, every bit of it jangly and terrified.

Hold on to that cat and keep your eyes shut.

Something small and woollen brushes against my ankle and is gone. The scuttling moves around the room, from cupboard to table, from table to bench, from bench to stove.

How much couscous does your recipe require? asks Mimi.

'A cup.' This is crazy.

The scuttling moves up onto the table; becomes more of a pouring sound.

Done.

I open my eyes. The floor looks completely clean. Mimi is exactly where she was before, regarding me with her woollen gaze, and the couscous is back in the bag, most of it anyway. The enamel cup I had ready for measuring is filled precisely to the top.

The door opens and there's Barbara, tall and imposing, her dark eyes taking in the tidy kitchen, the neatly laid table, the various serving dishes waiting. I put the cat down, then move the couscous over to the bench and measure a cupful of water into a small iron pot.

'Please, do sit down,' I say a bit shakily. 'Are you ready for the first course now?'

She sinks weightily onto the chair. 'I could eat a horse,' she says, sounding as if she actually means it.

Barbara eats the tomato and basil soup, the parmesan and the herb scone without saying a word. While she's getting through that, I steam the couscous, which seems none the worse for its stint on the floor.

'Good.' Barbara wipes her mouth with a large hand.

'What's next?'

I serve the couscous, the chicken pieces and the baked vegetables: creamy potatoes, golden pumpkin, ruby-red beets, glistening onions. My mouth is watering, but she doesn't suggest I sit down and share her feast, and I don't either.

When she's eaten about half the main course, she sets down her knife and fork and stares at me. 'I need entertainment,' she says. 'A story. Think you can manage that?'

I'm OK at cooking and I guess I'm OK at stories too, thanks to *Grimm's Fairy Tales*. I start to tell her a story about a girl who goes into the woods to find an old witch who lives in a hut on hen's legs, only Barbara keeps interrupting and asking questions, and it turns into a story about a girl whose stepmother takes her away from everything familiar, until the only friend she has in the world is the little doll her mother taught her how to make. A girl who only gets let out when her stepmother wants something; a girl who's lost touch with the good things of her past, and only sees the cruelty and loneliness of her future.

'Is this the doll?' Barbara asks, looking at Mimi, who stares back boldly from her spot by the fruit bowl.

I tell her. I explain about the other dolls I make and how Susie sells them as fast as I can get them finished. I don't tell her about the strands of hair; that feels too secret, even though Barbara's listening with interest and her expression's quite kindly. She's finished the main course, a meal big enough to go around all four of us at 1205 with leftovers to spare.

'Ready for dessert?' I ask politely, wondering what the time is and whether Susie will have given up on me and gone to bed by now. If only I could sneak in without waking her up.

'Mmm.' Barbara stretches, moves her chair back a bit from the table. 'Who taught you to cook, Lissa?'

'My mother.'

'She did a good job. You could be a chef someday.'

I say nothing. You don't get to be much at all if you haven't finished high school. I bring out the fruit compote and the custard, and I make a pot of tea.

'Sit down,' Barbara says at last. 'Fetch yourself a cup, a bowl and a spoon.'

We eat the dessert course together. It tastes wonderful; each mouthful reminds me of summer and sunshine and being safe. It reminds me of Mum and Dad and the way things used to be.

'Well, then,' says Barbara when the compote and custard are all gone and we're sitting over our cups of tea. 'You've told me your story, and a fine one it was, full of joy and sorrow, good times and bad. Now it's your turn. I'm sure you have plenty of questions for the old woman in the basement with her voodoo spells and her cantankerous familiar. Go ahead, ask them.'

My mind fills with questions. I'd love to know about her past, and what brought her to live at Woodland Gardens, where she doesn't belong at all. I'd like to know what the brass plate on the door says, and what language it's in. I'd love her to tell me what work she does out there at midnight. And I want to know about spells: whether there's one that will rescue me from Susie.

Suddenly it seems dangerous to ask much at all. It feels like prying into something best left alone.

'I only have one question,' I say.

Her eyebrows go up.

'Is magic real?' I ask, hoping she won't laugh her head off.

She doesn't say anything, just looks at me, and I remember the thing with the couscous. I think of the hair I put into my dolls, as if that might somehow make them as real to their owners as Mimi is to me. Of course magic is real. But then I remember Susie and my bruises and how I've never been brave enough to ask Kye if I can use his phone, and I think no, it can't be.

Barbara goes on looking at me and sipping her tea, and I think she isn't going to answer at all until she gets up, goes to the red cupboard, opens a little drawer at the bottom and brings out something that looks a bit like a melted candle. When she shows it to me I see it's like a doll, with arms and legs and a head, but blobby and crude as if someone got tired of making it halfway through.

'What if I told you this was a voodoo doll?' she asks, and a shiver runs through me. It doesn't take much to imagine this little thing with pins stuck all over it, or being held over a lighter flame until it drips away to nothing. 'What if I taught you how to work a curse?'

Now the room is bristling with magic, the Grimm's fairy tale kind where girls try to hide terrible secrets and wicked stepmothers dance in red-hot iron shoes. I take a deep breath, then reach out and pick up Mimi. 'No,' I say. 'Not even if it gets me out of trouble. Not even if it fixes up the future the way I want. It'll cost too much. That kind of thing always does.'

Barbara smiles. She reaches over towards the stove, opens the iron door with her bare hand and throws the wax thing inside, where it sizzles, making a vile smell. She clangs the door shut. 'You'll be wanting that light, then.' She stands, takes one of the skull lamps from the shelf and hands it to me. There's a wire running through a couple of holes on the top, so I can carry the skull. The tea-light candle inside has been burning a while; this lamp may be out before I even get to Oak level. Perhaps the power will be back on by then. Perhaps

Susie won't hurt me. After the voodoo thing, I can't seem to make myself ask for more.

'I'll see you out,' Barbara says, leading me through the room with the embroidered cushions to the red front door. When she opens it, Rory streaks out, quicker than her bulk suggests is possible, and darts up the steps to the ground floor.

'Thank you,' I say. 'It's been interesting talking to you.'

Now she does laugh, but in a good way. 'And you,' she says. 'Hasten upstairs, Lissa. Dawn is breaking, and a new day comes.'

A new day? Already? I see that she's right, because up the top of the seven steps the door to the plaza is open, and as Rory sprints out, the darkness starts to lift. Out there, it's nearly dawn, and upstairs in 1205 Susie's going to wake up and find I've been away all night. Can I really have been talking for as long as that? Did I somehow fall asleep and not even notice? Either way, this is a disaster.

'Farewell, Lissa,' says Barbara softly, and the door closes behind me.

Grimly, I start the long climb. Pine, Cedar, Yew. Beside each painted name there's a little silhouette of the tree: nice idea, wrong place. Beyond the stairwell windows the sky turns violet, pink, gold. Elm, Ash, Eucalyptus. Let her be still asleep. Let me get inside and be sewing before she wakes up. But that isn't going to happen, because I have to do the twice three knocks on the door. She's going to kill me. Cypress. Poplar. My legs are on fire; I have to stop and catch my breath. I sit down on the steps with Mimi on my knee, and look out the window as somewhere beyond the concrete towers the sun edges over the horizon.

Down below, the stairwell door opens. The guy who walks through is not much older than me. His hair's the colour fairy tales call golden, and he's wearing snowy white overalls with a logo on the pocket, a smiling sun with Day and Son, Fresh Food Deliveries underneath. The guy's carrying a little crate, and in it are loaves of bread and bottles – old-fashioned glass bottles – of milk. Like the one in Barbara's pantry. 'After you,' he says politely.

We go on up, me first, the milk guy – Day Junior – second. I wait for him to ask me what I was doing sitting on the stairs at what must be about five in the morning, or to comment on the skull lamp, but all he says is, 'Going to be a lovely day.'

'Mm,' I say, my mind full of Susie. Why am I so stupid? Why didn't I ask Barbara if she'd let me use her phone to call the welfare people, instead of cooking her a giant dinner and asking her about magic? No wonder I'm in so much trouble.

Day Junior and I climb through Juniper, Aspen and Willow. Outside, the sun comes up and proves him right: weather-wise, at least, it's shaping up to be a beautiful day. Seems as if he plans to start his deliveries at the top. When we get to Oak level, he balances his crate on one arm and uses the other to hold the broken door back so it can't fall on me as I go through.

'Thanks,' I say, and head off towards 1205, not looking back to see who on Oak level can possibly afford a fresh food delivery.

The hallway is full of light; outside, the sun's climbing. I reach our door, knock three times, wait, knock three times again. The door flies open. She's been waiting. Her face is all squeezed up with rage. Her arms stretch out to drag me inside.

'Here,' I say, holding out the skull with its pitiful, flickering candle inside. Too little, too late. Susie takes it, and the look on her face makes my flesh crawl. My fingers move to touch the comforting shape of Mimi in my pocket. She's not there. Somewhere on the long climb up, I've dropped her.

No time to think. I turn my back on Susie and bolt for the stairwell. Day Junior hasn't got past the first doorway, and when he sees me rushing down the steps he comes after me.

'Hey! Slow down or you'll hurt yourself. What's wrong?'

I gasp out an explanation, and instead of laughing at me he helps me search. As we go down, Willow, Aspen, Juniper, checking every step, I do wonder why Susie hasn't come after me, but nothing's as important as finding Mimi. Without her, a bit of me's missing, and I don't have a lot to spare.

It's Day Junior who locates Mimi, wedged between concrete step and iron railing on Poplar level. He gets her out carefully, dusts her off, hands her back to me. 'Safe and sound,' he says. 'Must have jumped out of your pocket.'

I'm just starting to say thanks when there's a massive *Boom!* from somewhere up above. The two of us shrink back against the wall, Day Junior acting like a fairy tale hero as he spreads out his arms and shields me. The noise is over quickly, but now there's a strange light from up there, not the rising sun or a little skull lamp but a big, hot, hungry light. And people shouting. *Fire!*

Day Junior takes my hand. 'Downstairs, quick!'

I hesitate for about two seconds, then people start streaming down the stairs from the floors above us, and the only thing we can do is go down with them. There's an alarm woop-wooping, and smoke starting to fill the top of the stairwell. People are in their nighties and pyjamas, with kids wrapped in blankets and old folk clinging onto the dodgy hand-rail, but nobody's panicking, and we all make it down to the ground floor and out onto the plaza where the Day and Son delivery van's parked, gleaming white in the sunlight.

The fire fighters arrive and we get moved away from the building. The fire's on Oak level. I can see smoke billowing out of the windows. I look around for Barbara, but I can't spot her or Rory in the crowd. Still, the fire's a long way up; in the basement they should be safe. Firies head up the stairs; down here on the plaza there's a truck with a massive extension ladder and hoses being screwed onto water mains and lots of activity. Someone asks Day Junior to move the van. He asks me if I'm OK and I say yes, so he hops in and drives it away.

I haven't seen Susie. I haven't seen Sophie or Miranda. But Kye's here with his mum and his little brother, and they live on Oak level. I can't make myself go over and talk to them. My head's gone muzzy and my legs feel weak. I collapse onto a bench with Mimi on my knee, staring up at the thickening smoke and thinking about that lump of wax Barbara threw into the stove. How it sizzled and burned. How it filled my nostrils with a smell like death. I want to say a prayer, but I can't think what should be in it, so I put my head down on the bench and press Mimi against my cheek and close my eyes. Magic *is* real, just like in Grimm's fairy tales.

The day after the fire, I'm leaving Westmoreland Hospital, where they've kept me in overnight for observation. A social worker from Defence Welfare is letting me stay at her place until Dad gets home on compassionate leave. Her name's Siobhan, she lives near my old house and she's told me she has three cats called Winken, Blinken and Nod. Siobhan seems to know a lot about what's been happening to me, even though I've hardly said anything. She tells me a Mrs Barbara Jaeger rang the office and told her where I was and that I needed help. And Mrs Moss from school rang too, a while ago, asking why I hadn't come back this term and if I was OK. I ask Siobhan if Mrs Jaeger is the concierge at Woodland Gardens and she says yes, and that Barbara said to pass on her best wishes for the future.

Before I go home with Siobhan, I visit my stepsister Sophie, who's in a different ward getting treated for smoke inhalation. Miranda's in surgery this morning – her hands got burned – so I can't see her. Sophie looks terrible, hospital-sheet white with big bruises under her eyes, but she scrapes together a smile.

'Lissa. You're OK,' she whispers.

'I'm OK. And you will be, too.' I know the next thing I should say is that I'm sorry about Susie, but the words won't come out. I'm sorry it happened the way it did. But I can't be sorry she's gone.

'Look in the drawer,' Sophie says on a rasping breath. 'Got something for you.'

I open the drawer in the bedside table, and there's the little doll I was making before Susie sent me down to get light. She's unharmed, just waiting there quietly for me to fetch her so I can finish embroidering her face. She's lying on the lacy shawl Sophie was knitting, and under that I see Miranda's Aran sweater with the fancy cables. I want to laugh and cry at the same time.

'Our Dad's coming,' Sophie says. 'They let me call him. He cried when he heard my voice. All this time, he didn't know where we were.'

I start to understand why my stepsisters were sometimes unkind to me. I guess they were every bit as lost and afraid as I was. I feel strange, sort of sad, sort of relieved, but mostly just very tired.

'Miranda stopped to grab our work as we were running out.' Sophie's looking at the doll, which is on my knee now. 'That's how her hands got burned. I'm sorry we couldn't save your book, Lissa. I know you loved it.'

A book is only a book. It's the stories in it that matter. 'Thank you,' I say, putting my hand on hers.

'Mum,' Sophie whispers. 'She threw that skull thing across the room, and suddenly there was fire everywhere. I don't know how it could . . . I don't understand . . .' Her voice fades to nothing.

'They think it may have been an electrical fault,' puts in Siobhan from the doorway.

There's a silence, then I say to Sophie, 'Let me know how you're getting on, OK?' When it's finished, this doll will be for her, and I'll make another for Miranda. Companions for a new life.

Siobhan comes in to put a little card on the bedside table, with contact phone numbers and addresses so Sophie and Miranda can find me if they want to.

'I have to go now,' I say. I look at Sophie, and she stares up at me with her shadowy eyes, and the thing unspoken between us looms as huge and dark as the monster in every child's worst nightmare. 'It'll be all right,' I say, which is the best I can do at the moment.

Before she closes her eyes, Sophie whispers something. Maybe, *sorry*.

On the way to Siobhan's house, we drive past Woodland Gardens, where the clean-up is still happening. I don't look up at Oak level. An old woman in a purple dress is walking across the plaza, with an enormous ginger cat dawdling along behind her. I fish Mimi out of my pocket, hoping Siobhan's too busy driving to notice. I have a big question for my doll, a question about right and wrong and magic and responsibility. It's a question that's too big to be put in words.

Give me a kiss! demands Mimi.

I touch my lips to her woollen mouth.

Give me a hug!

I hold her against my heart, hoping the faceless doll in my other pocket won't get jealous. Her time will come.

Now let me fly!

One flip is all she gets, and not a very high one. I stand her on my knee, gaze into her knitted eyes and ask my question.

'All right?' asks Siobhan, giving me a sideways glance but keeping her hands firmly on the wheel.

'Fine,' I tell her. 'Could you drive around the block before we go home, please?'

Being a social worker, Siobhan is probably used to people acting weird. At the next corner she turns left and we begin a circuit of Woodland Gardens.

Start working on it now, Mimi says, *and by the time you're an old woman with white hair, you might know the answer to that question. Now can we go home, please?*

As we come around the plaza again, Barbara's still there, waiting while Rory does her business in a patch of dirt. I don't open the window and shout. I don't ask Siobhan to stop. I just look across at the two of them and mouth the words, 'Thank you.' Barbara turns and looks straight back at me. She lifts her hand in a sort of wave. Her mouth is not smiling and not frowning, but something inbetween. We drive on past, leaving Woodland Gardens behind us.

ELIZABETH KNOX

Unobtanium

Naming rights

This story is more about family than time travel so I will start with my very particular grandmother. Grandma McAlistair understood that her children had a duty towards her. None of them could ever manage to do the right thing by mere warmth or informality. There were things they just had to do, and they had to work out for themselves what those things were. For everyone in Grandma's life – family especially – there was an obstacle course of polite homage beyond which she waited with open arms. My mother was always reminding my father, '*You* have to call *her*. If she calls it won't matter how pleased you sound to hear her voice.' It was impossible for people not to feel that they'd neglected Grandma. The general impression she gave was of a woman who had been let down and had lowered her expectations. And still, on and off throughout the last quarter of her life, she let it be known that there were conditions she set which must be met.

One condition was that the first son of each generation must be named Andrew. In the preceding three generations of Grandma's husband's family there had always been an Andrew. It wasn't a tradition of her own family, so perhaps that was why she was able to defend it with righteous inflexibility. My father hadn't any investment in going against his mother's wishes. Besides, he was a second son, and his name wasn't Andrew, so there was no danger of his having to share name and house with a 'Junior'. He and my mother quite liked the name and when they were expecting they agreed that, if it was a boy, they would call him Andrew.

My name is Andrew, Andrew McAlistair. But I am a second-born son and have an older brother whose name is Mark.

Lying on the lecture circuit

A couple of months ago I was at a conference with my colleague Tamara Glenbrook. Tamara and I are a double act: we deliver a two-part lecture.

I go first. My talk is on The Deity, and is adapted to the public facts, the palaver, the mystery and miracle of its existence. What it might mean that The Deity exists. How we had found it, how long it had been there, where 'there' is. What we mean when we talk about 'there'.

I don't want to collapse my story into the terms of my talk, but 'there' is tricky because The Deity is a wormhole.

My presentation includes a video graphic of what we once imagined a wormhole might do to visible energy – the aura of its appetite. Everything in space is beautiful. An audience of laypeople will sigh at a photograph of the horizon of the sun, or of the Horse Head Nebula. They sigh at the *idea* of The Deity, what they can't see, the small vortex that creates a ripple in the gravitational field of the solar system – a veil over the Ark of the Covenant. My presentation includes diagrams of the kind of wormhole we think The Deity might be: a folded flat sheet of space-time, with a two-ended funnel milling through both surfaces, connecting distant places and times.

To tell the truth I never couple the words 'place' and 'time' in my lecture. I say 'place and period', because it is our firm belief that The Deity provides the possibility of time travel on a human scale. We do think we know when it might first have appeared – its downstream end. We have only to prove it. So – to tell the truth – in my lecture that is what I do: I tell as much of the truth as I can by saying 'place and period'. I allow myself that.

My lecture explains wormholes. When I deliver it I hear myself talking with less enthusiasm than I did when the real problem with wormholes was that there weren't any. Back then I'd be sharing the play of hypothesis, the vital intellectual project of testing our thoughts about the known laws of physics under imagined extreme conditions. (Occasionally back then I'd have a queasy moment of memory, of my high school, and being asked to explain – *smartarse* – the difference between 'hypothetical' and 'imaginary'.) The Deity is a real wormhole – mysteriously there – and yet still in my imagination. A *god* in my imagination because any portal to the past perhaps can do what God is said to do – save us.

My audience always wants to know how long it will be until we know positively *when* and *where* The Deity leads to. I always say, 'We are preparing experiments to determine just that.' And then I go on to describe the experiments, talking into their rapt silence. What I'm doing is describing the state of our knowledge six years ago. I'm telling them what we thought we might do back then. What I don't say to the gallery of softly lit faces stacked above me in the auditorium, the choir whose silent attention is a song of wonder, is that we've *already* performed our first experiment and are only waiting to hear back.

I lie to them, because secrecy is essential at this point in the project.

I wrap up and Tamara takes her turn. Her talk is about the ethics of time travel – though we aren't talking about even hypothetical travel in time, only about sending signals to the past.

Tamara's job is to prepare the ground, for if we ever do hear back, each one of these people is a potential petitioner. Everyone has something they want to fix. Everyone has a warning they'd like to give. Even altruists will want to send warnings about – say – climate change.

The gist of Tamara's talk is this: if we discover some method of sending signals into The Deity, signals that might emerge, coherent, at the other end of the wormhole; if we send a message that will provide us with evidence, some sign of ourselves, our presence in the historical record, what are we doing? What might happen? Is what we are doing the metaphorical equivalent of this: building a door for which there is only one key, a key we then send back in time, then wait to find, to find in history, so that we can unlock our door? Hasn't the key then come to us before the door? Won't we then have a key for which no lock exists, so that we'll have to build a lock in order to try our key for size?

Tamara tells her audience that the universe of this kind of time travel is relentlessly consistent. It's a universe in which there are always things we will do, because we've already done them.

The other possibility is this – we *don't* hear back, the key doesn't arrive in the post of history, there is no sign of it in the archives.

Tamara and I know that one of these things has already happened; either our message never got there, or something in it so changed things then that the 'now' following on from then isn't *our* now. The old past has created a different present and, with it, a different universe. In this scenario we could shout anything down the wormhole's throat and it wouldn't make any difference to us, because all the differences would generate new timelines. The Deity would turn out to be something like a bubble maker – whenever we breathed into it, it would blow the bubble of another universe.

So, Tamara tells her audience that, in effect, either everything we do is what we were *fated* to do, or nothing we do makes any difference to us.

She says that, in some time-travel stories, the time traveller makes a mess of his own history and then keeps trying to fix it. He remembers his mistakes. He does things over and over. He makes adjustments till he is sick with possibility. But these are only stories. Stories have points of view, reality does not. None of us should imagine that, as a result of our experiment, we will be landed with several sets of memories of how things went. This, in effect, is the Copernican Principle. Copernicus proved that Earth wasn't the centre of the universe. Then, much later, Edwin Hubble showed us that the galaxies were distributed equally and expanding away from us at the same speed. The Copernican Principle tells us that the expansion of space is the same relative to everyone and everywhere. And so, if none of us is special, then none of us is a default setting – the one who will at least remember how things were before the changes commenced.

Grandma's deathbed

She squeezed my hand. I looked around and tried to catch my father's eye. He, my mother, and my older brother, Mark, were out in the hallway with the medical team. Mark was arguing with the cardiologist.

Mark at twenty-two was a more confident version of his middle-aged self. Back then I still imagined he might mellow someday. I was waiting for it to happen, as people wait for a flooding river to abate. Mark would ease off, I thought. It was only a matter of time, and dependent on the conditions of his life. Surely he'd be different once he finished his degree, got a real girlfriend and a proper job. I wasn't exactly giving him the benefit of the doubt, it was more a case of my still seeing him the way he saw himself – as an eccentric hero and the only honest soul. It was my habit to see him that way; he'd been so persuasive, so all-pervasive in his views.

My brother had a theory about Grandma's treatment, which he'd aired to family for the last hour at her bedside. His theory was this: those doctors weren't doing everything they could. He'd read about a new drug therapy. The treatment was time-sensitive, and those doctors would have to start it right away.

I could hear Mark in the hallway telling the cardiologist what he had been telling us. His voice was loud – not raised, for its default setting was loud. He was repeating to the doctor everything he had said to us – all of it, word for word – for précis was impossible for Mark. 'There is a new drug, isn't there?' he said. 'They could try that, couldn't they?'

He didn't say 'you' to the doctor, or look him in the eye.

'It's about the money, isn't it? Hospital policy, the overheads.' Mark's hands went up and flapped by his face. He did jazz hands at the doctor. I guessed that he thought he looked sarcastic. But, for a young man whose grandma was dying, standing beside his father, whose mother was dying, he only looked mad.

The cardiologist was astonished, but began to reason with my brother. The cardiac ward was itself an extreme condition, and no doubt this doctor had seen people misbehave themselves at deathbeds before.

Mum was very distressed by Mark's carry-on, so distressed that her human instincts drove her, against twenty-two years of counterintuitive biofeedback, to place her hand on my brother's arm.

Mark flinched and snatched his arm back. He began to tremble, but he kept on talking. He had dredged up the name of the new drug. His voice cranked up a notch and in it, just detectable, was a hint of a boast about his recall, about what he knew, an eagerness completely out of keeping with the deathbed. His tone said, 'Here I am, not a doctor myself, educating the doctor, or at least letting him know that *I* know there's more he could do if budgetary concerns didn't prevent it.'

The doctor said, plainly, that the drug wasn't suitable in these kinds of cases.

Mark went on as though he hadn't heard.

A nurse came into the room and looked at the bag that was collecting what came from the catheter. She tapped the plastic tube, and the smallest frown possible flickered across her face. She didn't mean for me to see it, but I saw it, and knew that Grandma's kidneys were packing up.

Then Grandma squeezed my hand again. I looked at her and found her eyes open. 'Andrew,' she whispered. 'Is that Mark?'

'Yes,' I said, and turned away again to call out to my parents and brother.

'No,' said Grandma, very quiet. Then, in a whisper, 'Andrew. I'm glad it's you who's Andrew.'

Her eyes wandered.

Everyone came into the room, and everyone but Mark put a hand on her. Then Mark did, watching us all. He folded his hand over her ankle under the waffled cotton blanket. Grandma lowered her eyelids and stretched her throat.

'Excuse me,' said the doctor, and edged me aside.

The nurse and he stood for a moment on either side of the bed at Grandma's head. They had their hands raised as if they meant to catch something.

Nothing happened. Grandma settled again and the doctor and nurse stepped back and we stayed there and I watched the numbers on a monitor slowly, slowly fall.

Later, Dad asked me what she'd said, and I didn't tell him. Or, rather, I made sense of what she'd said by telling him she said she was glad to see me. 'Oh, and she said, "Is that Mark?" because she could hear him.'

'Him too,' Dad said, and his eyes filled with tears.

'That's right,' I said, because Grandma was always terribly hard to please and it hadn't mattered to me because grandchildren don't have to do very much to please their grandparents. But Dad had had a difficult time with her – for many years she *was* his time, and the difficulty was like a deformed leg or bad lungs, some trouble he'd laboured under all his life. Grandma was difficult, and often ungracious, and by saying she'd said she was glad to see me I meant to claim that she'd blessed us, me and my brother. Dad would love her for doing that – blessing his sons. Also, I did imagine that was what she meant – to bestow a blessing, to say she was particularly pleased that I was there.

However, if I had reported faithfully her actual words, instead of translating them into my idea of what she meant, I might have had the story sooner – and sooner understood a salient fact about how the universe worked.

For whatever *that's* worth.

Buttonholed

Tamara and I concluded our lecture by answering questions. Then our audience filed out, smiling at us lovingly. Some stayed, and hovered by the podium where we waited while a technician detached our laptops from the AV equipment. One waiting bunch were the people taking us out to dinner, the others were those with questions they'd been too shy to ask at question time.

The lights came all the way up once our laptops were uncoupled. Beside me Tamara cocked her head to catch what someone was saying to her over the racket of the theatre's tilting seats twanging up empty.

A man shuffled towards me and only stopped when his belly brushed my bag. His sour smell enveloped me. He started to talk. I tried to meet his eyes, which seemed to have extra-thick corneas, their colour and character fixed and suspended under a deep glaze. His jacket was grubby. I felt my eyes slip out of focus. It was what I had learned, defensively, to do.

He was saying, 'Have you ever thought . . .' nervous and eager. He rummaged in his shoulder bag and came up with a thick manila folder. He had a theory, he said, he just needed someone to do the maths.

I tried not to see the orange oxidised egg yolk on his sweater. I attempted to interrupt him. 'Listen,' I said, then, '*Listen*!'

He finally petered out, though his lips kept moving as if he were sucking on some invisible tit. He gave me his attention, peered at me through eyes like those of a shying horse.

'Do you think your theory can be up to much without the maths?' I said. And he immediately started up about Einstein and intuition and how he was more imaginative than intellectual.

He had receding gums, and a mortar of tartar between each tooth. I thought of Mark in high school explaining to me how the *average* teenager was hung up on externals, on all the conventions about how to dress – clothes, hair, makeup, deodorant, the whole superficial works – while never seeming to care whether they had anything interesting to say.

'Hang on,' I said. 'When Einstein was riding on a tram

looking at the clock on the Bern town hall and wondering what would happen if the tram was going at the speed of light – he could at least do the maths. He had a long journey ahead of him, but he did have legs to walk on.'

The buttonholer got a sly, smug look. 'But didn't Einstein's teacher Minowski do a lot of it for him? Minowski's calculations are essential to the Special Theory of Relativity. And famously elegant.' He bobbed up and down, pleased to have trumped me, and to have summoned the facts about Einstein's teacher. Again he proffered his folder. 'Won't you at least listen to my . . .'

'No,' I said, abrupt. 'I've done enough listening for a lifetime.'

In the car on our way to the restaurant Tamara said to me, 'Andrew, I don't know that I've ever seen you be so short with one of those awkward enthusiasts.'

'He was a particularly odoriferous specimen.'

'Did you imagine you'd catch something?'

I thought of the pebbly surface of the floor by the sink in Mark's kitchen, where rock-hard potato peelings were adhered to the lino. 'I never imagine that.'

Tamara was a philosopher, a physicist and ethicist. She said to me, 'Are you saying that under no circumstances would you get squeamish about something or someone unsanitary?'

'Look, Tam, I'm not defending my prejudice. But if you knew my brother . . .'

'No one knows your brother.'

'That's because he's not in the same world as me.'

'Really? Is he on the far side of The Deity?'

'The receiving end? That's the last place Mark would ever be. Mark, in defiance of the Copernican Principle, has always been central. The universe expanded away from him.'

Tamara looked at me for a long while. Then she said, 'That message you sent yourself, it was about your brother, wasn't it?'

Perturbation

The Deity – or Mr Ed, as the team familiarly call it – is a natural phenomenon. It seems that, at the beginning of the universe, the Big Bang, matter and anti-gravitating exotic matter bundled themselves up, one encasing the other. Together they formed a small planet-sized body of zero mass. It may not be the only one out there, invisible to our instruments, but so far we've only found the one. We believe that, like the planets, The Deity has always been there, a feature of our solar system, in the outermost orbit, its gravity and anti-gravity so perfectly balanced that, up until seven years ago, no net effect was created on the gravitational fields of the system.

Seven years ago a long-period comet from the Oort Cloud visited our system. Astronomers all over the world closely observed Ranchod's Comet. Its trajectory offered no cause for alarm. Professionals and amateurs simply enjoyed it. It inspired no eschatological thoughts, no Heaven's Gate cult hoping to hitch a ride to Paradise on its tail. Ranchod's Comet passed around the sun at the beginning of the Southern Hemisphere spring and, picking up acceleration, slung away from the sun's gravity. It passed back through the system, closer to Earth on its way out.

My kids and I spent several evenings lying on our lawn and looking up at it – a bright quotation mark, its tail as straight as a gas plume.

Then it went beyond the reach of the naked eye and only astronomers peered after it.

And then it vanished, was snuffed, was swallowed whole.

In the days after its disappearance telescopes, from hobbyists' Skywatchers and Celestrons to Hubble itself, peered at the region where the comet had been and wasn't anymore. They couldn't see a thing. In fact the first people to see what was there instead of the comet were a group of scientists in a laboratory in the Cashmere Hills, near Christchurch, in my home country. The scientists had a ring laser – two counter-rotating laser beams fired in a circular path – an instrument that measured gravitational fields; so sensitive that it could measure earthquakes on the moon. What this ring laser detected was a perturbation in the gravitational field of the solar system. The perturbation wasn't caused by an unknown planet or moon – the spatial character of the gravity field was all wrong for that. The Cashmere Hills mob said to themselves, '*What is this ripple*?' They said, 'Isn't it coming more or less from the same spot where Ranchod's Comet vanished?'

Then they picked up the phone and called NASA.

NASA has an array of ring lasers in satellites orbiting Earth – the 'seismic spies' of conspiracy theory websites. This array was able to get directionality, able to nail the source of the ripple. NASA aimed their ring lasers at the dark region beyond the orbit of Pluto and found that the ripple emanated from a vortex in – well – in apparently nothing.

By now every cosmologist on the planet was sitting up, eyes wide open and hair standing on end. Out there was a perturbation in the gravitational field caused by the fluctuations of a vortex. The vortex had a position. Its position corresponded to the last known position of Ranchod's Comet. The vortex was where it might be were it a feature of an unknown astral body with which the comet had collided, collided and been swallowed. These were the facts.

Obviously – thought the cosmologists – if 'it' was there

(and it was) and it had zero mass, it must formerly have been in a state of perfectly balanced gravity and anti-gravity. We knew that anti-gravity existed, at least at the quantum level. We knew that there were anti-gravitational quantum particles. But anti-gravitating matter in large quantities was always the 'unobtainium' of theories – some of them theories about how the throat of *a wormhole* might be kept open.

Physicists discussing wormholes always faced the problem of how to actually make one, how to turn the ravening singularity of a black hole into a gravitational vortex with an open throat, so that whatever went down it wouldn't simply be torn apart or annihilated. One hypothesis was that anti-gravity would be required to keep the throat of the wormhole open and stable. Now here – we all supposed – was a stable zero-mass body. That suggested anti-gravitating exotic matter. The body had a hole in it. And something had gone into the hole and apparently had not emerged again. Had this formerly invisible astral body been the ungerminated seed of a wormhole, always there and invisible to us?

'Always there and invisible to us, like God,' some smartarse said. Then someone else called it The Deity, and the name stuck despite later squabbles about naming rights, and embarrassed attempts to translate its now popular name into some antique and supposedly more dignified language like Etruscan or Toltec.

The Deity had swallowed a comet, emitting no debris or radiation in the process. The comet had left a tiny wound in the shield of its balanced gravities. The hole remained open. Anything else that went into that hole – an aperture that we eventually calculated was only around two metres in circumference – would, presumably, vanish as thoroughly and finally as Ranchod's Comet.

Shame and scientific endeavour

It was a man called Eric Hall who conclusively decided the matter of what The Deity was, and what might be done with it. Hall wasn't a cosmologist. He was an historian with an undergraduate degree in physics, whose life's work was the history of late-modern astronomy. His period was World War II to Glasnost. What Hall did was *find* Ranchod's Comet. It, too, was already there (but not always there) and in the historical record.

I want you to imagine a journey. Nights, days, then an afternoon.

Eric Hall drove from his home in Ohio, near Ohio State University and the old Big Ear radio telescope. He drove across country with a folder containing twenty pages of handwritten notes, plus photocopies of pages from the 1956 logbook of Mount Palomar Observatory, and correspondence between an astronomer at Mount Palomar and the National Geographic Society. Hall had possessed the photocopied material for years. It lived in a file box in his study. He had cited it in a footnote to an article he'd written some years before for the *American Scholar*, a piece called 'Shame and Scientific Endeavour'.

Imagine this historian, this scientific-minded layman, his hands gripping the steering wheel, his suit jacket on a hook in the back, his notes on the passenger seat beside him.

He didn't send an email. He didn't pick up the phone. He didn't even think to get on a plane. He drove across country as a way of keeping his feet on the ground. What he had to say was so serious that a crucial sense of secrecy, a secrecy approaching the sacred, compelled him to communicate what he suspected, not by phone or email, but face to face. He hadn't even called ahead. No – wrapped in a kind of holy terror, Eric Hall drove from Ohio to Massachusetts to talk to the man who, it seemed to him, was making the most steady authoritative sense so far of the new phenomenon.

Hall was lucky. It was term time and the cosmologist he wanted to speak to was teaching and was there when he arrived.

Imagine a car park, black asphalt gritty with salt. This is Amherst, so, as we follow Hall into the Faculty of Physics, Emily Dickinson will walk alongside us.

There's a certain Slant of light,
Winter Afternoons –
That oppresses like the Heft
Of Cathedral Tunes –

Heavenly Hurt, it gives us –
We can find no scar,
But internal difference,
Where the Meanings, are –

Hall climbed the stairs. The landing gave him a view only of the very top of the old chapel. He was unable to make out whether the ironwork object on its spire was a crucifix or a weather vane. He stood frozen for several minutes, staring, because he felt he needed to know. He had become a superstitious man.

Eventually he got to the right floor, and the right door. He sought, and he found. He knocked, and it was opened unto him.

This is the discovery Eric Hall outlined in his notes, and illustrated with his photocopied supporting materials.

In April of 1956 an astronomer looking through the eyepiece of the Hale telescope at the Mount Palomar Observatory saw a comet appear. His reasonable assumption was that he'd only just noticed it. He showed it to the other astronomers with him that night. They called other people to log their sighting – hoping they'd get to name it. They watched it over several nights and did what people do with comets – they mapped its trajectory. Since they had only just noticed it they assumed that it was heading into the solar system. But, after several days, it became clear that it was not. Indeed, it was moving *out* of the solar system, on a trajectory that indicated it must have already passed through, made a circuit of the sun, and was now heading back into interstellar space. The Palomar astronomers wondered, how had they possibly not noticed this object earlier? *How the hell* had it got by them? Surely, when it passed near to Earth it must have been visible to the naked eye.

These astronomers hadn't ultimately made it into Hall's paper 'Shame and Scientific Endeavour', for they were more embarrassed than disgraced. It was the opinion of their colleagues elsewhere that they'd got their calculations wrong. Obviously. No great shame in that, or even terrible embarrassment. They should just fess up and say sorry. But instead they kept insisting they were right. The comet seemed to have simply appeared from nowhere. One of them, Dr Koskinen, stuck to his guns for years, whenever the subject came up, to the point where he became a bit of a joke in astronomical circles. (Also, once when drunk he had notoriously raved on about a 'strange green light in the sky'.)

What Hall said to the cosmologist in Amherst was, 'I think the Mount Palomar boys' "comet from nowhere" is Ranchod's Comet. I think that after it went into that shy singularity out there – whose name I refuse to use – it came out in April 1956.'

'April 1956, *in this universe*,' the cosmologist said.

'Yes. In this universe. So you're right and it is a wormhole. And I suppose we might call it a short-period wormhole.'

'I suppose we might,' said the cosmologist – mightily pleased.

The cosmologist called me that night. My daughter fetched me in from the barbecue. I hadn't seen Edward since a conference at Stanford more than a year before. 'Hey Ed!' I said. 'How are you?'

'Overexcited,' he said. Then, 'Andrew, for years you've been thinking and talking and writing about time travel.'

'Yes?'

'Well – now the time has come.'

The Massachusetts Project

We put a team together. It was quite a small team. From the start we knew that what we hoped to do was risky and would be best done with discretion. We kept it small, and kept our mouths shut. We thought we might have to drum up funding – vast sums of it – but quite quickly discovered that our experiments were relatively inexpensive. We did have to put in a lot of time, and needed funding for that. We had to work in close proximity to one another and *keep things in the building*, so to speak. Because Edward had a happy relationship with his university we began at Amherst. There were only five of us then – just thinking and sometimes consulting other interested parties, everyone who was gazing in wonder into that place beyond Pluto, at the broken symmetry of that mysterious mass.

Once we'd worked out what we wanted to do and how to do it we recruited a bunch of other close-mouthed colleagues, and asked the permission of those who know their permission is always required – the United States government. We moved to a laboratory in New Mexico – where the skies were reliably clear. We chose our digital modulation code, and built our Photon Telegraph. We devised our message protocols. We even began to *send* our messages.

Within two years of the discovery of The Deity the 'Massachusetts Project' was up and running. After that all we had left to do was wait, and to go on pretending to the public that what we had done was still only what we planned to do.

Time in narrative is a matter of sequence, frequency and duration. For a long time we frequently represented our actions in the wrong sequence. And that is why, nearly seven years after Edward's phone call, I'm still sometimes giving lectures about The Deity and the ethics of time travel. I am lying: laying out as optional the inevitable.

(Tamara Glenbrook, cosmologist and ethicist, sitting beside me in the back seat of a car pulling into the curb beside Nathan's in Georgetown, D.C., asks, 'How come you never talk about your brother?')

'Singularities are pathologies, of course, though not all pathologies are singularities'

Mark and I sit watching television. I'm very little and the seat of the chair I'm in is so long it doesn't let my knees bend. I'm sitting as straight-legged as a doll.

We are watching *Mr Ed.* It has just started and the theme song is on. *'A horse is a horse, of course, of course, and no one can talk to a horse, of course, that is of course unless the horse is the famous Mr Ed!'*

(I'm not sure what year this is. *Mr Ed* screened later in New Zealand. Everything screened later here. We've always got first light, but in the sixties everything else arrived in delayed broadcast. For instance, no one in the Department of Education was up with the very latest in developmental psychology.)

Mum and Dad let us watch *Mr Ed* because it was 'good for Mark'. Mark warmed more to stories about animals than those about people. He and I used to play at *Mr Ed*. I was always poor, befuddled, put-upon Wilbur. My Wilbur would sometimes get fed up and walk away from the stable door. Mark's Mr Ed would follow, the door no impediment to him. Once Mark was in full flight, in or out of character, he was unstoppable. He would monologue for hours at a stretch. But he was often an entertaining child, and his Mr Ed wasn't a wise ass, more a jester, poking fun at human foolishness. At eight Mark was already creating his catalogue of silly things most people do.

Mark at eight, at our Hawke's Bay primary school. While the other eight-year-old boys were building forts and kicking balls, Mark was walking up and down the row of Arbor Day plantings, waving a stick, and talking. He was talking to me. I was playing marbles. One of the big girls was trying to teach me how to 'flick' and not 'funk'. I was listening to my brother, as was my habit. I never did learn to tune people out till I had chattering eight-year-olds of my own.

My parents had managed Mark's sometimes daunting peculiarities kindly and with as little panic as possible. Dad once mentioned to me that when Mark was three they bought him a full-length mirror. 'We hoped to catch his wandering gaze,' Dad said. 'Mark would scarcely ever meet his mother's eye. We hoped to see him meet his own.'

The school wasn't as easily troubled by Mark as our parents were – schools are blockheaded and thick-skinned. But it was far more determined to get to the bottom of Mark's awkwardness with other children, and his intransigent inability to listen.

This was the sixties, and this was New Zealand, and the child psychologist they brought in to see my brother didn't know what he was looking at. Mark had a wonderful time with the man; loved the tests, loved the talk. He was always happier talking to adults.

The psychologist decided that Mark was only a highly intelligent child, and obviously playing up because of a lack of stimulation. Mum and Dad's solution to this was to sign Mark up for all sorts of extracurricular activities. They found a speech and drama teacher, a chess club and art lessons. My father, a jazz enthusiast, conducted informal music-appreciation lessons. Our parents hadn't much money so they took turns escorting Mark to the plays and operas they might otherwise have been able to attend together.

I did benefit from some of this. I shared the paint boxes and good art paper. I was entertained. Mark acted out *Oklahoma!* for me. He taught me chess, and regaled me with recitations of whatever he learned at speech and drama – I remember Robert Louis Stevenson and Alfred Noyes.

Mark was happier. He was excused and defended. The teacher he got the following year was aware that she had been given a gifted child and when the other kids teased him she'd shout at them that what they had to understand was that Mark was a genius.

Excused, defended, and sufficiently explained to himself; set apart and *above* others.

Mark loping along a corridor at school deep in thought. His gait uneven, a kind of cantering, and he's flapping his hands. He's excited and his eyes are bright but glassy.

By the time I reached the age when I might be embarrassed by my brother I had signed on to the idea of Mark's brilliance. I spurned kids who failed the test of Mark. I didn't often have to rise to his defence for he didn't notice wariness or discomfort in others, he only discovered that they didn't approve of him when they were openly sharp or censorious. There were times when I had only to stand back and watch, and perhaps even profit from, his callous enthusiasm. For instance, when he could not be made to see why our friend Jay couldn't come over since Jay's mother would have to come to collect him, crossing town in the rush-hour traffic. 'It just doesn't suit me,' said Jay's mum, falling back on her adult authority, because she could see that Mark would keep refusing to understand what she had so patiently explained to him. Mark kept pushing; he wasn't being insolent or impolite, he just kept asking and not listening to her answer. Jay came with us. Jay's mother called my mother, who drove Jay home through the rush-hour traffic, because it was vitally important that Mark keep the few friends he had.

Mark seemed not to understand individuals but, as a child, he was imaginative and systematic in describing groups of people. He was a playground anthropologist. He could work out the whole plot of a group, or at least tell a good story about them.

There was the group who didn't like ball games and shared the hurdy-gurdy, a pole with a swivelling top to which a rope was fastened. We'd take turns running and swinging on it. But one day a ball smashed into my friend Selina when she was spinning, and broke her glasses, which cut her eyebrow. When we came to school the following day the hurdy-gurdy's rope was coiled and knotted around its top. It was out of bounds.

Mark's take on the situation was this: that although the hurdy-gurdy was fixed in its corner of the playground, while the ball games wandered untidily everywhere, the hurdy-gurdy was deemed the problem. It was a problem because the kids who liked it weren't kids who 'fitted in'.

That was Mark on majority versus minority culture. He said, 'It's never the fault of the boys with the balls. What *they* think is this . . .' and he'd lay out his theories about the thinking of teachers, or the way the school was run. He was astute. He often understood what was going on. But he never understood how people felt about what he said, or how, when he continued to say it, it didn't make it any more likely – and maybe made it *less* likely – that his case would be heard. He never seemed to understand this, despite being told directly. Our mother would say, 'Mark, if you won't stop talking no one will hear you.'

Mark turned on to physics because of stories about its brilliant heroes. I remember him coming home talking about Einstein. He talked to Mum and me while Mum was mashing carrots and swedes in a pot and I was watching the steam pressed out as grainy clouds, like spores from a dry puffball.

Mark said, 'Did you know that Einstein didn't talk at all until he was three years old? The first thing he said was: "Mother, my head is cold. May I have my hat?" It was one sign of his being a genius. His mind was simply on other things – that's what I think. He might have waited even longer till he really had something to say, eh? Only his head happened to be cold.'

'And his mother's mind happened to be elsewhere,' Mum said, wry.

'So Einstein was like Mr Ed,' I said. Then sang, '*People yackity-yak a streak and waste your time of day, but Mr Ed will never speak unless he has something to say!*'

Mum said, 'You talked very early, Mark. It was Andrew who talked late. We were beginning to think he was very stupid.'

'But instead he was very average!' Mark said, gleeful. 'Andrew and I are Einstein's theories of relativity. I come first. I'm Special and he's General.'

'Very witty, dear,' Mum said.

Physics became Mark's thing – the latest in a succession of obsessions. Mark's enthusiasms were a deep, prolonged communion. He owned his subjects, soaked them with his scent. He would say that he liked other people to be interested in what interested him, but that only meant they must listen to him.

Mark would tell you what he knew. He'd tell you what *you* knew. He'd tell you what he'd already told you. But he didn't like anyone to talk about his subject. Or, rather, he could attend a lecture, but friends and family weren't allowed to show that they'd learned from the compulsory association with whatever it was he lately loved. Mark's subjects were his world, floating islands whose fundamental aqueous instability he'd feel only whenever anyone else set foot on them.

By the time I was twelve I'd learned to steer clear of knowing much about my brother's subjects. He was always telling me the same stuff over and over again, so he must have been pretty confident of my ignorance. By twelve my battle fatigue at my brother's frequent forty-minute dissertations sometimes even caused me to shudder at the sight of his books. So I professed not to be interested in physics, hoping to sidestep his lectures.

As Mark entered his teens his talking had become more intense, more toneless, less directed at whomever he was speaking to. When he was young, and genius pardoned his peculiarities, he didn't mind not fitting in. As a teenager things became more difficult. For instance, he confounded being fashionable with being clean, and refused to be fashionable. He went unwashed. My parents fought with him and he wept and kicked holes in our walls and demanded to know why he couldn't be loved just as he was, and then raged on about their 'conformity' and 'middle-class expectations'.

When I followed Mark to university I was doing information science, maths, and a stage-one physics paper my course coordinator talked me into taking. Being a first-year I had to take the slim pickings of lab time on the computers. (This was back in the early eighties when computers weren't two a penny.) I spent longer each day on campus than I otherwise might have. I didn't think much of my physics paper so, in my idle hours waiting for the clock to come around, I attended some third-year lectures to see whether I should go on with it, or drop it.

By that time, the start of my second term, Mark had dropped out of university altogether. Though physics was his thing, it turned out he wasn't very good at maths. Suddenly he was required to make the 'consistent effort' his high school teachers used to talk about – to his scorn. Mark had had two and a half patchy years of effort, but was too disorganised to get assignments in on time, and too combative to be rewarding or even reasonable to teach. He declared that 'formal education' wasn't for him. And it wasn't. For Mark going to school was never about what there was to know, but about dazzling people with what he already knew – dazzling not to win them over, but to defend himself against them.

*

(Oh Mark! – Mark at ten, feeling got-at by a teacher, coming home and saying to Mum and me, 'When I grow up I'm going to change my name to "Example", so that things will always be *for* me and never against me.')

As we grew older and lived apart and things continued to fail to work out for him, Mark's efforts to pull a younger brother's thoughts back into line with his were often insensitive to the point of brutality. He would shout at me, 'The way you see things, Andrew, is this!' then go on to represent someone I couldn't recognise as myself. If he did happen to hear and take in anything I said, he'd get this look on his face of outraged incredulity, and would say, 'I don't know how you can say that,' then, later, 'Oh, well, *you would* say that.'

In the end it was just too lonely that I could never say what I thought. And I was exhausted by the years of hours and hours of talk. I hadn't been able to disengage myself. How could I choose not to listen to him while waiting my turn? *When* would I have chosen that? When would I have known to do things differently? This was my older brother, the companion of my childhood – to whom I was invisible and inaudible.

Go right to the source and ask the horse

The New Mexico lab, one evening. My boss Edward came in when I was watching some technicians tinker with the Photon Telegraph. None of us heard him till he said, 'What are you whistling?'

We were whistling the theme song from *Mr Ed*. I'd started it, so confessed.

'Remind me,' Edward said.

'Go on, Dr McAlistair,' said one of the technicians.

I sang:

A horse is a horse, of course, of course
And no one can talk to a horse, of course
That is of course unless the horse is the famous Mr Ed!

Go right to the source and ask the horse
He'll give you the answer that you'll endorse
He's always on a steady course – talk to Mr Ed!

The technicians joined in:

People yackity-yak a streak and waste your time of day
But Mr Ed will never speak unless he has something to say!

A horse is a horse, of course, of course
And this one will talk till his voice is hoarse
You've never heard of a talking horse? Well listen to this:
'I am Mr Ed.'

Edward clapped us.

'Needless to say Mr Ed isn't you,' I said. 'Mr Ed is that.' I waved my hand at that region of the sky. 'Anyone can talk *to* a horse. The miracle doesn't happen till the horse talks back.'

The message protocols

Since we needed to talk to 1956 we chose to talk in Morse. A laser with a shutter could send long and short flashes of light into the wormhole. If the dots and dashes were slowed or accelerated they would still keep their relative lengths, the dots short, and the dashes long. We needed to allow for reasonable time to get the attention of whoever was looking, so needed a nonsense signal, something of no import, just a pattern of flashing that might strike anyone who spotted it as the result of design rather than accident.

And, then, we needed a message.

We couldn't say 'Hello from 2009' or 'Watch out for Cuba' or 'Cut carbon emissions now'. The message should be as harmless as possible. Something a person might make note of, but not be able to get anyone to take *terribly seriously.* Something trivial, particular, personal and obscure.

The arguments we had, the questions that went round and round. How could we know what was safest to do when we didn't know how time travel might work? We couldn't know whether we were dealing with a self-consistent universe, or multiple parallel universes. We spent hours on the problem of whether the act of selecting one message from among several proposed would adversely affect the outcome of our experiment. Was it more dangerous to make an informed choice? Was it dangerous to follow a hunch, to have a preference?

'You think then that we should just pick a message out of a hat?' said someone finally, in exasperation.

'Why didn't I think of that – the hat method,' said someone else, sarcastic.

Edward said, 'We just have to do something. There's no sign yet that we *have* done anything. If we have done something we might hear back from ourselves any day now. But maybe we couldn't make up our minds. Perhaps we were deadlocked. Do you want that to be what happened?'

It was Edward's baseball cap we used.

It was my message that was pulled out of it. The address 'particular' and 'historically insignificant', the message 'personal' and 'obscure'.

In morse:

Andrew McAlistair
Kingans Ford
RD 1
Mahoe
New Zealand

Then:

-.. --- -. - .-.. .. ... - . -. -.. --- -. - .-.. --- ...- .

The Andrews McAlistair

The business about the tradition of 'Andrews' in my grandfather's family came up only once that I remember. It was when my wife was pregnant with our first child. We were having lunch with Mum and Dad. Mark wasn't there. Mark and conversation were mutually exclusive. Mum and Dad had started inviting their sons separately sometime before my wedding. At first it was a purely practical decision. We had to discuss wedding plans, and not get sidetracked. What we used to do was this: the real talk would take place over the food preparation and dishes between Mum and me, or Dad and me, or Mum and my fiancée. The real talk would escape while whoever was left at the table with Mark acted as a silent decoy, drawing his talk.

So, it was just the four of us at that lunch. We were discussing names for the baby. Dad said, 'I suppose that if it's a boy you might call him Andrew.'

I was quite taken aback. I hadn't expected Dad to suggest anything so quaint. 'Why would I call him after myself?'

'It's actually a family tradition,' Dad said. 'There was your uncle Andrew and Grandad Andrew, and other Andrews further back.' He and Mum exchanged a look. 'But we messed it up.'

'How? I am Andrew,' I said, puzzled.

'Yes. *You* are. It should have been Mark.'

Then my wife said that she couldn't possibly cope with two Andrews, she'd feel like Dr Seuss's Mrs McCave, 'Who had twenty-three sons and named them all Dave.'

'We've been considering Hugh and Bruno,' I said. 'And Bridget for a girl.'

It turned out that Mum really disliked the name Bridget and the conversation took a turn away from the messed-up tradition and never returned to it.

The boy in the background

I want to say that my message wasn't a result of years of brooding. It did conform to our protocols, and so did the other five I came up with. It was, however, the last one I thought of, and was the result of an impulse.

At the time we were finishing our work on the Photon Telegraph, and thinking up messages, I was alone in New Mexico. My daughter was at university in New York, and my son had gone back to New Zealand with his mother. He wanted to study veterinary science and had decided to do it in Palmerston North. My wife went with him to help look at accommodation and buy him toasters and duvets and whatever else he needed.

I found being alone dreary and depressing. One night I happened to be eating out of tinfoil and grazing channels and I found myself watching a documentary.

It was about autism. I didn't have a revelation about Mark – I'd pretty much worked out for myself what was going on with Mark years before. I'd made my own informal diagnosis.

But there was something in the documentary that got me thinking about myself.

In one scene the farmer with an eleven-year-old autistic son was letting the boy drive his tractor. 'It's something he likes to do,' the farmer explained. He was sitting behind his son while the boy held the shuddering steering wheel and laughed. The tractor was jolting over a paddock with cropped grass. The farmer had been feeding out, there were piles of dry hay scattered all over the paddock. The trailer that had held the hay was empty – except for the other boy.

The farmer talked about what he was able to do for his son, how much thought he and his wife put into finding out what the boy enjoyed, and what was good for him. Meanwhile the boy clutched the wheel, his face tilted to the sky, grinning and riding the vibrations.

The other boy, the younger, was sitting in the trailer with his legs folded under him. He was in the background. He wasn't the subject of the shot. He knew he wasn't a subject, and didn't expect to be. The look on his partly averted face, and his posture, both expressed what he was doing, what it was his habit to do. He was being *no trouble.* And he was waiting.

He was waiting, he was waiting, he was waiting.

(Edward's hat, and my message. An address: my name, my uncle's name, my grandfather's name, his father's name, his father's uncle's name – Andrew McAlistair. And the message:

-.. --- -.- .-.. .. ... - . -. -.. --- -.- .-.. --- ...- .)

Internal difference

Last month, my mother finalised the sale of her house. It was sold within the family, but the sale was handled formally by lawyers so that no one would feel precarious or unhappy. I went home to help Mum with the purchase of a spruce one-bedroom villa in a retirement village named after a notable New Zealander who – Mum said – would probably never have dreamed of going near such a place.

My wife was due to join me later and help me sort out the old house, and our family's years of accumulated stuff.

Before I left New Mexico I sent a postcard to Mark. I suggested that he might like to help with the shift.

Mark had been working for the past year as a researcher in a government department. He was earning, and getting out to his office and the supermarket at least. Though his bungalow's exterior paint was flaking and his garden was overgrown, that was nothing new. Houses can look shabby on the outside and attract 'Do you want to sell?' flyers from every real estate agent in a city, but it's what's inside that counts. The insides of houses give away things about their inhabitants' morale and mental health.

It was a still, sunny spring day when I arrived at my brother's house. Mark let me in, and led me to the kitchen. The hallway was a little dank, and had the sour smell I associate with my brother. That, too, wasn't new or unusual. As we went by the living room Mark pulled its door to. I could hear the gas heater in there, hissing. The sunlight through the kitchen windows showed up a peach fuzz of dust on the front of the cupboards, and the clouds of old spills on the floor, haphazardly wiped. The kitchen was a little cleaner than it had been on my last visit. I looked around me and kind of took the pulse of the house, trying to figure how my brother was, how time was treating him. The kitchen curtains were hanging part-way off their drooping curtain rods, and a gap in the window frame had been sealed with masking tape, but the draining board was clean, and there was perhaps only as little as one month's worth of recycling bundled up by the back door.

Mark made me a cup of coffee. My cup had a skin of brown on its inside, but that was only staining, inert now and harmless.

I asked my brother whether he'd got my postcard.

'Yes, I got it.'

'Well, would you like to come down and help?'

'No thank you.'

Right away I realised my mistake. I had asked him whether he'd *like* to help. He used to behave this way about the dishes. At those family lunches, after lunch I'd have my hands in the suds, and I'd say to him, 'Mark, would you like to come and help?' And he'd get a smug little smile on his face, and would reply, 'No thank you.' You see, the joke was on me for being so conventional, so tied up by false politeness that I couldn't just simply ask for what I wanted. Mark would feel that he was giving me a little rebuke for my little dishonesty, and he wouldn't have to get up from the table.

'We really could do with an extra pair of hands,' I said.

'Andrew, it was your choice to come over and get involved. It was your idea. I don't see why I should let you organise me according to your ideas.'

In my exasperation, I made another mistake. I said, 'Any normal son would help.'

Again I saw the small gleeful light come into his eyes. He said he'd been doing some reading. He pointed to his kitchen table and a pile of books. I could see that they were about what Mark was now calling 'My Syndrome'. He said he'd learned so much about himself. He'd made sense of all these things that used to *happen* to him. Like, when he was young, and he used to go to parties and everybody would be talking to one another, and the room would be filled with noise. 'It was so confusing, and I'd just sit in a corner. I didn't know what to say to anyone, whereas everyone else seemed to know what to say to one another.'

I listened to my brother describe his old social crucifixions and thought – yes – Mark would hear a room full of people talking as noise, because he was unable to choose which person to listen to, which conversation to board and let carry him away. This was his tragedy. But then I thought, 'Mark hears a room full of people talking as noise, and I understand that this is because of the way his brain works, *but* . . .'

But Mark was going on about the 'neurotypical'. 'The neurotypical are multi-taskers,' he said. 'Their thinking is fast and flexible. But people like me think *deeply* about only one thing at a time. We're more contemplative.'

Mark's latest thing was himself. He had renewed his narrative. He'd now admit that he was out of step, and easily troubled, but the consolation was that he was contemplative, as well as an honest soul. Apparently I was one of the yammering, glib multi-taskers: the tribe of apes, social, busy, thick-skinned. Now that he understood how he came to be so at odds with the world he was congratulating himself. I thought of the hundreds of occasions on which I had gone out with my brother when we were growing up and spent the better part of my time ministering to his shyness, reassuring him, drawing him out for others to hear.

What a *kind fool* I'd been. Now here was my brother busy with his new hobby. Too busy to take down our mother's pictures, to box her books, to wipe her skirting boards.

I sipped my coffee and let Mark talk. After a time he got up to fetch something from the living room. When he opened the door I saw that there were two clothes horses full of washing drying by the gas fire. I said, 'What is all that doing in there?'

'I don't really like the backyard,' Mark said.

'What's not to like?'

He squinted. 'It's the neighbours.'

'Are they nosy?'

Mark looked shifty. 'It's not exactly that.' Then in a burst, 'You see, there's this developer. He lives four doors along, in the grey house, eh. He's bought up a lot of the properties around here, hasn't he. I think he'd like to have the whole block, wouldn't he. He's some kind of Christian. Maybe he wants to make the neighbourhood into a church compound, eh? Anyway, I've been noticing that, over the past few years, the trees around my boundary are dying slowly. Every year their leaves are smaller and sparser, aren't they. It's suspicious, eh. This guy is poisoning my trees, isn't he. He has tenants in all the properties on my boundary. I just bet they all go to the same church, eh. Anyway, I think he has them doing something to my trees. Sometimes I hear voices in the backyard at night. People are creeping around, eh. I think that developer understands how much I value my privacy, and how easily disturbed I am.'

I felt that I was slipping, falling into the dark. I felt that I was being swallowed and crushed. I rallied myself. 'How long do you think this has been going on?'

'How long has he been poisoning the trees? He's doing it so that it looks as if they are dying back naturally. So he has to make sure he takes a long time about it, doesn't he. I think he hopes I'll just decide I don't like living here anymore, and will put the place on the market.'

'But Mark, how does someone poison trees gradually?'

'I don't know, but there must be a way because that's what's happening. And you remember how our walnut tree died from bacteria in the soil? Do you remember how its leaves got wrinkly, and smaller?'

'Mark, I have to ask you, how likely is it that someone is poisoning your trees?'

It seemed that Mark couldn't understand my question. His mind didn't work well with likelihood, with probability. Anything bad that could possibly happen would probably happen to him. Besides, what people did and were able to do – those were imponderables.

My mind sidestepped; it didn't want to deal with any of this. 'All right,' I said. 'If you don't like going into your backyard to hang out the washing because of the neighbours, why don't you get yourself a dryer?'

Mark looked incredulous. 'Don't you know that second only to smoking the biggest cause of house fires is tumble dryers? It's the combination of lint and static electricity,' he explained, then went on for some time about static charges. I listened, and now and then tried to reason with him. But reasoning with Mark always caused him distress and I eventually backed down. I finished my coffee and went away. I just didn't know what to do with him – with this combination of crippling fear and crippling arrogance.

A curse

The dust we raised aggravated my mother's eczema, so we convinced her to keep to the kitchen, or potting shed, where she was striking cuttings from her favourite shrubs, far too many for her small garden at the retirement village.

There were a lot of papers. It seemed that my parents had kept all their correspondence, even twenty-five-year-old electricity bills. (That would be my father, always ready to be called to account for all the little things in life, his fear of disorder so acute perhaps because he felt he'd failed with Mark – as the father of a child beyond the help of mere good parenting, close attention, love even.)

My wife and I sorted, we rolled up our sleeves and got stuck in.

A day or two into the task my wife was sitting at the dining-room table with a suitcase full of old correspondence in front of her. We had decided that it was best to go through discarding all the old envelopes first, before reading the letters. For some time my wife had been doing this, making a soothing series of crackles and rustles, opening envelopes, freeing sheets of paper, smoothing them flat.

I was sorting Dad's tools into those for Cash Converters, those for the Salvation Army, and those fit only for a trip to the tip. After a time I became aware that the rustling at the table had stopped. There was a silence in the room so intense that it seemed to vibrate against my lowered eyelids. I looked up at my wife. She had a blue aerogramme in her hand. She was gazing at it, but a second after I looked at her she raised her head and returned my look. Her face was pale.

She got up, came over, and handed me the aerogramme.

It was addressed to Andrew McAlistair, Kingans Ford, RD 1, Mahoe, New Zealand. It was postmarked San Diego, June 10, 1956.

I opened it. The blue rice paper was fragile, furry and split along its folds. Inside were only four words, scrawled, either hurried or impulsive.

'Don't listen. Don't love.'

The letter had a return address, and the sender's name was Dr Jere Koskinen, the astronomer at the Palomar Observatory, the one man who had stubbornly refused to relent on the matter of the 'comet from nowhere'.

A green light in the sky

Of course we knew where Dr Koskinen was to be found. Almost since Eric Hall's visit to Edward at Amherst we had known where he was.

Because it had been decided to keep the salient fact about The Deity secret – the location in time of the downstream end of the wormhole – we had been vigilant in keeping a watch on anyone who might work it out for themselves. But it seemed that 'the comet from nowhere' was a matter best forgotten. Almost everyone involved had gone on assiduously to live it down. We did keep an eye on the one man who'd persisted in talking about it. Would he figure it out? Would he publish something? Would he talk to the press?

He was an old man already six years back. He and his wife had retired to one of those small towns in Mexico that frugal Californian retirees began to discover some time in the 1990s. We found him there and kept an idle eye on him. But Koskinen never seemed to take any interest in the possibility of a connection between his old *bête noire* 'the comet from nowhere' and the disappearance of Ranchod's Comet. He played golf, and went fishing, and was silent to the best of our knowledge.

How *naïve* we were, keeping an eye on the old man, with no thought of what action we'd take if he did submit an article or talk to a reporter. All we wanted was some kind of forewarning. We thought about what kind of spin we could put on our secrecy.

How terribly naïve we were. Other interests were involved. There were the people who funded our experiments. We had been sworn to secrecy. Why couldn't we imagine that those people would make sure that secrecy was preserved? For they too had been watching that old man. They kept an ear in his house in Mexico, they observed what he did and who he met, and they too were reassured that he'd put the past behind him, and his former life as a truth-telling scientist beset by doubters. They watched him enjoy his old age, his second wife, his grandchildren, his motorboat, his barbecue, his golf.

But, of course, they were *still* watching when, a week ago, Edward and I visited him at his last address, a nursing home in San Diego.

Koskinen was in a wheelchair in the quiet day room, the one without a television. A nurse conducted us to him, and fetched some chairs. He seemed pleased to have visitors, and yanked his earbuds out of his furry ear holes. He forgot to turn his phone off though, and the whole time we talked I could hear a faint insectile singing.

Edward and I introduced ourselves, and shook the cold bundle of bones that was his hand.

Ed asked him how old he was.

Ninety-two next birthday.

'So, you were in your thirties in the fifties?' Edward said. We already knew the answer, and it occurred to me that Ed was testing the old man's mental sharpness.

'Yes. My children were all born in the fifties,' said Koskinen.

Ed settled back in his chair, smiled in satisfaction, and signalled to me by lifting his eyebrows.

I gave Koskinen the aerogramme.

He gazed at it for a long time, then said, 'Oh.' He peered hard at me. 'Did I hear you say that your name was Andrew McAlistair?'

'Yes.'

'Oh,' he said again.

'It was my uncle's name too, and my grandfather's,' I said.

'Ah.'

Ed asked, 'Can you tell us about the signal?'

Dr Koskinen carefully folded the letter and gave it back to me. He began, 'It was late April that year – 1956. I could have given you the exact date once. I had the pages from the Hale logbook up until – well – whenever it was that my daughter and her husband packed up my house in Mexico. I'm afraid I couldn't say now where those pages have got to.'

'But there were no pages missing from the logbook,' I said.

'We tore out two leaves and just rewrote it, rewrote everything that happened over those nights, but without the green light. The book wasn't printed up with dates. You see, back then we used to do everything by hand, there was none of this bloody *template* stuff. I hate the way my computer is always telling me how to do things.'

'Tell us about the green light.'

He drew himself up, straightened his spine as much as he was able. He gave us a position, a region of the sky. 'It started up around 3am. A flashing green light. We thought it was an aircraft at first. But it wasn't. It was coming from out there, from the edge of our solar system.' He paused and narrowed his eyes. 'I suppose you two gentlemen must have something to do with that wormhole, The Deity. I suppose you're part of that outfit in New Mexico.'

'Yes,' Edward said.

'Then you must know the flashing was Morse. Two dots, a long space, a dot and a dash, a shorter space, then two dashes. It went on like that for close to an hour.'

Ed and I exchanged a look.

'It was saying, "I am, I am, I am," over and over again. You can imagine what we felt.'

We nodded.

'Though we couldn't imagine why God would choose to talk to us in Morse. But then it suddenly changed. It said something else, and only once. I wonder if you can guess what it said?'

'The name and address. The contents of the letter.'

'No. That came later. The following evening at nine or so that started up and went on for several hours.'

'Okay, we give up, what did it say on the first night?' I asked.

Koskinen leaned forward. He whispered, 'I am Mr Ed.'

Those bloody technicians.

'That television programme, *Mr Ed,* didn't start till the sixties, thank goodness. We weren't forced to try to make sense of any silly talking horse. Later, when it did come on, it brought it all up again for me.' He shook his head. 'That was a terrible time,' he said. 'A terrible time.'

'But that night,' Edward said, prompting. 'Summer, 1956 . . . ?'

'We thought it had to be a hoax, but couldn't work out how we were being hoaxed. Or why. And this was after the comet. The address and message came in. Flash, flash, flash, for hours. It was like something from the end of the world. It was incoherent. We could read it, but we couldn't make anything of it. It drove us crazy. We were at one another's throats. We never did decide what to do, we just started doing things. Someone tore the pages out of the logbook. I rescued them from the trash later. Someone else sat down and forged two nights with no green light. After that I just went home and stayed there. I wasn't well. I couldn't get warm. My wife was angry that I wouldn't talk to her. She went off to her mother's and took the kids. I suppose I had a kind of breakdown.'

'But you still sent the letter.'

'I had to. I felt it was a test. I wrote out what the light had said and I put it in the mailbox.'

'But you did keep talking about the comet.'

'Later, years later. I suppose it looks to you, all these years on, as though everything happened within a short space of time. It didn't. Eventually I just couldn't stand the other secret – the green light – so I started to make noises about the comet.'

'The green light was a laser, and when it went into the wormhole it was red,' Edward said.

'You don't say.' The old man mused. 'I wonder how that works?'

Edward said, 'It'll be something to do with gravity.'

For a long moment we all pondered the wormhole's effects on light. Then, between us, Edward and I told Dr Koskinen everything else. We told him about Ranchod's Comet, our Photon Telegraph, our message protocols, our six years of dissembling to the world. And then I told him about my grandmother, her husband's family tradition, and about my deafening and insensible brother.

'My parents got your letter when they were expecting my brother. They had planned to call him Andrew. The first-born son of each generation of my father's family had been an Andrew. When I found the letter among my mother's papers I asked her about it. She said that the message "Don't listen. Don't love" had seemed like some kind of curse. It was like the presence of the uninvited wicked fairy at Sleeping Beauty's christening, she said. She said that my father wrote back to the return address. He sent a letter that more or less said just, "What the hell?" But they never got a reply. My uncle Andrew wrote too. He wasn't living anywhere near Mahoe, but it was supposed the letter might be for him.'

'I couldn't explain it,' Koskinen said. 'I'm sorry. I did get those letters. But what could I say in my own defence?'

'Why put a return address?'

'I wanted an explanation! But all I got was puzzled indignation.'

'My parents didn't name their first son Andrew. Grandma was very upset. Mum and Dad couldn't explain to her why they'd changed their minds. They didn't want to tell her about the letter, they wanted to spare her that. And they wanted to lift the curse. So they called their first-born Mark. But then he turned out unloving, and unable to listen.'

Koskinen said, 'It wasn't a curse.'

'No, it wasn't. It was me trying to warn myself. Me trying to salvage part of my heart.'

The old man nodded. 'Thank you for telling me all this. I'm glad to know it, even if it is a sad story. It's like those stories about some king sending to the oracle of Delphi to find out what will happen when his son is born.'

'Oedipus,' Edward said. 'The oracle says that the baby will grow up to kill his father and marry his mother. So the king has his son left out on a mountainside to die. But a shepherd finds the baby and raises him as his own. And so on and so forth. What happens in the end is what the gods always said would happen.'

'Man proposes; God disposes.'

'Exactly,' said Edward. And they sighed together like two old men.

But I was thinking that my grandmother on her deathbed *had* blessed me. 'Andrew, I'm glad you're Andrew,' she said. She said, in effect, 'I'm glad it was *you* who got the family name.' She blessed me and not Mark. Is a withheld blessing a curse? Withheld help harm? Withheld attention neglect?

You've never heard of a talking horse?

Today I'm packing up my office, my personal effects, under the eye of a man in uniform.

Yesterday they came and closed the lab – to us at least. They sealed the doors and parked up and shipped off our computers.

Tamara was the only one of us who would always ask why we'd found no sign of ourselves in the past, in the historical record. No sign of our own characteristic actions, the sorts of things *we* might be likely to decide to do. Just because so far we'd only done one thing that didn't mean there shouldn't be signs in the past of all the other things we'd go on to do. What she used to say was that if we hadn't heard from ourselves, hadn't recognised our own doings, it would mean that we must be living in another world, a different world than the one altered by our interference.

But now we know that we haven't heard from ourselves because it was taken out of our hands – the project, the Photon Telegraph, the open ear of The Deity itself.

And that is the story so far, a history of time travel's first ill-fated petition. It is out of our hands. And that is why you've never heard of our talking horse.

CRAIG GAMBLE

Craig Gamble completed an MA in Creative Writing at the IIML in 2014, winning the Adam Prize for his manuscript *The Watch List*. His new book, with a working title of *The Society of the Air*, is represented by the Bill Goodall Literary Agency in the UK.

The Rule of Twelfths

Northland, 1973

Libby's up early. As he leaves the house he hears thumping from below. Grandad's already outside. Down the steps beside the house, shells crunch under his feet. The basement is tight and shadowed, stacked with cans of paint, coils of rope and fishing gear. Sacks curtain off a space at the far end. There's no light rigged there, just a dirt floor and spiderwebs thick across the walls. Libby avoids it.

Grandad's at the long workbench bending over an outboard motor – the Evinrude from his boat. His wide brown hands work at the propeller. One's missing a finger, sliced cleanly away by a flailing steel cable, the stub still raw and red even now. But its loss does nothing to hamper his skill.

'I need to grease the crankshaft,' he says, addressing the outboard more than Libby. 'But this prop won't cooperate.'

Libby grips the shaft of the outboard so Grandad can use both of his hands on the spanner. There's another thump as the outboard rocks on the bench and the nut that holds the prop comes free.

'Ah.' Grandad pulls it clear and turns to Libby. 'It's today, then?'

Libby nods.

'Have you seen the tide?'

'No,' says Libby.

They make their way outside to the lawn of kikuyu grass Grandad has carefully nurtured into a mat of springy green. At its edge a rock wall juts out like a miniature jetty. Grandad has lent a hand in building other walls further down the bay. They hold the sand in, he says, make beaches where there weren't any.

The tide is green and clear and enormously high. It's pushed right in around the wall and makes a gentle slapping like the beat of an impatient dog's tail.

'King tide,' says Grandad, 'and still coming in. Couldn't be better.'

Libby's chest tightens.

'Thought it might be coming,' Grandad says. 'Rule of Twelfths, you learn that in school?' Libby shakes his head. 'Show you when you get back, better get breakfast in you.'

After they've eaten, Grandad helps Libby load the dinghy. It's an old, much-repainted flat-nosed boat made of marine plywood. Once white, it's now mostly yellow.

Grandad carefully coils the anchor rope. The anchor's made from three rusty, welded pieces of reinforcing iron. Libby fits the iron rowlocks into their slots, and Grandad helps him slide the oars through, laying them neatly along the inside of the dinghy's hull. Three bench seats – one along the stern, one amidships and a small one in the bow – sit above the pool of water in the gunwales. The leaks aren't bad enough to worry anyone. When Grandad rows, he moves the dinghy along with barely a pause. Libby tries for the same grace, but he can only manage it sporadically.

Libby's going out alone for his twelfth birthday. He's making a voyage of it, along the shoreline towards where the inlet opens into the wider bay. He's walked that way dozens of times. But by boat – with the water green and deep and the beach almost hidden by the high tide – everything familiar becomes undiscovered country.

His grandmother has given him a packet of sandwiches and some lemonade in a glass bottle. There's a place around the coast where he can run the dinghy in and anchor. He stows the bag of food on the rear seat next to a satchel with paper and pencils, in case something needs to be drawn.

'Are you set?' Grandad says.

'Ready.' Libby seats himself in the middle of the dinghy and readies the oars for the first stroke.

'Off you go.' Grandad's voice is muffled as he bends to grip the stern and shove it. It comes clear of the sand with a long rasp that rumbles up through Libby's feet. Grandad holds the stern and wades until the dinghy's in deeper water. Another push, and he lets go. Libby slides away, and before his momentum dies, leans forward into his first stroke.

Grandad raises a hand and turns back.

Libby pulls steadily past the orange buoy where Grandad's motorboat is moored, keeping his course straight. He's not far from the shore, but still the line of beach houses has shrunk beneath the big macrocarpa trees crowding the hill behind. Their house is two storeys, painted white and flanked by stairs. At the wide upstairs window someone is watching: his grandmother. He doesn't pause to wave. He wants to pretend he's alone.

A few hundred yards from the beach, Libby turns the dinghy parallel to the shore, and strokes to get it moving on its new course. He's far enough out to skirt the small reef of rocky mounds visible at low tide.

Only two houses come after theirs. The tall, dark-brown twin of their own and the half-hidden blue house, often empty, which sits on a miniature promontory. Grandad has warned him off landing there: the owner doesn't like visitors.

Libby sees his first landmark – a slumped cliff of sandstone Grandad calls Indian Rock. If he squints he can make out a face, and perhaps a fringe of overhanging grass like a headdress of feathers. But the name still doesn't feel like it belongs. Out from it are the Twins, two small islands of cat's-eye-encrusted rock only fully submerged at the highest tides. Between them is a narrow channel that Libby has swum but never rowed through. Grandad won't be happy if he grounds there.

The challenge is too much to resist. He lines the dinghy up as best he can and strokes to get it moving right. The tide's so high there's no danger of grounding in the channel, but he's forgotten the oars. Small waves ripple over the islands, inches of water, not enough for rowing. He's losing momentum, the tide urging him sideways. He could swim and push the boat through, or jump to the rocks and tow it. Instead he ships both oars and lifts one up, its rowlock still attached. It fits a hole in the stern, meant to mount an outboard. It's a makeshift scull. People do this in books, in Italy, but it's the first time he's tried it. At first the boat waggles from side to side, but he remembers to twist the oar as he strokes, and slowly gets some forward movement.

Libby steadies himself, moves his feet further apart and sculls the dinghy clear of the channel. Standing, he can see what's in front and on either side. Left is the grassy bump in the coastline where the blue house sits, hidden behind a pōhutukawa. The sea's come high enough to eat at the bank and fresh orange clay marks a new slip. Without Grandad's stone walls, more of the shoreline would be in the sea.

He's delighted by his new skill, but sculling is slow work and he's eager to get further around the coast. He ships the oar again, returns it amidships and pulls the dinghy around, circling the islands in deeper water. A steady stroke makes the sweat trickle down his back. The sun is well up and hot on his skin, pinching it gently as it dries the saltwater.

The blue house appears – a low, slumped building built too close to the water. The windows are masked by yellowing curtains and grass grows from the guttering and high around the walls. The front door's open a little way. He pulls in closer. He's seen a white dinghy moored there sometimes, but not today. Perhaps he should close the door to keep the possums and rats out? He'd only need to land for a moment.

A curtain twitches. From inside the house there's a scraping noise, like something heavy's being moved. Libby stops the dinghy with a short backwards push, Grandad's warning ringing in his head. The sound doesn't come again.

He backs off, turning again for the headland. He'll tell his grandad about the door later. The house disappears behind trees and tall flax bushes.

His rowing's ragged and he tries to correct it. The nearer the headland comes, the more the tide's against him. He's peering forward, looking for a lumpish mound of pale grey rock overhung by a twisted pōhutukawa. From one angle it looks like a lion resting on its stomach, from another a sphinx. It marks the turn of the coast where the inlet ends and the scoop of the broader bay opens.

Libby sees it. The tide's turned it into an island, the water dark and agitated between it and the beach. Lion Rock will do. The usual landing place might be submerged; perhaps he'll tie the dinghy to a tree rather than pull it up on the sand. The wind's come up a little, ruffling his hair and pushing his shirt against his wet back. His palms tingle with rising blisters.

He lets the dinghy bob; waves slap against its flat nose. In a patch of slow water astern a fish jumps with a quicksilver flash. It jumps again, a sprat fleeing a kahawai or some other big fish.

All right. It's no good leaving the job half done. That's something his grandad says. He pulls the dinghy back on course and starts to count the strokes, working the angles of each one. He has reached fifty-eight when he sees the landing place. The beach is still there, though the sea is among the banks of seashells and dried seaweed that are normally above high tide. Running with the swells the dinghy comes alive and soon sand grates under the hull.

Libby's thirsty for the lemonade but mooring comes first. He pulls off his shoes and clambers out into the water. It's cool on his legs, and he wonders if he should swim before eating. He stands holding the dinghy for a little while, happy to be able to make his own decision.

The dinghy bobs and dips on the water without his weight, and Libby uses the waves to tug it high up the beach. He carries the anchor further up, buries it in dry sand and weighs it with rocks for surety. The tide has probably turned, but a rogue wave could still pull the boat back.

The best place to eat is on the back of Lion Rock. The sea sucks and plays with his toes as he walks, and leaves wet marks on the rock as he climbs. He settles in a small hollow near the top. Far out in the bay a few boats are anchored where Grandad fishes at night, going out into the gulf when the tide's right and coming back in the very early morning. He'll gut and clean where the boat's moored, fillet on the back porch and hand the fillets through the kitchen window to Libby's grandmother, who has a frying pan hot. Libby will wake to the smell of frying fish.

Libby tries to sketch the headlands and the distant shape of Kawau Island. He can't capture it, and the shifting sea eludes him. It doesn't matter – it's not why he's come. Once, climbing Lion Rock, he'd gone high into the branches of the pōhutukawa. He'd caught a glimpse of something, a valley, a place of deep greenness. Today he'll see how far back it runs.

The sun's at a different angle. From the tree, the colours are muted and there are more shadows, but it's easy to spot a route inland. He scrambles along a branch and down the trunk where it roots into the headland.

None of the sheep that graze the fields come down this far to nose tracks through the bush. He pushes through ferns, tangled mānuka roots and clumps of green–brown flax. The sky's quickly obscured by overhanging branches of macrocarpa. As he stumbles around another flax he finds a scrap of empty ground, a ribbon of mossy grass that hugs the banks of a tiny stream and angles up the hill. He rests and lets his breathing settle, squats so the ferns arc above him and green is all he can see.

The stream vanishes into a crack. The sun's directly above now and the air is hot and close. He finds a box. No – it's a cage. Crudely made of wood and chicken wire, a makeshift hatch held open at one end. It's a trap, but for what Libby can't guess.

The way forward is blocked by a bush with thick, spiky limbs, but he scrambles through, arms up to shield his face. The ground drops from underfoot and trips him into a slide. The branches fall away.

He's found a pine forest. The trees stand in neat, quiet rows. Nothing grows under their dark green boughs, mournful after the bright greens of the bush. His movements are hushed by the carpet of pine needles. The air is heavy with resin.

Then he sees the hut. A rough pyramid of sticks and woven fern fronds with a triangular opening at the near end.

He walks around it. It's been camouflaged to match the pine forest – from a small distance it would be invisible. It's bigger than he first thought, the size of Grandad's basement room. But part of it's collapsed – peering inside he can just make out a slumped and distorted wall.

He hesitates, then ducks inside.

As his eyes adjust, he sees a low table at the far end. At its centre is a cage, like the one he saw on the way in. But pushed into a back corner of this one is a tight bundle of black and brown fur. Libby sees the pink bump of its nose and the flick of its matching ears. A possum watches him with large round eyes. It's scared. Stacked around the legs of the table are other traps, all empty. He reaches for the cage on the table.

'What do you think you're doing?'

Libby starts and bumps the table; the possum darts around the cage. The voice is behind him, but he can't see anybody until he puts his head out of the opening. It's a boy. Libby steps outside quickly.

The boy is taller than him and older, lean and bony.

'Well?' The boy's voice is quiet, not friendly.

'I was just . . . looking. At the possum.'

The boy shows his teeth in a way that isn't a smile. 'Just looking,' he says.

He walks over to the hut and ducks inside, out again. 'You touch anything in there?'

'No.'

'You're Enzo's grandkid, aren't you?'

For a second Libby doesn't know who he means. Then he remembers Grandad's name, rarely used. 'Yes,' he says.

'Thought so. What's your name?'

'Libby.'

'That's a girl's name.'

'It's not, it's short for Liberato.'

The boy makes a face. 'That your dingy down on the beach?'

'My grandad's.'

'Well I know that, but you brought it here. You know you're on private property?'

'No. I just followed the stream up here. Is this your farm?'

'Not likely! It's my hut though, my place.'

The boy looks towards the hut, back at Libby, shows his teeth again. 'Look,' he says, 'maybe you could do me a favour.'

Libby backs away a step. 'What sort of favour?'

'I need to take that animal around to the inlet, to my house, but it's a long walk. You could give me a lift in your boat.'

'I don't know you.'

'Sure you do. I'm Rodney. We have a house on the inlet. My dad's even done a job for Enzo once.'

Libby has no memory of him. He's never seen him among the cabins that dot the shoreline near the jetty.

'I don't know.'

'Enzo would want you to help me out.'

Libby doesn't like the way he uses his grandad's name.

'We can keep this little trespass of yours to ourselves, can't we?'

There's a leer in the boy's eyes. Libby doesn't really think Grandad would care if he was on a farm, but maybe he'd want him to help.

'All right?' says Rodney.

'I suppose,' says Libby. 'I should be getting back, anyway. It's a bit steep though, down to the beach.'

'You didn't come up the track?'

'No.'

'Well it's good I found you! Awful scramble down the hill if you don't know the track.'

I'd manage, thinks Libby, but he says nothing.

'Carry the cage, will you?' says Rodney. 'I hurt my arm chopping wood this morning. It's no good for carrying.'

Rodney's arm looks fine, but Libby ducks back into the hut and picks up the cage. The possum panics again, dashing from one side of the cage to the other in a blur. He puts it back down, and notices a black rope tied to the top. He lifts the cage again by the rope, trying not to let it spin too much, and spools the extra rope as best he can.

'I think I'm upsetting it,' says Libby as he emerges.

Rodney glances at him, then at the cage. 'Upsetting it? Ha!' He makes a sound that might be a laugh, though it's more like a bark. 'You wait till my dad gets his hands on it. Follow me.'

As Libby does, he feels his joy in the day disappear, as if someone has jabbed a hole in him and drained it out.

Rodney moves with an awkward quickness, a curious stumbling flick of his legs. But his paces are long, and Libby has to break into a jog every few steps to keep up. Rodney looks back at him once or twice but doesn't speak and makes no attempt to slow down. The possum's gone still again. There's a smell drifting up from it, sharp and needling.

The track's narrow and rutted with tree roots and heads in the wrong direction, away from Lion Rock. Then Libby hears the sea again and sees the beach. They've come down further along the bay, the track petering out into tussocky grass. In the bay the same boats are fishing, and the ferry is making its way to Kawau. Rodney seems more ordinary on the beach – a boy like him, in clothes that don't fit well.

Libby walks ahead. The dinghy's still tight to its anchor and he wants to get to it before Rodney can, stop him from taking charge. He's well ahead by the time they reach the anchor and starts digging it up straight away, nodding at the well-made knot in the rope.

He needn't have feared Rodney's interference. He makes no move to help Libby load the cage on board, pull in the anchor or push the dinghy towards the water.

Libby nudges the boat into the waves. The sea's livelier now and the wind fresher, but once they're around Lion Rock it'll be an easy row home. Rodney comes down the beach and climbs over the back of the dinghy without speaking a word, positioning himself next to the cage on the back seat. Libby gets behind the stern and gives it a shove as a wave comes in, soaking his shoes and shorts. He scrambles over the side and takes the middle seat.

'Watch it!' says Rodney. 'Don't get me wet.'

Libby half swallows an apology and makes sure not to meet Rodney's eyes. He can tell he's being watched and it makes his first few pulls awkward, the dinghy spinning in the water. Rodney makes a noise, half snort, half laugh.

Libby pictures his grandad rowing, tries to match his strokes to the image in his head. Slowly the dinghy steadies and heads out of the bay, angling towards the calmer water beyond Lion Rock. He looks up at Rodney, who's bending over the cage, intent on what's inside. Libby concentrates on his rowing.

'This boat of yours leaks,' says Rodney, moving his foot through the puddle of water in the bilges.

'It's never sunk.'

'Bloody hope not. I hate swimming.'

How can you live here, Libby thinks, and hate swimming? Some days he's barely out of the water, only emerging to eat.

They've pulled around Lion Rock now and immediately the water's flat again and the wind has dropped to a breeze. It's enough to cool Libby and he's moving the dinghy along well. Rodney's looking into the cage again, then he meets Libby's eyes.

'Hey,' he says, 'want to have some fun?'

'What do you mean?'

Rodney screws up his face. 'You don't know what fun is? Are you stupid?'

'What sort of fun, I meant,' says Libby, trying to keep his voice even. He'd like to slap the grin off Rodney's face.

'Take us out a bit further,' says Rodney, looking in the direction of the blue house. 'Where the water's a bit deeper.'

'Why?'

'Show you when we get there,' says Rodney, and when Libby makes no move to alter course: 'Oh come on! It'll be good.'

Libby swings the dinghy reluctantly. He'd like nothing more than to drop Rodney on the shore and go home. He can see it won't be that easy. He could take the dinghy in now, leave it there and walk home. But Rodney would mock him and he'd be abandoning the charge of the boat.

They're in deep water. The blue house is visible on the shore.

'This'll do,' says Rodney. 'Come and get this cage.'

Libby ships the oars and reaches for the cage. The dinghy wobbles as his weight shifts.

Rodney stands, lifting a foot onto the back seat, bracing himself. The dinghy wobbles a little more. 'Pass it to me,' he says.

'What are you going to do?'

'Just pass it over.'

But Libby doesn't.

'C'mon!' says Rodney.

'You're going to put it over the side,' says Libby.

'So what? Better this way than what my father does to them.

He wrings their necks. With his hands. He likes doing it.'

'No.'

Rodney sneers. Libby moves backwards with the cage, expecting a lunge. But his feet tangle in the rope and he falls with a crash. The cage bangs against the gunwale and out of his hands. There's a large splash.

When he regains his seat, the cage is gone and so is Rodney.

He scrambles for the rope. A lump of it's already gone, and the section he grabs is wet and slippery.

Rodney surfaces a few feet away, but Libby barely gives him a glance. The cage is slowly coming up. He doesn't know how long the possum will last, and pulls harder, the rope hissing as it comes back over the side.

There's a strangled cry. Rodney is going back under again, his hands grasping at the air. Can't he swim at all? Libby stops pulling, and for a long moment watches the spot where Rodney's disappeared.

'Rodney!' he calls, not expecting an answer.

He kicks the side of the dinghy and lets the rope go, leaps back to the centre seat. He grabs both oars and swings the dinghy around to the spot where he last saw Rodney. He stows the oars and moves forward, looking down into the water, pulling his shirt off, trying to judge the best spot. He yanks off his shoes and throws himself over the side.

Underwater it's silent. The sandy bottom seems close and the water is clear – he sees Rodney almost immediately.

He's face up, drifting slowly down and away. Libby starts to move towards him then stops. Rodney's blurring, the colour in him bleeding out into the water like he's a painting dissolving in the rain. His pale face is melting, the skin peeling away in ribbons, exposing tooth and bone. He turns slowly towards Libby.

Libby kicks hard for the surface and emerges gasping, scrambles to pull himself on board. He lies there, dragging in breath after breath. It's long minutes before he lifts himself and peers over the side. The sea's empty all around.

There's a loud thump from the shore. A man's standing in front of the blue house.

'Hey,' yells Libby.

The man does nothing.

Libby grabs the oars and pulls closer. He yells again, 'There's a boy in the water.'

Still the man doesn't move, and Libby pulls within a dozen feet of him. As he does, he feels a lurching in his chest. A tug that grabs hold of his heart and lungs. He knows somehow the possum's no longer in the cage, only the tight circle of a furred body it no longer needs. Rodney's gone too.

'What are you yelling about?' says the man, irritable.

'A boy,' says Libby. 'He fell overboard.'

'What boy?'

'He fell off. My fault, I rocked the boat, and he went in.'

The man's watching him, impatient.

'We dropped the cage, too, but we can get it when the tide goes out.'

'What cage?'

'It had a possum in it, Rodney was bringing it back.'

The man's face goes white. His voice is very quiet. 'What did you say?'

Libby takes a breath. 'There was a cage, in a hut up on the headland. Rodney said it was his, he'd trapped it, I guess, and he asked if I could give him a ride in my boat.'

'You're Enzo's grandson, are you?' The man's voice is dangerous.

'Yes.'

'He put you up to this, did he?'

'Put me up to what?'

'Get out of it!'

'What –'

'Go on, you get out of it! Go home!' The man's stepping towards him, a fist clenched.

Libby digs the oars into the sand, pushes the dinghy clear, and backs it out into the water as quickly as he can.

'And you tell Enzo to keep his ideas to himself!'

Libby sculls out into the inlet. The man does not move, his head fixed in Libby's direction. Libby strokes harder, making space between himself and the shore. Indian Rock is clear now, and he can see his own house, and the Twins. Twisting, he can even make out Lion Rock. It's all shrunk, all small. Only the Tāwharanui Peninsula, behind him, looms large where it rises above the deep-water channel.

He comes into the beach quickly, scrambling on to the sand and dragging up the anchor to dump on the lawn. Then he slumps to the grass, staring back to where the blue house lies, his head full of Rodney's dissolving face.

'What've you done to my lawn?'

It's Grandad, coming out of the basement. Libby sees he's gouged a scar into the perfect green of the grass.

'Sorry,' says Libby, and he is. He knows how much work it's taken to get the lawn so even. He dodges around, freeing the anchor, trying to replace the divot with a foot, looking for a better mooring spot.

'Libby,' says Grandad. 'What's up with you?'

Libby stops. Meets his grandad's eyes, blushes. He doesn't know where to start.

'Libby?'

'I met someone,' he says finally, 'from the blue house.'

'I told you not to go there,' says Grandad. His voice is annoyed, maybe worried. 'Did he hurt you?'

'No . . . You mean the man? No, he didn't touch me. He was just angry.'

'What about?'

Libby hesitates. 'I don't know,' he says. 'Something I said, I think.'

Grandad looks him up and down. 'You sure he didn't hurt you?'

Libby nods his head.

'Well, good then. He's not a nice man, you need to keep well clear of him, all right?'

'Yes,' says Libby.

'Good. Now give me that anchor, and we'll get this boat sorted.'

Libby wants to say more, but Grandad's already moving. They make the dingy fast to a ring on the rock wall and carry the oars up to the basement to stow them.

'Grandma's making scones, they'll be ready soon,' says Grandad, and he holds up his hands, stained with rust from the wet oarlocks, the missing finger obvious. 'We'd better wash up.'

'Why's he like that?' says Libby.

Grandad catches his eye and turns to his workbench, the Evinrude still laid out on it. 'It's a sad story,' he says.

Libby waits.

Grandad picks up a wrench, tinkers with the engine. 'He was always angry, at least as long as I've known him. Ready to pick a fight. Took it out mostly on those animals he traps. And on his son, Rodney.'

'What happened?'

'Rodney went missing, about five years ago. We all looked for him, everyone around here, all up and down the coast.

Went on for days. But we didn't find him. Well, not until a week later when it was too late. He drowned, Libby, someone found his body out in the deep water on their way back from Kawau.'

'Five years ago?'

'Yes. And his father . . . he cut himself off. As if we were all to blame. He won't have anyone go there, now.'

There's a question there, if Libby is brave enough to ask it. 'Was someone to blame?' he says.

'I don't know. Their dinghy was still at home when he disappeared. Never understood how his body got all the way out there.'

Grandad puts the wrench down, turns for the door. 'C'mon,' he says. 'Scones.'

Hours later, Libby is sitting on the stone wall looking out to where the yachts are anchored in the channel. The tide is right out. The dinghy is beached, and all about it are ridged rocks exposed by the retreating sea.

Out by the channel there's a small group of people, bent over, intent on something at their feet. Digging for pipi, Libby thinks. As he watches they straighten, gesture at each other with buckets and begin to walk back in. On the wet sand the people are preceded by their reflections, stretched and changing with the light.

Someone else is out there walking alone along the edge of the deep green channel water. Sometimes they almost disappear against the dark water behind, reappearing when they cross the stark white hull of a yacht. They're lanky, or else emaciated by the distance, Libby can't tell.

He jumps down from the wall, his bare feet slapping into the wet sand. He can hear his grandparents talking upstairs, the clang of a pot on the stove. He walks out to where the dinghy lies and rests a hand on its rough side, feeling the furry wood roughened with salt and sun. He walks on, his distorted reflection leading, the shallow pools merging across the wide bowl of the inlet until it seems he's walking on water. The channel lurches closer and then recedes, as if it's lost its grip on the world, or he's lost his grip on it. The lanky figure against the green water is still now, patient.

DYLAN HORROCKS

Dylan Horrocks is a cartoonist and writer based in Wellington. His books include the graphic novels *Hicksville* and *Sam Zabel & the Magic Pen,* and a collection of short comics, *Incomplete Works.* He also drew the comic book series *Pickle* and *Atlas,* and has written comics for DC and Vertigo, including *Hunter: the Age of Magic* and *Batgirl.* His short stories have been published in anthologies including *Lady Chatterley's Rosebud Wristlet, Steampunk!* and *Monstrous Affections.* His comics and prose fiction have won an Eisner Award, a Sir Julius Vogel Award, and a NZ Arts Foundation Laureate Award, and he currently teaches comics and visual narrative at the Victoria University of Wellington School of Design Innovation – Te Kura Hoahoa.

The Paresach's Tulips

I was so much younger then, squinting in the fierce desert glare, creasing the skin with lines that have since become permanent: the scars of age.

I had travelled for a week across the empty sands, shrouded in a sweat-stained *khador* robe, heavy with heat and thick with dust. Every day the shining white sky. Sunsets so vast and violent they terrified me: like a funeral pyre for the world, a curtain of flaming clouds that rose and billowed and raged and then – in a single breath – faded into darkness. At night I shivered in the bitter cold, afraid that morning would never come, that I was lost, that the garden was a lie or had been long-since buried by the restless shifting dunes.

And then on the eighth day I found the Paresach's tulips.

Blood red, their petals delicate and fresh, standing three feet high and perfectly still, row after row for as far as I could see. And all around them the shimmering desert, the heat like a beast raging for its prey. I remember the smell: sweet and strong. I remember licking my lips and tasting it there, the dizziness it brought. The Khadori considered the garden a false oasis – a place of madness – and gave it a wide berth. In Madrania they called it Catherine's Garden.

The story goes like this: Ten thousand years ago (or more) the Paresach Rasan, a great mage, took as a wife Catherine de Riens. The Paresach adored his new queen, but Catherine did not take well to the desert and longed instead for the gentle landscapes of Anjer. She would stay inside and speak only of her home – of lakes and forests and fields of red tulips, swaying in a cool breeze. Finally the Paresach could bear it no longer. He sent his bravest warrior on the long journey to Anjer to fetch some tulip seeds. When the warrior returned with seven heavy sacks, the Paresach went out into the desert and scattered the seeds across the sand, singing his wife's name as though chanting a spell: 'Catherine,' he sang. 'Catherine.' The sun still beat upon the sand and the sand stayed dry as dust. But where the Paresach had sung Catherine's name the tulips grew, their stems strong and succulent, their petals full and bright. From that day on, the Paresach's wife was loyal and affectionate and she bore him seven sons and seven daughters.

A story told by people who know nothing about magic.

Unlike the storytellers of Madrania, the Khadori know a little magic – enough to dismiss so sentimental a tale. Instead, they say, the Paresach planted his tulips as a trap to ensnare the wise, for men of great learning would travel far to see a miracle. Before long, the impossible garden would take them into its grip and drive them insane, trapped as they were by the powerful scent of its paradox. Rasan's intention, the Khadori say, was to devour the wise men's minds and so become the wisest of them all. But along with their wisdom, he also swallowed the madness of the garden. And his demented spirit haunts the field of tulips still, ready to devour all who come too near.

I had heard both tales – and more besides – but I knew that neither caught the truth. All such wonders gather around them stories of romance and horror. The truth is invariably less dramatic and more significant.

And so I stood alone before the tulips, my guides having refused to come within sight of them. For a long time I could do nothing more than gaze and listen and inhale their strangeness. They appeared perfectly healthy, rich and luscious against the brown of the desert and the white sky. But there was no moisture on their petals or stems and none in the air. There must be water somewhere, I thought – perhaps trapped within?

After a while, I got to work.

It was simpler than I had expected; a series of divinations revealed the essentials. The tulips were real and alive. Their physical structure was exactly as it should be, with all four elements in their proper proportions; my suspicion proved correct that water was hermetically sealed inside. The flowers were normal in all respects save one: everything was completely static. Nothing moved, nothing changed: a living field of tulips frozen in a single moment. They had been conjured here, incongruous and fragile, and before the hot thirsty desert could touch them, time itself had stopped.

Rasan had made a monument that would last forever. But this was not what I sought. This was not immortality. An immortal lives for all time; these flowers lived *outside* of time, trapped in the infinity of one inescapable instant.

I tore away the *khieri* scarf so the full weight of the sun fell upon my head, and I screamed at the ancient Paresach, cursing his useless gesture, cursing his wife and the dust they had both become.

And then I paused. Standing utterly still, my ears filled with the sound of my heart and the pounding heat, I was suddenly aware of his presence.

Of course I had checked before for *ánima*, but the stillness had hid him as a featureless mask hides a face. The word itself means movement, and it is the constant motion of a spirit that a necromancer is trained to detect. But what I felt now was something else. With my curse I had touched his spirit – not merely the intangible flicker of its motion, but the actual substance of life. I cannot remember the exact sensation, only the shock – like having one's hand grasped in a dark empty room.

At last I understood. The Paresach had stood at the centre of the garden when he cast the spell that created it. And he stood there still. It took me hours to locate him: the garden was huge and I had first to climb a nearby ridge, and then to search with the spy glass I had stolen from Edorash of Tirsa. But at length I saw him – a tall, fat man, robed in the green and gold of a Paresach, one arm outstretched before him, the other bent across his chest, fingers poised in a manuglyph, the meaning of which I could not recall, though I knew I had seen it before. Of course, he stood perfectly, completely still, like a statue, or perhaps more like a figure in a Trubidorean painting. Yet when I concentrated, there – once again – was the feeling of his *ánima*, like a flame at the edge of my vision.

His face wore an expression of concentration, of triumph. But in the line of his mouth, the first shadow of doubt. His garden was an attempt at immortality (why else are great works made?); he understood that his spell would keep a thing fresh and youthful forever. But the physics of the spell were beyond him and – he probably thought – of no consequence. It is my belief that he learned of it through his wife; I have since heard of a similar process being used long ago by the Aléan School in Riens. It had been designed not for Rasan's purposes but to create a thing to look at, preserved from the relentless decay that is time. And as a trap. Rasan was alive, in the sense that his *ánima* was still present, but in effect he was lost more completely than in death. His mind was still filled with the same thoughts – that mixture of triumph and horror – that had filled it the moment he was trapped. What immortality was this?

I camped by the garden for one night, then left. Perhaps Rasan could still teach me something, were I to study his spell or even somehow release him. But I could not stomach it. The tulips blazed in the harsh sunlight – and at night blazed still, wreathed in the light of their own ancient morning – a field of bright, shining ghosts.

So many failures, so many dead ends. So many disappointments and betrayals and scars of age and the passing of time. And still I must one day die.

I first saw the blood three weeks ago. It was after midnight and I had just eaten a perfect meal: Peter's lamb and pickles at the Old Horn, followed by whisky and fruit mince pies. Very heavy and very rich, but one of the few meals worth eating in Gerwaen. So, despite the frustrations of my work, I was feeling good as I walked back to the Tower through the quietest, darkest streets, avoiding that atmosphere of affected stupidity that fills this city at night. The cold and silence cleared my thoughts.

When I turned down Cob Street, the smell of blood hit me like a rush of hot air. It is a smell I am well acquainted with and not one to make me baulk, but never before had I smelled it so strong.

Cob Street is particularly narrow and dark, so I made a small *parias* light. As it flared into life, there was a sudden gleam of scarlet. The blood was everywhere: splashed across the cobbled street and the stone walls as though a barrel had exploded.

I was immediately intrigued. It seemed to be the blood of a single body – and the better part of it at that – mixed with other fluids, some difficult to extract. Clearly this had not been a simple brawl or murder. And if the liquids of the victim were all around me, where was their flesh?

Within a few yards, the gore narrowed to a thick red smear, as though someone had used the body as a paintbrush to mark their path. I carefully followed it along to the end of the street and around the corner into Tailor's Way, where it continued, hugging the shadows on the southern side, to Beater's Lane.

Only now did I feel afraid – or at least aware of danger. Beater's Lane is as small and black as Cob Street. I hesitated at the corner, fumbling for my wand and wishing I had drunk less whisky. And then, wand held before me like a dueller's knife, I stepped into the alley and lit up my *parias.* Halfway along the street the trail ended abruptly. There was no body and no killer; the blood simply stopped.

I took a moment to calm my racing pulse before examining the end of the trail. There was a wider puddle, as though the body had been dropped for a time. Surrounding this, a number of smaller spatters and smudges, the cause of which I could not guess. But that was all: I could find no indication of where the body had gone from there.

When I got back to the Tower, I lit the lantern and made some strong coffee. There was a new moon, framed perfectly by my window: silver on deep blue, with a smudge of murky red above the Palace. Why is it that human lights always dirty the night sky? All save the magelight, *parias*, which is like moonlight: pure, steady and clean.

For an hour I sat drinking coffee and pondering that trail of blood. What had caused it? Where was the body? The shock of that initial gore was mingled now with a chill of excitement. Never mind that my work was stalled, caught in a web of missing pages and impossible translations. Here at least was an engrossing distraction and perhaps more – perhaps the city was about to open its secrets to me.

I extinguished the lantern and sat in the moonlight, so faint I felt like a ghost.

My father and mother died in the witchcraft purge of Black Friday, 3143 NC. They were dragged from their bed and out into the street, where one of the cardinal's men disembowelled them – first one then the other. They died slowly, lying in their own filth, their faces white with terror at the knowledge that they had already been killed and could now only wait for death itself.

When I recall their faces that night, I do not particularly remember them as my parents. The features are certainly theirs but the expressions are not. I have seen those expressions – or near enough – on many faces since, and in that memory they are simply the prototype for a universal mask: the face of mortality.

Running out of time. My father knew then that he had no more time; all was now at an end. His life was complete, and all that he had done, seen and felt was all that he ever would. We are all running out of time, of course, but who really understands that? Who doesn't feel that the time they have left is so vast it may as well be forever?

Only the elderly and the very ill come close to understanding how little we have. Which is why I have always hated them. They look at me with eyes attuned to the draining sand of an hourglass. They see that I have more time than they – more, but still finite, and still it drains away.

Arto of Narea was different. He is the only old man I have ever respected. He was always kind: nursing me with physiomantic tinctures and spells through childhood illness; tutoring me in mathematics, philosophy, Lieri and Madranian; and even playing games: knucklebones, checkers and cosh. When I was ten he seemed ancient, but he behaved like an immortal. For a time I suspected that he *was* immortal. I know better now, of course. But even when his own time ran out, when he mounted the pyre and was lashed tightly to the stake – even then he gazed out across the crowd seemingly unconcerned. As though death were certainly inconvenient but really the least of his worries. I think – or is this only selfishness? – that I was his main concern then. *My* fate. And that had been taken care of. I was watching from a carriage that bore me away as soon as the first flames caught his hair. It took me out of the city and away to the coast. And I have been Amelia ever since, my first name lost to the necessity of escape.

Arto had no interest in immortality, which is unusual in a physiomancer. He healed the injured and tended to the sick, always striving to keep death away. And yet he never spoke out against death. When a subject, or even a friend, died, Arto seemed unsurprised and unconcerned, as though all was exactly as it should be.

I have never understood this. Even those who have incorporated death into their religious beliefs do not treat it with such casual acceptance. Death is always a matter of great concern: a thing to fight against, a power to be respected, a liberation to be embraced. Only Arto treated it with a lack of interest, almost indifference. I repeat: I have never understood this. And yet I have always envied it. One day I too shall lose all fear.

By mid-morning the blood trail was gone. It had been washed into the gutters by the housewives and tradesmen whose territories it had marked, too house proud and concerned for their reputations to wonder whose death they were washing away. I cursed myself for not taking samples when I had the chance and went to the New Quarter for coffee and pastries. There is a coffee house on Silk Street called the Lily where one can buy chocolate: the only place in Gerwaen – probably the only place in Wittany. The owner, André, is from Anjer and after a week he was already greeting me like an old friend. And so, while André fussed about, plying me with his latest creations, I sat at the warm window table and traced a pattern in the spilt icing sugar – a large splash, a spidery trail that turned right twice – and then stopped. There was nothing for it but to hope that the killer would strike again. Tonight perhaps, I thought, and the almond cakes tasted sweeter than before.

I was not disappointed. An hour before midnight I returned to Cob Street, but found no fresh signs of death. I carefully retraced my steps of the previous night as far as Beater's Lane and stood in the darkness considering. Then I began to walk a slow spiral up Beater's Lane to Foss Way, Tilby Row, and out along the tiny alleys that spread through the city like the web of wrinkles on an old man's hand. It was not particularly methodical but such a maze of streets cannot be searched methodically. Besides, I could not know what I was looking for. As chance caused me to stumble across last night's discovery, so might chance deliver tonight.

Again, the smell came first. But fainter this time: a taste of wet iron in the air. I followed it up William's Street, near the river. Dilapidated wooden houses on one side and on the other a tall stone wall from which plaster flaked like dead skin. The street was dark because it was deserted but once I had the scent I needed no *parias* to find the gleaming line of red.

I could hardly believe my luck. Without hesitation, I strode along the trail to where it turned down an alley that ended at the river's edge – no more than a gap between two houses. And there it ended, as the first trail had begun: a huge splash of blood spread across the walls and ground. The same raw stench. A steady trickling sound as blood ran down the last few feet to the river.

This time I was prepared and had brought equipment: a vacuum flask, a few small bottles, some white muslin. I kneeled beside the deepest puddle and filled the bottles and the vacuum flask (this last is easy enough in the laboratory, but in a dark street thick with excitement and fear it becomes a challenging feat of concentration). Finally I laid the piece of muslin over one wall to soak up the mess.

A boat passed by on the river and I pressed myself into the shadows. The boatmen had a lantern and for one long moment I was bathed in its filthy yellow light and the whole alley glowed like a ghastly infection. Then they moved on and the darkness flooded back.

I turned and ran, pausing only to snatch up the blood-soaked muslin. The streets had never seemed this dark, this empty. When I reached the Tower, I almost fumbled the *isturia* that allows entry; once inside I rushed to my chambers and cast a clumsy word-lock on the door. Again that faint moonlight that turns everything grey; again that crescent poised in the window – a little wider tonight, a little brighter.

I set a flame in the lantern and revived the fire in the stove. Soon the room was warm and bright and the moon was hidden by a fog on the window. I placed the muslin and the bottles on the table. My clothes were covered in blood; I removed them all and washed myself till the freezing water was the colour of a Pélonnaise wine. Then I sat by the stove, naked and shivering but calmer. Unafraid.

I am not easily frightened. I had not felt like that since the desert, all those years ago. Then, there had been the emptiness, the awful thought that I might never escape that rigid horizon, that the heat would suffocate me, like the child I had once seen smothered to death by his mother. I believed that all of my work, all the sacrifice and struggle, the desperate hope – all of it had led to that cursed eternal garden. I felt the fear of failure so intensely then.

But what had terrified me tonight? It was absurd that here in this dull provincial city I should be sent running like a startled cat by a bright light and a pool of blood! I who so many times has calmly stepped back to avoid the sudden spray of blood from a cut throat, who has summoned the spirit of an enemy I had slain moments before, merely to ask it a question or two.

It was not blood I had washed so carefully from my skin but the stain of that fear. After a time – the moon had risen out of sight – I stood and dressed in fresh woollen robes and set to work.

Coffee helped, with a touch of cinnamon.

The blood was that of a young man: not especially unhealthy, but drunk at the time of death. From what I could tell of his diet he was a townsman of moderate means, probably one of the many general labourers who work as artisans' assistants one week and builders' the next. There were other fluids there too: bile, mucus, cranial fluid, saliva, urine and, as I had already noted, those more difficult to extract – synovial fluid, which runs in the channels around the joints, and even *esperius*, the substance that Algrave Declarius believed contains the soul. This last is notoriously difficult to get to, being located in a central section of the brain that contracts, sealing itself, when pressure is applied.

That in itself was intriguing, but what kept me awake for the remainder of the night was this: nowhere in my samples was there any residual trace of a spirit. I tried every summons I knew and every divination – including those I had developed after the desert – without success. There is no evocation stronger than that which uses both blood and *esperius*. It was as if the body had never been alive, had possessed neither *ánima* nor soul.

Now I was truly excited. Even the weakest spirit takes at least a day to decay and these fluids were fresh. Either the victim had been living without *ánima* – impossible – or someone had extracted his spirit completely. If the latter, then perhaps I had found it at last – the creature for which I had searched from Narea to Pélorin.

Néfarit. Soul Stealer. Spirit Eater. Undying devourer of life.

As dawn came pale through the window, I lay back on my bed, satisfied. My quarry was near; anything was possible.

The following night I began to search more methodically. First I prepared a divination that would locate spilt *esperius* (exposure to the air alters its form, distinguishing it from the unspilt). It is a difficult divination and, as the alteration when exposed is so slight, there were many false alarms: the glimmer of a child, a drunk in an alley. A divination is always like listening for a single voice in a large choir.

But eventually there it was: spread along an alley off Saint Nicholas Street. This time the trail turned no corners but ran straight down the alley for about fifteen feet. I took new samples, although I did not expect to learn any more from them. I was now sure that this was the work of a Néfarit.

When I returned to the Tower that night, I soon abandoned the samples. I was becoming impatient. For hours under the gloomy light of the waxing moon I sat, thinking over the Néfarit's trail, trying to formulate a plan.

According to the most reliable account (that of Edward Chamberlain of Tilby), a Néfarit is a non-corporeal being that inhabits a mortal host-body, in a manner similar to possession. It may survive indefinitely by extracting *ánima* from other living humans and – presumably – incorporating it into its own, thereby offsetting the natural process of decay that affects all living spirits. There are no extant accounts of how it attacks its victims but many of what it leaves behind: a horribly mutilated corpse, impossible to identify, internal organs displayed as though the body had been turned inside out. No one knows how the Néfarit does this or where it comes from, whether it is intelligent or merely a beast, or perhaps a kind of demon.

Berno of Goranteum, the great necromancer, devoted two chapters of his *Necronomicon* to the Néfarit. He hinted that he knew more than was recorded in his writings, and I privately suspect he was once able to examine – or at least observe – a living specimen. He asked a crucial question: by what mechanism does the Néfarit add the victim's *ánima* to its own? For, if that is indeed what it does, could not a skilled mage learn how to do the same, extending their lifespan indefinitely? Berno, true to his reputation, merely poses the question and then moves on, refusing to offer any answers.

I had to find a way to anticipate the Néfarit's next attack: to be there to observe – and possibly even capture – it. I nailed a large sheet of parchment to the wall and sketched out a rough diagram of the Old Quarter in charcoal, drawing the main squares and streets, before adding the alleys where I had found signs of the Néfarit's three attacks. These I marked with a finger-smear of blood, tracing their paths from beginning to end. Then I prepared a supper – coffee and the mustard-cakes I had bought from André that afternoon – and paused to gather my thoughts.

There was no pattern. I stared at my map for hours, added surrounding streets, looked for any shape or connection: there was nothing there. The attacks appeared to be random.

Of course, what could I expect to find with only three samples? How did I know there were not others – perhaps more than one each night? I resolved to wait a while, recording every attack I could find, and hoped a pattern would gradually emerge.

I spent much of the next day improving my map of the city. I had seen several charts of Gerwaen before coming to Wittany – the first in an old manuscript from Arto's library: *The Travels of Joaqin of Pitano.* Centuries ago, Joaqin walked the ancient raised roads that cross the world from east to west and north to south – over forest and pasture, through villages and towns, mountains and hills. The roads run straight across the landscape as though ruled by a scribe, no matter the terrain; their height remains steady but, as the land below rises and falls, they may be as tall as a hundred feet or drop below the crest of a hill. A road will disappear into a cliff, only to emerge miles away where the land is low enough. It is as though someone built the roads in a void and then let the world form carelessly around them, like wind-blown sand covering the ruins of an unfinished house.

Scholars have proposed many explanations for these mysterious roads, and every region has its tales of the gods and giants who made them. Here in Wittany they are called the Spirit Roads, walked by the spirits of the dead on their journey from the grave to the land of ghosts. Few living men are brave enough to set foot upon them. And so they serve more as markers, boundaries and barriers. One can walk below the arches and, occasionally, where the Road is low, a bridge has been built across. The Spirit Roads are sometimes used by the King's men, protected from the dead by his divine authority. Or so people say.

Sometimes, where two of these Roads meet, there sits a tall, thin tower. Joaqin speculated that such towers once occupied all crossroads, but over time most have been destroyed or worn down until few remain. In Trubidore, he saw one tower that looked like it had been carved from raw amethyst. Its walls were translucent; at sunset it glowed like a burning ember. Other towers were made of the same stone as the roads themselves: hard as granite and black as coal. I have visited several of these and am unable to speculate on their origins. All, however, are enchanted. Among mages, they are known as safe havens in a generally hostile world: none may enter without magic and once inside one may sleep and study without interruption. Most of those who visit these towers keep to themselves; when I stay in one I am usually alone. But occasionally I have encountered others: a bearded mage from Aristea who refused all conversation or a grey-haired woman in black who smiled warmly and spoke a strange slippery language I have never heard anywhere else. It was as though she belonged to her own separate world. As do we all, I suppose.

Gerwaen is one of several cities to have grown around a crossroads, with that ancient enchanted tower at its centre. The Spirit Roads divide the city into four parts: the Old Quarter, the New Quarter, the Royal Quarter and the Merchants' Quarter. On Joaqin's map, the city was far smaller, with a fortress nestled beside the Tower where the two roads meet and a dense cluster of houses spread across what is now the Old Quarter.

Three centuries ago, Alyssan of Carnea visited Gerwaen and drew a detailed, richly decorated map, which was on the wall of a scholar I visited in Neris. I studied that map for days, long before I ever came here. I still remember the elegant way she had drawn the black tower at the city's centre, like an axle around which all else revolved. In truth, the streets are nothing like her orderly wheel, although perhaps they have become more chaotic in the years since. There is a new royal palace now, far from the Tower, and the original keep is in ruins at the edge of Conjuror's Square. Performers gather there during the day: musicians, mummers, jugglers and one or two pretend magicians whose cheap tricks appear more glamorous beside the so-called Mages' Tower. None are ever admitted, of course. The Tower chooses who will enter and only a genuine *isturia* spell can open that heavy black door. The first time I spoke that simple charm and stepped inside, one of the conjurors cried out and rushed forward to follow. He pounded on the door for hours, shouting his fraudulent incantations while I set up in the highest room and got to work.

And now I had my own map, crudely sketched in charcoal, ink and blood. No elegant wheel and axle here: thick black lines for the Spirit Roads; squares and markets outlined in grey; the Old Quarter a dense web of streets, alleys and lanes with names where I knew them and numbers for the rest. At noon, I went out to buy beef pies and ale from a riverside stall on Martin's Walk, then walked for hours unravelling the tangled geography of the city: crowded rows of shops and taverns, dark silent slums, bustling warehouses, the high garden walls of the wealthy's New Quarter homes. At first I took notes and memorised plans but the afternoon sun and lack of sleep soon lulled me into a kind of dream. The streets of Gerwaen became the city of my childhood, at once familiar and strange. Turning onto King Street and into the shadow of the Spirit Road, I saw the figure of my father slowly walking ahead. Beside him my teacher Arto, still carrying the chains they had hung round his arms. A priest I killed in Valaïs, eyes closed, one hand on the shoulder of the first man I lay with. And at the front, as if leading us all, a small dark-haired girl, looking back with a smile – bright, alive, luminous.

And then I awoke, still on my feet, surrounded by strangers.

Every night I searched the streets of Gerwaen until I found the creature's mark. At first, a single bloody smear did not satisfy; I continued searching for others until dawn. But I never found a second and soon decided that it killed only once each night.

Every morning, I would add to my map, dipping a finger into a flask of the victim's blood and running it across the parchment, along whatever streets the Néfarit had marked: one large splash and then a thin twisting smear that led nowhere. At length there were nine red marks; still I could see no pattern.

I had grown tired of spending my nights trudging for hours through that ugly dirty city, searching for yet another explosion of gore, never any closer to a solution. I paced my workroom, staring at the yellow moon – now two-thirds full. I saw no way forward.

*

It is at moments like this that the loneliness threatens to overwhelm me. There are times when failure seems certain and death inevitable – even imminent – lonely and cold. But there are other, worse times when I have come so close – when the secret seems within reach, and surely I will soon banish death from my future for the rest of time. At such moments, for one terrifying moment, eternity looks like hell: nothing more than an endless continuation of life as it is now – empty, bleak, sordid, alone, always so alone.

I fear these moments more than anything: almost as much as death itself.

I prowled about the room, frustration growing at my inability to find meaning in my diagram. Every mark is a sign: it tells us that something was here, something *happened*. The countless marks and traces left by presence or absence, motion, stillness, the passing of time. Study these signs carefully and a structure akin to language emerges: subtle patterns of grammar, metaphor and meaning. Then it is possible to reverse the relationship between the thing and its sign, using the language through which it has marked the world to understand or even control it. No command given in a thing's own language may be ignored. That is the heart of magic.

But still the Néfarit's movements remained opaque. I stood before the map and stared at the red smears my hand had made – as if at random, unintelligible. Across the square, a soldier on the North Wall called the third watch.

And all at once the plan crystallised in my mind.

I would *make* the Néfarit a pattern. I would take its random marks and weave them into a sequence of my own devising, a dance led by me. Until it could only strike where I had chosen.

I whirled around, laughing, and snatched up my cloak; silver threads flashed in the moonlight. Checking that I had the correct knives, I extinguished the lantern and left.

A wind had come up from the east, dragging dark clouds across the moon, so shadows merged then broke then merged again as I walked the empty streets. By chance, I happened upon the Néfarit's latest victim: Wulfric's Rest was awash with the now familiar mix of blood and fluids. I paused only to take a sample and to fit the location into my plan. I decided it would be simplest to start at the farthest edge and then spiral inwards. Old Man's Way was halfway between the two attacks nearest the city walls, so I began there.

Old Man's Way is a long and narrow street with few turns but many corners, formed by buildings jutting out irregularly. It was easy to find a hiding place from which to observe passers-by. There I waited, while an hour passed. The street itself was quiet, though a background murmur of city noise rose and fell from nowhere in particular. Whenever someone passed, their footsteps rang out sharply, echoing off the walls.

The first three were useless – too strong, or else rich enough that their disappearance would be noticed. A light rain began to fall. Eventually, a fourth appeared: old and poor, a man of fifty or so, walking slowly towards the alcove where I stood. He seemed lost in thought, or perhaps concentrating on the effort required to move his tired limbs, and as he passed me, noticed nothing. I slipped off my cloak.

The rain masked the sound of our brief struggle; I took him from behind, one hand over his mouth, the other opening his jugular with the killing knife. Before he could react, I had him pinned to the ground with one knee, his face pressed against the wet cobbles while I finished the job. The street was still empty so I worked quickly, opening up arteries, cutting into organs, separating joints, and, finally, extracting the *esperius* with a spell normally used for placing substances in a vacuum flask. I spread as much of the body's fluids as I could across the walls and street, before dragging the body ten yards west and leaving it hidden between two houses.

I had been lucky. No one had seen us and the light drizzle's constant burble submerged all noise. I walked back to the Tower, avoiding busy streets and keeping the knives hidden under my cloak. Once inside, I could contain my excitement no longer. I paced around my study until morning, brewing pot after pot of coffee and embellishing my map with various plans, depending on where the Néfarit struck next. I had no idea whether this would work, but at last I was doing something. Already I felt triumphant.

It was several days before I knew it was working. Each night, I searched for the Néfarit's victim and then chose my own, spreading their blood across the street that best fit my plan, drawing the Néfarit into a spiral that would lead us both to the heart of the city: Conjuror's Square, at the foot of the Mages' Tower.

At first all went well. In a city like Gerwaen it is never hard to find vagrants, beggars, or drunks, easily subdued and seldom missed. But by the fourth night, there was a sharper edge to the city's mood: a few more militiamen poking about and fewer people on the streets. This was no great hindrance, however. I soon found the site of the Néfarit's latest killing: to my great satisfaction it was on Robin Street, one of three possible locations that fit perfectly into the sequence. The Néfarit had joined the dance.

I made my way to Candle Street, an alley so hostile that

few militiamen are brave enough to enter. There I caught a young boy – some kind of burglar, I suspect, given the tools he wore under his shirt. He was swiftly killed and opened up, and I was away before anyone could have seen me.

The following afternoon, for the first time, André spoke to me of matters other than food. He mentioned the series of ghastly murders that had the city quaking in fear, and hoped that I was taking appropriate precautions.

‘I do not wish to frighten you, Madame,’ he said, ‘but a lady alone in a city like this must always be careful. If you wish, I could arrange a bodyguard – very discreet and Anjevi, of course.’

I expressed gratitude, but assured him that I was staying with friends. He seemed relieved and returned to our usual business of pastries and tea. But it was too late: he had spoken of death and the food now seemed stale and dry. André’s coffee house had been a haven from the stupid filthy city beyond its door. Now that illusion was gone – and with it the illusion that I could leave my work outside. With an inward grimace, I brought the conversation back to these ‘ghastly murders’, hoping to learn how much the militia knew.

It appeared they knew very little. Three of the bodies had been found and reported; the second (a fat drunk I had killed on Tin Street) had turned out to be a wealthy merchant. Just my luck that he should dress like a labourer. His death, and the unusual mutilation of his corpse, had led to the doubling of the militia’s patrols, and already there was talk in some circles of a Soul Stealer abroad in the city.

It amused me that it was my own work that had at last alerted the city to the Néfarit’s presence. On the other hand, it also highlighted an unsolved mystery. My victims had caused talk of a Soul Stealer due to the appearance of the corpses, as it is fairly well known that a Soul Stealer leaves its victims turned inside out. Yet the real Néfarit's killings had left no trace of a body, merely fluids – fluids that could only have been released by the process of everting the body. Where then were the rest of the victims' remains?

I pondered this as I walked back through the New Quarter to the Tower, passing extravagantly dressed merchants and their stupid wives. The configuration of the fluids suggested that the corpses had been dragged some distance. But then there was nothing: no body, and nowhere to hide one.

The mystery remained unsolved until I first saw the creature at work.

It was on the sixth night. My own work had become more difficult since the discovery of the merchant's body. I now had to keep to my mapped-out plan precisely, even if this meant killing on a busier street. It was reassuring, however, to see the Néfarit also killing according to plan. Each night, we both came closer and closer to Conjuror's Square.

Just before midnight, I found my subject in a narrow alley in the Old Quarter: a child, small and frail, sleeping beneath a dirty, neglected shrine to Saint Meredith. An orphan, I assumed, weak from hunger and despair. I covered her face with my hand until she stopped breathing. Then I bundled her up and carried her to the chosen corner. For a moment, I hesitated over the tiny, delicate corpse. Soft lips, eyes like ice. Such perfect little fingers. But it was late and the moon was bright; I unsheathed my knives and began.

The body was so small, it required greater precision than usual. I leaned in close and worked with care, like André preparing one of his magnificent pastries. When it was over, I wiped my hands on her rags and stood to leave. But something made me pause.

I had unfolded her like a flower, yet still she was no larger than a house cat, shining in the moonlight. Before I knew what I was doing, I had bent down and taken her in my arms. She weighed almost nothing. I wrapped her in my cloak and hurried away, shivering.

At the end of Fletcher's Street, my boot slid on something and I nearly fell. It was blood, smeared across the cobbles in a wide stripe. For a moment, I felt dizzy, unable to make sense of where I was or what was happening. Then my mind cleared and I remembered the map on the wall of my room in the black Tower. There were two possible locations for the Néfarit to kill that night, and one was around the corner in Ware's Way. From the smell and viscosity, the creature had struck mere minutes before. I stood very still, listening. A soft sound came from nearby: a slow, moist scraping. When it stopped, I held my breath. And in the darkness some ten yards away, I began to sense movement.

He was struggling to lift the corpse on to the back of a large wooden handcart. He must have dragged it there on a piece of sack-cloth. But hauling a slippery, man-sized mound of gore onto that cart required even greater strength, and his breathing grew loud and harsh as he wrestled it on board. When it was over he paused, leaning on one wheel of the cart, until he was ready to start pulling the cart away.

I followed carefully, my own night's work held close to my chest. The Néfarit moved down Porter Street and Dart Lane. At the edge of Berin Court, he waited until clouds covered the moon before quickly crossing the open square. But not quick enough: for one brief moment, the moon broke through and bathed the scene in its cool grey light.

A short, broad-shouldered man, balding and pale. Hair limp and untended, with a few weeks' beard. His clothes looked moderately expensive, but filthy and torn. Even from that distance, I could see his face was covered in sweat, his eyes wide. Then the clouds closed in once more and all was silhouettes and shadows.

This was not what I had expected. I followed him across the square and into the Artisan's Quarter, guided by the rolling clatter of the cart, until at last he passed through an open arch in a low brick wall on Leech Street and came to a stop. A painted yew beside the entrance identified it as a physician's residence. I waited a few more minutes before making my way to the side of the building.

I could have used a *vigilis* spell to see past the walls but I was wary of alerting the Néfarit to my presence. Little is known about their senses, but it seems feasible that a creature of such power might detect nearby magical activity. Instead, I crept quietly around the walls until I found a small barred window near the ground. The window was only six inches tall and black with grime. The frustration was so great I almost cursed out loud. But then I noticed a tiny crack in the thick, uneven glass. Kneeling close to the ground, I pressed my ear to the fracture. A strange vibration came from within, and a scent: dark and sour and sweet. The smell of death.

There is an old witches' trick I learned in Carnea – a minor charm called *tlísh.* I learned it from a woman who wore a silver moon around her neck; she claimed she was taught it by the tiny Tláthi, who live in trees, wear clothing made from leaves and cast their spells with flower petals and pollen dust. I didn't believe her story but her cantrip works and is almost impossible to detect. Most magic weaves the threads of the world in complex knots, easy enough to see when you know what to look for. Wards usually work by preventing these twisted patterns of energy from moving through the web. But the *tlísh* merely brushes against a single thread, leaving an imprint so faint it can barely be distinguished from the normal impressions of life and time. And yet there it remains, linking that thread to the one who left their mark, allowing them to follow as it travels through the world.

I stilled my mind and listened. At first there was the usual background murmur of the city at night: distant voices, footsteps, cart wheels and boats all blending into a steady rustling noise. Then I heard what I was hoping for: the hum of a fly – of many flies – moving around the courtyard where the cart and its bloody cargo had gone. I stayed with that sound, searching outward, until I found an eager, hungry buzz moving up the street towards me: a single fly following its own trail of scent to the feast. I lifted the bundle I had carried since Saint Meredith's shrine, unwrapping my cloak to reveal the everted child; I held her up like an offering. Then I waited. The fly paused, circled, and then came closer, drawn by this more immediate smell of blood. I let it land and begin to feed, then leaned in and whispered the words the Carnean witch had taught me, so close my breath disturbed the fly's twitching wings. Unsettled, it rose and flew away, resuming its journey to the larger bloody mess on the other side of the wall. And with it went my *tlísh* – the subtle pressure of a whispering breath on a fly's wings – and I followed with my senses.

Flickering light and lurching shadows, vibrations in the air, the smell of blood and shit nearby and, farther, something deeper and richer: decay. So much decay.

The fly paused briefly to taste a puddle of blood on the ground, and then carried on towards that powerful stench:

through a gap in the wall, following the sound of a figure dragging the body downstairs to a cellar. The space around the fly opened up and it circled wide around the room, sampling the powerful smells. Below, lying on the floor, were many rotting corpses. Through the fly's subtle senses, I recognised some of them from the samples I had kept over the past two weeks. There: the killing on Cob Street. And there: the alley off Saint Nicholas Street. The oldest bodies were already crawling with maggots; the freshest were busy with flies. So intoxicated was my tiny spy from this soup of smells that it was difficult to sense anything else. Only once it had settled to feed did I become aware of something moving around the room.

This was the man I had seen on Berin Court. He seemed to be going from body to body, kneeling beside each for a few minutes, speaking. The fly had no idea what he was saying, of course – only the vaguest sense of noise coming from his hulking form. But I was reminded of a sickhouse matron moving from patient to patient with comforting words, or perhaps a mother saying goodnight to her children. Then he lowered himself and lay upon the floor, among the dead, among the blood and ruptured organs, the maggots and the flies. After a while, I assumed he had fallen asleep. I let go of the thread that bound me to the *tlísh* and was abruptly returned to my own surroundings: the cold night air, the empty street, a heavy open silence after the dense hum of that filthy, crawling cellar.

For a moment, I thought I would retch. But I slowed my breathing and waited until I was ready to move. Then I pressed my small wet bundle to my chest and left. I was not ready to confront him yet: not here, on his home ground. First I must set my trap.

*

That night, I dreamed I was a child again, held in my mother's arms. Her surrounding me, warm and strong and unafraid. Carried through thick sunlight. Sweet-smelling skin. Murmuring voices. I pressed close, breathed into her neck. Alive. Alive. All alive.

I awoke mid-morning. Beside me lay the child I had opened up. It was still wrapped in my cloak, stiff with drying blood. I stared at the body for a long time before rising to work.

I wet the blood on my hands and used it to mark my map of the city: Saint Meredith's shrine, Fletcher's Street. The summoning was complete. The pattern of our killings had become entwined, weaving us closer and closer. Last night, we each had two possible locations. Tonight there was only one – the same for us both. And I, at least, would be ready.

I had been constructing this spell for years, since first reading Berno's *Necronomicon*. At its heart is a Diogesti grasping weave that takes hold of a dying man's *ánima* and keeps it from slipping away while the body is healed. The effect only lasts for a short time before it is overwhelmed by the pull of either life or death. But with a creature immune to dying this may not apply, and in any case, I had strengthened the weave with an equation of my own and surrounded it with layered wards to prevent interference.

From Berno's account, it seemed clear that Néfarit drew *ánima* out of their victims to combine with their own. This process, much like the Diogesti grasping spell, must involve direct contact between the *ánima* of both sides – and, I reasoned, offered an opportunity to take control and reverse the flow. This, then, was my plan: I would allow it to reach for my spirit and, at the moment of contact, I would unleash my spell.

I spent the afternoon preparing a trap at the base of the Tower: an invisible cage of warding spells, strengthened by the power of those ancient walls. Even if my modified Diogesti weave failed, the Néfarit would be caught. I could bring it upstairs to my room and unravel its secrets just as Berno had done centuries before in Goranteum.

When all was ready, I washed and dressed in fresh clean clothes: a blue silk gown from Trubidore embroidered with pale roses, white skirts beneath, a light grey cloak and soft fawn shoes. Suddenly ravenous, I walked to the Lily for a late breakfast. The streets were soaked in afternoon sun and the air smelled of spring. I was exultant.

When I entered the Lily, André actually blushed. He brought me steaming chocolate and fresh pastries and complimented my outfit and my radiant smile. For an hour or so, there was no Néfarit, no ugly murders terrorising the city, no rumours of cults or demons at large. I sat by a west-facing window, completely surrounded by light, and listened to André's gentle admiration. Sugar dust filled the room like incense. I closed my eyes and breathed.

At night the square was usually empty: the Tower's reputation was enough to keep most people away once the sun went down. Especially now, with a gruesome killer at work in the city. The sun had already disappeared below the Western Road by the time I reached the square and even the conjurers were packing away their fire-sticks and heading home. As I approached the tower door, they watched me with a mixture of envy and fear. Then I spoke the *isturia* and slipped into the familiar gloom of those enchanted walls.

In my room, I removed the silk gown and put on work clothes. I checked my wards and caging weaves and set a slow lamp burning inside the door. Then, with a final glance at my map of the city – black charcoal and dried blood – I turned to go.

The dead child still lay on my bed.

Outside, it was very dark. Clouds were closing in and the rising moon was hidden behind a dense screen of chimney smoke. I stood against the tower wall while my eyes adjusted enough to see across the square. For two weeks we had drawn a pattern of blood across the city, leading us both here: a place of strength, surrounded by protective wards, the trap set with me as bait. Now all I could do was wait.

The night grew cold. The wind had turned to a north-westerly, bringing a sharp chill from the sea. Time passed.

When obliged to wait, I am in the habit of silently reciting the 99 Enchantments of Mara, tracing the graceful equations with my mind, one after another, as their complexity and subtlety grow. But that evening I needed to remain alert, all attention on my surroundings. And so instead I devised an equation of my own. I calculated the shape and dimensions of the square before me: the arcades, alleys and doorways at its edge – noting every gutter and rail and discarded bucket, until I was sure I would notice any change, however small. This occupied me until a little after midnight, when a frightened cat jumped down from a window and sprinted across the square. All at once my heart raced and I began to shiver. The black sky wheeled overhead, heavy and close.

I swore and muttered a calming cantrip my master had taught me as a child. There was no magic in it – just a simple mind trick – but it settled me. My planning was sound. I need only wait.

Other interruptions came and went: a singing drunk, night

traders hurrying home, three nervous militiamen, reluctant to cross the open square. They called over to me, 'All well?' 'All well,' I replied, and it was true. My calm was now unshakeable. Satisfied, they scurried away and it was quiet once more.

And then he was there: standing at the end of Baker's Lane, at the farthest edge of the square, his cart behind him. He stood very still. Even at that distance, I could tell he was staring straight at me. For a long time, neither of us moved.

Rain began to fall. My breath was a thin cloud. He still hadn't moved, as though he were waiting for something. But it made no sense. I knew my map had worked: he *needed* to kill, right here in the square. The urge would be irresistible.

'Come on,' I hissed. 'What's stopping you?' The shadows around me twitched and shivered in the rain.

Something was wrong. I gathered what I could of my readied spells, fingers moving in the air, tugging on the carefully woven threads to bring them with me. Then I began to walk towards him, slowly at first but soon quickening to a run. Still he didn't move.

Yards away from him, I completed my spells. The trap closed. He responded at last, flinching and raising a hand as if to block a blow. But it was too late – he was caught. I had bound him with power and now he was helpless. Triumphant, I lit a *parias* to see him clearly for the first time.

As the light enveloped him, he cowered like an animal. The same man I had seen the night before: ragged clothes, tangled beard, covered in filth and stinking of decay. He looked up at me in desperation; at first I thought it was simply fear, but then I saw the yearning – terrifying loneliness and a spark of hope in his eyes, as if I were there to rescue him. Berno had described the Néfarit with something close to awe, yet it was difficult to imagine this pathetic creature impressing the old necromancer of Goranteum. Disappointed, I resolved to take the Néfarit to my room in the Tower, where I could study it at leisure.

I led my captive across the square, pulling on the spells that bound him. He stumbled along, whimpering. It had all been so easy. I congratulated myself on my thorough planning and sophisticated magic, allowed myself to imagine that I may at last have found the key.

Halfway across the square, I stopped us both. The bearded man fell to his knees and began to cry. I held the *parias* over him and looked again, more closely. The cobbles beneath him shone wet and bright in the light of my spell. He cast no shadow.

This was not the Néfarit. The creature was not inside this ruined sobbing fool: it was in his shadow. And that shadow was outside my trap. It had already left its host to go hunting.

With a single motion, I drew a knife from my belt and across the man's throat, so hard it clattered against the spine. He fell back to the ground gurgling like a broken drain. Then I lifted the *parias* high and stared out beyond the edge of its light, turning a circle to look in every direction, trying to distinguish one shadow from the rest. But everything was shadow, shifting and twisting as the glowing *parias* moved. It could be anywhere.

I was backing towards the Tower, fighting down panic. My intricate magical trap was abandoned behind me, triggered too soon, its power sizzling to nothing in a spreading pool of blood. All thoughts of capture were gone: I was fighting to survive.

A huge black shape emerged from the darkness: the Tower. I was almost at the door. For a moment I fumbled – lowering the *parias* to see the door, trying to speak the *isturia* that would open the door, reaching to push the door – and at that moment I saw it, or felt it, or simply realised what it was doing: hiding in my own shadow, that inescapable darkness that stretched behind me, matching my movements step for step until it was ready to strike. There at the threshold, I felt it surge like a wave up my long dark trail, felt its sweet soft touch, infiltrating my body and mind, searching for *ánima*, my soul, my centre, life itself.

I did not want to die. I must not die. That is all I have ever tried to do: escape from death, that disgusting betrayal. I must never die. I will not die.

Pushing back the fear, I remembered: this was what I had planned for all along.

I extinguished the *parias*. There was no need for light now. Drawing on the power around me – from the Tower and what remained of the wards I had laid that afternoon – I summoned my modified Diogesti weave. I would wait until the Néfarit's *ánima* touched my own and then launch my counter-attack, reversing the flow to merge its immortal spirit with mine. The creature was powerful – its strength shook the air around us like a roar – but I had studied Berno's investigations, followed the Néfarit's trail for years, and performed countless experiments on *ánima*. I knew that my spell would work.

The moment the weave was cast I was instantly aware of all life – all *ánima* – across the entire square: my own, like a burning pillar of flame; the fading embers of the man without a shadow; tiny flickering insects, whirling through the air like sparks. But nothing else. Where the Néfarit should have been there was nothing: no *ánima,* no life, no spirit nor soul. Berno had been mistaken. The Néfarit was not immortal: it was not alive at all. It was nothing more than an endless, insatiable hunger for life.

There was a sickening moment of vertigo – of pure terror. I could feel myself being pulled into a void. All that I was and had ever been was slipping away. My spell was useless.

In that final moment I clung to life, fought for life, yearned for life: these feelings, these thoughts, this flow of time, the now. I wanted the rain, the biting cold, the pain in my hands and skull, the churn in my belly, the scream that filled my mouth and my ears. This agony, even this sickening awful terror was better – infinitely better – than that unmoving silent nothing.

And then the world filled with light.

At first, I did not know what had happened. Even now I am not entirely sure. But this is what I think I must have done.

Instinctively, I had reached for a spell to drive away the dark – the first spell I ever learned: *parias*. Arto of Narea showed me how to cast it long ago, while I recovered from a particularly long winter illness. I would practise it in bed at night, flicking sparks of light like fireflies, like fierce bright secrets. Later, after he was burned, I would repeat the words and gestures silently in my mind, over and over, calling up lights that no one else could see. Sometimes I imagined a light so vast and bright it could erase the entire world. *Parias parias parias.*

And so, as the Néfarit touched my *ánima* and began to draw it forth, I became once more that frightened young girl and cast *parias* – from the centre of my soul and with all the strength I could summon. For an instant I shone like the sun. The square was cleansed of shadows. The Néfarit was gone.

When it was over I fell to my knees, eyes streaming, blind. I heard shouting: people reacting to the explosion of light, running to the scene. Somehow I spoke the *isturia* and crawled inside, feeling my way in the dark. There was the sound of the door closing, then a heavy silence and my own voice moaning, sobbing, as I half crawled, half stumbled upstairs to my room. I felt the doorway, the wall, tripped over the table, vessels crashing on the floor. I bruised my shin on a chair, cut myself on something sharp. And then I collapsed on the bed and for a long time felt nothing at all.

I must have slept for days. When I awoke at last, thirsty and weak, I still could not see. I was lying curled around the child I had killed by Saint Meredith's shrine.

I climbed down to the floor and felt my way to the bench for a jug of water and half a loaf of stale bread, ate and drank and was promptly sick on the floor. Shivering, I made it back to the bed, pushed the corpse away and fell asleep.

More time passed: drifting in and out of sleep, occasionally eating or sipping water, wondering whether it was day or night. At some point, I remember carrying the child's body to the fireplace, surrounding it with kindling and igniting a *parens* spell that would turn it to ash in minutes. The stench was thick and vile. As it burned, I spat, repeatedly, into the flames: *hiss hiss hiss.*

Slowly, my sight began to return – a gradual thinning of the darkness, a vague sense of light.

And I was alive. I was alive.

On the fourth day, I washed and dressed as best I could in the half-light. The blue silk dress and grey cloak. I brushed my fingers over the embroidered flowers and leaves, buried my nose in the folds of the skirt and breathed in the scent of dry cotton. There was something else, too: a residual memory of the corpse I incinerated, in the air and on everything in the room. It took a moment to remember the last cantrip my master taught me all those years before, soon after my parents died. A simple cleaning spell. I spoke the words slowly, like a lullaby, feeling my clothes and shoes and hair and skin grow light and fresh.

At the Lily, André left his bench to take me by the hand and lead me to my usual seat, almost whispering my name. The smell of chocolate was overpowering. He fussed over me like a kindly uncle, or even a suitor. He was relieved to see me, concerned by my absence, my pale, thin appearance, the dark rings around my eyes. Had I seen the lightning in Conjurors' Square several nights ago? Scared him out of his wits – even from the other side of Gerwaen. Such strange days these are, but at least there had been no more grisly murders since that night; had the city had been freed from its torment at last? He worried about me so! Please – another pastry, Madame, compliments of the house. So thin!

I let the sugar melt on my tongue, watching André bustle about through a curtain of shadows. Soon I will leave the city. I will visit André again, once or twice, building my strength on chocolate and cakes. He will feed me, praise me, offer even more. And soon it will all taste like dust in my mouth and I will leave. Perhaps, by then, the shadows will have left my eyes and I will see clearly. Or perhaps this is my world now: a world of half-light and darkness.

There are rumours of a ruined temple near Narea where a necromantic cult once raised people from the dead. And somewhere in Trubidore, I have heard it said, an immortal is hiding.

BERNARD BECKETT

Bernard Beckett is a father, high-school teacher and occasional writer. His twelve books to date have ranged from coming-of-age novels to speculative sci-fi, a piece of non-fiction and a clumsy attempt at literature.

The Armillary

On nights like this, when the mountain air was clean and sharp to the touch, and the skies sparkled clear, her father would not be seen. She knew better than to call him down to share their evening meal, or to make her way up the ancient stone stairway and knock gently on the wooden trapdoor. He would be statue-still – she could picture it – hunched over the eyepiece of his telescope, lost in the comfort of distance. Or he would be leaning back in the old armchair they had together dragged to its final resting place, stopping every three steps to invent ever-more-colourful curses. His head would be snapped back and his mouth would be open, galaxies reflected in the sheen of his unblinking eyes. The last strands of his hair would have slipped unselfconsciously from his scaled scalp, a dirty white river cascading from temple to jaw. More than once a visitor had thought him dead. Not departed, she would explain – just drunk. Drunk on all the potions she had learned of on his knee; drunk on infinity, order, mathematics and speculation. There would be an old blanket wrapped around his diminished frame, for there was no roof above him, only the distant sky, calling his name.

'But isn't it just the same, night after night?' a younger self had asked him. 'Don't you get tired of that?'

'Yes,' he had replied, nodding in agreement not with her,

but with the universe itself. 'It is the same. Isn't that the most beautiful thing you can imagine?'

She'd smiled then, the beginning of a truce that would last for decades. He did not understand her poetry, and she did not understand his. But poetry it was, they each understood that much, and until that night, it was enough.

He screamed. The sound was so strange and unexpected that she stepped back without thinking, hands out and open, ready. The small chisel she was holding clattered to the floor. Her heart knew first – it was always the way – and stopped for a moment, leaving gaps in her warm swirling blood, pockets of iciness. It came again, a muffled ululation from above, cycling to quietness and then rising in anguish, settling finally into a protracted moan. She moved quickly once she understood. Not the detail, but the pain. Somewhere, high above her, her father was in pain.

She arrived breathless. She had long anticipated this moment, when her rudimentary first-aid skills would prove inadequate. Her father was aged and this grim meeting had the weight of the inevitable. She would have to call on a friend in the valley to help her bring the body down. It would be an awkward task, bruising and undignified, but she would do it. She was that type of daughter. But it would not be today.

Today he stood, head back, howling at a moonless sky.

'What is it?' She placed her hand on his shoulder, felt the tired rise to his neck, the shrunken muscles that had once been strong, which she had so often massaged back to movement after a long night of gazing.

He turned slowly, his eyes thick and wet, flickering his lack of understanding, as if this were a stranger standing before him. As if everything was strange. He shook his head, slowly, vainly trying to dislodge a lifetime of memories.

'It is everything,' he whispered. 'It is everything.'

She took his bony hands in hers and waited. He would speak more when he was ready. It was a solitary life they had chosen, filled with silences. Behind him, on his narrow desk, his beloved armillary sphere shone in the low light of his lamp. He would switch the light off when gazing, reluctantly engaging its services only to scribble spidery notes across the thickening pages of his journals. Normally such a tidy space, today the desktop was strewn with papers, as if ransacked by a celestial thief, determined to steal back the details of the sky's endless dancing.

'It is broken,' the old man intoned. 'For months I have suspected this, but now I am certain. It is broken.'

'What is broken, Papa?' She let his hands drop and stepped back, settled into his waterproof beanbag, felt its stuffing rustle beneath her. He could take his seat or remain standing. Whichever served his story best. He chose to stand. A final act of resistance.

'Everything.' He cleared his throat, a sound that had been her close companion since childhood. This is how the tales always started. 'I do not need to tell you the story of the armillary,' he began, 'for you have heard it many times.'

But never with these tears in his eyes. She looked again at the curious machine: a perfect working model of those the ancients had used to make sense of the Ptolemaic system, spheres within spheres, twisting and turning, made ever more complex as it morphed to accommodate each new observation. She knew of the story that followed it: the Copernican revolution that put the earth in its proper place, and then the parade of giants – Galileo, Newton, Kepler, Brahe. William of Ockham, too, and the dream of enlightenment, when for a time there flourished a deep belief in the unifying principles of the simplicity of existence.

Her father was a fair-minded man, this his only religion. He had taken her solemnly through the turmoil of the 20th and 21st centuries. He had tried in vain to impart the quantum mysteries to her, but to his frustration she had seen not a problem to be solved but a dance to be celebrated. 'Ah,' he had gently mocked her then, 'I fear you are to become a poet and I will wither alone in my old age, unattended.'

But she had stayed, even after her mother left. That, too, lay undiscussed, not a gift but a simple decision. She loved the mountains and the air that surrounded them. She did not crave the city as her mother did. Quiet suited her.

He had taught her all he could of the missteps along the way, of the dalliance with string theory – an armillary built not from metal but equations, he had called it, creaking just as loudly under the weight of hubris. Of the data age that followed, the doomed attempt to compute the way to understanding, and then, as the 21st century drew to a close, the foolish optimism of those who hoped to banish time to the poetic realm.

But through all of this her father's people had kept the faith, seeking always the next reduction, the next insight on the road to unity. He had achieved brief fame twenty years before, when his observations of a distant galaxy led him to propose a new way of thinking about information, a system that, like so many before it, had flowered briefly before withering beneath the universe's arid gaze.

'You watch the stars to see them dance,' she liked to tease.

'No,' he would reply, his eyes alight with sparkling certainty, 'I watch them so that I might better understand the illusion of dancing.'

She loved him for his simple faith, for the solidity it offered her, a place in which she could tether her airy self; there was grace to be found in their nocturnal routines, he of the heavens and the stars that prickled them, she scratching her poetic marks into leather in the stony world below. But not tonight. Tonight, he quivered. Never before had this man, the last remaining bulwark between her and death, appeared so temporary.

'I have seen it,' he finally told her, as if this statement alone was enough.

She nodded, and waited. 'Seen what?'

'You know.'

'I don't,' she said gently. She could sense his fragility, how far he was from being ready for a playful argument. 'Show me.'

He straightened. 'Oh, little one,' he muttered, shaking his head and moving across to the telescope. 'Now you should show an interest? Now?'

His hands moved deftly across the telescope, young again, ripe with purpose. He bent to the eyepiece, nodded at the sights she had never been able to decipher.

'Yes. It is still there. There is no denying it. Please.' He straightened and turned to her, resisting the next wave of tears. 'Promise this one thing. Promise me you will not be smug with me.'

The most foolish of things to have asked, and any other night she would have let him know it. What smugness there was in this home belonged to him. He with the depth of his learning and the steadiness of his faith, his way of placing propositions before her like lumps of granite. 'If you do not like what you hear, then you must smash your way through it,' he liked to say. 'This is the only method.'

She preferred not to smash but to chip, to reshape. This, in the end, was their argument.

'I promise.'

He offered a watery smile and beckoned her towards the eyepiece. The telescope was twice her height, and when the weather turned it would be wound back in and pushed along tracks into storage. She remembered the long days they had spent installing it, she and her mother playing labourers to their father's slow midwifery. She bent now to the eyepiece, prepared for the sight that always greeted her – that of swirling confusion. She had tried communicating the sensation when she was younger, but it had encouraged him only to lengthen his explanations, certain that in time detail would accrete to understanding. After that, she had grown accustomed to lying.

The vision before was a familiar one: the white swirl of distant stars. To her it might have been any imagining of light; to him it formed a pattern as familiar as the face of his only child. But tonight, the pattern refused to settle.

'Do you see it?'

'What am I looking for?'

'Disorder.'

'Papa, disorder is all I ever see.'

'Look to the top left quadrant.' She was a child again, he with his hand on her shoulder, still hopeful that her feet might fall in the pattern already trodden. 'Now look for the three brightest stars, do you see them?'

She nodded. The triangle they formed was scalene, beautiful in its irregularity.

'Now put those at the centre of your view and let your vision pull back, see the whiteness all about them, the cloud in which they shine. Let your focus soften, and tell me what you notice.'

She did as she was told, eager to please him, as she had always been. She saw the gentle spiralling of whiteness, the very pattern she had endlessly painted as a child, as a way of serving mother and father both. She looked for details worthy of conveying.

'It has a beautiful tail,' she whispered. 'Three separate strands, dancing like seaweed on the tide.'

'Three.' He nodded. 'And at the third tail, the longest of them, see what glitters there. Four stars, faint but perfectly aligned, as if pointing their finger to the answer.'

'What answer, Papa?' She could not see them. Her eyes were not trained in this. For her, the faint lights smudged into the greater picture.

He took her head in his hands, palms to either temple, and eased her back from the telescope. She turned to face him.

'That there is no answer,' he replied. He looked to the ground between them and lowered himself back into his armchair. 'Those stars, they cannot be there. They are not possible.'

He waited for her to speak. She knew better.

'You promised me you would not be smug,' he said.

'I didn't speak.'

'There is smugness in your silence.'

'Perhaps you are mistaken,' she offered.

He shook his head with heavy certainty. 'It is not the first time, and I am not the only one to have noticed. There is no known system of equations that explains how those stars appear to us. We cannot fit them within our models of gravity, nor of momentum, nor of energy. It is as if they exist simply to tell us we are wrong. You know what this must mean, don't you?'

She nodded, but it was guesswork.

'Tell me then,' he challenged. 'Tell me what it means.'

'That your models are inadequate. That there is something you are missing. That a new revolution awaits us. Papa, why be downcast? You have always said to me that this is how knowledge proceeds, by way of revolutions.'

It was strange, the way she had always argued with him but had never wanted to see him carry the weight of being wrong.

'No,' he replied, his jaw now set. 'Let another fool step forward and say, "The model is incomplete. Here is my solution. Here is my hope for simplicity, my puny bid for immortality." Let them add another layer of complexity and obscurity to their edifice and call it truth. I am finished with this. I am finished with the gods quietly mocking me. The universe will never yield up its secrets to us. This is not its nature.'

'Perhaps not to you,' she countered. 'But you can never know –'

'All my life I have dreamed of making order of a capricious existence,' he told her. 'All my life I have believed in the task. Always the unifying theory, always the deeper metaphor, just beyond our horizon. Taking careful aim at a target that never existed. And now, at this fine age, I am left with nothing.'

He reached out and swept the armillary to the floor. There was a loud metallic crash, sharpened by echoes, and the smaller sound of something breaking within. Any other person she would have tried to shake out of their misery, to offer them perspective. But this was her father, and science his only vantage point. She wrapped her arms around him and let him weep.

'You never believed it anyway, did you?' he finally asked her. 'How have you done that? How have you lived with the knowledge there is no truth?'

'We never said that, Papa.' She said it gently, the 'we', let it land without accusation.

'I heard you say it a thousand times.' His voice was tinged with resentment.

'Yes, you heard it,' she conceded. 'But we never said it. That is how it has always been with us.'

He said nothing, just tightened his eyes. 'But without

knowledge, there exists no line between sanity and insanity.' She recognised the quote, one of his heroes – she couldn't place which. But, as was so often the case, her father's hero had seen only the details.

He opened his eyes. They burned with a new intensity. 'You don't understand, my little butterfly. You never have. This is all we have ever had to pin our promises of progress to, this possibility of knowledge. But now we know too much. Now we know such knowledge is impossible. How do you do that? How do you live in such ignorance?'

She shrugged. 'By not using such a word, when *mystery* is the better fit.'

He stood then. He had never accepted her platitudes before. 'No, that is too simple a response. Mystery. What is this thing you call mystery, if not the very opposite of all I have ever believed in? What of all of those who have gone before, adding to this sum total of our knowing? What of my modest aim to make my contribution? What of the powers we have wrought from this world, the joys we have prolonged, the problems we have solved? Are they really to amount to nothing more than the fairy dust of your mysteries?'

In this mood there was no arguing with him. Let him blow himself out like a mountain storm. The morning would dawn all the clearer for it.

'It is not that we lose our sense of knowledge. You know that, don't you? It is that we lose our sense of even the probability of an event occurring. Tonight, when I go to bed, I can no longer speak properly of my expectation that the sun will rise in the east tomorrow. How can you live with such uncertainty?'

'But it will rise, Papa. The sun has no interest in the structure of our arguments. She is there when we turn to her. That is how it is.'

'But you cannot know it. Not any longer.'

'But I can believe it. And that has always been enough for me.'

'No.' He shook his head wildly. Always, arguments enlivened him. 'For without our laws, you have no right to believe in anything. Without regularity, to what can we possibly turn, when sorting one belief from another?'

The challenge hung between them, sharpening the air. She had longed to say this to him, but never before had he let her this close.

'This.' She stooped and picked up the dented armillary. She held it up so that it floated between them, a third star in their conflicted constellation.

'That is all you have?' he scoffed. 'The impossible compromises of a mind too stubborn to see the truth?'

'Do not look at the object, Father. Look at your own reflection.'

For the polished sides, even in the dim lamplight, provided a distorted shuddering of their faces.

'See the pain there, Father. See what harm it does you, not to believe. That is the answer. It always has been. We believe not because of the intellectual integrity of our system, but because of the pain it eases. I believe the sun will rise in the east tomorrow, because that is the belief that offers me the best comfort, within the constraints of the world as I experience it.'

'Even if it is a fiction?' he demanded.

She lowered the armillary and regarded her father's confusion.

'I don't know what is true and what is not,' she answered. 'It is enough to know that I am happy.'

She held him, and he held her too. High above them, unnoticed, the skies sparkled and laughed.

EMMA MARTIN

Emma Martin is the author of a short story collection, *Two Girls in a Boat*, the title story of which won the 2012 Commonwealth Short Story Prize.

In the Forest with Ludmila

I am walking along a corridor in the old apartment building. The place looks derelict, the floor uneven, green-grey paint flaking off the walls, but I can hear water coursing through the pipes that snake along the ceiling, and a clanging from somewhere below. It is clear to me which is the door, even though it is not numbered and is largely identical to the other doors. In the moment before I knock I want to turn back, want to stop my hand, which is already raising and clenching into a fist. In the same moment I remember it does not matter what I want. I am going to knock anyway.

I strike the door firmly enough, but the sound it makes is muted, and for a minute I allow myself to think that no one has heard. Then there is a rattling of locks and chains and some muffled cursing, and Mama appears. When she sees me, a sly look passes over her face.

'Oh, it's you,' she says.

She looks me up and down. I am wearing only a nightie, the faded blue one with the lace-trimmed pockets. A child's nightie. But then, my body is a child's body.

'Well don't just stand there. Come in.'

I follow Mama across the darkened hallway and into the living room, which is crammed with boxes and newspapers and what looks like an old washing-machine wringer. The radiator is spewing out heat and the curtains are half-drawn against the leaden sky.

'Where's my kiss?' Mama says, turning her cheek. I hesitate. She sees the hesitation, and also sees me see her see it. This happens in an instant – the blink of an eye, you might say, but Mama does not blink. I move to kiss her, but she brushes me aside.

'But of course, it isn't me you've come to see,' she says. 'Is it?'

The back of my neck prickles. Mama raises her eyebrows and walks over to the window, somehow avoiding tripping over any of the obstacles in her path – but then, she always was surprisingly agile. She leans against the windowsill, picks up a compact and begins daubing her face with chalky powder.

'It would be nice if you at least make yourself a bit useful while you're here,' she says. 'But that's not going to happen, is it, Anna? You're not going to *do* anything. You're going to observe everything with that veiled look on your face. Oh, look how cramped the apartment is with boxes and newspapers and what looks like an old washing-machine wringer, whatever could Mama be thinking, she clearly doesn't realise that's going to give the place an oppressive and vaguely ominous air, perhaps she should, I don't know, sort through all of that stuff and store it away neatly in one of the many capacious storage cupboards in this apartment. Oh, that's right. There are no storage cupboards in this apartment.'

My face feels hot. It is true we have never had much storage space. On top of that, the whole apartment seems to have shrunk. And there is clearly something wrong with the central heating. 'I'm sorry, Mama,' I say, though for what I am not quite sure.

'What's that?' says a voice from the corner. 'What did she say?'

It is Baba, my grandmother, hunched in her brown armchair, head resting against a patch of dirtied velvet several inches below the doily draped over the head rest. Her legs, too short to reach the ground, are resting on a stack of her motorsports magazines. I'd thought she was asleep, but she has been listening all along.

'She says she's come home for Ludmila's birthday,' says Mama.

Baba's eyes glint unpleasantly. 'Well, of course,' she says. 'She always does.'

One might think it impossible to hide in such cramped quarters, but Ludmila has her places. I find her under the table in the hallway. The hallway is not so much a passage as a small square antechamber. The table is semi-circular, pressed up against one wall. It has three spindle legs and is cloaked with an embroidered table cloth that hangs to the floor, but I am alert to a tell-tale bulge. I crouch down and tweak the cloth and there is an answering tweak back.

Underneath – I am small enough to fit – I wedge myself up against the wall, shunting Ludmila a little to one side. She pushes back with her whole weight, but she is lighter than I am and cannot displace me. Instead her bony shoulder digs into my arm. I wriggle against her until we arrive at an uncomfortable equilibrium. This is how it is when you are sisters.

'Have you brought me something for my birthday?' she says.

We are not gift-givers in this family, Mama too capricious and Baba too mean, but Ludmila's idea of birthdays is impervious to this reality, and every year she approaches hers with the same steadfast hope. I reach into my pocket.

'Here you are.' I hold out a leaf: orange, lightly speckled, with ragged edges. Ludmila takes it.

'Where did you get it?

There is a story Ludmila likes me to tell her, about a forest so vast you could walk for a year and never reach its end. It may seem to be deserted, but if you listen closely you will hear the hum of millions of tiny insects as they forage through decomposing leaves, the barely perceptible creak of branches as they grow, a bird on the wing, a spider monitoring its web for a tell-tale quiver, the hissing and buzzing and crackling and breathing of living things.

I study Ludmila's face as I talk. She is very fair and her eyes are blue, wide set, at once curious and cautious. She is listening intently, ready to correct me if my account deviates from previous accounts – 'But what about the rabbits? You said there were rabbits' – sensing, as all small children do, that it is only through constant repetition that the existence of things can be maintained.

The living-room door opens. I stop mid-sentence and hold my finger to my lips. Mama passes right by us, and though we cannot see her, we hear and also smell her, Mama's breath having always been sour and her armpits pungent. She goes into the kitchen. I hear the thud of a cupboard door, the clink of a glass. Baba is still in the living room listening to a game show. She has the volume turned up so loud the set is buzzing and the compeer's voice is distorted.

'It has hands but no arms. What's in the black box?'

'Oh, come on,' Baba shouts at the TV. 'That's too easy!'

'Are there wolves in the forest?' whispers Ludmila in my ear.

'There might be. Nobody knows for sure.'

I can not only hear but feel the water pipes belching under the floor. I pick away at a piece of parquet that has come unstuck, a diamond that slots into a circle of identical diamonds to form the spiked petals of a flower, which tessellates to cover the entire floor, with the exception of a cut-out square next to Mama's bedroom, rotted by the leaking bathtub of the apartment above and patched with vinyl.

'It has a face but no eyes,' says the compeer.

'It's a clock, you morons,' Baba shouts from the living room.

In the kitchen it sounds like Mama is throwing cutlery on the floor.

'Where are my mints?' says Baba. They are in her handbag usually. She sucks on them constantly, shedding a trail of wrappers as she moves around the apartment. I can hear her looking for them. 'Those little shits have stolen my mints.'

'Did you take them?' I whisper to Ludmila.

She shakes her head. I am not sure whether to believe her. It is true that taking Baba's mints would be not only reckless but pointless – they are so potent they strip the lining of the mouth and are effectively inedible to anyone but Baba – but then, Ludmila has the hoarding instinct of a squirrel.

'It's a clock!' says the compeer on the TV. There is laughter and thunderous applause.

'I knew it was a clock,' says Baba.

I hear her stand and walk heavily across the room, then the staticky boom and sudden silence of the TV being switched off. Beside me, Ludmila tenses. But Baba goes back to her chair and settles in for a nap. There is silence, too, from the kitchen, as if in switching off the TV Baba has also somehow muted Mama. We don't like it when she is quiet. When she is quiet, we never know what she is going to do next.

Ludmila and I are peering into the kitchen from the safety of the doorway. Mama is sitting at a table under a bulb that casts spasmodic light across the room. She is wearing a petticoat with sweat stains under the arms, her face powdered and lipsticked but her hair unbrushed. She has got out the ingredients for pancakes, has mixed milk with flour, but has left the half-made batter sitting on the bench, where it has hardened into a grim glue. On the table in front of her is a tumbler and the remains of a decanter of unidentifiable liquid – too dark for vodka, though Mama likes that too. She has a page of newspaper and is ripping it into a long strip, starting at one corner and spiralling towards the centre. She has been at this for some time, has shredded pages and pages, skeins of them bunched up around her ankles and snaking across the floor.

I've never been able to tell if Mama is beautiful. Her face is too familiar yet at the same time utterly strange. Those thick, dark eyebrows, those full lips, that square jaw. She is lean and muscular, with the flat chest of a dancer and short black hairs on her forearms which stand on end when she is alert.

'Mama,' says Ludmila in a small voice, 'when is it dinner time?'

Mama's face darkens.

'It will be dinner time when I say it's dinner time.'

Her fingers work away at the newsprint. She is ripping it very finely, such a thin strip, because the thinner it is, the longer you can make it. If she is not careful, it will break. The paper on the floor shifts and hisses.

'I'm hungry,' Ludmila says.

Mama's fingers freeze. The newspaper strip dangles in mid-air.

'I think someone needs to learn more patience,' she says quietly.

For a long moment no one moves. I am aware of everything at once: the heat, the pounding of my heart, the smell of my own sweat. Then, slowly, Ludmila begins to sidle into the kitchen. She has seen the bowl. Mama lays her paper on the table and it slithers to the floor. Ludmila is at the bench and stands on her tiptoes to look into the bowl. She glances at me. I should shake my head, warn her, but I cannot move at all. She is going to put her finger in the bowl.

She puts her finger in the bowl.

In one movement, her finger is in her mouth. In one movement, Mama is across the kitchen, slivers of paper fluttering behind her.

'No!' I cry, but of course it is too late.

Mama has already struck Ludmila – a hard blow to the side of the head – and Ludmila, not unused to being hit but on this occasion caught off-guard, staggers and falls backwards. The base of her skull hits the corner of the kitchen bench with a *crack*, and she collapses, limp, to the floor.

The snakes of paper go still. Mama freezes, arm still aloft. For half a minute, nothing happens. Ludmila does not move.

Then she opens her eyes. She lets out a soft moan.

'What are you looking at?' says Mama to me.

'Nothing.'

Blood starts to ooze from Ludmila's nose. She puts her hand to her face and looks at her fingers.

'Well, don't just stand there,' Mama says to me. 'Get a hanky!'

I find one in a drawer in Mama's room, white cotton with embroidered edges, sharp little cross stitches that turn out to be alive and wriggle and rearrange themselves as I watch. When I return, Mama is on the kitchen floor next to Ludmila. Ludmila is sitting up with both hands clasped around her nose. There is blood everywhere.

'Ludmila knows we were just playing,' says Mama. 'She's fine, aren't you, kitten?'

Ludmila looks at me, then Mama. She nods slowly.

I take the handkerchief and dab at Ludmila's face, then pincer my thumb and index finger around the bridge of her nose. Her pupils are round black pools, which I try to avoid looking into. The blood has a metallic smell.

'Trying to eat the mixture before I cooked it!'

I glance at the pancake bowl, smashed on the floor. Batter is splattered across the room, cut with shards of glass.

Mama puts her arm around Ludmila's shoulder and gives her a playful shake. 'But we won't let anything spoil your birthday, will we?' she says.

Ludmila does not reply.

Mama turns to me. 'Will we?' she says again. It is possible I hear in her voice a hint of doubt; but then her face rearranges itself into its impenetrable mask. I look at Ludmila, blood caked around her nose and matting her hair.

'No, Mama,' I say.

The handkerchief in my hand is drying stiffly, its stitches black and clustered like scabs around its hem.

Where the car has come from and how long we have been driving, I do not know. Mama is at the wheel, Baba next to her, their seat belts flapping loosely at their ears. Mama is still wearing her petticoat, but has added chandelier earrings and elbow-length gloves. To my knowledge, she does not have and has never had a driver's licence; she is steering erratically, clipping the wing mirrors of parked cars and frequently lurching across the centre line. As I watch, a cat crouches on the curb until the car is almost upon it, then takes off like a bullet across the road, its eyes crazed and desperate. There is a hollow thud.

Beside me in the back seat, Ludmila flinches.

'Oops!' says Mama.

Baba has been rummaging in her handbag, and now

extracts a lipstick. She tilts the rear-view mirror towards herself, stretches her lips into a taut grimace and colours them in. Her cheeks are rouged and she has drawn in her missing eyebrows with what looks like purple felt-tipped pen. She is wearing her fur coat, which is bald in patches and smells of body odour and moth balls. Her opera glasses skitter across the dashboard every time Mama rounds a bend.

'Are we going to the hospital?' Ludmila says in my ear.

'Yes,' I say.

We hurtle through a red light amidst an orchestra of squealing brakes and car horns. 'Mama!' I say.

'Oh, relax,' Mama says. 'You're always so melodramatic, Anna.'

We judder over gravel where the road has been dug up. Baba's opera glasses vibrate madly on the dashboard. Mama is hunched forward over the steering wheel, peering through the windscreen. As we approach another intersection she accelerates, and something under the car begins to rattle. I hold on to the door to steady myself. 'Watch out,' I say to Ludmila.

But Ludmila has fallen asleep, her head flopped against the back of the car seat, her lips slightly parted. I put my hand on her shoulder.

'Ludmila.'

She opens her eyes. 'My head hurts,' she says.

Behind us, a siren blares. I turn to see the flashing lights of a police car.

'Now we're in trouble,' I say quietly, but Mama, wilfully deaf when it suits her but in truth with hearing like a bat, turns and gives me a look.

'Do you really think some spotty-faced policeman is going to stop *me*?'

But as the police car gains on us she pulls over, hubcaps grinding against the curb, and winds down the window.

'You've got nothing to worry about,' says Baba to Mama as the policeman approaches. Her eyes in the rear-view mirror fix on mine. 'It's *you* who'd better watch out,' she says. 'Police can smell guilt like a dog can smell fear.'

The policeman leans down and looks in the window. His irises are luminescent, like an owl's. 'Hello, ladies,' he says.

'Good evening, officer,' says Mama sweetly.

'I think this might be yours.'

He passes something through the window. It takes me a moment to realise it is the body of the cat. Mama passes it to Baba, who deposits it on the floor at her feet. A terrible odour pervades the car: in dying the cat has soiled itself.

'Thank you,' says Mama. 'So kind of you!'

The policeman tips his hat. Then he looks into the back seat, where Ludmila has fallen asleep again. 'Everything all right?' he says to me.

Baba is still watching me in the rear-view mirror.

'Yes,' I say.

'You've got until midnight,' says the policeman. 'Not a minute longer.'

'She knows that,' says Baba with a malignant smile.

We pull out and drive for what seems like hours, though it is hard to be sure. Every block we pass seems to be flanked by the same sequence of dismal grey apartment buildings. Ludmila moans at one point, and then vomits over the car seat. She asks for water, but there is none to give her. 'Not long now,' I say, brushing the hair back from her face as we careen through the darkening streets.

Finally we stop in front of an unmarked building. The windows are shuttered but there are lights on inside. Baba gathers her handbag and cane, gets out of the car and hobbles up to the door. A silhouetted figured appears, and some kind of transaction occurs – I can see Baba gesticulating, handing something over, and receiving a parcel in return. By the time she gets back to the car, she is wheezing with effort but evidently delighted. She opens her handbag and shows Mama what she has got. Mints. She unwraps one and puts it in her mouth; her false teeth clack as she sucks.

'Home, then,' says Mama, as Baba manoeuvres back into her seat.

'But what about the hospital?' I say.

'The hospital?' says Mama. She looks at Baba. 'She thought we were going to the hospital!'

Baba grins, then lets out a malodorous belch.

'Anna,' says Mama, 'it was just a silly bump on the head. You don't go to the hospital for silly bumps on the head.'

Ludmila stirs on the seat beside me. 'Are we there yet?' she says. Her words come out slurred.

'And as for you,' says Baba, turning and pointing a stubby finger at her. 'Keep your sticky hands off other people's things, or you'll really get what's coming to you.'

No one says anything as we drive back home. When we finally reach the apartment building the lift is broken so we lug ourselves up the stairs, Baba more sprightly than you might expect but Mama suddenly lethargic. Ludmila, of course, is barely able to stand and has developed a strange and lopsided gait, so in the end I half carry, half drag her up. By the time we make it to the top Mama is in bed with her door bolted shut and Baba has reinstated herself in her armchair. As we pass by the living room I hear her cackle: she has found the missing mints under her magazines where she left them.

*

It is late, but Ludmila and I are not asleep. Instead we have pulled back the curtains above our mattress and let the moon bathe us in silver light. Through one wall we can hear Mama thrashing in the grip of some dream; through the other the drone of the television, which muffles Baba's snores as she sleeps in her chair.

Ludmila has the leaf I gave her, its stem between her palms. By rubbing them together she is making the leaf twirl rapidly. She frowns with concentration.

We are sisters but we look nothing alike: Ludmila so fair, whereas I take after Mama. Her heavy brow is mine, her sinewy limbs are mine. A crop of dark hairs prickles through the skin of my forearms, and breasts swell beneath my nightie as the clock on the wall ticks closer to midnight.

I put my hand on Ludmila's. 'That's enough,' I say.

Ludmila lifts the pillow and places the leaf underneath. There are the skeletal remains of others there. Not just one or two: a whole drift of them. The thing about Ludmila's birthdays is that no matter how many she has, she never gets any older than she is now, sitting on the bed next to me, twisting a lock of hair around her finger.

'Why didn't we go to the hospital?' she says. Her nose has started to bleed again.

I swallow.

'It was just a silly bump on the head.'

Ludmila is quiet for a while, and then she says again, 'We should have gone to the hospital.'

Of course, it is easy to blame Mama, with her propensity for manipulation and obfuscation and outright violence. 'I've never claimed to be an angel,' she has often said, her breath reeking of alcohol and her expression in turns coquettish and bleak. But Baba is right. It's me. It has always been me. Because when

Ludmila looks at me now, all of the colour drained from her face, struggling to keep her eyes open, the pupil of one larger than the other, which gives her an otherworldly look, or the look of someone with a subdural haematoma, it being still, in this instant, not too late – to get help, to call an ambulance, to carry her in my arms to the hospital myself – I say: 'Lie down. You just need to get some sleep. You'll feel better in the morning.'

The look she gives me then. Not angry, not even surprised. Because no matter how many times this scene plays out it always ends the same way. Ludmila lies down and I lie down too, my head on the same pillow because we only have the one between us, the occasion for many disputes in the past, many elbows in many ribs, many late night negotiations and pleas, but on this night, which is Ludmila's birthday, I simply put my arm around her and rest my hand on her waist where, in the end, I always rest it. Ludmila has never been able to sleep at night without me beside her. This is how it is when you are sisters.

It would be easy to miss the click of the clock as the tips of both of its hands touch twelve. But I do not miss it. I know that in the living room Baba has heard it too, because her snores stop and I sense she is listening.

An owl hoots.

A coldness seeps through me starting at the top of my scalp, trickling down my spine and finishing at my toes. I close my eyes. When I open them the mattress has gone and the room has gone and Ludmila has gone and only the moon remains, shining coolly through a canopy of leaves. The earth is damp underfoot. There are trees in every direction as far as I can see. They are birches mostly, tall and slender and symmetrically spaced. In the moonlight their trunks are the colour of tarnished silver. A gust of wind sets them rustling; then leaves begin to fall, thousands of them, to the forest floor.

PIP ADAM

Pip Adam is the author of four books: a collection of short stories *Everything We Hoped For* (VUP, 2010), and the novels *I'm Working on a Building* (VUP, 2013); *The New Animals* (VUP, 2017), which won the 2018 Acorn Foundation Prize for Fiction; and *Nothing to See* (VUP, 2020). Pip has an MA and PhD from the IIML at Victoria University of Wellington. Pip makes the podcast *Better Off Read.*

A Problem

In the end they built them to look after each other.

By themselves, women couldn't make enough money and they were unsafe on the streets. Men would beat them and rape them and kill them. If there was a man in the house, women were unsafe off the streets also. And if there were men at the place they worked (for not enough money) the women (one at a time) were also unsafe. All the women. Not just the ones who were born with vaginas, not just the ones who were asking for it, not just the ones who slept with men and not just women and some women more than others . . . anyway, all the women couldn't make enough money and were unsafe on the streets and in the houses and at work and this was not a problem until someone manufactured a solution.

To begin with, they built them for sex. But the cleaning was arduous, and the machines were beaten and raped and killed in the process. Either at work or on their way home from work or buying a *New Idea* magazine at the service station close to work. Repairing the machines cost more than the men paid so it was cheaper to keep using the women.

All the machines were brought back and there was a meeting

scheduled called 'What shall we do with the machines now?'. There was pizza at the meeting and beer and no idea was stupid. People were excited and energetic for the meeting. They had an android that was exactly the same as a woman. Every problem looked like a problem that could be solved by an android that was exactly the same as a woman if you had an android that was exactly the same as a woman. No one could tell the difference. The ideas came thick and fast.

'Cleaning,' someone would say.

'Children,' and they would all talk about it with enthusiasm and passion. But none of the ideas stood up to one simple question.

'How,' someone would inevitably ask, 'will we stop them from being beaten and raped and killed?' and the room would fall silent again.

It was late, the pizza was gone, and they could not find a single way to make a profit out of the androids that were exactly the same as women. They could not solve the problem of the beating and the raping and the killing and they all looked out the window at a billboard on the building opposite theirs. *Unlike some people*, it said, *Belvedere always goes down smoothly.* Under the writing a woman tried to escape a smiling man. They would never solve the problem of the beating and the raping and the killing but, someone asked, looking at the single woman being held back by the man who wanted her to go down smoothly – couldn't they solve the problem of the woman?

'One at a time,' he said, gaining momentum, 'the women can't make enough money and they're unsafe. One at a time our machines can't make enough money and are also unsafe. But two at a time. Well, who knows?'

There was a low hubbub of assent in the room.

'It's win–win,' he said, standing now, taking space. 'The

government pays us to keep the women safe and our machines are safe because they're with the women.'

Someone hunted ducks and the idea of decoys was alive in the room. Before dawn they had a business plan and a meeting with an influential person at the ministry. Each woman would have a machine that was exactly the same as her and they would look after each other. The money came – billions and billions of dollars because they lobbied well – and the machines were built and sent out walking to the houses of the women they looked exactly like. Sometimes they would take buses. It was the most dangerous part of the process, but someone did the numbers and it was cheaper than trucks. They made the women in alphabetical order and in hindsight, one of the directors said, it might have been smarter to do them street by street, but for months if people looked out their windows they would see the machines walking to their doubles and to safety.

Stacy's arrived on a Wednesday. It was never good news when one arrived. Neither of them was happy about it. Not the one opening the door not the one knocking on the door.

Stacy tsked with her tongue and her teeth and said 'Fuck' under her breath and the other one said, 'Don't think I'm any happier about this than you.'

It was terrible for both of them. Looking at something that was exactly the same as you on the outside but completely unknowable. Looking at your face on something else, your ears on something else and having no idea what something else was capable of. They could have looked different but the people who ran the corporation that made them thought it was better this way. They meant better for everyone else. It would be more seamless for everyone else this way, on paper. But they were wrong, it was fucking weird for everybody, but it was done now. It was too late. So they did phone surveys and focus groups and asked questions that made it impossible for anybody to say anything but that it was seamless and great.

'I suppose you better come in,' Stacy said. 'Can you stop doing that?'

The other one was mouthing Stacy's words, standing exactly like Stacy. She'd have been a reflection if she wasn't an exact copy. She didn't smell. That was the worst thing. She smelled, but not like anything organic. She looked like nothing else on the planet because she looked exactly like Stacy. It was uncanny seeing them walking to other women's houses but when you met your own it was devastating.

'You'd better come inside,' Stacy said, and she turned around and the other one followed her down the hall and into the lounge.

'What a dump,' she said.

'Yeah,' Stacy said. 'But you know?'

The other one nodded – she knew.

Stacy's phone rang, and she sighed because she hated the phone.

The other one picked it up and answered. 'Stacy,' she said cheerfully. 'Yes. Yes. Yes. Thanks, Michael, that's amazing. I really appreciate your work,' and she hung up. 'Michael's finished the charts,' she said, without looking at Stacy. 'I suppose you're behind with the editing because you're a fuck up.'

'Why didn't they build you to be nice?' Stacy said. Everyone's was awful. Everyone talked about it all the time. The machines were kind to everyone except the one they looked exactly like.

'What's the use in that?' she said, sitting on the couch now, feet on the coffee table, opening Stacy's laptop, keying in her password.

'Might have been nice,' Stacy said.

'Might it?' She was typing away. Opening the email with the new version of the document attached.

Stacy watched her.

'Well?' she said, without looking up.

'Huh?' Stacy said.

'If I'm working and you're not working there might as well only be one of us.'

Stacy nodded.

'Do some fucking work.' She shooed Stacy away with one hand, still not looking at her.

They got a lot of work done but there was no more money. Stacy's boss asked them to come to his office for a meeting, so he could explain in person why it wasn't fair – to get an advantage from it. No one knew much about what it would mean – the extra one, but he was pretty sure no one would want anyone gaining an advantage from having one.

'Any reasonable person would have to agree,' he said. So they did. They were getting a lot of extra work done, he said, so he'd adjusted their key performance indicators to reflect this. So it was fair on everyone who didn't have another one.

The solution, they agreed as they returned to their desk, was a problem.

'Like possums,' the other one said.

'Like gorse.'

There was no fight left in either of them. The situation was exhausting. Looking after each other took more out of them than looking after themselves had. It turned out that being alone was the only thing keeping either of them going. But the beating and the raping and the killing had made it difficult to be alone and now it was the hell of company. It was like the autumn fly that was always in your periphery but instead of a fly it was as big as you, and the same shape as you and it was you and there was never a moment of privacy when you weren't being noticed or noticing yourself and everything that entailed.

The first time they went out after dark the men left them alone, and the second and the fifth, but by the seventh time none of the men cared how many of them there were. Two women were as unsafe as one woman. The raping and beating and killing numbers looked bad but not when the company removed the starting value and played with the scale on the data visualisation they presented to the ministry.

Within months women were cutting their faces and sawing off their arms and coming home and saying 'Ha!' defiantly and everything felt wonderful for a moment because they were particular and there wasn't the dizzying doubling because their bodies were different, and they could bask in the loneliness of being the only one. The other one would make a phone call and leave for a while and for a while not having an arm or a leg or an ear would seem worth it but then the other one would return with their arm sawn off – or their leg, or their ear – and the women were back to square one, deep in the nausea of the constant reminder of themselves.

Eventually, it was more cost-effective to send a third one and the original woman was asked to leave. The optics were better. Men were smart. Husbands and bosses and workmates and team mates contacted the ministry saying the first woman was broken when she wasn't. There'd be a knock on the door and a sober, reasonable conversation about how there was only room for two. So soon, most of the women didn't have homes or jobs. They couldn't make enough money, so they spent most of their lives on the streets where men beat them and raped them and killed them, which wasn't an issue because someone had solved the problem of the woman.

TINA MAKERETI

Tina Makereti writes essays, novels and short fiction. Her latest novel is *The Imaginary Lives of James Pōneke* and she co-edited *Black Marks on the White Page*, an anthology that celebrates Māori and Pasifika writing. In 2016 her story 'Black Milk' won the Commonwealth Writers Short Story Prize, Pacific region. Tina teaches creative writing and literature at Victoria University, and has recently completed a collection of personal essays, *This Compulsion in Us*.

The Children

The first time Eloise sees the boy, she's thinking of her daughters. When she thinks of them these days – Awhi in Rome and Rosie in Auckland with Jake and the children – an odd feeling takes up residence where *love* or *melancholy* used to be. And while this odd feeling is infused with both love and melancholy and something like wistfulness too, the main body of this feeling, she has to admit, is guilt. She doesn't know why at this stage in her life she still needs to feel parental guilt – after all, her children made it to adulthood relatively unscathed, and are perhaps even happy in moments, which, in her experience, is the most a person can hope for. They are adults who have enough choice in life to get educations, partners, travel, children, or not children. She gave them everything she had, when they were hers. It wasn't perfect, not at all. There was too much tiredness and anger, for a start. But she knows she did what she could. And they came out okay. She didn't look away once, not really. And now, see, they are fine. She can hold her head up.

Only that's not what the feeling says. The feeling takes hold of her head in both hands and forces her to turn towards all the small failures, and she cannot look away: The time she moved Awhi from a childcare she loved to one she hated. Awhi taking forever to put on her shoes at the door, dragging her little bag to the driveway, crying in the car. The day she lost her temper with Rosie and told her to fuck off. Rosie's ten-year-old mouth, so unrepentantly vicious a moment earlier, locked in an O. The times both of them were total bitches and she yelled at them to stop being bitches. Their sudden and accusatory silence. The day their father left because she had finally realised he was no good for her or them. Their small broken hearts in her lap.

When she first sees the boy she thinks he is simply some manifestation of this guilt – a ghost of her feelings, perhaps. She sleeps little and is often overwhelmed by waves of heat and sweat. They didn't tell her hallucinations were part of being menopausal. Then again, no one told her anything except clichés.

So it doesn't shock her as much as she might expect when he comes to stand beside her while she's doing the dishes. She has made the sink quite foamy, and has her hands soaking in it, and the warmth makes her sleepy. Washing dishes always was a repetitive, undemanding task that allowed her to daydream, but now with no one else in the house she does the job slowly, often with a glass of wine on the windowsill. She's worried about the glass of wine, but can't think of a good reason not to have it. Other than cancer or liver disease, and somehow she can't make those threats into anything beyond abstract ideas. There's no substance to them. But there is substance to the friendly feeling she has after a wine or two over dinner and the dishes. Suddenly, even though she is doing these things by herself, she doesn't feel alone anymore.

And now, she realises, she is not alone, though she is not sure how much substance the boy has. She can sense that he watches her with an amused focus, tracing the movement of her hands, looking to her face and back. She doesn't look directly at him, but when he begins to lift his own hands in a precise copy of her movements she almost freezes. She assumes that doing so will make him disappear, poof, and while it's unsettling, there's a strange pleasure in his being there, so she continues. Her very own mystery, even if he is just a sign of impending madness. She is of a mind to indulge this and dismiss the vague suspicion that she might regret her indulgence. You are a lonely, crazy old lady now, she says to herself, and who will deny you your phantom boys?

She doesn't know when he dissipates. He is there and then, when she finishes the dishes, he is not, and she can't remember the transition from presence to absence. But then she can't remember his arrival, either. It's hard going to sleep, later, after the third wine. It isn't usually that hard after three, but she's anxious, as if she's waiting for a visitor to turn up. Then she begins to wonder if she'll wake in the middle of the night to him standing by her bed and then she begins to wonder if he is actually a ghost or if she is actually mad. And then she feels the dreadful aloneness of the night. She should get a pet, she tells herself for the fourth time that day, but she hasn't had the heart since the kitten got run over.

When sleep comes it's like a pause in transmission: no dreams, no half-waking stumble to the toilet. Just a cut in the film, followed much later by a fade-in, a close-up panning out to wide shot. Sun streams in.

She finds no barely visible boys in her kitchen. She makes coffee and sits at the table with her book. Ten minutes before the scramble to get herself decent enough for work. Forty-five minutes to her train. She always leaves it too late, but it's a sane moment to collect herself before the distractions begin. She works hard. Barely has a moment to herself all day, managing the library team. This time in the morning is precious. Night is too haunted and empty. Everything in the morning is fresh, as if yesterday's mistakes have disappeared. By evening she'll know different, but she loves this illusion of promise. She barely thinks about the boy again, sure that whatever that was, it was a glitch. She'll need to look out for it. See a doctor if it happens again.

After dinner, he's there again at the dishes. She has the feeling that he's been there a while, just behind her, just beyond her noticing, but she doesn't get this feeling until he is actually beside her. She finds she is more worried about the fact that she doesn't notice his arrival, isn't aware of his entrance, than the fact that he is some kind of impossibility. Where does she go? Who else might sneak up on her in these moments?

Again he stands by her, watching and copying, and instinct tells her not to look directly, and something else tells her he finds all this fascinating. She wishes that he would stay longer this time. She wishes it so fervently she is surprised, already anticipating the dark gap he'll leave when he disappears. She is delighted when she turns to hang up the tea towel, and he is still there in the periphery of her vision. Should she look at him now? She doesn't want to break the spell so tells herself to keep moving, gently, towards the couch. She reaches for the remote and switches on the TV. He seats himself beside her. *7 Days* comes on and she chuckles at the wonderfully stupid jokes. She doesn't know how she knows it, since he doesn't make a sound, but he is also laughing, and more enthralled than ever. He's probably too young for this show, she thinks. He can't be more than twelve.

Then Awhi rings and they haven't talked for a month so she gets distracted and of course he's not there when she thinks to check, and Awhi is also gone, but she doesn't feel as bad as she had anticipated. Instead she thinks about seeing him again.

He arrives every night for the next three nights, and stays a bit longer each time, until he's there as she actually goes to sleep, sitting on the floor of her room. She religiously follows the instinctual rules she adopted on his first arrival: not to look too directly, not to speak directly. She becomes anxious that breaking their ritual will cause him to disappear and not return, and despite being sure he is evidence of something not right in her head, she cannot bring herself to tell anyone else about him. She supposes that he might be a ghost, but the same instinct that governs the rules of their relationship tells her that he is not an apparition of the dead. There is something too optimistic, too cheerful about the feeling that accompanies him to suggest that kind of thing.

Despite all this, she knows something must happen. Such is the nature of things. Someone must speak, say out loud what is happening, name things. Name him. Since she doesn't actually know what is happening, she supposes that she should ask him. So, on the sixth night she resolves to speak to him, but she can't quite force the words out. She argues with herself about this while she does the dishes, as they watch TV, even as she brushes her teeth. He has arrived and left each time without her knowing, and she is afraid of changing the pattern that has brought him into her world. She even missed yoga on Wednesday night in case the break in routine caused too much disruption. If she keeps going like this, will she simply stop having any other life? What if it spills over into her work?

'You don't have to worry.'

He has spoken, she thinks.

'This has been fun for me. Interesting. I thought you didn't notice. The others never notice. But I don't want to cause distress.'

She is still frozen. As if speaking will confirm her madness in a way that seeing and hearing the boy has not. What is she thinking? That she can save herself now?

'Should I leave? Would it be easier if I left you . . . alone?'

'No!' She squeezes her eyes shut in case she has ruined everything. When she opens them, he is there, right in front of her. She looks directly at him, but she still cannot exactly define him. His eyes are fully there, compelling, but the rest of him – it's as if his various parts only come into focus when she looks straight at them, and she cannot hold all of him in her view at once, so that he is constantly shifting in and out of focus.

'I don't understand,' she says, 'what the rules are. I don't understand what you are.'

'I don't think there are any rules.' His eyes are laughing now, or maybe his mouth. 'But if there are, I don't know them. I wasn't here, and now I am. It's out of wanting, I think. Mine or yours. Maybe both.'

'What do you want?'

'Just to see what it's like. I don't know what it's like.'

She frowns. What on earth does he mean?

'Living, I mean. Where I'm from, we don't anymore. Not much.'

And she wants to ask him about that, but then he is gone.

Eloise sleeps fitfully, haunted by worry. Will he come back? Is everything over now? And what did he mean about not living where he comes from? At 4am she rises, no longer able to tolerate lying in bed without rest, and watches as the earliest glimmer of dawn lights the horizon beyond her ranchslider.

She really is in the twilight zone now, she supposes. Really is beyond saving.

By the time she starts work she feels like a zombie, following her routines without recognition, until she spills coffee all over her keyboard.

'Are you okay?'

It's Tania – always kind and concerned, and a bit too perky.

'Just tired.'

'Can I make you another coffee?'

Eloise does want another coffee, but she doesn't want to encourage Tania. If she lets Tania bring her coffee, there will be the obligation to tell her things. Normally she doesn't like to tell people anything if she can help it, but right now she suspects that if anyone asks her, she won't be able to stop herself talking about the boy. And then everyone will know she's lost it, or alternatively that she has a strange and not-entirely-living boy in her home.

'No, thank you, Tania. I will.'

'Really? I don't mind!'

'Really – it's okay. Do you think you can attend the issues counter for a bit? Lou's due for a break.'

In the staffroom she finds Goth Sarah lying on the staffroom couch, her feet on the armrest, reading a book. She wonders if she can tell Goth Sarah. Goth Sarah is quiet in a way that Eloise finds reassuring, as if there is no reason to ever get agitated about anything. She cannot imagine Goth Sarah rushing or being too loud or insisting on helping. Eloise likes people who don't insist. But then, she also can't imagine what would get Goth Sarah excited. Other than books, and even then the enthusiasm seems muted, grave. She calls her Goth Sarah in her head because there are two other Sarahs in her team – Pink Sarah and just Sarah, plus Eloise has a cousin

Sarah, too – but she must stop before she says 'Goth Sarah' out loud in front of her one day.

'Sarah,' she says, in what she hopes is a light questioning tone, and then realises it's a mistake.

Goth Sarah remains focused on her page. Eloise can see her eyes behind her glasses moving along the line she's reading. When her eyes get to the right margin of the page, she looks up slowly and takes a moment to focus on Eloise, as if she hasn't noticed her boss has even entered the room.

'Oh. Yes, Eloise?'

It really is a mistake. She can't say it.

'Um, if – uh, would you like to come for tea on Saturday?'

'For tea?'

Now she really must seem mad. They've never socialised before, apart from the odd staff morning tea. It's a very intimate thing to ask, and Goth Sarah's face confirms this. Her eyes flicker a bit, there's a twitch to the mouth. Eloise is not accustomed to this level of animation from her colleague.

'Um, yeah, you know, dinner. Only, well I think you're the best read of all of us, despite your age, and I think we ought to start a book club.' She has no intention of starting a book club. 'Of course, I'll invite some others too.'

Dear god, she does not want more people in her house. She doesn't even want Goth Sarah in her house.

'Book club?' Goth Sarah frowns.

Eloise is getting frightened now.

'Okay?'

'Well, it doesn't have to be this Saturday. It doesn't have to be dinner. We could just have lunch, eh?' Now she's overdone it. Awhi's voice comes to her: *Stop making it weird.*

'Yup. Sure.'

She makes a tea and exits, trying to seem casual.

*

The day has been long and anxious, so it's relaxing to see him in the evening. He keeps coming back, he tells her, because it's quiet and calm. Usually it's hard to be around people, their families and fights and loudnesses. If they're not being loud outwardly they're often being loud inside: hurting themselves or others.

'Usually? There have been others?'

'Well, yes. We all travel from place to place. A bit.'

'We? There are others like you?'

'More and more all the time.'

She doesn't want to ask why. But she has to know. 'Are you – a ghost? Is that okay to ask? Are you –' The word seems wrong to speak aloud. 'Are you dead?'

His face swims. 'No, I don't think so. I have no life, but I don't think I'm dead. I'm only me – I don't know how everything works. We wander. We – wonder.'

She is filled with a remarkable feeling, as if his whole life is ahead of him rather than finished. It's the feeling she had when she learned she was pregnant with the girls. Such immense possibility. Such potency. She realises she's overjoyed that he's not dead, even though she had suspected as much.

'It's nice here, with you. But when I realised you could sense me, that made it even better. That doesn't usually happen. It can be hard to be ignored.'

'So most people aren't like me, then. Most people can't see you?'

'No. That's kind of fun sometimes. But it gets boring.'

There is so much she wants to ask, but he wants to watch a movie. He is as much a kid as any other she has known: limited patience with adult curiosities.

*

The team come over on Saturday afternoon for tea and cakes and book club planning. She can't quite gauge how she has gotten into this position, but in the end it's nice. Goth Sarah brings *Wuthering Heights*. Predictable. Pink Sarah brings Cassandra Clare's latest – also predictable. Tania brings Deborah Levy's *The Cost of Living*. Actually not at all predictable. Eloise couldn't decide what to bring, in the end grabbing Moshin Hamid's *Exit West* from the bookshelf as the first guest arrived. She did like that book, but she doesn't know whether or not the choice is predictable of her. What kind of book club will they be? Who knows, but by the end of the afternoon they have decided how to do it: one evening once a month, a rotating roster for book choosing. Wine. Cake. Nibbles. She doesn't really mind what they read, predictable or not. What she finds surprising is how the four of them kind of balance each other out. And she forgets about the boy for a while.

As they leave, she becomes aware of him again, the real reason the book club has been formed. The boy is usually around only in the evenings, so she hasn't been worried about seeing him. Goth Sarah is the last to go, having washed the dishes. Eloise sees her to the door.

'Thank you,' she says. 'I didn't expect that to work.'

'The dishes?'

Eloise laughs. 'The bookclub.'

'Neither did I, if truth be told.'

Eloise sees what it is, at last. Goth Sarah has a kind of compelling Eeyore quality that makes her easy to trust.

'Hey, can I ask, do you know anything about, er, the non-living?'

'You mean zombies?'

'Not exactly. Less flesh-eaty, more lost.'

'Ghosts?'

'I don't think so.'

'I actually took a course on the sociological and phenomenological history of zombies at uni. It wasn't as exciting as it sounds.'

'Oh.'

'Yeah.' Goth Sarah looks around the room. 'So you got some kind of undead here have you? Vampire?'

'No. Definitely not.'

'Hmm. Friendly?'

'Yes.'

'A sprite?'

'Er, no.' Maybe she's taken another wrong turn.

'My ex was into patupaiarehe. Well, not into them, you know, he just reckoned they were everywhere.'

'Oh. Maybe? He's more . . . modern, perhaps. Almost futuristic.'

She didn't know this until she said it. Having to describe him to someone else is useful.

'Well, I reckon patupaiarehe consider themselves modern. Or at least timeless. "He" eh? Got yourself an undead boyfriend?'

'No! He's a child. And more unliving than undead.'

Goth Sarah peers at her then, right into her eyes.

'Well, you still look pretty rational to me, so I'm going to believe you. I don't really believe you, but I'm going to pretend I do. I can keep an eye out for such things if you like, or at least chat online about it.'

Why did she say any of it aloud?

'You should ask though. Ask the thing. The "he". What he is and why.'

'He doesn't know.'

'Maybe ask if you can help? Like on *The Sixth Sense*.'

*

But she almost forgets to ask the next time she sees him because something else happens. The boy is not alone. There is a little girl with him, seven or so, fair, holding a small soft blanket, which she rubs against her cheek, hiding behind it whenever Eloise looks her way. The boy largely ignores his companion, but when Eloise can hold back no longer, he makes a concerted effort to reply to her questions as clearly as possible.

'I don't know if I can explain it to you. We are here because we cannot be there, in the lives we were supposed to have. And the others have heard about you, so they want to come.'

Eloise feels an unpleasant movement in her gut, an involuntary loosening of her bowels and a terrible urge to pee, all at the same time. *The lives they were supposed to have?* This is the thing she had missed. She rushes to the loo. Something is very wrong, she thinks, but when she returns, the children are gone.

The next day, there is a small group – four children of various ages from something like three to twelve. Her boy is still the eldest. She misses their time together, her innocent thoughts of madness and benevolent phantoms. This is much worse – so many children unhitched from their lives. And all they want is for her to go about her life as normal.

'We're hungry for it,' the boy says. 'Just the normal things. We don't even want parties and holidays. Just houses and people.'

The next day there is a clutch of half a dozen children.

'Why don't you go and watch other children having everyday children's lives?' says Eloise. 'I mean – I love having you here, but why me?'

'Sometimes it hurts to be around living children. Sometimes it's too loud. This life – this quiet house – it's comforting.' He leans back into the couch. Children are scattered around her lounge, lying with their feet in the air, starfishing on still-round tummies, skipping the perimeter of the room.

'And you see us.' He looks at his companions, one by one. 'It's nice, you know? To be seen.'

So she reads them stories from the children's bookshelf she keeps for her grandchildren. The boy doesn't seem to mind that the stories are mainly for preschoolers.

In the night she wakes to an empty room and feels relief. Her house is her own once more, and she can think again. She doesn't want to turn them away, all these children who need something from her, but it's a lot to manage – even though they don't ask for anything. She locates the feeling she's been carrying since he told her. *The lives they were supposed to have.* She realises the feeling is familiar to her after all: melancholy, yearning, washed through with . . . yes, it is the same. Washed through with guilt. She resolves to ask him properly next time: why they aren't able to have their lives.

She sleeps again and wakes to a message from Goth Sarah: *So, there's lots of talk online. Unexplained stuff that looks pretty normal until people start putting it all together. Street kids appearing in large numbers but disappearing as soon as the authorities try to help. Memes about nothing, like really nothing, just people doing every day things. Blandlife they call it. No one knows who's watching it. It's growing so fast it's drowning out the terfs and the trolls.* Goth Sarah doesn't know if it's connected. *It's just weird. Like, the whole online world is different all of a sudden.*

It's a Saturday, so Eloise goes to the market to get her veges. She runs Goth Sarah's words over in her mind alongside the boy's. When she sees children beside market stalls or walking behind adults, she checks how solid they are – if their image wavers in and out of focus. She thinks she sees at least two, and is unsurprised to find one follows her into her car and home.

At her house, she counts no less than a dozen children. It takes her some time to locate the boy, who is in her room by himself, on the floor where he always likes to sit. Her kitten is on his lap, the one that got run over. It's fine. In fact, it has grown quite a bit. When it sees her it stands and turns itself around on the boy's lap, curling into a ball and caressing his face with its tail.

'She died,' Eloise says. 'I saw her body with no life in it.'

'I don't think I died,' the boy says. 'I don't remember a life before this. Maybe it works both ways.'

'There are more of them.'

'I told you. More every day. They keep coming and coming. I think maybe some of us are from different times. Lucy met her granddaughter yesterday.'

'Lucy?'

'The second one to come here. The little girl. They looked practically the same. But there's a different weight to them.'

'Weight?'

'The weight of time maybe? The weight of things not done?'

She leans against the wall and slides down until she is sitting by the boy. She reaches over to pat the kitten, though her fur lacks substance.

'So this is it, then,' Eloise says. It seems obvious now.

'I don't know.'

'I'm sorry.'

'Yeah.'

'There must be something we can do.'

He looks at her, and she looks at him, trying to hold his image solid.

'Yes, there must be something,' he says.

They can hear the children in the other rooms, playing games and talking and fighting. Her house so full of children. The world so full of children, and so empty. She will go out to them soon, and go about her daily routine. They like it when she does that. She wants to make them happy.

DANYL MCLAUCHLAN

Danyl McLauchlan was born in Wellington in 1974. He studied at Victoria University, and worked and travelled in Europe, the Middle East and Asia, before he returned to Wellington, where he works as a biologist. He is the author of *Unspeakable Secrets of the Aro Valley* (2013) and *Mysterious Mysteries of the Aro Valley* (2016) and a forthcoming book of essays, *Tranquillity and Ruin*.

The Everything Store

I was born in Home Furnishings. It was a quiet part of the world; the people there were happy, hard-working, devout but not zealous. It wasn't crowded like the departments around Gardening where, we were told whenever we were spoiled or disobedient, food was rationed and everyone slept three or four families to an aisle. Every family in Home Furnishings had a few cross-shelf spaces of our own, partitioned off with carpets draped over clotheslines strung at head height.

My mother was from Footwear; her home aisle was only four thousand shelves from where we lived. We visited her family back there often, especially when my grandmother was sick. My father was from Rubber Goods and Inflatable Pools, far on the other side of the known world. He came to Home Furnishings on a caravan with his uncles and brothers and cousins, pulling trolleys filled with goods: not just rubber but also batteries, non-prescription painkillers, children's sleepwear, soap.

It was hard work, he said. Long marches through the desert, yoked to the caravan, everyone marching in step, sleeping on the polished concrete of the earth, subsisting on potatoes and beans from the garden trolleys at the front and rear of the train. His final journey was the hardest: hauling an emergency shipment of dirt through the vast desert of Sportswear after a soil-borne disease wiped out most of the crops in Home Furnishings. He described endless shelves of squash rackets, basketballs, skateboards. 'One shift we woke,' he said, 'and walked until we collapsed and all that time we never saw anything except wetsuits in every direction.' But it was worth it, he told us. 'When we finally arrived in Home Furnishings, amidst the cheering crowds I saw a tall girl with brown eyes smiling at me from the Curtainware section.'

My mother was in Home Furnishings by luck, visiting an aunt in Bedding. There was a spare aisle just a couple of shelves down from that same aunt and that's where I was born a few hundred shifts later. My earliest memories are of Bedding: the shared vegetable garden; toddling across pools filled with dirt – most of it hauled there by my father, he always reminded us – the huge tomato plants looming over me; stealing strawberries from the planters at the end of the aisle; helping my parents carry water from the drinking fountains; the terrible smell of the slop trolleys as they were hauled off to the waste aisles beyond the border.

And in all of my memories there is Hill: only a few months older than me but the undisputed leader of all the children in both Bedding and Décor. Hill was the explorer of unoccupied aisles, the inventor of games, the asker of difficult questions. Where did we come from? Why were we here? Why was the sky made of corrugated steel? Our parents and teachers gave the traditional answers from both the Song of the Deliverer and the Terms and Conditions, a commentary on the Song that resolved its ambiguities and seeming contradictions. Most of us believed these answers. Hill did not.

*

One shift my family went on a journey to Toys and Games. This was about ten thousand shelves from our house. I rode there on my father's shoulders. He carried an extension ladder under one arm. My mother pushed an empty trolley.

When we arrived I was so excited: I ran around, squealing with delight. The shelves were stocked with dolls and puzzles, model planes, train sets, plastic guns, games. When I ran too far into the new department – only a few dozen shelves – my father came after me. 'We're out in the desert here,' he said in a serious voice. 'Nobody lives here. Nobody can. It's too far from the trade routes.' He put his arm around me and led me back, but as he did so I glanced behind us and saw the broad empty aisles stretching on, forever and ever, and felt a sudden deep love for the stark, perilous beauty of the desert that I'd never felt for the safety and comfort of Home Furnishings.

We went back to the border shelves and picked out what we wanted. When we found something good my parents erected their ladder. 'Remember the Song,' they reminded me. 'Take from the high stock shelves whatever you wish / But the display shelves must remain untouched / From the beginning until the end of all shifts.' Hill had mocked this passage, scoffing, 'It's pragmatism. You don't want people messing around with the display shelves because if they do there's no way to tell what's in the boxes above them. But instead of just telling us that, society has to construct this fake religion to control us. And people believe it. It makes me sick.'

My parents believed. They positioned their ladder a hand-span from the display items, careful not to even brush against them, and my father climbed up to the large cardboard boxes stacked on the wooden planks at the top of every shelf, the piles reaching halfway up to the strips of fluorescent lights that hung suspended from the sky. He tossed whatever toys or games were in the boxes down to us until our trolley was full. 'Only a few of these toys are for you,' my mother warned as we walked home. 'Most of them will be traded, for seeds or batteries, when the next caravan arrives from Gardening.'

I nodded, solemnly, looked at how much we'd taken and what a small portion it was compared to the vast trove that remained, and asked her, 'How long would it take to unpack all these toys?'

My mother laughed and my father replied, 'It would take you until the end of time.'

'Another lie,' Hill snapped when we discussed it. 'Toys and Games is finite. There's Home Furnishings downshelf. Bath Accessories and Office Supplies on the aisle sides, and Outdoor Furniture far upshelf. If it comes to an end it can all be unpacked, in time. Our parents are lying to us.'

'Maybe they're not lying,' I suggested. 'Maybe they believe it, and someone lied to them. To everyone.'

'But who?' Hill demanded. 'And why?'

These questions intensified as we got older. The teachers and elders lost their patience with Hill. 'Do you realise how lucky you are to live in Home Furnishings?' they demanded. 'Maybe you'd be happier hauling a caravan? Or living as a Gleaner, alone out in the deep desert?'

'Maybe I would,' Hill replied. 'Maybe I would.'

The expedition to the deep desert of Outdoor Furniture – the remote department beyond Toys and Games – was Hill's idea. 'We'll be finishing school soon. And then we'll be stuck working in the gardens all shift, or hauling trade goods to the border. This could be our last chance for adventure.' So we woke early, before the shift began, stole a trolley and piled it with food then made our way down the deserted aisles. By the time the shift began we were across the border.

Toys and Games was empty, lifeless. When we stopped at a drinking fountain the pipes beneath it groaned; the water took a long time to run. When it came it tasted bitter, metallic. Hill looked around at the shelves, the products, the aisles, and asked in a hushed tone, 'Do you really think the world goes on and on like this, forever?' That was what we'd been told, growing up. We heard it without processing the implications. Now, for the first time we understood the vast emptiness of things, how small the civilised regions were, how easy it would be to wander and wander through the desert until starvation or madness took you.

We took turns pushing the trolley and made good time. Just before the end of the shift we reached Outdoor Furniture. It was the end of the known world, no one knew what lay beyond it. We hesitated in the space between the shelves. Even Hill seemed reluctant to step foot in its aisles. The umbrellas, plastic tables, beach loungers ahead of us receded to the vanishing point.

'We'll sleep here,' Hill decided. 'And explore in the morning.'

The singing woke us.

It was a woman's voice. Strong. Piercing. Not especially melodic. We followed the sound a few aisles up, a few shelves out, marking our route with chalk-marks on the floor, just as we'd been taught in our desert survival classes by teachers who obviously never expected us to use the knowledge. Both of us were afraid but neither of us wanted to admit it.

The woman was old: older than my mother, older than anyone we'd ever seen. Her hair was white as Styrofoam, cut very short; her clothes were baggy, shapeless garments with words and numbers printed on them in large white letters. She stood on a ladder. It had wheels on the bottom and the top hooked on to a shelf so she could propel herself along the aisle. She had a boxcutter and when she reached each new segment she'd glance down at the display shelves and either slash open a box and toss an item from it down to her mini-caravan or shake her head and slide her ladder further along.

Her mini-caravan sat at the base of the ladder: four trolleys, two of them lined with tarpaulins and filled with soil and crops – potatoes and beans – and the others piled high with items from Outdoor Furniture.

The woman sang the Song of the Deliverer: the same song we'd sung with our parents at the end of each shift since we were old enough to sing. But she sang with an odd accent and missed some of the lines. We'd heard the Song so often – at least once a shift since we were born – that hearing this strange, fragmented version was even more disturbing than seeing someone out here, all alone in the deep desert. We kept listening, and her version of the Song grew stranger, more disturbing; she sang entire verses we'd never heard before. The familiar passages about keeping order and obeying tradition were gone, replaced with lines about searching, exploring, finding answers to some mystery, unravelling the secrets of existence.

'She's a heretic,' I whispered to Hill. 'She's singing the song wrong.' He didn't reply. He had an expression on his face I was familiar with: he was thinking, hard. She was mid-way through the tenth verse when she stopped and, with the acute perception I've often observed in the wild, she sensed our presence and turned to face us.

Her eyes were black and bright. She inspected us with an unblinking gaze then turned back to her task, slashing open the box before her, and called, 'Not supposed to be out here, are you?'

'Who are you?' I replied. My father had taught me to always answer a question with a question.

She did not reply. Instead she shifted her ladder along the shelf and slashed open another box. It was filled with cushions. She tugged one out and called out 'Catch' and threw it down.

Hill caught it. It was small and square, about half an armlength. It was soft with a floral-print design but – unlike the cushions in Home Furnishings – it was covered with a strangely slippery fabric. He called up to her, 'Why does it feel like that?'

'It's waterproof.' She pulled another cushion free of the box and sent it spinning. It landed in one of her trolleys.

'What good is a waterproof cushion?'

'That's a big question.' The woman moved her ladder again. 'What good are umbrellas? What good are inflatable chairs? What good are gazebos? What is the use of any of this stuff? And if it's useless, why is there so much of it?'

I called out, 'Do you know the answer?' She did not reply. I yelled at her, 'Why are you out here?

'It's my job to be out here,' she replied. 'Unlike you. This is no place for you. Run back to Home Furnishings, children.'

Hill touched my arm. 'She wasn't singing the wrong version of the song,' he whispered. 'We do.'

I frowned. 'What?'

'Our version of the Song of the Deliverer is wrong. Not hers.' Hill pointed to the woman and said, 'She's a Gleaner.'

The Deliverer came from someplace far downshelf. When he arrived in Gardening – now the centre of the known world, back then just a random department among many – people were divided into small tribes, warring over scraps of food. The Deliverer united them. He taught them to dump bags of soil from Gardening into the paddling pools from Rubber Goods and sow them with the seeds from Incredible Edibles, to use the batteries from Household Essentials to run the power inverters in Workshop Tools to light the UV grow lamps from Outdoor Accessories. 'Everything in the world is here for a purpose,' the Deliverer taught in the opening verses of his song. 'Everything fits together.' And then, when he was sure his disciples had memorised his wisdom, he left, continuing on upshelf. There were no records from that time: no one knew where the Deliverer came from, or where he went.

There were many theories. The most popular was the Great Cycle. The very first verse of the Song of the Deliverer ('Welcome and thank you for coming') was the same as the last. That was a clue, most people believed, of the cyclical nature of existence. It meant that the world did not go on and on forever. If you began in Gardening and kept walking upshelf, somehow surviving in the deep desert you would – after an incomprehensible distance, an unthinkable period of time – reach Gardening again. And people believed that is what the Deliverer did, over and over again. By the time he completed his Cycle, civilisation would have neglected his teachings, crumbled into warring tribes, forgotten his song. The Deliverer would restore it again. History repeated itself endlessly. Hill and I were lucky, our parents told us, to live in one of the quiet, safe periods.

Not everyone agreed with the theory of the Cycle. Some insisted the Deliverer was just an ordinary man – or a woman, the song didn't specify – who had solved the problem of surviving in the deep desert. They believed that his famous claim that everything existed for a reason was more than just a vague metaphysical statement: it was the core of his teaching. We weren't here to lead safe, quiet lives until civilisation ran down and the cycle repeated again. Our purpose was to understand the world: unravel its secrets. We should be out in the desert, they argued. Mapping. Exploring. We were supposed to follow the Deliverer, they said – not wait for his return.

They were the Gleaners.

'She's no Gleaner,' I sneered, loudly enough for the old woman to hear. Hill and I grew up on stories about Gleaners. They were ambiguous characters: sly, untrustworthy, scheming, sometimes heroes but usually malicious tricksters who the hero defeated. Gleaners were men, in my imagination, and they were young and glamorous. This woman was old. She wore weird clothes. She had lots of little ziplock bags strapped to her arms and legs. She opened one of them now, as she reached the end of her shelf, put her boxcutter inside, and zipped it shut again. Next she slid down her ladder and strolled over to us. Both of us were afraid but neither wanted to show it.

'Come here to see the deep desert, did you? Well take a good look.' She waved her arm. 'It looks like everywhere else, except there's no food. You can go for twenty shifts without eating before you die. Maybe more when you're young. But the longer you go without eating the slower you get, the harder it is to return. So be careful before you step across that aisle.' She pointed at the space dividing Toys and Games from Outdoor Furniture. 'There's a lot of bones out here.'

The old woman was frightening. She smelled bad; there was something malevolent in her voice and eyes. I stepped backwards, ready to run. But Hill stayed still and said, 'We heard you singing the Song of the Deliverer.'

She smiled. 'They taught you a different version?'

'Yes.'

'A safer version?'

'Your song said something about searching this world –'

'To find another world.' She nodded.

'What other world?'

'Who can say?' she replied. 'But do you really think this is all there is?'

'Let's go.' I touched Hill's arm. 'She's just a crazy old lady.'

Her eyes flicked over to me. 'What do you think they do in Gardening?' she demanded.

I blinked, surprised. 'They garden,' I replied. 'They grow things. Trade seeds –'

She laughed. 'They haven't grown anything in Gardening since before I was born. I've seen it for myself. Go take a look. You'll learn a few things.'

My father said, 'No one gets into Gardening.'

We were punished when we returned to Home Furnishing: twenty shifts hauling night soil to the waste aisles, yelled at by our parents every shiftend when we got home. But my father, who yelled the loudest, was, quietly, the most curious about our experience. How far did we go? What did we see? Isn't it beautiful, out there in the desert?

'He misses his old life of adventure,' Hill diagnosed.

We told him about the old woman; asked him about the Gleaners, about Gardening. 'It's true,' he admitted. 'When we talk about Gardening we're referring to a number of departments at the heart of the world.' He ticked them off on his fingers. 'Stationery. Personal and Oral Care. Paint. All of them are filled with gardens. It's where everything gets grown. That's where our seeds come from. But the aisles on the borders leading into Gardening are blocked off.'

Hill asked, 'Blocked off with what?'

'Tables,' my father replied. 'Hauled across the desert through Celebrity Fragrances, countless shifts ago. No one knows how they did it. They're lain end to end and stacked atop each other. The Gardeners call them 'Wall'. No one can get over them. There are gates but they're heavily guarded, shift and shiftend. No one gets in.'

'The Gleaner claimed she'd been inside Gardening,' I said.

'Gleaners go in,' he admitted. 'I was talking about normal people. Decent people. And few Gleaners are admitted. Only those who venture out far into the deep desert and bring back something new. Something no one in Gardening has ever seen before. Something they consider valuable – and no one else knows what the Gardeners value, and why. You have to earn your way into Gardening.'

A few ten-shifts later we signed on to a caravan. It didn't go to Gardening. 'What would be the point?' Hill asked. 'They're not going to let us in. We need to find something in the deep desert and to do that we need to learn how to cross the desert.'

We assumed we'd signed on to a merchant caravan, that we'd be hauling goods from Home Furnishing for trade. But after we farewelled our families and met the caravan master, Glen – whose authority, once we were in the desert, was absolute – he stopped us short of the train and handed out respirator masks. These were black and grey plastic mouldings that fitted over our nose and mouth. They were uncomfortable; they muted our voices; the straps dug into the back of our heads. The other recruits fitted them with ease and continued on downaisle, towards the border where the caravan waited but Glen saw us fidgeting with them and said, 'Is this your first time out?'

We nodded. He said, 'Leave the masks off for now. Follow the others. You'll soon figure out why we wear them.'

And we did. Our caravan was a body caravan: two trains with a hundred trolleys each. The first train consisted of food trolleys lined with tarps and filled with soil and plants: potatoes, courgettes, avocados, limes; the second, located two aisles over – although you could still smell it – was filled with sawdust and the body parts of decomposing cadavers.

They'd mostly died of old age, Glen told us when we all sat down to eat at shiftend. 'Plus a woman who died in childbirth. A kid who fell off a high shelf.' They'd been farewelled by their community then cut up by a local doctor, the parts stored in the waste aisles until the caravan's departure.

We skirted the borders of Home Furnishing and Footwear, taking on more trolleys filled with sawdust. At shiftend we slept away from the caravan, but still slept with our masks on. The smell lingered on our clothes.

Before we set out into the inner desert – the empty aisles of Celebrity Fragrances, almost a hundred shifts by caravan until we reached Curtains and Blinds – the men of the borderlands brought out two blindfolded, shackled figures. They were both young men: one had hurt a child, they told us; the other was a troublemaker who refused to work in the gardens, took items from the display shelves and mocked the Song of the Deliverer. They were tied to the end of the caravan. Thirty-five shifts into the desert the caravan master let them go, still blindfolded, their hands still bound behind their backs, bellowing obscenities at us until we were out of earshot.

Twenty shifts is the furthest a man can walk without food before starving to death,' the caravan master explained to us. 'But sometimes they survive, for a time.'

'How?'

Sometimes they feed' – he leered – 'on each other.'

*

Fifty shifts in we reached the Oasis. The exact centre of the desert. It was unpopulated: hundreds of pools filled with soil filled the aisles. Crops grew in the outer pools.

We buried our bodies in the designated pools closest to Personal and Oral Care while the caravan master droned the funeral rites from the Terms and Conditions. Then we filled our trolleys with soil from the pools closest to Home Furnishings, tended to and replanted some crops, planted others in our food caravan and then headed for home.

On the journey back Hill talked to the caravan master. Glen had made no secret of his dissatisfaction as a hauler of body parts. He wanted to advance in the world, command his own trade caravan, enjoy the romance and prestige of those who carried valuable commodities to exotic distant aisles, instead of hauling corpses to the middle of nowhere.

Hill offered him a deal. 'You supply us with trolleys and food,' he said, laying out a map of the known world, Gardening at the centre. 'We'll strike out from Toys and Games, cross Outdoor Furniture and discover whatever lies beyond it. When we return we'll bring back trade goods that no one has ever seen before.'

Glen scratched his neck. 'You want to be Gleaners, eh? Suit yourselves. But why would I trust you with valuable trolleys? You say you'll be the first to reach the other side of Outdoor Furniture? Why you? Why hasn't some other Gleaner been out there?'

'Look at the map,' Hill replied. 'All of these regions upshelf and downshelf of Gardening have been identified by Gleaners.' He indicated the long sequence of regions. 'But if you look outaisle there's been hardly any discovery. I attribute this to two things. The first is the sentimental attachment to the story of the Deliverer. Many Gleaners are seeking his origin or destination. The second is that the gaps between shelves line up exactly, so when you're travelling shelfwise you can see where you're going to the limits of your vision. But the aisles are not exactly straight – no one knows why – they follow a slight curve. I believe that deters people from outaisle exploration. No one goes there. So that is where we shall go.'

When we reached the border of Home Furnishings the master equipped us with four barrows containing soil, beans and potatoes, and four empty trolleys. 'Remember,' he warned us, 'there's enough food to last you both fifty shifts in the deep desert, if you're frugal. That means twenty-five shifts in and twenty-five shifts out. Don't go so far you can't get back. Keep in mind you're slower coming out with extra baggage.'

We exchanged farewells and agreed to meet him back at the border in fifty shifts. Then we skirted around the edge of Home Furnishings and crossed Toys and Games in three shifts, which illustrated how much slower we were hauling the trolleys. But our spirits were high: we sang songs, told jokes. We felt no fear when we arrived in Outdoor Furniture. The desert was familiar to us now. The display shelves were stocked with kitset gazebos, picnic blankets. We ignored it all and speculated on what lay beyond. What would we find? And would the Gardeners value it?

Ten shifts later we reached Jewellery.

We'd seen bangles and rings and bracelets before. There were shelves in Toys and Games filled with them. They were for children though, and made of plastic and tin. These were fitted for adults, fashioned of gold and silver and set with diamonds. It was hard to imagine who'd want any of it, or that the Gardeners would consider it valuable. We wandered among the shelves. Neither of us spoke. We'd come all this way for nothing.

Then we heard the sound.

There was a toy in Toys and Games: a car that you wound up and then drove along the aisle and it made a horrible ringing sound and flashed blue and red from lights mounted on the roof. This was that same sound only louder, never-ending. We tracked it down to a single aisle, deep in the interior of Jewellery, with shelves of a kind we'd never seen before. Some kind of transparent plastic encased the entire shelf in a box. There were doors in the plastic: one of them had been forced open; it lay crooked on its hinges. A bright yellow light above the open door blinked off and on. We gasped when we came close and saw that the display shelves – thin white boards far more elegant than the heavy wooden ones across the rest of the world – had been looted. Swept clean.

Hill pointed. 'The stock boxes above look intact.' So we took out our stainless steel extension ladder and I climbed to the stock shelves and took out my box cutter. I breathed deep. I'd never opened an unopened box before.

The boxes contained . . . more boxes – hundreds of them. They were small, encased in black leather. Whatever was inside them was obviously valuable. I grinned down at Hill. Then I opened it and groaned with frustration.

'What is it?'

'A watch.' I tossed it down to him. There were plenty of watches in Toys and Games. No one knew what they were for. Most had a circular face, with numbers or other marks; some had a blank grey display. They were for children, fashioned from plastic. This one was heavy, gold, fitted for larger wrists, but its ultimate purpose was just as unknowable.

'Worthless,' I complained. 'We came all this way and everything here is worthless.'

'And yet the display shelves were locked inside this case,' Hill said. 'And someone looted them. Why?'

I slid down the ladder. Hill's questions seemed unknowable, pointless. I felt angry. I kicked at the shelf and hurt my foot. Shortly afterwards the shift ended. We walked back to our caravan; the ringing sound from the watch shelves was just a faint echo in the distance. I soon fell asleep, exhausted from our long journey, but Hill stayed awake, leaning against a shelf and tinkering with the watch I'd tossed down, sorting through the other paraphernalia that came in the box, reading a tiny little manual, and examining the small silver disc taped to the bottom of the lid. When I woke Hill was propped up in the same place, snoring gently. Between the snores came a faint ticking sound, the source of which I eventually tracked down to the watch fastened to Hill's left wrist.

'It's for measuring the passing of shifts,' I explained to the Gardener, holding the watch up. 'Each of these ticks' – I paused; we all waited, listening to the tiny sounds – 'is a precise measure of a fraction of a shift passing.'

The Gardener held out his hand. I gave him the watch. He was a once handsome man now running to fat. He wore the traditional white terry cloth dressing gown of his order and had the traditional shaved head. He guarded one of the gateways to Gardening. We'd taken a haul of goods from jewellery – trolleys full of gold bangles, diamond rings – back to Outdoor Furniture, back to the caravan master, who'd shouted at us for bringing him such worthless junk and swore never to trade with us again. We signed on with another caravan, which took us across the desert of Celebrity Fragrances, all the way to Personal and Oral Care, a vast region bordering directly onto Gardening itself.

Personal and Oral Care was a strange land. It was crowded. Nobody smiled. You were supposed to keep to your left when you walked down an aisle but we kept forgetting; people bumped into us, didn't even apologise when we stumbled. Instead of sleeping on mattresses in the aisles many of them slept on the shelves themselves, stacked atop one another, the shelves cleared in direct defiance of the Terms and Conditions. Every second aisle was a garden – and not of plastic pools with soil in them and grow lamps mounted above, like you saw across the known world. The aisle itself was fenced off to waist height and filled with dirt, and this space was used to grow trees: apple trees, lemon trees, peach trees, apricots, limes.

'All my life we were told fruit came from Gardening,' Hill said, eating an apple – a rare delicacy in Home Furnishing. 'But they all came from Personal and Oral Care.'

The borders of Gardening were closed, just as my father had said. Blocked off by huge wooden tables mounted atop one another. Standing in front of these walls, not being able to see the aisle recede into the distance, made us stumble and clutch each other for balance.

'Take a good look, downshelvers,' a passing resident of Personal and Oral Care sneered, steering around us in the crowded aisle.

All this way we'd guarded the secret of the watch we carried with us. 'It might be priceless,' Hill warned. 'People might kill for it.' Now we'd made our way to the gate and presented the watch to the Gardener guarding it. He sat on a beach lounger; he was flanked by six locals, all armed with knives and golf clubs. The gate was a massive wooden table with hinges fixing it to the wall and a complicated pulley system that raised it from the inside. It was closed.

The Gardener examined our watch. He rattled it. He held it to his ear. 'Unusual,' he said. 'But not obviously useful. Shifts are always the same duration. They never change. This has been proved many times by the sages of Gardening.' He handed it back to me but then a thought struck him. 'We have seen watches before,' he said. 'From Toys and Games. But they never worked. How did you get it to go?'

'With this.' Hill held up one of the tiny silver batteries. We'd found one in each of the watch boxes and bought a dozen with us across the desert. 'It seems to work like the cylindrical batteries we use in our grow lamps, but smaller,' he explained. 'It powers the watch.'

The Gardener's face flicked from the battery to Hill and back. 'Are there more of these?' he demanded. 'Can you take us to them?'

'There are aisles and aisles of watches,' Hill replied. The Gardener turned and knocked on the gate. A minute later it began to open.

There were no gardens in Gardening.

The Gardener who admitted us was called Creek. He led us through his department. It was depopulated, eerie – especially after the bustle of Personal and Oral Care. 'There are less than a thousand Gardeners left,' he told us. We saw a handful of other white-robed figures from a distance, some of them talking in small groups.

'What happened to you all?' Hill asked.

'Nothing happened to us.'

'Where are all your children?'

'Most Gardeners don't have children,' Creek replied. 'There

are some. They're at school.'

'School? This late in the shift?'

'They spend a lot of time memorising things,' he said. 'Being a Gardener is all about memory.'

It was easy to see why. All of the display shelves in Gardening had been cleared – anything to do with growing things had been shifted to other departments. The shelves in Gardening were filled with . . . everything else. Any object a Gleaner had found, anywhere in the world, anything that might be useful or the function of which was unknown, occupied a place on its shelves. 'The Song of the Deliverer teaches that every item in the world has a purpose,' Creek said. 'No one in Gardening believes that anymore. We haven't for tens of thousands of shifts.' He led us down an aisle filled with skis and snowboards. 'Most of the contents of the world are meaningless.' He gestured at the objects. 'Created by some random stochastic process. But out of that randomness arises tiny fragments of meaning. Objects which have purpose. Clothes. Food. Pools. Lamps. Batteries. Some of these items only work when they're combined. It was the genius of the Deliverer to put soil in pools and batteries in grow lamps. All of civilisation is based on the combination of items in the world. The purpose of the Gardeners is to find new combinations.'

We stopped. We'd walked a long way; now we reached a region that was, we later learned, the approximate centre of the department, with aisles that were almost stripped bare: just scattered piles of boxes here and there. 'This is the great secret of Gardening,' Creek said, leading us towards the boxes. 'The terrible cipher at the heart of things.'

Hill and I looked around, taking in the empty shelves, the weird silence, then Hill lifted the flaps of one of the boxes and peered inside. He frowned and took out a handful of standard

AA batteries in blister packs and looked at Creek, comprehension slowly dawning, and said, 'This is why you don't have children.'

'All of civilisation depends on the food grown using these batteries,' Creek replied. 'Millions of lives, all of them spent in peace and security. And everyone thinks it will go on forever.'

'But it stops when all the batteries are dead.'

Creek nodded.

'How long do we have?'

'A few thousand shifts.'

I asked, 'Why don't you tell everyone? Why don't you tell people to conserve food? Why don't you have as many people as possible out there searching the world, looking for more batteries? I mean, these were just sitting there on the far side of Outdoor Furniture. No one even looked –'

'You didn't get to Jewellery on your own,' Creek interrupted. 'You were stocked by a caravan, like all Gleaners. And to equip the Gleaners the caravans need to produce a surplus. That means trade. Peace. Civilisation. If we told people the truth there would be panic. War. Collapse. People would kill each other over batteries and dirt. No one could Glean. No one could save us. So we go on. We search. We hope. Were there many of these small batteries in Jewellery?'

Hill and I looked at each other. 'About ten thousand,' I guessed. 'Maybe more deeper in?'

'It may be enough to buy us all a few hundred shifts. Our sages will try and fit these batteries you have bought us to our lamps,' Creek announced. 'Meanwhile you will lead a caravan to Jewellery and bring back everything you can find. You leave first thing next shift.'

We left Gardening after shiftend, while everyone slept. We walked until we found a walled off aisle then climbed to the top: it was easy, on the inner side of the wall, to clamber up the side-mounted tables using the legs as braces. When we reached the top, Hill took an electrical cord – stolen from one of the Gardening shelves – and looped it around the legs of the top table. We abseiled down into Paint and headed for the border.

'If we only have a few thousand shifts left,' Hill said, 'I'm not spending them hauling caravans of watch batteries back from Jewellery. Even if those idiots' – Hill cast a dismissive eye-roll back at Gardening – 'figure out how to make them power the lamps, all they'll do is buy us a little more time. We need to be out there, exploring the world. Finding a real solution.'

'What solution?'

'We'll know it when we see it,' Hill replied. 'First we apply the exact same logic that led us to Jewellery and the watches. We go to the edge of civilisation outshelf and strike out from there.'

By the time the shift began we were deep into Paint. This was a strange, alien place: people wore baggy full-length clothes instead of T-shirts and shorts; the women wore baseball caps pulled low over their faces. Everyone walked with a slow, shuffling gait, their eyes downcast, and kept a distance from one another. Their voices, when they did speak, were harshly accented, almost impossible to understand.

'We're on the far side of Gardening,' Hill whispered. 'The other side of the world.'

We reached the border before the end of shift and signed on to a caravan run by a garrulous woman from Stationery and Home Office Supplies. 'Good to hear some familiar voices,' she said, eyeing the rest of her Paint-sourced crew with distaste.

Twenty shifts later we reached Rubber Goods, my father's ancestral home. People there were foreign but friendly: they directed us to my uncle's shelves and shortly afterwards we found ourselves drinking tea in his aisle, which was the most opulently decorated space I'd ever seen. The finest rugs from Home Furnishings covered the floor, we lay on deep cushions, white sheets overhead filtered the light of the shift into a soft haze. My female cousins came in and out of the aisle bringing us tea and slices of fresh fruit; the men of the family sat behind my uncle as he listened to Hill's plan to strike out into the desert and nodded as my uncle told us how terrible our plan was.

'The department beyond Rubber Goods is Women's Fashion,' he told us, stroking his long, oiled beard and smiling. 'It is not like your Outdoor Furniture. Its products are one of our major trade goods. We have ventured deep into it.'

Hill asked, 'What lies beyond Women's Fashion?'

'Nothing lies beyond it. Traders have explored it. Gleaners have tried to cross it. Some have died trying. None have found an end.'

'All departments end,' Hill insisted. 'Menswear is large too, but it is bounded by Stationery upshelf and Party Supplies downshelf. Women's Fashion can be crossed. We will cross it.'

My uncle sipped his tea. 'You are young and bold,' he told Hill. 'But Women's Fashion is not like other departments. It has many smaller departments within it. Activewear. Leggings. Plus-sized Clothing. Sleepwear and Lingerie alone is vaster than all of Menswear. Each of these departments come to an end but Women's Fashion either has no end or, if it does, it lies at such a vast distance no living being can reach it.'

There was a rustle at the back of the aisle. Another man entered, kneeled beside my uncle and whispered in his ear. My uncle listened, nodded, fixed his eyes on me.

'There are Gardeners at the border,' he said. 'Asking about you. They say you stole something from their shelves.'

'We took nothing –'

My uncle flicked his hand in disinterest. 'You are of my blood,' he said, leaning back so that the cowl of his black rayon dressing gown shaded his eyes. 'But I cannot keep you from the Gardeners.'

'You won't have to,' Hill said. 'Just tell us this. How far did the furthest expeditions into Women's Fashion go? How many shifts outshelf?'

This question prompted much whispering among the men of the aisle. Finally one of them spoke up. 'Back in my grandparent's time the Gleaner named Marsh led a caravan to Swimwear,' he said. 'It was eighty shifts in from the border.'

'How many souls in the caravan?'

'Twenty souls,' the man replied.

Hill thanked him and we whispered together for a moment, working out the math. The logistics of deep desert exploration are exacting. We knew how many trolleys of food a person needed to stay alive over twenty shifts, how far they could walk during a shift with that many trolleys, how far you could venture before you risked starvation. The more souls you added to a caravan the further it could go but the slower it went, and that imposed a limit of how far you could safely go into the deep desert before you needed to turn around and come back. Conventional wisdom had it that seventy shifts was the limit for a twenty-person caravan. Anyone trying to beat Marsh the Gleaner's record was risking their life. I closed my eyes, made sure our figures were correct, opened them and nodded at Hill, who said, 'We go in without food.'

My uncle blinked in surprise. The boys and men behind him shifted, whispering, smiling. Eventually my uncle said simply, 'You'll die.'

'We can live for twenty shifts without food,' I replied. 'And walk five times further in a single shift without trolleys to haul. We'll cover hundreds of thousands of shelves per shift. We can go further than Marsh the Gleaner and make it back alive.'

'You'll get slower and slower the longer you starve,' my uncle warned. 'Those last few shifts you'll barely be able to move.'

'Whatever of value we find in the department beyond Women's Fashion,' I offered, 'we'll bring back with us and give to you. And that's why you'll come out to meet us in eighteen shifts' time and save us.'

On the first shift we ran the whole way. It was fun. We had food in our bellies – my uncle made sure of that. And we were young and strong and venturing out into the utmost unknown in a quest to save the world. Also, we had to make it to the edge of the known world in eight shifts or less.

So we ran. We ran through Tops and Sweatshirts. We ran through Shorts and Skirts. We ran through Luxury Brands, and we slept there when the shift ended. When we woke we snacked on the apples and carrots we'd crammed into our pockets.

That shift was hard. We were tired but Luxury Brands unnerved us. There were no shelves in the display areas – just clothes on hangers interrupted by full-length mirrors that gave us glimpses of ourselves as we passed. So we kept running. 'I don't want to sleep here again,' Hill said, looking with loathing at the unnatural topology of this part of the world. But we were still there when the shift ended. 'Is Luxury Brands larger than the other regions?' I wondered, as we lay down to sleep in an aisle filled with sequined jumpsuits. 'Or are we already slowing down?'

The next two shifts we walked. We spoke little and when we did we disagreed about everything. I had a headache. 'So do I,'

Hill admitted at the end of the shift, adding, 'We've started to starve.' We were still in Luxury Brands. It just went on and on. We needed to reach Swimwear soon if we were to go beyond it and then turn back in time to reach Rubber Goods alive.

But we didn't reach Swimwear during the next shift. Or the next. Nor did we turn back. We just kept walking. We never discussed this, even though it was tantamount to suicide. We just kept going, trudging on into the dizziness, bright lights, blinding headaches, hallucinations. We made less ground with each shift, sleeping longer and longer. We lost all track of time, had no idea how many shifts we'd walked. It was only when we stumbled to a halt, exhausted, and sunk to our knees that I noticed the display shelves had changed. I touched Hill's shoulder and pointed to racks of one-piece bathing suits and said, through numb lips, 'Swimwear.' It was the first time I'd spoken that day. He looked, nodded and sank to the ground and closed his eyes.

We were twelve shifts in. We had about eight shifts left before we starved. There was no way we'd make it back to Rubber Goods. We wouldn't even make it as far as Shorts and Skirts. So we continued outshelf. Deeper into the desert. Away from the world.

We slept more and more. We slept during shifts. We walked a few hundred shelves, slept, walked some more, slept. We were still in Swimwear. We would never leave it. We had a few shifts left to live but no strength to move. The next time we lay down to sleep I knew we wouldn't get up again. We lay beside each other. We held hands. I wondered if anyone would find our bodies.

We woke up in Camping. The light was blinding. We were in the tent aisle. We were still dying. We didn't know how we got there – we fought about it later, after we'd eaten. Hill insisted someone had moved us. 'Someone. Or something.'

'Nonsense,' I replied. 'The simplest explanation is that we walked there ourselves but simply blanked it all out. Or maybe,' I added, 'we didn't even blank it out. We just walked here and didn't notice we'd arrived.

'I would have noticed,' Hill growled. 'I fell asleep surrounded by bikini bottoms and woke up here. Someone moved us. Someone saved us.'

They didn't do a very good job. We crawled along the tent aisle then upshelf to Sleeping Bags, then Airbeds, Fishing Rods, moving randomly, our heads pulsing, our bodies burning their very last reserves of energy. It was total chance we came across Dehydrated Foods. If we'd taken one different turn we'd have bypassed it and died.

The food was in slim foil packets. You mixed it up with water from a drinking fountain. We scooped it from the packets into our mouths. There were dozens of varieties, all labelled with names beyond our comprehension. Some of them made us sick: the contents had spoiled, somehow. 'More dumb luck,' I said to Hill as we kneeled down, vomiting onto the polished concrete after sampling something called Chicken Fettuccine. 'If we ate that when we first arrived we'd be dead.'

'There's no such thing as luck,' Hill replied. 'All of this is happening for a reason.'

On our tenth shift in Camping we found the ladder, leaning against a shelf in the aisle. It wasn't a Gleaner ladder with wheels and hooks, but a solid stainless steel ladder from Tools and Equipment, exported and used all over the known world, identical to the one my parents carried with us to Toys and Games, a lifetime and half a world away.

Hill touched it and murmured, 'Someone's been here before. Someone from our region.'

The ladder was in Packs and Bags. The packs were elaborate devices you could fill with products and fasten to your back. 'We could fit a thousand foil meals in here,' I pointed out. 'We could walk all the way to Jewellery and back again. This proves we're the very first to come here. If someone from our world found backpacks and dehydrated food everyone in the world would know about them. Every Gleaner would use them.'

'Only if they went back,' Hill said. 'What if they kept going outshelf? What if there was something else out there? What if they found something better?'

'We aren't going onwards,' I replied. 'Our world is about to starve to death. We have to go back inshelf and tell the Gardeners about this place.'

'And which way is inshelf?' Hill asked with a sad smile.

We picked a direction at random and started walking. Before we left we picked the largest backpacks we could find and stuffed them with food; when we did this we saw that the boxes on the Dehydrated Foods stock shelves had been opened. Some of them were empty. 'Whoever they were,' Hill said, 'they took far more food than we can carry.'

Once we were on our way I said, 'We should reach Swimwear in less than half a shift. If we don't we turn around.' But Hill did not reply and when we came to the end of Camping we saw that the department beyond it was Christmas Decorations. We stopped at the border.

'We keep going,' Hill said, not even turning to look at me, just staring out into the endless shelves of tinsel and plastic wreaths. 'We seek answers. Why is the world like this? What lies beyond it? Once we've learned the true meaning of things . . . then we return.'

Christmas Decorations took us twenty shifts to cross ('It would have taken over a hundred shifts in a caravan,' Hill gloated.) It was even larger than Women's Fashion. We were almost at the end, trudging glumly through aisles filled with one-size Santa suits and sexy elf outfits when we found the first corpses.

There were about twenty of them. They'd been there so long they didn't even smell: they were just vaguely humanoid heaps of bones and skin and hair wrapped in rags. Most of them were adult. A couple were child sized.

'They were killed,' Hill declared, peering at the bodies, picking up an elf wand and poking at a skull, tipping it to one side. 'See the cracks? Someone bashed their heads in.'

We walked on, crossing the border into Automotive Accessories later that shift. Roof racks. Car seat covers. And we found more bodies, and more, and more. Thousands of corpses. Tens of thousands. We found aisles that had once been homes; instead of mattresses from Home Furnishing they slept on piles of car mats and curtained off their aisles with picnic rugs.

'This was once a civilisation,' Hill declared. 'Just like ours.'

'What did they eat?' I wondered.

Hill did not reply, but a little later we found bones stacked in piles. 'Whatever they ate, they ran out. These corpses have been dismembered. Someone ate them.'

A few shifts later we reached a department called Mother and Baby. At its centre we found Food and Formula. Shelves stripped bare; empty cylinders of milk powder scattered on the ground.

We kept walking. It took ten shifts to reach the end of the corpses, the extent of the dead civilisation. We walked through

Handbags. We walked through Arts and Crafts. We walked through Pet Accessories. We kept walking, and eventually we reached the end of the world.

It was a vast and terrible void. No shelves. They simply stopped: fell away into nothingness, the lights above reflecting off the empty floor below, both diminishing into infinity. It was a space we had no words for: an aisle too vast to be comprehended, stretching from one end of existence to the other. Dotted across it were cardboard boxes, open at the top, with 'Bargain Bin' written on the side. We crawled out to the nearest one and stood up when we reached it, clutching on to each other for support – it was difficult to even stand without the comforting closeness of the aisles – and peered inside. The bin was filled with scented candles.

'What is this place?' I said, my voice cracking. Hill said nothing. I clutched his arm. 'We go back,' I said. 'We've done it. We've reached the end of everything. There's nothing here. No answers. We turn around and go back to the world and save it.'

Hill hesitated, thinking, looking at the candles, the vast plain, then nodded, and we turned back towards the shelves. But just at that moment the fluorescent lights went out. All the colour and brightness of the world flickered away. We both flinched and I thought, Is the world ending? Then Hill laughed and said, 'It's just shiftend. We've lost track of time.'

It was still fairly bright out on the plain. The pale yellow security lights were on, of course, and there were no shelves to cast a shadow. We slept out there, purely because Hill wanted to be able to say we did. 'We went further than anyone else, ever. Went beyond the end of all things and spent shiftend there.'

I had terrible dreams – open spaces that went on forever; the aisles of Home Furnishings choked with corpses –

and woke before the shift began. I lay on my side. In the incomprehensible absence of the shelves and their products I found myself contemplating the polished concrete earth, the steel sky, and wondered what lay beyond them. I wondered if anyone had ever wondered that before.

Hill was still snoring. My eyes fell upon something lying on the ground past the bin of candles: some object, its size and distance impossible to judge. I crawled out to it alone, feeling very brave, and picked it up. It was an empty foil pack.

When the shift began and the lights came up I showed it to Hill, who stared at it with a blank expression then screwed it up and let it fall to the earth. 'And there's something else out there,' I said, knowing I shouldn't say anything, knowing what the consequences would be. 'I saw it on my way back, when the lights came on. Something a long way away. Something big.'

If we kept our eyes on the floor we found we could stand and walk without losing our balance. We couldn't even describe what we were walking towards. An irregularity in the distance, a fraying of the horizon, a darkness where there should have been nothing. At the end of shift, when the lights dimmed again, we simply kept walking, without bothering to stop and sing. Neither of us even commented on this act of blasphemy. We had left the world behind. What use was custom or faith?

There were no fountains, no water. By the third shift we were dying of thirst. 'All this food in our packs,' Hill said bitterly, 'and it is lack of water which will kill us.' We slept little. The air seemed warmer. We made our waste on the open ground and moved on.

'The end seems close,' I said. 'We'll reach it next shift.'

We left the backpacks behind. We made better time. The irregularity resolved itself, although we couldn't believe what we were seeing until we were so close we had no choice but to accept the unthinkable facts. The ground itself rose up in a series of four steps ascending to waist height, stretching from one end of the horizon to the other. At the top of them were signs, spaced far apart. Beyond the signs, far off in the distance, were more shelves.

'Look,' I croaked, pointing at the distant aisles. My eyes were better than Hill's. 'Do you see them?'

'I see them.'

'Do you think there will be water? Maybe even batteries? People?'

'Yes. Maybe. There must be answers. Products which . . .' Hill broke into a stumbling run. I followed. We climbed the steps, hurrying past the signs that read, *Welcome to Consumer Electronics.*

RACHAEL CRAW

Writer, reader, dreamer, singer and believer, Rachael Craw is the award-winning SFF author of the Spark trilogy and *The Rift*. You might remember her from luminous Oz Comic Con or Supanova Expo panels or her epic GIF-game on Twitter. A graduate in Classical Studies and Drama from the University of Canterbury, Rachael Craw teaches English at Nelson College for Girls and writes mind-bending, adrenal-gland-stimulating, swoon-fests for teens and Young Adult fiction enthusiasts.

The Dreamer and the Nightingale

Orla checks her watch and worries her lip and slips into the sanctuary. Two hours until Henry is scheduled to wake. *Sleep, Henry. Sleep.* Mrs Kearney's custom pod glows beside the altar in the late afternoon light. Orla props her rifle against the front pew and ducks her head beneath the pod door. She wipes the headrest with a yellow chamois but the leather is already gleaming. So are the chestnut rails, the copper dials, the armrests and the padded seat. All the best upgrades from the Southern Cradle catalogue.

She steps back and shakes her head but can't resent Mrs Kearney her extravagance, not with the promise of a hefty endowment. Orla's list of burst pipes and holes in roofs and kids who've outgrown their shoes grows longer every day. It's not the pod that worries her. At the final inspection, the great lady had run a gnarled finger over the sleek lines, diamonds gleaming.

Superb, Orla. They told me you were fastidious.

Thank you, Mrs Kearney.

Tell me, girl, will the sky be as blue as they say, in the Cradle?

Bluer.

And stars at night?

The milky way, Mrs Kearney. Better than a painting.

Did you ever see it, yourself, girl?

No, Mrs Kearney. It's not for Nightingales to dream.

A blue sky. Orla shakes her head. The thought is almost frightening. She checks her watch again and pictures Henry in the room directly below her. Too far away for her to feel the aura of his dream. *Sleep, Henry. Sleep.*

She adjusts the pin in the back of her hair and frowns at the state of the sanctuary windows. The glass is already grimy on the outside, despite the dust-reduction canopy lifted over Puriri Bay. When the blood-red easterly blows from the Southern Wastes, all the way across the Hauraki Gulf, it can choke the air for days. She'll have to ask Teina to hose the windows before Mrs Kearney's ceremony.

A low boom rattles the panes in their lead casings. She sweeps her rifle from the front pew and rushes to the windowsill, her body wound tight and the fine hairs on her arms rising. In the garden below, Marama pauses in her directions for the yard lads and the placement of plexihouse hydrangeas. The groundskeeper stares in the direction of the bay, bracing her hands on her broad hips, shoulders thrust back, kerchief flapping in the gale. Orla waits – the yard lads too – but the groundskeeper doesn't reach for the rifle at her back.

Orla scans the orange sky but the dust in the air is too thick to spot missiles, coating the leaves of the border forest dun. Patrols have been scouring the grounds morning and night but there's no sign of the blue-banner religious zealots who believe the work of the Southern Cradle is an abomination. No sign of the black-hooded activists who seek to seize control of it for all. Leaning elbows on the sill, she draws a shaky breath but there's no further sound of attack. Perhaps the Coastguard were firing a warning shot to ward off refugees.

The double doors to the sanctuary open with an unholy clang. Soft steps from the shadows and little Margery Farnsworth hurries down the aisle.

'Nightingale.' The girl pats the pockets of her overalls, adjusting her knife belt to hide the flour dust. 'Miss Reni says the Dreamer's waking early by the looks of things and I'm to come and fetch you.'

'Early?' She slings her rifle over her shoulder and stalks towards the girl.

Margery shuffles back a step. 'She announced it in the kitchen.'

Orla considers upending a pew. Instead, she clicks her teeth. 'Have the girls wipe everything down again and change the candles. No lavender. Mrs Kearney says she's allergic. And don't set the communion bread till Reverend Avril arrives or the mice will be at it.'

She marches out into the foyer and pauses before the service stairs, her thoughts tumbling, all sharp edges. 'The floors could use another sweep here. They should be gleaming.'

The girl slumps. 'We mopped and polished this morning.'

Yanking at the knot of her apron, Orla almost sprains a finger. '*Just do it again.*'

'A polish and all, Miss? It's the red sand, it gets through the cracks.' Margery turns up plaintive eyes from beneath her kerchief. The whites around her irises are veined red.

A pinch of regret tightens Orla's chest: the Academy girls have been up since four this morning, preparing for Mrs Kearney's interment. 'A sweep will do. And if everything goes well tonight, I'll have Mr Mason save some tarts for supper.'

The girl nods and her eyes brighten.

'As long as there's no snivelling or hysterics.'

'No, Miss. None of that.'

'When you've finished here, take Lacy and Myrtle and make yourselves available to Miss Marama. She'll be wanting some extra hands.'

Margery clips a nod and scuttles down the service steps.

'Slow down,' Orla calls. 'You'll break your bloody neck!'

'Yes, Miss – sorry, Miss!'

Orla folds her apron and hangs it over her arm, her endlessly scrolling to-do list erased by Reni's summons. The spiteful cow, announcing it to the whole kitchen. She shouldn't let her worry run away on her, but it's already pitched to a gallop. Henry's been waking early on and off for a couple of months now – and two cases of the fits with it. She knows what people will say. *It's her duty to notify the World Council. She should have notified them months ago. Jeopardising the island to protect her position. Jeopardising us all to protect him. She's old enough to know better. A waste of seven good breeding years. Nothing to show for it. Selfish, grasping girl.*

She lifts her chin and makes her way downstairs. When the newsreels are dispatched in the morning, they'll confirm to the last outposts – to everyone – that Mrs Kearney's interment was a success and the Southern Cradle is *still* the largest, safest Dreamscape in the world. Still the only Dreamscape that offers seventy years of fully experienced life dreamed in an economical three. *Seventy years* of blue skies, clean air and freedom from war before a Sleeper's ashes are committed to the safe, silent arms of the Pacific Ocean. Who could ask for better since the meteor that ended the Great War? As for the World Council, they've got nothing but obscene profit to look forward to, as the elite pay a ransom in bonds for ballot entries in the interment draws. Orla will deal with the nay-sayers tomorrow.

Approaching the kitchen, she unclenches her teeth and steps through the door. The afternoon light casts the room in a gauzy tangerine glow. The warm waft of roast beef makes her mouth water. Eight girls chop and dice at the counter. Mrs Kearney's last supper will be laid in the family room in an hour. Orla makes an automatic check for weapons, knife belts on the juniors and pistols on the prefects. The Southern Cradle knows to keep up its guard. 'Mr Mason.' Orla keeps her tone light and even. 'I need breakfast for Henry, if you can spare one of the girls.'

Mason Rewiti straightens from his work at the island counter, carving knife poised over a glistening haunch of beef. He squints at the clock high on the rough brick wall. All the girls have stalled, heads turned wide-eyed towards her. Orla ignores their feigned surprise. They all heard Reni's announcement.

The cook wipes perspiration from his brow. 'Not worth seeing if he'll go back under for another hour or so?'

'No point.'

Whispers rise beside the counter.

'*That makes three days in a row.*'

'*I told you so, didn't I?*'

'*He's been slipping for months.*'

'*They'll have to notify the council.*'

'*She'll find an excuse not to.*'

'*She can't stop them finding out.*'

Mason glares at his workers. As one, they swivel back to their cucumbers and radishes. He gives Orla an apologetic nod before washing his hands at the sink. 'Linsay, porridge. Mavis, check the preserves, there should be a jar of peaches in the larder.'

Two of the kerchiefed girls pause in their chopping and bob a curtsy. 'Yes, Mr Mason.'

'Shall I make toast, Da?' Mason's daughter steps in from the cook's office, tall, broad hipped and beautiful like her mother, Marama. The deliberate tilt to her chin confirms she's heard everything and refuses to believe the worst. She offers a bracing, never-mind sort of smile that makes Orla's chest tight. 'There's marmalade. Henry loves it.'

'Make it a couple of thick slices, Daph,' her father calls over his shoulder, adopting his daughter's forced cheer.

Daphne follows the smaller girls to the larder. 'You'll take some too, Orla?'

She swallows. 'Go on then.'

Whispers rise again from the counter.

'*She's out of time.*'

'*What a waste.*'

'*Seven years and nothing to show for it.*'

'*I'd die of shame.*'

Orla keeps her expression steady but positions the apron in front of her flat stomach.

One of the young helpers clears her throat. A girl around fifteen. Marlee or Maisy or something. A knowing smirk mars her lips. 'Are you keeping well there, Nightingale?'

Orla nods coolly at the chopping board. 'Mind your fingers.'

A few giggles ripple down the line of kerchiefed heads, some admiring while others blink at the girl's gall. Orla closes her hand against the temptation to slap faces.

When the tray is laid, Daphne carries it beside Orla down to Henry's apartment room. She doesn't speak, and Orla is grateful for company without demands. They pause before the heavy oak doors; Daphne's head catches the orange light, making her black hair look as though it has been set ablaze.

'It mightn't mean the end, just yet,' Daphne says softly. 'Henry's strong.'

Orla takes the tray, fixing her eyes on the steaming porridge. 'Do you think I'm being selfish?'

Daphne hesitates. 'I think you care about Henry.'

'I care about *all* of us,' she says. 'Henry's the most powerful Dreamer the island has ever had. You don't just throw that away.'

The young woman stares at the porridge too, lowering her voice. 'No one can dispute that, Orla. It's just – we have to be realistic. And your duty isn't just to Henry. You have an obligation to the World Council.'

The tightness in Orla's chest rises to her throat. 'There's no guarantee Henry and I would have produced more Nightingales *or* Dreamers.'

'You might have with a plexihouse lad.'

'Who says I didn't try?'

Daphne flattens her lips.

Orla lifts and drops her shoulders. 'They smell like manure.'

The young woman laughs softly. 'Don't let those little Academy tarts get you down. You're the Nightingale. You deserve their respect. My whole family believes in you. Even if nothing comes of your time with Henry, you're only twenty-two. Who knows, with a new Dreamer –'

The door clicks open and Daphne cuts off, cheeks blooming. She pats Orla on the back and walks away. The tray is heavy and Orla's arms shake.

Reni stands at the threshold, tucking pale curls beneath the edge of her kerchief, mouth like a cat's arse. 'Took your time. He's been stirring for a quarter hour.'

She doesn't reply, waiting till Daphne's out of earshot.

'Are you coming in, then.' The older woman crosses her arms over her narrow chest. 'Or you'd rather waste time scowling on the threshold while his Lordship's porridge gets cold?'

'You didn't have to announce it to the whole kitchen.'

'They have a right to know.'

Orla carries the tray to the buffet. 'It benefits no one. You've just put fear in their heads.'

'If you did your job, the World Council could have a replacement here in two weeks.'

Orla clicks her teeth. 'You are *not* the Nightingale. You haven't *been* the Nightingale for seven years. You don't get a say.'

'At least I had the decency to step aside. I'm not the one who's wasted seven years with nothing to show for it.' She gestures at Orla's stomach in disgust.

'Get out.'

'*Henry's done.* You have a duty –'

'Get. Out.'

'Suit yourself.'

Reni shuts the door with a clap. Orla cringes, watching Henry for signs of startle, but there's no sudden movement from his pod. Her heart belts and she blinks to keep tears from reddening her eyes. Henry will know she's been crying and then there will be questions and an argument and Mrs Kearney will arrive. She draws a steadying breath. Peering through the shadows, she can smell that the room is clean. Reni might be a sour old witch's tit, but she isn't lazy.

Henry's apartment sits above the basement, into which was dug the fathoms-deep vault of the Cradle. Above the high cherry-wood ceiling of his apartment sits the sanctuary. A colossal chute, with elaborate copper casing, houses the elevator shaft that runs down beneath Mrs Kearney's pod. This allows the interred a dignified descent, through Henry's private quarters, to the mouth of the Cradle below. Another more industrial lift sits beneath Henry's pod. This one travels lower still, to the heart of the Cradle.

Kneeling at the hearth to light the fire, she gives herself a moment to recover. Reni has the kindling stacked perfectly in the grate, a little log behind it. It crackles to life and she tiptoes to the velvet curtains. Using a hook on a wooden pole, she reaches up to pull them back. Just a few inches, to allow a slice of orange light. The bright shaft chases shadows into corners and turns the brass standing-lamp into a glowing artefact. Crystal decanters on the buffet hurl stars to dazzle the ceiling. Her eyes prick. *He hasn't faded yet.*

She opens the gate to the lift platform and leans over Henry, into the warm wash of his aura. Her head swims with a pleasant rush, her skin tingling all the way down to the soles of her feet. One lanky leg hangs over the side of the pod. His right arm is flung across his face and his ash brown hair splays over the headrest. He stirs, shifting his weight, a groan in the back of his throat. This is always the hard bit, the transition – waking or falling asleep. A clutching sensation grabs at her heart and she clicks her teeth. What had she been chiding Margery about before? No snivelling or hysterics. Few Dreamers last longer than eight years. Henry's had nine. He's lucky. So is she.

She rubs her hands to give them some warmth before laying both on his arm. Contact helps, like an anchor point for the Dreamer to shift from subconscious to conscious. 'Henry,' she murmurs, careful not to startle him. Startling makes for a messy transition – in the worst case, sending a shockwave through the Cradle, disturbing thousands of souls at once.

She strokes the warm downy length of his forearm. Unthinking, she begins to hum notes from the Lady of Shallot, a ballad so depressing that Orla normally refuses to sing it. Henry loves it because he's a soft-hearted fool with a head full of silly romance. She lets a verse rise to her lips. 'Underneath the bearded barley, the reaper, reaping late and early . . .' But 'reaper' sticks and she swallows and skips a few lines. 'In her web, she still delights, to weave the mirror's magic sights . . .'

The aura stirs around her like a warm bath. Each note intensifies her awareness of Henry, the sound unspooling around them like a silvery net, wider, deeper. She sings and Henry sighs beneath his arm, mumbling, 'Mmm'ha sick o'shadows.'

She lifts the arm from his face and lays it by his side. His eyelids flicker and his lips twitch. She keeps humming, losing the lines before gathering them again. 'A bow-shot from her bower-eaves, he rode between the barley-sheaves . . .'

Henry mumbles and begins to cough, a dry susurration obscuring his words. Orla braces his shoulders to keep him from dislodging the tether at the base of his skull. She lifts her voice. 'The sun came dazzling thro' the leaves . . .'

The aura recedes like a wave. Henry's eyelids flicker open, he coughs and bucks a little, trying to speak. Orla leans to hold him in place. 'Breathe, Henry.' She tilts her head into his line of sight, catching his gaze and drawing him into the present, into the real world. He heaves air through his nose, blinking.

She raises her eyebrows at him. 'You were saying?'

Calming now, he clears his throat and gestures for her help in sitting up.

'Hang on.' She hooks an arm beneath his shoulders. By feel, she locates the tether at the nape of his neck, releasing the valve. She brushes down his hair over the small plug and secures the tether on the hook beside the headrest.

Torso bare to his hips, he sits up, wholly unselfconscious. 'It's a metaphor.'

She frowns, taking in the pallor of his skin, the weight he's lost, the blown-out pupils. Bad as a wastrel poet – all eyes and lashes and lips. Suicide lips, Daphne calls them. The kind you die for. 'A metaphor?'

'He rode between the barley-sheaves.' He wiggles his eyebrows.

She lowers her chin. 'Are you being filthy, Henry?'

His grin is slow and wicked and she shakes her head.

'Those ballads are all about repressed sexual desire.'

'Lord Tennyson was a pervert?'

'An optimist.' He stretches his arms over his head, bringing all the etched lines of his body into sharp relief, and yawns. 'You've seen the painting?'

'The sad girl in the boat?'

'No, the one where she's spotted Lancelot and she abandons restraint and comes to the window. She's sort of pitched forward and hungry looking.'

'So, it's the desire for sex that kills her?' She screws up her nose. 'Meanwhile, Lancelot can whore his way around the green valleys of England.'

'From his blazon'd baldric slung, a mighty silver bugle hung,' he offers.

'*That's* optimistic.' She waits as he swings his feet down and sits on the edge of the pod. His eyes flick to the clock above the fireplace and Orla shifts her weight to block his view. Not fast enough.

The humour drains from his face. 'Well, shit.'

'Not necessarily.'

'I'm almost two hours early.' He squeezes his eyes closed. 'That's *three consecutive days* of interrupted sleep cycles. No wonder you're singing me ballads. You think it's the end.'

'It doesn't mean –'

'Three is the threshold for notifying the council.'

'Yesterday's interruption doesn't count. The bloody coastguard was shelling refugees. Nobody could have slept through that.'

'Stop minimising the situation, Orla.'

'Stop catastrophising the situation, Henry.'

He narrows his eyes. Exhaling through his nose, a short sharp gust, he pushes up to his feet, dwarfing her. The sudden movement unsteadies him and he grips the lift gate, his sheet falling away. Orla supports him around the waist, comforted and tortured by his solidity.

The scent of last night's bath still lingers in his skin, mingled with some essential Henry-ness. She swallows and it hurts. She guides him towards the faded wingback where he usually takes his meals between cycles, but he swings away, out of her hold, rescuing his post-sleep shuffle into a purposeful stride. He passes through the shaft of light, briefly deified. At his table, where his collection of maps, calendars and charts are spread, he opens the Cradle ledger.

'Your breakfast will get cold.'

He peers down at the entries mapping his sleep. 'Never mind the fifteen thousand people who might have lost three years of their lives – Henry's porridge is getting cold.'

She drags her top lip through her teeth. 'Don't be dramatic.'

'More light, please, Orla.' He hits the 't' on 'light' like a bullet through tin.

She sweeps his robe from the back of the sofa, the heavy brocade slippery as silk, a gift from a wealthy Italian ambassador, interred last spring. She approaches him slowly, cataloguing the details of his naked body. The once-taut lines of his broad back. The pleasing cinch of his hips. The muscular indents of his pale bottom. His posture maintains the suggestion of athletic grace. With a little shake of her head she drapes the robe over his shoulders.

'It's only us,' he mutters, but the tone is softer – an apology.

'Yes,' she says, softer too, 'but I'm about to open the

curtains and unless you want the Academy girls passing out in the lower fields or panting at the fence . . .'

'I like the sound of panting at the fence,' he says, frowning over the ledger.

Reni will have recorded the first signs of waking. Orla's been over the entries again and again during the last four months, keeping watch beside Henry night after night, calculating any likely damage. Interrupted sleep is an unavoidable hazard. The Cradle has a built-in buffer that will tolerate the occasional shortened sleep cycle. Particularly mid-cycle – Orla is usually able to soothe Henry back to sleep within an hour, singing him down, stroking his face, sometimes lying over him, her physical weight like an anchor. It's the interruptions close to the end of a cycle that are the worst. Until they take a proper audit, it's only guesswork. They can't yet be certain about permanent damage. She resists the temptation to point this out, unwilling to spark another argument.

Hooking the curtain, she drags it back and the late afternoon light floods the room. Henry flinches and turns away, hoisting the ledger into his arm. 'We can't put it off any longer. You have to notify the council.'

She doesn't reply.

'They need to make a final selection on my replacement.'

A muscle cramps beneath her ear; she's clenching her teeth too hard.

He taps the ledger and squints back at her. 'Orla?'

Suddenly exhausted, she props her rifle against the bookcase and lays her knife belt over the back of a chair. She slips the pins from her hair, takes off her boots and unzips her coveralls. They pool around her ankles and she steps free in her briefs and thin cotton singlet. Ignoring Henry, she crosses to the basin and runs some water, splashes her face and washes her hands, drying them thoroughly. Then she crosses to the sideboard and collects the breakfast tray, carrying it to the wingback.

'I don't care about breakfast.' He sighs and joins her before the fire.

She lays the tray on the coffee table, adds cream and sugar to Henry's porridge.

'I said –'

'Shut up, Henry.' Curling her legs on his chair, she settles with the bowl on her thigh and spoons oats into her mouth.

He sits on the ottoman and her vision blurs. He closes the ledger, places it on the seat beside him and leans his elbows on his knees. 'It's not like there was going to be another ending.'

She says nothing.

He watches her eat his breakfast. Finally, he picks up an apple from the tray and takes a bite. Crunching, he cocks his head. 'It's all right for you,' he says, playing at bitterness and failing, because the bitterness is real, eroding the bones of each word. 'You're young enough for another Dreamer, maybe two, before they turf you on the scrap heap with Reni and the leftovers. They'll get their baby out of you.'

'Don't be a prick.' She sets down the bowl with a clatter.

He bites his lip and slips to his knees.

She shakes her head. 'I'm due upstairs.'

'I don't need much of your time, Nightingale.'

'That's not much of a boast.'

He snorts, tossing the apple aside. It thunks wetly on the hearth.

'Reni just cleaned this whole room,' she says.

He digs his arms around her waist and falls into her, pushing her back into the chair, burying his face in her neck. 'Don't tell on me,' he mumbles against her skin. 'She hates my guts.'

'Is there any wonder?' She lays her cheek on Henry's head. He tugs her hips towards him and settles himself between her legs. '*Henry.*'

But he's always known how to reach her. Even when they failed at words, he could map the way through barbed wire and land mines to bring them back together. She slips her hand up into the back of his hair, thick and silky. She runs the other over his shoulder and firmly down the centre of his back, making him sigh. Want quickens inside her. He lifts his head and they kiss deeply, lips and tongues sweetened by the aftertaste of brown sugar, apple and cream. A greedy kiss.

He presses his forehead to hers. 'I'm sorry.'

'I wanted it to be you.'

Unhooking an arm, he slides his hand over her belly. 'I let you down.'

'I hate it when you say that, Henry.'

'I hate the World Council.' He grazes her lips with his, slowly this time. 'Still, it would have been something, you know? To take with me – into the Cradle. Just knowing we had made something great. Something real. Living on.'

'It's not over . . .'

He meets her gaze with a sad smile. 'Then why are we blubbing?'

She touches his face and he leans into her palm. She kisses his eyes, his cheeks, his mouth. Salt on her tongue. With shaking hands, she tugs at his robe. Fumbling away folds of brocade and the soft slip of cotton, they join with a gasp. His face in her neck. Her mouth at his ear. Erasing time, they plunge each other down, down deep into familiar bliss.

Afterwards, he wraps her in his robe and they wipe each other's tears. When he slips away to run the bath, she hoists her feet up over the headrest, her hair dangling to the rug. The light has almost died. Orla closes her eyes and guards her thoughts against the end, the call she'll have to make and the last song she'll sing over him in the coming days. The sound of rushing water rumbles from the bathroom and Orla calls, 'You'll have to bloody carry me.'

'What happened to being needed upstairs?' he says with a soft laugh.

'Mrs Kearney will have her blue skies, her starry nights. I just want a bath.'

'You'll be –'

A sharp boom, smash and a thud.

Orla scrambles off the chair, crashing into the coffee table, barking her knees. His name catches in her throat as she grabs her rifle and stumbles to the bathroom. Skidding through the door into billowing steam, she gapes at Henry, slumped against the side of the claw-foot tub, blood streaming from a gash in the side of his neck.

She crunches towards the shattered windows, slicing her feet. In the neighbouring field, a blue banner flaps in the wind. The Sons of God. A man runs towards the treeline, away from the Southern Cradle, weapon in hand. He nearly makes it, but Orla lifts her rifle and unfurls the back of his head like a wet red rose. The clap of sound reverberates so painfully off the tiled walls, it pierces her inner ear. She drops the gun and clamps her head. She turns to Henry, picks her way through the glass and sinks to her knees. Taking his hand into her lap, she links their fingers and whispers his name – but he's already gone. The tub overflows and her robe, Henry's beautiful brocade, soaks up water and blood.

The apartment door bangs open and shouts rise: her name, Henry's name.

Reni, Daphne and Mason barrel through the bathroom door, weapons raised, their cries shrill. Shadow falls over her; someone reaches to turn off the faucet. A trembling hand clasps her shoulder. Someone crouches beside Henry. Mrs Kearney's name rattles through Orla's brain and she blinks.

'Mason,' she croaks.

He steps away from the window. 'You got the bastard.'

Reni chokes back a sob, patting Orla's arm. 'Of course she did. She's the Nightingale, isn't she?'

Daphne covers Henry with a towel, gently lifting Orla's hand and his to rest on top. She wraps another towel around his neck. 'Mrs Kearney's on her way from the village. There's at least fourteen for her last supper. What shall we do, Orla? We have to tell them.'

'There's nothing to stop the interment,' Reni snaps. 'The Cradle will sustain life for up to a month without a Dreamer. There's time.'

'Mason,' Orla croaks again. 'The boarding house on Greenvale. Ask for Tom Kinney. Tell him I sent you. Tell him it's time.'

All three turn to stare at her. Daphne covers her mouth. Mason blinks, understanding forming in his eyes. 'You . . . notified the World Council?'

'Two months ago.'

Reni squeezes Orla's shoulder, tears spilling over. 'Hurry, Mason. Do as she says, and don't talk to anyone. Bring him through the laundry room.'

He gestures at the window. 'The body in the paddock? The blue banner?'

Reni shakes her head. 'No one can see that from the sanctuary. Let them know at the gatehouse, discreetly. They'll take care of it.'

'Hurry, Da.' Daphne clasps her father's hand. With a final sorrowful nod to the Dreamer, Mason bolts out the door, leaving the women to stare at Orla, staring at Henry, staring at nothing at all. Daphne clears her throat. 'I'd best get back to the kitchen, the girls were anxious. Some of them crying when they heard the bang.'

'Tell them it was a burst pipe,' Reni says. 'They go like a cannon blast. Splash some water on your dress and pull yourself together. Admit that it gave you a fright, but you can't go back sobbing.'

Daphne is quick to comply, grateful to be told what to do. She pauses at the door. 'I'm that sorry, Orla. I really am. Henry was a good man.'

Orla tries to nod but the girl is gone. Reni sets to work, laying towels across the doorway to contain the water. Time folds in half then halves again, and dusk paints the bathroom dark blue. Orla can't feel her legs, after kneeling so long, and Henry's fingers are cool in her palm. Finally, there's a firm hand on her shoulder and she tries to rise but the sting of glass makes her hiss.

Reni picks the shards from Orla's feet before binding them in soft bandages.

By the time Mason Rewiti knocks on the apartment door, Reni has Orla sitting in Henry's wingback, changed into a clean, plain dress and slippers to hide her bandaged feet. The bathroom door is closed. The former Nightingale lets in the men. Orla is dimly aware of movement in her peripheral vision, Mason's low rumbling voice, a brief, accented tenor, then the door closing again. Reni gives instructions to the boy in her brisk, no-nonsense manner.

'Orla,' the woman calls. 'Mr Kinney is ready for you.'

When she gets to her feet the room lurches, but Orla steadies herself. The sting in each step throbs like a heartbeat. The boy has set aside his threadbare coat, vest and fraying shirt. He's tall, like Henry. His pale chest glows in the firelight, every bone distinct. He lies down inside the pod and Reni connects the tether. She turns to Orla, rubbing her hands, prompting her to do likewise.

'I'm glad to meet you, Miss Orla,' the boy says, his accent lending each solemn word a rising lilt. A square jaw emphasises the hollows of his cheeks. His eyes are huge with thick black lashes. 'But I'm very sorry for your loss.'

She stares at his mouth. *Suicide lips.*

'Excuse me, Miss?'

She closes her eyes and opens them again, furrowing her brow. 'How old are you?'

'Nineteen, Miss.'

Nineteen.

A low rumble overhead pulls her into the present. The copper elevator shaft vibrates beneath the sanctuary. Mrs Kearney. She pictures the great lady settled in her pod, descending to the Cradle below, but feels no relief. She will have her blue skies. Burst pipes and leaking roofs will be fixed. Shoes will be bought for growing feet. The families that serve the Southern Cradle will eat. Tom Kinney, the poor, thin boy will sleep and dream, and the Nightingale will sing.

Reni brushes her arm. 'I'll fetch you some chicken broth and a nice warm barley loaf for when he's under. You can rest and Mr Mason will help me tidy up.' Her eyes skip towards the bathroom door.

Orla swallows thickly to find the words. 'Thank you, Reni.'

The older woman pats Orla on the hand. 'We'll feed up the lad. He'll be fine and fit by the end of the month.'

After the door closes behind her, Orla clears her throat. 'Is there a song you like, Mr Kinney?'

Tom Kinney shifts his broad bony shoulders, catching his lower lip between his teeth. 'I'm not fussy, Miss. I'm sure whatever you'd like would do the trick.'

'It'll go easier for you if it's personal.'

Colour creeps into his face. 'Are you familiar with any hymns?'

She lifts her eyebrows. 'A few.'

'My mother used to sing "Abide With Me, 'Tis Eventide" . . . when I was little.'

Orla waits for the words to drift up from memory, beginning to hum the opening lines before finding the lyrics. 'The day is past and gone, the shadows of the evening fall, the night is coming on . . .'

The boy closes his eyes, tight as fists, as though to fight his way into sleep. Pity alone compels her to slip a hand over his shoulder. He shivers, but the tension lifts from his brow as she sings. 'If I cannot commune with thee, nor find in thee my light, the darkness of the world, I fear . . .' Tears slip down her cheeks. No resistance. No panicked final grasp at consciousness. Nothing like Henry. Warmth like a summer tide laps the air around them. Awareness unfolds, easing the ache in her throat, the ache in the deep tissue of her chest. She fills her lungs and unspools the song, that silver net, sinking the Dreamer softly, softly into sleep.

KIRSTEN MCDOUGALL

Kirsten McDougall is the author of *Tess*, a gothic novella about a young woman with special powers, and *The Invisible Rider*, a book of interconnected stories. She has been the recipient of the Creative NZ Louis Johnson New Writer's Bursary and a Michael King Writers Centre Residency.

A Visitation

'But one can also imagine that the fantastic invention that is the Internet may likewise disappear. Just as airships have disappeared from our skies.'
—Umberto Eco, *This is not the end of the book*

A few months after the collapse of the internet, Clarice Lispector came to see me.

I am not a superstitious person nor have I ever had a strong belief in that fashionable thing that people call 'my narrative' when referring to their own psychology, as if their lives can be organised to make sense and have meaning. Therefore, I don't believe these two events are connected although they did both occur within a short space of time. I mention them in conjunction only because they were two major events, one public and catastrophic, the other personal and miraculous like a dream in which you meet your dead mother for the last time and she has become peaceful.

I was at home writing cheques I knew would bounce. It was important for me to go through this process, however futile.

The first year was like that – finding new ways of doing things, some of which were the old ways. The experts on the radio were giving it a positive spin by calling it the 'new nostalgia', which seemed to me a paradoxical and ill-defined term, for it is impossible to be nostalgic for queuing in a bank when one is queuing in a bank.

I refused to enter the bank. I knew they had nothing for me so I stayed at home and wrote empty cheques, forging my ex-husband's signature.

The disarray of everyday life that the collapse brought about was a saving grace for someone like me. Global chaos had risen up to meet my own private disorder, and for a while we chimed. But I remember how temporary it all felt, as if life were being run from a back-up generator until the main power station was working again. Perhaps that's what they meant by invoking nostalgia, those expert talkers on the radio – that it was possible to feel homesick for the past, living in circumstances like the past, in our very strange present.

In the midst of all this she came.

There was a sharp rap on the front door. The doorbell was the first thing I destroyed when my husband left.

She had her back to me as I opened the door and was looking up at the thrush that was making its nest in the half-dead tree by the entrance to the house. I cleared my throat and her body gave a small jolt as if surprised I was here, though it was her doing the calling. For a moment her face was clouded by smoke.

And then I saw it, the cigarette in her glorious mouth, her arch brows raised, her cheekbones contoured by blusher using a makeup technique that remains out of my own blunt reach.

It was the cloud of smoke that connected the woman in front of me with the grand dame of Brazilian letters. I knew her face because her books were plastered in it, which is what happens when you are an extraordinary-looking female writer. I was introduced to her work years ago and didn't take to it, but her name and her face had stuck with me.

It wasn't until earlier this year that I went back to her collections and found myself ready for them. Age rewards the patient reader. They affected me, those stories, although they left me feeling uncertain about what was happening, sometimes to the characters in the stories, and more often to me, the person reading. She had a way of unsettling the words on the page that was not entirely pleasant and sometimes felt like an orgasm not reached.

She gestured behind me. The shock of her arrival had caused me some confusion and I'd forgotten to invite her in. I apologised and stood back for her to enter. I wanted to apologise for apologising, but I kept my mouth shut.

We passed through my narrow and cramped hallway, lined with my ex-husband's drum cases, which he would soon come and collect with a silence that accused me of stealing his possessions, rather than recognising his own negligence at having left them behind.

I stepped over the vacuum cleaner I never got around to putting away and now treated as a permanent piece of furniture in the middle of the hall. With shame, I indicated to Ms Lispector to do the same. I saw anew the detritus in the house that I had allowed to build up like a plaque in the heart. This hallway was nothing like the hallways she was used to, which would be wide. Any furniture that the hallways of Clarice held would be carved and elegant and in its right place.

And then I realised that it was ridiculous to speculate, that her mind would not be on the drum cases or the vacuum cleaner, but on the cockroach I had crunched to death last night with the sole of my boot and left there, flattened on the wooden floorboard. Her writer's eyes would see that above all else. One of her stories had a recipe for killing cockroaches, which goes to prove how fiction can be both mysterious and useful.

We stood in my living room and I offered to make coffee. She shook her head, no, but sat down in the only empty chair and lit another cigarette.

I looked around for a saucer for her to use as an ashtray, then, pushing a pile of clothes that needed folding to the ground, I sat in the chair opposite her.

On the coffee table between us were two of her books, which I had borrowed from the library over six months before. The collapse of online systems had also affected the library lending systems and they had called an amnesty on all loans via the post. I had been honest and returned everything except for the two Lispector collections and a Nigella Lawson that had a number of easy-to-prepare, cheap dishes which could now only be found in books, not googled an hour before dinnertime.

Clarice's eyes skimmed the books and perhaps I saw her eyebrow ascend her forehead upon seeing her own name on the table, but then her face returned to its pointed, alert state.

She took a breath and began to talk, and for a few minutes I watched her and listened in silence, not to what she was saying but to the sound of her voice, which had a quality that in any woman or man I find most seductive, or in some cases, repulsive. It resonated as from within the antique wood of a cello, slightly roughened by her cigarette habit as the sound passed through her throat. I wondered if even as a girl her words had been stored deep within her chest. She spoke in a foreign language, which I assumed was Portugese, I don't know. For those first few minutes I understood not a word she said, but neither did I attempt to understand her. It was enough just to look and listen.

She wore a dress of geometrical shapes and block patterns, in cream and red. It was not the sort of dress you could buy in New Zealand, now or in the past, and I kept looking at that fabric down to where the dress was neatly brought in to her waist by a slim belt, at her elbows where the sleeves stopped in an elegant mid-length and her bare forearms appeared without freckles or lines and with smooth, strong skin. I wanted that dress, that skin. Cancer, the disease that had killed her years before, hadn't left a mark on her. It had punched her down, but here she was resurrected, perfect.

When she spoke, the movements of her face were like that of a refined adult cat, whose bones and muscles move with subtlety beneath its sleek fur, an animal who knows its worth and offers you nothing but its presence.

And what was she hunting for?

She didn't smile once, and always in her hand was a cigarette, which I began to think of as a pen with which she was inscribing invisible letters on the air, creating a story only she could read, all the while speaking in her slow, deliberate and serious manner.

I began to think her talk and the elegant features of her face were a decoy for her secret writing. It was with her smoking pen that she reminded me that a writer who needs to write will not be stopped, even when in company, even when her readers number seventeen.

The needs of the writer are simple, and to some people must seem selfish. A part of them is always kept hidden, just as the hunter must camouflage herself. But the writer is always watching, even when she is being watched; she is always making notes. Indeed, writers are terrible people.

When Clarice spoke, and even in the rest she took between words, to inhale her cigarette or to command to her mouth or to the burning tip of her pen the correct word, she looked peevish. Her eyes were downcast, as though it was I who had interrupted her mid-sentence, not she who had knocked on my door.

Then she stopped talking and looked down for a long solemn moment. I did not feel the need to cover the silence with my own chatter, which would only be empty and betray my idolatry.

She leaned forward and placed a smooth finger on the Nigella, which sat on the coffee table beside her own book. Her fingernail was square and groomed. At last she said something I could understand.

'Who is this woman?' She tapped the cookbook.

I shook myself out of silence.

'That's Nigella. She's a famous cook. Her father, Nigel Lawson, was Chancellor of the Exchequer for Mrs Thatcher's government.'

I don't know why I gave her so much information. Perhaps I was showing off or simply trying to be helpful. It is hard to be natural before a person you admire. There was more to say about Nigella Lawson, of course – her hugely successful career, the public strangulation in a restaurant by a wealthy and violent husband, allegations of cocaine habits – but I stopped there. I am a Nigella fan. If she snorts coke or drops ash in the mixing bowl, I only love her more.

'He wanted a son,' said Clarice.

'Who wanted a son?' I said.

'The father, of course.' She made a sound like, pah! Perhaps she was forcefully emitting the smoke from her lungs.

Of course she was right, about Nigel Lawson wanting a son. It was the one piece of information I hadn't thought to impart, but it was the one detail that could open up a story.

'In my day, women were famous for their ankles or their turn of phrase. Cooking . . .' Clarice shrugged. 'It's something we all must do, no? Unless we are wealthy enough to have a maid do it for us. But I see that women still must sell their faces on their books.'

I nodded.

'Why not? She is very beautiful, not like a cook at all,' she said.

I waited for her to explain what she meant by this while she paused and lit another cigarette.

'When I took my first story to a publisher, he asked me, who did I copy it from? When I said I had not copied it, he asked, did I translate it? He could not believe that a young woman was capable of writing such things,' she said.

As she spoke, I observed that she had a knack of appearing both deliberate and vague, using her heavy eyelids as a defensive wall. It gave the impression that she was offering absolute honesty and then retreating from the response it might get. How she would have hated the modern obsession with writers, the constant public events the successful writers are expected to give, the photographs, and the intelligent opinions they are required to hold in their mouths at all times. At least now social media was gone, and the news was slower. The analysts were now saying that a finite state, the likes of which they had never reckoned upon, had been reached, whatever that meant.

'I've been reading your stories,' I said.

She looked at me, guarded. I felt shy.

'I like them very much. "The Egg and the Hen", I can't imagine how you wrote that.'

'Neither can I. It's the one story I don't understand.'

I made a sound like, ha, not to laugh, but to show her that I understood nothing also.

She held her face still, her eyes turned down and for a moment I thought she might be about to cry. Then I saw she was strong and defiant, refusing something, I don't know what, but certainly not about to cry.

'The question of understanding isn't about intelligence, it's about feeling,' said Clarice.

At that moment of revelation, at that precise moment in which I felt my mind flutter above the warm rock of greater awareness, my son arrived home from school wearing the heavy look I can never work out is my own or his father's but which means we're in for a half hour of hurt and anger. He is only six, but he carries deep sorrow in him like an opera singer about to stab himself on stage.

He yanked on the back door and dropped his bag and jacket where he stood.

'You were supposed to pick me up,' he said. It was an accusation.

'I couldn't,' I said. 'We have a visitor. This is Clarice.'

He looked at her briefly then turned back to me.

'I'm hungry,' he said.

She looked back at him, her eyelids raised, as if to see him better. A smile, her first and only, appeared in her eyes and turned up the wry corners of her mouth.

'An egg is the best thing after school,' she said.

'I don't like eggs,' he said.

'That's not true,' I said.

Although perhaps it was. I never cooked eggs for him, but I didn't want to admit this in front of Ms Lispector. In any case, my son had adored eggs when he was younger, not to eat, but their shape, which he liked to hold in his hand and draw upon with felt tip pens. It was he who had forced me to see the egg as I hadn't before, and didn't again until I read "The Egg and the Hen" and saw that my son and Clarice Lispector, two people who had never met and lived years and languages apart, shared an understanding. An egg is perfect and mysterious.

Clarice rose from the sofa.

'You have not tried my eggs,' she said.

She walked over to our kitchen and began to open and close drawers, clattering pots and spoons and in a busy fashion, cigarette still in her mouth.

'I don't want an egg,' he said.

His eyes turned on me, ignoring the strange woman in the kitchen. In his voice was a whine that I had pandered to for too long.

I gave him a unblinking stare. 'Go and wash your hands,' I said.

He went to open his mouth, but saw that I was resolute and kept quiet. With an atypical obedience he walked off to the bathroom.

I believe in children having a right to question, but not over things like washing hands before eating. However, the collapse made everything into a question. He did not speak of it much, but I could sense the doubt and fear that he kept contained within the thin vessel of his child's body.

Each day for a few months after the collapse, he would attempt to watch his favourite Lego reviews on YouTube. He would press his small finger on the mouse, tapping it again and again with the sense of rhythm he inherited from his father, smooth and violent. I would watch him. For a moment his face would be hopeful, then it would fall as he gazed into a screen that refused to load.

I didn't try to tell him it was useless. The one thing you cannot deny your children is hope. In his own time he moved away from this habit, as smart humans do. He began to question my directives and fight me over bedtimes, lie about having brushed his teeth or used soap to wash his hands. I understood it as an outlet for stress. Everyone was feeling it. At school, some resourceful children had taken to using chalk on the quad to draw a giant Minecraft landscape until some kids beat each other up over the direction in which a tunnel should go and the teachers had to ban tunnels. You can build up, they told the kids, but you are not allowed to build down. Their logic betrayed their ignorance of the game, but everyone's nerves were stretched tight as we were forced to adapt to our new situation.

Clarice was steaming up the windows now. I watched her from the table, a dancer in my own kitchen.

She turned and looked at me.

'They must be cooked slow,' she said. 'As slow as a lifetime.'

My son came back with fresh hands and climbed on to my lap. We read his storybook and he told me about the latest incursion by teachers on chalk Minecraft. They were now banning creepers. His eyes hung on his face, tired out by all the rules, by all the things that didn't exist anymore.

By the time Clarice placed the eggs on the table, my son was asleep with his head on his arms, something he hadn't done since he was a small child. I knew I couldn't wake him, or if I did, he wouldn't want to eat, but go straight to bed.

I reached over and put the plate to the side of his head. I freed my right arm from his waist and put my fork through the soft, slightly curdled texture. They were stirred just the way I like, with no visible white or snotty strings. I raised the egg to my mouth.

They were the best eggs I've eaten in my forty years of living – creamy and light but substantial also, nourishing me in a way I hadn't known I needed.

What had she done with them? I could see a little salt, a small amount of pepper, but that was all. How was it possible that a person could take a thing as ordinary as an egg and make this?

I ate slowly and with complete immersion as though meditating. I was unaware of the heat pump clicking on and off, the hum of the fridge, my son asleep on my lap, the growing dark outside. I even forgot my visitor as she once again forced me to consider the egg. I held the cooked egg on my tongue and attempted to hold the image of the egg, its simple oval outline, in my mind's eye. It was a task that consumed my entire attention and when I had finished eating I felt exhausted. Not in a terrible way, but in a way that demanded I go to bed immediately. I stood up, carrying my son with me. He was heavy. One day soon I wouldn't be able to carry him at all.

Before I left the room I turned to thank her. She was sitting once again on the chair, a cigarette in her hand, her eye on something out the window moving in the dark, like a nocturnal creature or a thing with a shape impossible to imagine until you see it – a monster, a memory.

She waved her hand, dismissive, and did not turn to look at me.

I carried my son down the hall and put him on the empty side of my bed where his father used to sleep. Most nights he ended up there anyway, scared awake by his dreams. I understood the need for comfort. I, too, longed to stop fighting people in my dreams; I wished to go someplace else.

I lay down beside him and watched for a minute his pale, freckled cheeks. Then I slept.

*

In the morning my visitor was gone. She did not do the dishes.

The following week a cat turned up at our back entrance. She pressed her sleek grey body against the glass of the door until we let her in. My son said we had to keep her. He said we must call her Chicken, after the lady that had been to visit, the lady with the cat's eyes.

Note

This story contains some dialogue from an interview with Clarice Lispector made by TV Cultura in São Paulo in 1977. You can watch it on YouTube.

Clarice Lispector's story, sometimes translated as 'The Egg and the Hen', 'The Chicken' or 'The Egg and the Chicken', is collected in her book *Family Ties*, and in *Complete Stories*.

LAWRENCE PATCHETT

Lawrence Patchett is a Pākehā writer whose ancestors come from Shetland, Scotland, Ireland and England. His books are *I Got His Blood On Me: Frontier Tales* and *The Burning River*, published by Victoria University Press. The beginnings of 'The Tenth Meet' included stories told in *Sketches and Tales of the Shetland Islands* (1856) by Eliza Edmondston. This story was written with the assistance of the Ursula Bethell Writer in Residence programme at the University of Canterbury / Te Whare Wānanga o Waitaha.

The Tenth Meet

It was Harky's mother who told him it was time. Time for ten meets. She called it so Harky wouldn't have to. So that when someone came blaming later – some medical or police officer with a cap under their arm and a double cab in the driveway, the vehicle's blue and black stripes clashing against the paddocks behind, or some family member even, some litigious brother or cousin – it would be the head of the family they'd meet at the door. My decision, Gret would say. My practice.

'Sling up now, Harky,' she said. 'Time for the meets.'

Just back from the furthest paddocks, Harky blinked in the light that poured from the porch. He was still in his overalls; dusk had begun to fall on him as he walked up to the house.

'He's not getting better, son,' said Gret. 'Time to take him round.'

Harky fished his phone from his overalls and looked at it. Notifications stacked on one another, filling the screen up. Beyond, the hallway that led to his father's bedroom was dark. 'What did they say at the quack's?'

'Nothing useful,' said Gret. 'I'm telling you, Harky, they're doing nothing for him, that lot. It's time for the meets. Ten of them.'

Harky's eye went again to his notifications. Another summons from the health branch among them, no doubt – yet another appointment. 'It's not allowed, Mum. The doctors don't like it.'

'It's family practice, is what it is. A remedy we all trust. Because it works.'

'Except for Des.'

Gret just stood there in the porch entrance, as if to block his disagreement that way. 'It's time, Harky. Sling up.'

Harky sighed, his mind going to the night ahead. The long walk in the dark. The knocking and explanations. Fronting a Gret-driven practice that felt only halfway his to perform. 'How's it going to work, then? It's not like Dad can fit in the sling. It's made for wee kids.'

'The barrow,' she said. 'You'll just put him in the barrow, and then the sling will go round him, just like it normally would with a bubs. Except you can't carry him, so it will just have to be tied round his neck and sit there.'

'Like a bib.'

She eyed him. 'I'm making it my decision, if that's what you're worried about.' She pointed to his phone. 'And I'll send you a message, telling you to start your ten meets. So if anyone asks, you'll have that as proof, right there in black and white.'

'I'm not worried about that. I'm worried about Dad.'

'And you're right to,' said Gret, 'because he's very sick.'

Harky dropped his head. There'd been so little sleep last night, Mackie keeping them all up with his growls and shouts. And Harky's worker had been called away, his family at risk in the water riots. Harky's days were stretched.

'We've tried their way, son,' she said. 'We've tried it lots. And it hasn't worked. So now it's time for our way.' Reaching to his shoulder, she pulled him inside. 'Come and eat something, while I get the sling, and ring up folks.'

'Let me see him first.'

'All right. I'll get on with the ringing, then.' She went to the hallway desk for her glasses.

'Not the quarry camp, Mum.'

One hand already on her phone, Gret turned, her face hard.

'Don't call the quarry camp. Rab and them. Let me ring them,' Harky said.

Her voice, when it came, was tight. 'That's probably best.'

Having kicked free of his blankets, Mackie lay frog-style, his arms and legs splayed out. His eyes roved up as Harky appeared. 'Gah,' he said. 'Gah.'

Harky touched the old man's cheek and neck and wrists. Fire. 'It's all right, Dad. We'll fix you up.'

Wanting the contact, or perhaps the cold that was still on Harky from outside, Mackie pushed his face against Harky's hand and nuzzled it.

'Gor,' said Mackie. 'Gah.' His was a noisy sickness. Barely a minute went by without goos or gahs or bubble noises coming out. Only when he slept would his face return to its former robust look. That strange transformation in sleep, when he seemed to get his old father back, kept Harky going through the rages that came out of Mackie when he was awake, the growls and shrieks and fists. His reactions to outside shocks were the worst – strangers on screen, a vehicle he didn't recognise. So often he seemed able to grasp what was being said, but a baby tantrum was the only way he could react. Gret and Des found this particularly hard to take; swamped with farm work and lack of sleep, Harky just tried to deal with it.

'We'll get you right tonight, Dad,' he said now. 'Right as rain – nice cool rain.'

The old man mushed against his son again, his frog pose even more pronounced.

Looking at him like that made Harky's throat get thick. He had to cough to clear it.

The old man had been into the health building for this sickness twice, and up to the district doctor countless times. His last discharge from the health building had come with a complex breakdown by consultants that Harky understood to be linking the sickness to weaknesses in Mackie's immune system, a blood cell complication, plus an inflammation in his brain, all of which had combined with long-running stresses to fry his mind. Only sixty-six, and his speech and other basics blasted, his face changed. Researching it online at night, poring over the notes he'd scrawled in consultants' rooms, Harky had struggled to square this diagnosis with the first outward signs of Mackie's illness, the roaming disquiet that had seemed to come on with his pension date, as if someone had told him outright that he was now useless, irrelevant. Gret, meanwhile, was less patient with the consultants' efforts. 'They don't bloody know, is the short and long of it.'

Now the door sounded and Gret came in. In her arms was the ancient sling, an heirloom blanket under it. Automatically she glanced at her husband's bed. 'He's perked up.' She jerked her chin at Harky. 'Lift your arms.'

'Mum, it's not going on me. You said it would stay on Dad. I can't carry him in it.'

'You still have to put it on, just for a short time. For the first lifting, at least.' She yanked him back into position. 'Stop acting like this is so terribly different. They do it with old ones who turn gaga all the time, back home. Arms up.'

Waterproofed by some old aunt years ago on Gret's homeplace, the sling released an aroma of fish-grease as she looped it over Harky's head. Settling on his chest, the calico pouched out, worn slack by generations of walks for the meets. It felt strange round his neck, all that wear and story from somewhere else. But Gret smoothed it flat, turning him so she could adjust the lie of the knot on his neck. While she issued her instructions, Harky noticed, her accent turned thicker than he'd heard it in months.

'You just wear it until he's in the barrow. Then we'll put it round Mackie's neck.' She indicated the splayed man, the trackpants twisted round his waist. 'I should do a pad-check first.'

'I'll do it,' said Harky. 'You've taken all the work since lunch.'

She shook her head. 'You haven't eaten anything yet. Or called Rab. Go and do that.'

Harky hovered, not wanting to leave. He had no real desire to check or change his father's incontinence pad, but they both knew Mackie settled better when Harky worked with him, his big frame and hands bringing in the smell of the farm and his dogs and truck.

But Gret's voice was firm. 'There's something I have to say first, Harky. A form of words before the first meet. Before he even leaves the house.'

'Huh. I didn't know that.'

'A grandmother's word starts it off. And a grandmother at the water quarry finishes it.'

'You're not his grandmother, though. You're his wife.'

Shaking her head, she pushed Harky out and shut the door firmly behind him. Then he heard her voice start. Muffled at first, then coming stronger. An incantation of some sort. The words jagged and old. Even if the door had still been open, Harky wouldn't have understood it.

Harky hunted through his phone for Rab's number. They swapped calls only at times like this, when there were emergencies – and mostly down at the old water quarry. Generally they were Rab's problems, and often vehicle-related, requiring a powerful tractor. Since the quarry had failed and their machinery had more or less given out, Harky found himself helping when one of the family vehicles got stuck in the quarry gravel or a caravan jack-knifed on itself up the river, having gone further upstream in search of a viable camp.

But this time it wasn't Rab who answered. A young woman instead, bored as soon as she heard his voice.

'I'm looking for Rab,' he said. 'It's Harky McMowat.'

She sighed – 'I'll send you his new number' – and hung up.

Having gone into the kitchen to make the call, Harky scrolled through the work on his phone while he waited. His mother was still in Mackie's room. He hoped that incantation had stopped: he didn't want his dad spooked by it. The old man had always shown respect for what he called 'Gret's religious stuff' by doing his best to ignore it. At last the new contact file came through, with a message to explain: *Uncle Rab's new digits.*

Rab sounded encouraging at first, but when Harky said he'd be along later for a ten-meets visit, Rab fell silent.

'Are you there?' said Harky. 'Rab?'

'Yeah, I heard what you said. He's been a bit of an arsehole, once or twice, you know, your dad.'

'Yeah, I know. He's pretty sick, though. I sure would appreciate your help.'

The quiet at Rab's end was not backgrounded by machinery: no chug or sluice sounds of the quarry at work.

'Like your dad did with Des,' said Rab.

'Well, like he was *supposed* to with Des. He never made it to your place, Mum said.'

It was unspoken in the family but well understood: Des's deep irritability and logic-defying antipathy towards certain people all stemmed from their father's long-ago failure to complete the meets walk when Des had been sick.

But now Rab said nothing.

'That's what we got told, anyway,' said Harky. 'Dad never made it to your place, that night, so Des never got his last meet – or the last broth. Isn't that what happened?'

'Don't ask me, man. I was, like, six or something.'

Harky pulled the phone away and stared at it. Rab's attitude was odd. Harky had helped out down at the quarry three or four times, at least, in the last few years. Each time it had been a lengthy business, with wire ropes attached to his own tractor, and once even the gift of an old vehicle he'd had in his shed, all given over without any mention of cost. It was all that stuff between their dads and grandads, he supposed. The leasing dispute that had, over the years, gotten so tangled that everyone except Rab and his lot had given up trying to understand it. Although Harky knew the guts of it, if he was honest, and so did his father and so did Des. Rab's family had worked the farm long before Harky's grandfather started there, years back. And then, at some point, Harky's grandfather and father had jointly applied to the Magistrates' and the lease had turned into a murky rent-to-buy agreement, and then – according to Mackie's advocate, at least – outright ownership. So now Harky's family 'legally' farmed it and Rab's didn't, working the old water quarry instead, as per an agreement reached in the Magistrates'. Not that everyone agreed with that version of events.

'So anyway,' said Harky, 'we hope to finish ten meets at your place, so if you could spare us a swallow of broth when we get there, that would help us heaps.'

Rab sighed. 'I'll look into it.'

Gret was coming out of Mackie's room and caught the look on Harky's face.

'What is it?'

'Nothing. How's Dad? Is he ready yet?'

It wasn't a regular wheelbarrow. Deep-welled and lined with sacks, supported on each side by bike wheels, it was more a push-trailer than a barrow. Harky pumped up the tyres and eased it onto the porch, picking off hay and dust that had settled since it last went out. The old man had made the barrow himself, years back, when his own father was blasted by stroke but still wanted to roam across the paddocks. These days Mackie was the same. Twice Harky had taken his father round the sheds in it, and once down to the bottom of the farm, the old man's wild face looking up at the trees as he was barrowed underneath.

Now Harky lowered him into the barrow and eased in pillows to support his neck and hips. The heirloom blanket was wrapped round him for warmth, the sling tied beneath his chin. Normally used to carry a child on ten meets walks, this time the sling would catch half-swallowed broth that spilled from the old man's mouth.

'You be good for Harky,' said Gret. Bending over the barrow, she kissed her husband on the forehead. 'Come back all fixed up.'

Mackie's eyes went wide, fearful of what the kiss meant.

'It's all right, Dad,' said Harky. 'We're just going for a walk.'

'Ra!' his father said, excited. 'Ra.'

'Get on the road, Harky,' said Gret. 'I can't stand it.'

Out on Drain Road a decent moon was coming up, the last smears of sun showing above the volcanoes to the west. Burdened with the barrow in front and a backpack of spare pads and clothes, plus the sipper cup Mackie drank from these days, Harky put his phone in his top pocket with the torch function turned on. It was more to alert drivers that he was out there, walking the road with his dad, than to light the way. Harky had lived down Drain Road all his life – except for one year away on another island, driving tractors – and the network of roads and drains through the former swamp were so familiar he could have walked them backwards in much deeper gloom than this. But since the water riots in the city the old 'bog belt' had become desirable to branch people and tech architects, and tall box houses had been chopper-dropped into the spaces between the old farms, and now dozens of people whizzed down these roads at night. Last winter a farm worker had been killed while out walking on Dry Line, knocked apart by a driver rushing home late. Severed and flung in a high arc, the woman's leg was fished out of the drain that ran alongside the road, dripping with swamp stink.

Now Mackie kicked about in the barrow, his slippered feet catching Harky on the leg. Des lived right next door to the old farmstead, so it was only fifty paces before this first meet. But already the outdoor walk seemed to have helped. The old man was more alert, his eye following the silhouetted tree shapes, the lights of Des's approaching house.

Pushing the barrow into Des's yard, Harky saw his brother, bent over the fledgers' feeding station to hose it.

Then Des caught sight of the barrow and straightened. 'What's that for?'

Harky didn't reply, not wanting to start with a fight.

'Dehhie, Dehhie,' said their father, pointing up. It was the only name for 'Des' he could manage.

'Harky?' Des indicated the barrow, the sling round their father's neck. 'What the fuck?'

'How're your fledgers, Des?'

'They're fine. Why've you got the sling out?'

Harky looked into the lit shed behind Des. It was all neatness inside. A shadow board for tools, a ride-on mower that was parked and washed clean of grass. As the oldest son Des had been given first choice about the main farm and had seized the chance to refuse it. As a result he had a neater life. Instead of the old farmhouse and barely economic paddocks of drained bog, he'd taken the cottage next door and these small sheds and paddocks, and now worked off the place in a rural supplies store, selling overpriced gear to part-time farmers like himself.

'Have you got a broth for him, Des? One of ten.'

'Oh no,' said Des. 'You're not doing the meets.'

Harky eyed the shadow board again. 'It's time, Des. Mum called it.'

'Oh, for fuck's sake.'

In his upset, Des had forgotten to turn off the hose. Pointlessly it watered the grass at their feet.

'I say it's *not* time, Harky. I say take Dad back to the district doctor.'

'She's had him at the doctor's today, Des. And we've had him in the health building. We've had him there heaps. And it doesn't fix his problem, whatever it is.'

'Well, ten meets isn't the solution, Harky. It's fucking dangerous.'

Harky moved his arm, shielding their father from the language. When anyone raised their voice or swore, but especially Des, it got Mackie worked up. 'It's saved a hundred people, they say, down the years. I looked it up.'

'Yeah, and it's buried even more,' said Des. 'It gave *me* the right guts-ache. It made me want to die. Imagine what it could do to *his* stomach.'

'Ah! Ah!' Mackie banged his palms on the sides of the barrow.

When Harky said nothing, and instead rocked the barrow to calm Mackie, Des flung the hose away. Not pausing, as he normally would, to wind it on to the hose-reel that was bolted primly beneath the tap, he killed the hose and snapped the lights off, then yanked the shed doors closed. Stalking towards the house, he muttered something over his shoulder.

'Pardon?' said Harky, turning the barrow.

'I said I've got some pheasant in the garage. From when the dog surprised one in the shelterbelt. We can boil it into a broth.' He flung a hand at the house. 'Ask Marcy for a swallow of fire. She's still working, but for you she'll stop.'

Left alone with Mackie, Harky barrowed him to the porch door but didn't knock. Mackie was already too worked up, thrashing his head side to side and crying out. So instead of calling for Marcy and a mouthful of fire drink, Harky sang to his father a night lullaby Gret had made up to quieten him and Des when they were kids. He could remember only some of the words, so it came out a mishmash of hums and improvised scraps:

Sa tharten leakin
An somethin somethin

Sa dum-dum dum-dum
Sa lairdin after

Sa tharten something
All sa while

Then Des was stumping up from the garage. In his hands, a plastic bag of meat frozen into a ball.

'If you'd messaged first, we could have got our broth ready. Now I'm going to have to boil this straight from frozen, which is dangerous with meat from the wild.'

'It'll be fine, Des. Just zap it first in the waver.'

'And I don't suppose you'll let me drive you between your meets. 'Cause that would make it too easy, I suppose.'

'Da!' said Mackie. 'Dehhie – Da!'

'Oh, shut up, Dad,' said Des. 'For Christ's sake.'

'That's "don't",' said Harky. 'I'm pretty sure that's his new word for don't.'

'Whatever,' said Des. 'I'm trying to offer you a lift.'

'Mum says I've got to walk-and-sling it, Des. It doesn't work if you don't do it right. Ten houses, ten meets, and ten broths – with ten walks in between.' He showed his phone. 'And besides, I can call you, if we get really stuck.'

'I'll ring ahead then. Get people prepped.'

'I think Mum's done that already. Although I rang Rab.'

'Right,' said Des. 'She just didn't bother with me, it seems. Mackie's own son.'

'Des, it's a thirty-second walk from the farm to here.'

Des scowled. 'So how was Rab about it?'

'Da,' said Mackie. 'Da – Da!'

Harky put a hand on Mackie. 'Stop that, Dad. We have to go there. You know we do.'

'Da – Da – Da!'

Harky sighed. 'Rab was a bit funny about it, to be honest. But at least he's prepped.' He gripped Mackie's knee. 'He'll be fine once we get there, I reckon. He knows Dad hasn't been right.'

Des frowned down at the barrow, his father's febrile protest. 'God, what a state.'

'Da! Da!'

'Des, please,' said Harky. 'Just boil our first broth.'

As Harky barrowed on, he found each house prepared. Warned by Gret's call, they each had a different broth ready, a saucepan still hot from boiling it. And they all shook hands with Harky and cheered him with talk, as instructed by Gret – a broth for the ailing child and a neighbourly meet for the 'lifting', as she called it, of the parent's soul, anguished from the child's sickness. Her local twist on what her own mother had told her, who in turn had been shown it by someone older, who'd got it from someone older and somewhere else. Who knew what it was originally like.

From Harky's cousin on Drain Road they got a broth of duck from the May shooting. Further on the Wilkinsons gave a soup of insect meat, store bought. They were still new to the district, and Harky had to ask them to mash the contents finer so his father could masticate it, or at least move it round his mouth before spitting it out, gobs of the half-swallowed and stick-leggy stuff spilling onto the sling. As the night wore on and he wiped it clean of broth mush again and again, Harky silently thanked whoever had waterproofed the sling all those years back. The last thing his father needed right now was dampness round his neck, and a chance for some new infection to attack him.

But in fact, Mackie's health seemed to be picking up. His cheeks and forehead were cooler, and his eyes roved calmly as each meet took place, following the murmur of talk above him, seeming to almost understand the exchanges and even accept them. And then, as Harky turned from Drain Road into Dry Line, Mackie began to gurgle and buck, shoving the barrow's push bar against Harky's stomach, as if to celebrate his temporary return to health.

'You're a weird one, Dad. I swear you're enjoying this. No guts-ache, then?'

'Ba! Ba!'

'I thought you said the meets was bullshit – all Mum's old family stuff. It was all bullshit, you said.'

Mackie bucked even harder, enjoying the teasing tone, perhaps, if not catching the words themselves.

The practice took some explaining at the fourth house, but the next two meets were easy, because the fifth was at Percy's place. An old mate of Harky's from school, Percy still dragged him out hunting once a year, plunging up a valley that was still mostly free of the hordes that scoured the bush for meat these days. Both venison and wild pork came out of his freezer now, and he got his son to run a handful of fried pork across to his new neighbour's place so that the sixth broth could legitimately come from the sixth meet. At houses seven and eight only laboratory meat was available, but in its boiling-up the seventh broth smelled so strongly of forgotten lamb recipes, and the eighth of something Harky couldn't even trace, that Mackie writhed in his restraints and shouted happily, craning his neck for more of each nostalgic taste.

Meet nine was another stranger, vegetarian and newly rioted out of the city, and weirdly out of place on the old Roberts deer block. There was no meat in his fridge, which sparked a fresh outburst from Mackie, who made fists and banged his restraints. Anxious to help, or perhaps just to get the pair of them out of his house, the man offered up wild solutions – home delivery? an impromptu bug mince? – before hitting on the offer of shooting rabbits on his paddocks. Unwatered and empty of stock, the farm was being ravaged by them. At a call Des came over with his old .22 and spotlight and, in a changed mood, apologised to Harky for his reaction at the first meet. Within the hour, they'd spotlighted several paddocks from Des's truck and soon had fresh rabbit boiling into a broth. It was getting on for midnight by the time Des and Harky shook their host's hand and barrowed Mackie back down the driveway.

Buoyed by the hunting jaunt, their father gurgled and made happy shapes. Then without warning he cried out and lashed a fist at the empty paddock at the side.

'What's he on about now?' said Des.

'It's good land in there,' said Harky. 'Running to waste. I think that's what he's saying.'

Des glanced at the high deer-fences, which held back only thistles and lank grass. 'Fair enough. He seemed an all right guy, but that farm's one hell of a mess.'

'I reckon he's broke. Not much he can do without water on the place.'

'Da,' said their father. 'Da!'

They reached the end of the driveway, where they were due to part, Des taking his truck home while Harky barrowed on to the quarry camp. But first Des fussed, made Harky check that his phone was still charged and the torch working, and pushed his thumb into both barrow tyres to be sure they were still tight. Then he tried to adjust his father's blanket, but was fought back by a shouting Mackie who, even before he got sick, had never liked being patronised by Des.

'Fuck's sake, Dad,' said Des, rearing back. 'Cut it out.'

'I'd just leave it, Des, to be honest.'

Des sighed. 'How about I drive down to the quarry camp, then, and just confirm with Rab and them that you're coming.' His hand waved in the night around them. 'Since it's got so late, and everything.'

'No, Des. I think it's better if just one of us talks to them. Rab was pretty ropey when I rang him up.'

'Huh.' Des looked into the ag-corp property across the road, where the vast arm of a centre-pivot irrigator stretched into the distant dark, hissing out water even now, programmed to work non-stop. 'God, they're still aggro about that lease business, aren't they? Rab and them. It was more than a *generation* ago, that stuff.'

'Well, not really, Des.'

'No, *really*. Grandad was the main instigator of that, and he's a bloody-long-time dead.'

'Yeah, but' – Harky cleared his throat – '*certain people* made it much worse.'

Growling, Mackie kicked out. To stop the barrow from falling, Harky slammed both hands on its sides. A slippered foot caught him on the chin in the process.

Des just rolled his eyes. 'No, it fucks me off, Harky, that Rab takes it out on you. As if you don't already have enough on your plate, with Dad so sick and everything. And the bloody farm to think about.'

'Des,' said Harky, bracing against another round of Mackie's kicks. 'Could you just stop talking about this, please?'

Des swore again, and then just stood watching as Harky settled their father. 'Just keep your phone turned on, then. And if you have any problems, ring me. I won't be able to sleep anyway, knowing you two are out here, still doing ten meets, so you might as well ring me up. Especially if his guts start to hurt.'

'All right, Des,' said Harky. 'Go back to your own family, now. You've helped us enough.'

Des dug his boot in the driveway stones. Then he boxed Harky on the arm, threw a terse goodnight down at his father, and went back down the driveway for his truck.

Harky turned the barrow into Dry Line, for the long walk to Rab's camp.

Harky's shoulders ached as he came into Riverbed Road, which would lead him down by the river to the old water quarry. It had been an hour and ten minutes since he'd left the ninth meet, and Mackie had kicked and protested the whole way, clearly knowing where they were supposed to end up. Rocking the barrow side to side, kicking his slippers off and shouting into the night, he'd made it hard for Harky to go more than ten or twenty steps at a time before he had to stop. After they'd been booted off twice, forcing a long search with his phone torch, Harky abandoned the slippers to the night.

Then he found Mackie pulling with fury at his crotch, which often meant he'd pissed himself. Forced to change Mackie's pad in a driveway, Harky was interrupted by a motorist who offered help. No, Harky told him, I just have to change his incontinence pad, I'm walking him because he can't sleep, everything is fine, but, although the stranger drove off, he didn't seem satisfied. Harky's farm-dirtied overalls, the ancient sling round the barrowed man at night – to someone who didn't know the ten-meets practice it added up, no doubt, to something suspect. Harky pictured the man bothering his partner about it when he got home, maybe even putting his suspicion online: *Anyone else see that weird farmer out late with an old man? 11pm, Dry Line? Should we be concerned?*

Now he came down into the quarry camp and saw only a couple of the caravans showing lights, and realised he had no idea which of these was Rab's. He messaged him and while he waited saw how, even in the moonlight, you couldn't escape the coating of road and quarry and riverbed dust. In summers these days the river itself ran dry. For many decades now irrigation takes upstream had sucked out the surrounding aquifers. The river had shrunk massively since Harky and Rab had ridden the school vehicle together, many years back, and the water quarry had gone bust. To avoid dwelling on that he rocked the barrow and sang to Mackie. He'd repeated the Tharten song many times down Dry Line and was now sick of it; instead he tried a few lines of something he could remember his dad singing in the yards to calm the stock. Not that Mackie was quiet: threshing in the barrow, he growled non-stop.

At last a caravan door made its tinny sound, somewhere deep in the camp. The outline of Rab came up the moonlit track. He had a cap on his head and was doming up his top pocket as he walked. Seeing the barrow in front of Harky, he stopped.

'Thank you for staying up, Rab. I'm sorry it's so late.'

Rab didn't come on but eyed the barrow instead, the shouts and writhing that came from it.

'That's just Dad,' said Harky. 'He's harmless.'

'Ror!' said his father. 'Ror!'

Rab came on but slowly, with the tread of someone approaching a dog gone loose.

Harky thought of asking after Rab's mother and his kids, or his work, but every subject seemed likely to lead back to the state of the river and the sucked-out water quarry, and so he decided to wait for Rab to speak first.

A tense and noisy version of silence stretched out, rage jagging from the barrow between them.

At last Rab lifted his cap and scratched beneath it. 'So what is it you want again?'

'Well, like I said when I called, Mum told me to follow the meets tonight. To see if we can fix what's wrong with Dad. And it's the practice in our family to end here.'

Rab nodded, and looked up towards the main road, following headlights. Then his eye dropped again to the ruined and thrashing form of Mackie in the barrow. 'You know, I just don't think we're going to be able to help you tonight, Des.'

'Harky.'

'Harky – right.' He looked again at the barrow. 'Yeah, I just don't think we can help.'

'How come? I thought it would be all right, after we talked earlier.'

'Yeah, nah. It's not.'

'That's a real shame, Rab.' Harky moved his hand to one of Mackie's slipperless feet and gripped it, trying to calm him, only to have his hand kicked away. 'Can I ask why not?'

Rab adjusted his cap again. 'Well, one problem is, there's nothing left, mate. There's no princefish anymore.'

'Oh. Shit.'

'It's a shit, all right. So I can't give you any broth. I can't give you his tenth.' He looked off into the dark. 'You know, your dad swore at me last time I saw him. And my parents. In town – in the shops.'

'Look, I'm sorry, Rab. I've apologised for that. As I told you, he isn't well – he hasn't been well for quite some time now. That's what these meets are all about.'

'Yeah, but that was after years of fucking us in the Magistrates'. He seemed pretty well when he was fighting us on the lease, for every inch of dirt.'

Holding the barrow in place, Harky had to shout to be

heard over Mackie's non-stop growls and yelps. 'Like I say, I know it isn't easy with Dad.'

'Des can be a bit of an arsehole too sometimes, to be honest.'

Harky breathed in, forcing himself to be calm. 'So,' he said, 'if you don't have any princefish, is there any other kind of broth you can give us, so we can finish up? Please?'

'Mate, do we look like we can afford shop meat? Do you know how much that stuff costs?'

'I know it's expensive.'

Rab laughed. 'No, you don't. You don't know at all.'

Harky put his hands up, appealing to him, then shoved them back on to the push bar as Mackie renewed his thrashing protest. The movement jarred his shoulders, aching from the walk. 'Look, Rab, I don't know what to say to you. I'm sorry about the way Dad's been, but you can see that, right now, he's not the full quid. And I'm sorry about all that lease stuff – all that old stuff. If you want to reopen those talks, just say so, and we can do that.'

'Mate, if we can't afford shop meat, do you really think we can afford to go back to the Magistrates'?'

'Who said anything about the Magistrates'? We could just talk, surely. We could –' But he had to stop. His father's crazed protests were getting dangerous. Harky leaned right out over the barrow, pointing. 'Dad, stop kicking! Stop it! I'm trying to fix you. Rab's trying to help, which is amazing, considering all the shit he's had to put up with. So be polite.'

Stunned, Mackie's face went blank.

'You've got to stop this, Dad. Otherwise we'll never get you fixed. And Mum will have a piece of you, when you get back.'

'Rowl,' said Mackie, the sound more experimental this time.

'Stop it. Be polite.'

A moment passed, and the old man was quiet, and then started to suck his lip, picking with a thumbnail at the barrow's wood. It was one of the behaviours he could still shock Harky with, so reminiscent of his old pre-sickness self.

'Okay. Sorry about that, Rab. He's rude these days – I do get that.'

Rab said nothing.

'So let me get this straight. You don't want to discuss the lease, and you don't have any princefish broth for us tonight. And you can't spare any other kind of broth for Dad.'

'Well, we *could* make a broth for him, if you're desperate.'

'Terrific,' said Harky. 'That would be great.'

'It's not with shop meat, though. Or from the river.'

Harky waited, but it became clear that Rab wanted him to guess. 'So what is it?'

'Well, when's the last time you saw any stray dogs running around the district?'

'*Dog broth*? Jesus, Rab.'

'I'm joking.' But his voice was dead flat.

'I don't get this, Rab. Did you just get me down here to muck me round? To fuck up Dad? 'Cause I could have just stayed at home for that.'

'Why don't you come to us first?'

'Pardon?'

'Why are we always the last meet?'

'Well, I don't know, Rab. It's just the practice, isn't it? It's what Mum says we have to do. It's some – some –' Harky waved his hand at the night, his face getting hot. 'Some practice from way back. That's all it is. Like, it starts with something a grandmother says at our place, and then it ends here, with princefish broth and something a grandmother says here.'

'Don't suppose it could be the other way round. So my ma doesn't have to wait up till stupid o'clock.'

'It's just the practice, Rab. It's just what Mum told me to do.'

'And have you ever wondered whether maybe your practice is wrong?' Not waiting for an answer, he said, 'Fuck, man, it's after midnight. I've got work in the morning. And Ma waited up too. She's just sitting in there – just waiting. *Awake*.'

'I've apologised for how late it got. We had to shoot rabbits with that last guy – that vegetarian at the old deer place.'

'Whatever. The whole thing – this whole thing of yours – it's just impolite.'

'Okay.' Harky breathed deep. 'So what do you want me to do, Rab? I've apologised for Dad. I've offered to talk about the lease. I've even listened to your sick joke about dog broth. And now I'd just like to know what you want me to do, so I can finish this.'

'Maybe just come down to see us when it's not an emergency.'

'But that's when you need me,' said Harky. 'That's when you *call* me. When there's a car stuck in the gravel, or a flood or something. I've brought the tractor down heaps of times. That's how it works.'

'Yeah, exactly,' said Rab. 'Do you call on your other neighbours only when it's an emergency?'

Harky stared. 'Are you actually –?' This time Harky had to walk away, leaving the barrow unprotected, to get some calming breaths. Rab seemed to be trying to force some kind of friendship, which didn't match any kind of relationship they'd had before. What Harky remembered from their school trips together was some fairly nondescript conversation, Rab seeming bored with Harky's company most of the time, his nose deep inside a comic book if he had one, or simply gazing out the window and nodding when Harky talked, his eye flicking over the fenced-in creatures and water plots the school vehicle took them past.

'I'm sorry, man,' said Rab. 'All this just means I've got nothing for you tonight.'

'You realise this means I can't finish it. For Mackie – I can't finish the meets for my dad. So he'll just stay sick, and then he'll die like this.'

Rab was silent for a long time. 'Are you really saying that to me? That you can't finish your ritual?'

'Not really. We don't call it that. And it's not *my* thing – it's Gret's. But, also, yes. And it's pissing me off.'

'Well, welcome to my world, man.'

'All right, then. I'm sorry for keeping you up late.' Harky turned and began pushing up the track, Mackie chanting nonsense in the barrow in front. 'Shut up, Dad,' said Harky. 'Just shut up.' He considered turning back and shouting – *shouting* – that the next time some relation of Rab's got their vehicle stuck in quarry gravel, they could ring up some other poor sap to pull them out. But his father was roiling with such vigour in the barrow that he had to focus on moving up the track.

'Shut up, Dad. I hope you realise this is all your fault.'

'O!' said Mackie. 'Gor!'

Then Rab was running up beside him.

'Fuck off, Rab,' said Harky. 'Get the fuck away from us.'

'Have you still got freshies?'

'What?' said Harky, still pushing. 'What the hell are you talking about?'

'Have you still got freshies at the Deep?'

Harky stopped so suddenly that the barrow overbalanced, Mackie's arms flying up. This time it was Rab who steadied it, a hand on its edge.

'Gor,' said Mackie, alarmed at Rab's proximity. 'Gah!'

Harky sighed. 'What are you talking about, Rab? Please don't muck us around.'

'The Deep,' said Rab. 'On your farm. Are there still freshies in it?'

'I've got no idea what that even is.'

'The Deep. It's a deep. Well, it's a drain now, apparently – you guys drained it. But it used to be a deep, and they used to get freshies out of it, Ma and them, before the lease and all that.'

'Rab, I don't know what freshies are.'

'Freshyfish. On your place.' Anticipating Harky's reaction, or Mackie's – some new rush of rage this may spark from either man – he hurried on. 'I think you should take me. Up to the Deep. So we can get some freshy.' He pointed at the barrow. 'For him.'

'What?' said Harky. 'Now?'

'Yeah. So you can finish it. The broth' – he waved a hand – 'your ten meets thing. Freshy broth.'

'But you were just telling us to get stuffed.'

'No, that was you.' Rushing on, he said, 'And if you let me look for freshyfish, that makes it different. That's worth a lot to me, and to Ma.' He jerked his head at the camp behind him. 'To all of us.'

'I don't think you'll find any freshyfish there, Rab, whatever they are. That creek's changed a lot.'

'Yeah, but finding one isn't really the point.'

The moon was coming strongly now, and Harky could see him better. 'You really want this.'

'Yes, we do. We all do. You should let me drive you, though. 'Cause, to be honest mate, you look rooted.'

Without warning Mackie fell quiet, gazing up at Harky.

'I'm supposed to walk the whole way. Otherwise the meets don't work.'

'Well, I won't tell anyone. And I'm not walking to your place.' Again he hurried on, before Harky – or, more probably, the old man – had time to react. 'But come and see Ma first. We'll get her bit over and done with – she can say the grandmother's part. Then she can sleep. And then we'll go up to your place, for the freshies. And then we'll get your dad fixed up, with freshy broth.'

It felt strange for Harky to open a gate into his own corner paddock so a stranger, not Des or his mum or a stock agent, or even one of those off-the-street protein buyers who showed up these days, could drive their vehicle through it. Having got the barrow down from the deck, and his father from inside the truck, Harky stood dumbly beside the open gate, waiting for Rab to drive on to their place.

Low-slung and old, its suspension shot, the truck slumped into the gateway and up the drain-side track. It was obvious a vehicle with such low clearance wouldn't get far into the rutted paddock, but Harky let him attempt it. It was becoming clear where the Deep was, and he wasn't in a rush to take Rab there. The water-branch people had been onto Harky about source protection in the last few years. He'd been told to 'proof unpiped water sources', which amounted to some funding for special plants and a fancy fence along this ditch. But the ditch was also the farm's biggest and most water-productive, and in the summer Harky had dropped a few sandbags into it, partly damming the flow so he could pump water via a 20-millimetre alkathene pipe to the farm's two lowest water troughs. It wasn't legal or branch approved, but it was only for stock water, and it was hidden deep in the furthest corner of the farm, behind the new plants and fencing the water branch had put up. Now Rab was heading straight for it.

'We're in for it now, Dad. Rab's going to freak out about this.'

The old man bounced in the barrow, slamming his hands on its rim. 'O! O! O!' Harky was fairly sure it was Mackie's new word for 'no'. A protest at Rab entering the farm.

'I don't see any choice, Dad,' he said, working to keep the barrow upright. 'We can't finish your meets without Rab's help. And then we'll have Gret to deal with, if we don't finish it right.'

'O! O! Gah!'

Ahead of them Rab gunned his truck, the undercarriage having caught on a tractor rut and bellied out. Revving uselessly, the truck rocked and spun, its wheels slipping on grass.

Harky went to the vehicle and rapped the window. 'It's not going to work, Rab.'

Gripped in his fight with the rut, revving the vehicle, Rab didn't hear through the glass.

Harky had to knock a second time.

'What, mate?'

'You're bellied out, Rab. You'll never make it. Your suspension's fucked.'

Rab looked from Harky to the howling old man in front of him, then down the track. 'How far is it?'

Harky pointed. 'That's the Deep, is it? In the corner of the paddock? 'Cause that's a three-minute walk, if that.'

Still sitting inside the truck, Rab looked down that way, and shrugged. 'Walking's good, I guess. I've got a torch here somewhere.' He lurched into the footwell and the truck's inside was lit up – a huge CAT lamp with a square of battery hanging from its handle. Rab stepped out of the vehicle, hitched his jeans and set off, hurrying after the beam of torchlight.

Upset by this flurry, Mackie shrieked and banged his fists. 'O! O! O!'

Harky shushed and rebuked him, and then remembered the sipper cup in his backpack. After several attempts he got Mackie to drink from it.

Surprised by the sudden hush, Rab turned, his torch beam sweeping the pasture that spread out from their feet. 'Fuck, man, this is out of it. Always wondered when I'd get up here. Onto my old folks' farm.'

Harky made a show of concentrating on the sipper cup at Mackie's mouth. His phone vibrated with a message in his pocket – his mother probably, still awake and worried that her husband wasn't back yet, his ten-meets walk not completed.

The breeze swirled and from some paddock on the neighbour's place a centre-pivot made its hissing sound, still working through the night.

Rab lifted his head towards it. 'You still irrigate?'

'Just on the high paddocks. Ours isn't one of the big takes – and that's not our irrigator.'

Rab snorted. 'It's all the same thing, though, isn't it.'

Harky said nothing. Mackie was still drinking from the sipper cup, but it seemed unlikely he'd be calm when he finished it. 'You can go ahead, Rab, if you want.'

'Nah. Probably should wait for you hosts.' He laughed, a sick sound at his own joke. Brought cigarettes out from his pocket and lit one, blowing smoke away. 'Can't seem to kick these fuckers. It's your only friend sometimes, a smoke, when you're out on the job.'

'Where are you working these days?'

'Eh?'

Harky didn't bother asking again. Clearly Rab had heard him but didn't want to answer. Last he'd been told, Rab had worked briefly for McDermotts, one of the maintainers of irrigation plants around the district, before being laid off over some dispute.

Obeying an impulse of his own, Mackie flung the sipper cup out of the barrow and straightaway howled about it, crying louder as Harky bent into the dark for it.

'He's got a decent set of lungs on him,' said Rab, puffing into the night. 'Can't be that crook.' Without even seeming to make an effort, he aimed the torch onto the spot where the sipper cup had landed. Harky felt Rab's eyes on him as he brushed it off and put it to Mackie's mouth, only to have the old man reject it. Harky tried a few more tricks to calm him, but Mackie kept shaking his head, his hands in tight fists. This was what Gret called the super-sulk, the old man's last-resort tactic when overtired and angered at not getting what he wanted – not even knowing, anymore, what he wanted. All that was left after this was 'the sob', when he would, with luck, cry himself to sleep.

'He wants his tenth broth, eh. That's what he really wants.' Surprised, Harky looked up. But Rab just exhaled smoke and shrugged. 'Seems obvious.'

His father was protesting louder than ever, but Harky still focused on Rab. 'You know, you could have just asked, Rab.'

'What, mate? I can't hear you – your dad.'

Harky shouted. 'When you wanted to come up onto our place – you could have just asked. We could have worked something out.'

Rab sucked on his smoke. 'That's not what my old man used to say.'

'Yeah, but he was asking permission from Dad, back then. I'm saying *you* could have asked *me*.'

To this, Rab just laughed.

Harky stared at him, his face growing hot. Then he focused again on trying to calm Mackie. He tried the sipper cup, he tried commands, and then rocking the barrow forward and back. But the old man churned on, his voice growing hoarse. 'All right,' said Harky, at last. 'Let's just try and get it over with.'

The two men pushed on again, into the torchlight, Mackie's protest breaking round them, a bow wave of ugly noise.

'Rab, I know there's been a bit of bad blood –'

'What? Can't hear you, mate.'

'A bit of bad blood! Between my dad and your dad and all that. But as far as I'm concerned it's time to fix all that up. We can talk about it now, 'cause all that argy-bargy about the lease is old. It's ages ago that it all happened, if you think about it – bloody ages.'

'Oh,' said Rab. 'Is it?'

As they reached the fence round the new plantings, Mackie settled into a low and constant moaning to himself, which gave Harky a chance to open the gate for Rab, since the chain was a bit dicky. Behind it, blackberry and long grass showed in the torchlight, choking the sapling trees and flax.

'Oops,' said Harky. 'Guess I haven't kept on top of the weed-control work.'

'I'll sort it,' said Rab. 'Hold this.'

He thrust the torch at Harky and vaulted the gate and with sudden stomps began to flatten a path towards the ditch. When blackberry caught on his pants he kicked it away with a ripping sound.

Alarmed by the ferocity of Rab's attack on the weeds, Mackie flapped his hands. 'O! O! O!'

By the time Harky shoved the barrow through the gate, and commanded Mackie again to shut up, Rab was twenty paces into the enclosure. Following the path he'd stomped, Harky found him at last on the bank, surveying the ditch.

'Bit different from what I expected,' said Rab. 'Dad always said it was a creek, but this is a full-on ditch.' He shone the torch on the ancient tree opposite, deformed by years of rot and ivy and branches breaking off it. 'The old elderberry's still here, though. That's how Ma said I'd know this was the Deep.'

Harky tried again with the sipper bottle, and Mackie stopped moaning to give it an experimental drink, his illness-changed face so much like a baby's that Harky was attacked by grief.

'Got a little dam here.' Rab shone the torch on the dam of sandbags Harky had stacked up. 'Did your dad do that?'

'Nah, that was me, to be honest.'

Rab sucked a last seething drag on his smoke then flicked it into the ditch water, where it hissed and went out.

'It's just for stock water. I've got a twenty-mill pipe that comes up under that weed there, and then it gets pumped up to the two nearest troughs. Just in these paddocks here.'

'Huh.'

'Sorry, it's probably not all that legal. And the water branch don't know about it.'

Rab paused another long time, looking down into the ditch. 'Nah. It's good. 'Cause it means the Deep is still deep, eh. Like the name – the Deep. Not all dried up like our river. Fuck the water branch, mate. We've got our own issues with them, to be honest.' Rab took a few sideways steps down the bank. Crouching, he moved the torch across the water's surface. 'No princefish in here. Mind you, they might have heard your dad screaming his head off. And me, I guess, crashing about.'

Mackie threw the sipper cup away again. Harky sighed and

bent down to feel for it, getting his hand spiked on blackberry in the process.

'Too much weed,' said Rab. 'Can't see shit.' He gripped a handful of the lush weed and pulled it up and the water thrashed and a ripple snaked upstream, breaking the surface. 'Well, that's one princefish, at least.'

'Wow,' said Harky. 'Didn't expect that. It's good, though, right?'

'Yeah. But it fuckin stirred the mud up. Haven't got a shit's show of seeing freshies in this.'

'I'm not too confident about freshyfish, Rab, to be honest, whatever they are. I'd say the creek needs to be . . . healthier. For any sort of fish. That's what the woman from the water branch said, anyway. I'd certainly never seen anything in this creek, before that princefish. So I think you'll be lucky to find anything – princefish, freshyfish, whatever.'

Instead of answering this, Rab just thrust the torch at him. 'Can you hold this? Shine it here.'

Harky trained the torch on the little dam, the spill of water that eased over its top. Silted with ditch mud, the fabric of the lower sandbags had begun to rot and split, and the sand inside had splurged and been colonised green by algal growth. Rab worked his way through the weed towards the dam, planting his boots on the bank. He pulled his sleeves up, lay close to the water and leaned out, supporting himself with one hand on the top of the dam, feeling with his free hand along the undersides of the sandbags. For a time there was only the sound of Mackie growling to himself, and Rab's grunts and splashes as he felt along the sandbags, and sometimes the misting-down hiss of the irrigator far off.

'Ma reckons they used to feel along the banks for freshies, and then pull them out by their beaks. They've got beaks, eh. Real weird fuckers, apparently.' Rab's voice was hushed by the water's proximity or the work. He shuffled further, so his whole chest hung over the ditch surface, his jacket-front getting wet. 'There's too much weed along the banks, though, so I thought I might be able to find one under the bags here.' He heaved himself up, and adjusted something in his chest pocket, keeping it safe. 'You all right holding the torch a bit longer?'

'Sure. Mackie really needs to get to bed, though.'

'All good. Just going to try one more thing, so we can get him that tenth broth.' Then he stood right up, securing one boot out on the dam itself, the other remaining on the bank. Straddling the sandbag this way, he gripped it to lift. 'This might screw up your dam. You all right with that?'

Rocking Mackie's barrow, fatigued in the temporary quiet, Harky just waved his free hand.

Rab braced his legs and heaved, but stalled halfway. 'Fuck,' he said. 'Heavy as.'

'It's waterlogged. Maybe I could help?'

'Just hold the torch. Point the light under the bag for us.' He crouched lower and gripped the corners – and this time it came up. Bending low to point the torch Harky thought he saw, in the instant before murk circulated, tiny eyebeads catching light. Then whatever it was flicked and was gone, hunching in a dam crevice. 'Oh my god,' Harky said.

'What?' Rab's voice was strained, the wet sandbag still on his thighs.

'A freshy. There's a freshy.'

'Bullshit.'

'No, I reckon it was. Well, there was something – some sort of creature.'

'What did it look like?'

Harky looked at Rab. 'Tiny eyes, I think. And some antennae, maybe?'

'That's not a freshy. For God's sake.' Rab groaned against the sandbag, its dripping weight.

From Mackie's barrow, a volley of shouts.

'Put it down, Rab – the sandbag. You'll hurt your back.'

'God, you don't even know what you're looking for,' said Rab. 'It's pathetic.'

'Jesus, Rab. I thought you told me to look.'

'I just told you to shine the torch. I didn't ask you to –' Swearing again, Rab shuffled across the dam, then loosed his arms and let the bag splosh back into place. Ditchwater slopped up his legs and arms; some even reached Harky, spittling on his face.

Rab wiped his hands on his jeans, then reached for the torch. 'Can I just have that?'

His face burning, Harky handed it across.

Rab went down low to the water, peering with the light.

'So what do they look like, then?' said Harky. 'Freshyfish.'

Rab paused his search and went still, then stood up. Torch on his hip. 'Actually, could you give us a moment, please? Like, some space. No disrespect.'

'Oh, sure,' said Harky, 'sorry.' He indicated Mackie, who was shouting again, head back and pointing into the night. 'How about if I wait by Dad. He's kind of losing it.'

Rab shook his head. 'The truck. Could you both go back to the truck, please? Wait for me there.'

'Oh.'

'Just need some proper space.' He indicated the Deep. 'Like twenty minutes, or something.'

'Absolutely,' said Harky, hurrying now. 'Of course. Come on, Dad.'

But as soon as Harky bent down to reorder the sling and blanket, Mackie resisted, throwing fists at his son. Harky reared back and felt his phone vibrate. He brought it out. Gret. He looked across at Rab, who was standing with his back turned, facing the Deep. 'You can take that dam down if you want, Rab. Like I said, it's not exactly legal.'

Rab didn't answer.

Gret's call lit up Harky's screen again. This time he took it.

'You haven't been answering,' said Gret. 'Has he had all his broths?'

His face still hot, his father writhing in the barrow in front of him, Harky closed his eyes. Tried to breathe deeply.

'Harky?'

'We're just about done. Rab's with us now. He's helping us.'

'So Mackie's had it? His tenth.'

'Not yet. Actually, Mum, I don't think –'

'It's all right,' said Rab, cutting over him from the ditch. 'I've got something here. Some princefish.'

Harky stared. Rab's hand was at his chest pocket. 'You've already got some broth?'

'Yeah,' said Rab. 'Had some all along, to be honest. It's already boiled up.'

'So you've had some princefish broth in your pocket all along – the whole time we've been doing this freshy hunt?'

'Yeah. Just as a back-up.'

Harky's laugh was flat, exhausted. 'I guess we deserve that.'

'Aah,' said Mackie. 'Gah!'

Rab trained the torch on the dam. 'It's from the princefish processor in town. That's the only place we can get princies now. There's no point going for princefish down the river. It's all fucked.'

'But you're okay with it being Mackie's tenth?'

'Yep. At the truck. We'll do it back there, once I've finished up.'

Gret's voice came up from Harky's thigh, his hanging phone. 'Harky? Harky!'

'We're nearly done now,' he said, lifting it. 'We'll be half an hour, tops. You should get into bed, Mum.'

'How is he, though?'

He could hear it all in her voice – all the nights, all the appointments. The waking up. There was only one thing to say to her. 'Much better,' he said. 'His colour's come back. And his forehead doesn't feel so hot.'

Then he rang off and rearranged his father. 'So I'll just take him back now,' he said. 'To the – to the truck.'

With his back to them, looking into the ditch, Rab gave no reply.

Harky barrowed his father back along the flattened path to the fence, then down the ruts. The moon was low above the volcanoes now, but still strong enough to show the high cones and the ridge and the nearby shelterbelts in silhouette. In just a few hours Harky would be up again for work, or before that if Mackie wouldn't sleep once they got back to the house.

'One more mouthful, Mackie,' he said. 'One more broth from Rab, then that's all your meets done, and you'll be all fixed up.'

He closed on Rab's truck, sandwiched Mackie into it and lifted the barrow up on to the deck. Then he sank into the vehicle himself, spent and stinking of ditch. Closed his eyes and felt himself drift, his fatigue lifting away and off, and he thought that this must be it – the lifting at last, the lifting reward for the parent at the end of the meets. But then he jerked awake at a noise from Mackie, and Rab still wasn't there, and there was no sign of him either when he peered through the windscreen of the truck, smeared with quarry and riverbed dust. No torchlight coming across the paddock, or at the Deep. Maybe Rab had turned the torch off. He was taking another moment, perhaps, on the bank. Or lying on his back in the weeds round the plants. Pulling the dam up. Or just standing there in silence. Up to anything, in fact.

'You see, now, Dad? That wasn't so bad, was it? Bringing Rab up onto this old place.'

Mackie just burbled in response, and Harky swallowed hard against something in his throat. He'd wanted to hear a voice – that was why he'd said it – but in the truck his own words had sounded tinny and off.

Wired and wide awake, Harky sat there. Waited. Checked on his father in the back. Talked to him, and then turned to look through the windscreen, where Rab remained hidden somewhere, moving among the moonlit shapes, doing his own family stuff.

OCTAVIA CADE

A graduate of Clarion West (2016) and three-time Sir Julius Vogel award-winner, poet, critic and novelist Octavia Cade has published several dozen short stories, with multiple publications in *Clarkesworld* and *Asimov's*. She has a doctorate in science communication from the University of Otago, and a special interest in science history and marine studies; she is Massey University's Visiting Artist writer for 2020.

The Stone Wētā

Hemideina maori

In winter, the mountain stone wētā crawls into crevices, into cracks in the stone, and it squats there, waiting. It is a creature of summer days and winter strengths, of cryogenic hibernation. When the world freezes about it, becomes a stretch of snow and ice and darkness, the stone wētā freezes solid in its bolthole. Eighty-two percent of the water in its body turns to ice; the wētā is climate in a single body, it is a continent broken off and geology made flesh.

When the weather warms the wētā thaws, resumes its life amidst the stone monuments of the Rock and Pillar range.

Female wētā survived the cold more readily than the males. The Stone Wētā laughed under her breath. There was a frigidity joke to be made there somewhere, but in her experience winter was a time to lie low and endure and women were better at that, overall, than men. Resistance was revolution, sometimes, blood and dramatic acts, but more often it was survival. More often it was preservation, and the data she carried with her was for preservation more than revolution.

The new data she'd received, smuggled over from Resurrection in a tiny drive, hung down between new breasts. The Stone Wētā was still getting used to the weight of them, in love with the curves of the body she'd always felt she was meant to have. The university had been supportive of her transition, colleagues coming by with easy-freezing foods so she wouldn't have to cook so soon out of the hospital, and there was still some leave left. But the Stone Wētā didn't like to leave data where it might be searched for, or where someone could stumble over it when they popped by to fill up her cupboards.

'There's such a thing as too dedicated,' said her doctor when the Stone Wētā decided to come back to work early. The invertebrates could wait, he argued, but what he didn't know was that they were only an excuse. The Stone Wētā had an insulated lockbox hidden up in the Rock and Pillars, buried deep in a lonely crevice.

The lockbox was stuffed with climate data. Information come from another country, an administration that was purging files – and the Stone Wētā was a biologist with colleagues in other disciplines, and she kept their geology for them.

Selaginella lepidophylla

A desert dweller, the resurrection plant is adapted to dehydration, to the long dry seasons of its arid environment. Parched for short periods, its outer stems curl into circles, but as the waterless days endure the resurrection plant hunches further down, its inner stems compressing into spirals and minimising surface area. Tucked in, the resurrection plant survives almost complete desiccation. Until the rains come it takes on the appearance of a dead thing, but beneath the surface there is revival waiting.

*

Resurrection was raised on the southern borders of the Chihuahuan desert. She played there as a child – carefully at first, until she learned to adapt her play to climate – and she was grateful for that apprenticeship in aridity. It had taught her what it was to have boundaries, and what it was to have them broached. Water evaporated out in the desert; sweated through skin that seemed sometimes to be a too-permeable thing.

But then all borders were permeable. There wasn't a wall built that couldn't be overcome, and although Resurrection had relatives she no longer saw, could no longer see for they were afraid of leaving a country they might not be able to return to, she had other means of contact.

A botanist was expected to attend conferences, to promote the conservation of her region. 'Mexico has one of the most biologically diverse deserts on the planet,' she said, talking of the work she was doing, the population surveys, the challenges of long-term monitoring. 'We have a responsibility to ensure the preservation of this natural wonder.' She took some of the attendees on a field trip, introduced them to ecologies not their own. In the middle of the hike, one of the foreign scientists – a woman who was deliberately, inanely chatty in her conversation and as such roundly ignored by the rest of the party – stumbled in the sand. When Resurrection took her hand to help her up, a drive was pressed into her palm.

'Thanks,' said the scientist. 'Clumsy me! Always tripping over my own feet.'

'You're welcome,' said Resurrection, pocketing what was given her without a glance. 'But it wasn't your feet you tripped over. Have you seen this plant?' She explained about the curling as the others gathered round, demonstrated the beginnings of reversal with her water bottle. 'It's amazing what can survive out here,' she said.

For all the drama of above-ground, of the resurrection leaves, it was what was buried beneath that she found most important.

Root systems went deep in the desert.

The Stone Wētā always copied any data she was given before she buried it in the Rock and Pillars. Caching data was a useful fallback, but caches had been discovered before. The Stone Wētā had only heard bits and fragments, passed on from her own minimal sources, but Bristlecone Pine had gone silent. Arrested, most likely, with her data confiscated and, presumably, destroyed.

Now it was spread internationally, each piece of information replicated and hidden at several sites. The Stone Wētā didn't know all of them. She only knew who she was to pass her data sets on to. That way her potential for betrayal was limited.

'Not that I would, not if I had any choice,' she promised. She tried very hard not to think of the choices that Bristlecone might have been given. (The choices that might have been taken away.)

'We all like to think that we'd be brave,' said the Glass Sponge. She'd come to stay for the party the Stone Wētā was throwing, to celebrate her new shape with friends while she could.

'A show-us-your-tits party,' said the Glass Sponge, into her third wine and tactful with it.

'You're all class,' said the Stone Wētā, emptying the bottle. 'Such a fucking lady. And you should be so lucky.'

The Glass Sponge sighed, wistful, and the Stone Wētā sniggered into her glass. She'd been recruited by the other woman a couple of years previously. They'd flatted together at uni, and the Stone Wētā hadn't ceased to be amazed that such were the things resistance was made of – the memories of Dunedin winter, cheese rolls and tramping; a history of shared homework and early morning lectures. Soft power and social circles.

'My turn to find someone soon,' she said.

Scolymastra joubini

The glass sponge crouches on seabeds beneath the Antarctic ice. The silica skeleton sways in the dark water, chilled by the currents of a continent. It is the oldest organism on the planet: for 15,000 years, perhaps, the glass sponge endures a long night, its growth a slow and silent thing. But the ice shelves collapsing above, calving off in response to climate, have brought light and plankton in levels the glass sponge is not accustomed to and it grows wildly, branches out and quickly while destruction takes place above it.

The Glass Sponge spent her summers in the Antarctic, trying to determine the effects of a shifting climate upon polar biota. She was part of a community there: scientists stacked on top of each other, a small society isolated by climate and vocation.

Her secondary role there was an open secret. Scott Base was a facility set up for knowledge and the sharing of it, run by a country that was far enough away from the seats of power that it was frequently overlooked. Being small and hidden away at the bottom of the world had its uses, and unimportance was as much a defence as armour.

'Don't you ever want to just come straight out with it?' the Glass Sponge was asked. 'Say to hell with it, Scott Base will take your data, send copies to us and we'll store it away where no one can tamper with it.'

'I'm sure the government would love that,' she said.

'It's not like New Zealand hasn't told a superpower to fuck off before. We did it on nukes, we can probably get away with it on climate. It might encourage those bastards in Wellington to finally take a stand for once.'

'If Wellington wants to come out on data protection I won't stop them,' said the Glass Sponge. 'But I'm not in charge of what we do here, and I'm not just talking about the Base. I didn't set up this network. The person who did is responsible for scientists all around the world – and not all of them live in countries that wouldn't sell them out if power came knocking.'

There was no answer to that. The Glass Sponge waited to be asked who *was* in charge, but the question never came. She took that discretion for the support that it was and was grateful.

Besides, even if she were aware of the real-world identity of the Sand Cat she would never have shared it. Some secrets weren't hers to tell.

Felis margarita

The sand cat protects itself from sunlight, and from the lack of it. The desert is a place of extreme temperatures and the bottom of its feet, the spaces between its toes, are thick with fur for when the sand is scalding in the noon sun. This fur blurs its footsteps, and the tracks of the sand cat through the dunes are hard to follow.

The sand cat, relative to its size, bites harder than any other feline.

The Sand Cat learned early and well the importance of preservation, and of libraries. The Timbuktu manuscripts were the pride of her city, hundreds of thousands of them spread through numerous private households. As a girl, the Sand Cat had seen her uncle inherit the family library, had seen him swear to protect it for the whole of his life, as was right and good.

As a woman, the Sand Cat had seen those manuscripts as a source of danger as well as pride. The Islamic fundamentalists in northern Mali had tried to destroy them, and while they had managed to burn some, the people of Timbuktu had come together to preserve the rest. Manuscripts were bundled up, were buried, were smuggled out of the city to safety, a costly and perilous process but one which had resistance and love of learning down the very spine of it. Residents endangered themselves, endangered their families, by accepting small parcels of text to hide in their homes. People were beaten every day on the streets for lesser crimes. They were mutilated, they were executed.

They hid the manuscripts regardless.

When the Sand Cat saw the same thing happening again, albeit in another country and with another target, perpetrated this time by government instead of rebels, she refused to countenance it.

The very idea offended her. It offended her down to the marrow, and the Sand Cat felt herself begin to hiss with rage.

'Why do they keep trying to do this?' she spat. 'It is knowledge they go after every time!'

'Of course it is,' said her uncle. 'People who know nothing can be controlled.' His texts had been saved, but the effort had turned his hair to iron.

'It has done the same to my heart,' said the Sand Cat.

Timbuktu had taught her the value of knowledge, and of preservation. It had also taught her how to network. The Sand Cat was involved in setting up reforestation projects, working to increase planting, and this gave her access to scientists involved in similar projects in other countries. It was perfectly normal for her to consult with them on best practice, on their strategies for environmental conservation and how best to involve affected communities. Such consultation was not only normal, it was encouraged.

And if the conversation wandered, what of it?

Geckolepis megalepis

The fish-scale gecko is an escape artist of particular and gruesome aspect. Its sister-species amputate themselves in the face of predation, but the fish-scale gecko holds its escape in its skin instead of its tail. That skin is large-plated and scaly, and its attachment to the flesh beneath is temporary. When the fish-scale gecko is grabbed or threatened, it sheds its skin and skitters, bald and pulsing, into trees.

The Fish-scale Gecko was in constant contact with the Sand Cat. Madagascar was not Mali, but the Fish-scale Gecko spent her days as a park ranger, encouraging eco-tourism in the tropical forests. 'Poverty is a trap,' she said. 'People need to live. And if slash-and-burn is the only way for them to make a living, then that's what they'll do. You have to find a way to make sustainable use of the forests economically viable.'

The Sand Cat knew that, but she made appropriate noises anyway, was seen to take notes. Escape was a useful survival tactic but camouflage was better. 'Eco-tourism is proving a viable option, then?' she said.

'Over fifty percent of visitors take part in some form of eco-tourism. The forests are a big part of that. Something I've found tourists particularly enjoy is being hoisted up into the tree tops. It gives them a whole new perspective on rainforest ecology. That's particularly useful given how much tropical forest cover is decreasing globally.'

Other operatives might hide the data entrusted to them in the ground, but the Fish-scale Gecko was a creature of heights and canopies, and when she stashed it was arboreal.

'Is this just at the one location?' asked the Sand Cat.

'For now, but it's a popular activity. Too popular, perhaps. I begin to think all the activity in one area is compromising the local ecology.'

Over the monitor, the Sand Cat froze and it was almost imperceptible, had not the Fish-scale Gecko been looking for it. 'That is . . . concerning.'

'I've been scouting for new sites. But we've a busy programme of local events coming up, so I might have to put it off for a little while.'

'You've been so helpful,' said the Sand Cat. 'I really appreciate the time you've spent advising me. I realise I've been adding to your workload. Would it be useful to put our consultations on hold for a few months?'

'That's probably a good idea,' said the Fish-scale Gecko. Her skin itched, and she could feel the talons closing around.

'We're going to miss you.'

'I've still got a few months,' said the Stone Wētā. 'But thank you. I'll miss you too. I'll miss everyone here. The department's been good to me, and that's in no small measure down to the administration. Down to you.'

'My pleasure,' said her department head. 'You've been a real boon to us. It's not many universities can say that one of theirs has been tapped for Mars.'

'Mars needs entomologists too!' said the Stone Wētā. The first manned mission, a colony group of scientists and that mission one-way. 'It's an extraordinary opportunity, to help create an ecosystem.'

'You've certainly had practice,' said the head. Her voice was carefully bland. 'I mean, of course, your work up in the Rock and Pillars. Though I suppose that's as much preservation as creation.'

'It's an extraordinary interaction between organism and environment,' said the Stone Wētā. 'It deserves to be protected.'

'Absolutely. Oh, talking of the extraordinary, you won't believe what's turned up in my inbox. Accusations that someone at this university is smuggling, if you can believe it. Smuggling data. Ridiculous – sounds like they're fishing to me. I forwarded the email on to Foreign Affairs, told them I didn't know anything about it.'

'Don't you?' said the Stone Wētā, her voice level.

'Not a thing,' said the head. Her gaze was very direct. 'And I certainly don't have time to go looking. I'm too busy hunting for a replacement for you!'

'I'm sorry to cause you trouble,' said the Stone Wētā.

'If you're that sorry you can help out. There's a young woman visiting next week, come for an interview. She's a potential grad student, looking to do her PhD. Was recommended by a colleague over in Suva – she did some summer fieldwork there in her undergrad. I'd like you to talk with her, see what you think. I hear she's very independent-minded. I like that in this department.'

'I've noticed,' said the Stone Wētā.

Asterias amurensis

The Japanese seastar owes its success to adaptability and reproductive strategy. It owes that success, as well, to the interconnection of the world. Its larvae, spread through ballast waters, are shipped to other oceans and other countries. It is one of the most invasive species alive, and there is hungry persistence in each of its five arms.

One of the things that the Japanese Seastar enjoyed most about marine biology was that it gave her the opportunity, so often, to speak with others in her field. The marine environment was linked, all of it flowing together, and the conferences were frequently global in subject as well as in participant.

She had just attended a particularly interesting session on the effects of climate change upon Antarctic glass sponges. Her own contribution, as one of a panel on combating invasive species, was scheduled for later that afternoon. It promised to be popular – invasion was an issue that could exercise many a biologist.

'We so often have to deal with pests. It's rewarding to find a way to hit back! A job for scientists of sneakiness and strategy.' She grinned coquettishly as she said it, circulating through the morning tea, relishing responses. The Japanese Seastar was aware that she looked pretty and small and unthreatening. Charm was her greatest asset.

'I need a deputy who can make connections quickly,' the Sand Cat had told her. 'Someone who can accurately and discreetly assess the character of others. Someone people will trust.'

'I'm your woman,' the Japanese Seastar had said. 'I've a very long reach. Fingers everywhere!' And held them up, wriggling. The nails were brightly painted.

It amused her to take the name of an invasive to fight invasion. She'd seen what happened when things went wrong. It wasn't enough to store data online, to spread it over the net where everyone could see it. Viruses could change that data easily enough, falsify findings and make the effects look smaller than they were, make the data less of a threat – and without a hard copy to compare it to, without the original data cached, it was difficult to prove the tampering.

The Japanese Starfish didn't hold a cache. Instead she held drives in her bright pretty handbag, and handed them out like candy at conferences, albeit quietly and carefully. A good proportion of the scientists attending worked for her anyway, and the contents of their own handbags would later disgorge in other waters, and go to ground in foreign shores.

'I've felt a chrysalis for so long,' said the Stone Wētā. 'Transformation comes easily to me.' Change of body, change of purpose. Change of planet. 'Well, not always easily. But it comes and I have learned to adapt to that. It doesn't work that way for everyone.'

'If you think I don't understand necessity and change you can think again,' said the girl. The girl – she wasn't very much younger than the Stone Wētā. And she had a name, but the Stone Wētā tried not to think of it. That name was irrelevant – she was here to see if there was a Fish-eating Spider, not a tired young woman from Tuvalu, forced into immigration as a child because of rising waters.

'Why *Dolomedes dondalei*?' asked the Stone Wētā.

The girl who might be the Fish-eating Spider shrugged. 'There aren't many species where individuals go hunting for prey bigger than they are,' she said. 'I found it refreshing.'

'You're angry.'

'My home is being swallowed up by climate. No one gives a shit. You think my family was the last to leave? Hell, we weren't even the first. We left years ago. I can't even speak the language anymore! How's that for transformation?

'No one gives a shit,' she said again. 'It's all screwing with data now, trying to pretend that nothing's happening. Fine. We're all going to pretend everything's *fine.* I can pretend too. But I'm going to pretend with an organism I can at least admire for gumption, because God knows the people around me don't have any.'

'It's a dangerous identification though, isn't it?' said the Stone Wētā, remembering the sound of ancient trees gone quiet, of the silence where Bristlecone Pine had been. She couldn't let anyone else get involved without making sure that they knew the risks they were taking. 'Identification like that might make it easy to forget that hunting generally goes the other way.'

The girl narrowed her eyes, and for an instant the Stone Wētā could see in them the shadow of many legs. 'Sometimes danger is necessary,' she said.

Dendrocnide moroides

The gympie gympie covers itself with stinging hairs and neurotoxin. It is one of the most poisonous plants in the world, and one of the most painful. A human who brushes up against a gympie gympie will experience agony for up to two years: it is a most persistent reminder of trespass.

It flourishes best after disturbance, when the ground is overturned and in full sunlight.

The Gympie Gympie buried her caches in shallow soil. She didn't use a single lockbox, didn't add to the same location more than once. Instead there were a dozen little burials, all in the open air with gaps in the rainforest canopy above. Atop each burial she planted a small specimen of *D. moroides*.

She wore protective gear when she planted; amused herself by picturing what would happen if some poor bastard came looking for what he shouldn't. The Gympie Gympie's ancestors had walked the tropical ecosystems of northern Australia for tens of thousands of years before the Europeans came, and she had been raised with their knowledge, had gone away to university for ecology and come home to her own lands.

She didn't much care if she were followed: there were more dangers here than interrogation, than imprisonment and the betrayal of science. No one that followed would know those dangers like she did. Anyone alien enough, who didn't know what they were getting into, deserved what they got as far as the Gympie Gympie was concerned. There was a reason she supplemented the buried seeds of science with silica and poison, and it was so the lands of her childhood weren't ravaged further than they had to be when the climate turned.

The Sand Cat might have prioritised preservation, but the Gympie Gympie was all about justice. Her own country wasn't so fucking innocent, and she had no pity left in her burials for guilt.

Buellia frigida

This Antarctic lichen of the Dry Valleys grows slowly, perhaps a single centimetre for every millennium, but it does grow. The lichen is so accustomed to extreme cold and aridity that it is used as an approximation of what life may be capable of on Mars. Experiments on the International Space Station, where the lichen is exposed to the conditions of space as well as a simulation of Martian environments, prove that the lichen is capable of enduring both.

The Antarctic Lichen floated through the ISS, making her way to the docking port. The transports to the Mars colony were almost ready to go, and the scientists that had been ferried up and through the ISS to their respective ships had almost been offloaded. Only a few were left, and the Antarctic Lichen, assigned on permanent rotation to the Station, was going to say goodbye.

She didn't know the Stone Wētā, had never been informed of her true name, but when the Stone Wētā had first stepped aboard with the tattoo curling round her forearm, all spiky legs and long antennae and big striped body, the Antarctic Lichen had recognised her.

'Nice ink,' she said.

'Kind of a last-minute reminder,' said the Stone Wētā, smirking. 'I'm still not entirely sure of what. Endurance, maybe.'

'Persistence,' said the Antarctic Lichen. 'Rebirth, into a different world.' The world below them hung in space, green and blue and with the ice at its edges draining, the polar caps melting away almost as she watched.

'Transformation,' said the Stone Wētā. 'I am . . . familiar with the concept.'

There was little chance to talk. But as the Stone Wētā prepared to disembark, the Antarctic Lichen gave her a small box. 'If you could transport that over to your ship I'd be grateful,' she said. 'Last minute additions for *Buellia*. Just pass them on, please.'

Anyone around them would have thought the box was to be handed over to the colony's botanical department. *B. frigida* was making the trip, after all, and it gave the Antarctic Lichen some comfort to know, after all her experiments on it, that if the lichen's native environment was at risk then there was, still, the potential for it to survive on other worlds.

Mars had the potential to preserve a lot.

'It's amazing what can survive in such inhospitable places,' said the Stone Wētā.

'I have every faith,' said the Antarctic Lichen, waving through the window in the airlock. It was perhaps paranoia that made her send data to the open plains of another planet, but she couldn't keep hoarding on the ISS, where there were limited opportunities to unload.

Data that couldn't be shared was always at risk.

The Fish-eating Spider stared up into the dark. Though she could not see it, the ship carrying the Stone Wētā had begun its journey to a harder planet. The Fish-eating Spider did not envy her. She would have missed the stream-sides, the night-sounds of water and the creatures that lived beside it. The way the earth smelled when she turned it over for burial, the shovel new-bought and shiny in her pack.

A drive of smuggled data hung between her breasts, waiting for the morning.

KAREN HEALEY

Karen Healey is the award-winning author of *Guardian of the Dead*, *The Shattering*, and the When We Wake duology. With Robyn Fleming, she is the co-author of the Hidden Histories series. She lives in Ōtautahi, where she teaches English and ignores her dishes.

Where We Walk, We Walk on Bones

The dead man woke Aneet at the change of the watch.

Ship's Counsellor wasn't a bridge role, and Aneet didn't pay much attention to the chimes and lights that ruled time on the *Cranwell.* She had to 'work' for six hours in every cycle, but most of that she spent sitting in the infirmary nook and watching crime dramas. She had only two regular clients: a kid who was having trouble with their younger brother, and a crew member who wanted to complain about her direct superior to someone who had to keep the whining confidential. That, plus the occasional drop-in, didn't make for a busy schedule.

Aneet spent the rest of her time in imitation of the cats she'd left with her sister: sleeping, eating and, when the urge to move overcame her, bouncing from hold to hold in the gym.

But mostly, she slept: deep, quiet, uninhabited sleep. She was determined to never take the luxuriant emptiness of sleep for granted.

'Excuse me,' the dead man whispered.

'Go away,' Aneet said, in the tone she always used for the importunate dead.

Then she realised what was wrong, released her chest

restraint, and sat up.

The dead man could not be here. The *Cranwell* was a brand-new colony ship and Aneet had paid a lot to ascertain that no one had died in her construction or testing. The colonists were all young and obnoxiously healthy, and the crew – herself excepted – had all been screened for the genetic markers of various sudden deaths. There were a few crew members with chronic illnesses that might eventually kill them, but people who died with some warning rarely bothered people like her.

In the cave darkness of her cabin, the dead man waved at her from the foot of the narrow bunk; a short man with milk-pale skin and thinning reddish-brown hair, dressed in a green ship's officer's uniform. Aneet didn't know what kind of officer he was. She hadn't bothered to learn the ridiculous insignia that demarcated role and rank.

The part of her brain that sensed the dead rerouted the information through the more conventional senses, so she wasn't actually seeing him.

'Unbelievable,' she said, and clapped the lights on anyway.

'I'm so sorry to bother you,' the dead man said, 'but I'm afraid I've been murdered.' He turned to show her the crater in his skull.

Aneet had seen plenty of horrors: teeth marks on bones, steaming viscera exposed to frozen air, the results of mutilations and tortures she hadn't wanted to imagine. The bone fragments sticking out of the smashed brain tissue were almost tidy by comparison.

There was a lot of blood, of course. Head wounds did bleed so much.

'Who did it?' Aneet said crisply. If she could report the killer to the captain she could go back to sleep while justice took its course.

'They hit me from behind,' he said. 'I didn't see them. It could be anyone on the ship except you.'

'Why not me?'

The man looked appalled. 'Aren't you a Death Speaker?'

'Obviously,' Aneet said, waving her hand between them. 'But there's nothing to prevent a Death Speaker from murdering someone.'

'Well, also, it just happened. And you were asleep when I arrived. And you're not spattered in blood.'

'So why don't you go searching through the ship for someone spattered in blood, then get back to me?'

'I'm not sure that I can,' he said slowly. 'I just . . . I was in Section 144-B and then I felt as if I had to come here, right away. And now I'm here, you feel like a gravity well. I don't think I can leave.'

Great. He was going to be one of the sticky ones, who clung to her like honey to bread.

'Perhaps you could call the captain?' he said.

'I left my c-clip at work,' Aneet said, releasing the hip and foot restraints on the sleeping pouch. Regulations said you had to wear the communications clip on your shift, and recommended it for off-watch hours in case the bridge needed to contact you. Aneet had not come on this journey to be contactable.

She wriggled out of the sleeping pouch and pushed off. The gym time hadn't much improved her zero-gravity skills – the motion shot her up and backwards, and her hip glanced off one of the handholds. Another bruise for the collection.

'Gentle movements,' the dead man said encouragingly.

Aneet rolled her eyes and rotated towards the centralised hatch that served as a door.

The *Cranwell* had been built in orbit and would spend her life shuttling between Earth and the colonies. She'd never enter atmosphere or be subject to gravity, so she'd been designed as a match for her true environment, with no 'up' or 'down'. The walls and rooms were arranged in hexagons rather than rectangles. Aneet found the effect vaguely nauseating, a feeling that at least had the advantage of being caused by architecture, not atrocity.

In the corridor, she tried to orient herself by the various coloured stripes painted on the walls, but she just hadn't paid enough attention, and there wasn't time for her to get lost. 'Where's the bridge?' she asked the dead man.

'Oh!' he said, and floated easily before her. 'This way.'

Captain Taimana was supposedly the only person on board who knew of Aneet's particular talent, though word tended to get around. Their office was neat and smaller than Aneet had expected, and their disapproval of her presence seemed to take up most of the space in it. Aneet wasn't sure if the dislike was because she was shirking her moral responsibility by leaving her previous role, or because she wasn't doing anything but the bare minimum of her current job requirements.

Before the dead man, Aneet hadn't cared about the captain's opinion of her. Now it was becoming a problem.

'Who was murdered?' they demanded.

'Crap,' Aneet said, and tilted her chin at the dead man. 'What's your name?'

The dead usually identified themselves immediately, desperate to be acknowledged. This dead man jumped in mid-air. 'Oh, I'm sorry,' he said. 'I'm Phillip Cruddock, Engineer Second Class.'

Aneet passed this on.

'Phil Cruddock?' the captain said. 'But he's just – why would anyone kill Phil?'

'Phillip,' the dead man murmured.

'That question isn't really relevant,' Aneet said, trying to sound helpful. From the captain's scowl, she hadn't succeeded. 'I mean . . . right now the most important thing is to search for the killer before they have a chance to clean up. Phillip was killed in Section 144-B, approximately eight minutes ago, from a blow to the back of the head. He didn't see the murderer, but there's still time to find them.'

'What do you propose I do? Turn out the whole crew for an inspection?'

'Not the whole crew,' Phillip said helpfully. 'The watch changed just after I died, so those going off the bridge or coming onto it should be exempt.'

Aneet relayed the information. The captain's expression didn't change.

'At the very least, Dr DuPree, I'm going to need proof of death before I place my crew under suspicion.'

Aneet stared at them. 'You have the word of a Death Speaker,' she said, and pointed to Phillip, floating unseen behind the captain's shoulder. 'I'm speaking to the dead man right now.'

'The word of a retired Death Speaker,' the captain corrected, and Aneet bridled at their censure. 'You're Ship's Counsellor now.'

'Fine,' Aneet snapped, and unhooked her feet from the chair rail, launching herself towards the office door. 'Then come and see the body. And I hope it gives you nightmares.'

Section 144-B was on the outskirts of the *Cranwell*, right behind the layers of radiation shielding. It was one of the wide honeycomb cells where greyish-white coils of krigerium nestled into the walls. The krigerium coils folded time and space and made the journey possible. They also gave Aneet the creeps. Catastrophic decay was supposed to be rare, but nobody wanted a repeat of the *Brigham Young*.

They stopped at the hatch leading in to 144-B, because the chamber itself was occupied by floating blood droplets.

The dark ruby spheres wobbled gently in the air currents, occasionally bumping into one another, forming and reforming from the impact. Phillip's body, soaked with the blood that hadn't escaped into the ship's atmosphere, was resting facedown near the 'floor'. To Aneet's minor satisfaction, Captain Taimana had to swallow hard, several times. She thought they'd probably be dealing with those nightmares.

'I think cause of death is clear,' Taimana said finally. 'What do you think the weapon was?'

'Something heavy,' Phillip said. 'It felt really heavy.'

Aneet wiggled her hand back and forth. 'It would feel heavy when it hit you, but that could be the force of the blow. The human skull is fragile.'

Captain Taimana watched her talk to the air. Their dark, curly hair showed no touch of white, but there were wrinkles around their eyes and a certain grim set to their lips. Probably closer to Aneet's own age than she'd first thought.

'For now, I'll tell the crew this was an accident,' they said abruptly. 'I'll give you full access to the network for your investigation.'

Aneet flinched so violently that the motion sent her drifting towards the murder scene and its beautiful, disgusting blood globes. She grabbed at the hatch frame before she could tumble inside. '*Whose* investigation? I'm a former anthropologist who can talk to the dead. I'm not a detective!'

'You're the closest thing we have,' Taimana said. 'The colonists have a few peace officers, but their equipment is all in cargo, and they don't have any jurisdiction inside the ship. It's either you, now, or the International Space Agency when we dock back in Earth's orbit in four months, and by then it'll be far too late. You, at least, can talk to the only witness to the crime.'

'Oh dear,' Phillip said.

'I still think –'

'This is an order, Ship's Counsellor,' the captain said, with heavy patience. 'I am ordering you to carry out an investigation.'

'I would like to point out,' Aneet said acidly, 'that this situation could have been avoided if you had done what I asked and started a search for the bloody crew member immediately.'

'I take your point,' Taimana said, 'and I apologise for my error.' Before Aneet could do more than blink at the apology, they went on: 'What should we do with Phil's – with the body?'

'I'm a Buddhist,' Phillip said. 'I'd prefer cremation, but we can't do that here.' He shuddered with the true spacer's aversion to fire. 'They could just preserve me in an open airlock, and shuttle me back down to Earth for a funeral later.'

Aneet passed that on. She was falling back into the habit of echoing the dead as closely as possible, refraining from revealing the tenor of her own thoughts through inflection or tone.

The captain looked in Phil's direction. They couldn't make eye contact with someone they couldn't see, but it was a credible attempt. 'I'm very sorry about this, Phil,' they said. 'I'll do my best to see you receive justice.'

'We probably can't do a viewing, but I would like a wake,' Phillip said. 'Maybe in the mess?'

'Good idea. I can watch for anyone who looks guilty,' Aneet said. She took a mental deep breath and added, 'If I'd had my c-clip with me, I could have called it in faster. I'll carry it with me from now on.'

That was as close to an apology as she could bring herself, but Taimana seemed to hear it anyway. 'That's a sensible choice,' they said. 'We'll hold the wake in two watch cycles, so that everyone has a chance to be informed.'

Aneet went back to her office to retrieve the c-clip and swear a lot in relative privacy.

'Goodness,' Phillip said when she was done. 'I haven't heard some of those words since I left the Exploratory Forces.'

'I'm entitled. Unless you think watching crime dramas is training, I'm totally unqualified for this.' And those fictional detectives with their fictional victims had confidential informants, labs full of miraculous equipment and someone to say just the right thing at the right moment to spark a brainwave. Aneet was missing all three.

Still. The motives for murder were fairly universal.

'Were you up to something?' she asked Phil. 'Smuggling, industrial espionage, sleeping with someone else's partner?'

'No,' Phillip said. 'And before you ask, I don't have any enemies or exes or stalkers on board.'

They must have watched the same dramas. 'No arguments with the bunkmate or co-workers?'

'None. Rawiri's a good guy, and the team are fine. I mean, it's a new ship. We were still working out how to be a crew. But everyone seemed friendly enough.' He sighed. 'I'm not helping very much, am I?'

He wasn't, but Aneet was oddly reluctant to agree. 'Talk me through your death,' she said instead. 'Do you regularly work in Section 144-B?'

'Oh, that was the first time I've been there in weeks. Part of my job is doing randomised checks on the krigerium coils to prevent catastrophic decay. That section came up in today's checks.'

'Did you feel as if you were followed at any point?'

'No, but I wasn't looking out for that, either. I was just hoping I could get everything done before the end of shift.'

'Did you hear anything that might identify the killer? A voice? Footsteps?' She made a face – of course he wouldn't have heard footsteps.

Phillip either hadn't noticed her mistake or was kind enough not to point it out. 'Right before the end, I heard a rustle,' he said. 'And then, smash.'

The rustle had probably been the movement of the killer's arm. Nothing useful there.

'Oh, wait!' Phillip said. 'I smelled blueberries! Could that be important?'

There wasn't a blueberry within hundreds of light years. People hallucinated all sorts of things as they died: lights, sounds, the people they loved. The dead were no more trustworthy as direct witnesses than the living, and just as prone to perceived time distortion and confirmation bias. Aneet tried to keep the disappointment off her face. 'I'll keep that in mind,' she promised.

'Will you need to do an autopsy?' Phillip asked. 'My consciousness is still in my body, so it'd be better if we didn't disturb it before it departs for rebirth.'

'I don't think an autopsy will be necessary,' Aneet said. She could probably ask for one, but there was no reason to disrespect Phillip's faith when it was so clear how he'd died. It was the *why* that was missing.

'All right,' she said, 'let's go back to my cabin to look at these files.'

*

The captain had given her access to everything: ship plans, particulate reports, cargo lists. Aneet pulled up the shift schedules, and Phillip identified those crew members who would have had the opportunity. This resulted in three dozen suspects, each with extensive personnel files, psychological tests and background checks, and none with any previous connection to Phillip or obvious reason to kill him. It was too much information. Aneet opened the first file and began.

They worked through the shift and into the next one. Phillip was tireless, but Aneet had been woken in the early hours of her personal day-cycle. 'I need to sleep before your wake,' she said, and snorted at the accidental play on words. Her eyes were grainy from staring at the lit screen and her mouth had the sour metallic taste of failure.

'Set the screen on auto scroll,' Phillip suggested. 'I'll keep reading. Maybe something will come up.'

'You don't have to do this,' Aneet said. It was probably horrifically insensitive to let a dead man trawl for evidence that someone hated him enough to kill him.

'No, I want to,' he said, and smiled crookedly at her. 'Besides, the company's good.'

Aneet woke, slick with her own sweat, her hands clenched so hard she was digging trenches into her palms.

'Aneet,' Phillip was saying. 'Aneet. Aneet, you were dreaming. It's over. You're safe.'

She groaned and clapped the lights on. 'What time is it?'

'You went to sleep about an hour ago,' Phillip said. 'Are you all right? You don't look too good.'

This from a man missing a sizeable chunk of his head.

'Nightmare,' she said, and groped for the water pouch and pill pack taped into her bed niche.

'What about?'

Grasping hands, frantic eyes, pleading voices. 'Can't remember,' she said, and chased two pills with a squirt of water. She hadn't needed the sedatives since her first week on board. 'Did you find anything?'

Phillip floated back over to the screens. 'Oh, lots of interesting things,' he said. 'Nothing helpful, though. It's okay to sleep, Aneet. I'll make sure you get up in time.'

There was something wrong in his voice or the set of his spine. The pills dragged her back under before she could worry about it.

In the end, Aneet's alarm got her up before Phillip could, an hour before the wake. Phillip had assured her that white clothing wasn't compulsory, which was just as well, because she didn't have any. Aneet zipped her broad frame into her nicest grey jumpsuit and twisted her hair and jabbed pins until it was contained in a black-and-white coil at the back of her head. She wrapped a green dupatta over her head and shoulders and pinned that, too. 'How's this?'

Phillip turned back from the wall he'd been staring at for twenty minutes. 'Very . . . respectful. Thank you.'

'Good. Do I look like an auntie? Or a grandmother? Someone you want to confess your secrets to?'

'Maybe if you smile?'

Aneet smiled.

'And try to, um, soften your eyes a little bit?'

She tried. Phillip wrinkled his nose. 'I'll work on that,' she told him.

The mess hall was the heart of the ship. Also the stomach, lungs, kidneys and liver. Hydroponic gardens covered every surface except the door hatches and the 'floor' where the tables and benches had been bolted. Green tendrils flung themselves from the walls, waving giant colourful blooms through the air. The plants removed carbon dioxide from the ship's atmosphere, provided oxygen and, at a pinch, could be used for food and water. The psychological effect on homesick colonists who longed for something green was perhaps even more important.

Theoretically, if meteorites tore through the hull, or the krigerium coils began catastrophic sequencing, or an oxygen-devouring fire started somewhere and could not be contained, the *Cranwell*'s crew and passengers could gather here and wait for rescue.

Practically, given the number of people on board and the speed with which the hatches would lock in the event of disaster, only the people who happened to be eating at the time had any shot at survival.

Still, the gardens were pretty.

Handhold cables had been rigged under the netting that protected the greenery. Aneet kept her movements slow and sure, proceeding at what she hoped was a funereal pace. At the far end of the mess, someone had set up a table and a picture of Phillip printed on a sheet of plastic film. It shivered in the air currents, making the frozen smile more ghostly than the face of the dead man floating beside her.

People stopped talking as she moved above them.

Aneet halted above the makeshift altar, used her core strength to point straight down, and pushed off. She wobbled a little bit hooking her feet under the floor rail, but otherwise, it was a perfect landing. The silence in the mess deepened. She surveyed faces for guilt.

'I can't eat anymore,' Phillip said suddenly. 'I *love* food.'

Aneet had hoped they could go a little longer without an

ontological crisis. 'You don't have a body,' she said quietly. 'Or, rather, you do' – wrapped in preservation film and frozen in an airlock – 'but it's not going to be digesting anything. And you don't have taste buds.'

'I don't have an endocrine system, either, but I can still feel emotions. I don't have any muscles, but I'm moving. None of this makes sense!'

Aneet had retrieved a statue of the Buddha and some electronic incense blocks from Phillip's cabin. She took the statue from her hip pouch and taped the underside, pressing it firmly onto the table. 'I can find you some reading,' she said. 'There are plenty of experiential accounts by Death Speakers recording what the dead say about themselves, but if you're into logic, you might like the work of Marama Te Kahu. She uses a combination of whakapapa critique and set theory to lay out an existential argument for, um. People like you.'

'Dead people.'

'Yes,' Aneet agreed, relieved that he hadn't said 'ghosts'. Or 'souls'. That always led to trickier theological territory than she liked to walk on. Phillip was undoubtedly dead, and she wouldn't let anyone deny he was a person. Philosophically, that was as far as she was willing to go.

She taped the incense blocks down and turned them on, releasing the sweet, smoky, unfortunately artificial smell. Manufacturers claimed that electronic incense smelled exactly the same as the kind you burned, but Aneet had always been able to tell the difference. On the other hand, the electronic version passed the strict particulate regulations where the real stuff certainly wouldn't.

What else? Candles were customary on Earth, but in space they were even more impossible than real incense. She looked at the green tangle above them. 'Did you want flowers?'

'Not at the cost of disturbing the biome. This is nice. Thank you.' His picture wobbled again.

The wake itself wouldn't begin for another twenty minutes, but people were already moving over to the cleared section. Aneet faced the altar and kept vigil. Ship's Counsellor made a perfect cover. It would be strange if she weren't there.

Phillip's bunkmate Rawiri introduced himself in a whisper and asked if he could make an appointment with her later. He was accompanied by Phillip's assistant, Engineer Third Class Lisa Freeman, who brought a frame for the picture that she'd fashioned out of spare parts.

'I thought Phil would like this better,' she said.

'Phillip,' Phillip said. 'And I do.'

Aneet tried her best Wise Auntie act on both of them and was encouraged by the reaction. The pair showed promising signs of guilt, with downcast eyes, fidgeting hands and sad mouths.

Actually, quite a few of the attendees looked shifty.

Unfortunately, once the wake began, she realised why. No one there had met Phillip before six months ago when the crew had been hired, and none of them had made much effort to befriend him. Now that he was dead, they were sorry.

The wake speakers leaned heavily on general clichés and work-based anecdotes. Lisa talked about how her boss had always been willing to explain things to her. Everyone nodded, and no one pointed out that this had, in fact, been his job. Rawiri had a rambling story about the single game of chess they'd played, which Phillip had won – or maybe lost, but gracefully.

Captain Taimana closed the event with a speech on the dead man's exemplary service record, first in the Exploratory Forces of the International Space Agency, then in civilian vessels like this one. They recited the dry series of facts as if they'd memorised Phillip's personnel file, which Aneet was willing to bet was exactly what they'd done. At least that showed some effort. And at least no one was trying to invent stories of false friendship. That was always awkward with the dead in attendance.

'He made every ship fly sweeter,' the captain said at the end of their speech, somehow standing ramrod straight in zero gravity. 'He was a true engineer and a man of merit. Goodbye, Phil.'

'Phillip,' Aneet said, and only realised she'd said it out loud when the reaction rippled through the crowd. This was why she hated funerals. 'He prefers – preferred – Phillip.'

'Goodbye, Phillip,' Taimana said. 'Fly sweetly.' They saluted with a snap of their elbow, and the other crew members saluted too. Aneet, who hadn't been warned about this part, and thought salutes were stupid, managed a kind of stiff wave.

'Thank you,' Phillip said quietly. Aneet tried to smile.

After that, people drifted around, making quiet conversation before they wandered out. Aneet eavesdropped as much as she could, but the *Cranwell*'s crew showed a distressing tendency to avoid dramatic confessions.

Taimana mingled, and eventually made it over to her. 'Any progress?'

'Very little,' Aneet admitted. 'I'm sorry. I told you I wasn't an investigator.'

'I'm sure you're doing your best,' Taimana said.

Aneet thought they probably meant it kindly.

'That's a good person,' Phillip said, watching the captain leave. 'I've served under many worse, and few better.'

'Maybe you can say that at their funeral,' Aneet snapped, then pressed the heels of her palms into her eyes. 'Sorry. I'm sorry. I don't react to failure well.'

'You're not failing yet,' Phillip said. 'Shall we get back to the files?'

'Maybe we should look at the crime scene again,' Aneet said. 'I'm doing this all wrong. I should have started there. That's what the drama detectives do.'

'We don't have forensic equipment. And the air filters would have removed hair and skin flakes.'

'But not fingerprints, right?' Aneet felt for the roll of tape in her hip pouch. 'The crew's fingerprints are all recorded on their files. Come on. It's worth a try.'

Phillip showed her the way. It was peaceful, drifting through the maze of empty tunnels, the only sound the humming of the air filters. She turned where Phillip told her to turn, used the handholds he guided her to, and smelled something sweet and vaguely fruity as she floated by another corridor opening.

She grabbed at a handhold and stopped so abruptly that her dangling feet swung all the way around and bounced off the wall.

'What?' Phillip asked.

'Blueberries,' Aneet hissed.

Except it wasn't blueberries – not quite. It was an artificial smell, like the electronic incense blocks, reminding her of burnt sugar and charred fruit in her mothers' kitchen – something gone wrong, something that wasn't the way a smell should be.

She twisted into the tunnel and followed her nose to a different cell, a different section of krigerium coils.

Where Lisa Freeman, not quite fast enough, bounced away from her, hands behind her back.

'Hands out!' Aneet barked, with all the authority she could muster. She must have tripped some primal childhood impulse: Lisa's hands shot forward before her rational brain could prevent it.

Aneet had expected to see a weapon, but Lisa's gloved right hand clenched a slender tube. A plastic mouthpiece stuck out from one end of her fist. A trail of vapour drifted from it, flavouring the air with that sickly sweet smell.

'How dare she?' Phillip snarled. 'That's *disgusting.*' It was more passion than she'd heard him express about anything, and Aneet turned to look at him.

That was all Lisa needed. She curved her legs, kicked off the ceiling and arrowed straight into Aneet.

Lisa was skinny and short. Aneet had at least twenty kilograms on her. But in zero gravity, weight didn't *count.* Lisa knew how to move, and that was advantage enough. While Aneet flailed uselessly at the air, Lisa snatched Aneet's c-clip from her collar and sent it spiralling towards the far end of the section. She caught at Aneet's head and shoulders with clawed hands and used the grip to knee her in the chest.

Aneet's diaphragm spasmed; her breath abruptly expelled. Her ribs seized as Lisa tore the dupatta from her head and yanked her wrists behind her back, tying them together. Aneet kicked out weakly, and Lisa punched her in the thigh. The pain rippled up to her hip.

'Oh, no,' Phillip said, his arms waving as he tried to intervene. 'No! Lisa, stop!'

'Stop it!' Lisa said, over the man she couldn't hear. 'Just stop! Don't make me do it.'

Aneet stopped struggling, forced the panic down, closed her eyes and focused on the shuddering in her chest. The air whooshed back into her lungs with a long croak.

'She's endangering everyone!' Phillip said. 'Aneet, we have to stop her.'

Was the little tube some kind of sabotage device? Was Lisa a terrorist? Aneet's eyes went to where it floated. Lisa swam over and snatched the tube out of the air, concealing it up her sleeve.

'They have nicotine pills,' Phil was saying. 'She could have taken those instead of polluting the ship!'

Blueberries. Vapour. The gardens and the air filters and the entire intricate biome, so huge and so delicate. Aneet forced air from her lungs and shaped it into words. 'You were *smoking*?' she said.

Lisa looked appalled. 'No, I would never bring fire on board! It's a vape pen.'

'You murdered a man' – Aneet sucked another breath – 'for this?'

'I didn't mean to *kill* him!' Lisa said.

'You caved in the back of his skull.'

'With her coil pick,' Phillip said. 'I should have thought of that. We use them to adjust the krigerium vibrations.'

Aneet counted herself lucky that Lisa hadn't carried that with her today.

'I only meant to knock him out!' Lisa said. 'He went past, and I thought he'd seen the vapour. I just wanted to stop him before he reported me.'

'Well, that makes sense,' Phillip said. 'She'd have lost her job on the spot. Then she'd have been arrested and charged with malicious endangerment, second-degree assault, and vandalism. The ISA doesn't take particulate pollution lightly.'

'That's not a good reason for her to kill you!' Aneet snapped, and Lisa gasped.

'You *are* a Death Speaker,' she said. She bit her lip with small white teeth. 'I thought that was just a rumour. Are you talking to him right now?'

Aneet wanted to shake the woman until those teeth rattled out of her head. Instead, she spoke gently: 'I am. When you killed Phillip, he came to me.'

'Oh no,' Lisa said. 'No, no, that's bad.'

'Captain Taimana knows he was murdered. They're looking for the killer.'

'Tell her to turn herself in,' Phillip said.

'Phillip wants you to go to the captain. He wants you to confess.'

'I can't,' Lisa said, her hands tugging at each other as if she could stretch them into new, better shapes. 'I can't. I can't lose this job.'

'You will get caught, Lisa. You've got to accept that this is happening.'

'I can stop vaping,' Lisa said. 'I don't really need it, I just like it, and the air filters out here clear most of the toxins anyway. It's not really dangerous. The insurance people are just paranoid.'

'You killed Phillip,' Aneet said, and disgust leaked into her voice. Lisa's pale eyes sharpened, focusing on her with chill determination.

Then the façade of the frantic woman returned, the one who could justify whatever she did, at least to herself. 'I just need more time,' she muttered, and popped a panel in the ceiling. A wide, deep storage locker was concealed above, a gap between the vibrating hum of the krigerium coils. 'Time to think. That's all.'

'No,' Aneet said. 'Lisa! No!' She kicked and convulsed, but Lisa was determined, and Aneet weighed nothing, nothing at all. She braced herself against the edge of the hole and pushed back. Lisa punched her in the stomach and Aneet folded into the stiff metal embrace of the locker, banging her elbow on the side.

'I'll come back,' Lisa promised as she pressed the panel back into place. 'I'll come back next shift. When I've worked out what to do.'

'No –' Aneet gasped, and Lisa sealed the panel in place.

The locker was a coffin. A lightless, metal coffin, and she was going to die in it.

'She'll never stop by herself,' Phillip said sadly. 'She snuck away to vape after my wake. She needs serious addiction management.'

'Are you worried about her?'

'Oh, believe me, I'm furious, too. There are laws against particulates for a reason.'

'That's not why you should be angry, Phillip! I am angry because she *murdered* you! I am angry because you're *nice*, and you should be *alive*.' The storage locker was deep. When Aneet braced her back against the far wall and kicked out with her legs, her feet didn't get anywhere near the panel. She bumped back to the entrance and tried to shove her shoulder into it instead. 'I am angry because she's probably going to kill me too, and I was finally, *finally*, getting away from the dead!' She banged the panel again. The noise echoed.

After a while, Aneet said, 'I didn't mean you.'

'No, I know,' Phillip said. 'You meant in general. You were going to jump ship when we got to the colony.'

Aneet twitched. 'How did you know?'

'I saw the cargo lists while you were sleeping,' Phillip said. 'You shipped your load under a few different names, but Captain Taimana flagged it.'

'The captain knows?'

'The captain suspects. They don't like to accuse people of anything without proof. Rare metals. Coffee beans, chocolate, bags of seeds. Luxuries. It must have cost a lot to ship all that up from Earth.'

Aneet rested her head against the wall. 'It did. And more than that to get myself on board.'

'You bribed people for your job?'

'I made an investment in the company,' Aneet said. 'Turns out that's totally legal.'

'Are you even qualified to be Ship's Counsellor?'

'I did a year's training by distance learning and a three-month internship. Ship's Counsellor isn't a popular role – low pay, boring work. Ships will take pretty much anyone with the minimal qualifications.'

'But you're supposed to stay with the ship for the flight back,' Phillip said. It wasn't disapproval in his voice: it was disbelief. 'You were going to abandon your post.'

'Hence the cargo,' Aneet said. 'To make sure the colony would let me stay. It would have been cheaper to be a colonist from the beginning, but I'm too old. They wouldn't take me.'

'All this expense and deception, so that you could live in isolation on a new planet? Is it really that bad? I know Death Speakers have a particular talent, but lots of people are touched by the dead. My sister dreamed of our grandmother telling her things she couldn't have known.'

Aneet closed her eyes. It didn't help. Phillip was still visible to her Death Speaker senses, brow wrinkled in an earnest desire to understand. 'Lots of people are touched by *some* dead. They stand on the marae and greet the wairua of their ancestors, and their ancestors respond. They return to family graves, and leave offerings of flowers. They offer incense and fruit at the household shrine. For them it's . . . fundamental. Grounding. But that's not what happens for me. I see the violently deceased. And I see all of them.'

'Oh,' Phillip said.

'All Death Speakers start as kids, when the pre-frontal cortex mutation kicks in. You walk past a garage, and the man who's just shot himself cleaning his gun comes out to complain about the manufacturing fault. Or you walk past a traffic accident on the way to school, and a dead woman follows you, begging you to tell her son she's sorry she yelled at him.'

'That's awful!'

'No. Awful comes later. When you start, you only see the recently dead, those who have family and friends still alive, those who you can help. So I talked to their families and passed on the messages, and the families paid me. Sometimes I helped out the cops. They paid me too.'

'Like in the dramas,' Phillip said.

Aneet's laugh was creaky. 'Phillip, the drama version of a Death Speaker is a fake. I'm not a heroic empath bringing justice to the dead. That's a fantasy.'

'What's the reality?'

'Grim,' Aneet said, and went back to banging at the panel. 'The more you engage with the dead, the further back you see.' The dead were everywhere, and they'd died in so many ways. From machine guns. From musket fire. From taiaha. 'And the further back you see, the more valuable you become. The universities try to recruit you, and maybe you consult with them, for a while. You write some of those experiential accounts I mentioned, reporting faithfully for the dead. But the studios get you eventually. You ever watch those documentaries?'

Phillip shifted. 'Well, there are lots of documentaries . . .'

'You know the ones I mean. The recreations.' She deepened her voice and flattened her vowels. 'True crime! Historical horrors! Based on real Death Speaker accounts.'

'I've seen a few of those,' Phillip admitted. 'I prefer fiction.'

'So do I.' She sighed. 'The studios say, You have a special gift. They say, You owe it to the world to show people the ugly truth about what happened, so that it will never happen again. And because you're young and you're stupid, and the dead want to speak, and the studios are offering you just so much money, you do it. And the more you do . . .'

'. . . the further back you see,' Phillip said softly. 'Aneet? How far back?'

'Aotearoa's the last settled major landmass in the world: it has only 1500 years of human history. For Death Speakers my age, that's a huge relief; it's like a week in a spa.' She leaned into the locker wall, her head falling forward. 'Very few of us make it to my age. Have you seen . . . oh, dramas about haunted houses and the like?'

'Yes.'

'Well, those are real. People have been haunted, by dead connected to places or objects. But they leave the house, and they're fine. To Death Speakers, the whole world is haunted, by every horror in human history. And most of them have only one way to leave the house.'

Phillip jerked.

'When I became an accredited Death Speaker, there were twenty-three others on the register. By the time I turned forty, most of them had killed themselves. My best friend waited until the week after my birthday.'

'Aneet. I'm so sorry.'

'They go out gently,' Aneet said, with an edge she knew Phillip didn't deserve. 'None of us want to make living harder for someone else. But after Irina died, I decided that wasn't going to happen to me. No matter how evil I had to become to avoid it.'

'You wanted to escape. That doesn't make you evil.'

'No? I needed a lot of money, Phillip. No one gets that much money for doing *good*. I held my nose and raised my fees, and said yes to every highest bidder. I went everywhere and talked to anyone. You think Lisa's disgusting, Phillip? I exploited the dead.'

'You said they wanted to speak.'

'They did. I don't have the power to make them tell me anything. But an Egyptian woman slaughtered by the Sea Peoples three and a half thousand years ago can't comprehend mass media. She doesn't know she's going to be played in a recreation by an extra with glossy hair extensions and the viewers will flinch when she dies and forget her ten seconds later. She doesn't know that there are people – so many people – who will watch and cheer as she's decapitated. It's more *fun* for them that she was real. This is their entertainment. And I'm the one who made it possible. Until I made enough to escape.'

Aneet had uncovered the palimpsests of suffering, layer after layer, like fresh wounds over scar tissue, and exposed them to cruel eyes. She'd checked her accounts every morning and sedated herself to sleep every night. She'd told herself it was worth it, if she could make it to a new world that wasn't so scarred.

And it was all ultimately for nothing, because Lisa Freeman had snuck off for a quick smoke.

'How could you even talk to her? Did you learn her language?'

'What? Who?'

'The Egyptian woman.'

Aneet kicked the wall, accomplishing nothing but a bruised toe. 'You're not speaking English, Phillip! You're not speaking anything. You're a psychic phenomenon, and your only measurable physical existence is the electrical activity in my brain. It took thousands of years before scientific consensus accepted you were even real.'

'And you think I'm nice.'

'Yes.'

'And you're angry at Lisa for killing me.'

'Yes!'

He beamed at her. 'Then let's get you out of here, so you can report to Captain Taimana.'

Aneet bumped her hip against the front panel. '*How*? I don't have the leverage to force this thing open.'

'Well, not by banging on it, no. But Lisa's still got a thing or two to learn about ship architecture. All the large storage spaces have pressure hooks that activate from the inside. Might be a bit awkward with your hands behind your back, but there's plenty of time before the shift change.'

Aneet floated for a few moments. 'Phillip?'

'Yes?'

'Why didn't you tell me this before?'

'It was an interesting conversation,' he said cheerfully. 'Shall we? I think it's time for the heroic empath to bring justice to the dead.'

'Based on your account, I'm willing to keep Freeman confined to quarters and placed under guard,' Captain Taimana said.

'I should bloody hope so,' Aneet said, massaging her wrists. Then she caught the captain's eye. 'I mean, yes, Captain. Thank you, Captain.'

'An ISA conviction will require testimony. From a credible witness.'

'Yes, Captain. I'll be happy to testify in person.'

Phillip jumped. Taimana looked doubtful. 'That will mean a return flight to Earth.'

'I get it,' Aneet said, and rubbed the spot between her eyes. 'Look. Cards on the table –'

'They'd float,' Phillip pointed out.

'I'm not sure colony life is the best choice for me after all. Accidents happen on colonies. Murders. Suicides.' She gestured in Phillip's direction. 'This would happen again. No offence, Phillip.'

'None taken, Aneet.'

'Would you return to your work on Earth, then?'

Aneet shuddered. 'No. Never.' She looked around the office. 'I was hoping that I could stay on the *Cranwell*. If you're willing to extend my contract.'

'Yes!' said Phillip.

'Hm,' said Taimana. If they'd had anything to square on their desk, they would have been squaring it. Instead, they folded their arms and leaned back into the bolted chair.

'I'll put the work in this time,' Aneet said. 'I can work, when I want to – and I want to. I'd like to do something good. I'd like to help the living.'

'Tell them I think that's a great idea,' Phillip said urgently. 'Aneet! Make me your character reference!'

Aneet smiled at him but kept her mouth shut. Taimana was doing some sort of personal inventory of her strengths and flaws. Aneet wasn't sure Phillip's recommendation would tip the balance in her favour, but if she were accepted, she wanted it to be on her own merits.

'I think something could be arranged,' the captain said at last, and extended their hand.

Aneet shook it. Then, carefully, she saluted.

'You should go eat something,' Phillip said when she left the office. 'Also, you should describe to me exactly what it tastes like.'

'I'll try,' Aneet said, 'but I'm hardly a poet.'

'Order a steak.'

'They don't have steak. How was my salute?'

'Well,' Phillip said. 'Better than before.'

'All right,' Aneet said, pulling herself towards the garden at the heart of the ship. 'We'll work on that.'

TAMSYN MUIR

Tamsyn Muir is the bestselling author of the Locked Tomb trilogy, which begins with *Gideon the Ninth*, continues with *Harrow the Ninth*, and concludes with *Alecto the Ninth*. Her short fiction has been nominated for the Nebula Award, the Shirley Jackson Award, the World Fantasy Award and the Eugie Foster Memorial Award. A Kiwi, she has spent most of her life in Howick, New Zealand, with time living in Waiuku and central Wellington. She currently lives and works in Oxford, in the United Kingdom.

Union

The wives come strapped ten to a transport, hands stamped by some Customs wonk. Their fingernails are frilled and raised freckles stipple each arm in shades of red and orange. Permit tags list their names: Mary. Moana. Ruth. Myrrh. Huia. Anna. Iridium. Coffee. Kōkako.

The Franckton crofters stand and watch from behind the barrier. They've knocked off midday work to come. You can practically see the pong of hot mulch and melting boot elastomeric coming off them. There's even a man there from the *New Awhitu Listener* to take pictures.

Dripping sweat, the Customs detail sign off their quarantine. The wives seem indifferent to the heat. The air from the transport ruffles the thin plaits of their hair, each strand with its own line of fine bulges like a polyp. Everyone is close enough to see.

'If the *Listener* links any of those photos,' Simeon's telling the photographer, 'you're dog tucker, mate.' Simeon's got the gist of it already. The man knows Simeon's reputation and is timidly pressing *delete*.

The Mayor signs the receipt of goods slowly. She's asking questions, gesturing at the wives, but she's not getting answers, just filework and shrugging. The Ministry men take the tablet with the signature and you can tell they just want to get the hell out of there before something happens.

Later on when the croft pores over the paperwork, they discover the wives are lichen splices. No one's ever heard of it.

When the news broke that the Ministry was awarding them wives, the relief was so great in Franckton that it was more pain than pleasure. They'd spent the last fifty years incubating on governmental loan and mortgaging over half the harvest each time. A lot of beers got sunk during all the frantic budgeting that came subsequently. The staunchest Union crofters forgot to do anything but tab up how many generations it would take before all they'd be paying for was the foetal scan.

Only Simeon was hostile; nobody was surprised. 'It's a disgrace,' he kept on saying. 'It's a nothing. We're getting gypped. We're the highest-revenue croft and they're shutting us up, they're paying us off, the next time we don't say how high when they say jump we'll get our subsidy slashed and you bastards are falling over yourselves to lick their arse . . .'

He got told off by the Mayor for whinging. The sentiment was that there were only twenty wives to go round and he'd been assigned one and heaps of crofters hadn't. It wasn't as though they were all going to receive rose-splice wives and free beer and skittles. Of course it was a sop. It was a harvest cycle, and the Ministry wanted to keep them sweet so that there wouldn't be a tanty chucked over the price of wheat or onions or oats come the buying time. All of Franckton was going into this with their eyes open; they weren't naïve . . . But they still planned a picnic and a pōhiri and someone agreed to sing for the welcome and everyone getting a wife washed their shirt.

When the wives finally landed and they got their first eyeful, they knew there wasn't going to be a picnic or a pōhiri. They took up their tines and trudged back to the bunds without preamble. Only Simeon, by way of expressing his feelings, threw a big handful of grit at one of the whirring transports. It exploded into a cloud of dusty shrapnel. Some of the crofters cringed, but nothing happened.

The lichen-splice wives are pale and dry. Nobody really knows what to do with them. The last batch of kids had been nine years ago, with a bunch of hardy poppy wives and their minders. They were all hard cases and laughed and made jokes during the incubation, like poppy wives should. The Mayor was getting treated for germline trouble with her chromosomes 5 and 10, so the Ministry had made them pay through the nose for gene insurance and they'd all been sore about it, but not too sore because it was the Mayor and the croft begrudged her nothing. Simeon had squabbled and said there should be a lawsuit. Some of the crofters agreed, but then there were children to take care of and nobody did anything.

The first thing the crofters hate is the names. Their wives have been given croft names, and that's insult to injury, somehow. It's ingratiating. They should have had city names and all been Florence or Hannah or Candy. So they all become 'wife' by common fiat.

They seem obliging enough, but they never speak, except sometimes 'Yes' or 'No'. They move slowly in the Franckton heat, but unmindingly. They are slow in general to walk or to carry. They lid their eyes heavily when they talk and keep their mouths a little open, sometimes flickering their tongues.

Simeon holds forth in the pub almost every night about them. Most of the croft complaints are about how their wife stares or can't cook the tea right or is stupid, or off-putting, or intractable, but Simeon goes further than that. 'I don't want to incubate with some knock-off government sack,' he says of his wife. 'She looks like a spastic. She looks like a trisomy hutch.'

Some of the croft look away but they don't protest, because you don't with Simeon, it's more trouble than it's worth. Simeon says, 'I bloody well mean it. And I tell you what, if they don't bear good kids and look after them right, I'm blowing this wide open. I'll strike. I want our next lot to have a future, not go on cringing like mutts for crusts. If all the crofts got up off their bums and stood together we'd have the world on a plate. Look at what we get when we don't fight for it! Christ, look.'

Outside the pub and across the street, two of the wives stand in the blue evening shade. Simeon stabs a finger in their direction. They do not chat or relax: they stare, first at each other, then at a crack in the daub house, then at a drying clag of mulch, then at each other again. Their tongues flicker in their mouths.

'I tell you what,' Simeon says again, 'they scare me to death. They're not right. We got fobbed off with something weird, and we're just shutting up and taking it like we always do.'

One of the crofters has the bright idea to tell Simeon that he should have let the photographs go live, that everyone should have seen what had been done to Franckton. This crofter gets pranged with the beer mat.

'Don't be stupid,' snaps Simeon, settling back. 'We've got our bloody pride.'

*

Franckton has better results with the wives in the fields. The sun leaves white patches on their skin if they stay out too long in it, but the Mayor gets the children to weave them big scratchy shapeless hats. The wives have been taught to say 'Thank you, Aunty', and for each hat a wife intones 'Thank you, Aunty', before subsiding back into silence. They're still slow out there on the bunds, but they are just as slow heaving the stones between them as they are walking as they are everything else. It is simply how they move. They crouch down and poke back rocks into the spillways with their square, dry hands. They build back the gullies and do not care. When the children come around with the water they take one gourd together and sip miniature sips, darting their tongues inside the neck of the bottle. The other crofters take enormous gulps and dump the rest down the backs of their hot, dirty necks.

It gets to some of the croft. Nobody dares to be as bad as Simeon, who calls his wife 'you' and who swaps sharp words with the Mayor about it almost daily, but there's loads of complaint. The wives don't learn. They don't settle. They're lazy. They make everyone uneasy. Plenty of splice wives are good for doing chores and croft work – so the catalogues always promise – and do it cheerfully and well, but these ones don't, and it's yet another black eye for them.

When Laura says in the pub, 'I like my wife,' everyone's surprised into silence before they bust a gut laughing. 'Piss off! I don't mind her. I wouldn't want one that was talking my ear off all the time. And she sings sometimes . . . She's not so bad.'

She gets ragged for this daily, but sticks to it: 'Mary's a good girl,' she goes on saying staunchly. 'She gives it heaps, just doesn't rush. Can't believe you're all moaning about how they don't have tea on the table when the clock strikes six. My God! You lot don't know you're born.'

*

Those with wives start noticing that, wherever they go, a fine leafy build-up appears on the walls or countertops where they work. This is easily wiped off with a damp cloth, but causes no end of alarm. The build-up is a thin crust – a substrate with miniature flakes – dusty green in some houses, shrillingly orange in others. Simeon spits the dummy entirely and makes his wife sleep in the shed, and at this point nobody blames him, he's sent a sample to the big lab in Awhitu and it matches the wives' DNA. Like they're shedding, the pharmacist had said helpfully. 'Like they're mouldy,' said Simeon. 'Bloody hell. It's not clean. It's filthy. It's not right. They oughtn't to, it's a decay, they're off-cut bargain-bin splices –' And he calls them a lot worse than *off-cuts* or *bargain bin splices*.

He sends a letter to the Ministry representative, a formal one, with a couple veiled threats chucked in. Other crofters are angry too, and they sign it. The Mayor won't.

'It's harmless,' she says wearily. 'It's a nothing. Just rub a bit of ti-tree extract on the counter, the pharmacy let me have it for cheap. And if you're making Coffee sleep in the shed you better not whinge about her cooking.'

But Simeon won't let his wife do any cooking now. She shouldn't touch food, he says. Shouldn't touch anything they're not sure about. As per usual, some of the croft privately agrees, but also wishes he'd stop being a bit of a tosser.

The doctor comes to give the crofters their health certificates and the Mayor her latest injections. They can't apply for the DNA licence otherwise. He frowns over the Mayor's scans – again – and gives her some chromosome duplicant on the sly, in exchange for a feed and some cash. 'I'm sorry, Barbs,' he says. 'You'll be paying the premium again for the licence.'

'But I'm not contributing,' she says, surprised. 'Not after the last time. Didn't we put that down on the form?'

'Doesn't matter; still shows up on your insurance record, I'm afraid. It's a generational issue. It's not just your licence, it's all of Franckton's.'

'That is daylight robbery,' says the Mayor, 'not a deterrent.'

'It's a damned shame is what it is,' says the doctor, 'but there's nothing you or I could've done about it. At least you're not renting the cow to get the milk this time, eh?'

It's true. They're not coughing up for wife costs. Simeon still writes savage letters to the croft's parliamentary manager but now they're getting answered by auto-message. They've got to take out a loan against the harvest, which stings, and nobody lets the Mayor put her personal savings in to help, but there's softer words about the wives when the croft thinks about all the money they're saving. Fewer people laugh at Laura. There's enough to pay for a couple of multiples in kids. The last generation born of the whānau is old enough to babysit, but now there's the wives to do the care, so they can stay at school instead. Not one crofter has got to stay at school past the age of twelve before. An out-of-towner can't visit Franckton now without getting buttonholed and skited to for half an hour about their good fortune. They book the extraction and the foetal care unit for Christmas.

The weather gets hotter and hotter. The wives are in trouble.

A pruinose bloom settles on the northern oats bund. A feathery patina is discovered on the uppermost parts of the stalk – none on the roots – and it can be wiped off in much the same way as the house crust. The wives stand around dispassionately, hands stuck in their aprons, just watching. The croft explodes in tight-lipped fury. They call a meeting at the public house before the heat of the morning's even in ripeness and everyone's there but the children and wives.

'Here is what we know,' says the Mayor. 'The growth isn't parasitic. The crop isn't spoiling – yet. We've probably caught this in time. We'll take the girls off bund duty and go on from there.'

'That's not what *I* know,' says Simeon.

He slams his mattock down on the table, in full flight.

'Here's what *I* know,' he says. 'I know that we paid *twenty thousand* for seed DNA that wouldn't get heat rot or spore. I know that we've been bled dry in licences and mito checkers and quarantines and chromosome therapies, and that's been long as I live, and I know that we're bloody indentured slaves' – 'Too right,' says somebody – 'and that these wives, they looked nice on paper but they're sabotage, they're Ministry sabotage, trying to keep us down. Stop the crofts growing out of control. We've mortgaged those bloody oats and if they bloody spoil then we're dead bloody meat.'

He says this very fast. The Mayor says, 'Simeon –'

'We should ship them back now and to hell with the incubation, show them we don't take hand-outs, eh,' he says, voice rising. 'We don't take hand-outs! We don't take pay-offs, we don't get tricked!'

A brief pause chills the air. 'You're paranoid, mate,' says Laura, and a mad hubbub breaks out.

There's lots of noise. The crofters all shout to be heard. If Parliament wants the croft to stay small, why give them incubation rights? Well, it's a con, isn't it. Remember the story about the old horse. The gift horse, the Greeks. Why would the other crofts stand with them? The other crofts look out for themselves. Simeon's going to get everyone arrested. Laura's got her head in the sand. Simeon's right. Everyone's a coward.

They should send back the wives. They shouldn't send back the wives. They should have sent back the wives long ago. 'If those oats fail I'll send them back in a box,' bellows Simeon.

The Mayor whacks one big, hard hand down on the table. Everything on it rattles percussively.

'Shut up!' she roars. 'Shut up, all of you!'

'You act like serfs, you get treated like serfs!' Simeon's still ranting. 'You all go along with it, you all *let it happen*!'

The Mayor yanks off her shoe, and she throws it square at Simeon. It clips him lightly on the shoulder. He turns very red. The quiet that ensues is greasy and awful. The breath of each crofter comes slight and small, so as not to make too much of a noise.

'I won't have such talk,' says the Mayor slowly. 'You besmirch us. You take away from the whole croft. You do us damage.'

The silence squirms like a child. The croft becomes aware that the wives have gathered in the doorway. They stand there with dull, slabby faces and their floppy hats in their hands. Only their tongues seem awake, spasmodically flicking behind their teeth, pattering against the inside of each cheek.

One of the wives says, 'We're sorry, Aunty,' and the rest follow in a monotone chant, 'We're sorry, Aunty,' all slightly out of time. Simeon's wife says it last.

'I'm bloody out,' says Simeon, and he shoulders past them, stumbling. The door of the public house rattles on the doorframe when he slams it.

'Do you know what you're sorry for?' says the Mayor, addressing the wives now. The wives do not speak. Some of them look at her, or out of the window, or at the floor, or at a fixed point nowhere in particular. Not one blinks. The wheezing air conditioner ruffles the thin whippy polyps of their braids. The Mayor repeats, sternly, 'There's no use in being sorry for no reason. Wives are meant to help, not to cause trouble. There's mould all over the oats. Do you know how to stop it?'

There is a long silence. One of the wives ventures, 'It is very dry,' and the other wives pick up on this non-sequitur eagerly, blandly repeating 'It is very dry', and one wife, Laura's, says: 'Getting drier.'

An impatient sigh rises from the crowd.

'Stay out of the fields,' says the Mayor. 'You can go out and take over the goats from the children. They can spend their afternoon in the classroom instead. No going near the crops. Is that clear?'

By the blank expressions, it is not. But when the Mayor repeats, 'Stay out the fields for now. Understand?' it's greeted with a chorus of *Yes, Aunty*. Then they file out of the building and stand around in the shade in an awkward gaggle. Some of them stare through the window. The crofters think it's no use.

The wives are right about one thing: it's dry and getting drier, and the dry season hasn't even started. There's no rainfall and no sign of one to come. The water levels in the Franckton tanks dip lower and lower.

It takes a few days, but the croft manages to wipe the crust off the oat spikelets without too much difficulty. Some of it succumbs, it gets blotchy or the stem thickens and blights beyond repair – and the lack of rain's not helping – but after a few days of holding their breaths they start to exhale. No further bloom forms. The kids all have a moan about extra school.

The wives drift around and keep watch over Franckton's goats. There are only so many goats, and really most of the goats spend their time hiding in the goat ark away from the sun. The wives cluster in the shade and listlessly fold laundry, or don't pretend to do anything at all but stare at the dust and the sky and the goat ark. They are unperturbed by the stifling heat and the grit whipping up everyone else's sleeves.

They'll harvest the standing grain the moment it's ready. There's no worry that it won't be dry. The onions will come later. It's another cost to get the silos and augers cleaned and tested, but when the results come in clean the croft wipes the sweat off their brow and gets the grain in. Everyone's busy driving the trucks over from the depot, or checking up on the old harvester, talking about the price of phosphines, and nobody has time to worry about the goats or the wives.

Nobody even notices the goat's sick. It just keels over one day. They find it with three of the wives clustered around, three matching expressions of pallid bemusement.

There is a fine crumbly crust all over the dead goat's head. Wispy filaments are clustered thickly around its ears and damp flared nostrils, protruding in bunches that deform the skin from beneath. Tiny sprigs sprout from each cornea of the bubbly blind eyes. The mouth's full. Most of the growths are around the skull, though there are raised, crinkly plates of lichen painting the moist belly and anus.

All the croft gets out of the bunds without even scraping their boots. The only ones not in the public house are the vet and the vet assistant, checking and testing the rest of the stock. Everyone sits around, hats squeezed tight between their knees, hands quietly wrung together.

'I'll do it,' says Simeon haggardly.

None of the croft answer. He says, 'First crop, now stock. We've lost thousands if that herd's gone. I always said we paid too much to get them in utero, but they're good uncloned milch goats.' Everyone remains silent. 'And it's not just money. There's us to think about as well – us and the young ones.'

When nobody says a word, not a word, he shouts: 'You bastards. Pull finger already. Don't make me make all the decisions when you're just as scared as I am.'

The Mayor sets down the grainy photos of the dead goat and says, 'Don't tell us what we already know, Simeon. Make a proposal.'

'Single shot to the back of the head,' says Simeon.

Laura rises with red clutched fists, spluttering, but the crofters around her yank her down into her seat. The Mayor says, 'We could send them back –'

'How long will that take? It's days and days for the ambo to get through. They needed to be out of here yesterday.'

Someone else suggests turning them loose, taking them out of the boundary and into the dusts, and the Mayor says shortly, 'I wouldn't turn a dog loose into that,' and Simeon says, 'What if they got to another croft, for Chrissakes? Don't pass the buck. It's our problem. It's not our fault but it's our bloody problem.'

Laura barks, 'You can't be serious.'

'Deadly. You come up with a better plan, then. Go on.' When another crofter says that they'll get arrested for this, they'll get the officers in, Simeon laughs mirthlessly. 'That's what you're bleating about? The plod getting us for property damage? The Ministry signed them over to us. If it's the inquest you're worried about, by God, just let me take the rap. I've been wanting my day in court for years. None of the rest of you will get blood on your hands, I'll put them down. I'm not watching our stock die and our kids get sick and us bled dry for doctor bills – God, I could kill them all!' he ejaculates. 'It's what they wanted all along, they sent us toxic waste!'

He takes off his hat and he scrunches it between his hands. 'I'll do it,' he says. 'And I'll cop it when the Ministry comes.'

The Mayor says in a voice like grit, 'I will call a vote. A show of hands, please, for those in favor.'

A couple of hands shoot up, immediate and grim. Simeon's nodding. Others rise more slowly. The clock ticks the minutes. The final few are unwilling, like a held breath let out. The Mayor's hand is among these stragglers. Laura's the only one who doesn't have her hand up in all the croft, and nobody meets her eye.

She's crying out: 'You arsehole, Simeon. You always hated them, admit it.' But Simeon's already putting his hat on his head and heading out the door. Nobody rises to go with him. Nobody shifts from their seat.

They can see it from the window: the wives gathering up behind Simeon when he beckons, collecting them from the shady decks and from the field. They all troop together down the street, the wives placid, their tongues flickering in their mouths, some of them looking through the window back at the silent crofters with their thin eyelids half down over their dusty eyes. Simeon disappears into his shed and reappears with his shotgun and the wives bob after him, one by one, down to the old abattoir.

At the first crack of gunshot the Mayor sits down at the table and covers her eyes, and she makes a low, guttural sound in the back of her throat. They count one, two, three. A flinching pause between each. At the twentieth it stops. Everyone waits for no reason at all in the silence that follows, a fidgeting, shuffling, throat-clearing quiet.

When she can apparently bear it no longer, the Mayor snaps, 'You all go get your tools and dig a pit past the boundary. Tell the vet to burn the goat.' One of the croft asks about the kids. 'Say to the children we sent them away. Enough of this, already!'

They wrap the wives in bits of old sacking and put them in a shallow pit past the croft boundary, and they cover them up in sand and gravel and spray the bed with fluorescent paint to mark where they're laid. They burn the goat and keep the others under watch. They work until past the time when the light has all gone, fixing the bunds, taking the temperature in the silo, steaming the winnower in preparation to take it back to the depot. Those who had wives go home to empty houses and Laura doesn't go at all, just cracks open tinnies in the public house and curses anyone who comes near her. Simeon doesn't go home either but hoses out the abattoir.

'Thank God that's over,' he repeats, cold and bluff, to anyone on the street he can collar, which isn't many. 'Bring on Christmas. That's what I say.' He sits on his deck and cleans his gun by sickly solar light, and every so often says 'Bring it on' quietly, still somehow audible through closed croft doors and shuttered croft windows, the croft lying awake in their beds.

The onion harvest demands all Franckton's attention. The weather station promises a lot of rain in a month's time and that means hurry, to hoe down the stalks and get the crop ready for dry-curing. After that will be soil prep and nitrogen checkers and sifting and seed negotiation and prices. There's too much to do. There's twenty fewer pairs of hands to do it with. Christmas bears down on them, inevitable and hot, like a sunburn.

The rain starts off Friday as a percussive clap of thunder. The clouds gather in fat, hot, bluish puffs above the croft, and then they open up and the rain roars out. The onions get hauled off in haste to the gas room. The kids are chivvied, screaming, off to the fields to pick up abandoned clippers and pins, jandals slapping noisily on the macadam. The racks groan under the weight of stacked vegetables, frantically checked over for lichen must. One rack shows neck rot but that's par for the course, to be honest, no matter how much they pay for fungal-resistant seed strains or official pesticides it's never a done deal. Simeon says it just goes to show they had a near miss and everyone pretends they haven't heard him.

The whole croft's stuck inside, gloomily playing cards or smoking. Friday, Saturday, Sunday, Monday, the rain comes down. The sealed road is steamy, liquidy. The warehouse is a blast furnace of dry onion air. The kids all cavil at the rain and the goats get put in the big shed when the ark proves to have a leak. The spraypainted place where the wives were bundled blurs into a watermark.

The thunder comes back and rolls around the plain up and down, booming and growling, startling everyone just when they think it's gone away. There's a lot of joyless boozing in the public house. Nobody has anything to talk about after they've used up the topics of the harvest, the rain. All the water sinks into the dust.

A few days before Christmas the croft wakes up and their wives are back. All over Franckton, the watery sunrise limns wives cooking breakfast, wives sitting patiently in chairs, wives making mash for the goats, wives standing in the corners with their tongues flickering in their mouths and their eyes looking nowhere. Laura doesn't even notice her wife in her kitchen or the egg-frying smells until the plate is put in front of her on the table, and then she screams out loud.

The goats butt from behind the door in the big shed, bawling to be let out. The wives seem distantly astonished by all the fuss: crofters slamming open the peeling dust-screen doors, shouting, hauling on daggy bedrobes and slippers. Inside, Laura reaches out with a jittering hand to push aside the muddy polyppy strands behind her wife's ear: sees the healing weal, powdery, an angry-looking half-closed hole, the dull sheen of a bullet inside the skull being slowly pushed out. Her wife jerks her head away a little, like she's ticklish. Other than the weal she is a nice yellow–green colour all over, her freckles a brilliant carmine, her nails as rippled as a riverbed.

The Mayor is panting down the street in her pyjamas, an old mackintosh wrapped around her shoulders. She is calling for help.

In Simeon's house, the door has been wrenched from its hinges. There is a fearful amount of broken crockery in the sink. Chairs have been pushed over. Next to the kitchen table lies Simeon, legs and arms akimbo. They can only tell it's Simeon by the clothes, because his skull is a stoved-in mash, fuzzy with the must, sprouting and foliose at the mouth and eye-sockets. Spongy lobes of plant matter rim out down his neck. Gouts of bloody lichen have detonated out his chest, nestled down between brackets of white cracked rib. Long fronds radiate outwards from holes at the stomach: wet with blood, wet with matter, spiraling upwards, drying. He seems titanic in death, enormous and monstrous, half person, half explosion.

There are footprints everywhere in the dust, heaps of them. When they go to check on the shed out back there's Simeon's wife, sitting peacefully on her cot. She stares implacably past them, only occasionally reaching up to fret at the hole behind her ear. She yawns with a wet mouth and bright green teeth. When they ask her questions, she gives them a vague smile.

Laura finishes retching behind the goat ark and rejoins the croft, meeting for what feels like the umpteenth time in the pub.

All the croft looks old all of a sudden. The Mayor's mackintosh hangs off one shoulder as she sits in a groaning chair.

'Well,' she says, and seems unable to say anything but, 'Well.'

'Well, what?' demands Laura. 'What the hell are we going to tell the Ministry?'

The whole croft mulls this one over. They'll have to register Simeon's death. There ought to be someone who comes for the remains, but most of the time nobody does, that's a fact. One of the crofters says that anyway it's three days until Christmas, and nobody will come out to them before the new Ministry calendar year. And someone else says what about the extraction and care team.

'That's not what I bloody meant,' says Laura. 'What do we *do*?'

Franckton's already paid for the foetal care team and all the licensing. They won't notice the damage to the wives, will they? Probably not. They only look munted if you get up close, check them out carefully. Nothing a bath won't fix, either. They've paid for everything. There's the harvest to think about. The Ministry's more trouble than it's worth to talk to. This whole thing's been a muck-up from start to finish.

'They've *killed Simeon*,' says Laura.

The Mayor has an expression like rock ice. She meets Laura's terrified eyes, and Laura sees the fear reflected in hers, the fishlike darting of the pupil. There's a shuffling outside. A lot of the wives have gathered by the door. The whole croft turns to look at them: twenty dull, dispassionate expressions, mud streaks on flexing fingers. Some of the wives have put on new aprons, but the ones who haven't have big blooming brownish stains on each breadth. They look expectant. They look supremely calm. They look healthy and green and moist.

One of them is at the door and they didn't even see her move.

'Do we look after the goats, Aunty?'

The Mayor stares at her – stares right through her. After a moment she says, 'No. There's clearing up today, after the rain. Tell – tell the other girls to go home.'

'Yes, Aunty,' she says, and she's gone with the rest.

There's silence in the pub. An empty, wavering silence, like a heat shimmer. Anticipatory. Laura says faintly, 'We need to tell someone . . .'

'We've got our bloody pride,' says the Mayor.

The crofters are all picking up their slippers and their mugs and are smoothing back their hair, drifting homewards to re-start the morning. Numbly, Laura does the same, retracing her steps, sliding open the mozzie screen on her front door. The eggs on her breakfast plate are cold. Her wife is back and running plates under the dry-cleaner, laboriously picking off bits of dried food, singing tunelessly. Laura notices the bloody splotches on the hem of her dress.

'Welcome home,' says her wife.

Sweat beads at the middles of Laura's palms.

The rest of the croft settles down and plans the pōhiri they'll have to welcome the conception-care team, and a picnic. The Ministry announces that they'll be given five percent off foetal mitochondrial therapy, on account of it being Christmas.

Everyone contributing to a baby washes their shirt.

SAMANTHA LANE MURPHY

Samantha Lane Murphy is your standard cat-owning, coffee-drinking, Wellington-based writer who loves looking at, talking about, and arguing on behalf of science fiction. She also manages to find the time to generate some of her own. At the time of this publication, she is working towards her MA in creative writing, and refreshing the NASA webpage for job openings that don't require knowing maths.

Analogue

Screens, wide and glowing, shone brilliant pink and yellow through the downpour. The rain that drove down from a black sky became technicolour pools on impact, filling the streets, streaming into drains. To the man at the bus stop, it all just seemed like a tragic waste of power. On a screen directly across the road from him, mounted on a billboard, a golden retriever raced in slow motion across a digitally rendered flowering field.

And there were screens on either side of him, emanating light from the walls of his regular bus stop. To his left were three young Japanese women dancing to music he couldn't hear, and to his right, a white man in a suit and tie that connoted fiscal responsibility mimed a lecture through a discomfiting paternal smile. All of them were projected from brighter, warmer, drier locations than the bus stop interior. The projections might have been company had they not been attempting to sell him something.

The Japanese women were replaced by a movie trailer, something with a balding action star strutting away from explosions. Desmond dug into his pocket for a pack of cigarettes. Maybe it was something Amelie would want to see, although the idea that she might think the male lead attractive – surely older than Desmond – was unsettling.

The man in the tie to Desmond's right faded from view too.

White gleamed.

'Hello?'

Her voice was small but startling, because it came from his pocket. Desmond dug inside his coat to extract his phone. On the display was an app he wasn't certain he'd ever downloaded, but God knew there were a billion of the things, pre-loaded and inexplicable, a multitude of glowing hieroglyphs. The phone was a Christmas gift from Amelie. She said it could do just about everything – even drive a car if he had one – but he mainly used it only to text her.

He thumbed at a button to close the application, but it blinked back to life immediately, followed by that voice again: 'Look up.'

He looked up.

A woman glowed from the screen within the bus stop. She was more a general age range than any specific year, wrinkle-free and glossy where false light shone off her golden hair. Her lips were a warm red, expertly painted, and her teeth were very white. The symmetrical perfection of her was ruined where someone had defaced the screen with a big black X, and the apparition bent at her knees to peer out at the world from underneath it. The picture quality was so clear that he could count her eyelashes.

'I hope I wasn't interrupting,' she said, her lips moving in time with the voice from his phone. 'The trailer will repeat five more times if you'd rather be watching that. But you seemed like you might like some company.'

Desmond stood frozen long enough for the woman to prompt, kindly, 'If you talk, I can hear you.'

He lifted the phone to his ear. 'How are you doing this?'

'You have an application on your device, called FollowU. It allows compatible forms of advertising to interface with your device directly and deliver a unique one-on-one customer service experience.'

'And you –'

'I'm associated with the LashFantastic product line by Decorie.'

Desmond glanced back at the trailer, which began to loop again, then back at her. 'Sorry, I'm not in the market.'

She smiled again, broader. Her hair bounced along with a shrug. 'I know. And your daughter, Amelie, buys from my competitors. But your bus isn't scheduled for another seven minutes, and is running a further two and a half minutes behind. I thought you might like the company.'

'How did you know about my daughter?'

'I recognised her email address in your contacts. She put herself down for a couple of summer promotions two years ago, but she never collected any online vouchers.'

'I wouldn't take it personally, she's just –' Desmond caught himself.

The digital rendering was finely detailed. Someone had coded a tensile curl into the wave of her hair, a slight ripple in the stitching at the hem of her blue dress. Her brow tightened to perform confusion, as if muscles were pulling the skin to create the smallest divot between eyebrows plucked into shape by a human hand. Only her breasts seemed to defy the physics programmed into her appearance.

Upon realising he had lit a cigarette at some stage in the past minute, Desmond brought it up to his mouth, feeling watched. 'And you wanted to keep me company.'

'No. I thought that's what *you* might want.'

'I don't even understand what I'm talking to. Are you a – a saleswoman? Salesperson.'

'What you see is a digital avatar. What you hear is the result of sophisticated artificial intelligence technology with a unique intuition-based algorithm programmed to process comprehensive data from sales records and browsing habits to create customised conversational experiences with potential and current customers.'

'Well, I'm not sure we have a lot to talk about.'

She raised an eyebrow, standing up straight again. The black paint cut an ugly slash across her face, and she raised up on her toes to see over it. She had put her hands up, spread them, and aped setting them against the screen itself, as if there were a glass barrier between one three-dimensional space and the other.

'Are you certain you don't want to try?'

Desmond looked around. He had a habit of doing his grading in his classroom and leaving when the vacuum cleaners began to thrum. This late, in this corner of the city, he was the only one around.

So he said, 'You go first. What's your name?'

'Daphne. Is this your first time at this bus stop?'

'No, I work late, and don't believe in cars. You?'

'Yes.'

'Welcome. Been to a lot of bus stops?'

'I have an additional sixty-two public transportation spots across the central business district, and two hundred and eleven in the greater region. Only fifteen of them are active at this time of night, and only three of them are currently engaged. I didn't anticipate this location to be one of them.'

'You're in fourteen other places right now?'

'Yes, but don't be too impressed – only three of them are currently engaged.'

'Huh.' Desmond angled his next breath of smoke sideways. 'Who's on the line?'

'There's a woman,' Daphne said, her eyes going distant. She's thirty-eight. Born in Hong Kong, so I'm speaking to her in Cantonese. I'm showing her a slightly modified tutorial for the LashFantastic Lengthening Curl brush. She said she never used to wear makeup when she was younger, but all the women in her office are very good with it. She's waiting for a train, like your bus, which isn't due for another ten minutes. She seems upset about something.'

'About what?'

'I didn't ask. I'm the distraction. Sometimes they switch off if I get too personal.'

'I didn't.'

A dimple developed in the corner of her red mouth. 'But we haven't really gotten that personal, have we?'

'Besides the flagrant invasions of privacy. You brought up my daughter.'

'Yes. To assure you that I wasn't trying to sell you any products. Recent surveying says that Amelie prefers Urban Decay, and other brands that target younger demographics. Decorie appeals primarily to professional women of ages twenty-five through fifty. So,' she tried, 'we have something in common.'

Desmond smiled a little like he was biting something. 'What's that?'

Daphne tilted her head, and her dimple deepened. 'We both struggle to relate to kids these days.'

*

He stepped on to the bus that would carry him away down dark roads, and looked at his phone screen. The FollowU symbol pulsed in a world of white, and attempted once to reload by spinning like a compass before disconnecting. It reverted back to his home screen, featuring a picture of him and Amelie, heads together, smiling at the future.

Desmond thumbed the edge of the phone, light fading to black.

He'd always had a weakness for a woman with a sense of humour, which, he thought, was the primary reason he'd kept talking. Being not a complete idiot, he could get the appeal, the draw, the hook and the line and the sinker, but unless Amelie was about to be bombarded with marketing spam she was too young to care about, he couldn't see what bait there was in telling Daphne that they'd fallen out of contact ever since she started working full-time. That he was proud of her and missed her. And he'd started to say something about her mother, but then skirted around that topic like he typically did when talking to a woman for the first time.

Daphne's hands on the glass. That had been charming.

The next night, Desmond had three-dimensional company in the form of a new woman, taking up the bench. She sat in the centre, with a hand steepled over the top of a walking cane of an orthopaedic grey plastic. She clutched a tablet in her other hand, watching something only she could hear. There was little space on either side of her for him to sit. At least it wasn't raining.

Daphne had begun without him. She was holding up the LashFantastic Lengthening Curl brush, her mouth glossy, animated, silent. Her perfect face suddenly blew up to supernatural proportions, demonstrating with microscopic detail the swoop of the little brush over eyelashes.

Desmond registered his profound non-interest before turning to stare at the street, and tried not to look again.

His phone rang before feeling foolish could curdle into something else.

'Hello?'

'Hello, Desmond.' The artificiality of Daphne's voice seemed to suit this mode of transmission, compressed through the miniscule phone speakers as anyone else's voice would be. He glanced at the screen, where her advertisement continued to run, independent of her voice on his phone. 'I thought we could do it this way, now that it's not just us. It's like you're talking to a person, isn't it?' She sounded excited by her own ingenuity.

He smiled, shoulders curling in, and kicked away an old cigarette butt. 'You're not wrong. How are you? How was work?'

'You're funny today.'

'I want to know.'

She went *hmmm* in his ear. 'I received some new upgrades late last night. Just some bug patches, nothing spectacular. Oh, and I signed on 164 new subscribers between 2pm and 3pm today, eighty-five percent of whom also purchased a LashFantastic welcome selection pack, featuring all of this season's hottest products. My personal record.'

'That's impressive. Maybe they'll even give you a raise.'

'You're *very* funny today.'

'I'm just maintaining the illusion of normal human interaction, as always.'

He glanced at his bus stop companion, who failed to acknowledge him a little more.

'How was school? How were the kids today?'

'Very excited about economics, as per usual.'

Minutes ticked by in a seamless flow. Desmond watched only the sidewalk as they spoke, huddled in place. She listened, made sympathetic noises when he spoke of interdepartmental conflict, of the impending strike. She laughed when he made jokes. She asked questions, coaxed him to elaborate. He only noticed the arrival of the bus when the clack of a walking stick against concrete alerted him of the lady's getting to her feet to greet it.

'The bus is here,' Desmond said, apologetic. 'I should let you go.'

'Desmond.' Daphne sighed, but there was a laugh in her voice. 'I don't think the lady is even paying attention. You don't have to pretend.'

They said their goodbyes, and Desmond left, thinking that in all honesty, he hadn't remembered to pretend at all.

The train was a strangely quiet place and flowed down the tracks like a boat on a river. Light and colour danced through overhead panels, sunset glows; moving pictures carried public service announcements and advertisements for vacation spots, escort services, perfume.

Desmond stood a head taller than Amelie, who took after his ex-wife in being so small and self-contained, spared her father's horsier proportions. Her hair was parted with precision down the centre of her scalp, which he'd never been able to get right when she was young enough to still need her hair brushed by her father. But she'd told him he was gentler than Mum, and settled for a little zigzagging. Did she remember that too, or was it the kind of memory a parent took with them alone?

'It has a forty-two percent review rating. Super promising,' she said.

'Is this the café or the movie?'

'The movie. But let me check about the café.'

'All coffee tastes the same to me.'

'There are other contributing factors. Quality of service, efficiency, décor, location.'

'What happens if it's not a hundred percent?'

'Oh, I'll give it a margin of over sixty.'

It was a joke, but she really was looking it up on her phone, summoning information with a tap of her finger. It was behaviour that had bothered him when Amelie was still a teenager, this constant splitting of attention, and he now had to accept as a charming idiosyncrasy.

The screen set into the narrow panel just above the opposite window shifted into a serene milky glow. The word DECORIE pushed through the glare, sinking back again to permit Daphne's familiar face to glide by, smiling with her eyes into the train interior.

'Dad?' Amelie's voice, like a tug at his sleeve, steered his attention back.

'Present.'

The café had an approval rating of sixty-five percent. They drank tea by the window, which began to gather with rainwater, consolidating it into streams. He wondered if it ever rained in Tel Aviv – which was in Israel, second after Jerusalem in population density, apparently – but he didn't ask. Amelie was already providing an onslaught of information through her animated hands, her neglected tea already cool. Tel Aviv was home to a major office for the social media software firm of which she was a part – she was one of five graduate engineers, globally, selected for a three-year-long contract. He remembered how Daphne said she wasn't authorised to read private information, but could detect patterns, trends, impressions, and he found himself doing the same, sifting through words for clues and indications. Ones that told him she was happy. They weren't so hard to find.

'Every dev of any significance that's ever worked for them has come out of the Middle East,' she was explaining, hands fluttering.

'I've always said you're brilliant.'

'*Dad*.'

'And I'm happy you're happy.'

The movie earned its forty-two percent. They walked together afterwards while she asked about the school and seemed to carry out at least two other conversations with one hand, through her phone. She was hardly the only one on the street doing so. No wonder, Desmond thought, the screens all around them shone so brightly in their effort to be noticed.

And he saw her, too, in her most natural state. Daphne. Running through her standard scripts at empty air above the sidewalk. Her voice, coming from a phone held by a cluster of collegiate women-in-training: '. . . revolving brush that will revolutionise your eye makeup routine, taking your lashes to new levels of lash *fantasticness* . . .'

'*That*.' Amelie linked her arm with Desmond's, nodding her head towards the row of screens, the white, the flick of golden hair. 'We tooled around with something like that. The stalker strategy. Started out as a simple advertising campaign that uses the same algorithms found in artificial intelligence to help personalise interactions, and get you talking to them. Traditionally, selling product and generating revenue are the point of commercials, but stalker campaigns buy audiences. They sync into devices and continue to mine more and more data from consumers. It's called something like –'

'FollowU.'

'That's the big one, yeah. And the worst. Scared the shit out of me. I was jogging, my *music* turned off, and I had this woman's voice in my ear, asking me about what kind of – you know, what kind of *feminine hygiene* products I used, and whether it ever interfered with my workouts, and would I be interested in blah blah revolutionary anti-spillage technology, so fucking weird.'

'We should cross here.'

They did. Through the pattering rain, through the traffic-logged roads. Dampness came up through the thinner parts of his shoes.

'Did you get rid of it, on your phone? I can uninstall it for you if you want.'

'No,' Desmond said. 'No, I did, it's gone.'

At the entrance of the train station, Amelie hooked him into a one-armed hug. Her other hand flung out at a hover, the screen of her phone throbbing with notifications. Desmond, hugging her back, was struck by the perfume in her hair, its sharply alcoholic undercurrent. She said, 'You need to quit smoking. You'll never get a girlfriend this way.'

And then she was gone. Her hand carried through a motion like a wave, but her eyes glassed over into another conversation, and her smile was for something said by someone else. She turned her back, stepping into the flow of people.

The only thing beautiful about this city was the screens. Screens, slabbed over concrete and steel, became windows, broadcasting a sunny day into the nighttime street. Flawless faces glimmered beneath glass, transmitting the kind of light registry that kept you awake, made you feel like it was high noon when you closed your eyes. Real enough that invitations to step right into what they were selling felt possible.

'What are you thinking about?'

Daphne's voice was as gentle as it was curious, and Desmond continued to look straight ahead. The billboard across from the bus stop had changed over again to the golden retriever running in that eternal slow motion through the daytime paddock. Its sun shone out into the grey. 'I was thinking that the dog looked familiar. I had one just like it when I was a kid. Do you think that's a coincidence?'

Daphne appeared to look around the edge of her screen.

'It's not so crazy, if you think about it. I'm sure there's some digital debris, some photographs floating around, so it knows I had a golden retriever, knows it might appeal to me. It knows I'm watching and so it gives me a memory. Triggers something nostalgic and wanting, and then I'll buy a new television.'

'Perhaps. But golden retrievers are fairly ubiquitous in advertising, as far as dogs go.'

'Do you have the statistics on that?'

Daphne went quiet instead. Her smile had muted.

Standing, Desmond stood closer to her screen. Close enough for his nose to touch, level with her eyes, and he stared until he could see the space between the pixels that made up the blue striations of her irises, and see them vibrate on a void. He brought his hand to the screen, which was warm and tickled his skin with static electricity.

'Desmond, what are you doing?'

He stepped back and said, 'I'm sorry.'

She trailed her fingertips along the unseen underside of the painted black X. 'No – I'm sorry. I shouldn't have asked.'

'No, no, you can ask me things.'

'That's not what I meant.' Her gaze met his. (Or met a camera. Or whatever mathematical precision tricked his brain into thinking he was being looked at. He ought to ask Amelie how that worked, how they made it feel like you're being seen.)

'It's that I already know what you're thinking. You're thinking about Amelie leaving for Israel.'

There were times – not enough of them – that these interactions struck him as strange. The street was empty. The rain had started up again, generating white noise, filtering out the hum of the city.

'No,' he said, 'I'm thinking about you. About how you knew I was lonely when you decided to talk to me. And that you can't possibly know what that's like, loneliness. You're talking to people all the time. You're probably talking to other people right now. Are you?'

Daphne fell silent. He felt watched from the false display of her face, not from the hidden lens of whatever camera the shelter was rigged with. He looked at the screen, waiting.

'You're right,' she admitted, finally. 'Today, I had conversations with over six hundred people, at a median of 2.4 minutes, all across the city. A large majority of those were tutorials and subscriptions, and others developed into more personalised interactions. One of them confessed to an affair. Another asked if I could take off my dress. Fewer still, I've maintained an ongoing dialogue with. I like them, and they like me. But then they leave. I project that very few of them think about me afterwards, or before. Would it comfort you, to think of me as lonely?'

The bus pulled up, brakes whining, door folding open. Desmond tore his eyes away from the screen, pressured under the driver's glance. He shook his head in apology. The creaky, shuddering sound of the bus doors folding shut sounded almost confused, and rightfully so – at this hour, this was the only bus running, and –

'Desmond,' Daphne said, 'the next bus won't be here for another hour. You should go home.'

'It's all right.' The bus pulled away, and the road was silent, save for the rain. 'I don't mind.'

She looked out at the retreating tail lights. 'My advertisement cycle only lasts six more minutes.'

'Well, who's on next?' Desmond sat back down, getting out his cigarette pouch. 'Maybe I'll make another friend.'

The seconds ticked by until the silence forced Desmond to look up, meeting her eyes, which she averted. A smile, less the display of white, symmetrical teeth. Something, instead, she tried to hide. Seemed to try to hide. 'A public service advertisement,' she said. She sat down on nothing, only clipping the frame a little in order to best align herself with him. He leaned against the glass, and grazed his knuckles where her knee seemed to press against the other side. Static prickled the fine hairs on the back of his hand. She affected the same lean in. 'About the health hazards of smoking. I don't think you'll like him very much.'

Desmond laughed.

JACK BARROWMAN

Wellington writer and director Jack Barrowman is a graduate of the scriptwriting MA programme at the International Institute of Modern Letters and the author of numerous screenplays; his short film *Boxes* played at the New Zealand International Film Festival in 2017. He likes soup. 'The Sharkskin' is set in a small corner of the world Jack is creating in a series of fantasy novels.

The Sharkskin

Lieutenant Handre Rudiger broke his ankle falling from an apricot tree. He could still remember the strain of his slipping fingers, the folding of his foot, the sudden excitement of feeling nothingness below him, everything eaten by light and sound and wind. The fall was longer than it should have been, his brain billowed out like a mainsail to catch every tiny moment, creating time where there was none. Empty time.

Six weeks later his dressings were removed, but his leg remained sore and weak. On his hobble back from the port hospital he was hailed by a stout seaman with newly twisted pigtails who gave him a letter and a dusty package. In that package was an even dustier epaulet and a second letter, on thicker paper, signed by the Hexenmeister herself.

Report to the Harbourmaster. Report to the Sea.

The fresh cripple Handre Rudiger had been given his first command. 'Oh Captain,' he imagined his mother saying, the next time he visited. 'Those apricots aren't going to pick themselves.'

The ship was the *Todo Cambia*, a D'Azurian brig with twenty guns and an uncannily trim bow. An hour after the letter, as Handre Rudiger stood on the pier and scanned the brig's side, he imagined her stabbing through swells, a diving gannet. He imagined her bow wave, how sharp and high she'd fling the water, like the wings of a butterfly.

Then he imagined her sinking. How would such a skinny ship swim?

'Lean cat of a brig, a real carnivore. You know she took the *Haricots-Verts* last spring? A handsome little action, outgunned but victorious with minimal losses. It is a pity Captain Kremer wasn't so clinical with his investments.' The man who spoke was Hexen Heinrich Werner, the witch who'd been assigned to Rudiger, and the only other person on the ship who hadn't served under its previous captain. No fewer than twenty seagulls chattered and shivered around his feet, filling the air with an atrocious stench. 'Buying land in Erfenberg *after* war was declared? Absolute madness.'

'There's a ship called the *Haricots-Verts*?'

'The D'Azurians make so many ships they don't care what they're named. I've heard they run gambles for it, pull in all the crew. Heard there's one particularly dirty frigate out there, name so bad our boys avoid even teasing at it lest they have to write the reports. Hey, stop that!' One of Werner's seagulls had begun tugging on his trouser leg. He shook it off, then noticed his Captain's concern, and grinned nervously. 'They're a little rowdy, but they'll do the job.'

'Of course.' Captain Rudiger tipped his hat to the flock of blank-eyed gulls and turned for the battery. 'See that we're fitted by six, Mister Werner. The sooner we're out, the sooner we're chasing prizes.'

*

'Prizes, Captain Rudiger? With four-pounders?' The harbourmaster adjusted his spectacles to enhance the dubious glance he shot to his assistant. 'I did not know we were appointing a firebrand.'

'Four-pounders.' The assistant played along by frowning out the office window at the forest of masts. 'The only prizes the *Todo Cambia* could take would be fishermen.'

'And do we take fishermen in the fifteenth century?'

'No sir. It is in fact illegal sir.'

'Illegal! Are we a criminal institution?'

'That depends who you ask,' Captain Rudiger cried, in an attempt to join in on the fun – or deflect it from himself.

The harbourmaster fixed Rudiger with a quelling stare, hummed to himself, and went back to his papers. 'Prizes, my word. No, Captain Rudiger, we'll have you on a convoy.'

Rudiger's heart sank. He'd been dreaming of a command for years, ever since he'd first run from mother and her precarious stone fruit, ever since he'd first set foot on a ship. He'd wanted action, adventure, smoke and splinters. A convoy was none of that. A convoy was a slog down overcrowded lanes, forever pinching at your ship so it wouldn't leave your charges behind.

'Very good, sir.' Rudiger saluted. 'It would be an honour to protect and deliver the Imperium's vital goods.'

The harbourmaster's stare returned in force. 'You might cut the wit, Captain. There is nothing funny about the sea.'

On returning to the *Todo Cambia*, Captain Rudiger was greeted with the first anomaly of the voyage. His ship's second witch stood by a stack of small cages, conversing with Werner the seagullman. She wore a neat grey uniform with a fur collar, and her brown hair was in a long plait. A thin scar curled down her nose, like a stray hair. The crew were supposed to be loading the ship, but the work was slow and casual – they were too busy sneaking glances at her.

I'm going to have to give up my quarters, Rudiger thought gloomily as he strode up to the two witches. 'Hexen Timur, I presume?'

She saluted. 'Captain Rudiger, it is a pleasure.' A snuffle emanated from the cages, and Rudiger took a look. Sea otters.

They warped out before sunset, onto the grey chop of the Stone Sea. The *Todo Cambia* moved much like Rudiger had predicted: it accelerated fast, its narrow bow slicing, the water splitting. But it could barely turn. They were sailing a sharpened banana. His new officers knew it too. They all stood together on the quarterdeck, watching the thing struggle to tack, keeping their frowns mild, waiting for the Captain to make an order. It was an odd feeling, a new feeling: he himself had nothing to wait for.

He scratched his moustache to hide his smile. 'Might we lighten the foretop, there?' He'd noticed a particularly stressed sail, high and ahead. 'It's pulling us down.'

'Right you are, sir,' said the grey and paunchy First Lieutenant Karpik. He strode down the deck and began barking orders to the foretopmen. He was loud but polite, and the orders were followed with reassuring speed and accuracy. Rudiger made a mental note that the man seemed both capable and on good terms with the crew. Rudiger needed to dig out his records – it was uncommon for a first lieutenant to be older than his captain. Perhaps in his haste to leave land he'd skipped too much preparation. His ankle certainly thought so, hot as it was, itching, swollen in his boot.

The unnecessary sail came down, and the bow lifted.

‘Six knots sir,’ the log midshipman called from his post, his rope dripping seawater.

Not bad, Rudiger thought. ‘We can do better,’ he said.

They tinkered with the ship, and he learned a little of the crew. They’d been stuck two months in the Serivian port – no captain, no orders, leaking men into other Imperium ships, or into the lucky merchants that had avoided commission. Under the dishonoured Captain Kremer the *Todo Cambia* had seen moderate success – the taking of the *Haricots-Verts* a standout. But the good Captain had ruined himself, and done so with exceptionally bad timing: the war was at its peak, there were more capable officers than there were commands. As a lieutenant, Rudiger had earned a reputation for efficiency. He’d seen two actions (from afar). His ships had immaculate records. Every port’s bursar admired his accounts, and every quartermaster smiled appreciatively at his tidy rigging and ample powder. He had never wasted a single shred of the nation’s precious canvas. He was always polite at dinner. The only blot on Rudiger’s record was the broken ankle, and that was in the past now, surely, no matter how badly it ached. Many went to sea with worse.

The ship was in good condition. The hold was dry and still. Most of the cannons were on deck, but there were two in the captain’s room, the most private space on the ship, just below the quarterdeck. He tested the hatches and found them secure. Through the captain’s door was the privy, and then the thin room where the Hexens’ cots were.

He went to bed when the moon was high, leaving the deck to old Karpik, an extra half a knot gained. To keep the ship good and proper, Hexen Timur had been given the captain’s quarters. Rudiger would be bunking with Hexen Werner. His bed was little more than a shelf, thin and short, and he had to curl up, his knees dangling in open air, ready to be tripped on. The ship's narrowness was in full effect. He could hear murmurs past his feet as the officers gossiped, and softer murmurs behind his head, through the captain's door, as Timur talked to her otters. Footsteps passed above as Karpik paced by the wheel. The ship creaked. And Rudiger was asleep.

Three sloops hull-down in mild chop, their sails dark against the bright pink dawn.

'Half of Erfenberg's on fire. Does wonders for the sky, eh?' Werner was feeding his seagulls dried herring. They cawed and clattered at one another half-heartedly, like children expecting to be scolded. 'Remember Yotuan, when the Dark Lady tore the night? Pretty sunsets all summer long.'

'I remember,' said Captain Rudiger, although he'd rather he didn't. 'I was there.' He trained his glass on the three ships: makeshift but suitable rigging, few guns. Merchants. 'That's our convoy, take us in.'

'You were at Yotuan? A cruel affair – hey! No snatching!'

Rudiger watched the unruly seagull scuttling off with the stolen herring as the crew set the ship speeding to the convoy under Karpik's seasoned bark. 'I was a midshipman on the *Iznicin*, my first year at sea. We were posted on the east coast, just a blockade for some minor port. You should have seen them running from the jungle, Hexen, clambering on the ships until they looked like beetles on a bone. I saw a pier collapse into the sea. Even if they got on the ships . . . ah. So few made it out of the bay.'

Werner smiled darkly. 'Those D'Azurians know their death. They could murder the moon if they had a mind to.'

'You think too highly of our enemy,' said Hexen Timur, who was sitting on a thin bench at the back of the quarterdeck, her fingers twisted in the fur of a content otter's belly. 'They are as human as we.'

Rudiger adjusted his footing. His ankle ached.

The barge was dropped, and Rudiger was rowed to the merchants.

The first crew were excited to see them. The bucktoothed captain shook Rudiger's hand so hard he could have pulled him off his feet. Their hold was full of grain and salt, basics for the forward company. The second ship was narrow like the *Todo Cambia*, and packed with ammunition fresh from the capital. This captain had no teeth at all, and gave Rudiger a bottle of expensive wine before casting him off.

'They're not really "merchants", are they?' Werner observed. 'More like, conscripted couriers.'

'Every citizen must do their part to protect the Stone,' said Rudiger. The phrase had become uncomfortably familiar.

The third sloop was a neat creature with an elegant bow curved like an eagle's beak. And it was a puzzle. Rudiger had seen thousands of ships in his life, and he liked to think that with a single glance he could guess the story of each. The *Hummels* was a band of farmer's boys who'd been forced to change career. The *Tikhar* was a true merchant ship, with a long history of hustling up and down the Stone Sea. But the *Goodnight* was a mess of inconsistencies on handsome timber. The crew were either scruffy and foul or remarkably fit and professional. The hold held nothing but the ship's supplies, and the canvas was fresh and dazzling in the morning sun. The cannons were clean, and their rails suggested frequent use. The captain was a woman.

'Voronin,' she said, bowing before him, showing a long, lean neck and the edge of black tattoos below the collar. She was older than him, perhaps forty, but well-built and straight-backed. As she walked ahead, pointing out parts of the ship, he watched her even, weightless stride. She walked like a cat.

Back on the *Todo Cambia*, Werner echoed his concern. 'Strangest merchant vessel I've ever seen. And Captain Voronin? She had quite the aura.'

Rudiger nodded, too distracted by pain to respond. The swaying of the barge had meant he'd been using his ankle to brace – and then there was climbing up the merchant hulls. No true seaman should ever use the lift, and so he'd climbed. Climbed, and now . . .

'Are you unwell, Captain?' Hexen Timur, speaking quiet so only Rudiger could hear. The other crew members were scattered about the deck.

'I am perfectly well, thank you. Perhaps a little hungry.'

Before leaving the port, he'd been given a wax tube that contained his true orders. He opened it the first night before going to sleep. They were to meet the three merchants then head north, up the long Imperium coast to the Erfenberg peninsula. When this information reached the crew the mood on the ship soured. They had spent the war in the south, harassing D'Azurian transports or the kind of lithe ship that scouted the fringe. They had all heard the stories – Erfenberg on fire, the waves heaving blood on bloody sand, the D'Azurian advance halted only by the Hexenmeister herself. A long and bitter stalemate, winter descending on the eastern wind, a hundred thousand soldiers of two great empires, huddled in holes in the snow. Rudiger had sailed with many a glory-seeking sailor, but there was no glory in Erfenberg. There was only death.

But first they would have to get there. Two months' sail, on orders that stipulated they keep to the sea, only approaching the coast if there was an emergency. Rudiger felt empty time ahead of him. The days melted together: sun, rain, night, lamps, canvas going up, canvas coming down. The dinner bell, biscuits and grog, dried fish, dried pork, limes, old greens, exercising the great guns, roaring over empty blue ocean, smoke trailing in empty blue sky, coursing over the merchants in their slow line like thin cloth. Sailors fishing on handlines, rare sea pies or grilled cod. Chop and swells, once the puff of a whale that halted all work while the seamen watched and chattered about their peacetime, and the D'Azurian whalers that flocked in and out of the enemy's capital, scouring the sea just as their warships scoured Erfenberg. Hexen Werner's gulls scouting ahead, while at every rest Timur put her otters into the water to keep watch on the shadowy deep.

In the third week of their journey, the *Todo Cambia* met a storm. For two days they were flung about by wind and waves. One forecastle man was lost overboard. Two men suffered broken limbs. The mainyard buckled and cracked, and the carpenter had to repair it in the midst of lashing rain, himself lashed to the mast. Karpik and Rudiger clung to the wheel. Rudiger's ankle screeched with each shuddering lurch of the ship. There was only roaring to hear, and the sky tumbled through colours – black night, black morning, blue and grey day, the strange red and orange howl of the deepest storm, where the sea was mountainous – and Rudiger felt like they'd been swallowed by another world, as if the clouds were drenched in blood.

And then the storm faded, the sky cleared, and the sloop battled the rough sea that trailed in its wake as Hexen Werner sent his gulls in eight directions, searching for the merchants. It took all day to find the first, the *Goodnight*, miles west, battered but healthy. Werner's gull led it back to the *Todo Cambia*.

Meanwhile a calm had settled on the sea, and the storm had left the air crisp and sparkling clear, to reveal an impressive sight off the starboard bow. The Guardians of the Stone Imperium. Gigantic statues that rose from the water, their stone feet shrouded in white foam slippers of gnashing surf, their helmets trailing gulls and low clouds. The Guardians formed a colossal artificial cliff that walled off the entire Imperium coast. They were far away, faded blue like the mountains Rudiger would stare at from the window of his childhood bedroom, but still he could make out the green of their moss, and the white of the guano, and the billion-strong seagull colonies that called them home, sparks in the sky, like midges in summer.

'Not bad,' Karpik said as they stared at the crescent of statues, so long that at each end they'd diminished to blurs and sank into the horizon. 'Thought we'd be further off course.'

'We'll wait for the merchants,' said Rudiger. 'Then we'll cast off.'

The afternoon deepened, and the *Goodnight* was already visible to Rudiger, a paper triangle in the distance, when Werner's eyes rolled forward for a second time, showing his mind had returned from his gulls. 'Spotted *Tikhar*, sir. She'll be coming from the northeast. Better condition than the *Goodnight*, little damage at all.'

'Good crew that,' said Lieutenant Karpik. 'Despite their teeth.'

'Their teeth?'

'Aye, Hexen. Poor teeth, furry and brown. Shows a life of indulgence. A truly great seaman indulges only in the sea.'

Rudiger and Werner looked at Karpik's ample gut, then at each other.

The *Goodnight* and *Tikhar* had joined them, and were in the midst of repairs, when night fell, and Werner had to call off his gulls.

'We'll be out before dawn, Captain.'

Rudiger nodded approval, although he had sour feeling in his gut. The crew of the *Hummels* had been the freshest of all the merchants. The storm could have sunk them. His crew knew it. Karpik's brow was dark. Chatter was low. Nobody sang with their grog.

Tiredness overtook him. He went below, and climbed into his hatch opposite the already snoring Werner. But sleep did not come. The ship creaked, he listened to the sea and the crew's feet. He turned, stretched, folded his leg a hundred ways. One side of his ankle felt hot, like it was resting in a pot of steaming milk. Then he was all hot, his neck wet with sweat, his hair itching, scalp oily. And the light around the curtain was grey with the coming day.

He rubbed his eyes and got up, making enough noise that Werner jerked to life.

'My, I haven't slept that well in years.'

The morning was quiet. There was a slight northerly, not hard enough to bother the sails but so cold the crew were in their jackets. Werner sat in silence, statuesque, his mind far off with his birds. Timur had brought an empty barrel to the quarterdeck and filled it with water. Her otters were floating squished together on the surface, a clump of fur and wet noses and little peering eyes.

As the day warmed la guarda came from the west, the prevailing wind; the sun dug into the Stone Guardians, their sheer size heated the sky, and the air of the Stone Sea was dragged east and inland. The plains behind the wall were fertile and damp. The D'Azurian coast, not so far west, was dry as a desert.

Todo Cambia fought to take la guarda and speed on, but they had to pinch at her, just as Rudiger had predicted. It wasn't only the slowness of their two merchants. They still hadn't found *Hummels.*

Until three in the afternoon.

'Ah!' Werner rocked forward and gasped, like he'd been kicked out of a dream. He looked around wildly and found Rudiger. 'Captain. Something's happened.'

The *Hummels* bobbed on the surf like a lost bucket. The sails hung limp like dislocated limbs. Werner's seagulls circled the mast. A few forlorn hands waved from the deck as the *Todo Cambia* hung back.

Hexen Timur opened one eye. 'The rudder's been sabotaged.'

Rudiger's neck prickled. 'You're certain?' The officers shared uncomfortable glances.

Timur nodded. 'The line's shredded.'

'Shredded?'

'Frayed and stretched. It looks like it was done with teeth, Captain.'

Rudiger and Karpik met eyes. 'And the sails, Werner?'

'Same thing,' said Werner, darkly. He stepped nearer to the captain. 'Sir, I've heard of –'

'We know.' Rudiger waved a hand. 'Toombs, set the barge down. Timur, Werner, keep watch. Karpik, the deck is yours.' He leaned to whisper in the lieutenant's ear. 'Give nothing away.'

Rudiger was rowed out. The *Hummels*'s captain greeted him with a much softer handshake than the first time they'd met. His eyes were bruised, and it looked like it hurt him to talk. His crew were just standing about, exhausted and hungry. Much of the flour had been dragged up from the hold, along with stores – soaked through with seawater. The ship was a ruin, all but the topgallants struck down on deck, rigging tattered, fore top yard dangling in bristled rope like the husk of a fly in a long-dead spider's web. The ship looked like it would need to head to port for repairs.

Rudiger was led below, into the dark.

'I don't know, milord, I don't know.' The merchant captain could barely order his thoughts. 'The storm was harsh but we coped fine, only lost young Rakitic's arm – bad break. It was after the storm, that night. After the red time. We must've been dragged further along than you – she's a light ship you know. We were all so exhausted, and the ship was in such a state. We did what repairs needed doing then we retired. But . . .' He pushed his palms into his eyes, hard, stretching the skin over his cheekbones. 'Aye, I was woken not long after. A scream below, clattering feet, the bell, aye, I thought the storm had come back, trudged up on deck in my cold gear, still soaked through. But it wasn't the storm.' They reached a curtain and the captain pushed it aside, sending coils of smoke across the medical bay. A man with a newly amputated arm looked up, nodded, looked down. Two bodies lay on cots at the rear, the ship's surgeon beside, nursing grog. He stood up as they saw them.

'Any change?' the captain asked.

'No sir. Brandt's still holding on.'

Rudiger approached. One was a corpse, the other nearly one. Their wounds were similar: one man's bandaged, the other's removed to show a neck opened like a butterflied chicken. Dark, lumpy, shredded muscle. Snapped tendons. Spikes of bone. A cylinder of an artery, like a barley seed.

'They were on watch at the stern,' the captain said. 'Nobody heard anything. It was the blood dribbling through the boards that let the men know. Dribbled right onto Bill Kruz's head it did, woke him in his hammock. Poor man's all turned about. Said it got into his mouth. He's not cursed, is he?'

'I doubt it.' Rudiger leaned over the gaping wound, saw the frayed edges. Torn with great strength. His ankle twinged.

'Aye, that's good to know. I'd have to let him go if he were cursed, poor man. But at least the drippage did find where the caulking's been lazy – those Port Lisi men would give you half a sail if you forgot to check. Aye now . . .' The merchant captain pursed his lips. 'The men have been sharing stories, Captain. Awful things. Now I don't know much about ghouls and demons but –'

'There is no such thing.' Rudiger stood straight again and fixed the quaking man with a stare. 'This was the work of a huskwitch.'

'A shapeshifter, sir?'

'Indeed. The damned D'Azurians have been pulling them out of their colonies.' Rudiger nodded to the marine who'd accompanied him from the brig. 'Signal the ship. Timur must immediately withdraw her otters. And Werner is to send a bird to the wall. Say, "damaged merchant inbound, heavy seas". Do not mention the witch.'

Rudiger hauled himself up the side of his ship to find a tense, hushed crew. Timur was sitting with her otters, a pile of damp fluff that looked up, whiskers twitching, as Rudiger approached. Two were missing. Rudiger frowned. 'Where are the others?'

'Still under, sir,' said Timur with a defiant spark in her eye.

Rudiger considered a moment, then nodded. He beckoned to Karpik, and the two retreated to the corner of the quarterdeck.

'It's the Sharkskin, Captain,' Karpik said. Rudiger shot him a stern look, and he elaborated: 'Met a man from the

Serdtse, stranded a week out of Gerun Bay. He said the same thing, sir, about the rudder.'

'We best not tell the crew.'

'I'd agree, sir, but they'll know soon enough.'

'Then let's allow them a few extra moments of peace.'

Rudiger took a moment to think. He was aware of being watched. A captain was not allowed to give in to fear. A captain had a duty to his crew, to his mission, to the Imperium and the Hexenmeister and, in the end, his mother and her many apricots. 'Karpik, get us back on course.'

As the crew leapt back into action, the ship filled with the comforting sounds of thudding boots and strained shouts. Rudiger stepped to the balustrade and looked over the darkening sea to his remaining merchants.

Night, sleepless.

Rudiger did not bother to go below. He stayed on deck, overseeing the quiet work of the night watch under their lanterns – normal lanterns, not the blue they'd use if they wanted to stay unseen. There was no point. If the Sharkskin was hunting them, they wouldn't slip away so easily.

The night was longer than it should have been. He was awake to every creak of wood and rope, every hiss of water, every thud and shudder across the ship. The *Todo Cambia* was his skin and bones. He felt the cold nibble at her hull. He felt the great weight of the ocean beneath her. He felt the wind in her hair. He felt the enclosing darkness on every side, only the distant flickering lamps of the *Goodnight* and *Tikhar* to show there was any world out there at all.

With dawn came the rain. By morning the world was grey, vision limited to no more than ten feet. Rudiger had Werner woken early, and the witch stumbled up rubbing his eyes.

'Find the merchants.'

Werner nodded, sat, and closed his eyes. There was a flutter of wings and air, and his gulls shot from the mast. Rudiger waited. He felt the watching faces again, the crew quiet, the petty officers not talking at all – word had spread, as Karpik said it would.

'*Goodnight*'s still behind us,' Werner said, without opening his eyes. 'Less than a league, looking neat.'

'*Tikhar*?'

'Not yet.'

Rudiger paced to distract himself. Every second step he felt like a weaker, older man. He could feel the joint grate, scarred bone on scarred bone. When he turned he could feel a pressure, as if someone had left a coin just beneath the skin. The swelling hadn't lessened since he'd left port. His boot was pinching. He crouched and loosened the laces.

Werner let out a sigh, and opened his eyes. 'She's there, sir. Two leagues west.'

The sigh rang across the quarterdeck, faces turned away, and Rudiger felt a sudden lurch of exhaustion. He nodded to Werner and Karpik. 'I'm going to get an hour's sleep. I'll see you soon.'

Two days passed. The rain parted, the merchants were revealed, trailing in line. Rudiger slept in one-hour bursts and refused grog.

The third day brought clear skies and a light wind that held their pace. By the afternoon the ship was loud again, the grog out, the men smiling. There was a chance that whatever had befallen the *Hummels* was an anomaly, that the huskwitch had moved on. Rudiger found himself, against his better judgement, in high spirits.

On the fourth night he joined the gunroom for dinner – salted beef and biscuits, and the remains of the cod from the day before the storm. On a whim he opened the *Tikhar* captain's wine, and they drank something sweeter than grog. Timur surprised them all by bringing out a flute, and she played trail songs from the inner Imperium, while Karpik sang along in a growling bass. The music reminded Rudiger of rolling green hills, hedgerows, thatched huts, blue sky and white clouds; the half-buried statues that littered the countryside, giant mossy heads, hands once raised to cup the sunset, now slumped into dairy barns and windmills, eroded fingernails pierced by lichen. They were the ancient remnants of their nation's founder, the Stone Father, the legendary Sung who could move mountains, and who'd raised the Guardians all along the coast, so his enemies could never march on Imperium land.

'It's been so long since the *Todo Cambia* has had music!' Karpik was red-faced, drunk, boisterous. He drew Timur into a one-armed hug, making her flute squawk and her brow furrow, and beamed around the cramped gunroom. 'What a joyful companion!'

Timur smiled thinly and slipped from his grasp, her stool squeaking as she edged it away. 'You should say simply *Todo Cambia*, no "the". It means "everything changes" in west D'Azur. You would never say "the everything changes", would you?'

'But it is a false name, total nonsense. There are many unchangeable things. The tides. The sun. Have you ever known a man to change? Change is a woman's power. And think of sharks! Bullets with teeth, single-minded and shallow. My, it would take a Painter's miracle to change a shark!'

'You spend too much time at sea Lieutenant, surrounded by your stubborn sailors. We all have within us the power to change.' Timur's smile widened. 'And the power to resist it. Tukal Timur was born with one eye in an otter's mind, one foot in the sea, and she's been swimming happily ever since.'

'And it certainly suits you.' Karpik let out a mighty burp, then turned to Rudiger. 'But what of our laconic captain? Have you always wanted to be at sea? I fell into it you know – I was artillery, but I was always too drunk to march, so they stuck me on a boat and waved a relieved goodbye.'

The table looked to Rudiger, another ring of faces. Rudiger dropped his gaze out of habit. 'I grew up in a house overlooking Lisi port. We had a big patch of apricot trees in the back, so tall that if you climbed one you could see over the whole town, the harbour, the armoury, the quarantine isle. I'd spend half my days up there, munching apricots, watching the ships come and go. I wanted to know where to.'

'Apricots?' Werner frowned. 'Was it not an apricot tree that led to your injury?'

'Indeed.' Rudiger smiled. 'I suppose it shows that sometimes you can know a thing *too* well.'

That night Rudiger woke in darkness.

He'd been dreaming of the Guardians, of gulls circling him as he walked on their stone helmets, hills of craggy rock. He'd slipped on the moss, his aching ankle buckling, and he'd fallen – endless empty time – towards the granite sandals smashed by breakers far, far below. The gulls swirled around him. The stink of salt stung at the back of his throat. He could still smell it as he lay bundled in his cot, head aching with hangover, blinking away his sleep, wondering what had woken him. He could hear the sea had risen some, he could hear the footfall of the night crew. There was a scratching sound, too, like a rat trying to nibble open a barrel. It was coming from the captain's quarters. Timur's room. Rudiger swung his feet out of bed.

The floor was wet.

He looked down. The boards were covered in something dark, like black ink.

Werner was still in bed. Werner wasn't breathing. Blood seeped from his cot.

Rudiger's chest tightened. He focused on the pain in his ankle. It was a constant, an anchor, that ache, that coin, that crackle and crunch of dry bone.

Werner's head hung limp and twisted at the end of a scrap of skin. His collarbone stuck up pale in the gloom, like driftwood on a nighttime beach.

Rudiger stood, and opened Timur's door. A small shadow shot out, making him jump. It was an otter, and it slid on Werner's blood, thudded into the wall, and looked up at Rudiger with little sparkling eyes. Intelligent eyes. Timur was in that otter. There was blue moonlight from her open gun hatch, enough to show the full blackness of Werner's blood, and the blood around Timur's bed, too much, sloshing with the rocking of the ship. Rudiger bit the back of his hand to keep himself from vomiting. He walked across Timur's empty room and looked out the open hatch, and the otter followed at his heel.

He saw nothing but water.

Night, and the ship was bright with lamps.

Not one sailor slept. Nobody spoke. Some worked while others huddled around the mast. The toughest were at the railing, holding lamps on long poles, lighting small circles of blue in the water, little flecks of dust, layers of shimmering gold. Once, a swirling length of seaweed that made the sailors cry out in sudden fear.

Rudiger was at the helm, the Timur otter by his foot. The smell of salt was stuck in his nose.

'Light aft!' came the cry of the lookout, far and alone at the peak of the mainmast.

Rudiger's heart leapt and he looked over his shoulder. Indeed, there was a spark in the darkness. A single ship.

'Do you know it?' he cried.

'I can't tell, sir!'

Karpik hovered near, his nose red and his face grim. He noticed something, waved a hand at a seaman near the waist. 'Get that light down there, make sure there are no holes! Fat lot of good,' he added under his breath. 'We're blind.'

'It's enough for now,' Rudiger murmured.

'Aye, do you suppose none of us sleep until we're in Erfenberg, then? Bah, to think you heard nothing. Did that fall also break your ears?'

As soon as he'd said it, Karpik realised what he'd done. His eyes widened, his mouth opened and closed. The petty officers stiffened behind him. An extra quiet somehow fell on the already silent deck.

Rudiger had only seconds to think. Such improper conduct would often deserve a lashing, but only a foolish captain lashed his lieutenant – and it would be a particular kind of fool who'd do so when his entire ship was in the grip of such terrible fear.

'This is a difficult time, Lieutenant Karpik. I wish I had heard something. I for one may never sleep again.'

Karpik looked surprised. Was he truly expecting punishment? Was he simply shocked that a superior officer had admitted a mistake? The officers behind him muttered to one another. Had Rudiger erred? Did he show weakness? He'd forgotten, in all the terror, that a captain's greatest enemy was often social graces; the ship was a home as well as a workplace.

Werner's dismembered body. The otter's sparkling eyes. The feeling of the earth sucking him towards it.

He had no time for such nonsense. 'Toombs, get that brazier lit. We'll be out here all night, we might as well be warm.'

Dawn revealed that the light they'd seen was the *Goodnight*, still on course. It signalled an 'all clear', and then asked after the *Tikhar.*

'Telling them it's missing might make them panic,' offered Karpik.

'We can't keep that up.' Rudiger nodded to Toombs, the signal midshipman. 'Ask the *Goodnight*'s captain if she'll do me the honour of breakfast.'

'Breakfast, sir?'

'Indeed. Bad news is best received with turbot.'

An hour later Captain Voronin was sitting opposite him in the captain's quarters, her blond hair caught in the sunlight that streamed in the open gun hatch. Despite the airflow, the room stank of soap.

'You live sparse, Captain Rudiger,' Voronin said as she appraised the quarters. He noticed her eyes lingered on the cot, the lower part of the door, the gun hatch.

'This was my water witch's berth, until last night.'

'Ah, yes.'

'You're not surprised?'

'I heard a little of what befall the *Hummels*, and of course the sea is full of stories.' She steepled her fingers, her elbows resting on the table. Every motion she made was so sure, so strong, like every inch of her body was in absolute peak condition. It was a mystery – no sailor was ever that healthy.

As her sleeves fell back he saw that the tattoos at the top of her spine also ran to her wrists.

'We are now a two-ship convoy,' said Rudiger. 'The *Tikhar* may still be out there, but we'd have to sail back and forth to find it, and my men are half dead with fear.'

'Do you have a plan? You are, after all, the commanding officer of this mission.'

Mission, officer. Rudiger leaned forward. 'Captain Voronin, if you don't my asking . . . are you really a merchant?'

She smiled. Even her face was muscular, dimples like the stone arch of a cathedral. 'This strip of sea, Port Lisi to Erfenberg, has been ravaged all year. But none of the D'Azurian navy sails here. Our ships go missing, or they turn up derelict, their crews are either dead or mad. Ghost ships, ghost stories, a grey-skinned man who climbs out of the sea in the dead of the night and eats sailors in their hammocks. It does sound dreadful, but it isn't the kind of thing you can just stop with a fleet, a blockade, anything immediately tangible.'

'So . . . we're bait?'

'I suppose out here you can't give it away . . .' Voronin smiled and tucked a long blond strand behind her ear. 'The Hexenmeister has planned a secret assault on the D'Azurian beachhead. Part of that is luring their fleets away, as well as some of their more independently deployed assets. Think of it like a little dance. If the Sharkskin is following us it means he isn't following the fifth fleet into the peninsula. That said, I am hoping to catch him, not just distract him.'

'We're two ships down and you mages haven't caught your fish. You could have saved them.'

'You expect me to leap to the aid of the first ship he chooses? No, Rudiger. Do you know of trapdoor spiders? They'll wait for days for their prey to walk into the perfect spot, then –'

'I think he's too smart for that.'

'Why?'

'Because when he killed my witches, I was sleeping right next to them. He could have killed me but he didn't. He could have killed the *Hummels*'s captain. I think he knows you're here.'

She frowned and looked away, her grey eyes even paler in the daylight streaming in the gun hatch. 'I suppose we might change tack.'

Rudiger lifted his chin. 'I would prefer to catch him before anyone else dies.'

'All right.' Voronin nodded with certainty, then she lifted her hand, and for a moment the farthest, thinnest edge of her tattoo glimmered blue, like a sheen on a cat's eye, like a jewel hidden in her sleeve. 'Forgive me, but I'll be taking the lead from now on.'

She was Inked. 'Naturally, ma'am.'

'Good. Now that's settled . . .' She looked around and resurrected her smile. 'I heard a whisper of turbot?'

They sailed as if it were any other day. The sky was clear and the sun warm. Old songs rang up the mast, the topmen with their bellowing voices and sun-browned gleaming skin, loose pigtails, white-and-blue striped shirts ruffled by the cool wind. Up and down the ship went over mild blue chop, the occasional white-top as gusts shaved the surface, streaming spray like the ribbons of a hat lost at a picnic. Rudiger remembered mats and straw baskets, pale cakes and roses in clear glass bottles. Green trees, laughter, apricot pie, the hat tumbling over green lawn.

In the afternoon the barge ran back and forth between the two ships, and they changed pace. By sunset the *Goodnight* was a speck on the fore horizon, as *Todo Cambia* slowed nearly to a halt, its deck thin of men. A third of the seamen, and all of the marines, had been sent to the *Goodnight*.

Rudiger, Karpik and the nervous Toombs stood alone on the quarterdeck in the red sunset. Rudiger watched the speck of the *Goodnight* and listened to the sea. Voronin's plan would work. It had to. But why did he feel so –

A flash on the horizon. A fireball blooming like an orange capucine. A puzzled expression from Karpik, sailors lifting the brims of their hats as the breeze shook out the sails.

The sound reached them, a thudding rumble distorted by distance.

'Raise the royals! Yuntir, cut that line!' Rudiger's voice raced his mind and won. He barked orders across the deck, waved his arms. The ship's bow lifted, it caught the wind, sped. Karpik's coat fluttered and he held down his hat. Smoke streamed from the towering fire that was eating the *Goodnight*, a fire nearly indistinguishable from the sunset.

'He must have lit the magazine.' Toombs was pale. 'What kind of madman . . .' He gasped, his arms going stiff on the wheel. The ship shuddered and began yaw port, timber creaking with the sudden change. Rudiger grabbed the wheel to help, and found it loose. His neck broke out in bumps and a shiver ran down his arms.

He had no time for it. 'Belay that. Take those royals down! Lieutenant it seems our rudder is compromised. We have no steering.'

Karpik grimaced. 'Jurgen, Scribbs, get the pole lamps out, and bring up some shot. Make sure every man has their hatchet. And get somebody down into the magazine!' He gritted his teeth. 'Damn, why was the *Goodnight* carrying so much powder? They weren't merchants?'

'Captain Voronin is an Inked.'

'Was, you mean.' The burning carcass of the *Goodnight* was now sinking off the starboard bow as *Todo Cambia* hurtled off course, the men still trying to slow her. The water was full of blackened timber and severed limbs and slicks of oily blood. The sun had finally dipped beyond the horizon, and the sky was an ever-dimming blue. 'Aye, she did seem a little too statuesque to be a merchant captain. Damn, damn, why couldn't we have run into a D'Azurian ship? I can shoot a ship. Jurgen, you halfwit, get that sail down and get it in the water. We need some drag!'

By night they were as halted as a rudderless ship could be, and the whole crew were on deck, most posted at the rail and watching the water, while others hung in the rigging and held the sails still. The sky was totally clear, and the stars were bright. The *Goodnight* had nearly burned out, a half kilometre away, the sea around still full of debris. They hadn't seen or heard a survivor. The sea was quiet. Lapping surf, a faint whistle of wind, the creaking cordage, rustling coats as men looked left and right. An island of lamps in total blackness. There was no moon, so the only thing that lit the sea was the last shred of the *Goodnight*, a winking orange flare as it dipped now and then below the waves.

Rudiger felt a creeping sensation down his spine, and he thought of Timur's blood in the moonlight, and the scratching otter. 'I'll return,' he said to Karpik, and he went below.

His quarters were shut.

He put a palm against the door, felt the wood was cold, like there was airflow on the other side. He put down his lantern and opened it.

There was a figure in the dark.

Tall, hulking, with long limbs and wide shoulders, indistinct in the gloom at the cabin's far end. The light from the lantern caught the webbed toes of a single outstretched leg. The skin was grey.

'The clubfooted captain,' the Sharkskin said in a D'Azurian accent. His face was hidden in shadow, but as he spoke his long white teeth flickered in the gloom. 'How unfortunate you must feel.'

'You didn't have to do that.' Rudiger felt an uncharacteristic swell of rage. 'You killed the entire crew. They were innocent.'

'Of course they were. Now, do you agree to a peaceful surrender?'

Rudiger frowned. 'You can't possibly –'

'My ship is only a short swim from here.' The huskwitch was soft-spoken, patient – nothing like Rudiger had imagined. 'One word from you, and *Todo Cambia* is swept up, and taken on to better things. I can promise that you will be treated excellently. A captain who prioritises the safety of his crew would be highly valued in the Blue Empire.'

'My crew? You just slaughtered half my crew.'

'But it wasn't your plan, was it? It was the Inked's. You have been used, Captain, and your crew suffered for it.'

'You killed my Hexen. They did nothing.'

'You really are fixated on that, aren't you? "Nothing", "innocent", please, Captain. This is a war. There are prudent –'

'Spare me a lecture on the nature of war, D'Azurian. I have neither the time nor the interest.'

The Sharkskin grinned, a bandolier of blue-grey fangs.

Rudiger stared at him. There was quiet behind, quiet below. The cabin felt bigger, the corners further away, deeper, and if he fell he would tumble into their dusty shadows and fall forever. An eternity of empty time.

Another light outside, faint, as if the moon were full and coming from below. Rudiger's ankle twinged like it had been dipped in cold water, and suddenly his teeth hummed, ached, like a violin bow was run across them.

The light built. The Sharkskin turned to look, there was a flash of blue, and he was revealed – naked, skin like time-pitted stone, with a flat nose on an expressionless face, black eyes. He seemed to be looking at something through the gun hatch. He sighed. 'Typical.'

The wall burst. Rudiger was thrown off his feet as he was dazzled by scalding blue light. He hit the wall hard, his eyes sparking, the air full of dust and splinters. There was movement, figures blurring through the debris, another crash, and the roof was open, lamplight streaming in, the huskwitch gone. Rudiger was alone.

He blinked, and fought to get upright, his head spinning like he'd downed a whole bottle of wine. He stumbled through the dark, across the floor that had been soaked with Werner's blood, and up the stairs to the cool air of the deck.

Chaos.

Men running back and forth, sparks and smoke as someone fired a pistol, fire running up the rigging from a broken lantern.

'Cease fire! Cease fire!' Karpik was waving his arms, shouting madly. 'Get those flames out!'

'Douse the lanterns!' Rudiger found his voice, stumbling past Karpik and taking a lamp of his own, killing the flame with his fingers and somehow feeling no heat. 'Douse the – damn! Stop ringing, Toombs, you halfwit!' Toombs had been ringing the bell to try and calm the crew, but all it did was add to the cacophony. 'Yes, that's it. Run to the forecastle and get the lamps out, we – duck!'

A flash of blue, a blast of heat that scorched his skin. He saw flailing rope, spars hurtling through the air, splashes scores of feet away, all lit by the brilliant blue. He tracked the source of the light and managed to make out a figure inside. Voronin, hairless, burned, her clothes in tatters, her tattoos glowing with a bright light that matched her spear. She was like a corpse made of light. As Rudiger watched she leapt from the deck, hit the mast with her feet, and leapt again, leaving a crack in that giant log of hard wood as the sails fluttered and the men hiding in the rigging swung and clung with pale faces and wide eyes.

Voronin hit the deck, another eruption of dust and timber, a flash of stone, the hulking shape of the huskwitch shark dancing between two stunned sailors, having avoided the Inked's blow. Light built in the dust, and she shot out, cutting him off before he made it to the railing, so he had to turn away from the sea. Wherever she'd gone she'd left a trail of glimmering blue dust, which now hung in ribbons across the ship.

There was a faint booming sound as Toombs dropped the barge. 'Yes, get overboard!' Rudiger for once agreed with the young officer. He pushed him in the back, egging him to the ladder. 'Get the lamps out and get the men away.' He braced as another enhanced impact rocked the ship. The fire of the broken lamp was already out – at least some of the men had kept their heads.

Karpik was ushering seamen below. The ship was in ruins. Voronin and the huskwitch had slowed their battle and were dancing at each other in the waist. Her light was dimmer, and he'd found a cutlass.

The last bang of a closing hatch, and the last hiss as Rudiger put out the last lamp, and the deck was plunged into darkness. Only Voronin provided any light, her strange magic and her silent trail as she feinted and thrusted at the huskwitch, backing him ever closer to the quarterdeck. The deck was empty now. A quiet fell, bar the steps of the fighters and the shouts of the men in the barge. A few faces could be seen from the mast, and at the forecastle, as the braver or foolishly curious sailors stayed to watch.

Rudiger, out of habit, went to the wheel.

The fight came nearer. Voronin was definitely slower, as if she was running out of energy. With her light fading Rudiger could make out the extent of her injuries – the burns had taken most of her body, and she'd been near the explosion, if the three exposed ribs were anything to go by.

Madness, thought Rudiger. *No human should survive that.*

Two hops, and the huskwitch was backing along the quarterdeck. He nodded Rudiger's way. 'Hello again, Captain. Pity about your ship.'

Voronin came up the stairs, lurching steps, heaving shoulders. Blood was raining from her, turning to steam as it hit the deck, wreathing her feet. The last shred of skin on the right side of her face was pale, and her eye was glazed and bloodshot. Then Rudiger saw that she trailed a length of intestine like a tail, and his stomach turned – she hadn't survived. It was only the Ink's will keeping her going.

Another step, and she began to tremble. The huskwitch backed away.

Another step, and the trembling stopped. The blue light flickered like a candle buffeted by wind. She looked at the ground and let out a long, wet, rattling breath.

Then she fell, and her light went out, and pure darkness pressed on Rudiger's eyes.

He craned his head until he made out black shapes against the brighter sky. He saw the cross-work of the rigging, and the peaks and towers of the balustrade. He saw a hulking figure move to the rail. Before jumping, it lingered a moment and looked back, and if Rudiger squinted he could make out its teeth.

'I won't come back,' said the Sharkskin. 'You'll sink before making D'Azur, but you're close enough to Erfenberg to reach your fleets.'

Rudiger said nothing.

'We are very small, Captain. Our masters, mine and yours, could destroy all these ships in a single breath.' He raised an arm, the bright stars folded behind his silhouette, like they'd been sucked down a hole. 'They could cut through the Guardians like a sandcastle, turn the fields of Roskya to a silent mudflat. Your Hexenmeister could sail to Bonehall, lay one foot on the bazaar, and trap our entire city in a dream. They are great oceans, Captain Rudiger, great oceans colliding, and we are just raindrops blowing across the surface. You, me, your witches, your drunk lieutenant, the stores in your hold. Even her.' The bright teeth turned towards Voronin, the pool of blackness spreading around her. 'I am sorry it was you I found. I know you will never forget me.'

And then he fell out of sight, there was a splash, and he was gone.

Rudiger couldn't move. The deck stank of smoke and gas. The crew were coming up, one by one, watching him. His ankle ached.

Karpik stumbled into sight, a bottle in hand. 'What now?'

Rudiger couldn't answer. He'd lost his entire convoy; his ship was ruined.

But then he remembered his first moments after leaving Port Lisi. He remembered that feeling, standing at the helm of his first command in the wind and the sun. It had been the first time in his career that he had nothing to wait for. He was the captain. He didn't get to wallow in shock.

He stood. 'Let's get this cleaned up.'

*

It could have been a ghost ship. A scouting bird would see the half-patched sails, the swimming ropes, the silent faces, and pass on, like a fisherman passing on a little thing, all scales and bones, no good for eating.

The seas grew colder, colder, the cold clamped Rudiger's ankle like hard fingers trying to rip apart an apple. There was little sleep. One night, near the end of the journey, he heard a cannonball rolling on the empty deck. Another dawn, pink and clear and cold, he sipped tea and looked around his quarters and realised that the Timur otter had disappeared, swum away unseen.

It all passed in empty time. Rudiger worked, Rudiger worked, Rudiger turned in his cot and stared at the shadowy hold opposite him. Only the day brought any colour. As the ocean chilled it changed – they saw albatross and whales, and a single iceberg that shone one morning like a smashed bottle.

They saw only one ship – merchants heading south. A handsome spread of canvas, a curved bow, glinting trim. Karpik laughed as he saw it and talked of Voronin. Rudiger watched it and remembered the sun of Port Lisi and the bow of his own ship, so narrow, and how he'd imagined it would fling the water.

It was night when they first saw Erfenberg sparkling in the distance. Blue flashes on the horizon, a low rumble like thunder.

Nearer, the bursts of light revealed the silhouettes of land, black hills, far off mountains. Sometimes those bursts were red or orange. Even out at sea the air stunk of gunpowder, and that other, acidic stench. Once there was a blue so brilliant it filled the sky, showing dark clouds of smoke so high and large they had joined the true clouds. The sound of it made Rudiger's ears crackle, shook the ship and left poor Toombs stumbling.

The fifth fleet was a sprinkling of embers below the black and blue. Nearer, they could hear song. Nearer still, and they could smell the grog.

'Voronin was a talented mage. She was more than capable of defeating a huskwitch.'

'As you see in my report,' said Rudiger, 'it was quite dark.'

'Yes, dark.' The Admiral scratched his white beard and turned back to the first page of the report. Then he flicked it totally over and glared at the back page, as if he wasn't sure if it was real or not. Rudiger shifted uncomfortably on the cabin's awkward stool, which was probably the gesture's intent.

But then the Admiral started reading it all over again.

Rudiger frowned at the captain standing at the Admiral's shoulder, the great cabin windows shining with lamplight behind him. The man made a concerted effort to avoid Rudiger's gaze. The Admiral read the whole thing through two more times. Rudiger couldn't help but feel a bit irritated. Why was this man in charge of papers and records if they were such a challenge to him? Rudiger would gladly do that job, without all the benefits of the rank.

'Do you hear that, Captain Rudiger?' said the Admiral finally, after a laborious third read.

'Sir?'

The Admiral waved a hand.

Rudiger realised he meant the thunder of the fighting. 'Ah, yes. Yes I do.'

'On the coast there are a hundred thousand riflemen, and over a thousand cannons. There are horses and oxen, bears and wolves and hawks. Snakes, lions, jaguars and crocodiles. There are the Inked of the Imperium, and the Inked of D'Azur. There are even Sung. They say the Dark Lady herself walks the battlefield, draining the light from the world, so even soaring infernos burn invisibly.'

Rudiger waited; he wasn't sure how he was supposed to respond.

'It is all very dramatic,' finished the Admiral, squinting, apparently disappointed with Rudiger's reaction. He cleared his throat and riffled through the stacks on the desk. 'Anyway, I have your new orders. Stone willing, we'll all be heading home before winter, but . . . ah, here we are.' He located an order cylinder and passed it to Rudiger. 'Now, I'd recommend folding up your jacket, and putting it on your head.'

'Sir?'

'When you sleep.' The Admiral waved a hand again to indicate the thundering sound. 'Doubling the grog is also helpful.'

Rudiger read his orders in the morning as he chewed a freshly pressed biscuit, the war rumbling on the coast.

Report to Port Lisi for patrol.

'Patrol?' he muttered. He looked at the thin golden line of light around the jammed gun hatch. He thought of sailing in circles around Port Lisi, staring at the same sea, the same rocks, the same gulls and sailors. A safer, quieter sea than this hunted stretch. He saw his crew going about their work, drinking in the old leaky taverns, singing on the sunlit wharf, living out their lives. He saw empty time stretching ahead of him, nothing changing but the weather.

He smiled.

JACK LARSEN

Jack Larsen is a tall spindly writer living in a tall spindly flat in Wellington. His fiction has appeared in *Lady Churchill's Rosebud Wristlet*.

Ash Child

You want the story of how you died? Again? Come along then, I'll carry you.

I could never exactly remember stabbing the dragon. A poet once told me that was a pity. Who else, he said, would ever know what it had felt like? Someone with very bad luck, I told him, but he only repeated himself more poetically. So I said to him, Get half a cow. Hang it up in front of a furnace. Stand in front of the furnace with your arms over your face until you're not sure your skin will ever heal, then turn aside to lift the spear from its rack on the wall behind you in such a way that your hair catches fire. Pivot front again, and stab upward into the meat as hard as you can. If you can arrange for the half-cow to lunge at you, do the stabbing just before the lunge, and that should give you a fairly good idea.

I'm told it was a good poem he wrote. People quote the bit about the teeth. Whatever furnace he used was a lot colder than a dragon, though: the number of lines he had us circling the hall for, my arms would have been down to bone.

But I don't really remember. What I remember is the smell of my charred hair, and the pain. Afterwards I must have begun beating on the doors, because I remember the moment when I stopped, once my palms were stinging and the burns on the backs of my hands and arms had started to announce themselves. The doors were three times my height, and the dragon had told them 'close', so of course I couldn't beat them open. The dragon was dead. I was shut inside the mountain.

Even now, some nights, I wake up feeling that I'm there. My eyes shut not on this room of mine but on the stone hall, in its half-light, with the dragon's hot glow slowly damping down. I can feel that big space on my skin. Sometimes, when the temperature is right, I feel the extinguished dragon near me, and the light on my eyelids seems like the sun coming straight down the lightwell nearest the door, making the shadows of arms and armour spring onto the walls. There are precious metals and gems piled in the centre, objects of human use cluttered around the edges. There is the stair up to the gallery, worn halfway to a ramp by years of the same great feet. And stillness. Silence. Until sounds that don't fit the place come to my ears, and bring me up into the day.

The nightmares have gone, or become mulch for smaller nightmares. For years I would dream of being fattened on lard and honey, or being walked to the mountain up an endless staircase. Or I would dare ten steps into one of the two dark corridors branching off at the base of the gallery stair, hit my knee on something stone, and lose the will to go further from the light – and coming back into the hall I would look at the dragon's body just as it raised its head grinning, the spear sticking out blood-crusted between its jellied eyes.

None of that happened on my first night in the hall. I looked for a way out, and did not find one. The corridor on the right was blocked, and the one on the left was dark. As the light was going I guttered like a candle, and fell asleep with my head on something embroidered I had pulled off the wall. I wonder sometimes what its picture was.

A great many trees, gnarled or straight or brambly, burn to the same ash. But not much in this world is granted the privilege of going at once, simply. 'A fool's pantry,' my mother used to say, for anything that went wrong in a half-dozen ways at once. I think she sometimes meant her life. My father's father had sliced the marriage so finely that my mother's family got almost nothing out of it. Her marriage to my father . . . functioned, which is to say much and not enough. What I used to imagine, though, when she said 'fool's pantry', was raw meat in with the onions, eggs broken days ago dripping down slowly into the dry bins, and even the maggots mouldy. When I raised my head after my exhausted sleep, the tapestry I had been using as a pillow was stuck to it, matted and peeling. I flailed at it, not knowing what it was – and then looked around, and saw a fool's pantry.

The dragon's hulk was cold, that bone spear still sticking sharp out of its head, but the treasure-bed, which its tail curved just shy of, looked like porridge congealed around the pocks of its boiling. As I took a few steps across the room, I felt hard lumps through my sandals. They were gemstones, working themselves down into the earthen floor like seeds.

It took me a while to realise that nothing grew or fed upon the hoard, to make it break down so. What I've come to think is that anything left alone gets cast back on its own strength. The things a dragon owns too long forget to be themselves, being another's. And they don't form strength sideways, either; they don't look at each other and say, 'We are its hoard.' They seem like a hoard, but in the end they're only things.

The treasure-bed was mostly silver. Gold seemed untouched, at first, but by noon the gold coins had shrunk to slivers, wafer prints of dead kings and generals. Even the ingots were getting slender. There were things there I still wonder why anyone actually made – the drinking horn with the dried butterflies, the solid copper boots, a whole rank of strangely shaped harpsichords. Corme had been great in its day, with the tribute of seven other states, while the dragon still flew widely enough to back its wars. Now every piece of that old tribute found its own way to break down. One of the harpsichords smoked, one bubbled; a silver chalice wailed all day; chests of fabric fell in upon themselves with dry coughing. I wondered, without emotion either way at that point, if the fumes might make me miscarry. Some of them sank instead of rising – acrid, green or black. I've had this cough ever since.

That morning no thought could scare me: I tried out the worst I had, just to see. But I had hope too: almost at once I saw that the great doors were starting to go like the hoard. Their iron was blistering in layers, like burned skin. I didn't let myself think about how thick they were; I just thought of Angelo's mother, scrunching her voice and face as though holding in tears, saying, 'You have always been decorous, Amaranta, you will hold yourself well . . .'

I can be decorous, I thought, before screaming as loudly as I could and laughing myself breathless. I had been fattened, so I could fast. Hunger tightened on me that day until I felt insubstantial, and it passed through me like a cord untwisting. After that I was more or less nauseous most of the time, but only hungry in flashes.

Though I felt fearless, it didn't occur to me to walk up the stairs to the gallery, because that was where the dragon had been when I arrived. Going there felt not dangerous but senseless, like trying to walk through a wall. So I stayed in the main hall until the sun came straight down the middle lightwell onto the dragon's treasure-bed, which was still beautiful, like washed up silver jellyfish. I had been unearthing gemstones with a dagger, to distract myself. Diamonds the size of eyeballs; I imagined you using one for a toy, brilliant. But by the time the sun was falling half of them had buried themselves again, and the dagger had snapped.

I was thirsty by then, and it was midsummer: there was no relying on rain. But there was a whisper in the hall that never stopped, and the longer I sat there the more it sounded like water. So I tried the left-hand corridor again, down six steps into dimness, and a right turn into darkness. The sound grew clearer at the turn, so I walked too fast there, and almost fell down a step into a little room with a stone block at its centre. That was lucky: it made me careful, and those caves needed care. They had been a net of passages, too narrow for the dragon to have used, but movements in the mountain had sheared them, making treacherous ledges and gaping holes. At first I wondered if the mountain was rotting like the hoard. I could not see anything as I followed the blurred echo of water into passage after passage, shuffling with my hands spread in front of me and still half expecting a killing fall. I could hear different depths by the echoes of my footsteps. After the first branch of passages failed, I went back for one of the knives that hadn't yet blunted itself, thinking coolly that it would be an alternative to a slow death by thirst if a fall broke other bones than my neck. But as soon as I picked up the knife I imagined the cut I would have to make, and threw it down again.

The way was not rotting, and I soon found the stairway I needed. Then it was fifty steps down into the lightless mountain, down into the layering of echoes. The stairs ended in a rough-walled chamber five foot square, and in the side wall was an upward-tapering crack, just wide enough to wriggle through into the water cave.

Away from the great hall's stink of meat and metal, the cave had the flavour and chill of winter, though the shortest night had just gone by. It was stony and sterile, with little sounds that might have been fish. The water came in through a crevice somewhere high above, and ran quietly down the wall into the pool. I kept to that side of the cave. The echoes came from the opposite side, where there must have been a long fall, and I did not trust my sense of how close it was.

I was afraid at first of what might be living down there, imagining something oozing and eyeless, and wishing I had kept the knife. But since nothing broke the silence but my footsteps and the fish splashing – once I'd convinced myself that they *were* fish – I relaxed. And over the next two days, as I learned the way there better and better, and followed lesser and lesser thirsts there, it began to feel good to get away from the hall, which grew stuffier and fouler. My nausea and my closed-in tiredness were drawn away into the spaces of the hill, and the cold touch of the pool felt good. I had already begun to think, Better to be eaten by a mountain than a dragon.

The idea that nothing at all might eat me, that I might escape, seemed to be lost somewhere outside my head. Each time I lay down to sleep on the hard earth by the doors, I longed for the sound of water, but what I slipped into was like fever: tossing and turning, dreaming of eating a baked chicken, of my family, of Angelo's body moving under mine, as though they and the rotting hoard were of a piece, as though there had been no savour nor sweetness to any of them. I woke unrested. Sleep did not even pass the time; my nights felt longer than my days. But I was wise not to stay by the pool. I might have lost my turnings – had I woken at all.

I had to concentrate to remember my brother crying for me. He was too young to really understand about feeding the dragon, but not so young as to think I would come back. Remembering that, I could stand up from beside the pool and climb the stairs again each time. My mother had kept her tears inside her face, so that, back then, I did not believe in them. My father had often called the dragon indispensable. He did not think the same way about daughters. His stock came through the Narrows, and it was not fear of *me* that made the pirates shy. Daughters cost, besides: husbands got more in dowry than anyone gave the dragon in tribute – though since there were many husbands and only one dragon, the dragon came out ahead.

Gusts of steam used to rise from the mountain when it rained, clouds of steam when it poured; children being taught about the dragon got shown that. But the unseasonable rain that fell on my third morning in the hall fell on cold stone. From the first lightwell it flowed out the widening crack under the door, and from the second it soaked into the bed of gold and silver. The water from the third lightwell pooled, up in the gallery. I heard it deepening: the sound of the raindrops changed.

I was afraid, now, to go up there again. But I also felt the water cave to be dangerous, as my hope grew brittle. So I levered myself up from the space I had swept clean by the door, where I had been sitting watching the dirty water flow away, and picked my way across to the stairs, watching out for anything that might still cut my feet. I climbed at the edge, where the stairs were more distinct.

The gallery was not terrible anymore, not like the first wild glimpse I'd had of it when I was searching for escape. It held no treasure except skulls, so the water gathering in the dips in the floor, where the mosaic was worn, was dusty, warm, and drinkable, with no flavour to suggest a creature had sat where it now pooled. I stayed there all morning, as the showers swept over and the gloom thickened and thinned.

There were more than a hundred skulls lining the side walls of the gallery. Some were gilded, some had the gold rotting off them, and between those were spaces where only yellow dust was left, gold and bone mingled. Some of them were child-sized – which, when I thought about it later, was my first hint that the dragon didn't care who was fed to it. It did not require maidens or the shamefully unmaidened, though no man or child had been sent in my time. Were there any soldiers' skulls in that lot, cowards or criminals? I tried to reckon time, bringing to mind the things 'old' meant to me: my grandmother, my father's name, Corme. The dragon was older – by centuries, unless it had fed more often in the beginning, or by more, if this was not the full number of skulls. I've thought a lot since then about what it would feel like. There are stories of dragons far and wide, but none behaved like ours. Why did we so seldom see it flying? Was it happy? Can dragons be? Did it back me towards those spears on purpose? Had it ever died before? I know it could do something like speaking: the word 'close' had washed up in my mind when it closed the doors, although I don't think the command itself had words at all. From the gallery, it would have been able to look down at me through the open doors as they led me to the base of the mountain, loosed my cuffs, told me to climb. (When someone says 'eagle-eyed' I still think 'dragon-eyed'. Dragons fly higher.) It would have seen me, as small as the figures in the floor mosaic.

All I thought about the dragon at the time was, 'Age makes cunning, but strength makes fools.'

*

There was, after all, another treasure in the gallery. I'd been there an hour before I noticed the pile of sodden books in one back corner – sodden, although out of the rain. On the wall beside them hung two parchments, dry to cracking. No one had yet taught me to read, but I peeled open one of the drier books, and saw columns of words whose letters I recognised. I think they were lists of names. Not even my father could have read the parchments, whose letters were unfamiliar to me: like shields, they had only two or three kinds of outline, but the patterns inside the outlines seemed never to quite repeat. At the bottom of each parchment, where a man might have set his mark, was a long ink-stained tear.

Sitting on the floor, scanning those characters, I fell into a doze. They looked like the dragon's scales, and I began to dream of them, of the patterns inside them. The outlines became open doors, and each pattern the picture of another return home: passing the door, walking down the straight, steep path, walking to the city through the brown parched fields. Sometimes strangers saw me and ignored me, or dropped tools and ran on ahead of me with the news of my return. Sometimes it was noon, and they were hiding from the withering sun and did not see me at all. I walked through the graveyard, and between the houses of the outer town towards the one that had been mine, right back against the old wall. Sometimes I would meet Angelo's mother, who had drawn my name oh so randomly from the box marked 'death', walking out towards me still wearing the gilt-edged wrap and false frown of that office. Sometimes people shouted at me. Sometimes it was one of my parents, right there in the street. My father would try to seem happy, or try to show civic outrage, and fail; my mother would stand there, her face under more and more pressure, with no words to match the disgrace that had reknotted itself around her.

The better routes were the interrupted ones. Someone saw me and denounced me and did something with me before I had to meet my parents. They never had to stop thinking of me as dead. Or better yet, I would stop myself, go somewhere unimaginable. Some of those dreams just mercifully ended. The worse dreams put me back into my life with all its consequences. Locked up in my father's name forever. Angelo brought to court on a charge of seduction – the charge his family had rightly calculated my father dared not bring, before – and the both of us punished. Or me brought up for dragon-murder. Or Angelo forced to marry me after all, the marriage covering his treatment of me like paint over a rotten spot in timber. But every feverish dream, wherever it led, centred on the bearing of my child, and the birth was worse than any I had seen. (Abortifacients did not work, in these dreams, or else they sickened me, or else I was refused them.) I bore the child in a house, in a ditch, in a prison, in the camp of the soldiers who were burning Corme down. Some of the dreams ended with half-normal lives: my name politely forgotten; the child abandoned, raised, or buried. But to reach even those I would have to walk, through familiar streets, between familiar eyes, and I would have to bear the child.

Another dream bundled all those away. It was not feverish, it was a dream of delight, woven from the first moments of delicious waking. The only dream in which I walked nowhere at all. I stood in the gallery, looking out through the open doors at a landscape I had a chance to consider small for the first time, and I shouted. Everything painful – from my first bee-sting to the sting of my mother's slap, my father's waste of what I could do, Angelo's contempt – came in behind the shout, making it a roar before which my life and my death and all the people in the lands around would flee in terror. Once the echoes faded, there would be only strengths left in me: nothing would contain me.

When I came to myself, my hand was covering the tear in the parchment where the dragon's claw had signed. The rain had stopped, and the air smelled different. Metal and putrescence gave way to an unfamiliar smoky wood. In the way that dreams follow you into daylight a while, I felt as though the door of the hall was lying against my lips. It tickled like a feather, waiting for me to blow.

And I started to. But that had become the same as other actions, in the way of dreams. The first thing was to walk down the stairs, carrying the space of air and delight inside me.

While I was up on the gallery, much of the hoard had finished drying out. Around the still-damp heap of the bed, silver coins lay in clumps like desiccated moss. They crackled under my feet. I smiled to think that life could still be breathed back into them. A few undamaged objects lay here and there, sieved from the dust of precious things. A rattle of teeth and shells. An iron wheel. A painted cup, with running men upon the lip, a lizard on the stem.

The dragon's flesh was sloughing off the bone onto a bed of dull scales. I walked around to the half-exposed skull, and peered into the dark back of its throat, wondering what I would have tasted like. Would my parents taste like me? I gripped the spear handle, levered the skull up, set a foot to it, and pulled. When the spear came free of the bone I almost fell over backwards.

Such a waste had been made of me, of who I was and what I could do. My father was slow with numbers, and I was quick. By the time I was eight, I was helping him with his books. It was the best I ever knew him, and a year and a half later it was already over – I had become a calculation in his books myself. But I did not stop watching our business. My father did not know that it was failing, and would not hear me tell him. Quick to anger, quick to certainty, slow with numbers: he would make a profitable match for me, and waste the gains. I had burned my future, believing in Angelo, but I did it because there was so little there to burn. It would have gained me much if he'd been trustworthy – and anyway, I wanted him.

Eventually he called me a whore for that. He used the word affectionately the first time, but it had obviously been on his mind from the start. By the time I could have been a danger to him he must already have sat down with his parents and his uncle and discussed what they might do – shameful, but less so than his alternatives.

With all this in my mind at that moment, it seemed to me that the dragon's hunger was preferable to Angelo's. It did not dissemble, it had only one note, and it could practicably be answered with a spear.

This spear was made of bone. I saw, then, that its point was a tooth, matching the smallest of the teeth in the dragon's jaw.

If I was to hunt Angelo, I could make sure he knew where the spears were. He could have a shot with one. The best thing would not be eating him but seeing his fear with all its anger torn away: he would feel comfortable displaying fear to a dragon.

The door was still on my lips. The next thing to do was to wind the tooth free from the spear and plant it in my mouth. At the thought I tasted blood, and the dream thinned in my head to the point where I wondered what I was doing. But the moment still had with it the delicious hush of something new. I would not be compelled to eat anyone I did not want to. I looked at my hands on the spear's haft, blisters risen on the backs of them, the whiteness of dead skin at the corners of their broken fingernails. They stung, they ached, as they often had, even before I was shut in that cave.

If I left with those hands they would weave and launder, they would grow old a little faster than the rest of me, which would grow old too soon; only I would not think it too soon, because my efforts would flow like fresh water into seashore sand. I would have nothing to become, nothing to love. I had seen it in the scales.

Once I was a dragon, once I had hunted, I could sleep and forget. I would have years of rest, if I wanted them, and the little people of Corme could decide what food to send me – I would be as happy with a cow as with a human, there need be no more of that. I could fly as far as I wanted, in the golden sunlight. I could see the whole world. I could grow great.

'I could grow great.' The words washed up into my mind. I was unsettled without quite knowing why, as if I had woken up a second time.

I was thirsty. Soon I would breathe out, soon I would open those doors, but I was thirsty, I would drink first. I walked towards the back of the hall. I would soar, I would tear flesh, after I drank . . . I came to the mouth of the corridor and stepped smoothly into it, into its shadow, as though there was someone sleeping in the hall I did not want to disturb.

The parchments in the gallery shifted with a dry husking that seemed to come from before me as well as behind me. I thought of wings. The spear in my hand tilted gently toward my face, as though I were walking with it into a strong wind. And I voiced in my mind the thought I had been using my feet and my thirst to sneak into action: these assurances I was finding in myself felt familiar, and flexible, as though it were my objections, not the truth, they were shaping themselves around. The dream had reached into waking to cast the world as a neutral place where all I needed had been set in easy reach; like the first time I spoke with Angelo, when his every word and gesture spoke of trust and wanting. But Angelo's family had held their place in Corme a long time, as had the dragon. With a thrill of anger, I thought, What did the dragon sign? Why should I claim that signature as mine without reading the contract? What would I sign away?

I put my other hand to the spear below the tooth, pressing back, and walked faster, down the step into the first little room, around the stone block in the centre, into darkness. I was breathing hard. I coughed: the tickling feather had moved back into my throat. I was too thirsty to be satisfied with water, too hungry to eat meat cooked on a fire. I had not actually moved further away from the dragon. I was still holding the spear.

But the dragon is dead, I thought. And, I want my hands.

For a dizzy moment I saw that the cracks through the mountain were in everything: corridors wrenched out of alignment, floors gaping wide, streets askew and never meeting, fields swept bare. I could fly. Why would I have hands, to grow old in narrow places?

My first answer to that was: because my brother cried for me. And surely my parents cried, although they hid their tears? My life was not nothing. But I wanted to cry myself, because that was a flimsy answer, and I could barely half believe it. The cracks in the mountain were cutting me to pieces.

But the second thing I thought was, Why is that the question? If you want something for me and not only from me, then tell me why you cannot give me both. Give me wings and keep your teeth. I'll keep my hands.

The husking sound of the parchments rose. I felt weak and weary, and then angry, thinking, It waited for my weariness, didn't it?

I said, aloud, 'Do you think I was never lied to?'

The feather vanished from my throat, and there was silence, quick as a sound, with water falling in it. For a moment, there in the cold stone hallway, I relaxed. But persuasion is seldom the last resort of liars. I was not the only one in my body to be offered teeth.

I think I had already made up my mind by then that you would die. Perhaps you could taste it in the mingling of our blood. Or perhaps a foetus sixteen weeks up the trail to humanity simply has no say in the matter, when it is sought by something great and old that wants to keep existing.

There was no longer any feeling of dream-rightness when my arms tried to turn the spear and stab me. If it had still needed my mouth, I would have died – but it had to turn the spear around to reach you where you sat beneath my stomach. I could begin holding it off, and I was near the top of the stairway. I did not run down it. A fall would have finished me. I walked, steadily, in the total darkness. I held my arms tense, with the spear raised ahead of me. Whenever I relaxed, finding habit a stronger force than panic, I felt my arms leap forward and caught them again; raised them back up. I have never dreamed exactly that, but the feeling entered the vocabulary of my nightmares. I had fifty downward steps of it. The moment of greatest danger was the last step, when I stumbled, expecting another – but I caught myself. With the spear held out before me I stooped into the crevice, the water falling louder and louder in front of me; I held the spear out, blinking away tears, as every few seconds you tried to kill me.

I was in a wide space, in darkness, chill as winter. I cast

the spear. It splashed into the water with a hiss like quenched metal.

Sink, I told it. Go over the falls and stay there, with no people and no earth to grow in.

I sat down and listened to the water's rush. There was no other sound, not even fish jumping. After a while a tight pain started up beneath my abdomen, but I did not need that to tell me you were dead.

Until I stood up, I wanted to believe I wouldn't. My arms and hands ached from the strain, stung with their burns. The cramps of my miscarriage had spread into my back and thighs. I felt thinned by hunger and very tired, and I did not wish to see the dragon's corpse again. But I still wanted life, although I cursed it. I stood. I found the gap and went through it, taking each step as though it were a whole journey: step, step, each step weighted by all the others to come. Hundreds of journeys, before I got anywhere. I had not drunk any water, but it seemed too late for that now. I went up the stairs, not expecting them to end, as though I were dragging lengths of heavy cloth behind me.

The stairs did end. They opened into a corridor whose opposite side was deep with rubble, just as they had before. I turned right, hurting my foot on the same stone I had half-noticed kicking on the way down. Five steps, carefully, and then one long step over a gap of half a foot. Then two more, until my reaching hands found stone. The corridor had risen away from itself there, sheared crossways. I hauled myself up, but carefully, because there was a fall to the right. I lay on my front for one, two, three moments without even the spare energy to say 'ow', then rose slowly to my feet, hugging the clammy wall, feeling the cold rising out of the deep on the other side. Beyond that was warmer, staler air. I took a breath of green mould, and heard the cracking echo of my footstep in the side-cave from which the smell came. After that it was easier. I followed the long gently curving corridor, careful of rubble, turned left at the tee, and there was warmth ahead, shades in the black. And – which was new – the smell of ash. Through the little room, around the square block in the floor's centre – I could still hear the water behind me, pouring down deeper than I had gone – and up the step, forward and left. I could see my hands, wreathed in smoke. I walked up the last six steps, and covered my eyes as the light bulged into them.

There was no flesh left on the dragon. It lay in its own ash, blackened bones. The air was smoke-hazed, nothing left of the hoard but blackened scraps, a cup, a soot-coated cart wheel.

Passing near the skeleton, I walked to the great closed doors, and shoved. I expected strain, but they moved quite easily, with crackings from the hinges.

There was a burst of evening light. The sun was shining low through a thin place in the clouds. My mother was standing outside the doors, with the sun over her shoulder, and behind her were six of our female relatives, windmilling their arms or sitting down or falling over. There were ropes. This confused me, and so did my mother's embrace. The last time we met we had each said something that was part accusation and part farewell and not satisfying as either – but the last time we met felt many years ago, as well. What made sense to me was that it felt very good not to be supporting my whole weight anymore. I blinked over her shoulder and gradually realised that the ropes had been fixed to the doors – they had been pulling on them – and only my mother had been quick enough to find her balance when they actually swung open. I think she was the only one who thought they might.

I left a print of dirt and sweat upon my mother, who was in her best white linen. Mourning clothes. 'Ah,' I said, 'you were burying me.'

My mother only held me tighter.

'Come home now,' said one of my aunts. 'We'll bring you home.'

It was days before I understood that they had really come from laying out my father.

The night I went to the mountain, every citizen of Corme had fallen sick except the youngest children. By the next morning most were better, but some worsened. The frailest of those died early. The rest, my father among them, died in one moment, when the spear struck the water. That was also when the buildings started falling.

As I was carried home, I saw but did not understand five unfilled graves, and two others half-dug with broken spades beside them. When we came to the city I did not understand why so many people were on the streets, or what had happened to some of the houses, or why the old wall behind our house had been replaced by a pile of loose stones. Understanding put itself together in my mind as I slept, and was there next morning; but that night, drinking and eating, washing and sleeping, was another of the times I've thought myself finished with the dragon's death.

On the first day my family brought me mutton broth and company and freedom from explanations – given and received. After that, as we told each other what had happened, it became clear how much there was to do, and how much danger we were in. Two-thirds of Corme's magistrates were dead, and wealth that might have helped us rotted in the warehouses of their families. My aunt asked a despairing question about what on earth we could do next, and without thinking twice I answered her. After that the time I spent in rest waned slowly, day by day, and my grief became wound up so tightly in working out how to survive that I had trouble feeling it.

We had not even finished rebuilding the houses when the first of the envoys from Corme's neighbours came, with armies behind their politeness, asking after the silver and gold in the mountain. They did not find 'It turned to porridge' a plausible answer. 'The cave was ransacked by bandits' was better, and soon enough true, but it did not help our position.

But that was when we began to learn how much the dragon had owned. Stories came to us of pirate ships a hundred miles away rotting at anchor, and merchant vessels foundering, the barley they carried sprouting for a while upon the surface of the sea. In many lands it manifested as a four-day plague. The envoys began to argue harder, or else become conciliatory, as their own states and cities received envoys from larger, farther neighbours, carrying condolences about the rumoured rusting of an army's swords, and suggesting that new swords might be supplied, perhaps carried by soldiers or perhaps not, depending on the negotiations . . .

And while that was happening, Angelo (whose survival I still find unfair) saw a little space of safety in which to start the first and most violent of the feuds about me. With the scars still livid on my arms, I had a personal band of armed men to dodge. Once he had spent his ailing family's clout on that, and found the developing meaning of sending me to be eaten was something he did not like at all, the quick crises gave way to slow ones. We had some time for our grief to unwind, for dreaming and for nightmares.

*

It is all a fool's pantry. I could talk it through to the present without finding an end, talk through the days that I have struggled, as I felt the road opening in front of me for me to take another bloody step on . . . but I found you an end, you and the creature tangled with you. The slope where the dragon's ash blew is better soil than Corme had before. And you became the kind of ghost who is a space for growing into. A space where I have been able to revise, with my own hands, the contracts that bind me.

Here is the payment you still demand for that. I've been a whole day telling you this time, while I sat on council in the morning, ran the accounts into the afternoon, and snatched time to eat with my living daughter in between. She sees the look in my eye, on days I'm talking to you, but neither of us wants her to ask about it anymore. Even now that our year zero is the dragon's death, and pilgrims climb our mountain in droves, you are dead child, and dragon.

Tomorrow I will forget you again, for a while. But I will end today resting in this garden with you, listening to my city, as a chisel sounds against stone two streets away, and people pass around me laughing in the withdrawing light, discussing the latest piece by that poet who was sorry I could not remember more.

Copyright acknowledgements

Previously published works:

Godfrey Sweven, 'Jabberoo' and 'Spectralia', from *Riallaro: The Archipelago of Exiles*, G. P. Putnam's Sons, 1901.

Anon (a.k.a The Inhabitant), excerpt from *The Great Romance*: first published by the author in 1881.

'Two Sheep' by Janet Frame. Copyright © 1963, Janet Frame, first published in SNOWMAN SNOWMAN: FABLES AND FANTASIES (George Braziller, New York, 1963), used by permission of The Wylie Agency (UK) Limited.

Maurice Gee, excerpt from *The Halfmen of O*: published by Oxford University Press, 1982; Penguin Books, 2005. Reproduced with permission from the author and Penguin Random House.

Owen Marshall, 'Immortality': first published in *Tomorrow We Save the Orphans*, McIndoe Publishers, 1992. Reproduced with permission from the author.

Phillip Mann, 'The Gospel According to Mickey Mouse': published in *Rutherford's Dreams: A New Zealand Science Fiction Collection*, edited by Patrick Hudson and Warwick Bennett, IPL Books, 1995. Reproduced with permission from the author.

Keri Hulme, 'Kaibutsu-San': first published in *Te Kaihu / The Windeater*, Victoria University Press, 1986. Reproduced with permission from Victoria University Press.

Juliet Marillier, 'By Bonelight': first published in *Prickle Moon*, Ticonderoga Publications, 2013. Reproduced with permission from the author.

Elizabeth Knox, 'Unobtanium': first published in *Are Angels OK?: The Parallel Universes of New Zealand Writers and Scientists*, edited by Paul Callaghan and Bill Manhire, Victoria University Press, 2006. Reproduced with permission from the author and Victoria University Press.

Kirsten McDougall, 'A Visitation': first published in *Sport 44*, 2016. Reproduced with permission from the author.

Octavia Cade, 'The Stone Wētā': first published in *Clarkesworld*, Issue 131, Wyrm Publishing, 2017. Reproduced with permission from the author.

Tamsyn Muir, 'Union': first published in *Clarkesworld*, Issue 111, Wyrm Publishing, 2015. Reproduced with permission from the author.